UNCOMMON WORLD

THE COMPLETE EPIC QUARTET

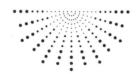

ALISHA KLAPHEKE

Text copyright © 2018 by Alisha Klapheke
Cover art copyright © 2018 by Merilliza Chan

All rights reserved.
Visit Alisha on the web! alishaklapheke.com

Library of Congress Cataloging-in-Publication Data
Klapheke, Alisha
Uncommon World/Alisha Klapheke. —First edition.
Summary: The fierce women of the Uncommon World defy all odds to defend the ones closest to their hearts and save the best parts of their wild world.
ISBN 978-0-9998314-2-7 **(FOR PRINT VERSION)**

[1. Fantasy. 2. Magic—Fiction.] I. Title.

Printed in the United States of America
10 9 8 7 6 5 4 3 2 1
First Edition

❀ Created with Vellum

To Amelia, Aidan, and Daniel, for all the great ideas

WATERS OF SALT AND SIN

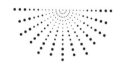

UNCOMMON WORLD

CHAPTER ONE

A breath before sunrise, the sea was a half-lidded eye, pale blue and white beyond the town walls and lemon orchards. The sea and me, the only two awake this early.

Or so it seemed when I climbed to the roof of the tavern. The streets were only dark mud and shuttered windows. I should've been out scouring, looking for a fallen dumpling or a bit of orange-spiced chicken. But I couldn't help myself. The glimmering saltwater winked at me and I gave it a lazy smile.

"Soon," I whispered before heading back down.

I had to finish the rope I'd labored on all night, because though magic was good for a lot of things, unfortunately, twisting coconut fibers wasn't one of them.

My hands used to bleed when I did this kind of work. Not now. Now my palms were like moving stones, pressing, rolling over the two sections and twining them around one another until they were long enough to tie off a sail.

My younger sister Avi snored lightly on our straw mat in the port tavern's undercroft. I opened her hand. Someday—if I managed to keep her alive until someday—those angry blisters would disappear and she'd have rocks for hands too. I touched the area around the worst of them gently. Though she was fourteen, I rubbed her arm like Mother used to do when we were little. Soon enough, she'd be beside me on the sea, rushing to finish our day's work before night fell and the salt wraiths came. But she didn't love the risk, the delicious challenge, or the waters like I did.

"Kinneret?" Avi's eyes opened, red and bleary.

"No. I'm Amir Mamluk," I joked, pretending to be the steel-eyed woman who held the town in her ruthless grip, only a few steps below the kyros in power. "I am in disguise as your sister so I can enjoy the pleasures of low-caste life. What's first? Prying barnacles off the hull or watching my hard-earned silver disappear into rich men's pockets?" I clapped my hands like an idiot as Avi laughed.

"You're a madwoman, Sister." She looked past me to the light. "You should've shaken me awake sooner. Did you get your sailing papers stamped?"

I waved her off. "I will. Tomorrow."

"All right." A black spot marred the edge of her grin. She'd lost a tooth last week. The empty place looked wrong next to the pretty yellow-brown hair she'd inherited from Father.

Avi leaned over to touch the shells she hid under her side of the mat. She didn't know I knew about them, so I stood and turned away, giving her a moment. It was her own ritual and whatever gave her peace was fine with me.

Gathering the fibers I hadn't used last night and the new rope, I forced a worthless tear back inside my eye and tried not to hear her little whispers.

"Mother. Father. The kitten. The cat. My broken bird."

She'd found a shell for each of the ones she'd lost. A curving one with ridges, as dark brown as our mother's skin had been. A spotted one for Father. He would've liked that. He'd loved the unusual.

As I tied on my sash, the tiny bells jingling, she drank from the bucket and wiped her mouth with the back of her hand.

"Eat that bread there." I jerked my chin at the stool that served as our table.

"What about you?"

"I ate with Oron late last night," I lied. I was a great liar, but I didn't rejoice in it. Lying was the skill of the desperate, something I intended to stop being as soon as possible.

"He actually ate?" Avi said around the nub of bread. "I thought he was on an all stolen wine diet."

"He wishes. Said so right before he went down to the boat." This time of year, depending on the crowd at the dock, my first mate sometimes slept onboard to protect our only real possession. Harvest brought a lot of strangers who wouldn't worry about consequences.

4

Smiling, Avi shook her head and handed me the bag of salt I kept tied to my sash. I shook it, felt its soft bottom. There was enough for some Salt Magic if we ended up needing it today.

"What shipments do we have?" Avi asked.

"None. We're scouting new port locations again."

"Hope it goes better than last time. Is Calev going to predict our weather for the trip?" Avi grinned.

As a member of the native community of Old Farm—and the chairman's son to boot—Calev was born high-caste, raised to oversee his people's lemon orchards and barley fields, and basically treated like a kyros around town. The brat, I thought, but a grin tugged at me.

Despite his powerful family and his position, he had the hardest time predicting weather, a child's first lesson on a farm or at sea. He just couldn't seem to gather the clues hidden in the thrush's song, the clouds' sudden curl, or the moisture in a breeze. Seriously, he was rubbish at it. His eyebrow twitched when it frustrated him and it was—

"You're the prettiest when you smile like that, Kin."

I shoved Avi gently. "Shut up, you. Come on. We need to go."

My relationship with Calev was complicated. And dangerous now that we neared the age of adulthood. Avi really did need to shut up about it. At least until I found some way to snake my way into a higher caste.

I unlocked the door and held it open for her, pretending there wasn't a pile of both human and animal waste we had to step over. Soon, the middle-caste merchants would open their booths in these dirty streets to trade goods and gossip under the white-hot sun.

Ugh. There was the sailmaker's son. He was still burned over the deal his father gave me when Calev came along to buy our new sail.

"Kinneret Raza the Magnificent, friend to high-castes." He pretended to whisper, but his words were plenty loud. "But only if you have eyes and a backside like that Old Farm boy Calev. For him, she pretends that bag of salt at her sash is for seasoning food. It's a miracle he doesn't see you for what you are. Witch."

A ringing filled my ears. If the wrong people heard him, we'd wish our only problem was finding something to eat today. "The real miracle is that pest birds haven't nested in your continuously open mouth, between your rotting teeth."

His gaze lashed out at Avi. "Soon I won't be the only one with an Outcast's mouth, witches."

I raged toward him. He lifted his leg to kick me off, but Avi jumped in the way. The tip of his sandal struck her leg, and she winced

5

"You better stop it," Avi shouted. "Or you'll be sorry." He laughed and went on as I bent to check Avi's leg. "It's a scratch," she said. "It's nothing."

"That horse's back end is going to be *nothing* if he ever touches you again. You should keep quiet when he is around."

"Oh, like you do, Sister?" She raised both eyebrows.

I snorted. "Well, I'm Kinneret the Magnificent, remember?" The ridiculousness of the title burned like a brand.

Avi put a hand on my arm and pulled me to standing. "You are magnificent to me."

I hugged her and felt her shoulder bones like driftwood under my arms. My temples throbbed. She was little more than a skeleton. A chill slithered down my back. How long could we live like this?

A woman who'd been Outcasted sat at the bend in the road, begging. Bells hung from her knotted hair, the edges of her dung-crusted tunic and sash, from every fingernail. The metal seemed to weigh her down, making her back slump like someone years older, bones rising beneath her rags. As a high-caste man walked by, his five bells lightly ringing, and in a series of rickety movements, the Outcasted woman tucked her feet under her to hide the scraps that used to be sandals. The high-caste whipped around and pointed at the Outcast.

In addition to never being allowed to enter their families' homes—or anyone's for that matter—they weren't permitted to hold a job, wear more than rags, or cover their feet with shoes.

At the man's gesture, the woman closed her eyes and removed her sad excuse for sandals, shoving them into the gutter. The high-caste nodded and continued on, obviously pleased with himself.

I'd heard the town's last amir caught that woman doing Salt Magic to win a boat race where the prize was a hefty bag of silver. But I wasn't going to let that scare me off what my mother had taught me.

An image of Mother's hands covering mine, salt glistening on our skin, blinked through my mind. I could be sly with the magic she'd given me. I could be clever with the way I used it. No one needed to know.

As we started toward the dock, a couple of high-caste women paraded by, their skirts clean and black and beautiful.

One sneered at Avi's skirt. "Filthy scrappers. Look at the blood on her clothing."

The other one frowned. "They were probably fighting like dogs."

Idiots.

I never bought anything that wasn't red just so no blood would show on me. But the high-castes were wrong. It wasn't fighting that normally brought the blood I hid. It was making rope, hauling sail, lifting, scrubbing, scraping. And I'd never let them see my blood.

As we continued on, Avi raised her chin like a proud woman twice her age. She should've had her woman's bleed already. It was lack of food that scared it off. I knew what came next. Her hair would go. The rest of her teeth, her skin.

Calev would gladly give us a loaf of bread or some lemons. But the questions I asked myself were always the same. What about tomorrow? And the day after that? I couldn't beg off him.

No.

I wouldn't let him bring us food every day like we were cripples. The thought turned my empty stomach and I kicked at the dirt. Mother and Father had made this life work. I could too. When the fevers had them, I'd promised I'd take care of Avi. Maybe I'd get another headland farmer to use us to ship surplus barley across the strait.

But that didn't put figs in Avi's mouth today.

"What are you doing?" Avi whispered as I walked up behind a woodcutter's cart.

Manure and fresh timber masked the scent of what was almost certainly a bag of barley cakes near the left wheel—the woodcutter's noon meal. I threw a tiny rock toward his horse's back leg. The horse jerked and the cart lurched to the side, the woodcutter shouting at his animal as I snatched the bag faster than a falcon can grab a chicken.

I ate one before Avi could argue, hurrying around the cart and hiding the bag in the folds of my skirt. Though she frowned at me during the entire walk to the dock, Avi ate her fill for once.

FISH LIVER OIL was both the worst and the best smell in the morning. Best because it meant I was near my boat. Worst because, well, it was fish liver oil.

The fisherman selling the stuff crossed his arms. "I won't give it for free."

"But you dump most of it anyway," I argued. "It's rancid."

"You need it. So I want something for it."

Of course he did. This was Jakobden, after all. A port town full to bursting with people who cared for silver and fame, and nothing as low as a generous spirit.

"Do we really need it?" Avi asked.

I whispered in her ear. "The stern stitching is begging for a coat."

I felt the coins in my sash. Four coppers. It was all I'd saved toward a better boat, a better sail, a better anything. Then my gaze dropped onto the bag in Avi's hand. There was one barley cake left. It would leave me without a noon meal, but the lack of oil could sink us under the wild waters of the Pass, the cursed strait we sailed every day.

Avi saw my eyes and handed me the bag. I held a cake out to the man.

"Fresh this morning," I said. "It's more than you deserve."

He frowned, then snatched the cake and pushed it into his sash for later. After he ladled some oil into our small, wooden bucket, we headed down the near deserted dock toward the red and purple boat our parents had left behind.

Sitting side by side on the dock's uneven planks, we took turns dipping our brushes into the foul-smelling oil and painting it over the coconut fiber stitching that held the stern in place.

Seawater slapped the space between the boat and the dock as I called out, "Oron!"

No answer.

"Why do we love him again?" Avi grinned.

"If he didn't handle sails like the Fire, I wouldn't…no…I'd still love him. The beast."

I didn't affectionately call him 'the beast' because he was both a pale-skinned northerner and an unusually small person—I wasn't a horse's back end like the sailmaker's son—but because of his taste for drink, his sharp tongue, and his tendency to nap like an oversized cat.

Footsteps pounded down the boards, and I turned to see an official striding toward us, his tunic and sash billowing in the wind.

Worry tied a neat knot around my heart. This might be about the rent and what I owed. It might be about any number of crimes. And the Fire knew, my word against a middle-caste's would be mouse dung to silver pieces.

Avi dropped her brush into the water and her lips pinched together. "I told you we should've gone for the stamp and seal."

I groaned as I helped her fish the brush from the water. These dock officials were the worst.

"Just Kinneret them," Avi whispered. "Like you did to the woodcutter."

"Hush."

"Sailing papers," the official spat, looking down at me.

Standing, I gritted my teeth and pulled my out-of-date papers from my sash. "Everything is good here." I held them to his face, then quickly folded them again.

He ripped them from me. "These are expired. You cannot sail again until you have an updated stamp. Report immediately to the town hall." Spinning, he hurried back up the dock.

"Guess I'll finish this up while you go," Avi said.

I didn't like how she looked. The skin around her mouth was pale. "I don't want to leave you."

"You have to. You know you do."

"I'll kick Oron awake first," I joked. Sort of.

He may've been the one who came to us in our worst hour, and close as an older brother or an uncle, but he still needed a good shove every once in a while.

She stood and wiped her hands on her skirt. "I'm fine. I'll do it. Go."

I had to smile. She sounded like Mother.

I rushed away, hoping she really was as strong as I thought she was, and praying my own stubborn will might be enough to keep us from the life of a dead-eyed beggar.

CHAPTER TWO

I walked under the town hall's arched doorway, passing a hand respectfully over the Holy Fire burning in the bronze bowl. Though I really didn't feel anything for the Holy Fire faith—the flames had never granted me any new ideas—everyone except Old Farms was expected to follow its tenets, and I certainly didn't want to join the Outcasted for such a small thing.

An Old Farm representative—with a beard that made him look like Calev's father Chairman Y'hoshua—came in behind me. Instead of passing his hand through the Fire, he slid his dagger across his finger and dropped a bead of blood into the bowl. He didn't even glance at me before pushing past to meet with one of the amir's officials near the front of the busy room.

I got in line to renew my sailing license as a man and woman wearing the red leather of the amir's fighters entered and paid the Fire their respects, their palms glowing for a moment and showing their faith. They moved on, squishing my toe with a heavy shoe.

"Don't worry about it," I growled out, rubbing my foot with fingers and thumb. "That was my least favorite toe."

The clink of silver coins and the din of gossip bounced off the domed ceilings and sloping walls, and my sarcasm was lost to the noise.

A flatbread seller's tray flavored the air with nutty cardamom and cinnamon. My stomach roared. I did my best to ignore the merchants' wives downing golden dumplings like every bite didn't cost what I made in two moons. Clenching my jaw and pushing a fist against my belly, I refused to feel hungry. If only my stomach would obey orders.

When I finally neared the front, Old Zayn shuffled in the door, a hand on his scanty beard and his gaze zeroing in on me. He lifted his shaggy brows and waved. As usual, he'd remembered something, and judging from the gleam of crazy in his sweet, old eyes, it was a doozy of a something.

Sweet as he was, I didn't have the sun for that. I had to get out of here before my landlord found me and decided I needed one less finger. Giving Old Zayn an indulgent smile, I waved back and held up my palm, meaning I'd talk in a bit. My all-too-numerous caste bells jingled, and the merchants' wives sneered. Putting a hand over my bells to quiet them, I imagined myself as kaptan of the amir's gloriously enormous, black-sailed ship, and gave the snooty crowd a pirate's grin.

Someday. Somehow. I *would* change my caste.

But I had to laugh at myself. A young woman, two steps from starving, daydreaming about running the town leader's ship? I was crazier than Old Zayn.

Berker Deniz, a middle-caste ship kaptan with as much charm as a bleeding blister, crossed the tasseled rugs. His feet kicked the hem of his silk tunic and a weasel's smile cut across his mouth. He didn't make eye contact, but headed for me like a dog on a scent.

"Move back, low-caste." In the mess of people, he tried to step in front of me. It was his right to do so, by law.

An itch I could never scratch started up under my skin. Considering I'd helped free his barge from the rocks last moon, he should've let me keep my place. I pretended not to see him. From the corner of my eye, I watched his face flush. It made him even uglier.

I was glad for my darker coloring, a blend of every blood that had lived in Jakobden and even across the Pass. When I blushed, no one noticed.

"You're just like your mother was," he said. "No honor."

I whipped my face to his. "What do you know about my mother?"

He grabbed my arm and pulled me back, taking my place in line. The merchants' wives eyed me, their ten, tidy bells shining from their sashes, marking them as middle-caste. One whispered something to the other, and my cheeks burned as I jerked away and settled for the spot behind him.

"Go ahead and argue," Berker hissed. "I'd love the officials here to order you to kiss my feet in apology."

Breathe. Breathe. I wanted nothing more than to throttle the beast and force him to kiss my flying fist. "I'll move up someday and people like you will be sorry," I whispered.

He laughed under his breath. "I saw you and that high-caste boy together at the docks last night."

I sucked a breath as Calev's face blinked through my mind.

Berker snorted, glancing over his shoulder. "Just as I suspected. You lust after him."

My face was hot as coals. "He is not…"

The room grew hazy.

I grasped for Berker's sleeve to stay upright. Lack of food was making me lightheaded.

Berker's mouth dropped open, then twisted into a grimace worthy of his sliminess as he stared at my fingers on his fine tunic.

"I scout port locations for Calev's people," I said, letting go quickly. "That's all. My twice great-grandmother was Old Farm."

"Interesting you would bring up an Outcast as part of your argument."

How did he even know that?

I mean it was public record, but still. Besides Avi and me, who cared that a long ago woman had an affair with one of the amir's house slaves and was Outcasted. How much did Berker know? Did he also know she lost her children to Quarry Isle, where her bloodline slaved until Father proved his worth at a testing—alongside Mother—and that Old Zayn paid for their rise to low-caste?

Why did it seem like Berker was always at my back, biting at my heels? For a grown man, nearly as old as my father would've been if he were still alive, he acted like an overgrown and seriously annoying puppy. A puppy that could ruin my life.

"Calev isn't always visiting me by the docks," I said. "His father sends him to Old Zayn to learn weather. We aren't doing anything taboo."

Berker dusted his striped sleeve and sea salt fluttered to the floor. "Not yet."

He was referring to our fast-approaching coming-of-age. "We're only associates."

"Well, it didn't appear that way when I saw you. Sometimes I wonder if you low-caste scrappers almost want to be Outcasted."

Our local ruler, Amir Mamluk, claimed keeping upper-caste bloodlines strong—making certain only highs bred with highs and so on—kept the right people in decision-making positions in Jakobden and the surrounding area.

A view worth its weight in dung.

"Sounds like you know a lot about my low-caste mother. How is that, when you've always been a middle-caste barge kaptan?"

"Your parents and I were on the slave island together."

The breath went out of me. My expired license crumpled in my fingers, the wax seal biting my palm. I knew Old Zayn had taken my parents from the island to apprentice on his boat, but that was about all. I'd never heard about Quarry Isle and Berker. My parents had mostly kept their pasts to themselves.

"What are you talking about?"

"Your mother was a liar with no honor." My hands shook.

"You're just like her," he said. "Being dishonorable will get you nowhere."

My mouth popped open.

Maybe this was why he made sure to push in front of me and gossip about me to his fellow middle-caste kaptans. He'd known and hated my mother for some invented reason. My teeth ached from clenching my jaw. No way he was right about my mother. He was the liar.

"You must earn your way to the top, like me," he said.

"Last time I checked, middle-caste wasn't the top."

His eyes bulged, but he smoothed his tunic along with his features. "I nearly forgot. Didn't you once run a shipment for that new grain farmer on the headlands?"

"That's my biggest run each moon." I didn't like where this was going.

"My apologies. I'll be running his goods from now on. He had a bumper crop and needs more than your little raft."

Panic rose and fell over my back. We had to have the money from that shipment. My knuckles pressed against my skin as I fisted my hands. And did he say *raft*? My beautiful, reliable, sturdy, brave craft had been my parents' boat. It was the cleverest one on the Pass. But a lot of good it did me if I didn't have enough clients.

The license official raised a palm to Berker. "Good day, kaptan. We have important matters to discuss."

Before joining the official, Berker hissed, "Remember where you belong, Kinneret Raza." He frowned at the bag of salt hanging from my sash, beside my dagger. "Salt Witch."

Praying and giving salt to the sea was an older practice than even the amir and her fighters' Holy Fire prayers. Why was one practice perfectly fine—expected even—and the other taboo? The only big difference was they used fire to develop new ideas and I used salt to alter current and wind patterns. It wasn't cheating any more than other prayers.

"I am here to pay for the removal of a bell," Berker said to the official. He held a handful of silver coins high and spoke loud enough for the world to hear. "Please consider my request."

13

I made a gagging noise. I couldn't believe Berker was moving closer to the top. If he made it to high-caste, he could buy and sell land, take the first fruits from every harvest, and have an even better view as he looked down his squid nose at me. But surely that would take him an eternity. That was a lot of silver.

The license official smiled, and with a lot of extra hand-waving, removed a bell from Berker's pale orange sash.

Berker retrieved two more handfuls of coins from his bag. "I would like to remove four more bells. Please consider my request."

It was like the wind had dropped to nothing on a busy shipping day. I could barely breathe. I certainly couldn't move.

The license official went to his work and everyone, except me, stomped their feet in praise.

Berker now wore five bells on the shoulders of his tunic. He was high-caste.

The license official raised his rough voice. "I have the distinct honor of announcing that as of today, Berker Deniz is the new kaptan of Amir Mamluk's ship!"

My legs became seaweed, and I caught the wall to keep from falling.

All around me, congratulations rose toward the painted ceiling. Sandals pounded the floor tiles.

A mean laugh snapped from my lips. I shook my head, picturing the ship's tall sides and its sails big as the night sky. Fire burned through me. My gaze lit on the fine linen and silk of everyone's sashes and the deep blues and blacks of their tunics. Their sandals without holes and fleshed out stomachs and limbs.

They didn't see the injustice, because they didn't want to.

I shook, my teeth grinding, and the bells of my sash jingling. My dreams were broken, cracked at mid-mast and beyond repair.

Words spilled out of me. "The lack of bells doesn't make someone a good kaptan. He may be high-caste, but he's a high-caste idiot!"

All heads turned, and before I could worry about what I'd done, the guards rushed forward and shackled my arms with their iron-strong grips.

CHAPTER THREE

"**L**et me go." I tried to peel their fingers off as the room erupted into hissing and whispers.

"Stop struggling, low-caste," the guard on my right said as they dragged me toward the door. "Don't want to work off all the tasty bits. Our prison rats are sadly underfed."

Before I could make a colorful remark about feeding his generous backside to the vermin instead, Old Zayn scurried over.

"Please, let me take her," he said in a clear voice. Everyone froze, then looked from him to the license official. "She's not been right since her parents' death. Neither her nor her sibling. Nor her sibling."

People called Old Zayn mad because he repeated himself. He might've been. But I was fine with his madness—it was always tempered with kindness and a flood of childhood memories. I was especially fine with his madness if it rescued me from this mess.

"They died over five years ago," Berker snapped. I squeezed my hands tight.

"Have mercy." Zayn bowed awkwardly. "I'll make certain she doesn't speak out again."

The official frowned. I was going to rot in a cell.

"Please," Zayn pleaded. "It's harvest. Time of plenty. Be merciful." He made the sign of the Fire on his forehead.

"Fine then." The official ran fingers over his beard, the Old Farm representative standing beside him watching everything. "But if she causes trouble, the amir will hear of it, and her life and yours will be in Amir Mamluk's hands."

While I waited by the door, Old Zayn secured my updated sailing papers. Seas, I had Calev's kind of luck today, catching Old Zayn in one of his lucid moments right when I needed him. The old friend ambled over, thrust the documents into my sash, and pulled me into a corner. His wide tunic sleeves almost covered his raisin hands.

"Thank you, Zayn." It wasn't enough, but it was all I had.

He'd risked his own freedom to keep me out of trouble.

A smile ghosted over his whiskered face. "You're like your mother, but ten times worse. You'll never settle for a small life, will you? Will you?"

More about my mother. My heart gave my ribs a nudge at the memory of her bright eyes and strong voice, but I didn't have the sun for this. I had to go to that farmer and get back his business.

"I need to—"

"Wait," Zayn said, looking at the line of people past the elephant tusk.

No one was peering at me anymore. They'd gone back to their lives. Berker had disappeared.

"Ayarazi exists," Zayn whispered.

The strange word echoed through me like a song I'd forgotten.

"That's a children's story." I touched his arm gently. "Mother and Father used to tell me about it. The lost island of silver is filled with pretty horses and green grass and a mist that'll freeze your toes off if you don't clean your dinner plate and wash behind your ears. It's a myth; a sweet, exciting one, but a myth just the same. Now, may I walk you home?"

His eyes flashed. Intelligence lived in their cloudy depths. And maybe a dash of anger. "Did I seem out of my wits in there?" He jerked a thumb toward the license room.

"No," I admitted. "But you come and go..."

A seed of maybe sprouted in my mind. Ayarazi—*moon land* was what the amir's fighting sailors called the lost island of silver—didn't exist, but maybe he knew of another island, a place I might sail to and find silver or copper coins in ship wreckage or something of the sort.

"I made a promise to your parents," he said.

"What?" This was the first I'd heard of this.

"I promised I'd watch out for you. You're set on rising above your status," he said. "Aren't you?"

My gaze flew to his face, and I imagined Calev's shining eyes, his jet hair, his hands. "More than anything."

He nodded. "And you want more for your sister and that dwarf you pity…"

"Pity? Oron—the best sailor I've seen and I've seen a load—has saved my life and Avi's about a thousand times. But go ahead and pity him." I could picture him, tying back his thick locks of purposefully tangled hair and looking up at me with his face of scars and sarcasm. "Oron loves silks. Adores northern ice wine. But pity? Pity is his absolute favorite."

"Yes," the old man said, smiling, misunderstanding me completely, going on like I'd said nothing at all. "I've watched you your whole life. With your fire, if you found riches, you'd put them to good use. Maybe you'd even marry well, marry him, and cease my worrying about you two. Outcasting is shameful. Shameful. One of the worst things the Empire encourages, in my opinion. As if your blood changes when you move up or down. Stupid. I should know…you two are meant for one another…remind me of your mother and father…"

My throat went dry. "Zayn. Please. Focus. What are you trying to tell me?"

He grinned. "My greedy, foolish cousin died. He never found the map. But you could. Now that he's dead and won't be coming after you with a rusty yatagan." He tapped the sore side of my head with a dirty finger that smelled like goat. "Smart girl. Smart girl."

"Zayn. Out with it. What are you talking about?"

"There's a story in my family. And in it hides the clue to finding the lost island of silver."

CHAPTER FOUR

Zayn's half-rock, half-mud home was a tumble of rusted fishing hooks, line weights like lead bags, and nets. The place smelled of charcoal and dirt. A hot breeze poured through the window where Calev often stood with Zayn, working on learning the weather's hints.

A moon after Zayn warned Old Farm of a hard frost and saved the lemon harvest, Calev's father sent the man a crate of the fruits, carried by his eldest son. Ever since, Calev visited regularly to work on reading the sky and earth for crop-killing surprises. I loved the arrangement because Old Zayn's hut wasn't too far from the dock.

Beside the window, maps smothered a spindly table. Some of the maps were drawn on yellow parchment, others on wrinkled paper, and more still scratched onto wide pieces of tree bark. Layouts of the sea, the borders of our town, and the swathe of rich land where Calev's people farmed along the southern edge of the jagged coast.

"What is the clue, Zayn? I don't have all day to gossip with you. Avi is waiting. You know how she gets." She was fourteen going on forty-five. Oron better have roused his lazy self to help her with the oil.

He made a tutting noise. "Sit. Sit. This is nothing that can be rushed."

A dingy hammock swung over the dirt floor. There was no evidence that this man was formerly high-caste. No silken tunics left over or fine furnishings. The only clue that he once scribed for the amir was the quill and ink pot sitting on the maps.

He gestured to a stool near the table and I took it, hoping I wasn't wasting sun being here.

Zayn ran a hand under his nose. "My cousin searched for the map every day. Every day, he returned to his home empty-handed. You remember seeing him once. I'm sure. A bald man, raging into and out of here. He said he'd murder you in your sleep if I told you."

"Hold on. What map? You have to explain this all to me." He had to be cracked. Ayarazi? It couldn't be real. He hadn't had family living here with him in a long while. But that's how his mind was, in and out, with days disappearing and reappearing. I did remember the cousin though.

"My ancestor was a scribe for the Invaders."

I blinked. "That was over three hundred years ago."

"He learned the Invaders knew the lost island of silver's location."

The Invaders hadn't attacked Jakobden in generations. They were from the far West and mainly ravaged the northern climes and the Empire's outskirts on that side of the world.

"He recorded clues," Zayn said, "and hid them in a wine jug that sank in a wreck along with my ancestors' employers."

"This…this is madness." I pinched at one of the bells on my sash, my foot bouncing. I needed to leave, to get on with my day. This was nothing more than daydreaming.

"Treasure hunting is not always so good for a soul. Dangerous work." Zayn picked a clod of dirt from the map and chewed his lip, making his beard stick out on his chin. "I don't have it in me to search. Takes a certain drive." He bumped a knuckle under my chin. "You have it, Kinneret. Inside you. Inside you."

I touched my bag of salt for magic and ran a finger over the fraying, leather ties. I did have that desire, that drive Zayn spoke of. I felt it, hot and unrelenting, in my veins, my heart, my head. I met his gaze.

"I'm sorry, Zayn. You're right about some things. About the caste system being wrong. That the lunar cycle would last an extra day last year. You always know the best place to catch those foul eels the high-castes strangely adore. But this? This is…I can't just take off into the waters on a story."

"Because you think you'll rise up on your own? How?"

I lurched back like he'd hit me.

Why was he trying to hurt me? Zayn had never been anything but kind, repairing our sandals when his hands were working right, passing gossip to me about which farmers might need a cheap grain transport. So why the meanness? He'd always been my friend.

"You know I'm right, Kinneret. Think."

19

Even if I kept scraping together every last bit we didn't spend on food or supplies, I'd never have enough to raise us all up. Thinking of my pitifully empty sash, I rubbed my temples and took a deep breath, my heart shushing with the most dangerous feeling in the world. Hope.

It couldn't be true. In 300 years, someone would've found it.

Wouldn't they?

I stared at Zayn's old quill and ink pot and thought about what my old age life might look like. Would I live in a hut with only wishes to keep me company, and dirt for a floor while some other girl wedded my Calev and had brown-eyed babies? My pulse beat in my ears. That feeling, hope, it tugged at my chest and spun a dream into my mind.

Calev and I dancing at a harvest celebration. Avi clapping to the music. In this imagining, my younger sister's skin glowed with health.

I looked at my arms and fingers, chapped and sun-scorched and bony. Hope. Was that all it took to risk looking like a fool, to risk wasting light to run after an old man's fantasy?

I never, ever wanted to see Avi brush the last of her hair with her fingers and come away with a fistful of sunny locks. I ached with all the tears she'd already shed. How could I stand more of them?

Closing my eyes, I whispered, "Say I did believe you. Say I was…up for this madness."

He stood, smiling. "Tell me again why you want it. I must be sure…the risk…maybe you should wait."

My eyes snapped open. I could at least try. If it didn't work out, well, I'd be no worse off.

"What's to wait for?" I was getting carried away by the idea of it now. I almost wanted him to stop me, to clamp a gritty hand over my flapping lips. "More of being kicked around? More of watching Avi starve? Tell me what you know, Zayn, and I'll do what I can for all of us."

I battled the possibilities back and forth inside my brain. A fly buzzed at my face and I swatted it away.

Breathing out his long nose, Zayn clasped his hands behind his back and stared into the pile of maps. "Just remember what you have, Kinneret Raza. Before you go off into the wilds, risking all—"

"I have nothing. I have a future in a boat with holes I can't afford to patch."

"It is decided then," he said.

He ran a finger along a map of the choppy waters I sailed daily. "The wine jug with the map will be somewhere near here. Where the current paints a teardrop on the surface of the water."

My skin went cold. "That's near the slave island."

Most slaves worked at Quarry Isle their entire lives, carving pale stone at night and sleeping a few day hours in a crowded pit they snidely called their Quarters.

Zayn told me they were whipped to bloody shreds when the slavers thought they weren't working hard enough. Food was nothing more than hard bread cakes, mealy and tooth-breaking. Father told me thirst had hounded his every waking moment there. "My skin was so different then. Like a dried barley stalk," he used to say.

Mother never would talk about it. When I asked her questions, she crossed her arms over her chest and just shook her head.

Thank the Fire, Old Zayn had rescued them from that hell by hiring them before I was born.

"Yes, it isn't far off at all." Zayn's gaze flicked to me. "As I said, there are risks."

"How do you know he meant that current? Just because it has the shape of a tear?"

His fingers pressed into my short sleeve. "I don't know. It is a guess. A guess. But I think it's a good one. And you're the only one looking for it now. I have no other family who has heard the tale."

A good guess. I breathed out and turned one of the bells on my sash. "Is there definitely a shipwreck there?"

He shrugged. "I've told you all I know. All I know." He scratched at his scalp.

I put my hand on his, and his cloudy eyes studied me. "If I find it," I said, "I'll give you any part of it you ask for."

Waving his hands, he shook his head. "No. I have a season or so left in me. I don't have the sunlight to weather a change in status now. Not after all these years."

Before I could leave, my skin prickling with excitement and my thoughts whirling, Zayn pulled a coin-sized compass from his sash and handed it to me. The bronze was warm from his body.

"Stop and note your course from time to time." He smiled. The young man he once was peered out between his wrinkles. "You are capable of doing this, but remember, it's your choice. You can return if you don't cross too many boundaries. Too many. Too many. After that?" He held out his hands.

"After that, I'll be rich. I'll have all the choices." I went to the door, opened it, and squinted into the white sun.

"I hope so," Old Zayn said to my back as I walked away. "I hope so."

CHAPTER FIVE

Silver. Loads of it. More than I could picture in one thousand of my low-caste, spit-on, calloused dreams. It would be raw. It could be cursed. But it would be ours.

Heading away from dockside, I padded down the baked dirt road toward Calev's home. Fallow fields of yellowed weeds chittered in the breeze beside stretches of barley. The sun would reign for another five hours. I had to move fast.

At the first of Old Farm's low, stone walls and wide-reaching fields, I eased past two men in calf-length tunics embroidered with lemons. I'd seen them with Calev's father many times. Their noses wrinkled at the bells on my sash and made them ugly.

I grinned at the men, teeth and all. Their Old Farm scorn couldn't touch me. Soon, I'd be wealthy—rich enough to buy a feast for my sister and Old Zayn. And I'd be on my path to becoming a full-ship kaptan, lord of a real ship, its hull heavy with bright lemons, bundles of barley, rainbows of silk.

Old Zayn might be softheaded, but I didn't think so. The details of his tale were too specific to be imagined. I had one life to live, and by the Fire, I was going to take it by the tiller and steer.

Passing through the estate's wooden beam entrance, I touched the ridged surface of the blue-striped shamar yam shell nailed to the supports. It held a written prayer, and I hoped some of its magic would soak into me. Maybe Old Farm practices like this had helped them survive the Quest knights' takeover, then the line of kyros since. It certainly couldn't hurt to embrace that kind of power.

At the edge of a shushing barley field, the earth's scent in my nose, I skittered to a halt.

Calev reined in his chestnut horse and waved, tossing his leg over to dismount. The warmth of the ground spread up through my feet and into my legs, stomach, and every inch of me. The harvest sun extended a beam over Calev's obsidian hair. Two workers nodded at their chairman's son. I breathed too quickly, willing my heart not to explode and expose my deepest secret.

I was in love with my best friend.

And he couldn't know until I had the silver to buy my way to high-caste. Only then could he consider me. Only then could I dream of his fingers drifting along my cheeks and his mouth dusting mine. I shivered. But I had to wait. I would not make him an Outcast by dragging him into a caste-breaking romance that would be taboo the moment we came of age. He'd never be allowed to enter his family's home again.

The coming of age thing was stupid. I was already a woman. I'd been one for a while. Calev was every bit a young man. At least the late timing of the old tradition gave us more sun to be together.

Beside the fields, Calev spoke to a man and a woman, his voice a lighter rumble than his father's. "...and take the seasoned wood to repair the first storage barn. The cowshed doesn't need it now. Not with this weather." He held up his hands toward the blue sky and turned his red-brown eyes to me.

As the workers hurried to follow his request, he gave me his smile like a First Sun gift, so much better than any spice cake or present wrapped in fine paper.

"Kinneret." He took my hands, and I looked at his. The land lived in bits and pieces under his short nails. I grinned. Such a land lover.

The two Old Farms he had been talking to furrowed their brows at our show of caste-free friendship, and after giving Calev a respectful nod, continued on. The elders tolerated our closeness because we weren't yet of age and also because I once saved Calev's life.

When we were both seven years, accompanying our parents at the bustling dock nearest Old Farm, Calev fell into the water. He couldn't swim —silly Old Farms didn't teach that until the children were ten years. I'd been swimming since I could breathe, so I dropped into the salty sea, grabbed him under the arms and dragged his skinny self to the rope ladder off our boat.

The elders would keep on tolerating us, to a degree, until our Age Day in one moon. On that day, everyone aged one year, and Calev and I would be eighteen. Adults. After that, if we were seen doing anything more than everyday business, we'd be Outcasted.

Calev tightened the deep blue headtie that rested above his eyebrows. The sturdy sandals he liked to wear on my boat stuck out from the bottom of his tunic. "Could we go on a quick ride before the port-scouting trip?" He ran a hand along his horse's nose.

My mind threw out pictures of Calev's lean body in front of mine, sitting in his green tasseled saddle. I almost felt the barley tugging at my skirt like paupers' fingers. There was no Berker anywhere in sight.

But we didn't have the sun for a ride.

I squeezed his strong fingers in mine. "We need to leave now. And it'll take…" I tapped my lips, thinking. Who knew how long it would take to find the map? Maybe hours, maybe much longer. Zayn's instructions would get me to the spot, but with weather and the possibility of the shipwreck moving over the last hundred or so years…

If I told Calev seven days, he'd say no. One, and he might not warn his father of his absence. "Three days. At the most."

He smoothed a hand over his head. "Three? I told the council we'd be at sea just one." Looking over his shoulder at the fields, he grinned. "It's harvest."

"Not yet."

"Almost. And my father—"

"Let your brother handle it."

His brother appeared from behind a painted wagon near the tool shed.

"Eleazar," I said, "Calev has something to tell you." I jabbed a thumb at him.

"I do?" Calev asked, laughing.

"You do." I pulled him two steps up the path toward the side of the fork that led to the sea. "Come on," I whispered. "I need you."

From shallow water spearfishing to creeping onto full-ships to climb rigging, he'd always been with me. I didn't need a lucky frog's leg like other sailors. I had Calev ben Y'hoshua, eldest son of the chairman of Old Farm—the most profitable stretch of ground on the amir's sprawling lands. Everything Calev smiled on grew wings and flew on to greatness.

"All right, Kinneret. I'll go. But you might have to take me on as a crewmate when my father throws me out."

"Ugh. An Old Farm sailor?" A laugh flavored my words. "It takes you way too much sun to get used to the swells." I pretended to be sick, bending and coughing.

With a gentle punch to my shoulder, Calev broke away and clasped his brother's arm in both his hands. "Father knows I'm leaving. It's been approved. I'll just be gone a little longer. Three days at the most."

Eleazar mumbled something and his jaw tensed.

Calev shook his brother's arm. "It'll please our ship's kaptan. You know Kinneret is good at this. Come on."

The side of my mouth jerked up. It was a good lie. Their kaptan, old as the sea itself, knew I was a master at navigating the Pass. He'd never admit it, but when I'd been caught going through his maps during a visit to see Calev, he'd told me I didn't need to spy. That I already knew the best routes.

A frown ran over Eleazar's freckled bottom lip. "I don't know…"

Thoughts of silver mounds, Calev's mouth, and every kind of exotic food I'd ever wanted to eat swirled around in my head. My life could completely change. I grinned, imagining Avi's happy smile. "The weather will change soon. We need to go. Now."

"Fine," Eleazar said. "I'll tell Father. As usual."

A shadow of guilt crept into my gut, but I pushed it down.

Wearing a butter-colored sash, a girl with the prettiest, darkest eyes walked out from behind the shed. Miriam. I wasn't proud of it, but anger and jealousy blazed under my skin.

She didn't smile but nodded once to Calev. He straightened his blue and yellow sash and coughed.

The skin over my knuckles burned as I fisted my hands tighter. They'd be married in a year if something didn't change.

Eleazar raised his eyebrows. "Maybe you should tell your Intended about your plans."

Calev closed and opened his eyes, then smiled at her.

I willed my heart to keep beating. That smile. I was the one who'd found that smile first. Not her.

She peered back at him, her chin tilted prettily. Pretty, pretty, pretty. High-caste, high-caste, high-caste. My teeth ground together. I looked at the fields, wishing I was a blind woman so I couldn't see her beauty. I was well aware that my smaller, lighter eyes were mere field flowers next to the black roses she blinked at Calev.

I tugged Calev's arm. "We need to go now."

"If it's so pressing, maybe we should enlist my horse." He had a point.

We bid them goodbye and mounted up as I did my best to push, shove, and smash the image of Calev smiling at Miriam out of my mind.

Calev had tried multiple times to talk to me about his father and Miriam and how all that happened, but I made it clear I didn't want to hear about it. The more the situation was mentioned, the more chance of it becoming real. In my mind anyway.

Seated in front of me, Calev kicked the horse with his heels, bumping my feet. "Don't worry about it, Kinneret," he whispered. His breath smelled like lemons. "My father is so busy with harvest preparation, he won't even ask them about me. Not until they need me. Which shouldn't be until five or so days from now, if I'm guessing right."

I looked skyward. He didn't even realize why I was grinding my teeth into nothing. At least Miriam and Calev weren't hennaed yet. The Intention ceremony hadn't yet been performed. I still had a chance. Not much of one. But still.

The horse's hooves ate the ground between Old Farm and the dock. I reveled in the feel of Calev, warm and strong, against my stomach, legs, cheek.

When we'd hopped off, Calev slapped the mare to send her home. She was used to our comings and goings.

"What's this about?" Calev asked. "I'm all for avoiding harvest prep—it's exactly as appealing as a hug from Aunt Y'hudit—but usually I know what kind of adventure you're dragging me into."

Smirking, I eyed the sun. "I'll tell you when we're on our way."

The hill slanted down to the dock where my craft bobbed in the jittery water.

Calev blew out a breath. "Last time you surprised me," he held his groin protectively, "...ugh, those spotted leeches..."

"No leeches, I promise. You'll love this trip."

"That's good," Calev said as our sandals slapped along the dock's wooden boards. "I'd take a bucket of Aunt Y'hudits over those disrespectful creatures."

I threw him a spicy grin. "You didn't lose anything important to the blood-suckers, did you?"

He grinned like a thief. "I'm fully equipped. Don't worry."

I felt like I'd sailed over an enormous swell.

Following me, Calev leaped onto the swaying deck. His feet barely missed the glass Wraith Lantern that would protect us if we didn't make some sort of landfall before sunset. Avi had sewn a new fist-width wick for it yesterday. Her long fingers were perfect for lacing the wool, iron, and pale malhatc fibers in sets of seven, three, and five.

As Avi untied us from the dock, I raised the stone anchor. The coconut-fiber rope scratched familiarly against my palms, and salt-scented water dripped from its coils.

Avi pointed to the hull. "Oron is asleep again." She hugged Calev. Her head used to bump the hilt of Calev's curved dagger, but now, she stood as high as his shoulder.

After hauling anchor, we lowered the poles into the bay's water and pushed our way into the open water of the twisting, cursed strait. The sea here was cursed, but I loved it all the same. The waters were like a prickly friend who always had something interesting to say.

Looking at the ridge of rocks and the narrow openings leading to our destination, I grinned.

"I don't like that look, Kinneret." Calev lowered his pole onto the flat planks of the deck, which made a hollow sound because the only thing below was Oron.

I set mine down, and Avi helped me tug the halyard and hoist the gaff to the mast top. Our lateen sail spread like a triangular gull's wing.

"Tell me where we're going," Avi begged, smiling.

I breathed the salt air in, loving the way it pulled at my curls. Directly in front of us, the Pass was empty of other boats. A feeling shivered through me, a tease of a freedom I didn't have. I couldn't use Salt Magic to make silver appear in my palm. But by the Fire, I could sail my way to it. I forced my features into a vicious smile, a scorching grin forged to burn through anyone's doubts, even my own.

"I will tell you. Just not yet," I said.

Calev shook his head. "Let no one say you know nothing about theatrics."

My skirt brushing my ankles, I left Avi and Calev on either sides of the tiller and used the strong josi line to force the sail into a tip toward the bow.

With the canvas like a second sky above us, we sailed close reach, at an angle going slightly into the wind. With my eyes trained on the sail and the water beyond, we sped into the Pass. Behind us, the stone wall around Calev's home faded into the distance.

I was finished with the tease. I wanted real hope.

"We're going to change our caste." I released a glance like an arrow at Calev.

The wind lashed a few loose strands of hair against my cheeks as Calev frowned, thinking. The sun glowed through the sail's dark purple fabric, casting a shadow like a bruise. Calev's tanned hand perched on my shoulder and his frown morphed into a grin.

"Are we becoming the pirates we always wished to be? If so, you probably should've brought a few more weapons. Maybe a monkey. I always wanted a monkey."

Avi laughed and chewed her braid. Fourteen was too old for hair-chewing, but I wasn't going to talk her out of any childlike habits. She could do as she liked as long as it made her happy in this harsh world.

Oron crawled out of the hull. "Flying Seastingers, people. Must you squawk like birds? What do you have against a man taking a well-deserved nap?"

Calev fought a smile and ran a sun-browned hand over Avi's hair. "Well-deserved, Oron? Don't tell me you've been sneaking around doing kind things for the masses?"

Oron grabbed for a skin of wine at his sash. As a dwarf, and three hands shorter than Avi, Oron had to look up into Calev's face. "There are more ways than one to deserve a nap." He took a hefty swallow of his stolen beverage. "Kindness to others is one, yes. But you must also consider the pursuit of a pleasant life as a valid goal. Don't you agree?"

"We have big things to discuss, Oron," I snapped. "Perhaps naps should wait for nightfall." I gave him half a grin.

"Sorry, my dear. But night is reserved for actual sleeping."

"Why I put up with you is the world's greatest mystery."

"Here I thought the mystery was whatever you all were discussing so very, very loudly." Oron plucked what appeared to be a rumpled golden dumpling from his sash and handed it to Avi. I wondered who he'd stolen that from.

Oron gave me a look that reeked of suspicion. "What was this about monkeys and pirates? If you're planning a celebration with said folk, I'm in."

"It's us who are the pirates, she says." Avi grinned.

I shook my head. "Not pirates. We're treasure hunters." That wasn't quite right either. "No, not hunters, really. We won't need to hunt. I know the way. We're going to retrieve a map to the lost island of silver."

Calev and Avi's mouths fell open, and Oron simply stared.

I nudged Calev aside to take my place at the tiller. "Ayarazi exists, and we are going to be the ones to claim it."

CHAPTER SIX

O ron's wide brow furrowed. He rammed a thick finger into his ear and jiggled it. "Did I hear her correctly?" He looked from me to Calev.

"Old Zayn told me where to find a map to Ayarazi."

Oron blinked. "When will I learn that a day with Kinneret Raza is never dull?"

The wind lagged, then gusted. The sail snapped grouchily as we rose over a swell and dipped down again.

Oron hurried to adjust the sail, his skilled hands moving faster and more sure on the line than anyone I'd ever seen on the water. When he'd first come to work for me, right after the fever took Mother and Father, I'd known he was a special person because who would offer to work for basically nothing? Only the kindest of souls. I almost felt like he'd adopted Avi and me. I hadn't known then how amazing he was with the sails. I sure as Fire knew now and I'd never let him go, no matter how much I joked.

Calev clutched the boat's side, his knuckles whitening. "What are you talking about?" He was a little green around the lips.

I gave him the tiller and brought him my skin of ginger water. "The lost island of silver."

"But that's not a real place." Avi's throat bobbed as she looked down the road of water at the rocks like broken-down carts. The biggest of the obstacles were Tall Man and the Spires.

"I heard it is," I said.

Calev took a swig from my water skin. "From who?"

"Zayn."

Calev grinned. "So the kind, but seriously very crazy old man realized how much you'd adore a chance of riches with a side of possible death and/or mutilation and offered this information."

Oron tipped his head. "Nicely put. Only brushes with Death himself sate our Kinneret here."

I shrugged them off. "It's not all that risky."

Calev squinted at the sun and held out the water skin to me. "At least this insane adventure is happening during the day."

Avi shook her head, all cynicism and muttering. "It's still dangerous." She eyed the upcoming black shapes jutting from the sea.

"We never come close to hitting those rocks, Avi," I said.

"Your idea of *close* is oceans away from mine," she hissed as I took the tiller to navigate.

As we dodged Tall Man, the boat's lee side heeled a bit more than I liked. I pulled the tiller windward, balancing her out.

"Even if it was night, Calev," I said, "we have the lantern's magic."

The domed and vented object sat behind me, lodged in a space between the tiller's housing and the side. I ran an absent hand over its glass surface. Father had made the lantern from a high-caste's discarded vase, and Mother had taught us how to weave the special wick. For as long as I'd been alive, the combination of the two had kept us safe from the Salt Wraiths, the evil spirits of those who'd died at sea.

"Lanterns aren't magic," Calev argued. "They're science. It's proven their light repels the wraiths. But repelling isn't always enough. Wraiths can be smart."

I ignored his all-too-common, close-minded view on the line between religion, magic, and science. To me, they were just different words for the same thing.

"Mother wouldn't have let this opportunity go by," I whispered, more to myself than to them. Berker's ridiculous slur about her being a liar wafted around like a bad smell.

Avi's steady gaze flicked to me. Her eyes were focused like she was about to pounce and rip my throat out. Mother and Father had always called it her *lion look*. She might not have been so good with Salt Magic, but my sister had her strengths. Determination being one of them.

"But we don't need an island of silver," she said.

"Speak for yourselves, dear friends," Oron said. "I need all the silver to do all the joyous things." He spun in a circle, jumping once and wiggling his backside.

Calev jerked his chin. "I'm with Avi. You don't need riches. Kinneret, someday you'll be the most successful small craft sailor on the Broken Coast."

If I didn't starve first. "Yeah. A successful ant in a field of horses," I muttered. "You don't know what it's like to have people push in front of you. To be refused service at the market because of bells."

To watch the boy you love be promised to a girl only because of her caste.

Maybe Miriam would be eaten by wolves on her northern trade trip with her father.

Calev frowned and glanced at Avi. I let the matter drop and smiled at the thought of Miriam running from very hairy, very toothy beasts.

To lessen our speed, we worked the halyard's pulleys and lowered the spar holding the sail aloft. After a good bit of tiller work and a few prods to the rocks with our poles, we made it through the Spires. Water splashed over the deck and wet our feet as I watched for the next obstacle—Asag's Door, a powerful eddy that had definitely earned its spirit-monster name. Another scattering of barely visible rocks sat at its end.

Not a league ahead, a sweep of lighter water showed where the door's current swept southward.

"The map lies near Quarry Isle." My voice came out louder than I'd wanted. "It's under a teardrop-shaped current."

Oron faced me, frowning, then looked around the boat, like he was searching for something. I rolled my eyes skyward at his drama. "Where is your note of permission to pass from the oramiral?" he asked, blinking his big eyes.

The oramiral was the kyros's second cousin. He was also totally and completely mad. The kyros let him reign over Quarry Isle and forced our amir to put up with the way he treated the slaves she took in wars with borderlands. It was a kink in the caste system, to be sure. Slavery was meant to prove mettle, not destroy the body and mind. It was an honor to have served. Only pure bloodlines of the desert race and the respected Old Farms were permitted to thrive outside the system.

"Did the amir herself give you leave?" Oron demanded. "Or perhaps, her new kaptan, Berker?"

"You heard about that?"

"When I'm not languishing in the arms of Lady Grape, I get around." He tweaked his ears with his fingertips. "These are not merely fantastic ornaments on my gruesome head."

My gaze traced the familiar lines around his mouth and the tilt of his eyes. I remembered, four years ago, when those eyes noticed the gaff break from the mast. He'd caught most of the sail and its support before it could land on Avi's small frame. He was the reason she could still walk.

"You aren't ugly," I said to Oron.

"Definitely not," Avi said.

"Not the point of this discussion, my dears."

Calev smiled. "Oron, your face is nothing less than legendary."

I glared at Calev.

"Don't aim those vicious eyes at him." Oron grinned.

"I didn't intend it as an insult," Calev said.

"Of course not," Oron said. "I like legendary. Makes me feel as if I really do belong on a boat with a madwoman who insists on sailing to an island born from the dreams of sailors."

The ancient wine jug was there, hidden under the water. I could feel it in the salt hiding under my nails and flaking from my cheeks.

Oron eyed me. "So we're simply going to sail right up under the oramiral's nose to the spot near the slave island where the goat man indicated and snatch some map?"

Avi made her way to my side, her eyes searching mine.

"It shouldn't be in the oramiral's waters," I said.

"A teardrop current?" Oron scratched at his tangled hair. "I know the place. It's dangerously close to his disgusting Quarry Isle. I'd argue it's past the boundary."

I always stayed well away from that section of the Pass. There were plenty of ways to ship goods and passengers from our lands, across the waters, and back again without nearing Quarry Isle.

"It'll be fine, Oron. We won't cross the boundary."

"But if you're wrong, and we do, he might not honor your bells. Or the fact that you're my employer. In fact, he'll surely nab me since I have no bells at all and am pretty obviously not Old Farm or of the desert race." He displayed a pale arm with a flourish.

"I said it's fine. We're staying in the free waters. No one will become a slave today."

Oron huffed. "As Kinneret wills, so shall the world move."

Avi chewed at the end of her braid, her eyes worried. She had to keep her nerve. I had to make this move.

Calev tapped his chin. "Avi, it'll be a few until we get there. Want to play?" He held up his hand and wiggled his fingers.

I mouthed a *thank you* as they began playing tally win. They waved hands over their laps and stopped at a count of ten. Calev displayed seven fingers, Avi two.

If I didn't change Avi's caste, along with mine, she'd lose Calev and it'd be like losing a brother. As he smiled at her, I knew he felt the same way about her. She was the sister he didn't have at home.

"Ah ha." Avi clapped once, but her eyes stayed tight, her lips pinched in worry. She pointed at Calev's fingers. "That's nine. Odd. My choice. You owe me a lemon slice."

"After all our suns playing games, I owe you lemons enough to fill the Pass," Calev said.

Avi worked at a laugh. "If we find the island of silver, I'll build a castle for my fruit. Every day you can visit and play tally win and drink lemon honey wine."

"Paradise," Calev, Oron, and I said in unison.

Avi smiled, enjoying our ongoing joke. She came up with wild imaginings and we judged them either hells or paradises.

"A pirate ship filled with monkeys," she said.

"Hells," we responded.

"A silver gilt pirate ship only slightly crowded with tiny monkeys who smell like flowers and obey our every command."

"Paradise!"

Oron looked to his sandals, smiling, and adjusted the josi line so the sail captured more wind. Avi went to help or really, it seemed, just to lean a little on Oron. He patted her arm, then squeezed it gently, and the shadows around his eyes deepened.

I kept my hand on the worn wood of the tiller, willing everyone to stay positive.

Eyeing the direction we headed, Calev brought his knees to his chin. His sandals, hidden beneath the drape of his tunic, ground salt and dirt into the decking as he fidgeted.

"The men on the slave island would've already found underwater clues to Ayarazi if there were any," he said quietly. "The oramiral used a hundred of his prisoners to scour the sea floor when they first sent him down."

From what I'd heard of the man who ran the quarries, he wore his honorary military title oramiral with a killing sneer. What had he done for the kyros to garner that cushy post?

"I don't think the oramiral knew what he was looking for." And I did.

Frowning, Calev turned toward me, then rubbed at his stomach and swallowed.

Poor thing. The Lord of the Harvest humbled. "We're looking for a wine jug." I dragged my gaze from the angle of his sharp chin and back to the sea.

From the front of the boat, Avi held a hand up to block the sun gliding over the green waves and soaking the air. A spray of water soared over us.

"It holds a map."

"Who knew a wine jug could be put to even better use than its original purpose? Color me impressed." Oron's words were as sour as those lemons Calev owed Avi.

"Kinneret." Calev jumped up. "The rocks."

I growled and jerked the tiller, bumping him back and out of my way.

The rocks churned the water, whitening it to the color of a wraith's shadow. I'd missed my mark, and we needed to reverse course and go around Asag's Door the other way. The tiller fought me.

"Avi, ready to jib!"

When Avi, Oron, and I had hands on the sheet's lines, and Calev was at the tiller again, I kicked the knot holding the sheet in place. It slipped from its wooden knob and the line ran through our hands. The sail whipped up.

"Pull the tiller to starboard," I commanded Calev.

"But won't that—"

"Do it."

He did, and when the sail's tip flashed over the spar, we tugged the sheet and brought the sail into place. The pouch at my belt was heavy with salt. If this didn't work, I had options. Magical ones. I didn't want to use Salt Magic around Calev, but if worse came to worst…

We made it around the eddy and its rocks. Avi tugged her sash back into place and her bells jingled.

Calev sucked a breath. "That was…exciting."

Oron edged a step away. "Please don't vomit. High-caste food stains."

I squeezed the tiller, wishing Oron had a much, much smaller mouth.

A ship appeared, and unfortunately, it didn't look like it was harmlessly toting lemons and wine. My stomach dropped.

"Did we pass the mark?" Oron's voice was wary.

Beyond Oron's head, sails the hue of sickness rose like the wings of an ancient flying lizard. The craft moved at a speed I'd never know unless I found Ayarazi and its silver.

Avi rushed over and handed me the spyglass. Through the tube, I saw a tall man at the prow. His yellow tunic billowed over his broad shoulders. I went cold all over. Was it the oramiral? He was rumored to be as handsome as he was cruel. His closest men were supposedly chosen for their height, so maybe it was only them and not their master.

"They're only running to the coast. They're not interested in us." My pulse ratcheted up.

Oron began to sing, slow and quiet, as Calev put a hand on Avi's back in a brotherly way. I adjusted our course, watching my sail and those of the oramiral's boat.

The craft drifted closer.

Calev pulled his dagger from the silver sheath hanging from his green sash.

No. Today was a lucky day. I had Calev. "It's not necessary," I said.

The dagger wasn't bigger than my hand and its hilt and sharp edge were decorated in intricate calligraphy. This was a piece of jewelry, not a weapon. Old Farms were known for their skills with daggers, but it was about ceremony, not killing. Calev was an innocent. And by the Fire, today would not be the day he saw blood.

"They only want to know why we're here," I said.

Avi trembled against me. "Shouldn't we try to sail away from them?"

"We couldn't outrun them on my best day, Sister." I wiggled the bells on her sash, then shook the ones on my own red one. "We remember so they remember."

It was the old line. If one's family had served, one should not have to serve again. It was respectful to have been a slave, then rise to middle or high-caste. Falling into slavery again was seen as a complete and total failure. A failure to rise, to survive, to swim strong in life on the Broken Coast. Was there any chance the oramiral would hold to the old line?

Closing his eyes, Calev inhaled, his chest rising and falling.

Oron pinched his lips together.

What would Father or Mother have done? I ran a finger over the sickle-shaped scar on my forearm—all that was left from the fever blisters that made my sister and me ill, but stole life from my parents.

A spot two fingers past our view of the oramiral's ship undulated with an odd current. It was the teardrop shape in the water. The spot Old Zayn had told me about. Excitement fluttered through my chest. "There's the place. The teardrop."

But no one responded, their gazes locked on the other boat. Was the oramiral's ship getting closer? Or were they turning her?

Something stung my ear and I touched my lobe. My fingers came away bloody. An arrow. I blinked, unbelieving. "They fired on us."

The arrow had missed me, going into the sea.

Oron swore. We all ducked low.

"It was just a warning shot," I said, desperate to be right. Everything was going to be fine. It had to be. My blood shushed through my veins.

Oron grabbed the lucky frog's leg hanging from the cord at his neck as the oramiral's ship leaped over the waves, coming at us now with frightening speed. The sails arched into the sky, impossibly big, dangerously close.

Calev urged Avi toward the hull. Her braid trailed her like a lit fuse and Oron disappeared behind her into the darkness.

"I'll tell him who I am. They won't make trouble with me." Calev's firm hold on the dagger turned his farmer's fingers into a soldier's hand. But he was no fighter. It was all a ruse. A rich boy playacting. "I'll tell him we're on a fishing day trip," he said. "You go below, too."

"I'm not hiding. Besides, if I can see him, he can see me." I tied the tiller off and tugged my blade from my sash. The beads of steel on the hilt gripped me back. "Drop sail. I'm not leaving without my map. You're right. They'll listen to you. And I'm not leaving."

Calev's wide sleeves fell back as he hauled the sail in, showing his lean muscular arms, browned from working outside. "You don't really want to argue about boundaries with the oramiral's men. They're—"

"Lay down your weapons, trespassers," a voice boomed from a speaking cylinder.

The owner of the voice hung from the oramiral's sails like a long, slim monkey. He flipped and landed next to his mates, most of whom wore the same slave bell contraption as he did. Metal circle around the waist of his tunic and his chest. Bar attached at the back, reaching past the head where the noisemaker clanked with every move. The slaves, dressed in fine, yellow silk, like the monkey-faced leader, drew back crossbows while the more ragged slaves, in gray tunics, nocked arrows. Together they formed a wall of flashing metal, wood, feather, and muscle, the one with the speaking cylinder in the middle.

With eyes like scorched wood, Calev raised his dagger. His arm brushed mine. He was beautiful, even in his terror. His gaze jerked from slave to slave, but his hands were steady. One strand of hair hung over his finely shaped lips.

I put my hand on his arm and lowered his weapon. "Just talk to them."

He squeezed his eyes closed and nodded. Avi sneezed from the hull and Calev took my hand.

"Bring them aboard," the leader said.

The biggest men of the bunch threw grappling hooks, and my heart snagged on a beat. I ran at the flying links, as if I could somehow stop this, but the hooks dug into the side of my boat like Kurakian fanged snakes. The slaves tugged the attached ropes, and Calev grabbed me as our boat surged toward the full ship.

"I'm Old Farm." Calev pushed himself between me and the three men leaping onto the deck. "My father is the—"

A slave threw an arm toward Calev's head, but Calev stopped the blow with his forearm, surprising me with his speed and power.

Avi screamed. When had she come back up? The wind gusted, and the sad piece of twine at the end of her braid tumbled into the waves.

I pushed her toward Oron's pale face. "Get back down there."

Oron stood at the hull's small opening, hand open and ready to catch Avi.

"Too late." The second man grinned, standing on starboard, then hopped down, grabbed Avi by the arms, and dragged her toward the side.

The world grayed for a beat.

Then I tore at Avi, trying to get a hold. "Didn't you hear him?" I shouted at the second man. "He's Old Farm. You can't treat him like this. The chairman is his father, associate to Amir Mamluk of Jakobden."

The slave kicked me in the stomach. The strike stole my breath, and I fell into Calev and Oron, who struggled with the other two slaves.

The slave threw Avi to his crew mates on the oramiral's ship. "We're not doing anything to the Old Farm, as long as he doesn't get in the way. We're just taking this one to punish you for crossing into forbidden waters. You're lucky we're not coloring the sea with your blood and hers, girl." He spat.

Dodging the spittle, I scrambled to my feet. My stomach clenched, heaved. I had to get Avi. "We're not in your master's territory. These are free waters."

From the side of the boat, he reached down and grabbed hold of my hair. Fire lashed from my scalp and down my neck. He threw me back and my elbow cracked against the mast, shooting sparks up my arm.

He and his crew mates rushed to their ship, tugging the hooks free on their way.

No. This wasn't going to happen. They couldn't take my sister. "I won't let you do this." Sweat bled down my cheeks as I fought my way to standing. "That girl's family already served. She has the bells to prove it." My voice was snake and storm and desert and it wasn't nearly enough. "You must give her back." I threw myself toward the larger boat, but couldn't make the jump. I fell against the side and tumbled back onto my boat, hitting the wood with a series of smacks and loud knocks I, for some reason, didn't feel. With Calev's help, I scrambled up again, dizzy. They had her. My Avi. My sister. My dear, kind, smart little love. I shrieked, hot and cold coursing through me.

"You'll regret this," Calev hissed at the men, his face carved into angry lines and ferocious shadows. "The oramiral will never sell another piece of stone in Jakobden."

But they didn't care.

The ship roared away.

With scratched and bleeding hands, I clutched my rolling stomach, tore at my hair.

I had to be asleep. This could not be reality.

A small cannon shot boomed, and after a puff of black smoke, the snarl of ripping fabric filled my ears. My ribs like firebrands and my head a pincushion, I stared at the triangle of my sail. Right in the middle, a circle of sunset sky marred the deep purple. Threads danced from the hole like flames.

"Come back again," the slave's voice spun out of the speaking cylinder and through the air , "and we'll take the lot of you. Best of luck with the Salt Wraiths!"

I fell to my knees beside Oron and Calev, who stood at the mast. Fear showed itself in the way they held themselves, the way they didn't breathe, the way they looked at the ruined sail.

Night was coming. We had no sail. And my Avi, my sweet sister, was gone.

CHAPTER SEVEN

"We'll go to my father. He and the others will rescue Avigail." Calev stared into my eyes. His hands lifted like he might try to hold me, but he dropped them.

Y'hoshua ben Aharon might help. Maybe because I'd saved Calev's life when we were little. Maybe because I had a little Old Farm in me. Maybe because he didn't treat me like he did other low-castes. Maybe maybe maybe.

I stood dumbly, shaking and trying not to scream.

A memory of Mother teaching Avi to weave the wraith wick flickered in my mind. Mother's hand reached across the tiller to help my sister add another row of iron-laced threading. We'd bought the stuff after a trip to Kurakia, where Mother's sister, Aunt Kania Turay, lived.

Visiting her tower house and farm felt as unnatural as walking on my hands. The sea hardly played a role in her days. I could never live as a Kurakian. I'd pulled at the neck of my shirt, feeling choked just thinking about a life without the sea.

"Keep the sevens of the outer part heavy on the iron," Mother had said that day long ago.

Avi had chewed her tongue as she worked the fibers into a neat braid.

"You're good at this," I said.

She smiled up at me and the sunrise glowed across her baby-fine skin. "I'm going to show Calev. You should do your magic for him."

Mother's eyes pinched a little at the sides. Then her face cleared. She touched my hand and Avi's. "You both have talents that will serve you." A spark glittered in her eye as she walked with me to the low-sided sea salt tray she'd left out on the dock beside our tied-down boat. She scooped a handful into the pouch at her sash. I did the same.

"Today, as all the women of our blood have done," she said, "you will learn to call the sea's wind."

I shivered like someone had dusted me with the waterflakes Calev told me fell from the sky in the North.

Father arrived and helped a man load our hull with lemons, and we set sail.

Leaning against port, Mother dipped elegant fingers into her salt pouch and they emerged sparkling white, a contrast to her warm, dark skin. The wind kicked its feet and helped the sea take some of its lifeblood back, the salt dancing up and out into the waves.

"I think the sea's wind is already here," I said.

"Ah, but it is up to you to ask it for a favor. Not easy when the sea is full of spirit. Now you will say this prayer—"

I took my own handful of salt and let the salt drift away.

"Hear me, sea.

Feel my will.

Bend the wind so we may reach another land."

The deck swooped under my feet, and Mother and I grabbed the side. Avi squealed and ran to Mother as Father called from the tiller.

"Kinneret Raza. Take care with your prayers."

The water licked at the boat like a thirsty dog and the air wheeled us around so that the sail pressed against the mast in a foul, aback position.

After we'd worked into a good tack again, Mother took my salt-rough hands in hers.

"You have great magic in you, daughter. Respect it. Learn first. Then it will be a help instead of a hindrance."

"But you like trouble."

"There is a difference between trouble and danger." She smiled sadly and turned away. "I suppose you'll have to learn that for yourself."

The memory dissolved.

The horror of now clawed its way through me. I gripped my skirt in shaking hands.

"It isn't getting any brighter out here." Oron's voice was barely a whisper above the water lapping and the clink of metal trappings.

He was trying to keep my mind off Avi. I looked at him, wanting to see that unmovable strength Oron's eyes usually housed, but tears wet his eyelashes.

Calev shut his eyes, took a breath, then opened them. Fear and determination swirled in their walnut depths. "We'll get her back, Kinneret."

I swallowed and stood on weak-kneed legs. "She won't survive long enough to participate in the testing for the apprenticeships. She's so frail. I never thought...I should've...I need to make a plan. Gather allies. Something."

The purpling sky told me we didn't have the sun to properly repair the sail. I went straight for the salt in my bag, hating what I knew Calev would think of it.

He stopped me with a hand, his gaze sliding to the salt. "Can't we just fix the hole?"

I gave him a look. "We'll sew it up as best we can. We'll use the Wraith Lantern when the sun falls. But we'll need the magic. Or we'll be out here all night. And I don't think you want that."

Calev grimaced. Though Old Farms weren't in charge of Outcasting anyone, they didn't like Salt Magic any more than the rest of Jakobden. They deemed it low and uneducated superstition. But Calev wasn't just any Old Farm. He was more.

I studied his face for clues. "You had to know I use the salt."

He eyed the sky. "I did, but I hoped it was only that once."

"At the cape during the storm?"

His dark eyes were honest, his mouth a frown. "Use what you need to, Kinneret."

"It's no different from your prayers." I was pushing him, but it had to be done.

"Is that really how you see it?" His voice was gentle, earnest. My eyes burned, but I willed those tears back inside my lids. If I cried now, I wouldn't stop and I'd be pointless to everyone.

Calev swallowed. "It's forcing your will. Our prayers show respect, use the proper language. We don't demand immediate displays of power like Salt Magic does. Even the Holy Fire is more humble than the salt. They at least wait for wisdom. There are no demands or heavy requests."

"It is the same...I..." I stuttered, my eyes swimming. "Calev. This is the skill my mother taught me. She used to cup my hands in hers and I remember watching her lips move in and around words and smiles. When I use the magic, it's like she's here again, holding my hand, her voice in my ear."

Touching the raised embroidery on his sleeve, I blinked and blinked again. "You have to agree—I need this now." I didn't know why I wanted him to be okay with this. But somehow, it seemed important that he was behind me.

He gave me a sad smile and put his fingers over mine. They stilled my shaking a little. "I'll try to understand," he said. "For you."

"That's all I ask."

Oron was already lowering the damaged sail.

Boards set loosely in place around the tiller gave us a place to sit out of the uneven and oftentimes damp bottom of the boat. I drew out a box of sewing supplies from under the wooden planks.

I'd call the sea and persuade it to move us the way we needed to go, get Calev and Oron safely to shore, then let my tears come, my rage overtake me, and my fear for Avi strip me to bare bones.

Shoving those thoughts to the back of my mind, I kept my hands busy by threading the stout bone needle.

Using a strip of extra cloth, we sewed the hole closed as best we could, fingers working against the setting sun. When the moon did come, it hung low in the sky like an old man's cloudy eye. When the cloud swam away from the orb, the brightness scattered gooseflesh over my arms. If a Salt Wraith came now, we would be trapped in its shadow, Infused, our minds twisted to lust for blood and death.

Helping Oron and Calev hoist the gaff and position the sail for beam reach, I stared into the darkening waters and pictured Avi's fingers wrapped around a quarry pick.

"Kinneret." Calev shook my shoulder, and I blinked. "We must go," he said. "How can I help?" His voice broke on his last word and he swallowed, his throat moving.

I realized I was standing there like a fool. Sucking a breath, I pointed at the bow. "Keep watch for rocks. Call out if you see anything." I didn't want to say wraiths.

Oron took the tiller. "I'll keep her even." His quiet voice chilled me. He didn't sound like himself at all.

"Thank you." I joined Calev at the bow.

The wind was nonexistent. We were becalmed. I forced a breath out of my nose. We'd never rescue Avi if the oramiral's men caught us or if we killed one another under a wraith's control.

The salt from my pouch was dry. Dry worked, but not as well as salt touched by fresh sea water. Blinking a strand of hair from my eyes, I bent, scooped a handful of cold water, and dashed it into the small bag.

Sprinkling a fistful of the dampened salt into the wind—more than I'd ever used—I cooed a sea prayer.

"Accept this gift, bold sea.
Breathe life into our sail.
Draw your currents near."

Was there a limit on the sea's patience? Maybe not.

The air, raised by the Salt Magic, shushed gently past my face, and the boat lurched forward. Calev slipped, and I caught him, hearing a thud from the tiller.

Oron had rolled off to one side. He swore as he righted himself. "My mother's third—"

"Where did you learn to talk like you do?" Calev's knuckles whitened on the boat's side, but I didn't think it was from Oron's foul mouth. His chin lifted as he scanned the thankfully empty night sky.

"Watch our lean, Oron," I said. We were heeling to leeward. A little more and we'd be thrown into the water.

"I was raised in a roadside brothel by a mother who fancied traveling theatre players," Oron said to Calev, his words whipping toward us as the wind rose even higher, and we sped forward. "I speak the tongue of the wicked and witty."

To keep our conversation off what had happened, to keep myself from jerking the tiller from Oron and turning us back and raging toward the oramiral to battle for my sister and lose, I picked up the distracting thread of talk.

"Surprised you never heard that one," I said to Calev. "It's his favorite line."

Moonlight slipped over Calev's hair. It rolled down his skull and sat on his broad farmer's shoulders like a death shroud. I tightened my sash's knot and pulled my sleeves lower on my arms.

"I'll take the tiller now." I moved to aft.

Asag's Door was quieter, though white caps still curled around the bases of the rocks. With the gusts and Oron at the sail, I pulled the tiller and guided us through the Spires. It was low tide now. The boat responded to me, shifting under my body like a horse. The sea had listened and sent us wind and soon we'd be home. If the Salt Wraiths let us be.

Calev came to the tiller with me and Oron moved to watch at the bow.

Calev tried to laugh. "Oron and I haven't had the opportunity to talk as much as I would like."

This was ridiculous, us trying to be brave and making jokes. Black shadows and streaks of moonlight used my imagination to turn the water and rocks into a slithering beast waiting for us to make one wrong move.

"He has the best foul language. I could pick up some tantalizing bits from him to shock Eleazar," Calev said.

I tried to smile, but all I could think was right now Avi was being led up the steep side of Quarry Isle. They would fit a bell contraption around her waist.

How were we going to persuade Calev's father to use his influence to get her back? Old Farm had never interfered with the oramiral. At least to my knowledge. It hadn't come up. Being people of the land, all Old Farms, except their full ship kaptan, stayed clear of the sea. Similar to my aunt's people in Kurakia, across the Pass.

Avi. My brave little Avi. How are we going to rescue you?

A grin trembled on Calev's lips but fled when Oron made a choking noise near the mast. We jumped up.

"They're here." Oron pointed to the western sky.

All the blood in my head drained into my feet. Salt Wraiths.

I whipped my flint and dagger out of my sash. We had to get the lantern lit. Now.

Calev held the Wraith Lantern's miniature door open. My flint sparked onto the wick, but it didn't flame.

A swooping noise like a tree limb swinging through the air stung my ears. The sparkling white of one Salt Wraith whisked between the moon and us, but far enough away that we could barely see it. Its soul-and-mind-possessing shadow didn't touch us, but it soared closer. I dragged the flint over the dagger again. The wick caught fire and blazed bright. Calev slammed the opening shut to keep the wind from putting out the strange flame.

Seeing the orange, black, and silver flickers, the wraith reared and disappeared in the distance.

Hanging the lantern on the mast's hook, Calev sighed. "That was too close."

"It might come back." As I made my way back to the tiller, I studied the fire encased in the glass. A flash of silver rose and fell, then a glint of orange.

"We need to squeeze into the hull." Feet first, Oron lowered himself through the square opening.

"We won't all fit in there." I raised my gaze to the sky.

"I told you we needed an on-deck compartment for ropes and water," Oron called out of the space. "If you'd let me buy the wood to build one, you could've tucked me in there. Being lesser in stature might be an advantage. Who knows? In one hundred years, we small people might be the only ones left."

A look dark as the Expanse's greatest depths crossed over Calev's face. "Let Kinneret in there first, coward."

I looked at Calev's hands as he stood beside me. "You're trembling too," I said. "I wouldn't cast labels around so easily."

"Courage isn't not being afraid," Calev said. "It's standing and fighting through your fear. Protecting those you love." His eyes softened. "Not that I have to tell you."

My heart skittered through three quick beats, and I looked away.

"I'll go down if I think it's necessary," I called out to Oron. "Someone has to get us home."

Whispering the sea's words over and over again under my breath, I worked with the magic to veer and tug, push and pull our craft toward Tall Man, toward home. Calev stayed by my side. The lantern's sunset light flickered over his cheekbones and his forearms. He looked made of flame.

Stars pierced the velvet sky. The moon watched, its candle-white glow melting onto the sea. Eventually, Oron climbed out of the hull. Calev stared at him, eyes slitted.

"Oron, will you see to the prow?" I asked. The tiller vibrated against my hand, a current fighting our direction. "I want your eyes on the waters."

Rubbing his small hands together, Oron nodded but didn't exactly hurry to his post.

"In case you decide to condemn me for cowardice, you should know I witnessed a wraith Infusing an entire full ship's crew," Oron said to Calev. "And yes, I can feel that scornful glare through the tunic on my back."

"What happened?" Calev asked.

The sail billowed in a gust and the ropes pulled against the blocks. The pulleys knocked against the mast like hammers.

Staring out at the sky, Oron crossed his arms over his chest. "A flock of nine came."

"Nine wraiths?"

Nodding, Oron said, "They spun around the vessel like the skin of the moon had been peeled away and tossed into the wind. The emotions whisked over me though I was a good league away on another boat. Rage, the desire to inflict control...it was..." He bent his head. "When the wraiths left, I watched their Infusion lights leave the sailors' mouths and leak back into the sky. We boarded their ship—I rode with a fishing crew then—there was nothing left alive. Men had hung themselves from the boom, their bodies swaying with the movement of the sea, their tongues swollen, eyes popped clean out. Blood covered the decking. I slipped in it. Drew up against a pile of men who'd either fallen on their own yatagans or been murdered by their Infused crew mates."

He ran a hand over the fat tangles of his hair.

"So when I go to the hull, you'd be wise to follow. We should all squeeze in there like happy sardines."

The whooshing sound returned. Calev looked to me. Oron swore. Another wraith.

The whispering began. Hissing, sighing, moaning in my ears.

I covered my head with my hands and the remainder of the salt I'd used rained onto my face and hair.

Oron was already back in the cabin. Calev grabbed my arm and dragged me toward the tiny space. We'd never fit. Besides, someone had to make sure the lantern didn't fall over or go out. If it did, the wraiths would swamp us and cover us in their whitewashed shadows—their way of possessing mind and body—and it'd all be over. We either had to be under the shadow of a solid roof in the hull or swamped in the Wraith Lantern's light.

I snatched the lantern and crawled into the hull behind Calev. Turning, he pulled my back against his stomach and wrapped his arm around me to help me hold the lantern up. His fingers lay on mine, his hips pressing into me. Both of us were shaking against one another as the sounds increased. Oron had to be suffocating behind us. The air was hot and moist with our breath. Our feet stirred up the pungent scent of old lemons and last year's barley, remnants of the shipments we'd made over our lifetimes.

We lifted the lantern as the wraith came screaming toward us. The light spun a web of colors over my forearms, but this creature was strong and some of its power crept under and over the flickering orange and silver. Emotions flooded my mind, rushing in like boiling waves, filling in every crack of my thoughts, my heart.

CHAPTER EIGHT

I tried to scream as Calev's hand fell from the lantern. He yelled, but it sounded far, far away.

Anger. So much anger burned, burned, burned in my veins, my hands, my head. Wild sadness, too. Then I was falling, and the sea was a gaping hole beneath us. A mouth. A well. An abyss, far under the earth's crust.

We would fall forever.

My hands slipped and moonlight darted into our hiding place, breaking the nightmare hallucination. I jerked the lantern up again, my fingers burning as I squeezed.

"Kinneret!" Oron shouted, then moaned.

Seething, swirling, my hands were not my own. I bit down on my lip, bringing blood to wake myself. I refused to be Infused. Their shadow wasn't touching flesh. I was fine. Fine.

Calev's hands found my sides, shaking but firm. I closed my eyes, soaking in his warmth like it would save me. His body pressed against mine. Every bump, curve, bone, and breath of him kept my heart beating, held my mind in check.

"Come closer," he said through gritted teeth.

The wraith screamed.

His body jolted.

"We can move back farther..." He breathed the words along my neck, making me shiver.

Another wave of blood lust washed over me. My breath hitched. I couldn't cry, because if I fell apart now, we'd be lost. They didn't know how to use the salt, and we were still too far from shore for swimming. The currents would take us to the Expanse. There'd be no coming back.

I whispered the sea's words again, chanting them into the rise and fall of the wraith's emotions. The boat surged, close to the wind, the sea answering me, the Fire helping me.

It wasn't working. All I could see was blood and hate roared in my ears. Then, as suddenly as it had come, the feeling eased, cooled, and lessened. I could breathe again. The sweeping sounds receded, and the anger drew away. The wraiths were leaving.

I collapsed, leaning out of the hull's opening. Calev helped me the rest of the way free and pulled me to standing. His tunic smelled like sun-warmed earth and crushed lemon leaves. I buried my face in his neck, wishing he would always be my safety, my place to come home to, instead of becoming that Old Farm girl's Intended.

"Near death experiences do lend themselves to salacious behavior, but do you mind waiting until we reach the shore?" Oron found his feet and dusted himself off. "Unlike my dear old mother, I'm not open with all things love. I rather like to be included when such activities are afoot." He peeked around Calev's arm, his brows raised. He took my hand in his, kissed it kindly, and pressed it to his forehead. "You were so close to it and still you didn't succumb. I'm not half the man you are, Kinneret."

"That's the truth," Calev said quietly.

My heart grew a little at their praise. But Avi's face flashed through my mind. I wasn't half the woman she'd someday be. I would rescue her. Doubt wasn't even in the same universe as me.

A sapphire cloud smothered the moon, promising rain and a veil of protection from the wraiths' infusing shadows. The mainsail had come loose and it flickered like a serpent's tongue, but with a bit more magic and a few more prayers, we sailed into Amir Mamluk's most southern port on the Broken Coast.

We were home.

The boat bumped the docking and Oron tied us down with Calev's help.

"I'll go to the amir. I've brought some of her surplus across the Pass, and a few passengers. Plus my low prices bring all the kaptans' charges down. Well, once in a while. People like Avi and me are good for Jakobden. Right?" I pressed a hand against my pounding temple. "I'm lying to myself, aren't I? Why would an amir care about us?"

Calev's normally smiling lips twisted and he stared down at the rope in his hands.

"Tell me something good." I knocked the tiller into its resting spot and climbed out to stand beside them, my heart shushing blood too quickly into my fingertips.

"No, maybe you're right. It is in her best interest to have talented Pass sailors." He met my gaze, his eyes steady as the horizon. "But shouldn't we try to talk my father into helping us first?"

I sighed, feeling like I held a sack of oats on each shoulder. He was certainly very careful not to say *my high-caste father*. A bitter taste stung my mouth. But his suggestion was a wise one. And it wasn't his fault he'd been born high and me low. It'd never been his fault.

"Yes," I said. "We should."

"That'll be entertaining," Oron said as he leaped off the boat and followed us up the hill. "The chairman of Old Farm might teach me a few new naughty words when he learns his eldest tangled with the oramiral and now the whelp who started the whole thing wants his help."

I stopped. He had a point.

"Shut it, Oron," Calev said. "Come on, Kinneret. He'll listen. He has accepted our friendship."

"He gave up and let you sneak around town with me. It's all been jokes and being children together. This is different. You think he'll be okay with risking his life and his people's lives to get a low-caste sailor's sister back? Hmm. I know he's a good man, Calev, but...I don't know."

We took the bend in the dirt road and headed toward Old Farm.

Calev studied the ground. "I trust my father."

"Oh, I trust him too, Calev," Oron said, walking with his chin held high. He touched the shamar yam at Old Farm's gate before each of us did the same. "I trust him to say 'Absolutely not.'"

Calev bunched Oron's tunic in his fists. "Maybe you should go back to the tavern and sleep off your mood."

I put hands between them. "He's right, Oron. Go on. It won't help me make my case if you joke around the whole time."

His lips parted, but he kept silent, shaking his head violently. "Fine. Go on. Be fools. It's not as if I've ever been able to change your mind on anything, Kinneret Raza."

He stormed back the way we'd come, a chunk of my heart going with him.

Calev touched my elbow, his dark eyes were black in the night.

With a sigh, I walked on with Calev. His father would either help or he wouldn't. We had to at least try.

Passing the ritual bath house, carved from a rock outcropping, I inhaled the scent of ceremonial oils and fresh water. Old Farms bathed there once a moon.

Last cycle, hidden in a tall basket, I'd watched Calev participate in the ceremony. He didn't understand why I was curious, but to me the ceremony was foreign, mysterious, something to be studied and treasured. He claimed it wasn't so mysterious, that it wasn't such a huge deal.

But if the ritual was taken from him, if he were Outcasted for getting too close to me after our Age Day, he would miss it then. He might deny it now, but I'd seen him coming up out of the sacred waters. His wet hair showed the shape of his skull and highlighted his large eyes, his nose, and his perfectly lobed mouth.

With his smile, he looked like a creature from the heavens, perfectly glowing and peaceful and happy. A black-robed soul-teacher dripped golden oil over Calev's naked head as he stepped forward. His white tunic, a second-skin over his lean chest and flat stomach, bled water onto the stone floor.

The experience had stolen my breath.

Now, as the square shape of the ritual bath house faded into the dark behind us, I wished I could go there and be blessed. I wanted to be reborn, stronger and wiser, ready for what was coming. But I wasn't Old Farm and I had to find my own path to a blessing.

Fatigue tugging at me, I followed Calev under the cedar lintel and entered the whitewashed stone walls of the Old Farm group house. Clay oil lamps set in triangular niches gave the room a yellow glow. Y'hoshua ben Aharon, Calev's illustrious father, sat at a long table with three other men and two women. Calev's brother, Eleazar, brought his father a leather-bound book, pointed to one of the pages, and said something about barley.

Y'hoshua untucked his beard from between the table and his stomach. "Talk to Ezra. He'll know how to handle it."

"Father." Calev stood in front of the table, his voice taking on what I liked to call *Lord of the Harvest tone.*

Everyone in the room paused to look us up and down. We were a disaster of torn clothing and rising bruises.

Miriam came forward, spindle-stick in hand, and whispered Calev's name. Her wide gaze drank him in, and I hated her more at that moment than I ever had an innocent person. It wasn't her fault she was set to be the one to share his bed and feel his kisses.

Her lips were thin though. I bet her kisses would be as delightful as mouthing two nasty, little eels.

"Where have you been?" Y'hoshua pushed away from the table, knocking over a bowl of black figs. He put his hands on Calev's shoulders. I hadn't realized Calev was the same height as him now. "Are you injured? Who did this to you? The harvest should've begun today at sunset."

"Surely not," Calev said. "The harvest wasn't ready. I checked just before I left."

"It's my fault." My bells jingled as the people seated at the table spoke to one another quietly. "I took him out on my boat. We sailed near Quarry Isle, and the oramiral's men took my sister as punishment for coming too close to their territory."

Y'hoshua's hands fell to his sides. "But you're not seriously injured, my son?"

"No, Father, I'm fine, but Avigail—"

Y'hoshua pulled Calev toward his room. "Then you must make ready for the ceremony." He pushed him through the double doors, still talking as he turned away. "You will lead the first ceremonial cart. You have the best voice for the singing, my good son."

He was chittering about the harvest ceremony? Now? "We need your help, Chairman Y'hoshua. Didn't you hear me?"

Calev's father wove through the crowd, back to the table where four people at once talked about the harvest feast and about the family who'd earned the honor of driving the cart carrying the first sheaves of barley for the blessing.

"Wait." Calev tried to follow Y'hoshua, but a woman with thick eyebrows held him back.

She chattered to another man while they removed his sash and dagger. "Your harvest tunic is the perfect shade. It will set off the gold of the ceremonial scythe."

I swallowed a bitter taste in my mouth and stood straighter. What could I say to get these people to stop fooling around with clothing and be serious?

Calev looked at me, his jaw set, as the eyebrow woman tugged his headtie off and replaced it with one the color of a harvest moon. Taking the woman by the arms, he gently, but firmly moved her away.

"Give me a moment, Rachel," he said, marching toward his father in the adjoining room. "Father. Please, listen. We need to go after Kinneret's sister now. The oramiral—"

Y'hoshua's face grew stormy and Eleazar backed away. "No, we do not need to go now," Y'hoshua said. "You have a responsibility to your people, Calev."

"As if I don't know that, Father." Pain colored his words. "I'm proud of who we are. We are the kind of people who help others. If you'll just send a group to Quarry Isle—"

"We have never, in over five hundred years, harvested without the chairman's eldest performing the ceremonial blessing. You have a vital role to play, Calev. We will do what we can for the girl after the harvest."

My heart shot into my throat like a cannonball. "After the harvest? She could be attacked for her portion of food while we wait. Strangled while the others sleep. Children are found dead all the time—especially smart ones who stand to gain apprentice spots come test day. The oramiral lets it all go to chaos. You know this."

"I know how life on Old Farm is." Y'hoshua's voice was a crack of lightning. "We have an agreement with the amir and her lord, the kyros. Dealings with the oramiral are a part of that. Believe me, I detest the man. I visited the quarries once." His eyes brightened like he had a fever. "And never again, if I can help it. The man...he..." Y'hoshua gritted his teeth. "At every quarter meeting, I argue against his treatment of the slaves, how he should free them after seven years as we do, but the amir will not agree to it. And I will not push her. If we don't make our way of life our top priority, we lose it." His cheeks above his beard flushed. Calev looked ill as his father pulled him close to his face. "We haven't held on through Quest knights, kyros, amirs, coast raiders, and northern men by losing our focus for those foolish enough to tangle horns with men like the oramiral."

I choked on a sob, stunned. Calev called my name. Turning, I pushed through the crowd of Old Farms and headed for the door. As I fled from the house, a voice snaked through the chaos.

"...she's going to turn him into an Outcast. I know it."

My sandals pounded the dusty path as I ran toward the town gates.

An Outcast.

I imagined Calev in a torn tunic shoveling muck out of a horse's stall. Beyond the stable, he stares at a window. Candlelight illuminates the shapes of his father and brother laughing and handing food across the table. His gaze drops to his bare, dirtied feet and he thinks one name. *Kinneret.* But I wouldn't do that to him. I would never try to pull him away from his people or urge him to forget what they held important.

But somehow, some way, I had to get Avi back. My lungs burned and tears pushed at my eyes, wanting to fall.

That man. Y'hoshua ben Aharon.

I'd thought of him as a step-father of sorts. He'd given my parents and myself a fair amount of business—sending surplus grains to ports down the coast—despite how his people saw us and our ways. I couldn't believe he didn't care about Avi at all. He knew Calev was close to us. It wasn't as if he didn't know every time he sent his son to study with Old Zayn that I would most likely be there. But our relationship with Calev wasn't enough to put us above a harvest celebration.

A tear leaked from my eye and I dragged a quick hand over it, erasing it. Fine.

I'd go to the amir on my own. I'd remind her of the constant service my parents and I'd provided for Jakobden's trade and economy. It probably wouldn't work. She'd probably serve my impertinent head to the kyros on a silver tray next time he came to visit. But I had to do something.

The massive doors into town were rough under my fists. "Entry!" I shouted up at the man in the tower.

Leering, he cranked the gate open a slice, and I slipped through. "Hurry up, scrapper," he called down.

Calev ran up behind me, his hair tangled and his sash still missing. "Kinneret."

When I walked on, he grabbed my sleeve. "Wait," he pleaded.

"I'm going to see the amir."

"You can't. It's late. She won't see anyone right now. Let alone…"

"Let alone a low-caste like me?" I laughed meanly.

"That's not what I meant."

"It is." I turned and rubbed more salty tears from my face.

Calev let out a growl of frustration and began mumbling under his breath. "He loves to dress me up and show me off, but he never listens when it's important."

He was talking about his father.

I took a breath. "He does sometimes. Like when that soul-teacher died and you named his replacement."

"Okay. Once, he listened. He probably had Isaac in mind for the position anyway. Kinneret." He touched my sleeve. "Tomorrow, we can go to the amir together." His words hummed like a good drum. I closed my eyes, reveling in their comfort.

"All right. Tomorrow." It was selfish. Dangerous. But we could handle it. I wouldn't do anything that would show my feelings for Calev. We'd just make a reasonable argument, touching on Avi's future contribution to the amir's town and maybe play on her pride. The oramiral took one of her people without proper cause and all that.

In tense silence, Calev walked me to the tavern's undercroft. I gave him a quick nod before shutting the door to his concerned face. I didn't want him to see me cry any more. If I was ever going to be respected, I couldn't weep like a child. Even though everything inside wanted nothing more than to crumble against Oron's snoring form and do just that.

As I lay down to sleep, Oron rumbling at my feet, I sighed. I shouldn't have snapped at Calev. He didn't think I was less than him because of caste. When we were still children, he'd struggled with it, but he'd risen above the prejudice.

A memory tugged me away from my cold, dark fear for Avi.

When Calev and I were ten, we stole a bowl of tatlilav from the old tavern's kitchen.

In that memory, Calev had held the container of fermented mare's milk in both hands. "I could've bought this, you know."

I'd shamed him with a look. Even then, I'd been good at that.

He had stared at his sandals. "I'm only saying…"

"Stealing is more fun and you know it."

Taking the drink from him, I gulped the almond-tasting alcohol. It warmed my throat on its way down.

"True." Grinning, he took the bowl back. When the horse milk touched his tongue, he spat and made a face like he'd just tasted dung.

"Not your favorite, huh?" I said. His face was too funny. Like a rooster who'd had his tail plucked.

The tavern's back door banged open, and Calev and I yelped as the hefty keeper shouted, "Ah!"

The tatlilav ended up in the dirt, the bowl overturned beside a set of broken wagon wheels.

"What is this?" the keeper demanded, his gaze on Calev. I stood between them. "You can't prove anything."

"I wasn't talking to you, scrapper. Witch." The keeper made a circle on his forehead with his thumb, the Fire's sign.

My cheeks burned hot as the manure-scented, summer air. "My father is Old Farm's chairman," Calev said. "He…needed a drink and—"

Furious at the keeper and my own humiliation, I pushed Calev back a step. "His father will pay for the tatlilav."

Ten-year-old Calev scowled at me. "I was talking to the merchant."

"So?" I crossed my arms.

"Step away, low-caste, and let the Old Farm speak," the keeper said.

My gaze flew from the man to Calev, who didn't look like himself at all. Haughty. Proud. Separate.

"Yes, low-caste," Calev said, his chest moving up and down too quickly. "Don't interrupt."

"What?" I was going to be sick right here, on their feet, on my feet, on that delicious bowl of tatlilav we'd dropped.

Calev's face fell. He put a hand on my arm. "I'm so sorry. It's just you always interrupt... and I thought maybe—"

The keeper growled, but his eyes had gone soft. "Go on, the both of you. Before I change my mind and have your hands lopped off."

I started to argue, but Calev pulled me down the dusty road. "Mind your companions, Old Farm," the keeper called out.

At the town gate, Calev urged me into the wall's shadow, his eyes bright in the darker space. People passed, on their way to the market, to their homes, to business, and all their faces seemed to turn to us and wonder why someone like Calev would be talking to someone like me. I shuddered.

"Say you forgive me." Calev was pale. His hand tightened on my arm. "Please."

My stomach twisted.

Calev leaned his forehead against mine. His eyelashes were so, so long, and his breath was warm and soft. "I don't care about castes and you know that. If anything, you should be high and me low. I'm the one who forgets my own mind the second we get in trouble."

I thought of his grimace after tasting the tatlilav. "You can be pretty dumb sometimes."

"Often," he said.

"Daily."

Leaning back, he held up his hands. "Deserved."

"But only when you're awake," I said, eyeing him.

"Are you finished?" he asked.

"For now."

The memory faded as I rubbed my forehead. Calev wasn't perfect, but he was good. I closed my eyes, thankful I had him on my side.

My throat tight, I reached under the bedding on Avi's side and retrieved one of her collected seashells.

My heart snapped like it might break into two. I clutched my shirt, breath hitching as the tears I'd fought poured down my cheeks.

The shell's outer surface was sharp and rough, bitten by the shore rocks. But inside was unmarred, smooth and fragile.

If the oramiral destroyed my sister's sweet soul, he was as good as dead. I'd murder him slowly, painfully.

I was still plotting when dawn burned through the cracks in the door.

CHAPTER NINE

Soon after dawn, I met Calev at the tavern and we headed toward the amir's manor house. We passed the Holy Fire worship house and its minarets. The design was meant to mimic the look of Akhayma, the Empire's capitol city made up of stone peaks that held up a sea of fabric. The Holy Fire worship house's lovely, spindly towers seemed to hold the sky up, making a tent of blue above us. Despite the beauty, I was on edge. Avi was waiting for us. I had little chance of persuading the amir to help. As we walked, Calev gave me information about the amir and the way her mind worked.

My sandal crashed into a mud puddle. I growled and swished my skirt, slinging brown onto the vegetable seller's cart and interrupting Calev's stream of advice.

"Eh!" The veg seller threatened me with an onion, then with a respectful nod, offered the vegetable to Calev.

I was too tired—body and soul—to care about a veg seller's slights. My elbow and side throbbed from the fight with the oramiral's men. And it was nothing compared to the chill of Avi's absence.

Calev veered left, out of the way of my muddy stomping. His hands were scratched up and one was swollen and red. "The amir, of course, honors the Holy Fire, but it's not a true priority to her," he said very quietly so no one could overhear. "She only really believes in battle tales, high-caste bloodlines, and her treasury."

"I'm going to work her pride."

Calev grinned. "We could even throw in some of the slanderous remarks the oramiral's slaves made against her."

"They didn't—oh." I smiled, whispering. "Yes. I must've *forgotten*. We told the oramiral's men they shouldn't take a Jakobden citizen without the amir's approval, and they said *The amir can approve this*." I made an obscene gesture.

Calev choked, almost laughing. "That might be taking it a shade too far."

A high-caste man, a hooded falcon perched on his arm, blinked at us and stopped mid-stride. "Old Farm, you should demand the low-caste walk behind. Don't shame your family."

Face clouding, Calev started toward him like he was going to fight him —not a winning plan. Before he could make whatever wonderfully brave, albeit asinine move he wanted to make, I dropped two steps behind.

The falcon's owner moved on and Calev heaved a sigh. "This is why you didn't go with me to the archery contest," he whispered over his shoulder.

"Nah. It's your insufferable company," I said, my humor falling flat. The breeze pulled the hem of Calev's tunic back toward me as we started forward.

It's not like I'd wanted to skip the contests the amir held for the harvest. Calev always nudged elders aside so I could stand beside him and actually see the competitors' yellow and black fletched arrows hit the targets lined up along the horse track.

But we couldn't do that anymore. It was too formal of an event for us to appear together. His father would never have approved. Not anymore. Worse, someone could report us to the amir. Someone like Berker. Then Calev and I both would be well on our way to being Outcasted. I couldn't put Calev in that position for a contest. I wouldn't threaten myself either.

"We're growing up. We're not knee-high anymore. I won't be the reason you're Outcasted."

He stopped and faced me. "That's not going to happen."

"Calev. Think about it. You, an Outcast? It would kill you."

I stared into his honest eyes, thinking of him sitting beside his father and Eleazar as they brainstormed ways to curb root rot. I'd been there, waiting to speak with Y'hoshua about what ports he wished me to visit. Calev had pounded on the table, pushing his points as his father argued with Eleazar bouncing between the two stances. But they'd broken into joking before it could turn into a fight.

If Calev were Outcasted, he'd never be allowed in his home ever again. At best, he'd be with the livestock, mucking stalls and sleeping in the open. At worst, he'd be on the streets along with me, begging.

"We need to fight the system," he said, eyes blazing.

The anger in his eyes made my chest swell, but I had to tamp it down. Rebellion had to wait for another day. "Think I don't know that? But first, we save Avi." I waved him to walk on, so I could trail him like a pathetic little donkey.

I couldn't wait for Ayarazi. Silver in my hands. The world at my feet.

"We will," he said. "I promise you. When this is over, I'll demand that my father listen."

"We need a back way in to fight the system. Something subtle," I said. "Someday we'll figure it out. If you yell about it, everything will be ruined."

Calev blinked. "Did you just suggest being subtle?"

"Told you we're growing up."

He smiled. "Sure."

"Thank you for doing this." My tears reflected in his eyes, and I looked away.

"Avigail is mine too," he said. "My family. You know that."

A light glowed in my chest. His *family*. I remembered how quickly they'd become friends when she was small. Once, when Calev and I were eight, I'd dragged him from Old Zayn's weather lessons and down to the boat. Father was arguing shipping prices with a farmer's agent who pointed at the marks on his wax tablet. Father did pretty well hiding his shock at Calev being there. The agent pulled off his straw hat, frowning at the bells on my sash. Calev took my hand and I squeezed his fingers, my pulse beating in the tip of my thumb.

A muscle in Father's jaw twitched. "They're young yet," he said quietly to the agent on that day so long ago. "Now about the grains…"

The agent put his hat on and went back to arguing.

Onboard, Avi hurried over. "Kinneret, play the shell game with me."

"I have things to do, little girl."

"I'm only three years younger than you."

Calev took one bright shell. "How do you play?"

She stole the shell back.

"Come on," Calev said. "I'm good at games. At home, I win all the time."

That didn't surprise me.

"Well," Avi started, "you throw the shells. Like this." She tossed them into the air. "Andguesshowmanylandupsidedown—four." The little crescents and circles clattered onto the uneven decking, only two of the four showing their shiny insides. "I win." Her eyes narrowed. "No one beats me."

She threw the shells again. "Six," Calev called out.

Avi glared. "Five."

All six shells landed belly-up and Avi's mouth dropped open. "Kinneret is right. You are lucky."

Calev put a hand on her shoulder. "Will you play with me every time I visit?"

Avi grinned. "Deal."

I shook off the memory. I had to focus if this little impromptu meeting with Amir Mamluk was going to accomplish anything even remotely good.

The walls of the amir's manor house loomed above us. They were made of the cloudy, white stone from Quarry Isle, the sole product the oramiral exported, the material Avi began cutting and hauling last night.

Chilled to the core, I walked faster.

I wondered if I was about to stride right into a death sentence. Although it wasn't technically a law, low-castes never pleaded their case here. Forcing myself to think positively, I rounded the corner and followed Calev into the amir's courtyard. Smoke from a fire crawled into the blue morning sky, and a slave tethered a dun mare to a post outside the mud-brick stables.

At least the amir didn't force her slaves to wear the high bell over their heads. They wore a large, copper one on a metal ring around each ankle. Three more slaves carried baskets of what looked like mushrooms and olives from a storage shed. Like worker ants, they made a line, each one eyeing me—the obvious intruder in my many bells, just one measly step above their status.

Where Calev's home was a simple but large stone structure, the amir's enormous place rose three full stories above the churned earth and layered stone of her courtyard. Made of the same white rock as the outer walls, the house boasted arches with orange stripes over a patio done in mosaic tiles. Manning the arched openings, two fighters wore onion-shaped helmets that pressed one strip of metal along their noses. Long, sharp yatagans hung sheathed at their sashes beside the ten bells that marked them as middle-caste.

I glanced at Calev, wondering for the millionth time what it would feel like to be an Old Farm and free of the system of slave, worker, warrior, leader. As part of their ancient agreement with the kyros and his amirs, Old Farms were considered high-caste from birth, though they didn't have to wear the bells. They'd worked hard to make themselves indispensable to Jakobden by working the soil in ways that were as much magic as my salt prayers.

When Calev—recognized here from his father's dealings with the amir—received a nod from the guards, we walked into the cool receiving hall.

The absence of the sun's soaking heat made me shiver. An ozan sang quietly of an ancient warrior's battle at sea, his voice warbling like a bird's. Men and women in silk draped the lower half of the walls like curtains. We waited at the door near the Fire in the bronze bowl. The flames flickered and sent the smell of oil into the air. Calev pricked his finger with his dagger and dropped his blood into the Fire. I passed a hand respectfully over the dancing orange and blue, feeling the heat on my skin.

Inside the main section of the receiving hall, Chairman Y'hoshua sat at the end of a long table, opposite the amir. Tapestries covered the top half of the walls. Colored threads wove together to show former amirs' conquests of borderlands, fleets of boats fighting the Great Expanse's waves to search for foggy, lost lands like Ayarazi, and bloody battles with western Invaders.

"You agree to our terms, Amir Mamluk?" Chairman Y'hoshua said.

Calev sucked a breath, frozen in the act of sheathing his dagger. "I didn't know he was here."

"Obviously." This wasn't good. Y'hoshua would stop our supplication before it could even get started.

The amir cut an imposing figure, dressed in red leather the color of blood. I loved the color red, never bought or stole clothing in a color too far from it, but this was a darker shade. Deeper. I swallowed.

She regarded Y'hoshua's beard with cool eyes. "I agree to all except the price of your barley."

"What should I do?" Calev whispered.

"It is a fine crop," Y'hoshua said, "and will make a great deal of silver in trade for us and for you."

"I will not pay like a trader." The amir's braid pulled at her light blue eyes. She cocked her head. The single, pure silver bell at her forehead—tied to a thin strip of leather similar to Old Farm men's headties—reflected the arched windows' morning light.

"Maybe you should get in there," I hissed back, ignoring a house slave's shushing noise.

The amir was too light-eyed and fair-skinned to be of the kyros's race and born high-caste, so at one point in her family's history, one of her ancestors had served as a slave. Now, she ruled this area, with only the kyros outranking her and far enough away to be more dream than reality. I was keenly jealous of the power she held in her manicured hands.

"You hold those lands because of my generosity, and the generosity of the kyros's ancestors," the amir said. "Do not forget, Chairman Y'hoshua ben Aharon."

My stomach twisted. I hadn't expected to like her voice. But it was beautiful. It rang like the bell she wore and made me want to hear her sing.

"I would never forget, my lady. And I thank you for meeting me here."

In the past, the ruling amir met the Old Farm chairman in the fields. Before Amir Mamluk, no Old Farms were permitted in her household. They were welcomed into town and highly respected in agreements and trading, but not allowed here, in the home of the highest ranking member of the kyros's ruling class.

Y'hoshua's face was like carved stone. "But, as I said, it is a fine crop."

"One-third finer than last harvest?" she countered.

Calev stepped out the shadows. "Yes."

The house servant sputtered and quickly announced us. "Calev ben Y'hoshua of Old Farm and—"

I poked the man and shook my head to keep him quiet. My presence only added problems. I wanted to stay in the shadows for a bit longer, see how this panned out. The servant's face darkened. He looked ready to throw me in a cell.

"We remember so they remember," I said quickly, drawing my gaze to his bells, then touching a finger to my own.

He took a breath and nodded slowly. "The amir might not like this. You must be quiet, and still."

I nodded.

Y'hoshua's loud voice rang through the room. He stood. "Son?"

Calev bowed to the amir, then gave his father a nod. "Amir Mamluk, what my father says is true. This barley is indeed one-third finer. My brother Eleazar ben Y'hoshua developed a new way to fight root rot and the crop grew more golden than in years past. If you cannot agree to the number my father has set, perhaps we could agree on last year's price plus one hundred extra workers—your fighters or any men or women you see as fit—to weed our fields after spring planting."

The servant beside me made a little *Hmm* noise of appreciation.

"Pretty quick, isn't he?" I whispered to the servant.

Y'hoshua turned an impressive shade of red.

The amir's eyebrow lifted as she stared Calev down. "It is a delicate balance we set here."

Calev stood straight under her burning gaze. "We are thankful for that balance. Gratitude sings the loudest note in our ancient ways, my lady."

"And we know how Old Farms love their old ways." She grinned like a fox and her fighters laughed lightly.

Y'hoshua and Calev bowed their heads a fraction, and a small smile drifted over one side of Calev's mouth. I hope he enjoyed the moment, because I'd bet his father would strap him good later. No way Y'hoshua would let this slide. Proving my point, he glared at Calev and his nostrils flared.

The amir stood, shoving her chair back with a screech. Y'hoshua hurried to echo the movement, though his chair made no sound.

"We are agreed, Chairman Y'hoshua ben Aharon."

Calev and Y'hoshua made the Fire's sign, forming a circle on their foreheads with their thumbs. The amir copied the gesture.

Now was the time to bring up Avi. I willed Calev to read my thoughts, but he acted like he was going to leave with Y'hoshua, waiting as the amir called for her scribe. The Holy Fire flickered in its bronze bowl and sent out a snap.

Looking at the now empty table—the amir and the chairman had gone to the scribe's podium to sign their agreement—I tried, and failed, to imagine a world where someone like me could sit there. How much silver would it take to make Salt Magic as acceptable as the Old Farm ways and the Holy Fire?

Calev was waiting too long to broach the subject of Avi. I had to speak.

I untied my salt from my sash and bent, pretending to adjust my sandal as I tucked the bag into the corner away from the servant's prying eyes.

Not waiting on the servant to announce me, I walked into the room.

CHAPTER TEN

T he house servant called out.

"I'm Kinneret Raza, Pass sailor," I squawked, saving him the effort.

Y'hoshua's eyes narrowed as the high ceiling grabbed every smacking sound my ratty sandals made and threw it back at the tiled floor.

Amir Mamluk had taken a seat in a tall chair on a raised platform.

I bent at the knee and raised an open palm to her in respect.

The amir looked at Calev's father. "Chairman Y'hoshua ben Aharon, is this another of your surprises?"

"No, my lady." His face was stormy. "I don't know what brings Kinneret Raza here."

"A low-caste sailor…" The amir wasn't even looking at me and I still felt the threat, all the possible words she could utter and ruin me.

Maybe I should've planned to tell her about the map to Ayarazi. The tales about her ruthlessness could've been false. She might believe me. Calev said there was no chance of her taking Old Zayn's tale as truth, but maybe he was wrong.

"I am sorry for the interruption, Amir Mamluk," Calev said with one of those smiles of his. The amir smiled back. Someone would have to be dead not to smile back at Calev. "But we do have another topic to discuss, if you are willing. It is a matter that needs immediate attention."

The amir's eyebrows lifted, but I couldn't tell whether she was angry or interested. "Immediate?"

Y'hoshua raised a palm and the amir turned her attention to him.

"Yes, Chairman Y'hoshua ben Aharon?"

"The sailor has had an unfortunate run-in with the oramiral. I do value the sailor's talent. Even young as she is, she has scouted two new ports for Old Farm. She is very skilled. But her current situation is nothing that concerns my son."

It was like hands pushed down on my shoulders and I had to fight to stand.

Calev's eyes flashed. "It does concern me, Father. And the amir, too."

"Yesterday," I said, "we sailed past Asag's Door, near Quarry Isle, and Oramiral Urmirian's men boarded our craft and abducted my sister, Avigail Raza."

Leaning back, the amir rested an elbow on the arm of her chair and adjusted the leather collar of her military vest. "I believe your father is correct," she said to Calev. "This should not concern you. Now, Chairman Y'hoshua ben Aharon, you may leave and I will have a little talk with your son."

Y'hoshua nodded curtly at Calev. "He does seem to think he has this in hand." And with that, he left.

A buzz reverberated inside me. I spoke louder. "I have brought many of your noble visitors safely across the Pass from Kurakia, Amir Mamluk, and I run many of the merchants and area farmers' surplus goods. My sister will follow in my footsteps to become another valuable member of your township. We work under the protection of your fighters, for the good of your township." I wanted to add the slurs Calev and I had thought up, but the words didn't want to come.

The amir's fingers lighted on the snakeskin sheath of her personal dagger. Her nails were stained with orange spices I'd only taste if I found Ayarazi. "The work you do, it is coppers to me. Have you ever kaptaned a full ship for any of my tenant farmers?"

"No..."

Shaking his hair out of his eyes, Calev took a small step forward. Burned silhouettes of tiny lemons and barley stalks decorated the edges of Calev's sash. That article of clothing alone cost as much as a cartload of grains. The amir's gaze followed the shining hem, an approving smile ghosting over her mouth. I stood taller. Calev had thought out what would impress her. He was truly doing his best to help Avi.

"My lady," he said, "Kinneret Raza runs surplus for the headland farmer Matan..."

I winced. "Actually—"

The amir slapped a hand on her throne. "Do not interrupt those higher than you, sailor."

My face burned as the amir looked again to Calev.

"You see, Calev ben Y'hoshua? You shouldn't encourage this one with your admirable kindness. She grows too bold for her station. It could mean trouble for the both of you." Her icy gaze nipped at me. "This one has talent. I've heard as much. But she would do well to earn her silver and rise in the accepted way, avoiding overly close association with upper-castes until she is ready. You know the kyros requires me to protect high-caste bloodlines. You must not mix unless the low is proven and rises, or you will both be Outcasted."

Calev went gray around the mouth, and I shivered.

"With my condolences on the young girl—one should not begin as a slave, then return to it after honorably working—please go on your way and give my best to your father, Calev ben Y'hoshua."

Just like that, she threw Avi's life away.

My heart choked as the amir motioned to the servant to lead us out. Her ozan began singing of her great-great-grandfather's journey to the North.

Frozen, I longed to blurt out my knowledge of the lost island of silver, but in this painfully formal room full of narrowed eyes and high brows, I couldn't say it. It wouldn't matter. None of these uppers would believe me.

I imagined Avi's small, thin body curled into mine during the night, her open-mouthed breathing. Where did she sleep now? In the open air slave quarters on Quarry Isle, along with a mass of others, men desperate and women angry. They'd probably already taken her tunic from her. They would steal her food. She wouldn't be able to fight back in such a crowd. They'd take everything she had.

I looked frantically at the approaching servant, then at the amir. We couldn't leave yet. I couldn't just give up.

The word left my lips and I couldn't begin to stop it. "Please."

The ozan didn't quiet down at my plea. The amir didn't turn toward me.

Calev's gentle hand warmed my arm. He gave me a smile, then raised his voice. "Kinneret will be the Old Farm kaptan for the next shipment of barley. Old Farm is confident in her abilities and what should be a quick rise in caste."

What?

He held his fist to his neck. "By my word," he swore, "or my throat's blood is yours, my lady."

The ozan's tune fell away.

I put my head in my hands, feeling like the world rushed around me, overwhelming and all too real. A throat's blood oath. It was binding until one or both died. If Calev didn't follow through, the amir would slit his throat in front of everyone in Jakobden and Old Farm and not even his chairman father could do a thing to stop it.

But I forced my chin up. This was my chance to help Avi. I couldn't take on the oramiral without the amir's fighting sailors, ships, and coin. Calev had thrown his life into the deal. I pulled in a breath of the manor house's spicy air. I had to back him up now. There was no other choice, as mad as it was.

"It is true, my lady," I lied.

The noblewoman stood. She was taller even than Calev's father. "When I hear from Y'hoshua ben Aharon's own mouth that this girl will kaptan his ship, that she has the protection of Old Farm, and therefore my own protection due to the old agreements, you will have the coin and fighters you need to take your sister back, Kinneret Raza." Her smile said she knew that would never happen. "I hope you are wise in this choice, Calev ben Y'hoshua. A public execution of an Old Farm would be dramatic indeed."

Blood lust colored her features.

The room spun as we followed the servant to the courtyard.

The ozan's lilting voice carried more tales of heroic deeds. As we walked, he sang of a man slaying enemies with a lion fighting at his side.

Outside the manor house walls, I raged ahead of Calev. "A throat binding, Calev? And how do you think I'm going to kaptan your ship? Your father won't even bend his precious harvest schedule to save my sister's life." I kicked at a basket of leeks and a girl in a white hair wrap swore at me.

"It's not as simple as a change of schedule, Kinneret, and you know that. It is about a holy ritual. It's not matter of mere inconvenience."

"Yes, it is."

"No. It's not. If we wait on the harvest any longer—and there's no way they'll harvest without me at the ceremony—we will lose crops, which means less food for everyone on the Broken Coast and beyond."

"I don't care if it means less food." I grabbed his tunic. "Don't you get it? She's probably the youngest slave. She'll be stepped on, pushed down. Or worse. There are men there, Calev. Desperate men, out of their minds. I have to go after the map to the island."

"The oramiral's men could take you too."

"I don't care. I have to try."

"I know, but maybe we should wait and think about this."

"Really? Wait on what? Silver is my only card to play. Your father is no help, or if he does help, it'll be too late and Avi will be—"

He covered my hands with his. "Kinneret. Calm yourself."

I pushed away from him. "Ooo, using your big man voice, huh?" I huffed and started my raging down the road again. "Save it for your field workers. There is no chance your father will agree to me becoming kaptan of the Old Farm full-ship. The only answer now is silver and lots of it. That's the only way I can save Avi and you. I'm sailing out now. Today. The wine jug with the map is out there, waiting for me. If I find Ayarazi on my own and return with the purest silver the amir has ever seen, she'll flay the oramiral alive if I ask it and Avi will come home again."

"Can't you wait one day? I will persuade my father to hire you. The old kaptan loves you and—"

"It won't work, then I'll be behind a day with nothing to show for it. Besides, you really think your father is going to let you walk out of Old Farm when the harvest ceremony over? He'll want you there for the full harvest. You know the fields. And you're better at getting everyone to work their tails off than anyone else. If I were him, I'd want you there."

"He will want me to stay, but I'll sneak off. Eleazar will cover for me."

I lowered my voice as we came to the town gate. "You'd leave right after the ceremony? Even if you know I'll use Salt Magic for this trip? Because I can't simply wait for a good wind. Avi is dealing with only the Fire knows what this very second. The men there will take more than just her share of food."

"I will leave as soon as I can. I promise you. I love Avi too." I wanted him to come. He was my good luck.

My rage cooled as I stared at his face, full of his promise. His throat bobbed, his skin smooth, the same skin the amir would slice open if I didn't kaptan Old Farm's barley ship.

"Will you wait for me?" he asked quietly so no one would hear.

I pressed my lips together. I needed all the luck I could get. Finding the map would be easier if I had another diver. Oron was terrible under the water.

"Yes," I said. "I don't like it, but yes."

"Come to the ceremony tonight."

I couldn't do that. His father was furious with me and I with him. Besides, the word Outcast echoed through my mind. "No. I need to ready the boat." I touched his hand quickly. "I hope your rituals go smoothly. I'll meet you at the dock tomorrow."

Before I could turn and see his dark gaze following me, before I chanced those eyes urging me into more trouble, I stalked down the road. Zayn's words played in my memory again and again like a prayer chant, promising a good life for Avi and me.

CHAPTER ELEVEN

O ron was drunk. Aboard our boat, he swayed on his wide feet, one sandal tucked inside a circle of extra rope and an eye swollen shut from struggling against the oramiral's slaves.

"I'm not worthless, my dear, um…my…Ki…Kin…"

"Kinneret," I correctly smartly.

I held up a hand to block the early sun. My bruised cheek thumped with pain, but the rest of me had stopped hurting as of this morning. I was still in a mood though. Calev hadn't shown yet and I wondered if his father had anything to do with it.

"I was going to say that," Oron said. "I needed a second to think."

"Get off the boat, Oron. I have places to be. Avi isn't lounging in a kyros's tent. I have no sun for your nonsense." I swallowed against the fist in my throat.

He plopped himself onto the rope and crossed his arms. "Fine. Stay aboard," I said. "But keep out of my way."

By the time I'd hauled anchor, his snores echoed off the boat's sides. I looked down at him and sighed. He didn't usually drink so much this early. I supposed he was worried about Avi and handling it in his own way. A stupid way.

As I let out the sail, someone shouted from the hill beyond the dock.

Calev.

His tunic flowing at his sides, he ran down the path and pounded up to the boat. He grabbed the side before I'd floated a foot off.

Tossing a sack and himself over the side, he said, "I'm sorry I'm late." He frowned at Oron. "Having trouble holding your alcohol again?"

"It's not for holding. It's for drinking, silly," Oron mumbled, turning over.

"Did you tell your father about the oath?" I asked Calev. I shuddered, and rubbing salt between my fingertips, whispered to the sea and edged the tiller, a motion more familiar to me than walking.

Calev watched me work the magic with a wrinkled brow. "No. You thought I would?" He handed me a wheat cake from his bag and tossed one to Oron.

"Ow." Oron scowled, then noticed the cake lying beside him. "Ooo." He gobbled it up and closed his eyes again.

"I didn't know what to think," I said. "It's not like you make a throat's blood oath every day."

Oron whistled like a sick bird. "This is getting interesting. Maybe I should consider consciousness…"

I glared. "You're not as funny as you think you are."

Calev leaned toward me. "The oath won't matter when we find the island. The amir just needs to be convinced you're worth her time." He grinned and my heart flipped.

Oron wiggled his fingers. "Oooo, listen to the optimist."

With Calev standing beside me and not judging me for using Salt Magic, and the sea like green glass beyond him, something bright like hope sparked in my heart.

On alert for the oramiral's ship, we made it to the Drift before the sun had fallen two more fingers away from the horizon.

Talking with Calev, Oron managed to make himself useful on the sail's lines. "So, let me get this straight. You promised the amir that our girl here was set to be the next Old Farm ship kaptan in hopes that the amir would consider Avi as a person worth rescuing."

"That about sums it up," Calev said.

"And the amir is waiting to hear from your father on this, even though your father knows nothing about it."

"He'll agree to it."

Oron snorted. "Delusional. And they don't even have drink to blame."

"We're assertive," I argued.

"Even if it kills you?"

Calev and I answered together. "Exactly."

"Did Y'hoshua punish you?" I asked Calev as I dropped the stone anchor off the side.

He looked at the water. "No."

"Well, that is one thing, hmm?" Oron tied the sails down.

"Not really," I said. "When he waits to punish him, it's always worse. So he didn't say anything during the harvest rituals?"

"Not a word," Calev said. "Acted like nothing even happened."

Not good.

AFTER DROPPING the stone anchor off the side, I skinned off my shirt, skirt, and sash, leaving my small clothes on. Calev peeled his tunic from his back and I averted my eyes from his bare chest and the loose short pants that hung on his hipbones. I couldn't sit around and enjoy the view. It was time to find the map.

Avi needed us. And she needed us now.

The sun-drenched water below the boat glowed like spring grass and lemon peels. As we searched, the light stretched fingers down through the open water, all the way to the broken boards of yet another sunken vessel.

All day Calev had been amazing at holding his breath under water, amazing for a non-sailor, that is. But his lungs were no match for mine.

Before I could crawl, I'd been in the ocean, chasing fish, learning the tide's pull, becoming a Pass sailor. It was why I never feared the rocks or the storms. They were a part of me as much as my own shortcomings—quick anger and stubbornness.

Kicking my bare feet through the chill water, fighting the Pass's rough hands, I swam through a hole in the side of a ship even older than the one we'd already scoured. Calev would likely need to go up for air very soon.

In the ship's crumbling hull, barnacles like rotten, boiled potatoes sat on stacks of cracked crockery plates. Mostly, the space was empty. The sea had claimed what the looters hadn't wanted. There wasn't a wine jug in sight.

Near a long stretch of what used to be part of the deck, the boat's figurehead angel stuck one wing out of the mounded sand, its stone feathers gone green and black at the edges. Past that, a small, walled-in area —probably the kaptan's room—held the skeleton of a bed, a fork, the encrusted remains of iron lanterns, and an astrolabe.

Where was my wine jug? Where was Avi's ticket to freedom? Sadness welled inside my chest, pushing and more painful than the need for oxygen. I had to get to Avi before it was too late.

There was a tug on my toe and I turned to see Calev pointing up. Dying light drifted through the broken vessel's decking and striped his face. Tiny bubbles huddled beside his fine nose and in the cleft of his chin. He gestured to his chest. He needed air. I nodded, and he twisted, swimming back to the boat and leaving me in the wreckage.

The tides would turn soon, making it that much harder to swim and sail against the sea's push to flow out to the Expanse. It also meant another sundown, another day, and with it, Salt Wraiths. I had to hurry.

We hadn't checked the tumble of wood to the right of the kaptan's quarters. Oron was waving the signal stick at me under the water, but I ignored it. Swimming through a cloud of algae-eating creatures no bigger than dust motes, I ducked under the leaning parts of a doorframe. A table, only two legs remaining, hogged the space. A lead plummet rested in my distorted shadow. I tucked it into my top. If I could manage to clean it up, it'd be better than the one weighing my sounding line now. The four transoms of a Jacob's staff poked out from under the table. I didn't want that. It was iron, and only the Fire could make use of it now that it had been under the sea for so long. I'd have to keep using my old wooden one to measure the angle between the horizon and the sun or the Far Star.

Oron and Calev had to be panicking by now. Hot fingers tore at my lungs.

Just one more look.

Letting the water tug me to the dark corner behind the mapping table, I reached out my fingers. Then a warm hand snatched my ankle. I nearly inhaled the entire Pass.

It was Oron, his hair like squid tentacles around his wide face. He waved a frantic hand for me to follow. With one glimpse at the unexplored corner, I finally obeyed my lungs and my friend, and headed to the surface, my feet like a tail behind me.

"Didn't you see the signal?" At the surface, Oron roughly wiped ocean from his face and hefted himself up the hook-topped ladder that Calev held steady against starboard.

The signal stick—berry-dyed and beaten to bare spots like a bad donkey —sat on the side of the boat, dripping wet. Below the ladder, I treaded water and pulled air into my neglected lungs.

"I want to go back down," I said.

The sky was the orange of Kurakian chicken and the purple of spiced wine, the memory of the last like pines and flowers on my tongue. I bit my lip.

Closing my eyes, I hated myself. I was a monster for thinking of my stomach, rather than Avi's.

"We still have sun," I said.

The sea lurched me sideways, and I grabbed the ladder, my legs flying in the water.

"No." Oron leaned over the side of the boat as he worked himself back into his tunic. "It's nearly sundown."

Calev, on the other hand, was taking his tunic off again. "I'm going with you. This is no time for cowardice."

I smiled sadly and dipped under the choppy waves to wait for him.

Like an arrow shot into the water, Calev dove into the sea. For me. For Oron. For Zayn. For Avi. And I loved him for it.

Where would I be without Oron and Calev? I might've found the map on my own, but it would've been so much harder. I wished I could do something for them, but nothing that wasn't stupid came to mind. Anything said wouldn't be enough. I didn't have any items to give them to show my gratitude.

Calev came up in front of me and grinned. It took everything in me not to wrap my arms around his neck and press my mouth to his. I wanted to kiss the tiny scar at the side of his full lips. Instead of making a complete fool of myself, I dashed through the water, aiming for the map room.

THE LIGHT in the underwater room was no longer a diffused, golden glow. Because the sun had fallen, swimming into the small area was like walking into one of Oron's blue glass gaming pieces. Like my shadow, Calev stuck to my side as I maneuvered past the table and the tools to the corner. Praying for the absence of eels, I felt around the darkness.

Smooth shapes. A tube—ah—the neck of a vessel. Two of them. Two jugs.

Sharp nests of twigs surrounded the containers on their broken shelves. Seeing what I was about, Calev pressed forward to help me uncover our finds.

No large cracks marred the jugs, at least none visible in the twilight. As we tucked them under our arms and kicked back to the boat, I spared a thought for what might actually be left of a map that had lived in salt water for three hundred years. Probably depended on how it was stored and sealed as well as what it was made of. Parchment. Vellum.

The Quest knights used vellum, calfskin, for religious writings. My father had taught me that much in our talks between spearfishing and sail-mending. He'd explained the kyros had faith, but his views differed somewhat from the Old Farm's religion, and also the Quest knights, who'd controlled Jakobden before the map's existence. The details of everyone's belief systems was lost on me, but I remembered Father's description of Quest knights' holy writings, words ringed with paintings as colorful as Meeka Valley flowers. So if the map was important to them it would probably be vellum too. Did it last under water? I doubted regular papyrus did, being made of plant material.

Oron helped us one by one into the boat, his big eyes drawing a line between the jugs and the darkening sky.

I squeezed the ends of my curling hair, hurrying so I could tug my skirt and shirt back on. Something about being half naked near a similarly half naked Calev made me feel very, very dangerous.

"What do you think the map is made of?" I asked.

Popping his head through his tunic, Calev opened his mouth.

Oron cut him off before he could say anything. "I see you're finally wondering what could possibly survive three centuries under water."

Calev ran his hands along his skull to press the water from his dark head. I tried very hard not to stare at the angle of his jaw and the slender bulge of his arm muscles under his damp tunic sleeves.

"The map is likely parchment," Oron said. "Made from animal skin. Not papyrus." He hurried over with me to the jugs. I was glad his gaze wasn't worrying over the sky anymore. He was focused on our goal now, like me.

I lifted the first gritty container. It was heavier out of the water. A blackened plug clogged the jug's mouth.

Oron raised a hammer. "Shall we crack it open or do you think we can get the plug out in a more graceful manner?"

I jerked the metal tool out of his hand and knocked the neck of the jug, breaking the top from the container. One of the handles, embossed with a Quest knight rose, came off along with the neck and rattled along the deck. I peered inside the jug.

Darkness.

My heart in my stomach, I looked up at Calev and Oron. "It's empty."

Oron twisted, then shoved the second sea-grimed jug into my hands.

It was empty too.

Knees shaking, I stood. Was Zayn wrong? Or was the right container still out there, under the waves? I looked out over the orange-tipped waves shining in the lowering sun.

"Kinneret," Oron said. "We need to get to shore."

Calev set a gentle hand on my arm, his fingers cool and damp. "We can come back tomorrow."

I nodded.

Night peered out of the East. Oron began tugging the anchor up, his fingers white on the rope. Dripping arms and legs of water, the rope marched from the Pass like a line of regimented fighters. I couldn't blink. I just stared, Avi's braid in my mind's eye.

Calev stepped closer.

Hugging my arms to myself, I tried to stop shaking.

This was one more night added to Avi's time at the quarry. One more night in a slave's bell brace. A shudder crashed over me. One more night surrounded by people who would cut her throat with a sharp flake of stone for her share of bread and oil.

I spun and knelt near the jugs. What if the map wasn't parchment or papyrus? What if I'd missed it? What if was an object or something I hadn't thought of yet?

Upending each container in turn, I shook them out to check.

Nothing.

"What is it?" Calev asked, probably thinking I'd lost my mind. Oron let the sail out. "I need your salt work to get us moving, Kinneret." He frowned at the pink sun sitting on the waves.

"Now."

I raised the hammer and smashed both of the jugs.

"What are you doing?" Calev asked. "We need to get back to shore. Becoming Infused out here won't help Avi."

Ignoring him, I shuffled through the pieces. The first container's insides were like the outside, red-brown and unmarked, nothing like the ones in the amir's hall that were blue glazed and covered in lotus flowers and phoenixes.

I lifted a big section of the second jug's body and flipped it over.

Blue.

I held it up to Calev, struck dumb.

He wrinkled his nose. "Why is the inside glazed?"

White scratches interrupted the color someone had painstakingly slicked inside before firing the thing in a kiln. There was a long line and several notches like tiny mountains. On the left, a snaking strip of white. To the right, another.

My mouth went dry. I smiled and laughed as the world seemed to open up in front of my eyes. "This is the map."

Oron appeared at my side. "And I am the kyros. And Calev is my pet donkey."

I glared. Calev glared.

Oron held up his hands. "I thought we were having a bit of pretend to ease the pain of crushing defeat."

I pushed him out of the way to find the rest of the pieces. Not that one. No. This one was blue, but not marked. Ah.

"Look." I held the bit I'd found against the other marked piece. They fit like lovers. The new section showed a thumb-sized triangle. I ran a finger over the serpentine lines. "This is Jakobden. This, Kurakia." Touching the tiny mountains, I said, "This is the Pass." My finger found the triangle. "And this. This is Ayarazi."

Oron's hand went to his mouth and Calev made a sound like a sigh.

"You did it," Calev said. "You found it." He shook his head. "I knew you would."

I gave him my best smile because he deserved it. He looked away from my mouth and swallowed.

Tucking the map pieces into my wide sash, I stood. "Now let's get out of here."

CHAPTER TWELVE

The wraith came on fast.

Years ago, when Calev and I first began sneaking out together, we finagled our way onto Old Farm's full-ship right before dawn. The sun yawned over the fields and dock. With him behind me, I scrambled up the mainsail mast. It hadn't been easy. The night before had seen a strong rain and every climbing post along the tall beam was slick as olive oil.

Calev pointed out the dark backs of seals sloping out of the orange-tinted water and I leaned to look past the rigging.

I slipped. It was a long fall and should've broken my back like what happened to Abraham, former scout on the Old Farm ship. But even though the fall didn't break me, it knocked every bit of air from me faster than I could scream.

And now, in this breath, in this moment, the wraith was that quick.

That unexpected.

Though now I was nearly an adult, I screamed like I was a child again. We didn't have a second to scramble to the cabin or light the lantern.

A scraping sound leaked from the spirit's gray-white, sparkling shape. It looked like a flash of starlight, then took on an almost human form, became shifting sands of salt, sometimes with arms or legs or a mouth, but always with reaching fingers.

Its presence pinched at my reason, instead of smashing it like the other wraiths did. It was a pinpoint of a feeling. Clear. Strong. Focused. But, though the wraith's warped emotions were unmistakable, they remained nearly impossible to fight. It was like trying to dig an inking out of your skin.

Some wraiths were like this, subtle and intelligent. From the stories, they usually had specific revenge in mind and once completed would give up their Infusion victim.

A shiver rattled me.

Ranging high near the moonlit husks of clouds, the wraith's shape unfurled and snapped like a banner. Its emotion smothered us.

Oron stood staring, caught in his fear.

Wouldn't his blood look beautiful like a Kurakian scarf around his neck? the wraith said into my mind.

No, I answered back, silently, whimpering like a fool.

But he doubts you. Always doubts you.

The spirit talked on, convincing, luring. I sucked a breath, grabbed Oron, and thrusted him toward the hull. I turned to Calev.

Like a hawk, the wraith swooped low, then high, and hovered, ready to strike its prey. Its arms—wings now—were white smoke, tattered strings of diamond salt as it dove for my dearest friend.

My heart smacked my chest and I lunged toward Calev. The wraith shot forward, the moon poised dead perfect, a spotlight for this sick player and his tragedy.

Everything happened at once.

The wraith's moonshadow struck across the deck and glanced against Calev's bare foot.

Or did it?

There was no time to watch for the wraith's Infusion light, to see if it had soaked into Calev's body. I snatched Calev's sleeve, missing a good grip on his arm, and pulled him back, half a second from Infusion myself. I grabbed the lantern.

Wrestling the tangle of my thoughts and those of the wraith's, I rushed toward the opening to the hull behind Calev. Inside, I pressed into him and he shoved against Oron. None of us could hear, I was sure of that. The whipping sound of the wraith masked all other noises of the water against the sides and our breathing.

The pinprick, knife-slice of black thoughts bleeding into my reason, my shaking hands found my flint and knife. I set the lantern outside the hull's opening, on deck, and lit the wick with a speed I didn't know I had. Orange, silver, and black flames danced inside the glass, illuminating the decking, the mast, our lines.

I looked up.

The wraith was gone.

The night only held stars and the moon and the memories of clouds. No wraiths. Dropping my hands, I choked on a sob, my cheeks burning with shame at what I'd thought about blood and death.

I spun to Calev. "The wraith...it's gone."

He blinked and wobbled. He put a hand on the boat's side.

Was he Infused? Had the wraith crawled into him? There was no way to tell, really. The Infusion light was invisible until the wraith's revenge or blood lust was satisfied, slaked. Then the light would leave the mouth, vomited like a sickness.

My skin cold, I fisted a hand in his tunic. "Calev? Can you hear me?" My heart buzzed and flopped between my ribs like a beetle on its back. "Calev." I shook him hard.

Oron shouted too, his voice tight, his eyes white and scared in the near dark.

Calev's gaze fell past my face to the deck beyond the hatch, like he couldn't see me.

Oron pushed us both out of the hull. He held my fishing spear. "Get him off the boat, Kinneret. Throw him over. Now. A waste, a loss, a grief, but we won't go down with him."

I stuttered, then found my tongue. "Oron! Shut it!"

Calev raised his head. "I'm fine. Stop. Stop yelling." He pressed palms to his temples. "I'm fine."

But his face was green around the edges and pale everywhere else.

I put a hand around his wrist, feeling the comfort of his pulse beneath my fingers. "You're certain?"

His beautiful lips stretched sweetly, weakly, a sad excuse for his true smile. "I am." He touched his thumb to my forehead and smoothed a circle, making the Fire's sign in promise.

I closed my eyes. "Thank the seas."

Oron was frowning when I opened them again. "To shore, my fellow looters." He shook his head. "I've had my fill of thrills. I want nothing more than my mat below the tavern and Kinneret's consistent snoring to keep me company."

"We'll go to the amir in the morning." I hung the lantern on its hook. "If I show her the map and offer her a cut of the silver, she'll help me take Avi back from the oramiral. The map will win her over."

Calev nodded, but his mouth was tight.

"What?"

"I don't know how you'll keep her from taking it all, from claiming Ayarazi's mines and the horses the stories claim are there."

Oron laughed theatrically, his arms tucked around his stomach. "I like how you both believe the place truly exists. This is a fantasy, Kinneret. You place your faith, your sweet, foolish faith in fantasy."

"And what do you suggest I do? Sail up to Quarry Isle and just ask kindly for my sister with a bow and a palm to the sky?"

"Thieves we have been before, my kaptan. Thieves we could be again."

"Speak plainly, Oron. I'm tired."

"We could sail to the northeast end, where they never go because of the sea serpents, and sneak onto the island. We could call up a wave to distract them at the southern end and get our girl over the wall."

"Call up a wave? What do you think I am? I can't work the salt that well."

"You do it better than any I've ever heard of," Calev said quietly. His gaze flicked to the salt pouch at my sash.

"Old Farms are not exactly Salt Magic experts." I raised an eyebrow, said a prayer, and blew my handful of salt into the slow-moving wind. A splash sounded from port side—a night fish jumping.

Calev held up his palms in defeat. "Still."

Oron sat on the bench beside me. "Still." He looked up. "Or we could go to your aunt's. Perhaps she could help."

Calev raised his eyebrows. "The one in Kurakia?"

"No," I said, longing for the comfort of Aunt Kania's strong arms, which had always reminded me of the black roots of the Topa tree that grew in that red and dusty country across the Pass. "She'd be no real help in this. I will handle it. It would take too much sun to get there and for what?"

They let the matter drop, and we sailed roughly through the rocks and the swirling current. We took one hard hit against Tall Man, but otherwise remained sound as we reached the bay.

"Calev, you don't think the island exists? You think Oron's dumb plan is better?"

"No, but it'll be difficult to keep the amir running down the road you choose."

"You are the key, Calev." I squeezed my hands together as Oron caught the dock with his foot and lowered a bumper to ease the rub on my boat's side. "You will stand as witness to her promise to take only a portion. A third of what we find. She won't ignore your witness."

Tossing the anchor overboard, Calev said, "First, I have to make you Old Farm kaptan."

"That can wait." I had no clue how we'd solve that problem, but it had to wait. This was silver beyond imagining. The amir would at least hear us out.

We lowered the gaff. The stitches we'd made to repair the sail had loosened dramatically. It was a wonder they held at all during the trip. We'd fix it later. I didn't have the silver or the sun to resew it now. Oron rolled the sail and tied it as Calev and I ran hands over the side where we'd knocked against Tall Man. No holes.

After grabbing his patchwork sack, Oron jumped out of the boat. "Luck to you both. I'm to brew and bed." His stocky shape faded into the night-shadowed road that led to town where some sad drinker was about to misplace his beer.

Calev and I climbed onto the dock and lit a lantern. We sat, one set of knees touching to make a crescent of our legs, with the map pieces between us.

I ran my hand over the glazed markings. "If I understand this correctly, the island is hidden past the northern edge of Kurakia. If the scale of Quarry Isle is tuned to the scale of the Spires' location, Ayarazi should be at least three leagues from the farthest trade route I've ever heard tell of."

My mind flashed an image of the water separating Avi and me right now. The wind. Her arms tucked around her sides. The look in her eyes. I squeezed my own eyes shut and swallowed the invisible glass in my throat, pushing the worry and fear away to concentrate.

"I think you're right," he said. "Do you know anything about the waters up there? Don't they connect the Pass to the Expanse at some point?"

I pulled at my bottom lip. "The chill you feel sometimes on the Pass comes from that direction. The wind too, mostly. There's a good chance the waters will be even worse than those on the Pass. Blue. Cold. There are more rock formations the farther north you sail up the Pass, so it's a guess the area will be challenging to run. A lot of underwater threats."

Calev's brown eyes found mine. "Cold. Rocks. Northern wind and abandoned sea waters. It's beginning to sound like one of Savta's tales."

His grandmother told stories around the community fire at spring planting and at the harvest celebration. Skin like a raisin and a voice like wine, she totally pulled me in with the Old Farm legend about the frozen birds of the far North that thawed once a century when the poppymilk flower bloomed and released its enlivening pollen.

"Which story?" I asked. There could be something in the tales that helped us get through this. After all, we had all thought Ayarazi was only a legend.

His eyes, unblinking, raised the tiny hairs on my arms. "The demon Asag."

"The eddy in the Pass is named for that story."

"Yes. But this is more than just an eddy. Asag is supposedly a horned demon that controls rocks that hide in the sea. He can make the water boil, killing everything near him."

"Cozy."

"And if the possessed rocks and hot water don't ruin you, his hideous face will. It's said that if you look at him, you die."

A shiver slid over my back. "Any way to fight the creature?"

"I'll have to ask."

A ruthless amir grabbing for my silver.

My innocent sister twisting and screaming in the hands of a madman.

Salt Wraiths and legendary sea monsters.

I looked down at my hands, which suddenly didn't seem as strong as they'd always been.

Calev's hand covered my knuckles. "I've seen you sail through the Spires in the middle of a winter storm. You can do this."

I found his eyes. There was no trace of glazed madness from the wraith. He was my Calev. Solid. Blessed. So very, very strong in spirit and body. I squeezed his hand, not caring whether he read into the touch or not.

He leaned forward, a slight, small movement, but my heart betrayed me and danced like the violet nightwingers flying dazedly around his head. Purple nets of light lay over his straight nose and the sweep of his dark hair. Goosebumps tickled my legs, and he reached a hand up and ran his fingers down the back of my neck, multiplying the feeling. My ribs rose and fell too quickly. He would notice. He would know. Why was he touching me?

"Kinneret." He breathed my name like a prayer. "You are so much more than anyone else."

I tried for a casual laugh, but it bloomed into a sigh. "More?"

"Your drive," he said. "Energy. Your spirit. You are fire, my friend."

Friend. My heart died a little. He didn't notice, his hand leaving my skin, leaving me cold.

"We should go," I said.

My knees trembled from his touch as we started up the path, the way Oron had gone.

My stomach swam at a sudden thought of Avi. I had let worry for her drift away for a moment. I was lower than the dirt on the sole of my sandal. I had to stay focused. My good, sweet sister needed all of me.

Calev's gaze drifted back to the darkness of the marsh surrounding the shining rocks of the sea coast. The skin around his eyes tightened, and his lips parted like he might say something. "Will you walk me back to the tavern?" I tried to talk to him like I'm sure his Intended did, all shy flirting. I wanted to go back to talk of me being fire and his fingers finding new places to rest on my body.

His gaze snapped to me, his eyes wide. "Really? You haven't actually asked me to walk you home since you were eleven years. To steal honey from the brewmaster, yes. To sneak into the guardhouse, yes. But a walk under the moon just for company's sake?" He raised an eyebrow like a question mark. "And what is that voice you're using?" He elbowed me gently.

Heat pricked at my cheeks. I was foolish to push him. He didn't feel that way about me. Maybe if I found the silver, saved Avi, and became a full ship kaptan, but now, no.

"Never mind. I will meet you at the amir's gates at sunrise."

I stormed away before I could fall into the moonlit trap of his beautiful face and strong arms. It wasn't a snare laid for me anyway.

Calev called out, but when I didn't answer, he laughed and said, "Tomorrow, fire friend!"

Yes. Tomorrow. It all hung on tomorrow. Avi's life. My heart.

Silver, death, the sea, and me.

CHAPTER THIRTEEN

The amir straightened in her tall chair. My bag of salt safely stowed under a rock outside, I ran my hand over the bowl of Holy Fire and rushed to keep up with Calev as he approached the dais. We held up our palms in greeting.

"I'd thought to see your father when my men told me an Old Farm representative had arrived," the amir said in her bell voice. "No problem with your throat-blood oath, I hope."

I snorted. Her nasty grin said she hoped no such thing.

"Kinneret," Calev hissed out of the corner of his mouth. I threw him a glare.

The amir laughed. "You two are amusing. I'll admit that. But I hope you don't think of her as a potential Intended, Calev ben Y'hoshua. Even if she does take on the role of Old Farm's full ship kaptan, until she's paid to remove," she eyed my sash, "many bells, you must refrain from your body's obvious desires."

"No, my lady, I..." Calev stammered.

I wanted to turn into water and soak into the amir's expensive carpets.

"There are times," the amir said, looking down at her own hand and talking very, very quietly like she was being more reflective than actually making a statement. "When I think we should permit high-castes to do as they please. Not marry lowers, but perhaps simply take them to bed and be done with this sort of situation—if we could be certain no caste-mixed

84

children would come of the temporary union. My predecessors would've fought such a notion, but I take a clean view of the body's needs."

I bit my tongue. She knew nothing about us. Yes, I wanted his warm lips on my neck, but it was only an extra layer of beauty on our secret world.

"Don't sneer at me, girl," the amir said, finally acknowledging that I could take part in the conversation.

"No, my lady. I would never."

"Of course you would. Your kind love to sneer."

My *kind*. "You believe because I'm low-caste, rising only a handful of generations past slave, that I—"

Calev smiled like sunrise at the amir, blazing through my rant. "I will fulfill my promise, but today my friend Kinneret Raza has a proposition for you."

"Please no more supplications concerning this one's sister. I'm bored of this conversation."

"Don't you need silver to continue fighting alongside the kyros to increase his dominion?" I asked, my pulse galloping.

"What does a Pass sailor know of the kyros's business with me?" Her eyes went to the servant behind us. She was going to dismiss us.

Her singing ozan hummed a sour-sweet tune and took up his oud, ready to do his job by singing to ease the growing tension.

Changing tactics, I looked at Calev, smiled, then addressed the amir. "Forgive me. I know nothing about politics. I do know that a leader such as yourself would beat me if I didn't share my knowledge of a possible adventure worthy of all the poetry in the world."

The amir's face lost its hard edge. Her lips softened and her eyes widened. "Speak."

"I imagine if you braved uncharted seas and found a lost place full of silver, people would sing your songs for an eternity."

Her body didn't move, but her fingers gripped the chair's sides. "And what is this place, sailor?"

"Ayarazi."

Steel returned to the amir's eyes. "Calev, your friend has seen too much sun. I will hear your father's promise that she is Old Farm's kaptan by the end of this moon cycle, or I will watch your throat-blood enrich my soil." Clapping her hands, she stood.

I pulled the map shards out of my sash and ran toward her with them shining in my outstretched palms.

The fighters by her dais rushed toward me, helmets reflecting the window's light and their arm-length yatagans drawn and ready.

Calev shouted my name.

The amir stared down at me, but held up a hand to stop them from running me through. Her guards halted, and I lifted the map shards like a sacrificial lamb.

The curved tips of her leather boots quivered as she walked down the two steps to meet me. A smile cut through her mouth.

"Correct me if I'm mistaken, sailor. You believe this is a map to Ayarazi, an island only known from stories, an island filled with mystical horses, green forests, and caves lined in the purest silver."

My heart scratched up my throat. When she said it like that, in her ringing, polished voice, the whole thing sounded about as reasonable as wearing a fur coat in the Kurakian desert during high summer.

I blew out a slow breath. "Yes." A glint brightened her eyes. "And, my lady, I am willing to guide your ship and your fighters to the island indicated on this map for only one half of the total amount of silver gleaned."

"Half?" She looked to Calev. "Was this your idea?"

Calev whitened around the mouth. "No, my lady, but I do believe Kinneret Raza. She found the wine jug—the pieces there—in a wrecked ship not far from Quarry Isle. Old Zayn—forgive me, I don't know his family name—insists that his ancestor worked as a scribe for the Quest knights."

Calev filled her in on the tale. The amir listened with thinning lips.

The amir's gaze whipped to a dark back corner, where a man had come in. "We have three days until our trip to Kurakia, yes?" the amir asked.

It was Berker. Fantastic.

His mouth fell open as his gaze went from my torn skirts to my face. "What are you doing here?"

"Kaptan Berker Deniz, you forget yourself." The amir's eyes flashed.

Berker cleared his throat and the surprise left his features. "Yes, my lady. My apologies. We do indeed have three days until our journey to Kurakia. I do wonder if you are aware who sullies your presence."

I rolled my eyes and Calev's hands fisted at his sides.

The amir's fine brow wrinkled. "Enlighten me."

"This low-caste sailor is the one I told you about. She works to seduce the high-caste Old Farm, Calev ben Y'hoshua, into marriage. They've been caught together more than once."

My heart knocked as I looked to Calev, who was blushing furiously.

"Only talking," I blurted.

Calev squeezed his eyes shut and tilted his head back.

Why couldn't I keep my mouth shut?

Steepling her fingers at her trim waist, the amir said, "Kaptan Berker Deniz, I have spoken with Calev ben Y'hoshua on this, thank you. They are not yet of age. The boy knows I'd hate to see him become an Outcast."

Berker bowed. "Thank you for safeguarding our stronger bloodlines and more capable minds." His gaze slid to me.

Calev put a hand on my arm, holding me back.

Even if I died for it, I was ready to rip the man's eyes out.

Calev's fingers tightened on me. "Shhh," he said under his breath, though he looked as ready to go for the kill as me.

One of the amir's fighting sailors came from the back of the room and handed her a square of papyrus.

She read it quickly. "Kill the criminal," she said to the man. "I don't care if he is the kyros's third cousin."

The fighter strode out of the room, not once looking away from his destination.

The amir turned her attention back to us. "Be at the main docks at sunrise. Kaptan Berker Deniz, Kinneret Raza will aid you as we sail toward the legendary Ayarazi."

Berker's hands splayed like someone had dumped ice-cold water down his back. "What, my lady?"

It was my turn to smile. "I'm going to lead you and the amir's fighting sailors on a quest."

The man's mouth shut like a night flower exposed to sunlight.

I almost laughed.

The amir held up a finger. "Ah, ah. Not lead. Just advise."

Berker turned a fantastic shade of purple. "I assure you, the scrapper is lying, my lady."

The amir took a step forward. "Do not use slurs in my presence. Her family served their time as slaves. She is low, but that is all. Also, am I mistaken, Kaptan Berker Deniz, or did you suggest I cannot spot a lie?"

"Of course not. I only meant that you don't need her help. I can take you to the legendary island."

"Oh really? Then why didn't you already come to me with this life-changing information?"

I bit my lip to keep from laughing.

"If it's out there, I can find it for you, my lady."

"Enough." The amir adjusted the tie that held her sleeve in place. "She will advise. Unless she is found to be as unworthy as you seem to think her, Kaptan Berker Deniz."

Calev edged forward. "As to the matter of the riches the group will find, I stand witness that the amir will claim only half of the silver mined at Ayarazi with the other half going to Kinneret Raza, master of this expedition."

Berker's lips pinched together, making them whiten. The amir's hand didn't move to her throat.

"Will you not make the throat-blood oath?" My words peeked out of my mouth like scared children. "My lady?"

Berker sneered. "Don't be insolent, low-caste."

"Silence," the amir said. Her look boiled the flesh from my bones. "I will see you at sunrise." Her long tunic snapped as she twisted and strode back to her chair. "Make ready."

CALEV and I walked out of the amir's main hall and under the orange and ivory striped arches leading to her courtyard.

I leaned toward Calev. "She didn't make the oath. And what is your father going to do when he hears about what you're doing?"

"She'll hold to her word. She only believes an oath is beneath her. My father won't do anything. He can't get in the way of the amir's plans. Plus, this shouldn't take so long. Eleazar is covering for me, remember? They'll be so busy with the harvest, they won't have the sun to notice I'm missing."

"Maybe. But how am I going to get us through the Pass and beyond without Berker seeing my Salt Magic?" Or how our hands brush and my breath catches?

Chewing his lower lip, Calev said, "You'll think of something. You always do."

I pressed a hand on my forehead. "I hope you're right."

CHAPTER FOURTEEN

The amir's black-sailed ship floated like a wooden fortress at the northern dock. Its pennants, pinned to the top of the mast and the towering prow, flew with the wind, snapping. The amir's seal crouched on each one—a roaring black lion on a field of yellow, ready for a battle with the sea.

But as lovely as the craft was, it was not a worthy opponent for the sea's challenges, nor was the man who now kaptaned it. Berker. He would make all the same mistakes as the kaptans before him.

Sailing a fortress like this one, they tried to force their will on the waters, instead of working with its tides, current, and creatures. If this were my ship, I'd fit it with looser sails. I'd trim the sides, lessen its weight. It'd be a beautiful beast, strong enough to withstand the worst of storms and clever enough to find its way through the waves.

My mother and father had set the idea of the right kind of sailing in my mind. As we crossed the waters with the sun hot on our heads and the hull and deck bursting with fruit, sometimes with sacks of Old Farm's fine grain, or a few less-than-wealthy travelers, my parents had poured their wisdom into Avi and me. Let wraiths own the night with the pain they remembered from their lives lost at sea. Allow the current to take the boat four knocks east of the intended route, because it will ease the trip around that rock shelf. Listen to the wind to know when the storm will hit or when the sea will calm and need to rest. The Pass could be a friend, or at least, a respected enemy.

We stopped at the ramp leading to the amir's ship and stood behind a line of her infamous fighting sailors. I leaned right to watch them as they stopped, one-by-one, at the ship's Holy Fire bowl. Each passed a hand over banked coals that glowed like jewels. Pennants of smoke danced over their tall forms and the center of their palms glimmered as they bowed to the Fire. A few touched the center of their foreheads, acknowledging the Fire's potential to give them ideas.

I couldn't even imagine doing Salt Magic in front of so many people. My bag of salt was tucked inside my sash, away from judging eyes, but at some point, I'd have to use it. I only hoped when I did, everyone would be too busy to notice.

On deck, the fighters lined up on either side of the amir and Berker as we boarded the soap-scented ship.

At least they'd swabbed the deck properly.

"Try to remember this is the amir's ship, Kinneret," Oron whispered. "And neither she nor her ship are here for your examination."

I scowled at him.

"You might stay alive longer. That's all I'm saying." Oron shrugged.

Two men fitted a barred cover over a storage space near the prow. I peered in and a giant's sharp, metal finger pointed up at me. "What is that?"

"Mining drill." Oron flicked a hand toward the dark beyond the object. "There are probably five or so aboard."

Those would slow us down for sure. "How much do they weigh?"

"No idea," Oron said. "Calev? Have you used any on Old Farm?"

"We used a different sort on a new well, but I don't know much about them."

We climbed the stairs and stood next to the man-sized tiller wheel as the amir spoke to her assembled fighters. Each wore red leather jerkins similar to hers, but theirs jingled with five bells on each shoulder. Their black sashes secured daggers and yatagans, frog legs, and other charms. Some held battle axes with gold or silver heads meant to deflect blows.

The nearest fighter's axe was decorated with calligraphy in the shape of phoenix heads. Beautiful and deadly—much like its owner, a giant woman who would probably lop my head off if I so much as sneezed the wrong way. But that axe of hers…

"You want one, don't you?" Oron whispered up to me.

"I do." My hands never wanted to curl around my small knife and anytime I'd tried a yatagan, it felt too skinny. The handle of that axe wasn't too different from a tiller, and I knew exactly how to handle one of those.

"Just for you, I'll ask its owner where one might find another like it," Oron said, his gaze going up and down the fighter's body.

"Just for me, hmm?" I frowned at the woman's impressive bosom.

Oron shuttered his eyes dramatically. "I am the epitome of self-sacrifice."

"My fighters." The amir held her arms wide. "Today we embark on a mission to find Ayarazi, lost island of silver."

A wave of confused murmurs ran through the group.

"You will be richly rewarded if you succeed in following this... temporary kaptan's orders as if she were me." She held a hand toward me and my mouth didn't want to work.

Temporary kaptan?

"The title gives you more control, gives you rank. I've decided I'd rather have the one who knows the way fully able to order my sailors. Unless that is a problem?"

"No. It's...no, it's wonderful. Perfect. Thank you, my lady." Calev elbowed me, his eyes making my knees go liquid.

"Apologies, my lady." Berker looked like his bowels weren't working well. "But she is low-caste and I know for a fact she is a practitioner of—"

"Thank you, my lady," I said, the words coming like they belonged to someone else. My heart beat in my ears. This was my dream. Berker had never seen me practice Salt Magic. He had no proof. And I wasn't about to let him ruin this. I turned to the crew. "And thanks to her sailors who will help me steer this vessel to the northern reaches of the Pass. Haul anchor and tie up the mainsail. I will handle the steering on my own. We go!"

The fighters each drove one fist into the air and hustled to their stations at starboard and port, prow and stern. They were pieces on the playing board and I knew this game better than any.

Giving me a gentle squeeze on the shoulder, Calev spoke in my ear. "My Kinneret, kaptan of the amir's own vessel."

Shivers ran up and down my arms. Kaptan. His Kinneret.

I turned, and our breath mingled. The scar at the corner of his lips twitched like he was about to smile. My body thrummed, wanting him to lean closer, a breath nearer, to press his body to mine.

CHAPTER FIFTEEN

Berker's cough broke the spell. "The sun waits for no one. Let's see what the little nothing can do," he hissed quietly. "It would be sad indeed if the nothing was seen consorting improperly with an Old Farm. Sad if she were thrown to the hull with nothing to do but clean his chamber pot."

I gritted my teeth.

Calev leaned toward my neck and whispered, "Everything will be fine if you can hold that sweet tongue of yours."

It was good we balanced one another like this. When he wanted to leap into something stupid, I held him back. When I was ready to bite and ruin everything, he kept me calm. Well, he tried. I didn't like tucking my tail between my legs. *Little nothing.* We'd see about that.

Twisting away, I focused on the Pass to learn what the sea had to say about the coming journey. The water was smooth, but an inconsistent breeze whisked through the air and a current snaked beneath the glassy surface, ready to suck us down if I didn't steer the ship right.

I looked to Oron. He nodded in the direction of the wind and I took his advice, moving the wheel a bit so we sat a little more westerly.

Hidden in my sash, the map shards' edges pushed at a spot on my stomach. I welcomed their sharp corners, remembering their promise.

As we cleared the shelter of the deepest part of the Jakobden harbor, Oron nibbled a skewer of meat—Where had he found that?—and started a game of bones and shells behind me with two sailors who smiled at something he said.

"Only Oron could get fighting sailors to smile," Calev said, walking away to find somewhere to lend a hand.

Tunic sleeves pushed over his elbows, Calev rewrapped a rope with the woman who had the beautiful axe. She was even taller than the amir. Her attention was more on Calev's wiry arms than the task at hand. A hot arrow jabbed my stomach, but I pushed the jealousy down. We had no more sun to waste. I had to get these sailors moving.

I called out my first orders. "Take us fifteen knocks south before turning north."

"What?" Berker clutched an enormous key and a book with gold lettering down its spine. "That's hours out of our way."

The sun-warmed cedar wheel heated my palms. I took a fortifying breath. "How many Pass trips have you made, kaptan?"

"More than you," he spat.

I'd asked around about him, but he'd somehow cloaked his early days in Jakobden. He might've even changed his name, but that was a weak hypothesis of my own. I did know some things though.

"I heard you were a malhatc rope merchant before ever setting a sandal on a boat." I smiled.

His eyes widened.

"Didn't think I'd find out everything I could when I realized how this journey was going to go?" Fisting my hand, I put my thumb against my forehead, but instead of drawing a circle, the Fire's sign, on my flesh, I spread my fingers in a sudden burst, the dirtiest gesture Oron had taught me.

I heard Oron laugh from far off, but thankfully, no one else had seemed to notice. He had moved away from his game, taking a block from a fighting sailor's hand and adjusting the line. He waved to the sails and rolled his eyes. I was so glad he was here.

Berker gasped belatedly, shocked by my gesture. "Such manners. Suppose I should expect twisted, disrespectful uses of the Fire's sign from one like you. You will learn to behave, sailor, or you will be punished."

"Truly? By whom?" The Pass was moody today. The waves had risen, and they ate at our speed.

"The amir—"

"The amir put me here. I'd guess she won't care that I use the sign to shut your flapping lips. I don't think the Fire cares much either."

Leaving the sailor he'd lectured, Oron pushed his way between Berker and me. "Nor will the amir mind if I ask where the wine is kept. Now be on your way, other kaptan. I have much to discuss with my own lady here."

Huffing, Berker bustled off toward the amir, who stood at the prow with her hair in viciously tight knots. She held her shoulders back as if she could intimidate the sea. The woman was awful, but also kind of fantastic.

Unsteady on his feet, Calev came up beside us. "Rankling Berker again?"

Oron groaned. "Don't start, good luck charm. I haven't had a drop of wine, let alone an amount sufficient to help me tolerate your obnoxiously good nature."

Calev said, "Good luck charm? You're the one who works the least and manages to get the most food. Maybe I should tie you around my neck like a frog's leg." He plucked the last piece of meat from Oron's skewer and popped it between his lips.

Oron rubbed his chin. "It's not a bad idea. I'd have a better view from up there."

"What did you want to tell me, Oron?" I'd asked him to examine their wraith lanterns.

"They have five. They look well enough, though not completely glass like your mother's."

I wished we'd brought mine. Wraith lantern wicks were a complicated thing. Slight color switches at the third and seventh threading, or at the one-third or one-seventh mark across the wick's expanse, repelled wraiths more acutely, and kept them at a farther distance.

"They keep them in those small boxes, don't they?" Calev asked. The joking slant had fled his lips. He pointed to the dark wood containers poised along starboard.

The odd glint in his eyes told me that last run-in with a Salt Wraith still hung over him. Who could blame him? I'd screamed my face off last time. Only because I'd dealt with the wraiths so many times could I cast off the fear of Infusion afterward.

Once, when a small fleet of us low-caste sailors were shipping Old Farm surplus figs to a port just north of Jakobden's, two wraiths had attacked. My mother had lit the lantern's expensive wick with a grace and speed no one else in the world had. Father had Avi strapped to his back. We had tried to work the sail and get away, but the wraiths speared from the sky again and again, challenging the lantern's effect on them. Far enough from those who would threaten Outcasting, we all went to the salt. A woman in a boat nearby called out prayers and threw handfuls of white, but the sea was sluggish to answer her. Two middle-aged sisters in another boat huddled together and sprinkled salt over the side of their craft. The wind breezed toward them, but not quickly enough. One of the sisters had been Infused and nearly throttled her own first mate before anyone could lash her to the mast.

I had dusted our salt into the waves, and with one focused prayer, we slipped away, leaving the others to their fate. We were the only boat to get away without an instance of Infusion. For a good year after, the other small-boat Pass sailors had dipped their heads to me as if I was special. So even when I, just like everyone else, was scared to shaking by the wraiths, I still had a thread of confidence running through me.

"I wouldn't worry about where they store the wraith lanterns, Calev," I said now, shoving the memory away. "In this clear weather, we'll have no trouble getting them lit and hung before sundown."

He stared at the approaching rocks, Tall Man first, then the Spires, after that, Asag's Door. For a second, the healthy glow leeched from Calev's skin and hair and eyes. He looked like a bad fresco of himself, and my heart clenched to see it. I touched his arm, wishing we were on my boat, away from all of this.

The wish tightened my throat. I jerked my hand away.

No. I didn't want to be away from this. Being kaptan is what I'd wanted my whole life. I could save Avi as a kaptan. And Calev was strong enough to deal with wraiths. He had to be. I spun. The fighters worked the rigging, the sail snapped and caught, and the ship dipped in the increasingly rough water, then soared high again, my stomach lifting and making me smile. This was what I wanted. Regardless of the risk. Kaptan Kinneret. Equal to Calev.

"So all the lanterns were in good shape?" I asked Oron, double-checking for Calev's sake.

"I think so. But maybe you can take a look at the wicks and see if we should add a threes and sevens stitch." Oron frowned at Calev.

Calev braced himself against the ship. "I'm not worried, if that's what you think. I'm fine." He smiled, but it wasn't his good smile.

WITH THE AMIR'S men and women following my orders, I steered the weighty craft around the rocks. The wind at a nice angle, we tracked our way north. I wanted to find the lost island before nightfall. The map shards only gave the vaguest sense of distance. It was impossible to know if we could pull it off.

The sails billowed above us, and I pulled the largest of the shards out of my sash. Calev and Oron leaned over me to look. Calev pointed to a spot we'd see pretty soon.

"What do these raised ridges mean? Do you think they were put there purposefully, or are only a part of the pottery?"

"I think they show some sort of hazard." The wheel pulled at my grip. I tightened my grip and my bag of salt slipped from my sash.

Calev sucked a breath.

I grabbed the bag and tucked it back into place, checking to see if anyone noticed.

"Smooth," Oron whispered as a sailor walked by. He raised his voice. "I think these marks are creatures."

"If they are," I said. "There'd have to be an army of them." Goosebumps tripped down my back.

The scout shouted from the sky cup, his voice carrying from his perch at the top of the mast. "Ahead! Ahead!"

The yellow, sunny day seemed an ironic thing suddenly.

Directly in our path—and any path we could take with the wind the way it was—wrecked ships protruded from the white edges of the choppy water. Like dead starfish, the ships clung to what looked like dark reefs punching through the sea's surface.

Oron grabbed my arm and squeezed. Hard.

Any one of these ghost ships could reach out and break the hull. We'd be food for seastingers. We'd be doomed to rise as Salt Wraiths, twisting and hating for eternity.

"What do they do to Salt Witches at sea?" I asked Oron, my voice taut, almost breaking.

"Throw them overboard."

Calev stood closer. "You won't go down alone."

"I'm not going down at all. I'll die on this boat first."

CHAPTER SIXTEEN

Masts like broken fingers. Ragged sails twisting in the water. Prows, noses to the sun. Wide tillers, jagged from their tragedy. The water in front of us was a labyrinth of debris.

I imagined an errant, wrecked stern puncturing our hull and fighters sliding to starboard, panic jerking their movements. In my mind, a sail reached its triangle of fabric around our tiller until the mighty wood splintered and left us rudderless in the Pass. My head pounded. I went cold from forehead to foot.

And then I was in a memory.

Mother, Father, Avi, and I on the deck of my boat, the sky a green and black calamity raging toward us.

"There are days you must let the sea take you, Kinneret," Mother had said, her voice quiet but strong, like a yatagan slicing the air. "Let the water and the wind, the sea itself, guide you through. Those days, like this one, release your hold on the tiller and your gaze from the rigging. Let go."

The howling storm had raged over us that day. We'd lashed ourselves to the hatch, to the mast, to the side, watching nothing as the rain blinded us. A thousand, two-thousand seconds later, we drifted out of the clouds and wind and water, alive. Humbled. Reminded that the control we have over our lives only remains in our hands if we sometimes released it from our fisted fingers.

And now, I needed to do the same.

"Loosen the rigging on the mainsail!" I threw an arm toward the black swathe of fabric that pulled us through the water. "All sailors to the sides, positioning beams in hand!"

The fighting sailors had been frozen by the ship graveyard, but they turned, pointed helmets shining, to frown at me now.

"Don't just stand there, fools!" Oron was small in size but not in voice. "Your kaptan gives orders!"

I was already pulling salt from my pouch, hoping I could do more than I'd ever done with the magic and praying Berker and the amir would stay below. Calev shielded me from most eyes, his wide sleeves billowing around me. He watched me scoop a handful of sparkling white, then he nodded.

"Save us, my fire."

My heart rolled over. "I'll try."

I moved to the side, lifting my palmful. The sea grumbled around the dead ships and their rotting limbs. I took a breath. What prayer should I say? Why wouldn't the words come to me?

"Kaptan?" a sailor's wide eyes turned toward me as he struggled with the lines beside his friends. "Is that—"

The amir burst from the cabin door, Berker trailing her like a string on her tunic.

I growled.

"My fighters," the amir said. "Do as she says."

Calev said something under his breath, the sound of it harsh and sharp, unlike him.

The amir must've seen our situation from her cabin window. And now she'd see my situation too. Well, what did Old Zayn say? As well hanged for a chicken as an egg. The dead ships in the water loomed closer, raising threatening masts and broken hulls. If I didn't work fast, this would be over. I had no sun for more fretting. Ignoring everything else, I dusted the salt into the breeze and prayed, the words finally flowing.

"Sea, be with me.

Wind, please answer.

To take, to give.

Tumbling currents, push us, pull us.

Set us free."

Some of the salt ghosted into the water. Most of the sparkling white floated back and danced near the sailors' heads, before drifting over the sails and down to brush the amir's cheek.

Our gazes met and my blood pounded in my ears.

CHAPTER SEVENTEEN

H er mouth formed words I couldn't hear over the growing wind, but could see and understand. "This is your skill? You are no true kaptan."

The ship shifted under us, and we dragged our way past the first drowned vessel. Some of the sailors gasped. Two turned from the amir to look over the side, as if they could see the magic.

I raised my voice so it would carry like the salt, over the sailors and into her ears. "There are times when we must trust the sea to bring us through. It knows the way."

Oron put a fist in the air. "Yes."

My mother's words *Trust the sea* surged through my veins alongside her blood and the bond that no death could ever steal away. I dared the amir to try.

Among folds of Calev's linen sleeve, his warm fingers found my hand. I held tight, hoping his luck would soak into me. His unblinking eyes focused on the amir.

Berker and the amir strode across the deck as the sailors wasted time staring, positioning poles in their hands.

We drifted closer to the larger grounded ships with every breath.

"I told you she was no more than a Salt Witch." Berker laughed.

The amir's gaze slapped him silent. But then she loosened the leather collar of her vest and looked to me. "Sailor, stand down. Kaptan Berker Deniz takes control now."

We had no sun for this. "We will sink, my lady." We might anyway. I'd never pushed my skill with prayer so far.

She glanced at me, my skirts, my bells. "You've been given your order. Guard!"

A man with a red beard stormed up the three stairs to where we stood, pushed past Calev and Oron, who argued. The guard grabbed my arms, and everything slowed to a dreamlike pace as my mind wandered into varying possibilities.

Maybe I could use the salt to fight?

I'd never used salt against anyone. Unless you counted wraiths. But if I drowned this sun, Avi would die, by wraiths or by work in the quarry. I had no idea how a salt prayer would work to hinder or hurt a person. Maybe it wouldn't do anything at all. But my desire, my focus—as Mother had always called it—was certainly there, burning and struggling against the impossible situation. I had to at least try.

Avi was suddenly there, in that same memory of the night we'd escaped the two wraiths. Her cheeks were round as she peered over Father's shoulder, her legs still against his sides. I whispered prayers and sprinkled salt, and her mouth fell open as the sea answered me. Unlike my sweet sister, I was naturally good at focusing my will and creating strong Salt Magic.

Now was the time to see exactly how strong.

Rubbing the remnants of salt from my fingers, my skin burning under the fighter's rough grip, I whispered a prayer.

"Go true, winds on the waters.

You know me and I know you."

Calev's eyes widened.

Oron's leg flashed out as he kicked the fighter who held me in the knee. "Son of a whoring goat. Let your kaptan go."

Startled, the man let go for only a breath, then he held me again. The sky grayed like someone had drawn a curtain on the sun, and an air current curled around my legs, tangling my skirt.

The wind tugged me from the fighter's hands.

Rain like knives dashed from the ballooning clouds above the ebony sails.

The sea was listening.

The ship turned toward starboard, under my feet, heavy and lumbering.

Calev, Oron, the amir, and I—united in survival—took hold of whatever was closest. I clung to the railing near the wheel. Oron clutched the large bell hung for sounding arrival to the docks. Calev latched onto an empty rope's post toward port, the amir at his side doing the same. A fist of fighters fell to the decking. Some shouted to the Fire, to the power of the sea.

The boat listed to port, then back again roughly. Water lipped the edge, salt sea mixing with the fresh rain pooling and dragging across the smooth wood. A sailor slipped and dropped over starboard, legs in the Pass, hands latched to the rim like starfish.

I scurried down to help her back onboard as we twisted past the first of the larger wrecked vessels. A cracked beam reached over the gap between our ship and its own broken body, and I ducked, avoiding its wooden spines. The beam scraped the stern and turned our tail.

"Kinneret!" Calev was running at me, his feet slipping and his face white.

I tugged the fallen sailor's vest and pulled her onto the deck.

The rain went sideways as the sea steered us around another ship with its sails and bedraggled pennants like rebellious daytime wraiths in the storm.

The blowing rain clouded the amir's face. I couldn't tell whether she ordered more fighters after me or if she was simply clinging to the ship like everybody else. The black and silver lightning blinked over the clouds, then Calev was with me, his hand on my back, his eyes filled with fear.

The ship swung around to avoid two ancient dhows, twice the size of my own craft. Their lines hung from masts and splintered prows like saliva from a wild dog's mouth. Our ship veered close, too close. One snagged our prow and jerked us.

Calev pitched over the ship's side.

He disappeared under the waves even as my hands reached out pointlessly.

My mouth worked, trying to breathe, taking in metallic storm-rain.

Someone screamed. Another shouted.

Numbly, I thought, *You can't take Calev too. Please.*

Leaning over the ship, I spotted flesh in the water. Hands. Fingers, wet and pale, holding to a ridge of wood connected to the side of the boat. We lurched backward and Calev's head appeared, the sea releasing him for a second. Near the stairs, a rope and a float hung on a hook. Oron was there before I could finish my thought of grabbing it.

"Here." Oron tossed it, and I caught the netted float in both shaking, freezing hands.

There was no sun for more salt prayers. I threw the float, praying, hoping, wishing, longing for Calev to reach it, to be able to grab his one chance of seeing another day. This couldn't be our end. It couldn't be.

The Salt Magic worked the current of the water and helped us between another lost vessels.

But the float flipped past Calev.

He threw one arm out to catch it.

Missed.

In the crash of water, the float blasted back toward him. Letting go of the boat's side, Calev committed both hands to his attempt. Somehow—because he was lucky Calev—he caught it and hugged it to him.

I twisted. Fighting sailors gathered behind me, Oron with them.

"Pull! Pull now!" My throat was raw and my heart was bleeding.

The rope slid through my chilled, wet fingers, its coconut fibers cutting into my skin. With everything I had, I latched onto it and yanked, the fighting sailors doing the same.

Calev's face cleared the wall.

My heart knocked against my ribs. Oron and I tugged him aboard, and I fell onto his back as he lay forward and gasped. I cried and squeezed him, not caring if we wrecked now because he was here with me. He was here with me. Not gone. Not in the sea. Not lost to become a Salt Wraith.

The rain eased, and the sun leaked through the clouds as we passed the last of the dead ships. I stood, hands on my knees, my skirts wet and heavy, and smiled.

Thanks to you, sea waters. Thanks to you, Fire.

We were alive. We still had a chance to save Avi. Unless the amir decided she'd had enough of my magic.

CHAPTER EIGHTEEN

The Pass was a road of silk that night. Watching for wraiths, sailors lit the lanterns. The swinging patterns of orange and silver light almost made me forget the terrible spirits could come at any moment and Infuse us. That they could sweep over us, find a place not cloaked in magic light, and twist our minds so we set on one another like rabid animals.

On the small, raised kaptan's deck, the amir walked up to me, her eyes half lidded. A servant hovered near and offered her skewers of goat's meat. She took two and gave me one.

"Kaptan Kinneret Raza, you may spend the night below with my unit leaders, Calev ben Y'hoshua, and Kaptan Berker Deniz."

"Thank you."

It was unbelievable. I'd thought after the Salt Magic, she'd have me thrown into the hole to suffer the rest of the journey with the rats. My efforts to escape the ship graveyard outweighed my taboo magic. In her eyes, at least. But wonderful as her invitation to go below was, I couldn't leave Oron. Or the fighting sailors.

"I will be fine on deck, my lady."

Calev came out of the shadows, his lips tight and his gaze on the amir. "Thank you for your offer of safety, my lady."

I suppose he'd heard her mention his name.

"Will you sleep below then, Calev ben Y'hoshua?" I asked, using his whole name to show I understood the high-caste ways. I tried to keep any judgment on his decision from my voice. It was smart to take safety when it was offered, and the cabin would definitely be better than staying out here, despite the lanterns. Calev was important to our community. I understood. But it didn't stop me from hoping he'd stay out here with me.

He cocked his head. "Maybe later. For now, I'll keep you company."

"For planning purposes only, of course," the amir said in her bell voice as she walked away and disappeared belowdecks.

My cheeks heated, and my blood sprinted a lap around my body. "Of course," I answered before Calev could ruin things by defending our friendship to the amir. I'd had enough fighting for one day.

Oron sat on a barrel beside some sailors near the main mast. He'd found a gourd-shaped oud and was plucking the strings like a master.

Clouds masked the sky and blinded the moon. The lanterns were swaying stars that sent comets of gold light off the posts, the decking, and the fighting sailors' varied faces. Some were my age. Most older. Men. Women. Hair like copper, ink, sand. Their flesh was lighter than my own. None with Kurakian blood.

I touched Calev's sleeve. "Want to go down to the main deck?" I gestured toward Oron and the others, who were drinking now and singing sailing songs.

Calev's eyes flicked to the door through which the amir had disappeared and he flipped his dagger casually. Through the cloth of his salt-crusted tunic, his skin chilled my fingers, but his usual scent of sun-heated fields and lemons was a comfort.

"Come on," I said. "You need a little music."

Taking a breath, he nodded, sheathed his dagger, and let me lead him down the short staircase to the main deck.

Oron lifted his eyebrows in greeting as he strummed notes into the night to help us forget the wraiths and the loss of one of our sailors. Oron's smallest finger jumped up and down on the oud's thinnest string, making the instrument quirk high, then higher. I plopped onto a crate of what smelled like flatbread. Sitting next to me, Calev shook his head and moved his jaw.

"Water in your ears?" Other than a three-finger-long scratch down his forearm, he hadn't suffered from his fall overboard. If it'd been me, I'd have lost an entire leg to an errant seastinger.

A woman next to Oron began a haunting accompaniment on an eagle bone flute.

"My head…I feel a little off," Calev said.

I put my hand on his knee to stop his leg bouncing. "It's been quite a day."

"Quite." He gave me a quick grin and tucked his hair behind his ear. A dusting of scruff shadowed his sharp jawline, and my stomach dipped like I'd sailed over a swell.

The tall female sailor from earlier elbowed me. "If I had a man like him look at me like that, I'd have him up and dancing no matter the cost later. Besides, you're a kaptan. For now, anyway." She laughed quietly. "A wraith's welcome is always a surprise, the sea's embrace a cold one."

The traditional sailor's motto had me standing in a breath. Never before had the old words seemed so true. Life was short. I was going to enjoy myself. Just for tonight, while I was still a kaptan. It did Avi no harm for me to keep on living as we worked our way to rescuing her.

"Calev, will you dance with me?" I held out my hands, my heart shivering.

This was a line for him to cross. Maybe I could keep the kaptan status. A low-caste kaptan. Whoever heard of such a thing? But maybe, just maybe...

Plus, it was only one dance. It wasn't a proposal of Intention.

Calev looked up at me. The lanterns poured copper light over one side of his face. His eyes were that deep brown-red of good wine. The kind I'd only tasted when Oron stole a jug. The music, complex and drifting, swirled over our heads, but Calev didn't rise.

And there was Berker, a flash of too-bright silk in the corner, his lips poised to laugh at my public humiliation. I was sure he didn't view my status as anything but low.

I began to drop my hands. Flames enveloped my neck and chest.

Oron added words to his music and crowed so loudly that I knew he was trying to deflect attention from me to himself. Kind soul.

"He drew her in like tragedies often dooooo, his heart so black and his eyes so bluuuue. She would die before the sea drank the sun, but his smile would be worth it before it was done."

Then, in one smooth movement, Calev stood.

My heart answered his smile by reaching into my throat and attempting to push me, head first, into his arms.

I fought the urge. I'd gone this far. I wouldn't go further. He had to take the step.

"I'd like that, kaptan," Calev said.

And if it weren't for my sister's plight, it would've been the best night of my life.

Oron shaped his song into a tempting syren's call as Calev's arms circled me. He placed his hands, warmer now, on my back. His palms felt large against the curve of my waist. They sent a slow-moving wash of heat up my back and down my legs. Trying to breathe normally, I lifted my own hands high and flipped them this way and that like swallows at dusk. His gaze locked on my face, we stepped right, then left. His fingers tightened slightly on me and I swallowed, definitely not breathing normally. In rhythm with the leaping, colorful music, we turned as one.

Other couples joined in, bumping us here and there and smiling. A man held a wooden bowl of tatlilav to our lips, each in turn. The drink warmed my throat and loosened my arms and legs. A strand of Calev's hair whipped into my eye, and I laughed as we spun and spun and spun, my body held upright by his strong hands.

Calev's winded voice found my ear. He smelled a little like the salt of sweat and I found I didn't mind it. "They don't teach this kind of dancing at Old Farm." On the last word, someone jostled us and his mouth brushed my ear. I shivered and swallowed.

"N-No, I suppose not." I stepped on his toe and grinned as apology. "It's a trader's jig. Oron taught me."

Hearing his name, Oron tipped his head at us and finished the song with a trill of low notes that had everyone stomping their feet in approval of his skill. He set his oud aside and hopped from the barrel. "Calev, why don't you favor us with an Old Farm dagger dance?"

My mouth popped open. Did Calev know the traditional steps? I'd never thought about it. But he'd be a perfect dagger dancer with his long limbs and enviable grace.

A blush crept over his nose and cheeks.

I smacked his arm playfully, the tatlilav doing its work to make me bold. "You do know how, don't you?"

The man with the wooden bowl offered me another sip, but I waved him off. Oron motioned for the sailors to gather around, then threw two handfuls of salt at Calev's feet.

Berker snorted and left for belowdecks.

We made a wide, seated circle around Calev, who didn't appear to have a choice in this. If he knew how to do this robed-in-secrecy dance, we wanted to see it.

Calev put his palms on the deck's luminous wooden planks. "I don't know if this is a good idea, Oron."

Was that the dance's starting position? I'd heard tales about it. But even though Calev was arguing this, he at least didn't seem haunted like he had earlier tonight.

A long-faced sailor leaned in. "We won't tell."

Another agreed. "This may be our only chance to see this. Would you rob us our vision of the Fire's weapon?"

Good-natured laughs followed. Old Farms, the native people of Jakobden, claimed their dagger skills were why the Bahluk conquerors—the amir's people—permitted them to keep their lands. Today, three-hundred-sun-circles later, we knew the real reason. Silver. The Bahluk conquerors and the kyros that employed them enjoyed the silver brought in by trading Old Farm lemons and barley. None had been able to mimic Old Farm's perfectly sweet, but achingly sour fruits. And Old Farm's barley never wilted in the worst of droughts. Although Calev had surprised me with his speed and agility already on this voyage, his people's strength came from wisdom and careful planning, not physical prowess. The dagger dance was ceremonial, not martial.

"I think it's a fabulous idea." Oron grinned. "You'll either make us laugh at your ridiculousness, or everyone will swoon, wondering if your coordination translates to the bed."

Whoops erupted over the deck and I went a little lightheaded. Calev cocked an eyebrow at all of us, then looked at me.

"What do you say, Kaptan Kinneret?"

A light like the sun glowed through me. Even if it was ceremonial, I wanted to see it. Their rituals tugged at me like the sea.

"Please, Calev ben Y'hoshua, son of Old Farm," I said, "dance for us."

With the smile that could heal all my hurts, the smile that promised we'd get Avi back and keep the amir from taking Calev's throat-blood by making me kaptan of Old Farm's ship, he closed his eyes and began.

With a grating sound, his palms smoothed along the deck in front of him until he was nearly lying face down, then with a movement that seemed impossible, he leaped into the air and landed in a crouch, his dagger drawn with a speed I had only seen in animals.

The group gasped, but quickly quieted as his arm arced, making an invisible line with the dagger before thrusting forward, spinning, thrusting back, and whirling one foot in a high kick that had to be more distraction than attack. Calev's foot stomped once, hard, his eyes flashing and his hair swinging. His feet made a thousand small steps, his dagger like a minnow in the waves of his sweeping tunic.

I didn't breathe once.

The dance took on a dreamlike quality. Wide arm movements. Dramatic slashes. Impossible kicks and defenses against imaginary conquerors.

I was no longer on a ship. I was no longer a sailor.

I was a Jakobden native, one of Calev's ancestors. I was leaping from trees to slice a Bahluk's yatagan hand. I was spinning, the ties of my traditional headtie snapping and the sun on my blade blinding another bell-adorned attacker. I dug a bare foot into the ground and the scent of fertile earth and tannic, syrupy cedar rose into the air.

Calev stopped, bowed, and the spell broke. His dagger hung at his sash.

The sailors sprang into the air, feet stomping, mouths shouting.

My knees quaking, I went to him. "Calev. I…Calev."

He bent toward me, but instead of kissing my lips, his mouth went to my forehead, to my hairline.

I couldn't stop my hands from wrapping around his body or keep my heart from breaking with want. I was a shivering, ridiculous mess. If he could move like that, he could fight. If his stomach and mind could handle the horror.

"Kinneret, thank you," he said. "I haven't enjoyed a night this much ever in my life." He pressed his lips to my head again and my eyes closed. I wished he could be with me, like this, every day. He hadn't kissed my mouth yet, but maybe he would.

The night was still dark and heavy with promise.

But during another trader jig, the ship halted in a way that told me the night's promise had nothing to do with anything as pleasant as kissing.

CHAPTER NINETEEN

I broke away from the knot of sailors who'd joined me in dancing while Calev told stories near the brasier's glowing coals. Lit orange, his face rumpled in confusion at my sudden movement.

The deck jerked under my feet. Calev and Oron flew to me. "What is it, Kinneret?" Calev asked.

"I don't know…but it isn't good."

The ship had gone still again. Maybe we were lodged on a rock.

"What is that smell?" Oron's wide nose wrinkled.

The stench hit me. Stale salt water. Old fish. Blood. Swallowing, I took a struggling breath, wishing I didn't need air.

"Why are we stopped?" Oron asked.

I ran to the side and leaned over the railing. Black rock jutted from the sea and crowded around the ship, gripping it, holding it still in the battering waves. "We're stuck on an outcropping."

"We've run aground," a stocky sailor said.

"But our last depth reading…" The ship shuddered. This wasn't only an unexpected reef. This was something…more. I turned and faced my sailors. "Take up your weapons!"

Heat rose from the water, steaming against my arms and making the ends of my hair curl more tightly.

Calev pointed. "It's boiling. Kinneret, the sea, it's boiling." His eyes went wide, and the waves lashing at the ship gurgled like black stew in a cauldron.

I couldn't speak. I'd seen many horrors on the Pass, but never this.

Fish, some small as a fist, others larger than our hull, floated to the surface with dead eyes and cooked, white flesh. The smell was overwhelming. The stocky sailor and the rest made the Fire's sign on their foreheads, ran hands over the Holy Fire, praying and holding tight to battle axes, bows, yatagans, and lucky frog legs.

Oron grasped my arm. "What is this?"

Calev and I looked at one another. In unison, we said, "Savta's monster. Asag."

"To the cannons," I called out. "Everyone else, to port side and starboard."

The amir's men and women rushed belowdeck to the cannons and hurried to the sides of the ship.

"Raise your bows, your blades!" I shouted. "Get into position, then close or shield your eyes. Aim for the sound. Use the noise as your target."

Calev nodded. "She speaks the truth. Quickly now, cover your eyes. Use your sashes, or a strip from your tunic."

My pulse drummed in my temples. "A demon will rise from the water. If you look at it, you will die. Listen to its screams and aim true, aim high. Stay side by side so we don't injure one another. Courage, all."

A pounding noise echoed from under the ship. We rose into the air, then were dropped harshly.

My stomach dipped and my breath caught. A shrill ringing poured through the night.

Calev, Oron, and I ripped strips of cloth from our clothing and handed them out to white-faced fighting sailors. We found two bows and three quivers full of black-fletched arrows. I was glad Calev and Oron both placed in the amir's archery competition in the past.

A quiver at my waist and a bow in my hand, I ran to the amir's room, pounding down the stairs, knowing my life was ruined if she didn't make it through this whole and sound.

Before I could knock on the leopard carved into her door, she pulled it open, her eyes like tatlilav bowls. She held a gold tipped bow. The yellow and black fletching of her arrows stuck out from the quiver at her waist.

I handed her a strip of cloth for her eyes. "My lady, the monster Asag is rising. He controls the rock of the seabed and holds your ship. You can't look at him."

Berker came up behind me. "Asag is a story. The low-caste lies. We've run aground."

"Then how do you explain the dead fish, the boiling water?" I spat.

A vicious smile spread over the amir's face. "We will shoot toward its noise." She pushed past Berker and I, and strode onto the deck, tying the cloth I'd given her over her eyes. Winding around the ropes and sailors and masts, she never took a bad step.

With Berker at my back like a malevolent shadow, I found Oron and Calev.

The seawater over the starboard side collected into a bubbling mountain. Two night-black horns, glossy and twisted, broached the surface.

I shut my eyes.

The demon rose, making a sound like glass breaking, roaring out a cacophony like one thousand men being flayed alive.

"It is your Salt Magic that's brought this curse," Berker said.

"Your mouth is the curse. Now find something to do. Cannons, fire!" I shouted over the din, my throat burning. My order was echoed, and the weapons below boomed from the ship's windows, shaking the deck.

As I pulled the bowstring back and wished I'd spent more time practicing my aim, hot tears seeped from my eyes and hurried down my cheeks to hide under my chin. A vibration pounded in my feet.

The rocks. The rocks he controlled were moving.

A sailor called out, and I tried to turn to see who had fallen, who was screaming over the scream. There was just so much noise. My lungs shuddered as I sucked a foul breath of fish and death. Someone bumped me. Calev said my name from a few steps away, and then the amir's voice was beside me.

"I will end this demon," she hissed as her arm moved against mine.

She fired arrow after arrow, her string whipping the air beside me.

I tried and failed to keep up with her as Asag's rocks rolled the ship roughly to starboard, then seemed to let go. We bobbed and floated free, the deck moving beneath my feet, as the demon shrieked, rising like the moon over the boiling, deadly water. I heard splashes and shouting. Someone, maybe more than one, had fallen from the deck.

"Fire!"

Again the cannons boomed, fewer this time. It had to be frightening to reload and light them while peeking from under a blindfold.

The ship lurched.

The screaming ceased.

A rhythm like a hand drill buzzed from the center of the deck. Asag's rocks were drumming their way into the hull. We had to end this now or we would all become wraiths.

Out of arrows, I kept my eyes to the decking as I rushed to starboard and yanked a whaling spear from the side. Careful not to look toward the creature, I spied Oron handing off arrows to fighting sailors. Calev shot the last one he had and lifted his headtie. His eyes found me.

"Take up spears," I called out to the fighting sailors. Flashes of pain blinked through my ears. The noise was unbelievable. "Wait for my word." I handed another spear to Calev and found the amir's side.

My spear was heavy and slick with seawater. The clank and drag of more fighters arming themselves with spears interrupted the demon's screaming. The grinding coming from the bottom of the ship halted.

"Now!" I threw the harpoon. Holding my breath, my pulse hammering in my throat, I prayed.

Asag let out another heart-shattering scream, sending me to my knees. The amir laughed, her foot dragging against my leg.

Then there was only silence.

I stood and opened my eyes.

Only a spill of what looked like oil and ashes marred the water's smooth surface. A dead squid and a school of boiled silver fish floated beside it.

The amir tore the cloth from her eyes, her bell ringing lightly. "I killed the demon Asag."

I could've argued. I knew in my gut that I'd killed it. But the amir's pride worked to keep her on my side.

"They will sing songs about this, my lady," I said.

She smiled, but I couldn't smile back. The deck held five dead fighting sailors, their eyes blackened in their sockets and their skin gray, slayed by the sight of the demon. More had fallen overboard when the rocks harassed the ship. Two corpses drifted past Asag's remains.

My eyelids shuttered closed, open. I spun to see Calev and Oron, hands clasped in victory like old friends.

Despite the loss, we had won.

THAT NIGHT, while a dark-haired, mostly silent fighting sailor named Ekrem manned the wheel and a crowd of others sewed the damaged sails, cleaned, and brought our ship back to a functioning level, sleep didn't give me rest like it should've.

I tossed and turned, never comfortable, drained, but strung too tight from the day. Giving up on sleep for a while, I stared at the busy sailors who moved like barley stalks blowing in the fields and took comfort in Calev sleeping sitting up beside me. Finally, my body gave out.

Avi found my dreams, and her pain turned them into nightmares.

Slender hands bloodied by work. An empty belly. A man's calloused finger tracing her jaw. Her shudder. A longing stare toward the Pass as she prayed I'd come for her.

I WOKE EXHAUSTED from my fitful sleep, my body trembled as the sails and the bruised light of morning came into focus. Oron, Calev, and myself had slept on benches beneath a cracked Wraith Lantern, too exhausted to fear anything anymore. I raised myself, slowly, painfully, and took a selfish moment to enjoy Calev's sleeping form.

His eyelashes rested in two crescent moons on his cheeks, and his fine nostrils edged out as he breathed. His collarbone was a smooth line above the zigzags of his tunic collar. I clutched my fingers to resist touching the skin there.

My longing must've woken him. Calev's eyes opened and I smiled.

"Good morning, Kinneret."

The sky was purple through the stitching in the jib sail. "To you also."

Oron snorted and rolled over as we made our way to relieve Ekrem at the wheel.

"Will you see what you can do to mend the Wraith Lanterns?" I asked the man, looking up, and up, into the fighter's stern face.

Leather braces covered his massive arms. He made the Fire's sign on his forehead—which I took as a *yes*—then he woke a handful of sailors to help him.

I claimed the wheel, my hands still shaking from the dream.

"Are you all right?" Calev asked.

An ornately carved, wooden box on a support stood next to the wheel. It held the compass and somewhat protected it from all the metal in the ship, metal that often disturbed its readings of our direction. Calev opened the compass box's lid and peered in. He gave me a nod to indicate we were on course. I checked the fact against Zayn's compass that I'd kept in my sash through everything so far.

My shaking stopped as I adjusted my hands on the wheel. "I'm fine. Just...nightmares."

Three fighters, two big like Ekrem and one more my size, but with nine times the muscle, approached and held up palms to me in greeting.

"Kaptan," the stocky one my height said. "What do you wish for us to do?"

"Loosen the mainsail. The wind wants it."

The Salt Magic had worn itself thin and I had to wiggle us around an outcropping of algae green rock to the East. The ship took an age to lip its way to where I wanted it to be. My boat would've already been around the rocks and halfway to the horizon.

"Why the frown?" Calev ran a hand lightly over a row of battle axes strapped to the wall.

Someone had cleaned the slime and blood from them. I was a weakling. After the demon's attack, I couldn't have cleaned one thing if the Fire Itself had asked me.

"The frown is because this ship lumbers like an old, fat man. He's always jostling into things and listing too far."

"Hmm." Calev put a hand to his mouth.

"What's so funny?" Hands on the wheel, I widened my stance and eyed him.

He shook his head. "Nevermind. You won't drag me into an argument, kaptan."

A rush of pleasure like lightning snapped through me at the term *kaptan*. I'd never get tired of that title. "I will drag you in and you know it." I half-grinned, half-scowled. "Now what are you laughing at?"

The stocky sailor rushed up the stairs and showed a palm to me. "Kaptan Kinneret Raza, our amir wishes to speak with you in her cabin. Her...other kaptan is there too." The man's mouth pinched like he'd sipped old tatlilav.

I had a feeling he wasn't too fond of Berker. Join the crowd.

I rubbed the tense rocks of muscle in my shoulder. "Any guess on the purpose of this meeting?" He probably wouldn't tell me. His loyalties were with the amir.

He leaned in and whispered, "The other kaptan sees you as a Salt Witch. I'd watch yourself around him. Stick to what happened and how you saved us and the amir will dance to your tune."

My shoulders relaxed and I couldn't fight my smile. I glanced at Calev, who raised his eyebrows.

"Thank you, sailor," I said. "What is your name?"

He sucked a little breath. "It's Ifran, kaptan. And I-I thank you for caring enough to ask. You know, when I passed my palm over the Holy Fire when we first boarded, the Fire gave me a thought."

"You are blessed," I said carefully. He seemed nice, but plenty of people claimed their ideas came from the Fire. Few really did.

"He told me you are good."

"He did?"

The sailor nodded.

I just stood there, mute, as the man hurried away.

Calev elbowed me. "I bet that made up for the old man ship a little bit."

"Yes. A little."

Wanting to think a minute, I called another to relieve my place at the wheel, Calev trailing me. I went to the ship's wide, copper salt pan, where seawater was exposed to sun and allowed to breathe back into the air, leaving the precious salt behind. It was mainly for cooking and salting the rare, edible fish we managed to catch, but of course, I had other uses for it. I scooped a handful and refilled my pouch.

This leadership, this charge, was what I'd always wanted. I'd longed for respect. A ship to kaptan. Equality with Calev. He'd danced with me last night. But now, staring at my hands and thinking of how much they looked like Avi's, all I wanted was my own craft and Avi on it, with Oron and Calev at my side in any manner they saw fit. I wanted safety. I toyed with the ends of my sash. The endmost bell was cool between my fingertips.

"Strange..."

"What's strange?" Calev nodded in a friendly way to the enormous fighting sailor with the beautiful battle axe, the weapon I'd envied. She was cooking some flatbread in a pan over the brasier. Her looks were very plain, ugly even, but orderly. Nose neat above thin lips. Eyes with very scant lashes sat a bit too far apart.

"I never wanted safety before," I explained. "I craved adventure. Wealth." My gaze flicked to Calev's strong cheekbones and chin, tanned from a life in the fields. "And...other things. But not safety."

"When did you last feel safe?" he asked.

It had been years. "At my aunt's home in Kurakia."

There was a time when I longed to flee Jakobden with Avi and live with Aunt Kania. But my life was sailing. My life was in Jakobden. I loved Jakobden's olive and lemon trees, and its Broken Coast, full of challenges. I had to be on the sea, my sea. It was home, where I'd lived with my mother and father. And it was Calev's home too. I couldn't leave him any more than I could stop breathing.

"You've never told me much about your aunt," Calev said.

"I haven't seen her in forever." Aunt Kania's tower house with its four-story mud brick walls lorded over her nearly barren field of cattle brown as dirt and chickens even browner. "She lives outside Kurakia's capitol. With far too many chickens."

"Can there ever be too many chickens?"

"If you can't get from door to yard without stepping on a dozen, you may have a few too many."

"I bet chickens make for soft stepping stones."

I cocked my head as we neared the amir's quarters. "Soft, yes. Quiet, no."

"Well, not the proud ones. But what about the humble ones, willing to sacrifice their comfort for yours?"

I snorted. "You're starting to sound like Oron." I knocked on the amir's door.

Oron appeared at Calev's elbow and threw his dreaded locks out of his face. "There is no such thing as a humble, quiet chicken."

Two lines formed between Calev's eyebrows. "Except those on your plate."

A laugh sprang out of me despite my sadness and worry. "That's horrible."

A voice rang out from the sky cup, high above the black triangle of the mainsail.

"Land!" the scout shouted.

I grabbed Calev's tunic, my fingers cutting into the fabric.

Ayarazi.

Running to starboard, I looked ahead. There, on the horizon, was an island that sloped like the back of a horse. It was too far to see the colors of the land, to judge it desert or forest, fertile or barren, a simple stretch of rock or a lost island of silver.

But my heart leaped at the sight of it. Until it disappeared.

CHAPTER TWENTY

I blinked. Then blinked again.

"Where did it go?" Calev ran a hand over his face and frowned.

A corner of the island came into view, but I couldn't discern its edges.

"Not good." Oron muttered something else and rubbed the frog's leg hanging from the string around his neck.

A mist thickened and gathered on the surface of the water. As the rising sun glowed orange on the fog, the island seemed to disappear again.

"This is why no one's found it." I began climbing the mast. I'd get a better look from the sky cup.

The scout peered down at me. "Kaptan?"

"I'm coming up. Make room."

A wind like glass shards tore through my hair and across my arms and cheeks. I tucked my head down.

Oron called up from the deck. "Just so you know, from now on, I am deemed forever correct in every assumption."

I scowled down at him. "And what assumption are you talking about now?"

Calev narrowed his eyes at Oron.

Oron crossed his muscled arms. "The one that involves frigid weather mixing with the hot and humid air to which we are accustomed and what it will do to us. The assumption that we are about to freeze our important bits off in the middle of a wet, cold nowhere with no opportunity for one last huzzah."

Looking to the sky for patience, I crawled into the cup. The scout scooted to the far side of the mast that ran through the middle of the perch, giving me a clear, or in this case totally unclear, view of where the island used to be.

"It's still there," I called down, looking again. "It's hidden in a weird reflection between sky and sea." I directed my voice at Ekrem who'd taken the tiller. "Keep our course trained toward the last sight of the land."

I'd thought it would be good to have a high view like this, a view my own boat never could permit, but it'd been worth nothing in this case. As the scout tripped in trying to get out of my way so I could climb down, I cursed this fat, old man ship again. I missed my boat. I'd already have been at the island by now.

The second my sandals hit the deck, my arms were stiff with cold and my hair crusted in ice crystals. Oron and Calev huddled with everyone else, around the brazier. It was ridiculous. One bumping the other. None getting enough heat from the metal bowl to thaw their fingers.

"I don't need everyone on deck. Go below deck and out of this weather. Except for you, please." I pointed at the stocky sailor, Ifran. "And Oron. Calev, would you give the amir my apologies for not answering her summons, and tell her to get her tail up here."

With smooth steps, the amir mounted the stairs and came to my side at the tiller. Berker walked near her, his eyes sour and sharp. A heavy cloak covered his shoulders, but the amir faced the biting wind like a sparring opponent, her grin sharp.

"Speak," she said to me. Her voice might've been like bells, but sometimes they were scary bells.

Berker's gaze traveled up and down as he studied me. Planning my death, no doubt.

I raised my chin and looked the amir and him in the eye. "I saw the island. It is approximately twenty-two knocks northeast."

Her elegant brow reached toward her headstrap and its grape-sized silver bell. "And the island is now…"

"It's there. I saw it. So did the others. This mist and the light are just masking it."

She pressed her lips together. "You saw this too, Calev ben Y'hoshua?"

"I did, my lady." Calev ran a hand up and down my arm and I shivered from both the cold and his soft touch.

Berker tensed. He'd seen the gesture.

Calev and I were getting brave lately. I didn't have time or brain room to consider what that might mean.

Oron swished back the last of a cup of wine. "The island was there, my lady. And if we're to find it again and do any silver mining, you might want to give us some more wine to keep our hands from freezing solid."

The amir's hand landed with a crack on Oron's cheek. My pulse thrummed in my fisted hands.

"Insolence," Berker hissed at Oron.

Oron straightened and wiped his bleeding lip. He gave a deep bow. Calev held me back.

The amir sniffed. "Is that the medicinal wine my physician dosed for your twisted back, dwarf?"

Seas, I wanted to punch the woman.

The amir looked like she believed Oron had a bad back about as much as she believed we'd seen the island.

Sneering, Berker took over the explanation. "He's taken more than three times the amount he was prescribed. But we've allowed it, considering his...condition."

Instead of being put out like I would've been if someone spoke about my stature like it was a disease, Oron beamed and headed back to the wine barrel to refill his cup.

The amir's jaw tightened. "If there is an island in the middle of this, get us there, Kaptan Kinneret Raza. I will be at the prow."

Berker remained, unfortunately, and the amir walked away, her head held high. Calev went with Oron to get a rag for his cut cheek.

The deck looked slicker. Ice. The wind died off and the sails drooped. We were becalmed.

"You're lucky the amir likes you, sailor," Berker whispered. "Don't get too comfortable. I will set everything to rights as soon as we find that silver."

I did my best to ignore that stupid grin of his. "Unless you freeze to death first, hmm? To the oars!" I ordered the sailors. A chill like needles pricked my throat and nose.

Calev returned. "The rowing will keep us warmer. So that's one good thing."

I grinned at him, shivering. "I can always count on you to find the light in the dark."

Leaving Berker to his plotting, Calev and I started toward the sailors leaving the deck.

The amir's voice stopped us. If I hadn't already been frozen, I would've frozen then. "Calev ben Y'hoshua, please keep me company here."

Berker was one step behind us. "Yes, you should keep yourself away from the low-caste vermin."

Calev spun. "She's not—"

I hit his arm gently and he squeezed his eyes shut. "Just go," I whispered.

I broke away and started down the ladder to belowdecks.

"Be sure to empty the chamber pots in our and the amir's quarters as soon as you can be spared," Berker said. "Calev ben Y'hoshua will dine with his high-caste equals now."

Scrambling down the ladder, I held my tongue. Now wasn't the time for angry words. Soon as I had some silver to my name, Berker was going to eat every single one of his insults. Hopefully, this show of dominance from the amir was temporary. I really wanted to use the salt to get us out of here, but I couldn't risk angering the amir even further. Maybe she'd come to her senses if I bowed to her will and Berker's for a few moments.

BESIDE THE FIGHTING SAILORS, I was pretty close to worthless at the oars. My wiry arms were nothing to their limbs of cedar. I pulled alongside them, and we tugged the ship closer and closer to the spot where we'd last spotted the island. The bitter mist sliced through the openings in the ship's sides, flaying us with a cold that rattled teeth and turned bones to ice.

We hadn't gone far before five men and women had developed a chill so debilitating that they couldn't row any longer.

"Kaptan?" A woman with red-brown hair similar to my own turned around on the bench in front of me. "Should we stop?"

"No. We must get through this. And the movement will keep you warm."

As the ship lurched slowly through the water like a wounded beast, worry scratched at my mind. If this lasted through the night, we'd all freeze to death. I'd forever be known as the low-caste kaptan who threw an entire amir's guard into the next life as wraiths.

"Pull harder. Your families need you. We need you. Be strong," I called out to the other sailors as I gripped the oar's worn grain and pulled, my shoulders moaning.

Oron appeared beside me, smelling like charcoal and wine.

"You could help, you know," I said, jerking my chin at the open spot beside me. Ash blackened his cheek. "What have you been doing? Sleeping in the braziers?"

"The mist is thickening."

I swallowed. "Not what we needed to hear, Oron. Here." I stood, my hands throbbing. "Take my place. I'm going to get everyone down here. More bodies means more heat."

And maybe seeing me would remind the amir that we did have some magic on our side if she was willing to accept it.

On deck, I acted as though I hadn't been brought down a notch by Berker's insults and the amir's treatment. Neither the amir nor Berker were around anyway.

"Everyone belowdecks," I ordered. "If we stay close together, we might keep from freezing to death. You," I pointed to the man at the compass, "stay and watch and take note of our direction as best you can. Watch for the sun. Climb to the sky cup to check for land when you deem it best. Switch with a crewmate when you need warmth."

I ran to the amir's quarters. The lady, Berker, and Calev sat around a rough wooden table laden with brass cups, shell bowls half-filled with figs, and wide plates of dried goat's meat.

"I ordered the crew below decks to stay together for warmth—"

"You've arrived at the perfect time to clean the table for us and the pots in the side chamber," Berker said.

I looked to the amir. Surely after all I'd proven, she would keep him from demeaning me like this.

Her gaze, cold as the fog outside these wooden walls, ran over my face and hands. "A bit of simple work may do you good. You don't want to forget where you've come from, sailor."

Would arguing make a difference? The amir held my gaze, demanding submission. Maybe now that she had a good idea of where the island was, she didn't need me. Taking a deep breath, I tucked my tail and went to work.

Calev's pained stare never left me as I cleared plates, scraped leftover bits into the bucket by the door, gritted my teeth, and tried to remember this was all for my sister. Calev had his part to play and I, frustratingly, had mine.

The amir, Berker, and Calev went to speak to the sailors, who flowed down the stairs opposite the amir's quarters and flooded into any available space around the oars, cannons, and sleeping quarters.

The last of them cleared the stairs' slats and I, bucket in hand, climbed to the deck. A skeleton crew operated the ship, Ekrem at the wheel and compass and a few others manning the lines and blocks.

The wet clouds of the mist danced across the deck like ghostly sails. My bones shook, and I gripped the bucket's handle tightly to keep from dropping it. My nails had gone blue at the tips. I should've been miserable, but my heart raced at the unfamiliar feeling of true cold. This was adventure. I smiled sadly, wishing Avi could be here. Well, if we survived this.

"Kinneret Raza." Ekrem's light eyes narrowed and he pointed into the white.

Blue, green, and black appeared between the plumes of cold mist. I dumped the bucket's contents over the ship's side and ran to Ekrem, a warmer air teasing across my chest and arms. Feeling crept back into my fingers and toes.

"My lady!" I shouted, leaning this way and that, to see if the colors were what we wanted them to be.

Ekrem said a quiet prayer. "It is Ayarazi."

The island materialized as everyone crowded onto the deck.

My heart pounded. I could hardly keep from jumping up and down like a child.

The sailors made the Fire's sign on their foreheads, and the amir cursed —though it did seem like a pleased variable of swearing. Calev and I joined hands briefly, releasing one another before anyone could see.

Waves crashed and sprayed water over a line of gray rock and bright coral. The island rose, green and cool, behind the barrier. Plumes of spray rose from a waterfall that graced a far-off peak. Near a blanket of purple growth on a low hill, a ridge of stone made a scar across an emerald valley. There was movement, tiny spots of dark in the landscape.

The coast's vicious teeth had one gap. We could fit. Maybe.

If everything went the way I wanted it to. If this fat, old man ship listened. If the salt heard my prayers. If I had all the best luck.

"Calev, I'm going to need you by my side. On deck. Every second. Without your luck on this, we are dead."

"But I'm not good luck."

I pinched his lips shut. "You are."

CHAPTER TWENTY-ONE

I gnoring Berker's loud muttering about what my status would be in the afterlife, I whispered over the salt. It dusted back to its home in the cold waters surrounding an island that, before today, had only existed in bedtime tales told in my father's rumbling voice.

"And the silver threads through all things on the island," my father had said long ago, adjusting the blanket so that Avi had more than the small amount I'd given her. I remembered watching fire smoke dance through the small hole in our hut's roof. "The color runs in the waterfalls, the rivers," Father said. "Grasses grow there, more than you've ever seen even in summer near Old Farm. The green is laced with the precious metal. A handful of grass would weave beautiful sashes for my little ones." He'd touched our noses, a press, each in turn. "Forget the wraiths, children, and dream of the horses there, every color. Pick your favorite and ride her across the sloping valleys and through the rivers, kicking up silver water."

My heart shied from the memory like a beaten dog. I missed him so much.

Now, the whites of the sailors' eyes showed as they put hands to the lines and stared at the rocks.

"Wait for the lag!" I called out.

Oron stood beside the mast, his gaze focused on the red leather jerkins surrounding him, making certain the fighting sailors carried out my demands in perfect harmony. He put his face to the wind and leaned into it. He was feeling the wind and the sea's intent. Oron was the best sailor alive, aside from me. We both felt the Pass and the Fire in the waters and wind like music and soft hands, urging and pulling. With him helping me, we might just make it.

I turned to say as much to Calev, glad to break away from thoughts of my broken family, but the spot behind me was empty.

"Calev?"

The stairs held only Ifran ordering another sailor to tighten the line that ran with its mates to the rippling black shell of the mainsail.

When I spun back around to check our progress toward the gap in the breakers shielding the coastline, Oron's hand was cupped at his mouth. I could only catch a bit of what he was saying.

"...tracking too far West...the fore lines should be..."

He was right. We were off. I'd been searching for Calev instead of listening to the sea and the wind. The mining drills weighed more than this ship should've been carrying. Poor old, fat man of a ship.

"Tighten the lines, but keep all hands on them. I need them fully released at my word," I called out over the deck.

Oron gave a quick nod and whipped around, gesturing and working the lines, moving like a moth between the glint of the metal and the white of the ropes, the fighting sailors buzzing and tugging lines around him. I eased the wheel around, feeling the tug of water below. We were at the mouth of Ayarazi's natural bay, with teeth on both sides—rocks poised to tear us apart. Please stay sound, fat, old man hull. Asag's rocks had nearly ground it open.

Where was Calev?

There, past Oron, at the far end near the prow. He walked up behind the amir, something in his hand. From my vantage point, the object was partially concealed by the whipping ends of the amir's vest.

I needed him here beside me. I needed everything. The ship shuddered as we brushed a rock and a wave splashed over the side. Sailors shouted and grabbed holds.

"Calev!" I bent my knees as the ship lunged through the tight gap. "Pull all lines tight! Hold on! Wait for it!"

Calev had dropped away from the amir, coming up against the side of the ship, braced on the wall. From his right hand, his dagger blinked at me.

My insides turned to ice. What was he doing?

"Kinneret!" Oron was at the base of the stairs, below me. "The sails?"

I counted silently to myself as the ship righted itself and readied to bump—hopefully a light glance—past the last of the rocks lining the gap in the island's rocky coast. My hand on my chest, I counted. One, two, three, wait…ten, eleven, twelve. I couldn't let the wind take us in a jerk to port or starboard. We needed no wind at exactly the right time.

Now. "Release the lines!" My heart clanked against my chest and my throat ached from yelling.

The sailors moved as one. The blocks wiggled as the lines ran through them. The sail billowed and the lines flipped into the air. The ship ducked like a tall man going through a doorway. We listed hard, very hard, to port, and I fell to my knees, my head smashing against the wheel.

Ifran screamed as water crashed over the deck in successive waves. I stood, but my legs didn't want to hold me. The ship seemed to go forward and backward at the same time. I knew that feeling. Whirlpool—a roiling swirl of deadly water. And we had no sails.

Beyond the ribboning current, the water eased onto a black sand shoreline. If we somehow finagled our way through this, we'd be on shore. But we couldn't catch wind fast enough to keep from being sucked under.

The salt would have to do it.

"Get the sails up. Go. Now. Now!" My throat burned from ocean salt and shouting.

Oron's face appeared next to mine. "Ifran split his head against the side." He turned and shouted directions to the sailors, who grabbed at the lines and caught them one by one.

My eyes searched for Ifran in the mayhem of the ship. I couldn't lose another fighting sailor. These men and women had risked their lives to follow me into this madness. Ifran had been brave enough to give me advice against the amir's wishes.

Ifran lay beside the anchor's launching hole with the angry whirlpool churning right below. His dark head was a mess of blood.

"Calev." He looked at me and blinked. "Help Ifran, please!" I shouted over the chaos.

I was fairly certain if it hadn't been for the ship's jerking and the blood, the white of bone and tendon would've shone through the wound. I ripped another strip from the bottom of my skirt and handed it to another sailor. "Take this to Calev. Tell him to wrap the man's head."

Calev did as I asked. Beside him, Oron leaned in and made the Fire's sign on Ifran's forehead to bless him.

"What is this?" The amir loomed over them, her voice loud, one hand on a tied line and the other on her dagger hilt. Berker stood at her side like an attack dog. "Stop wasting time with what is replaceable." She jerked a chin at Ifran's body, then looked to me. "Get us to that island, kaptan." With a booted foot, she shoved Ifran through the opening and into the sea.

My body buzzed, my mouth open.

Calev reached for him, but it was too late.

The amir whipped around and shouted at the fighting sailors to trim the fore stay sail.

A smear of black-red marred Calev's tunic and Oron's sash.

"This is a quest for silver," Berker said. "And you, Kaptan Kinneret Raza, are about to fail. Now get us to shore."

The ship spun like a child's string toy. The amir shouted in anger, gripping the line tighter as the water churned around us. Calev grabbed the side and Oron fell to a knee.

Only one piece of my mind was on keeping my feet. The rest of my thoughts swarmed around Ifran. He was lost to the sea. His spirit—lost and angry—would become a wraith, set to Infuse and get his vengeance on the living. And it was my fault.

The ship rotated again, and the sound of cracking wood snapped through the air. By my guess, we had only a few seconds before we suffered too much damage to make it out of this whirlpool.

Scrabbling for the salt in my pouch, I turned away from the amir and whispered to the sea.

"Release us, waters of salt and sin.

Let us breathe another sun.

Our lives await, and also, our kin."

The wind surged and lifted the nose of our ship out of the whirlpool, but it wasn't enough. The current sucked us down again and water swamped the deck. Fighters shouted out and everyone looked to me. But there was nothing left to do.

We all knew it.

We were going down.

Calev ran to me. "Kinneret, I should tell you—"

With a mighty lunge, the sea spit the prow upward. Every man and woman fell hard as the prow led the rest of the craft free.

Calev and I tumbled against a large crate. I regained my feet first, but he quickly joined me. The sky was blue and clear above us. The water roared.

Oron whooped and threw a hand into the air. "We're out!"

The fighting sailors let up a great yell of celebration, and the amir stormed into her cabin, obviously satisfied with the outcome but unwilling to offer any praise. Berker stood staring at Calev and me. His lip curled and he mouthed something I couldn't discern.

"Throw anchor." But with everyone nursing wounds from falling, my order was slowly followed. I began cranking the anchor's line out myself, Oron and Calev helping.

As the fighters lowered the sails, I finally took a breath.

In front of us, Ayarazi, lost island of silver and the key to my sister's life, rose like a dream made real.

CHAPTER TWENTY-TWO

The sand was soft as down under my bare feet. My sandals dangled from my fingers as I followed the amir and Berker toward the low, grassy perches of land overlooking the beach.

Disembarking from one of the small boats that took us from the full ship to shore, Oron threw himself to the ground and lay on his back. "Sweet land, I do not care if you are rich or poor, you will do. You will do."

Calev threw his head back and sucked a deep breath. The sun smiled on the hollows, curves, and lines of his throat. My fingers twitched. I wanted to run fingertips along Calev's smooth skin, to feel his pulse and know that he was all right.

The scent of the beautifully rich growth rose like perfume into the air. The grasses smelled like mint. "My father told me silver threaded through the grass on Ayarazi."

I bent to see for myself as the party moved beyond us, climbing the rise and entering a vast meadow. The blades of grass cooled my fingertips and a shiver ran over my arms. The place was colder than anywhere I'd ever been. Not frigid like that mist, but crisp—a shade colder than Jakobden's winter. Squinting, I plucked one blade and held it to my face. Tiny rows of sparkling silver ran through the veins of the plant and gathered at the edges to create a frame.

"Beautiful," Calev said.

I turned and handed the blade to him. "It is, isn't it?"

He smiled with half his mouth. "I wasn't talking about the grass, Kinneret." His gaze slid over my head and nose and chin.

My cheeks grew hot as Calev grabbed my hand. His eyes were honey and wine. My throat bobbed as I tried to talk, but his eyes, the cool breeze, and the promise of this all working out had stolen my words. He touched my cheek.

"Sailor," Berker barked from above. The amir and her fighters had gone on, so they weren't around to correct his address.

Calev's eyes sharpened. His head snapped around. "Address the kaptan properly."

He'd taken the words right from my lips.

Berker stared us down. "You are no longer a kaptan, scrapper. You led us here. It's over now. I'm the only kaptan on this journey." He began to walk away toward the line of sailors, heading toward the mountains. "Funny how the chill gets in your bones so quickly," he said over his shoulder. "Someone might die in such an unforgiving climate."

My temples pounded. That man.

Calev shook with rage.

"Don't worry." I squeezed Calev's fingers and climbed the rise to join our party, noticing that Oron was already snoring on the sand behind. "I'll have a fight with Berker before this is over. And I will win."

Calev leaped up behind me, and we started through the silvery green, the cold breeze in our hair. "I don't doubt it, kaptan."

A smile pulled at my lips as I slipped a rope from a fighter's pack.

The amir was leading the group toward the closest mountain. As we caught up, the scar of rocky ground branching through the meadow appeared to our left. I tugged Calev's sleeve and nodded toward it.

"I think we should look there first. It may open into the ground. Plus, it'll be easier to check for silver than drilling into a mountain."

"Let's go," Calev said.

The air, fresh as clean water, spun down the green mountain and swept over the valley where we ran. The grass whisked our legs, and a light shone inside me. The journey here had been so terrible that I couldn't help but hope we'd find the silver quickly and without too much trouble. If I showed the amir what she could hope to gain, she'd give me any amount of fighters and let me take the ship to the quarry to reclaim my sister.

The land sloped upward. Flat, gray rocks mingled with the grasses and led to the seam I'd spotted from the ship. Turns out, it was less of a seam and more of a set of openings into the earth. At the crest of the rise, the ground broke open. Two more such openings sat nearby. I went to the largest and peered inside, Calev beside me, breathing heavily after our run.

I passed a hand over the dark opening's walls, feeling a slimy cold. "I can't see anything. We should get inside."

There weren't any rocks near the opening for me to tie the rope around. I kicked at the dirt at the cave's open ceiling and my toe hit a root.

"It's from that elder there." Calev pointed to a needled tree a stone's throw away.

"Elder." I laughed. "You Old Farms."

"What?"

I shook my head. "Nothing. Think the rope will hold me?"

"Definitely."

I helped Calev with a double figure eight knot and made a loop for my legs as well. Thankfully, there were enough roots and drier ledges for grabbing and I made my way down without Calev having to hold my weight. In the dim, the rope pulled taut and I knew I had no more length for exploring.

"What's it like?" At the top, Calev got onto his stomach and his hair fell over his face.

The walls were a light brown, or at least what I could see of them was. A line of black ran crookedly through the rock ledges, giving me false hope.

"It's just a cave. No silver."

"Come on back up. We'll check this next one."

With a sigh, I maneuvered my way out of the cave and into the next. No silver.

After I laced the rope around a stump, Calev went down into a third crack in the island, but still, no silver.

I untied the rope and coiled it around my arm, my heart weighing more than a boat full of Ekrems. Calev rubbed my knee and gave me a half smile.

"I really thought it would be here. That black scar in the first opening looked right from what I've heard."

"We'll find it. I'm lucky. Remember?"

My heart lifted a little and I dusted myself off. My calves shook with fatigue, but I didn't want to stop looking. To rescue Avi, I needed the amir's fighters. And the amir wanted silver. It was both as simple and as difficult as that.

Calev walked beside me as we worked our way through the grass. The strands of light gray in the growth blinked teasingly.

Calev broke off a hunk of shining green-gray and sniffed it. "Is this the island's idea of a joke?" He looked at the blade closely, his eyes nearly crossing. "It's really just dots of gray on the surface. I was sort of hoping we could get a scythe out here and reap the rewards, so to speak."

I grabbed a piece and scratched at the silvery spots. "Don't get a big head. You're not that lucky." The sun had slipped off its zenith and a sudden image of Avi's golden-brown hair flashed through my thoughts. "How much silver do you think the amir will need before she agrees to send fighters with us for Avi?" I should've clarified that in our agreement.

Shrugging, Calev said, "I'd guess once we locate a seam and begin drilling."

"We never talked about how many would stay to mine and how many would come with us."

Calev clicked his tongue. He was more worried than he wanted me to know and my skin itched with the need to leave now. "You should talk to Ekrem about it. He respects you."

"He does?"

"It's obvious. And he might know the right way to bring it up with the amir."

"What's going to happen when your father figures out where you are?"

"We already talked about this. He can't do much of anything. She is the amir and she asked me to go."

I raised an eyebrow. "How is he going to react? Will he get over it when you return home?" Home. Such a chaos of wonderful and horrible. I thought of awful Miriam and a muscle in my back balled up.

Then the ground dropped away.

I fell into the earth and pain ripped up my leg.

CHAPTER TWENTY-THREE

"Kinneret!"
I gripped at everything, anything, and my buzzing fingers latched onto a mound of wet earth and grass. My feet dangled above darkness. I'd fallen into the opening of another crevice.

Calev grabbed my wrists and helped me up, his eyes wide and his fingers strong. "Are you all right?"

When I'd maneuvered my way out, he patted my arms and my head, then held my face softly. I turned my mouth toward his parted lips. A shiver danced over the backs of my legs.

But a burning sensation drowned all the good and I looked down to see a tiny stream of blood leaking from my thigh into my sandal. I lifted my skirt a little and Calev knelt to inspect my wound.

"It's just a cut." I was lightheaded, but I wasn't sure whether it was from the fall, the blood, or because Calev's mouth was very near my thigh.

He cleared his throat and stood. "Doesn't look serious," he said, blushing.

It wasn't. Just a nip. I spun to face the crevice I'd so gracefully found.

"Should I tie the rope off?" Calev's head turned.

I bent and leaned over the yawning mouth of the cave. Plant life obscured most of the light, making the walls black. Calev moved behind me and a beam of afternoon sun hit the opposite wall and glinted back. Just a wink. Probably nothing.

"Do you see anything?" Calev asked.

"It's hard to tell." The surface inside alternated between smooth and rough. My hand slid over a slick spot and something sticklike stopped its progress. I ran fingers over the object imbedded in the smooth area. Its end curled like a fern's leaf and my heart danced.

"Silver."

"Where?" Calev pushed against me and shoved his hand into the opening. "Ah! I feel it! In some calcite crystal, I bet. Like the mine between Jakobden and the capitol."

"This shallow, it won't be that much labor to free it. A shaft dug. A pulley system. Picks. We don't even need those drills. We'll have to set up a smelting station. Nothing we haven't seen. There are people enough in Jakobden who could mine it and work it into useable pieces." I stood and pulled him to his feet. "You'll help me, won't you? I'll need you to make an appearance now and then to keep the amir in check."

I was already seeing Avi rescued and our lives moving into a place of full bellies and smiles and respectful nods from the men and women I'd sailed with during this trip.

"Of course." Calev grinned. "This is amazing. I never thought…Ayarazi."

A herd of horses in every color of a northern autumn forest pounded past us, whipping us with the force of their passing and shaking the ground under our sandals. Burnt ochre. Yellow and orange. Deep purple like my sail. Their tails and manes snapped like pennants as they galloped, the sun flashing from the silver hiding in the white and brown of their hair.

The look on Calev's face was pure joy.

We had done it. Found the lost island of silver. Grabbed the only chance to save my sister.

A laugh bubbled out of his mouth, and he covered his face with one hand, shaking his head in disbelief. Another laugh, and the deep sound melted over me, warming me in the brisk air.

My mouth wanted to taste his neck, and my body longed for the heat and strength in his arms. I wouldn't make the first move. He knew how I felt now, surely, and I wasn't about to make a fool out of myself even if it was all I could do not to leap onto him. His hair lifted in the breeze, and the sun reddened his browned cheeks.

"Kinneret," he whispered, taking my hands in his. His lips forming my name was worth all the silver under our feet. "You slay sea demons, fight storms, sail like none other, and work magic in a way that makes it holy rather than the abomination so many want to deem it. Why do you even bother to be my friend?"

He laughed, but at the word "friend" my chest clenched like the air was suddenly poisonous. I forced myself to breathe normally. Avi needed me. Even more than Calev did, it seemed.

Shaking a little, I pulled my hands away. "I need to show the amir the silver. Avi needs me now."

Calev's brow and mouth torqued out of line. Then he nodded slowly and followed me toward the slash of red-clothed fighting sailors heading up the hills.

When the group was within hearing, I called out to the amir, wondering where Oron had gone. "We found the silver!"

The fighters spun, eyes wide, and shouted. Everyone began talking at once, patting my shoulder and Calev's, and offering congratulations.

"Well done, kaptan!"

"I didn't doubt you'd be the one, Kaptan Kinneret."

"Thank you." I showed my palm to each in turn and handed out smiles like gold dumplings at an Age Day celebration.

The fighters parted for Calev and me.

"Do you want me to talk to her?" Calev asked. "Because I don't think you do. She is a vicious woman, but she respects you. She doesn't seem to care that you used Salt Magic. You got us through with only a few losses."

"No. I'll talk to her. I-I can't believe what she did to Ifran."

My mind speared me with images of Ifran and the handful of other sailors we'd lost. Their faces, pale, bloodied, shocked by Death's arrival, would never dissolve from my memory. I pressed a fist to my throat, making my own throat-blood oath.

"I will never forget those we lost," I said. "I will say a prayer for them every day I sail the Pass."

Calev blinked and made the Fire's sign on his forehead, his thumb circling the center of his headtie.

It was the very least I could do for them. How was I going to face the woman who'd kicked Ifran into the water before he was even dead?

I could barely stand to look at her proud gait and the back of her red leather vest. I wanted to make her pay for what she'd done, but she was also Avi's savior. I couldn't take the amir down without also destroying Avi's chance to escape the quarry. My stomach curdled and I gritted my teeth. There wasn't a thing I could do about it.

For now.

The amir walked, back straight and head held high, about ten knocks up the foothill. My feet began to complain. Then my head. My stomach. The excitement of everything was fading in my fatigue. I didn't want to waste sun eating and sleeping. But soon, I'd have to listen to my body, or it would shut down.

At last I was at the amir's elbow. Berker walked right beside her.

"My lady." My throat was dry and I could barely talk. I needed rest and water. "The silver is just there."

I pointed as she stopped and looked at me, disdain clear as the sky in her eyes.

"What do you know about silver mines, sailor?" Berker wrinkled his nose.

The amir faced him. "You will call her kaptan, Kaptan Berker Deniz."

"But, my lady, that was only a position for our journey here. That time is over. She should know her place."

"Enough," the amir said, her bell voice cutting instead of pleasing.

Berker's throat bobbed. "Yes, my lady."

Calev and I exchanged wide-eyed looks. I fought a mean grin, then decided to let it loose. Forget Berker. He deserved the treatment he received.

Pointing the way we'd come, Calev squinted against the sun. "Do you see the outcropping on that far slope, below the mountain with the waterfall, my lady?"

"I see it, Calev ben Y'hoshua." Lines formed around the amir's mouth as she frowned. She took a very deliberate breath. "Did you spot the metal yourselves?"

Nodding, I said, "In one opening, raw silver sits in calcite. It's an easy site for a mine, my lady, and one that'll make the both of us very rich." My voice sounded hollow on that last word.

Calev whispered in my ear. "Are you unwell?"

I smiled, my mind whirring. "No, I'm fine."

Calev spoke to the amir about traditional mining methods, and my thoughts turned inward.

Though I was more tired than I'd ever been and desperate for food and water, I actually felt as though I'd been healed of some horrible sickness. The gnawing need for silver, wealth, power and status, it was silent inside me. I had Calev, at least as a friend, and Oron, and with the silver and the amir's help, Avi's safety. Once I had my own quick and sturdy boat under my feet again, I'd be complete.

I studied my hands. They still looked like my own. My hair was still red-brown and unruly. A strand bounced back after I tugged on it. I appeared the same on the outside, but inside I had changed completely. I was no longer a ravenous fire, needing kindling and something to devour. I was the steel made in the fire, hard and strong, but quiet until the sharp edge was needed. And though things seemed to be trotting along the path I'd forged, I had a distinct feeling I'd call out for that cutting blade inside me very soon.

CHAPTER TWENTY-FOUR

G rowing pink, the sun fell out of the blue sky and hid shyly behind the jagged mountain peaks of Ayarazi. I rubbed my sleep-crusted eyes and sat up from the carpet of grass near the silver outcropping. The amir had insisted on seeing the silver herself before she would believe our story, so while the crew repaired the damage the ship had sustained during our trip, Calev and I led her around. Satisfied, the amir had called us together to eat. Finally. Most had fallen to sleep soon after.

For a part of our meal, Oron had crafted a salad of greens he claimed were safe to consume. Said they were the same ones we had at home, only smaller, tougher. I'd enjoyed the fresh food, a contrast to the hard bread and slightly sour wine. None of the others, except Calev, had munched on Oron's creation. Calev had gone so far as to add a plant his Savta had once described in her stories as having a healing power to it. After the others had their fill of food and of laughing at our green-eating habits, everyone fell asleep, exhausted from the journey.

I smiled at Calev's sleeping form. He argued sometimes with Oron, but he was kind to the man, backing him up around the others. And though Oron claimed to love pity and the shower of undeserved attention it reaped for him, I knew he wanted true friendship. I hoped he saw that he'd found it in Avi, me, and now, in Calev.

Snores rose into the air around the camp, and I was glad of it. As soon as that sun came up, we'd be on the water, headed toward Quarry Isle and Avi. If the amir kept her promise.

I popped my knuckles and patted the salt pouch on my belt. I was ready for a fight with the oramiral. Maybe I'd get the chance to take a hand from the man. He needed something to remind him he wasn't the only power in the world.

My whole body was jittery. No way I could go back to sleep.

As the last of the sun's blush faded, an odd glimmer lighted the foothills and the spray in the distant waterfall.

I shrugged it off. The island was full of things I'd never seen before. Instead of the tiny, violet nightwingers we had at home, Ayarazi's evening air was colored by floating silver moths, big as my hand. The ocean crashed magnificently against the barrier surrounding the island, a louder sound than the Pass's constant grating against Jakobden's Broken Coast. And no night insects seemed to be coming out to sing. The nightwingers at home zipped near ears, a familiar sound. But here, there was only the occasional pounding of horses' hooves, the waterfall's rush, and the sea hammering the rocks.

The inland light glimmered again, and I found my feet walking toward its inconsistent illumination.

It was strange to be alone on land. I'd been alone on the Pass many times. But on land, I'd always had Avi, Oron, or Calev. I stretched my arms wide, inhaled the clean air, and said a silent prayer for my sister into the moonlight. The moon actually looked lovely when you didn't have to worry about Salt Wraiths. That was land's only advantage over water. The earth didn't talk to me like the sea did. It wasn't an extension of my own body and spirit and heart. Ayarazi was beautiful. Awe-inspiring. But I was ready to get back out on the water.

The land dipped down before coming to the waterfall, and as if it'd heard my thoughts on land versus sea, the thick grass tripped me. With both hands, I caught myself and cursed my stupidity for walking into the night with only the moon, enormous insects, and a mysterious light to keep me company. I'd walked a good forty knocks from where we'd camped. If I hurt myself way out here, it'd take Oron and Calev a long while to find me.

Nearing the waterfall, I tugged everything off, except my underclothes, and made my way through a heaped circle of moss-covered, round stones to the pool. The cold air brushed over my exposed skin and I shivered. Beside my sash with its compass, salt pouch, and dagger, I knelt on the rocks to wash dirt, salt, and sand from just the edges of my skirt, shawl, and shirt. I didn't want to get them too wet or I'd be shivering all night. As the spray found my cheek and neck, I gasped. I'd expected the water to be cold like the air here, but it was warm as sunshine. I rubbed my gritty clothes, scrubbing the journey off the ruddy fabric. My face was rough with salt and sand too. I needed a bath.

I slipped into the cloudy pool. Goosebumps exploded up my arms and a heavy sigh left me. Perfect.

A shape came out of the darkness, and my heartbeat shot into my ears. Lunging for my dagger, I held it up.

"Who is it?"

Calev's laugh rumbled from the shadows.

My eyes closed in relief. "You scared the life out of me."

He knelt beside the pool, a grin pulling at one side of his mouth as he took in my bare shoulders.

My cheeks burned. I tossed my dagger back onto the rocks and took a step back.

"It's warm. The water. I thought I'd take a bath." I swallowed.

"Not a bad idea."

Standing, he began to shed his tunic, pulling the long, now tattered fabric over his head. My heart lost its hold on any kind of rhythm, clacking wildly fast and slow and everywhere in between. It's not that I hadn't been in underclothes with Calev before now, but something about the moon and new environment made this…different.

Bending at his trim waist, he slipped off his headtie, his sandals. His chest and shoulders were smooth and curved with lithe muscle and bone. He straightened, his eyes going very serious and a cocky grin tweaking his lips.

It suddenly seemed as if there wasn't enough air. I turned around. "I don't know if this is a good idea, Calev…I…if we—you could become…well, I can't stop worrying…"

Water splashed and lapped around my crossed arms as I faced the waterfall, spray cloaking me.

"How about we stop worrying and enjoy this hidden moment on this legendary island."

He was right behind me.

Every inch of my skin caught fire, and I couldn't breathe let alone form a response to this insane statement. His hands found my arms, and he brushed hot fingertips from my elbows to my shoulders. I shivered. My stomach dipped.

"Kinneret…"

His lips rubbed against the tender skin on the back of my ear. A molten heat in me twisted high, snaking into my arms and legs. I couldn't take his chest against my back anymore or his breath in my ear. It wasn't enough. The golden heat wanted more. I wanted more.

We couldn't do this. I would not do this to him.

"Calev," I said, gritting my teeth, "you'll be Outcasted if anyone sees us. We were fools dancing on the amir's boat. I won't be your fun for one night, then left to pine for you."

He spun me around. "Do you really think that's how I feel about you? That you're one night of pleasure for me?" He swallowed, his gaze going to my lips. "Even if you weren't a kaptan now, which will please my elders, I would still want you forever. I know that now. I could never only be your friend."

"I'm not really a kaptan. The amir was humoring me to get here. Until I can convince your father to take me on as Old Farm's kaptan—"

Calev was shaking his head, smiling. "I don't care about all of that. All I want is you."

He braced my head in his hands and kissed me.

My fingers covered his and my argument dissolved into the mist around us. I pressed into the kiss. His lips tasted salty and sweet, warm and wet from the waterfall's spray. He drew my top lip into his hot mouth and let one hand slip around my neck, back to front. His fingers paused, moving against the pounding pulse in my throat. His stomach brushed mine and what had been a molten glow inside me became a raging storm of heat, uncontrollable, consuming. His skin dragged over mine, and storm-tossed my heart into a blind joy of red flames and whipping lightning strikes of pleasure. I pulled back, gasping and grinning, to see his smile, that smile I adored, and his hair, curled and dark and soaked against his beautiful, lucky head. Drops of fresh water dotted his brow and the side of his nose. He was a creature from another world, as foreign and alluring as Ayarazi itself. Before I could throw myself back into the kiss, a branch snapped beyond the pool.

My mouth went dry and my heart stopped.

The amir appeared out of the shadowed moonlight. Calev's eyes went wide and blank.

A fever gripped me and prickled against my temples and palms. I started to speak, to address her politely to cover our crime, but before I could utter a word, Calev dove under the water. He came up out of the pool to stand beside the amir.

Silver flashed from his hand.

It was so dark, so difficult to see.

The amir grunted, an ugly sound, and fell to the grass. Her feet jerked, she moaned, then went still.

A harsh cold slithered over my skin. "Calev, what—"

He turned, and a wavering light poured out of his mouth and dissolved into the night. The blankness in his features melted away, revealing his kind eyes and soft mouth. Blinking, he looked from me to what appeared to be my dagger in his hand. Blood dripped from the steel onto his shaking fingers.

Bile rose in my throat.

He'd stabbed the amir.

CHAPTER TWENTY-FIVE

My hand went to my mouth. "Calev."

Dropping the dagger, he stammered, saying my name, then hers, making incoherent noises. "I didn't do this. Kinneret. The amir is dead. I didn't…what happened?"

I was cold all over and not only because of the temperature. "You killed her. Did you plan this?" I couldn't think. My thoughts whirled, dark and slippery as eels.

Calev ran a hand over his wet, chilled head. "No. Of course not. But I don't even remember having that dagger. Why would I…"

With her dead, I had no one to send fighters to get Avi. Berker would take charge now and Avi would be left to die. He'd, at the very least, Outcast me for the magic and take a hand for good measure. Calev would be put to death for murder. Old Zayn would blame himself, even though it wasn't his fault. It was mine. And Calev's. But why?

My lungs fought for a breath that wouldn't come. "Why did you do it?"

"I'm telling you. I don't know what happened."

A black knowledge swept over me.

He'd been Infused.

The light that had left his mouth was a wraith's Infusion—the evil will that possessed those touched by a wraith's shadow.

Ever since that night on my boat, he'd been Infused. "It all makes sense now."

"What? Talk to me, Kinneret!"

The occasional darkness in his eyes, unblinking. The times he'd stared like Death itself at the amir.

I swam to the side and climbed out, careful to avoid the bloody dagger in the grass. Shivering, I picked up my skirt and used it to clean his hands, looking into his face.

He was pale. Too pale.

"Calev. Listen to me. You were Infused. Remember the night in my boat? When the wraith flew over us? Since then, I've seen odd looks in your eyes. You acted strangely toward the amir. I didn't know...it was always something quick, gone before I could realize..."

"Infused?" He swallowed, allowing me to keep holding his hands. "But it's been so long. Can it work that way? And why would I wish to hurt one specific person?"

I pulled away from him and picked up his tunic from the ground. Helping him pull it over his head, I said, "I've never seen it happen that way before, but I've heard of it. The wraith felt different that night too. Do you remember?"

He shook his head. "I don't." His gaze flicked to me, his eyes widening. "I don't remember feeling the wraith at all."

"That's not uncommon. Lapses in memory. No recollection of being Infused. The wraith, this one felt...intelligent. Sharp, focused." I dressed quickly, my pulse like a frightened rabbit leaping and screaming in my head.

Calev put his hands over his face. "Do you think it meant for me to specifically murder the amir?"

"I just don't know. But it seems that way."

"If Berker and the amir's fighters see this, if they find me here..."

"You're dead. Old Farm or not. We'll find another way to help Avi. Somehow. Some way." Moonlight draped like death shrouds over the sloping hill leading to the camp near the silver outcropping. "We have to get off this island before they wake up, or they'll take you to Jakobden for a trial. You'll be sentenced to death. First, we'll hide the body."

Calev looked to the sky and heaved a shuddering breath, nodding.

We put hands under the amir's arms and shifted her into a clutch of thickly leaved brush past the waterfall.

"They'll see that someone dragged something through here. Look at the mud," Calev said.

"We don't have the sun to worry about it. We have to go. Now."

His gaze followed my own over the meadow. That strange glistening, silver light undulated around a boulder near the first rise and over the camp.

"They'll never believe I was Infused," he said. "I wouldn't believe it. I would never believe the Infusion could be aimed at one person." He rubbed his face. "Fire, help me." Making the sign on his forehead, he trembled.

"We'll sneak into camp, wake Oron, and take one of the small boats from the beach."

Running alongside me through the damp grass, Calev took heavy breaths between his words. "One of the small boats? On the Pass? But they're even smaller than yours and they don't have sails."

"It's not as if you, me, and Oron can run the amir's ship. It takes twenty to do that. The small boat is our only choice. And I have Salt Magic." We'd probably die. But I had to give it a go. There was nothing else to do.

"What about a Wraith Lantern?" Calev asked.

I'd never been so cold. My fingers were ice, my feet frosted. "We'll steal one from the ship."

Muscles and tendons in Calev's cheek moved as his lips pressed together.

He was right to be scared.

WHEN I SHOOK ORON AWAKE, he shouted, "I paid you already!"

I slapped a hand over his lips. Calev and I looked from Oron to the fighting sailors and Berker. Surely Oron's broken dream and shouting would wake them.

But none stirred.

Strange.

The sun was already painting the sky and readying for dawn, and these fighters trained every day at dawn. But now their chests rose and fell in sleep. A few looked pale. Two at the edges of the camp ring moaned and held their heads in their sleep.

"Is everyone ill?" Calev whispered, his face blue in the almost-dawn.

We didn't have the sun to wonder about this miracle that might save our lives. I pulled Calev and Oron toward the path to the sea. "It doesn't matter now. Oron, there's been an...accident."

"Why are you tugging at me? What are you talking about?" Oron jerked his arm free.

"We've no sun to explain. Come. Please."

With a nod and one last look around camp, he followed Calev and me across the meadow.

The sea crashed, promising both challenge and escape. The full ship bobbed in the waters just before the whirlpool. In the shoreline's pale sand, the five small boats that had brought our party ashore lay like beached whales. Together we pushed the closest one into the lapping waves.

As we climbed in, Calev explained everything to Oron. Oron paused in rowing, and his oar nearly slipped out of his hands before he caught it. I took over rowing with Calev.

Oron frowned. "No one will believe this story, Calev."

The ship loomed above us, and I snatched a grappling hook from the bottom of the boat and threw it over the side.

"It also doesn't help that Calev has the throat-blood oath with the amir," I said.

Oron held the rope steady as Calev and I climbed. The sea gave a heave, and the rope slid across the side of the craft, catching on a porthole. It jerked under my grip and I clung to the ship, Calev and Oron swearing in chorus.

"Hold on," I called over my shoulder.

Calev still held to the rope, but he'd lost his foot-over-foot grip. The waves came in like a bully again, stomping against the ship. Somewhere far off, there had to be a storm stirring up the waters. I tumbled over the side and onto the deck, then I checked on Calev. He slipped a yard down the rope. His head banged against another porthole.

"I could use some help here." His words broke under the sound of the waves on the hull.

Oron fought with the rope, his weight shifting the small boat. "I don't think it's going to go well for your lucky boy if he ends up in the drink right now."

Yanking salt from my bag, I tossed some into the wind.

"Peace under the waters and above.

I wait for your will but send prayers still."

The sea eased into a quiet swell, gentling like a guilty horse, and Calev turned his face up, nodding thankfully.

"Hurry." I reached a hand down, and after three more upward thrusts, he grasped it and slipped over port side to land next to me. He rubbed his skull.

"You're all right?"

"Fine. Fine."

He was anything but.

With my dagger, now clean of the amir's blood, I cut the rope holding a large Wraith Lantern to the mainmast. Calev caught it neatly, the sun an orange hill at the edge of the sea behind him.

A shout echoed from the shore.

Berker and two fighters stood on the sand, a battle axe and a bow raised. The man with the bow suddenly doubled over, coughing. Berker wiped a hand over his own forehead like someone with a fever.

Calev gripped the lantern. "They're ill." The ship listed, but he bent his knees and kept his feet. He was becoming a sailor.

"Exactly what I was thinking." If they were, we'd have more sun to find a way around the whirlpool. But if the sailors were sick, what about Oron? He'd stayed the entire night with them.

At the side of the ship, Calev and I leaned over to check on Oron. He looked up with imploring eyes.

"Do hurry, sweetings." His tunic billowed in a gust of salty wind. "They're sending arrows in place of prayers this morning."

Proving his point, an arrow zipped past my head.

With shaking fingers, I tied the lantern onto my sash while Calev steadied the rope. I climbed down to Oron, and when my feet were in the teetering boat, I looked up. We were headed back out to sea. That frigid mist was going to hit us hard.

"We need a blanket," I called up to Calev.

Nodding, Calev disappeared, then came over the side with two hefty woolen bundles under one arm. Another arrow flashed past, grazing his leg and bringing a scant amount of blood to the surface.

My pulse tapped insistently in my temples, hurrying me, rushing me, warning me. "Throw the blankets down." I held out my hands.

Oron and I caught Calev's stolen goods with outstretched arms as more shouts rode from the beach and over the surf. We tucked the blankets under the benches. On the sandy shoreline, two more fighting sailors ran to join Berker. If I squinted hard enough, I could see gray around their eyes and mouths. Definitely ill.

Hmm. Gray. Silver.

A spark lit my mind as Calev's weight hit the boat. He and Oron grabbed up the oars.

"Did you see the strange light last night?" I untied my sash.

Calev rowed on the opposite side, across the boat's belly from Oron and me.

Oron's gaze flickered between the sailors on the coast and the whirlpool we headed toward. "The only thing I saw was the black behind my eyelids, a lightless heaven."

The sailors nocked arrows and raised their bows high. A bead of sweat dragged down my face. Berker probably hadn't found the amir yet. He most likely suspected we planned to tell another party about the silver.

There wasn't sun enough to talk about my guess as to why the fighters and Berker were sick. Calev and Oron would simply have to follow orders. "We have to go southeast and slip past the whirlpool. There might be a way to lip around it."

A volley of arrows splashed short of the boat. The sucking sound of the whirlpool reached my ears.

I caught bits of Berker's shouts. "...the whirlpool reaches too far..."

My oar didn't want to move in the water, and my arms trembled with fatigue. I felt for my salt pouch. Nothing but a bit of dust. I'd thought there would be sun to refill it.

The whirlpool's blue-green and white waters churned all the way to the black rocks of the breakers leading to the Pass.

"I think we can make it," I whispered, one hand in my pouch and one on the oar. A road of water, unmoved by the whirlpool's deadly current edged the path toward the breakers. If we could line ourselves up with that... I turned to Calev, my mind thinking twenty things at once. "Did you not see the light last night?"

He faced me, tugging his oar, his eyes tight. "I-I...no. Just you. I..." His words tumbled together and a red flush lay across his fine cheeks.

I was sure my own blushing matched his.

"Oh ho," Oron shouted over the water, "I don't believe you've shared all your adventures." He tried to smile even as he glanced at the whirlpool. His features tightened.

Still blushing and full of ripe fear, I joined Calev to help him row.

"What?" Calev asked Oron as he shifted on his seat. The look on his face reminded me of when we'd been caught leaping from the Old Farm stables' roof onto his father's favorite steed.

"Your color tells me even more than the fact that you can't sit still over there, young man." Oron laughed, then yelped as another volley of arrows zipped into the air.

"Hush, you two," I said. "There was a strange silver light around the island last night, around the camp. Only we three ate your greens, and we're not sick. I think the light is poison somehow. The greens must give us some temporary protection."

Oron twisted and lifted his eyebrows. "Though not from arrows, I'm guessing."

One of the sailors' shots hit the hull. The arrow's yellow and black fletching colored a spot not two fingers from Oron's elbow. His face whitened.

"We have to go back," he hissed.

I nodded, my neck tight. "The fighters are weakened. Maybe we can get back to shore, fight them off or trick them, and disappear into the hills. If I can watch the tides turn, I might spy a path past the worst of the whirlpool and plan a way out."

"You're the most valuable to them, Kinneret," Calev said, his flush gone and confidence giving his words legs again. "Because of what you did to get us here. You stand with me beside you and we'll wave a surrender."

His reasoning was a little flawed considering I was the one Berker trusted the least, but I agreed. We had no choice anyway.

"Reverse stroke, Oron. Calev, pull hard."

I worked too, and our boat swung around, putting our backs to the shore.

"The only surrender I know is the formal one done at the harvest contest at the amir's field," I said.

Visions of men on swan-necked steeds decked out in tasseled saddles flashed through my mind.

"It's the only one I know too," Calev said. He met my eyes. "Ready?"

If this failed and the fighters aimed well, this could end with our blood coloring the boat and Oron lost in the whirlpool, destined to become a Salt Wraith. He'd never have the strength to row out and he certainly didn't have the talent with magic.

I steeled myself, not allowing my hands to shake as Calev gave them a quick squeeze. My heart galloped through my chest.

We stood as one and raised our hands, one arm bent and angled toward the other in the sign of surrender.

CHAPTER TWENTY-SIX

"**S**urrender!" I shouted with Calev.

The sea lifted the boat and turned her west as we edged away from the whirlpool. On shore, the fighting sailors held their bows high, and the arrow tips glinted in the sun, poised to strike.

His voice contorted by the sea's noise, Berker shouted something. The fighter on his left let one arrow fly.

Calev shoved me to the boat's bottom and threw himself over me. My elbow hit a bench seat on my way down. Pain splintered my arm. The boards under me reeked of old ocean water and I argued for him to let me up.

On top of me, Calev's body jerked unnaturally.

He grunted, and the hand that clutched me to him loosened and fell limp. I pressed it against my shoulder to make him hold me, but his breath came out in a hiss.

A cold knowledge crushed me. He was hit. The arrow had found him.

Then Oron was talking. Shouting rose from the beach. We needed to get back to the oars. The current was pulling us toward the whirlpool again.

Trying not to panic, I eased my way out from under Calev, settling him, stomach down, in the boat's belly and taking his head in my hands.

"Where exactly is he hit, Oron?" My voice was strangely calm.

Calev's beautiful brown eyes fluttered open and shut. "I'm all right." He sucked a breath and his body shivered. "It's my side."

I couldn't breathe.

Oron had maneuvered his bulky self around an oar handle to view Calev from the back. Oron's tangled locks fell over his wide nose as he crouched to see the point of entry. Calev was trembling in my hands, his knees butted against my own. The boat dipped under us, the tide now taking us too close. Calev was in bad shape. But the whirlpool was about to eat us all.

I met Oron's gaze over Calev's heaving form. "We have to row. Now."

Leaping up, I grabbed the nearest oar. Oron did the same. The whirlpool was a slurping, sucking monster ready to devour us, more dangerous even than Asag because no weapon could force it to change course. My will drained away. It felt eerily similar to a wraith sweeping over me. Without more salt in my pouch, more strength in my gut, and more confidence in our chances, we'd never make it.

But though we rowed hard, it was as if we weren't rowing at all.

The current sped across our path, tearing a wide ripple between us and the shallow water leading to the shoreline. Calev made a noise. I dug my oar deeper into the waves and strained the wooden handle back. Every muscle in my arms and back and neck screamed.

We weren't going to make it.

"Kinneret. The salt." Oron's voice was dry and cracked. He knew I didn't have anything but dust.

With one last haul on the oar, I wedged the handle under my arm and struggled with the pouch strings. The boat tossed with only Oron to row it. Calev's arm dropped to the decking with a knock. He groaned. My blood screamed, my heart hitting my ribs painfully.

Not my Calev too. Please not my Calev too.

Salty grit under my nails and in my palm, I tossed what little magic I had into the air and shouted to the sea.

"Send us out.

Send us beyond.

We know not your depths.

We want not your charms.

Out, out, out, out.

Please, sea.

Please listen to me."

I grabbed the oar and slammed it into the water. The boat turned its nose a subtle fraction toward the sky. Rowing, heaving, and praying aloud, we dragged at the boat. The current fought us. The salt hadn't worked. I'd shouted my salt prayer. Anger never got anyone anywhere with the salt.

I closed my eyes and put everything I had left into one last tug on the oar.

Then the craft began to edge out of the current.

Tears or sweat or maybe both poured down my face. Oron whooped in joy, and with a few more pulls, the tide brought us ashore.

All my thoughts turned immediately to Calev.

Oron leaped from the boat and joined the others in pulling the craft out of the waves. One sailor vomited beside the boat. They were still suffering from the silver toxin.

Berker was snapping and lashing out commands I didn't hear or care about.

I dragged Calev up and put his good side against mine, his arm over my shoulder. He mumbled something. I kissed his forehead, not caring for even a breath if anyone thought anything of it. If they tried to Outcast him for this, I'd kill them all. Twice.

I supposed I should remove the arrow from Calev's back and staunch the bleeding. I draped his body, chest down, over a patch of blue-green grass. Like rain drops, blood trickled from the place where the arrow's shaft sunk into his skin, more of it oozing from the top of the wound. He panted like a dog with sun-stroke, his breaths short and labored.

Purple rings circled Berker's eyes—probably from the poisonous silver light—as he yammered on. "I didn't intend for the fighters to injure Calev ben Y'hoshua, but this is your doing, sailor. As soon as the amir returns from her walk, I will inform her of your attempt to steal away and find a new associate to help you take all the silver for yourself."

My jaw ached from clenching my teeth. At least he didn't know the amir had been killed.

The silent fighters beside him shuffled their feet and mumbled with one another, voices low and worried, faces tinged with gray and yellow sickness.

"No one wants to hear your blathering, Kaptan Berker Deniz." With my dagger, I pressed sideways into the arrow shaft sticking out of Calev's shivering back. The wood snapped and left a shorter length that would be easier to grab and pull.

Berker tsked at my words and stormed toward the camp, his tunic whipping around his ankles. The sailors stayed with us.

I looked to Oron. Sand cloaked his chin and shoulder. He brushed it away impatiently. "This is the worst sort of place to treat such a wound."

"But we're near the ocean." The sea had the most magic. Its salt would be Calev's best bet against this wound. I put a hand near the arrow. Calev's torn tunic was rough under my fingers and the patterns in it made my tired eyes flinch. "Do you think it's a good idea to take it out now? He's still awake."

Oron knelt. "He won't be when you do the job." He began tearing Calev's tunic away from the wound.

One sailor hissed sympathetically and two held Calev still.

I grasped the arrow shaft.

Oron unsheathed his dagger. "Hold it and him still while I make a cut."

I tried to keep breathing as Oron sliced the blade through Calev's skin, making a cut two fingers long.

Oron met my gaze. "I have to touch the arrowhead. I need to see if it's stuck in bone or bent from a muscle contraction."

I squeezed my eyes shut, then opened them and nodded.

Calev shouted as Oron's finger slipped into the bloody wound. Oron tilted his head, his tongue between his teeth, and Calev went limp.

Pulling his digit free, Oron stared grimly into the grass and sand. "It passed between two ribs. I think it may've nicked his lung, but we won't know unless he…"

"Unless he what?"

"Unless he stops breathing properly, smells of pus, and dies."

I blew out a harsh breath. I would focus on doing what we could, not what horrors might happen. "Now what do we do?"

Oron was eyeing the fighting sailors. "Since it's not stuck in bone, we can pull it free. But I need something to loop around it. Anyone have a length of wire?"

A fighter with a voice like a raven said, "Would fishing line work?"

Snatching it, Oron began muttering. "If he dies, Y'hoshua ben Aharon will have me in his fields working off the blood price until the sun goes black."

I tried to swallow, but my throat didn't want to work. "The fields aren't his."

"Oh, don't you start too. I know. I know. Old Farm belongs to all at Old Farm. Everyone is equal and all that." He snorted. "But you don't see any other Old Farm boys meeting with the amir, now do you? They exist in a caste system as we do. They're only more skilled at masking its uglier side."

He was doing his best to distract me with an argument.

I glared. "If Calev dies, we all work in Y'hoshua's fields until we die. It'll be one big celebration."

Oron worked the line into a loop and eased it into the wound. "Remind me to educate you further on what is enjoyable and what is not.

Considering this journey you were so keen to embark on, plus your take on working in fields, I feel you've quite forgotten the basics."

The arrow's shaft trembled from Calev's unconscious shaking, and my palms grew damp.

Oron held tight to the fishing line. "Take the shaft and when I call it, pull straight away from the point of entry."

My throat convulsed. "Aye, aye, kaptan."

Oron gave me a wry look. A breath later, he said, "Now."

We yanked the arrow from Calev's back, a wet noise making my skin cold and damp.

I dove back toward Calev and covered the bleeding wound with the torn square of his tunic. The sea blew behind me, pressing along my back like a friend's hand. Squeezing my eyes shut, I only thought of Calev's smile and how my heart swelled when I saw it. There were no words to this kind of desperate prayer. My heart thudded in my fingertips.

Oron kissed the top of my head like Calev's Old Farm soul-teacher.

The immediate threat over, my mind flipped from rescue to rage, and Oron misinterpreted the look in my eyes.

Keeping one hand on the cloth at Calev's back, he touched my shoulder with the other. "There's no blood from the boy's mouth. A good sign. He's only asleep from the pain."

But that wasn't where my mind was. Now that Calev was tended to—as best as possible in the situation—my rage rose to the surface. I spun and stood in one motion like Calev had in his dagger dance, and my eyes searched out the fighter who'd loosed that arrow.

I found him.

Dark hair. Light eyes. Very, very tall. Ekrem.

I paused. Wait. I liked Ekrem. I hadn't realized he was the one who'd shot at us. The truth stung. Next to him, the blond woman with the beautiful battle axe frowned.

"You." I raged toward Ekrem, pushing the others out of my way. Ekrem didn't back away from me. I shoved his chest. "You hurt the most important member of Old Farm. Your life is worthless."

They didn't know about the amir. I could use her shadow to scare him. I wanted all of them scared. Of me. Of us. So they'd help me with Calev and help me sail away to Kurakia.

The plan grew roots in my mind. Maybe my aunt could heal him. I'd seen her heal a man with a head injury that had left him sleeping for three solid years.

Ekrem frowned down at me. "You know I was under orders, Kaptan Kinneret Raza. Kaptan Berker Deniz outranks you."

Ekrem's stiff leather vest was hot under my gritty palms as I pushed him. "Well, when the amir hears of this," I said, "she'll have you drawn and quartered. Your head on a spike. Or you'll be sent to the quarries."

My hands fell to my sides, and all my energy drained out of me. The quarries. With the amir dead, how was I going to get Avi back? Maybe my aunt would think of a plan for Avi. At least Avi was probably still alive at the quarry. Maybe. Calev could die at any minute. He could be dead already.

The rage in me blinked away. I fell to my knees, knowing my shouting did nothing.

Ekrem offered a hand, but I pushed his fingers away. Beyond us, the whirlpool's eddies smoothed from white and blue-green into a dull blue. The sun was a white circle, just a finger from its zenith. The tide had changed and the whirlpool had calmed a bit.

I faced the sailors, my eyes specifically trained on Ekrem. Maybe his guilt would move him toward my goal. All had to be done before Berker returned either with news of the amir or simply with the trouble he liked to cause me.

I stood again. "When we left, we weren't trying to do anything against our agreement with the amir." It was true, but obviously since Calev killed the amir, it hardly made sense, but they didn't know that. "Kaptan Berker Deniz is simply misinformed. Now, I need two of you to come with us to Kurakia, if you will. My mother's sister is the only one who can heal this son of Old Farm. If he dies, I guarantee one of your number will die for it, either in the fields under the sun or by the amir's rough hand. Your amir will suffer too. The kyros also knows and respects Old Farm. He won't let the amir's mistake hinder his ability to make silver from lemon and barley trade. Now, who will row our boat and do their duty to Jakobden?"

The light-haired woman spoke up. "We must wait for the amir's orders."

Oron nudged me. "Kinneret, what exactly are you doing?"

"Stay with Calev. I have a plan," I whispered to him.

"We cannot wait," I said to the woman. "To wait means death for this Old Farm son."

Ekrem raised his blue eyes and nodded.

I took a breath. "Good. I need one more volunteer. We need two strong sailors to row. I have a Wraith Lantern. We'll be safe. I am your kaptan."

The light-haired woman cocked her head and breathed out through her nose. Then she raised her palm and bowed.

A weight dropped off my back. "Good. Your name, please?"

"Serhat, kaptan."

I nodded. "You two, lift Calev ben Y'hoshua. The rest, give up your water skins for our journey please and shove us off the shore."

Movement in the distance caught my eye, and my heart contracted. Someone was headed here. I licked my lips and hurried to take the water from the sailors who weren't coming with us.

"Hurry now, please."

Ekrem and Serhat, who'd mostly regained their healthy color, leaned Calev up and put their heads under his arms. They lifted him, and I tucked my shoulder under one of his thighs to help get him to the boat. Another sailor joined me, grabbing the other leg. The other two men took oars from the next small boat and placed them in ours.

Once we had Calev settled on the floor of the boat, we hopped out to push the heavy craft into the water. It took way too long to get the boat deep enough for us to board.

The people approaching were taking shape now, getting closer. Three? Four?

We jumped into the boat, and I held up a hand to shield my eyes from the sun.

Berker's bright tunic caught the light. A smear of darkness marred his sash.

Blood.

My heart stopped. That was the amir's blood.

They knew.

I spun to face Ekrem and Serhat. "Row hard. We must make the tide to steer around the whirlpool's tight fist."

Oron took up an oar across from me. As he raised his eyes to the beach, his cheeks fell flat and his mouth dropped open. "Kinneret."

"I know."

Thankfully, the sailors didn't seem to notice Berker and the others trickling onto the beach. Serhat rowed with eyes trained on Calev, who'd begun bleeding again at their feet. Ekrem kept his gaze on me, probably seeing how I measured up in this unconventional situation. The man probably wondered why he'd agreed to this.

I twisted on my bench seat, trying not to hear Calev's labored breathing above the splash of water and the wind whistling through the metal rings that kept the oars moving in the right place. The whirlpool remained smoother than when we'd first tried this. I had no more salt in my pouch, so I scooted to the side and cupped a handful of ocean. Throwing the water high, allowing the sunlight to sparkle through it, I called out a prayer and a wish and hoped it was enough. My tingling fingers and toes told me I was too worried to do proper Salt Magic. This would have to be mostly skill and brute strength.

Our craft touched the lip of the whirlpool's hungry mouth.

"Hard to port!" The boat rocked, but the current didn't yet have us. "More! I need more!"

We rounded the island side of the pool, going counterclockwise. The second we slipped from that arc, we had to row with everything to rip free and head to the opening in the breakers.

"Starboard. Row hard to starboard. Reverse on port. Go. Go!"

I tugged at my own oar, the boat shuddering and tossing under me. The handle stuck and the water drew hands over the oar's tip. I cursed and swore and gritted my teeth and hauled on the paddle until it, and the work of the others, finally pulled us another shift away from the pool.

At the gap in the black rock barriers and billowing waves, Oron and the sailors followed my directions like they could read my thoughts. My back and arms cramping, we dashed through the pass, unbroken.

That obstacle crossed, my gaze flew back to the shore's inky sand. Neither the amir's fighters nor Berker were there. Oron pointed behind and east of us. Berker and ten sailors had boarded another boat and obviously followed our lead in getting around the pool. There were more fighters than oars, and some drew arrows from quivers on their backs. They were slow to nock them. Berker's mouth opened wide like he was shouting. His hands jerked through the air as their boat crested an incoming wave near the gap. He fell back and only his head showed above the craft's side.

"He's trying to get them to fire," Oron whispered to me.

Ekrem turned. "They will not attempt to hit us, Kaptan Kinneret. I did not intend to strike the Old Farm. The wind took my shot."

Serhat nodded, her blond braid shifting over her shoulder.

I swallowed and cleared my throat. "Why won't they attack?"

"Because you showed loyalty to Ifran. The amir did not. Kaptan Berker did not. We value loyalty above all."

His words steeled my heart. What could I give Ekrem and Serhat for all this? I had nothing but a trip across the Pass to foreign Kurakia, a trip that would most likely involve thirst, hunger, and to top it all, Salt Wraiths.

Still rowing, sweat pouring down my back and temples, I did my best to look calm and deserving of his service and his mate's. "I will reward you in any way I can, though the prize may only be friendship and a place to lay your head at the end of all this."

Not taking his hands from his oar, Ekrem closed and opened his eyes, nodding his head in acknowledgment. Serhat gave me a grim smile and went back to her rowing.

"Kinneret," Oron said quickly, his eyes shining. "You have given me more tales than I ever thought to hold in my heart."

"It isn't over yet," I said. In the shadow of the boat's side, Calev's lashes drew black lines against his sickly pale cheeks. "Calev better live through it with us." A vice tightened around my chest and I gripped the side to keep from falling.

"My wish too, kaptan." Oron's voice was rough as the waters, his gaze on Calev's shivering body.

A frustrated scream burned to escape my throat and rise over the sea, but I fought it back and straightened my shoulders. I forced myself to ignore the struggling boatload of Berker and his fighting sailors behind us, and I gave the order to drift into the Pass's main current.

AFTER TWO DAYS of riding a current, Kurakia's coast, barely discernible at this distance, was a calligrapher's practice stroke on the eastern horizon. We had to reach its shores before Calev's body stopped fighting and I lost my best ally in my fight to get Avi back.

CHAPTER TWENTY-SEVEN

louds shrouded the moon and drew a blanket of pale blue over the looming shoulders of Kurakia's coast. My body shook with fatigue as the others took a break from rowing to sleep. With one hand on our makeshift tiller—simply an oar I held out the aft end of the little boat—I did my best to use the currents to direct us toward my aunt. The Wraith Lantern scattered light over my arm as I scooped another handful of ocean water, threw it, and whispered magic.

The white-black sea shushed against the boat, and I dipped fingers into the water, my heart easing just a little. There hadn't been as many rocks coming from Ayarazi to Kurakia, thankfully. It'd been two nights on the Pass, but it felt like an eternity.

A wet cough and a moan sounded from the bottom of the boat. Calev.

With a small rope lying wet at the bottom of the craft, I tied the tiller oar to the stone circle anchor sitting at my feet. Edging past Oron's slumped and sleeping body, I leaned toward Calev and touched his cheek. His skin was sticky and cold. He opened one beautiful eye.

Swallowing, he tried to talk for the first time since we'd removed the arrow on Ayarazi's coast. "Where...is that...Kin..."

I pressed my palm gently against his jaw, my heart seizing. "I'm here. You'll be fine. We're almost to my aunt's. She'll fix you. Just rest."

He'd managed to drink from Serhat's water skin earlier and worked down two bites of fish Oron had miraculously netted. That was a true gift. So many of the fish in these waters were poisonous.

Hope for Calev and Avi burned in me like wildfire, out of control and raging through any common sense I'd picked up through my short life. I refused to sleep, thinking if I let that fire rest, it might go out.

"Kinneret," Calev rasped.

"I'm here."

His eyes went wide and rolled before closing again, like he was trying to see the two sailors that surrounded him. "Do they know I killed the amir?"

I sucked a breath and touched my fingers to his lips. A prickling sensation ran over the back of my neck. Serhat slept, mouth open and her eyes firmly shut. To my left, Ekrem also lay still, but his chest wasn't rising and falling like a sleeping person. It was dark though. Surely he would've said something if he'd heard Calev.

Calev seemed to be sleeping again though, or lost in pain, so hopefully he wouldn't repeat his question.

At some point I had to tell Ekrem and Serhat about Calev's Infusion and the murder. Would they still value my so-called loyalty when they learned I'd helped their master's killer escape? If they rose against us, we were lost. We could never fight them off with Calev so badly injured. I couldn't carry him on one shoulder and flee or fight.

As I crawled back to the tiller, a Salt Wraith dragged across the moon.

Raising the lantern high, I hissed a warning to the others. "Wraith. Block your ears. Stay low."

The rest, except Calev, stirred and crouched on the bottom of the boat between the bench seats, avoiding the moonlight and the wraith's shadow.

This wasn't the wraith that had Infused Calev. This felt like ones in the past had, all raging, nonsensical hate smashing my reason into splinters. Gritting my teeth, I shook harder as the grating anger skinned me alive. Thank the Fire the lantern glowed strong and true.

Oron and the sailors winced against the wraith's attack, eyes shuttered and shoulders tensed in the light of the lantern. The wraith whisked its charcoal-white, glittering shadow over us, and Calev jerked awake. I crawled to him. His cheek pressed against the boat's bottom, and he gave me a small nod, reassuring me. A muscle worked at his jawline. He was feeling the wraith, as we all certainly were, but he was still him, still whole in heart.

Checking Oron and the sailors, I lay down, my head resting on Calev's tunic-swathed calf, and his sandal's edge butting into my belly. I breathed him in, pushing the angry thoughts out, out, out.

Finally, the wraith's shadow disappeared. The sky was clear.

"No more?" Oron scratched his head.

I sat up and squeezed my hands to try to stop their shaking. "All clear."

"Too bad. The whole Wanting To Kill Everybody thing was tamping the whole Our Future Is Looking Pretty Crap thing down really well."

I shot him a look.

"Kinneret," Oron whispered, his big eyes watching the fighters settle into their rowing. "This whole business with the yatagan-eyed wiseman and the golden axe-wielder," he nodded toward Ekrem and Serhat, "it's...we should've left without them. Not that I don't love the blond's looks of death. They're like rich dumplings that turn your blood to sludge as you grin and take another helping."

Sunlight crept over the hills of the Kurakian shoreline. Ease washed over me. We'd made it.

"Hush, Oron. Please."

"Pardon me for interrupting your moment with the sunrise, but we need to—"

"You did not tell us your truth." Ekrem sat up.

My hands strangled the oar I was using as a tiller.

Eyeing me without a hint of emotion on his rugged face, Ekrem tugged his vest into place and splashed a handful of water over the back of his neck. His voice was loud over the water shushing against Kurakia's red sand shoreline.

"I heard Calev ben Y'hoshua mumbling in the dark. The Old Farm murdered the amir."

I went cold as he and Serhat stood in unison.

"Yes, but..." What was the best way to explain this?

Oron raised his thick eyebrows in an I-told-you look. I curled my lip at him.

My oar slid easily from the water, but I dragged it slowly into its ring like it weighed four Ekrems holding nine Serhats. Oron and I began to row us closer to shore. He gave me yet another look, his lips pale and his throat moving in a swallow.

Both fighting sailors stood in front of us with arms crossed, pieces of their hair like whips around their stern faces. Their oars sat on their benches like a sign of rebellion. My stomach felt empty and full at the same time. If I didn't word this wisely, any chance we had to save Avi was over, not to mention the rest of our lives. There was precious little hope of rescuing Avi. What could we do? Even if Ekrem and Serhat spared our lives and stayed by our sides, what could five people do against the oramiral?

Nothing.

"Please. Just..." I didn't know what to say.

A shudder ripped through me. I pressed my lids closed and tears bled out of my eyes. I was losing Avi. And Calev. If the fighters didn't believe our story, Oron and I too would be killed.

What was the point of trying?

My oar slipped from my hands. I opened my eyes as Oron jumped in front of me and caught its handle before it could disappear into the water.

"Kinneret," he said softly, holding my oar with two white-knuckled hands, "you must move forward. If you don't move forward, the worst will happen. If you do move forward, it may not."

I took a jerking breath, wiped my eyes, and took the oar from him. The truth in Oron's words buoyed me. I had some strength in me still and I would use it for my loved ones.

"Before we left Jakobden," I said, looking around the fighting sailors to the Pass, to the challenges we were leaving behind, "Calev went with me and Oron to get the map to Ayarazi." My gaze flicked to Ekrem. "You heard about the map, yes?"

He nodded.

"After our dive, Calev was Infused. I didn't realize it then. He was still Infused on Ayarazi. The wraith ordered the amir's death. I watched the Infusion light leave Calev's mouth." Unblinking, I met their gazes, showing them the truth in my eyes.

From my periphery, I saw Oron nod across the boat from me, his eyes swiveling from one sailor to the other. Calev lay silent and shuddering between the bench seats at the bottom of the rocking craft.

Ekrem's chest expanded, and his vest creaked like a saddle as it stretched over his broad build. He exhaled very, very slowly.

I turned away from him to peer over my shoulder. The shore crept up behind us.

The sailor looked to his crewmate. He was asking her what she thought. It all sat on her shoulders. Calev. Avi. Oron. Me.

Serhat stepped onto her bench and leaped deftly over Calev.

"What are you doing?" If she tried to hurt him, I would die defending him.

She leaned into Calev's face, her body glancing against my back.

"He can't answer your questions now," I said. "When my aunt—"

The sailor held a hand up to my face, and I shut my mouth. She brushed a large hand over Calev's askew headtie. Her finger touched the line of pale skin that normally hid beneath the cloth. I tugged at my oar, twisted slightly in my seat. A word sneaked out of Serhat's mouth, but I couldn't understand it. Turning her fair face to me, her gray eyes found mine, and I swallowed.

Her mouth was a line. Her eyes were as cold as the mist surrounding Ayarazi. "If your aunt can heal him, we will talk then."

I took a breath and glanced at Oron. So we had no promises from Ekrem and Serhat, but we had time between now and their decision whether or not to avenge their amir.

I'd take it.

Giving Serhat a terse nod, I drew my oar into the boat and hopped into the knee-high seawater to drag the boat onto the shoreline. The others pushed and shoved along with me, sweat blooming on our brows. Already the Kurakian sun was a burning brand on my cheeks and arms. Sand squelched into my sandals, but I didn't mind.

We had made it to my mother's homeland.

CHAPTER TWENTY-EIGHT

Skirting the walled capitol city of mud-brick tower houses with their grass-topped roofs, we wove down the path cattlemen used to take their beasts to market. A small crowd of Kurakians surrounded us, their clothing bright with purple and red dye, but dusty. Calev rode my and the sailors' shoulders, and Oron led the way.

Oron elbowed a cow that was headed out of the city perimeter like us. "Get your massive hind end to the side, beast."

A woman in a one-shouldered dress and elaborately braided hair laughed with her friend.

The bare-chested cattleman at the cow's long-horned head gave us a scowl and chit-chitted at his animal to move it along more quickly. The cow bellowed, and the owner drew a whip from his loose pants and cracked the beast lightly.

Pushing the tentacles of his hair out of his face, Oron squinted at the horizon of scrubby Topa trees and dry sloping land. "How far away is your dear aunt's bastion of healing, Kinneret? Or have you tricked us all and are luring us into the Kurakian desert to die slowly?"

I took a heavy breath of spice and manure, then adjusted Calev's legs on my shoulders. Gripping his ankles, I tried to speed up. I could tell the fighters were keeping their pace slow because of me.

Oron's question sparked an idea.

I'd done my part to keep the fighters safe during the sun they'd spent with me. Maybe if I brought up a few of those instances, they'd be more likely to believe Calev's Infusion was truth instead of lie.

"If I'd wanted you dead," I said, "I'd have slit your throats as you slept last night."

We cleared the city's uneven wall and started up a steeper rise toward the countryside. A cloud of red dust spun into the air.

Ekrem coughed. "We're fortunate you stopped at simply slaying our leader."

Oron clapped one hand slowly on his thigh in applause. "For one normally so quiet, you certainly know how to craft a verbal strike."

"Striking is who I am," Ekrem said. "I am a hit. A cut. A slash. A blade and a bite."

I looked over Calev's leg at the fighter, then turned to see what his crewmate would say, if anything at all.

She raised her gaze from the patches of scrub grass along the path, to Oron's frowning face. "A kick and a cry of rage. Always, always, always coming for our enemies."

Goosebumps dragged over my arms.

I'd heard the fighters' creed before, tales about it from my parents. But I'd never heard it spoken in all seriousness by those who upheld its intent.

I had to win these two to my side. When Calev was healed—because I couldn't even think about my aunt failing in that—I needed these fighters to help me somehow rescue Avi.

Calev moaned.

My plotting dissolved into the sting and burn of fear. I rubbed my thumb over the bone at the bottom of his ankle. "Soon. We'll get you help soon."

The sun lashed its rays down on our heads and the bare shoulders of the Kurakian men who continued on the path to the next city. We went west and left the crowd. A Topa tree, resembling a hand rising from the dirt, crowned the next hill.

"There," I said. "My aunt's place is beyond that tree."

"Into the hand of the Fire," Oron mumbled, quoting the first kyros's three-hundred-year-old address to his conquered Jakobden natives. "I wonder...should we hope our young man here is delivered into that hand or left behind to fight with us?"

It was a good question. If Calev survived, he'd only live to be injured again if he stayed by my side like I knew he would. Was it selfish of me to wish for that?

"Oh, don't look too torn," Oron said, touching my sun burnt arm. "He would come with us no matter what you tried to do to prevent it. The man is quite in love with you, I fear."

My heart leaped and bumped into my ribs. After what happened at the waterfall, I'd guessed Calev did have feelings for me. But unless I survived this to become a real kaptan... Wait. He'd killed the amir. I'd been by his side. We were both doomed to die in the worst way if we ever returned home.

"What's to fear?" My voice trembled. "Who cares about caste anymore? It's not as if we can ever return to Jakobden. Calev's Infusion has set us on a path out of our home country. And I don't...I don't know..."

My words tripped and fell back inside me. For once, I had no real plan.

"Is this it?" Ekrem said.

"Yes. We're here. The ancient homestead of the Turays, my mother's family."

My aunt's farm looked much the same as the last time I'd seen it when I'd held my mother and father's hands with Avi trailing along behind us. A low, dirt wall surrounded scrub, three large Topa trees, the hen house on short stilts, a brick oven, and Aunt Kania's four story, mud-brick tower house. Dodging green-throated roosters and black-brown hens, we carried Calev through a gate crafted of sticks and knotted rope.

"You weren't joking about the chickens." Oron nudged an especially curious one away with his sandal. It clucked and spread its wings, flying the short distance to a hen house ramp.

Desperation for what to do about Avi and worry for Calev threatened to burst through my skin, but I tried to keep my voice light. I didn't want to douse the fire of hope inside me or the others. "I never joke about chickens."

Aunt Kania appeared from behind the second hen house, her skin polished as Topa wood, as Mother's had been. A basket balanced in the braids of her head. Above her traditional, red Kurakian scarf, her wide smile faded as she studied the load on our shoulders.

I wanted to run to her, to bury my face in the bright pink folds of her one-shouldered dress and breathe in the tangy scent of dust and the cool, green smell of healing ointments. It would remind me of Mother. I knew it would. It would be comforting and wonderful.

And a waste of sun right now.

"Greetings, Aunt. I'm sorry it's been so long." I held my palm up as we did in Jakobden, and she quickly dipped and shook her head in the Kurakian greeting. "My friend needs you. He took an arrow to the back. His lung might be injured too."

She tossed the basket to the ground and hurried over, her red linen scarf flying behind her like she had wings. "Get him to my rooms." Her Kurakian accent lengthened the vowels of the Jakobden tongue—the language everyone knew, the trade language, also known as the Common Tongue.

As we walked through the rough arches underneath the tower house and headed toward the ladder, I lowered Calev's legs and let the fighters manage him in the narrow space.

A lot of rushed instructions, sweating, and fretting later, we had Calev on my aunt's top floor.

Aunt leaned over him as he lay on her striped rug. We gathered around, a smelly group for sure.

One ear on his chest, Aunt listened and clucked her tongue. "Not good. Not good."

My skin went cold.

Oron grumbled something and walked to a corner, his hand over his mouth. Serhat and Ekrem helped themselves to a jug of water on Aunt's table and sat on her stools.

Aunt reached toward a set of shelves under her hammock near a wide, open window. Withdrawing a crock, she met my eyes. "He will probably die."

I shivered. Kurakians never did coat the truth with syrup. "But he's strong." I knelt beside Calev. His hair was soft, despite its sandy grit. His parted lips had lost all their pink-plum color. I drew my finger along their perfect edges. His breath was warm. "He's the eldest son of the elected leader of Old Farm."

Tilting her head in a maybe sort of gesture, Aunt said, "A strong bloodline. Will it be enough?"

Using a water skin and a fold of linen, she washed his wound. He stayed asleep, his face pale but not gray. Not the color of death. The unguent she tucked into the arrow's hole smelled like cinnamon and pepper and green plants. Taking a handful of salt from a pouch on her belt—a pouch much like my own—she began her magic.

Rubbing her palms together, her hands moved like fish darting up and down as she whispered prayers in Kurakian. I spoke nothing of the language. My mother had done her best to teach me. I had no talent for languages other than my own.

Sitting cross-legged, she rocked back and forth. The grass mat beneath the rug crackled with her movements. Dusting sea salt over Calev's back and into his hair, she prayed over and over, her words blending together and lilting like she was very nearly singing. I couldn't look away from her. The sounds. Her hands. The salt sparking in the light from the window.

"Does Salt Magic work on land?" I asked.

Aunt shrugged. "Who knows what truly works? Could be coincidence when things go our way. Could be prayers. Maybe magic. Some things I know work, but we do it all, just in case."

With a final word, she placed one hand at the base of Calev's skull and the other below his wound. I'm not sure if it was my fatigue or the fire in me, longing for his return to good health, but it seemed as if the air around her hands and his body shimmered.

Calev's back moved in one deep breath. A deeper breath than I'd seen him take in a long while. Since the boat, at least.

The fighters remained silent. From the room's back corner, Oron breathed entirely too loudly. Calev wasn't breathing loudly enough.

Aunt looked up at me. "Now we wait." She took my wrist in her warm, dry hand. "You rest, my niece."

If I slept, what would I wake to?

As Aunt stood, I grabbed a handful of her dress. I had to tell her about Avi. "I need to talk to you."

Wrinkles formed between Aunt's scant eyebrows and she eyed the rest of our party curiously. "You have a story to tell. I have Kurakian chicken to share. Wash, then we'll eat and you'll tell your tale."

Taking turns at the rocky, struggling creek outside Aunt's walls, we did our best to wash our travels from the creases in our arms and the backs of our necks. We hurried back to the tower house, following the spicy scent of the food she'd cooked for us in her outdoor oven. She'd laid a table fit for an amir near Calev's resting form. I crouched to run a quick hand over his clammy cheek.

"Don't stop fighting, my Calev, my luck, my friend," I whispered, my heart beating sluggishly in my chest.

Someone touched my back. I jumped and turned to find Aunt's kind face smiling sadly.

"He must indeed be lucky. To have such a friend as my Kinneret. You are your mother's lightning strike, her beating heart."

I swallowed. "I was."

Aunt jerked her head once. "No. You *are*. She lives in you and your sister."

The word turned me inside out. I fell into Aunt's arms. "The oramiral took Avigail. I was searching for Ayarazi, for a map Old Zayn had heard about. We ran too close to Quarry Isle. The oramiral's men boarded our boat and they took her from me. They took Avi to the quarry."

Her gasp jerked my head off her chest. "Ah, no. No." Her arms tightened around me.

"It's all my doing," I said. "All my fault."

She made shushing noises into my ear, and I tried to quiet, knowing I was making a fool out of myself in front of the fighting sailors.

Pressing her mouth closer to my ear, Aunt whispered, "It is not your fault. Tell me. Tell us all."

The dinner forgotten, we sat around the table as I poured out my tale of Avi and the map and our travels and the island of silver, coming back around to Avi. Oron's interpretations punctuated my descriptions.

"The oramiral's mind is not sound." Aunt lit a powdered stick of incense in the center of the table. The resinous scent of myrrh cloaked the musk of animals wafting through the open window. I hated that she used the expensive stick on us. It was meant only for the most important events. "The amir should take him from that island and put another in his place to run the quarry. It is a shame, really, that the madman has no one to care for him and keep him from hurting people."

Serhat's forehead wrinkled. "You don't blame the oramiral for the way he beats his quarrymen? The way he—outside of battle—steals men and women, even children, for slaves?"

Aunt stood, the folds of her dress slipping into vertical lines like a rushing river. Her eyes were sharp. "At least he takes them in his confusion and is not like you and your amir, who take slaves with clear heads merely because of battles won and lost."

The fighting sailors pushed away from the table, faces pinched. "You question our honor?" Ekrem's voice punched out and up toward the grass roof.

Oron hopped off his chair. He made a short wall between the fighters and Aunt Kania. I loved him for it "We're in a strange situation here, my friends. We won't agree on everything. Kinneret cannot tolerate too much spice in her dumplings, but I would bathe in it if given the opportunity. We must band together in the face of our differences to save this Old Farm innocent and Kinneret's sister."

"I don't believe the Old Farm boy is innocent," Serhat whispered, her words slithering into my ears.

I waved my hand and accidentally knocked over the incense. "He was Infused. You must believe me. Why would he want to kill the amir? The amir supports her people. A new amir may not." I wouldn't bring up the throat-blood oath he'd taken. They most likely already knew about it, but if they didn't...

Aunt's brow wrinkled. "What are you saying? Jakobden's amir is dead? This young man," she pointed at Calev, "slayed the amir? The one who managed peace between our country and yours?" She spun to face me. "Is this true? Was he Infused? Why was he alone with the amir on the waters?"

"He wasn't alone. And it was on land. The Infusion…it-it was different." I shook my head trying to think of a way to explain. "The wraith that Infused him felt sharp, cunning. It wasn't all wild rage. It was fingers in your thoughts instead of kicking feet. Calev didn't hurt anyone until he had an opportunity to kill the amir on Ayarazi. I was the only witness."

Her mouth pursing, Aunt walked on shaky legs back to her chair. She put her hands on the woven back and leaned in, breathing heavily. "Could it be?" she mumbled. "If it is, we might have a chance."

"Could it be what?" I asked.

She motioned for everyone to sit again. The sailors frowned and began to argue.

"Tut tut. Enough of this. What has happened is bigger than our arguments." She pointed to Oron. "The short one is right."

Pulling his tunic against his arm to show its shape, Oron's mouth twisted. "I prefer well-muscled, but go on."

Everyone leaned in to listen as Aunt began to talk. Aunt possessed the richest, most lilting voice. She eyed each one of us in turn.

"Have you heard of the Tuz Golge? It is most likely a bad idea to mention it in your Jakobden lands, but it is a tale of your amir. The one your friend slayed. The woman is, was, far older than she looked, I'm certain. The Luk warriors always did age well."

"She was old?" The amir's skin had possessed a few wrinkles, but she'd been beautiful still.

Ekrem nodded. "If your blood is purely Luk, you live much longer than most."

"Does that mean you and Serhat—"

"No." Serhat brushed the incense powder I'd spilled back into its dish. "We are of mixed blood. Desert race, northern blood, and Luk, of course. Almost all are mixed now."

Aunt Kania handed a bowl of chicken around the table. "Amir Mamluk once had a husband."

"He was taken to the quarries, wasn't he?" Oron licked his lips and tucked into the food.

"Yes." Aunt ran a thumb over the side of her mouth. She didn't seem to want to eat. Me either. "He gambled," she said, "and was sent to the quarries by his own wife, the woman who is now the amir."

Both fighting sailors shifted a little in their seats and frowned. They considered gambling a soul fault, same as families who'd never served as slaves, never ridden a horse, or sailed. It was akin to performing Salt Magic.

"You have no problem with my use of the salt," I said, wondering how they'd bypassed this soul fault of mine.

They looked at one another quickly, then Ekrem said, "You used it to save our lives. You have shown your loyalty to our crew mates. We decided we may be wrong about Salt Magic."

Oron snapped his spice-stained fingers and talked around a mouthful. "Enough about customs. Let Auntie talk."

"Most believe the amir's young husband died at the quarries, but he did not. He escaped."

"Escaped from Quarry Isle on his own?" Oron snorted. "It's surrounded by chalk cliffs and seastingers and the worst waters of the Pass. Not to mention the bevy of guards with those terrifying spears."

"Not impossible," Aunt said. "He is the only person I know of who found his way out."

My heart soared out of my chest and thudded in my heads and hands. I slapped my palms on the table, shaking the dishes and bowls. "If he escaped, so can Avi."

Aunt tilted her head and clicked her tongue. "Slow, my child. Slow."

"But if you know the story, you know how, right?"

"I don't know how he did it."

I sat back, closing my eyes against the pounding in my head. "Then why tell us? What does this have to do with anything?"

"The amir took a new husband, and though he did not live long, the man at the quarry heard of it. He escaped, only to die in the waters of the Pass."

"He became a wraith."

"The great and terrible wraith called Tuz Golge."

"And you believe Tuz Golge Infused Calev and forced him to kill the amir?"

"There used to be tales of Tuz Golge on our shores. Tales of the sky-clouding wraith the size of a full-ship's sail that would scour travelers' minds, looking for a link to the amir. But that was many years ago. Nothing has been heard of the wraith in a long time."

I dug at the wood grain of Aunt's table, eyeing the bowl of sea salt on the shelf beside the window. "He was waiting for an opportunity to kill the amir. It was revenge."

Ekrem stood, turned toward the back of the room, and ran his hands through his hair. "I trusted there was an explanation, but this?"

Serhat spoke softly. "You told us truth, Kinneret Raza. Your man was Infused. He is an innocent."

Her crewmate whirled. "And we have no one to punish for this outrage."

"I thought you hated the amir after what she did to Ifran," Oron said.

Ekrem put his hands on the table and faced Oron. "Disagreeing with her decisions is one thing. Murder is another."

"She all but murdered Ifran," I snapped.

Aunt pushed my bowl of chicken toward me like she wanted me to eat. "There is nothing now you can do to punish Tuz Golge. He has what he wants. A dead lover. But you can gain information from him."

"He could tell us how he escaped from Quarry Isle." The idea chilled my bones.

"Whoa, now." Oron got up and began pacing. The hot breeze through the windows tossed his hair and tunic. "Good woman, you expect us to meet with a Salt Wraith on purpose? To question the thing?"

Aunt grabbed his sleeve. "To save my sister's daughter, I do."

Oron closed his eyes. After a breath, he nodded. "For Avigail.

Sweet, strong Avigail."

Pressing my fingers into my temples, I inhaled the food's scent of orange spice and the incense floating around the room. I had to do this. I had to confront a wraith and speak with it. I looked to Calev, lying on the floor. I needed Calev to heal and be strong enough to help me.

"Tell me what to do, Aunt."

CHAPTER TWENTY-NINE

We decided not to move Calev for the night. Aunt and I washed him and wrapped him in a clean pair of loose Kurakian pants, leaving his back and his wound bare. I tried to sleep beside him, but all I did was stare at his eyelids and pray they'd open soon.

The others slept on hammocks on the other side of the room near the ladder leading to the courtyard. Aunt curled up in her own sling of netted fabric above the shelves. The night was noisy with cattle lowing, people snoring, and roosters unwilling to wait until dawn to give a shout.

Aunt had told me when the moon reached its height, she'd wake and show me the Salt Magic needed to converse with a wraith.

I swallowed. Never thought I'd need to know a horrible thing like that.

The moon glowed through the window and I stared at it for what felt like hours. Then Aunt slipped from her hammock onto a low stool and to the floor.

"Come," she said.

I took a breath and ran a finger down Calev's proud nose. I touched his lips, his bare shoulder. He was just so beautiful. The wound didn't look any better though. If anything, the puffy red around the entry had grown more swollen.

"Refill your salt bag first." Aunt looked to her bowl on the shelf.

I shivered under her warm hand and did as instructed. Prepared, we walked past the others in their hammocks. Oron grabbed my hand and I jumped.

"If you can, give that spirit a kick to the babymaker for me, kaptan," he said. Then he rolled over and resumed snoring.

A smile pushed at my mouth, but my lip trembled, and I bit it, holding back emotions that were both good and bad.

Aunt climbed down the ladder that passed through a hole in the floor, and I trailed behind, down one level, another, then the last. I marveled that the structure was made of only the earth. Each floor was thicker than two Orons placed side by side. When my feet hit dirt, I spun to see which direction Aunt had gone.

My pulse tapped nervously against my wrists. Aunt walked into the night, a stately column of bright fabric and braids, surrounded by the still shadows of her cattle in the moonlight. The night smelled like a storm, metallic and heavy, though no clouds plumed overhead.

Beyond her gate, we found a spot to sit beside the twisting trunk of a Topa tree. The old leaves, crushed under my sandals, smelled like vegetables. Cool, rainy, tart. Aunt pulled a handful of salt from her pouch and jerked her chin at me, her big, black eyes shining.

"You too."

Reaching into my bag, I did as she instructed, then sat with salt cupped in my hands like a baby bird.

With her free hand, Aunt removed the whip from her leather belt. It was her status symbol in Kurakian society. Finer whips, those with more tassels, more gems, more decoration, spoke of more cattle—the only measure of who you were here on this dry land. The whip snapped as she lashed it over her head. I jumped. I didn't have a whip.

"You will use your own physical representation of pride." Her white teeth showed behind a chilling smile. "Show the spirit your confidence, your core."

Her eyes closed, she began speaking low, murmuring words into the night. The hairs on my arms lifted. She laid her whip in her lap and clapped her hands together. The salt she'd held ballooned around her and hovered before falling like waterflakes to her nightdress.

Her magic was already working. This wasn't any small lesson on using the salt. She was trying something. Now.

"But there aren't any wraiths here," I said. "On land. I thought you were only going to teach me."

Her gaze flicked to my face, faster than her whip's strings. "If I do this right, we will hear a wraith, even at this distance from the sea waters. If you follow what I do on the Pass, the wraith will fly to your boat and you will not only hear its true words, but see its face."

Ice jolted through me. "The spirit's *human* face?"

Wraiths' humanlike form showed only white, crystalized shadows where the face would be. My flesh shrunk against my bones. What would it be like to look at a dead man's face? A dead man who'd been tortured through a death at sea? Through drowning? The very worst way to die?

Aunt didn't answer me. She hissed and mumbled in Kurakian, the rhythm of her words matching that of the night insects around us. "Rumrumrum, ruuuummmmm. Rumrumrum, ruuuuuummmmmm."

With salt-dusted fingertips, she drew a circle on her face, starting at the small, curling hairs escaping her braid and falling onto her forehead and going all the way down her cheek, across her chin, and back up again. She ran one finger along the inside of her lips. When she said something that sounded like "Nat-kooroo-turumtah," and her voice was no longer hers. Or, it was, but it sounded as though it belonged to someone five times her size, with a much deeper tone.

The insects went silent.

The wind rushed through the Topa in a sudden gust.

Though the sky remained clear, the air still smelled like a storm.

Invisible splinters pinched the skin around my spine and along my ribs as Aunt said another word. Another. Her voice rang in my ears. The prickling hit me again. The wind. Once. Twice.

Then I heard it.

The wraith.

It started as a noise so far-off, so quiet, I wasn't sure it was even a noise. Maybe my own heart or lungs, but the noise grew legs and ran into my head, thrusting a spear into my thoughts.

There were no words, only intent, specific intent that my mind shaped into words.

What do you want, Salt Witch?

"To hear your voice," Aunt said in the Jakobden tongue.

I have no need of you.

"We want to speak with Tuz Golge."

Do you wish to die? He has great power.

"This one here witnessed the Tuz Golge's vengeance played out on earth."

No business of mine. I leave you to it.

"Wait." Sweat broke over my scalp. There wasn't time to think. I had to learn how to do this, for Avi, for me.

Aunt held up her salty hands and nodded.

I raised my hands and threw my salt into the leaves of the Topa, into the night. Closing my eyes, I let the salt fall onto my face. Grains danced on my lips.

"I ask you to stay." My voice sounded strong and clear in spite of the fear of the invisible presence lurking around us. I opened my eyes.

The wraith wailed. A scream bellowed from the air and pounded against my skull.

"Tell us where we can find Tuz Golge. I must know. My sister will die." Tears burned their way down my cheeks.

My aunt stared at me. Her eyes went up and down my face and body as the wraith howled louder and louder. "Release him, Kinneret. I know what I need to know."

A frown pulled at my lips. "But we didn't know anything yet."

"Now, Kinneret. Release him."

I blew the rest of the salt lining my palms into the air beside us. "Go and find rest."

The wind gusted once more. The prickling sensation fled and my shoulders relaxed. The small part of the wraith that we'd managed to call over land was gone.

Aunt tucked her whip into her belt, stood, and offered her hand. One thousand questions in my head, I took it and started back toward the courtyard.

"Why did you let him go?" I said. "What did you find out?"

She made a noise like a hum. Mother had always made that noise and now Avi did. It was a noise like she was thinking.

"You are the strongest Salt Witch that breathes, Kinneret."

I stopped. "What?"

"You are. You held that wraith, made him cry out."

"I'm not a witch. I'm only using prayers. Using the salt the Fire gives us."

"Same. It is the same." Aunt frowned toward the chicken coop that sat just inside the fencing.

"Not to me."

Then she stopped too, her hand on the top of her stick gate. "Maybe that is what gives you such power."

"What?"

"Don't fret about it. You are who you are. I am who I am. It is what it is."

I rolled my eyes. Kurakian wisdom. More riddle than reason, Father always said.

CHAPTER THIRTY

Back at Calev's side, I let the tears come.

Everyone else was sleeping, so they wouldn't see my weakness. I simply lay there for what felt like days, praying and wishing and longing for Avi's voice and Calev's grin like a thirsty man on a salty sea. I didn't want to know what a wraith's voice sounded like and I didn't want to think about having strong magic right now. I wanted sunlight and freedom and everyone safe and happy. Avi and Calev were my fresh water, my life source. I had to have them back. Without them, I'd shrivel and die like a fish stuck on a shoreline.

"Please wake up," I whispered to Calev, my throat aching. "Aunt says we can control the wraith who Infused you. It knows how to get Avi out of Quarry Isle. Wake up and we'll go. We'll go get our girl."

A sob took my breath, and I sucked air through my nose, trying to keep quiet. I put a hand on Calev's forehead. The bare skin felt odd. Normally, he wore his headtie.

It was odder the way heat rolled off his skin and into mine.

I jerked away. No.

His cheeks looked like they'd been slathered with fat, waxen and swollen.

"Calev? Can you hear me?"

He was so hot. I lifted his arm to see where the arrow had punctured his body. A fiery red glared back at me and yellow pus leaked from the center.

The wound was going bad.

I ran to Aunt and shook her shoulder hard. "Calev's getting worse."

She licked her dry lips and blinked. "I told you he might die."

A spear went through me at her bluntness, but she smoothed my cheek with her rough fingers and I knew she was just worried too. I grabbed my shirt and squeezed the fabric between my burning fingers.

"You have to save him."

Swinging out of her hammock, she sighed. "He has to save himself."

With a stone mortar and pestle, Aunt ground bitter smelling herbs and animal fat into a poultice for Calev's souring wound.

For hours, we nursed him.

Poured fresh water over his lips, only to watch it dribble to the floor. Wiped his flaming face with cloths.

His eyes never opened.

I ran a fingertip over the slight bump in his nose, as familiar to me as my own features. He inhaled slightly, a ragged, weak breath and my own chest clenched, wanting to breathe for him, to be strong for him. I hovered a hand over his wound and heat blared through Aunt's wrappings. The skin around the strips of linen had reddened even more over the last hours.

Her herbs and our prayers weren't making him better, but that didn't mean I was giving up.

Please, Fire. Let me keep him a while longer. We still have so much to do. Let him see Avi safe. I need him to help me save Avi. Please. Please. Please.

My hands shook as I stared at him. His face became Father's, then Mother's, and I was a child again, losing my parents.

I ran to the window and threw up everything in my stomach.

It was all going wrong, so, so, so wrong. If I failed now, Oron would never stay here with me and my aunt. He loved the sea like me. Zayn would die alone, blaming himself for our end. My sweet, little sister was lost to a horrible, disgusting life at the quarries. I clutched at my hair, squeezing it to the roots and welcoming the pain. And now, I was losing my love, my Calev, my smile and my luck. My lungs fought a breath and I fell to my knees, Aunt's hands on my back and her whispers in my ear.

As dawn cut the room with light and Aunt took to her hammock, I curled up next to Calev, resting on his outstretched arm. His dry palm lay against my mine own, and I cried until I was an empty husk.

This entire trip had been for nothing.

I'd found silver I couldn't use. I'd thrown Avi from one hell into another.

I could never glean information from Tuz Golge. I hadn't even known

Calev was Infused. I was clueless, a fool, a stupid, stupid low-caste with no chance of the life I'd dreamt of. The bones in Calev's arm pressed against me. He felt like a dead man already.

I was an idiot and all of this was my fault.

CHAPTER THIRTY-ONE

T hen one of Calev's eyelids lifted. Gasping, I put a hand on his cheek. "Calev?"

His eye closed. I sagged, lying next to him. Seas, what could I do?

If it wasn't for Avi, I'd wait here with him forever. But Avi needed me to at least try to rescue her. I could never live with myself if I didn't fight for her. If I left now, would Calev wake up and not find me? What if...my eyes blurred...if he died while I was gone and only had Aunt, a stranger to him here during his passing, that would be horrible.

My chest wanted to split open. This was a pain worse than anything that an arrow or a yatagan could cause. It seared and gnawed and swallowed me whole.

Calev made a small noise.

I sat up.

He opened his eyes, blinked, then closed them.

I touched his shoulder. Was Aunt's magic finally working? "Can you hear me?"

It was little more than a hiss, but I heard the word. "Yes."

The room spun for a breath and I took a gulp of air. "You're going to be fine. You're strong."

"Fine?" he croaked, barely loud enough to for me to hear. "Not sure about that."

I laughed through tears, afraid to believe this moment was really happening. "Stay quiet. Rest. Next time you wake up, you can talk more. All right?"

He must've agreed because his eyes flickered once, and not long after, his breathing evened out in sleep.

Aunt's magic was healing him.

I don't know how much time passed as we slept there, but when I opened my eyes, I saw Calev's smile. Pale, weak, but real.

The wildfire in me rose and dried my tears. "How do you feel? Any better? Can you breathe well?"

I touched his shoulder, then pulled away. She'd healed him. The magic had actually worked. I could hardly wrap my mind around it. I was scared to say it aloud and risk it not being true.

Calev laughed quietly and winced. Moving so that his forehead braced against the stripes of the mat, he said, "I am better. Much, much better." He put his palms against the mat and began to push himself up.

Scrambling to my knees, I supported him. "You can't get up yet. Rest. Later you can get up."

With a nod, he let me lower him back down. The effort must've sucked him dry because he slept again almost immediately.

The gray light of dawn and Calev's rustling woke me later. He was trying to sit up. I lodged a hand under his arm, afraid to say too much and realize this was a dream.

"Don't rush it. I don't want you dying on me again." Fear sharpened my words.

Shaking his head, he braced a hand on his knee, and I helped him sit.

His wound was clean and smooth. Still red and a bit swollen, but healed. Aunt's magic was strong. I squeezed Calev's hand, then let go, knowing if I kept touching him, I'd throw myself at him like an idiot.

His ebony hair fell over one side of his face as he swallowed. "I need a drink."

I had to grin as I scooped water from the bucket near Aunt's hammock into a wooden cup and handed it to him. A part of my own thirst was quenched.

Now to find Avi and complete the answer to my prayers.

The bones above Calev's chest were sharper than they had been before his injury. His stomach, though still muscled, sunk in like a depression between two waves. He sipped the water I gave him, his throat moving as he threw his head back. I hugged myself to keep my arms busy.

He set the cup down. "Now tell me about this wraith."

I did.

And to refrain from staring at Calev's bare chest, to keep from crying with relief at his healing, I allowed my eyes to stray to the window's view. Behind Calev, night lightened into day. A purple-white glow laced the edges of the Topa tree where Aunt and I had spoken to that wraith, where I'd learned…what? That I could control a spirit? That I had enough Salt Magic to glean information from the legendary Tuz Golge?

I shared all this and more—everything—in hushed whispers with Calev. Before he could say anything back, Oron flipped out of his hammock and landed flat on his back.

"Creations of the Devil," he spat at the hammock, rising and dusting his hands.

Then everyone was awake.

Aunt scowled at Calev and patted at her braids, which had grown fuzzy during the night. "You should not be up yet."

Ekrem and Serhat eased out of their hammocks, the bells on their shoulders jingling, and looked Calev up and down. My insides going cold, I put a hand on my dagger. In a second, they could be on him and he could be dead.

"Ah," Calev said. "They know what I did."

My finger circled my dagger's cool hilt, and the wind from the window tugged at my curls.

Oron smirked. "That they do. I strongly suggest you explain your side of the story before they decide your handsome head would be a fine decoration for their sashes."

The sailors advanced on him, step by step. Aunt's room went from cozy to cramped.

Unhitching himself from the wall, Calev held out his hands and lowered his chin a little. "I had no fight with your amir. I hated what she did to Ifran, but aside from that, she was Old Farm's friend."

Ekrem's eyes were calm, but Serhat stared at Calev with death in her face. They traded a look, then Ekrem said, "Because Kinneret believes you, we do also."

Serhat's jaw tightened. She turned her head away.

Ekrem's words made me stand taller. I took my place at Calev's side, Aunt and Oron muttering at both ends of the room about how the sun wasn't even up yet.

"So you'll go with us?" The question was one I'd asked Calev so many times, the words so familiar to my lips. But I was far from anything truly familiar now. In Kurakia. Making plans to deal with a wraith. Asking loyalty from high-caste fighters. "To meet with Tuz Golge and break my sister out of Oramiral Urmirian's quarry?"

"We are your fighters now, kaptan. Command us at will."

Aunt made a shushing noise. "Never thought I'd see a girl with no cattle to her name command two of the amir's. If you've never ordered beasts, how are you to order men? Now, go down to the courtyard, let my animals out of the gate and wash yourselves to eat. Gather some eggs while you're there and gain some advice from those hens as you do."

Advice? From hens?

"I'll ready some oatcakes and dried beef," she said. "We'll treat the farmer's wound once more, then you can be on your way."

The fighters climbed down the ladder, Serhat's head disappearing from view as Oron walked over and grabbed my arm and Calev's.

"You're certain about meeting with the Salt Wraith? Calev, talk sense into her."

"I trust her," Calev said quietly. "And I'm not a sense-first man. I'm more of an adventure-first, challenge-obsessed land lover kind of fellow." He grinned.

I elbowed him gently, my cheeks warm, then patted Oron's hand. "There is no sensible way to do this. We have to grab this opportunity, this one small, dangerous edge on the situation, and go."

"Go?" Oron held both hands up. "Just like that?"

Calev and I nodded in unison.

Oron gusted out a breath and folded his hands behind his head. He turned away. "Foolish youth."

Aunt's steady hands urged us toward the ladder to do as she'd instructed. "Yes, small man. They're so ready to give up the short life they've had."

Oron stepped down the ladder, looking up at me. His wine-dark eyes were bright in the strengthening dawn. "I'm not so sure about your aunt's sanity, but in this instance, the woman is right."

"This is our life to live, Oron. And I won't do it without my sister by my side."

He swallowed loudly and continued down the rungs. "It's not as if I meant…all right then. But Fire help me, I do not wish to die on the sea or at the oramiral's hands."

"I know, I know."

I passed through the last floor before the courtyard. Dust from Calev's sandals rained on my head as he came down after me and I didn't dislike it at all. I was just so glad he was alive.

"I'm guessing that you, Oron, prefer to die in a feather bed with a woman's arms wrapped firmly around you," Calev said.

I leaped from the ladder to land in the courtyard, narrowly missing a hen who squawked her annoyance.

Oron grinned. "How well you know me."

Calev laughed and tucked his hair behind his ears. He had replaced his head tie and it was strange to see someone in an Old Farm style without a fine, embroidered tunic. The blue Kurakian pantaloons made him look taller.

Oron's mouth tucked up at one side. "I think I'll grab some eggs while you two...wash." He jerked his head toward the pump well that the fighters had left to open the gate.

Laughing, Calev and I zigzagged through chickens that brushed along our legs and beat wings at our feet. At the well, he insisted on pumping the water and allowing me to cup handfuls of lukewarm water to throw over my face and hands. I went ahead and doused my head too. The day wasn't going to grow any cooler and I was already sweating. Calev winced a little but managed to toss a handful at me. I got him back right in the eye.

Calev went quiet and still.

"What's wrong? Are you feeling your wound? Should I get Aunt?"

"It does hurt. But that's not... We shouldn't be enjoying ourselves while Avi is..." His throat worked.

Tears burned at the corners of my eyes. My chest caved in as I tried to keep breathing. "It's terrible. It's impossible. But we should laugh. She would want us too." I squeezed out the ends of my hair and kept my face turned toward the ground. The sadness in his eyes would make me cry like last night and we didn't have sun for that. "We need some smiles to give us strength for what we're about to do."

"I don't know why it always surprises me when you say wise things. After all our lives together, it shouldn't. You're right. If we're going to deal with the darkness of a wraith, we need all the light we can rouse."

I looked at him then. His black hair shuffling over his bare shoulders. His honest, red-brown eyes, the eyes that always held a spark of mischief. His hands on the pump, ready to help me with more water if that's what I needed. I pressed my eyelids shut and tried to sear the image of him on my mind. I never wanted to forget this moment. It was the light I would need to face the Tuz Golge, the creature that had twisted my good Calev into a killer.

CHAPTER THIRTY-TWO

That night, the moon opened its eye over the horizon and stared at us as we gathered on the Kurakian beach. The sea was the pale blue of ice, stretching out from the shore in one solid, clean mass under a steady wind. My heart ached to sail on it. I couldn't see our boat yet, but it was there somewhere. Tiny, and a sad, little thing to ride on into the night, but it would have to do. My hands clenched with the need to feel a tiller's worn, wooden grain and tug a coconut fiber rope. Beside me, white light cloaked the fighters' emotionless faces, Aunt's braids, Calev's wavy hair and strong nose, and Oron's smirk.

Oron put a fist under his chin. "I don't know if you've noticed, but that's not the boat in which we arrived, dear kaptan."

Aunt was smiling. The sailors made appreciative grunts and nodded, pointing to a wooden craft with two masts bobbing in the shallow water off the shore.

My heart jumped. "Did you do this?"

I squinted and the two lateen sails wrapped against the masts reflected a flash of pale moonlight. Long ties at the boom fluttered in the breeze.

"I have much," Aunt said, still smiling. "Cattle. A home. Chickens. And no children. No man. No woman. I'm glad to have the chance to help my sister's children."

She had bought us a boat. A very fine boat. I couldn't believe it.

Her lips tilted down at one side and she took my fingers in hers gently. She stroked the back of my hand with her calloused fingertips and the child inside me wanted more than anything to run back to her tower house and curl into a hammock.

"Get our Avigail safe," she said. "You can do it. I know you can."

My throat was hot and dry. "If I fail…"

Aunt tsked with her full lips. "It is not good luck to talk of that."

"We should have a shamar yam." Calev picked up two shells from the sand and studied them with a look of concentration. He tossed one down and cupped the other, his serious eyes meeting mine. "I don't have paper for the prayer, but I can speak one into its hollow and secure it to the mainsail with my headtie."

Aunt elbowed me. "You are right. He is lucky. He knows how the world works."

"Thank you. For everything."

I hugged her, my arms and hers tight and strong. She smelled so much like Mother, like dust, green things, and spices from this land that was foreign but also familiar to me. I didn't want to let go. I was dying to let go. Because every minute we waited, Avi spent another in the quarries.

Aunt thumped her hand on my back. "Go on now."

When I pulled away, tears wiggled down her beautiful, sloping cheeks. She wiped the moisture away impatiently, frowning.

"And the Wraith Lantern?" I asked.

Surely she'd thought of that. But if she hadn't, maybe we could get one at the market. Aunt had never been to sea. Kurakians hated the water. She might not realize how many wraiths roamed the skies. Though we meant to meet with one, more than that would be suicide.

"It hangs from the center mast." She gave a nod.

Oron looked impressed as we neared the craft, our feet splashing into the cool, rolling water. One sail ruffled loose like a woman's skirts. "Kurakian-style sailcloth," he said. "I haven't seen such handiwork since I worked on that northeastern trading ship."

"Kurakian craftsmanship on a northern boat?" I lifted my newly filled bag of salt from my sash to keep it from being doused.

Chest-deep in water, we made it to the boat. Aunt took hold of the fore and Calev went toward the back. Aunt had sewn a tunic for him out of one of her plain, dusky blue work dresses.

"The northeastern kaptan had a fondness for the women of this land." Oron hefted himself into the craft as we steadied it. "He appreciated their many…skills."

Calev snickered along with Oron and I threw a look at them.

Oron wasn't talking only about sailcloth.

Aunt shook her head and smiled, helping me up. Though I didn't need the assistance, it warmed me to have her hand at my back, ready to be there if I slipped. I hadn't had an older person take care of me since Mother and Father died. Unless you counted Oron. But he was as much trouble as he was help.

The fighters crawled aboard and gave Calev a hand up without exchanging a single word. How deep did their loyalty to me go? Was it really enough to forgive Calev for killing their leader? There wasn't much I could do about it, so I pressed the worry into the corner of my mind.

With one last wave to Aunt, we rigged the sails and tracked a line away from her tiny shape in the shallow waters. I'd never be able to thank her enough for saving Calev. If her idea to meet with Tuz Golge worked and we discovered a way to get Avi out, I'd be further in her debt and happy to be there.

Oron lit the Wraith Lantern while Calev whispered a prayer into the shamar yam and tied it to the mainmast. The orange, silver, and black flickers from the lantern's wick passed over their faces, illuminating cheek hollows, accentuating noses and whites of eyes.

The Pass was a wide road of white and black beyond our boat. I'd need to see clearly if we were to get to the place we'd first met Tuz Golge. We had to keep the lantern lit in case we had to deal with another wraith.

The moment I thought the word, one swept away from the moon toward us.

Ekrem took the lantern from Oron and held it high over our heads. The crystalized spirit drifted over our sails, its evil intent lashing against my thoughts like a desert lion's claws. Sweat dripped down my nose as I plugged my ears with my fingers.

Oron sat next to me, Calev on my other side. "Can't you control this one too?" Oron shouted above the wraith's sweeping noise and its accompanying hissing whispers of murder and rage. The whites of Oron's eyes and teeth were bright in the near dark.

"It will leave," I yelled back. "I'm not wasting any salt." The wraith pressed on my mind.

Fury.

Blood.

The taste of blood. Salt in my mouth. Flesh in my teeth.

I opened my eyes when something warm brushed against me. It was Calev. Fingers in his own ears, he'd scooted closer to me and his elbow touched my back. He lay his forehead against mine and I inhaled deeply, breathing in the scent of him—sun-warmed earth and lemons—to wash away the wraith's sour wrath.

The shadow dusted over us once more, then seemed to leave. The blood-lust was gone. I took my fingers out of my ears and looked at each of my crew in turn.

The fighters were hunched over, their heads brushing their knees. Making the Fire's sign on his forehead, Oron crossed his thick legs.

Calev gave me one of those smiles. "We made it through."

Warmth flooded my stomach and I turned away to focus on my words.

"The Tuz Golge's attack will be different from that," I said as we found spots to sit around the decking. "Some of us know how he feels inside the head. It's a sharp thing. Intelligent. Difficult to block out."

The headsail, the smaller of the two triangular sails, lagged a little. We needed to jib and track toward Jakobden's angry coast, and the wind was cooperating.

"Hopefully my Salt Magic will control it, but stay alert in case I fail."

At my command, Oron lowered the headsail and Calev and the fighters tucked it away.

"Take a line, everyone," I said from aft. "We need to jib. When I shout, let them run through your fingers." Everyone but Calev knew exactly what to do, but I didn't want to single him out, so I called out directions for all.

When I shouted, they did as asked, and the ivory sail flipped high over the mast. We took control again and brought the bottom of the sail back to the boat's side. We tied, Calev tying right alongside us like a real sailor. I smiled.

The only thing loud now was my heart. It shivered like a scared dog at the thought of how exposed we were and how reliant on the small lesson I'd had with Aunt. We were almost to the place where we'd seen Tuz Golge.

Black water lapped on all sides and the wind stayed steady. With Oron's clever help, Calev's good eyes, and the fighting sailors' strength, we easily wove around a high ridge of shining rock.

And at a calm stretch—as calm and open as the Pass can be—I started calling for the wraith.

Sitting cross-legged, across from Calev's encouraging face, I raised my dagger and carved a circle in the air about my head. I whispered the words Aunt had given me, "Raturookumruntarah. Rumininah. Rumininah. Buruqnahrumtilrirah. I listen. I understand your cause. I understand your cause. Speak to me, and I will hear you in your empty place."

The Kurakian words tripped out of my mouth and caught on my lips with quick turns in emphasis and hard sounds. It was not a beautiful language. It had only been my aunt's lovely voice matching the calming din of night insects. My own pronunciation lacked skill.

Would it work?

As Aunt had instructed, I began chanting the amir's name. "Mamluk, Mamluk, Mamluk."

Her former sailors' heads snapped up and they glared before blinking and seeming to resign themselves to the situation. They knew as well as I this was no time for anything except completing this horrible chore and living through it.

Then my head seemed to crack open.

Tuz Golge slipped into the mercury light over our heads. Roughly the shape of a man in a flowing tunic, the edges of his spirit-self leaked into the sky like spilled poison. The lightest part of him fogged the place his face should have been. His shadow, impossibly large, blotted out the moon and a sick light rained down, a fitting match to the twisting evil in our thoughts.

I went from enjoying the smooth beauty of Calev's skin to imagining the press of a knife separating flesh from bone. Blood in patterned lines down his cheeks and chin and throat. His eyes closed and he lifted his face, swallowing hard. Oron's voice called across the abyss of bloodlust, toward the man I loved more than any other.

"Kinneret." Oron's voice scratched against the wraith's planted thoughts. His fingers were in his ears, the sailors beside him, shaking and eyes wide open.

Sucking a salty breath, I stood. I tore my dagger across the wind that blew my skirts around my legs.

I would not let Tuz Golge take us here. I could do this.

I sheathed my dagger and took salt from my pouch. I spread the grit from the insides of my wrists, over my sleeves, and onto my collarbone, to my pulse points. The wind rose and tossed my hair wildly. The sea rolled as I knelt.

I slapped my hands together and shouted to the wraith. "I ask how you escaped the quarry."

Then there was hissing and nonsense. Garbled words—a mix of Kurakian and the Jakobden tongue. But behind the power, the hate, and the sharp mind, panic danced through the sounds. Uneven. Low, then loud. Realization flooded through me as the wind sheared against us and rocked us hard in the water.

Calev killed the amir. Tuz Golge owed us.

The boat righted, and I knew exactly what to say.

"Speak in this tongue," I said. The salt thrummed against my flesh like a thousand tiny hearts beating in the same rhythm as my own. "We have done your work. We have slayed your wife. You owe us obedience."

The hissing grew into snarls that matched the rising wind. Waves dashed against the hull, and Calev and I slammed into one another, grabbing for the mainsail mast. Oron and the fighters latched onto the sides of the boat, their faces like yesterday's ash. My salty fingers grated against the mast and one of Calev's hands and I pressed my forehead against his. He was whispering with eyes closed and one hand on the shamar yam. He was praying.

Nothing! Tuz Golge shouted into my thoughts. *I owe nothing!*

My words hadn't moved him like they should've. What was I forgetting?

The wraith's sharp intent pushed against my will, drowning it in darkness and pain and the desire to unsheathe my dagger and slide it along Calev's face to destroy the beauty Tuz Golge would never again possess.

I fisted my hands and pulled myself against the mast, squeezing it with my arms, trying to feel the boat under my sandals and the wood against my skin instead of the hate, the hate, the hate.

Calev's lips moved fast as nightwingers. Sweat became diamonds on his chin, tangled in the beard he'd grown over the last few days. He brought his hand from the prayer shell to his mouth, touched his lips once and began praying again.

The salt. Aunt lined her mouth in sea salt.

I ran my first two fingers along the insides of my lips.

My skin puckered as I shouted, "Yes, you do owe us, Tuz Golge. You will listen. I am Kinneret Raza, born on these waters, slayer of the demon Asag, conqueror of the lost silver island, and you will speak with me."

The intensity of rage and inky fingers of mind control flattened and cracked. My will, like a small orange sun, squeezed into the small, broken places, shining through the cracks in my thoughts. They brought memories with them.

Calev. Chin held high. Teeth gritted together. Determined face. His laugh at the well. The velvet of his hands on my waist at the waterfall. The feel of his lips, his mouth smiling against my neck.

And Avi. Strong, long fingers on the sail's ties. Stubby nails. The dimple in her otherwise fierce face.

I would be fierce for her.

For Calev. And Oron. And these two warriors who'd risked all to help us.

The orange sun of my will blasted through the broken lines of the wraith's twisting hate.

The wind settled.

Speak, Kinneret Raza. The wraith hung still as death over our heads. *What would you ask of me?*

Everyone stared.

"Is it talking to you?" Oron asked, taking a step.

The fighters relaxed their hold on the boat and put hands to the battle axe and yatagan at their sashes, as if weapons were any use against this threat. I gave Oron a nod and he stepped back again, crossing his arms. His mouth pinched up and Calev stared. He reached a hand out and I took it gladly.

I closed my eyes, let the salt thrum against my skin, and spoke silently to the wraith.

How did you escape the oramiral's island?

Why do you desire this information, sailor?

Tell me.

A laugh, dark and bitter like soured coffee. *I didn't. I died. In the waters. You know that.*

Tell me.

I gathered fallen bamboo on my treks up the stairs to the slave quarters. It is open air. But you know that. Your sister, yes? She hides in the shadows there? She slaves for the oramiral?

I wasn't about to bend and give him knowledge he had no right to. *How did you escape?*

I removed my tunic, ripped it down the middle, tied it to the bamboo I'd lashed together with rope I'd stolen from the guards' storage bins, and I created a glider.

Details.

I made a sturdy length of framed fabric and sailed off the slaves' castle walls into the air and down over the Pass.

My concentration faltered. A sail? For the air? But how would that work? How would someone catch the wind, then direct the fall with only a long strip of framed fabric?

Like someone had drawn a blade across the tie between my Salt Magic and Tuz Golge, the sense of the wraith left my mind and floated away.

The sky was clear of spirits and a bank of blue-black clouds had gathered. He was gone. I collapsed onto the deck. Bamboo and a tunic? That was the great information I'd risked everyone here to get? I wanted to scream and throw the entire sea at the creature who'd been so cruel. That plan would never work to free Avi from the quarries. My sister was lost.

CHAPTER THIRTY-THREE

C alev opened his eyes. "What did he tell you?"

It was then I noticed my hands were shaking. I hid them behind my back, but Calev grabbed them gently and rubbed the backs with his thumbs.

"You should be scared," he said. "There have been times when I've wondered whether you're human like the rest of us." He smiled grimly as he kept on stroking my hands, flipping them over and starting on the palms, massaging them now and pulling me closer.

It was a trick and I knew it, but I let him tug me into the circle of his arms. My shaking grew into a full-body tremor.

My mouth pressed into the soft blue fabric of the tunic Aunt had made him. His chest tensed under my lips and the strength there, both in muscle, and beneath that, in heart, gave me hope.

"I was afraid I wouldn't be able to handle the wraith. It was all on me."

"I know." He made soft shushing noises into my hair. "It wasn't sailing. Or anything else you've done before this sun."

He held me tighter as I felt a hand on my back. Oron.

"You did well, my kaptan," Oron said, peeking at me and smiling with tears in his eyes. "You used what your aunt taught you, claimed your status with the spirit, and gleaned information from the other side. Very well done. I would've messed my tunic and leaped overboard, so all in all I'd say the evening has been a resounding success."

Ekrem pressed fingers into his temples, shaking his head. Serhat glared like she was upset she hadn't attacked the wraith and Oron might serve as a good second choice of target.

I looked down at the X stitching along Calev's short sleeve. "But the wraith talked about things I didn't understand. I don't think it's going to help Avi."

"Maybe we can make sense of it." Calev stepped back, and I turned away to look out over the waters.

"The wraith said he made a sort of sail out of bamboo and his tunic. He jumped from the top of the slaves' castle quarters, and the sail helped him soar through the air, to the Pass."

"How would sticks and fabric hold a man?" Oron rubbed his chin. "And I think we should decide on where to make landfall. That brewing storm looks almost as threatening as Tuz Golge."

He was right. Those clouds, snipped and billowing, meant lightning, high wind, and slashing rain. But where could we go? Not home. We'd be questioned by the amir's men and women who hadn't left on the journey. They may have even received a rock dove from Berker by now and his message would tell them everything. Calev's father and kin would question him on his lengthy disappearance, his clothing, and his new scar even if they didn't receive a message from Berker. The story would come out, then what was left of the amir's retainer would strap us to horses and rip us to pieces.

We couldn't go straight to Quarry Isle. As much as I wanted to get to Avi, we had to plan if we were to emerge with her alive, instead of full of the oramiral's cannon shot and spears.

Ayarazi? Definitely not. Kurakia again?

"Kurakia is our only choice." I untied the rope that had helped flip the sail. "We'll use this storm-blowing wind to take us east."

But when we landed, what then? Tuz Golge's idea made no sense.

The wind gusting brightly, the storm chased our boat neatly back toward Kurakia. The speed made my blood sing through my veins. Normally, I would've been light and happy during such a successful sail, but now, no. We were racing to nowhere. I had no answers and was no closer to rescuing Avi. Plus, soon the amir's absence would be taken as something out of the ordinary. We'd planned on three days away. It had been seven. Maybe eight. Or nine.

I rubbed at my eyes, my knees dipping when the hull slapped the water. The kyros and Old Farm would send men and women looking for the ship. Kurakia was the closest known landing spot. Aside from Quarry Isle. And Aunt couldn't protect us. Her city-state of Lutambiarum would give us up without a thought. Calev's father might try to protect him. But maybe not. Calev had committed the crime. He was guilty. If they didn't believe us, he would be condemned to die. If they caught us here, no one would speak up for the fighters, Oron, or I. We were good as dead.

When we walked back into Aunt's courtyard, she waved, then proceeded to ask one hundred or more questions. I lost count. She steered us toward her house and began feeding us like we'd never eaten.

Hours later, I finished my bowl of Kurakian chicken and licked the orange spice off my fingers. Though my soul hung somewhere low as my feet, my stomach couldn't be ignored. Besides, I needed food to get my mind working.

Calev pushed his now empty bowl to the center of Aunt's table and leaned back in his chair. "A sail. For the air." He put his hands on his elbows and sighed.

Oron finished Aunt's remaining store of tatlilav and belched loudly. "Let's try it." He hopped up and slapped his thighs. "I've lived a good life. Strap the bed linens to me and toss me off the roof."

He started toward the hammock he'd been using, assumably to grab the linen sheet tangled in the woven coconut ropes.

I stood and snared his arm. "Though I'm impressed you've matured enough to offer yourself, we're not throwing you off things." I looked to Aunt and Calev for help.

The fighters were down in Aunt's courtyard, training with their beautiful, flashing weapons. No matter. They wouldn't care about Oron's impending doom.

Aunt cleared the wooden bowls from the table and wiped her mouth with the back of her hand. "You will find the answer, Kinneret."

Oron tugged his sleeve free from me. "We already have. Me. The roof. Fabric." He began flapping his arms like wings.

Calev laughed, though his eyes were sad. None of us could stop thinking of how long Avi had been gone now. "Oron, exactly how much did you have during the meal?"

Oron eyed him. "Are you asking about alcohol intake or would you also like to know food consumption for weight considerations?"

"I think he's talking about the tatlilav," I said.

He held his hands up. "Well, I want to be sure to provide such information as our Old Farm friend sees as necessary for tossing men from roofs."

Calev grinned.

Oron rubbed his chin. "I believe I imbibed around three bowls each of tatlilav and chicken." Patting his slightly round stomach, he added, "Just about perfect for a would-be eagle, I think."

"Eagle?" Calev said. "I'm thinking more of an overgrown, extremely ambitious chicken."

Aunt rubbed the clean bowls dry over her water bucket, laughing quietly.

I gave Aunt a quick hug, passed Oron and Calev, and started down the ladder. "Come on then, bird of questionable descent. We must check your wings." The ladder's rungs were smooth under my tired hands.

Oron, Calev, and I dodged chickens and pecking roosters and walked out of Aunt's courtyard and into the patchy grass of her fields.

"We'll sneak into the slaves' quarters. Then, because we'll no longer have surprise as our ally, we'll glide off Quarry Isle." I nodded, more to myself than anyone else. It was a ridiculous plan, but the only one I had.

"You're the kaptan," Oron said.

We were fools. "We need bamboo." I headed toward the creek. A clutch of green shaded a cow and her calf. The mother turned her head to look at us with big eyes. One of her arm-length horns brushed benignly over her young's bony spine.

Oron stepped behind Calev and eyed the cow. "Better not anger her. She could skewer and kabob us without moving a hoof."

Calev put a hand on the first group of stalks we came to. Their light brown lengths reached higher than the roof of Aunt's tower house. Lime-green leaves fluttered in the dry breeze.

"Has your Aunt cut any?" Calev asked as we snaked through the small forest. "Saplings grow right out of their harvested elders."

Oron chuckled. "Spoken like a true Old Farm."

"Yep." I pushed some fallen branches back to look for stalks at the base of a broken trunk.

Calev cocked his head and crossed his arms.

"Don't get defensive. It's just how you all are. You call mature trees and plants *elders*." A smile pulled at my lips as he raised his chin. "Old Farms see growing things as they see people."

Eyebrow lifted, Calev took a step toward another bunch of smaller trees and shrugged. "Our mindset has worked so far, wouldn't you agree?"

"Yes, yes, Lemon Prince." Oron took a small, green-handled saw from his sash. We'd borrowed it from Aunt's tool rack outside the henhouse.

Calev frowned as he cleared thorny brush away from the base of the head-high stalk Oron had found. "I don't enjoy that title, Oron, and you know it."

"That's exactly why I used it." Oron grinned in Calev's face. Calev glared at him.

"Be careful, chicken-eagle, this one will be manning our escape boat after we fly from the roof of the quarry slaves' quarters." I held the stalk steady as Oron ran the steel teeth back and forth.

Calev's gaze snapped to me. "What?"

"I can't risk the oramiral getting his hands on you."

"First, he won't take me. I'm Old Farm. Second, what makes you think I'm going to stay in the boat while you blast into the quarry to battle trained fighters?"

I stood and put hands on my hips. "First." I couldn't keep the bite out of my voice. "You are an Old Farm who murdered the amir. You don't need to borrow any more trouble. Second, you just try to keep me from going in there after Avi." My blood burned under my skin. "Just. Try."

Oron stopped sawing. "Whoa, there, kaptan. Remember who the enemy is here."

"It's the oramiral," Calev said slowly. "And I will not watch as you, Kinneret, pointlessly subject yourself to possible capture."

"Pointlessly?"

I gritted my teeth and stared at Calev, who'd risen and matched my glare. His red-brown eyes were on fire and it made my blood even hotter.

This was my rescue mission and my sister and my magic that had pushed us this far. He was not going to lash me to the mainsail to keep me safe like I was a child. I didn't care who his father was or how old his blood or how smart he thought he was.

"You think I'm pointless?" My voice coiled and raised its head like a cobra.

"Acting like you are a fighter is pointless when we have two actual fighters in our party. You are the sailor. You should stay in the boat. That's the safe choice. The smart choice. And you well know it, Kinneret. You're being obstinate."

My head was about to come off. My fingers itched and trembled. I wanted to lunge at Calev and shake him until he felt how impossible it would be for me to perch in safety a stone's throw from where my own sister was being held by the worst man in the world.

"Kinneret." Calev put hands on my shoulders and I couldn't breathe I was so frustrated. "Oron can stay with you. The fighters and I will rescue Avi if it's possible. If it's not, you being there will make no difference and only risk your life too."

Then we both went silent. Like the eerie quiet before a storm. Anger and love and frustration and everything we'd been through rushed through me, burning me, jerking me, setting me on fire. Calev's mouth didn't move. His eyes were black stones and his chest rose and fell like he was about to—

Oron put his hands between us and tried to push us away from one another. "All right now. You two are either going to fight or...well...we don't have the sun for any pleasant diversions, if you'll recall. No matter how long it's been coming," he muttered, finally succeeding in shoving us each back a step. "Now help me cut this tree so we can make the ridiculous wings."

I swallowed, my throat dry and scratching. "Fine."

Calev's jaw tensed and he turned back toward Aunt's house. "Fine."

WE ENDED up cutting five stalks taller than Calev and headed back to the courtyard to meet Aunt. Calev kept stretching like his healed wound was bothering him a bit. It was amazing the wound didn't still have him half dead and on the floor of Aunt's house. I wished I could heal like Aunt Kania.

She greeted us with a white-toothed smile. "I'm very interested in this. I have meditated and think this may actually work."

Oron tossed a hand up. "Oh. Well. She meditated. We must be on the right path then."

I elbowed him sharply.

"Ow!" He rubbed his arm.

With sweating brows and heaving chests, the fighting sailors gathered around our bamboo and a stack of fine, silk robes on a straw mat at Aunt's feet.

Calev knelt by the stalks and grabbed two, bent them. "They'll give and hold like the gaff that holds the sail on a boat, right?"

I nodded. "If we lash those two together, they'll be the size of the gaff on the boat you gave us, Aunt."

She held up a length of draping red silk. Sun glinted off its smooth surface and the wind lifted it briefly as the fighters each took a handful to spread it out.

"I can cut this to fit the framing." Aunt turned her head a little like she was considering where and how to make the cut.

"Will silk be strong enough?" Oron asked. Standing beside the fair-haired fighter, he fingered an edge of the rosy fabric and scratched his hair.

"Oh yes." Calev tied two of the stalks together. The muscles and tendons in his forearms worked smoothly, beautifully, like sailing ropes under his browned skin. "Silk is very strong. And light."

"Light being fairly important if this rig is meant to keep two people in the air for over four hundred yards or so," Oron said. He looked at Calev, then me, like we might start in on one another again.

"Why two people?" I asked.

"We have only so much of this expensive silk. And just four good stalks." Oron kicked the fifth, exposing a splintered edge on the underside. "Two for each glider. A fighter can stay with me in the boat, in case we're boarded."

"Stay in the boat?" Ekrem frowned. "We will infiltrate the fortress. We are masters of such maneuvers and should be involved in the recovery. I see that we will need to glide out. They'll surely know of our presence with the slaves once we're there. But Serhat and I should execute the plan."

Oron held up a hand. "If the oramiral's men see the boat and take it, then where will the rest glide into? A friendly seastinger's jaws? A relaxing Pass current that will take them down to a wraith's death?"

The sailor's mouth pinched up.

"He's right." I wanted to pick up on his thinking. I wanted to go in to get Avi. She'd be so frightened, so weak. She needed me.

"Oron and one fighter will stay with the boat. Calev, if you insist on going in, you and Serhat can come with me. I will fly out with her and Calev, you can fly out holding Avi's hands to the glider's supports. When thinking of weight, the plan makes sense."

Calev threw me a dark look, but nodded. "I agree."

Oron put a hand over his heart. "They agree. The impossible is possible."

"Cut here. Here. Along this place too. And you two," Aunt said to Calev and Oron, "saw the fifth stalk into two pieces. You can suspend the piece from the support frame for the handle as Kinneret explained in her plan this morning."

Aunt handed the silk off to the fighters who began cutting with silver shears in the places she indicated. Oron and Calev traded jokes as they followed her orders. Then Aunt took my arm and led me away, toward the well where a rooster strutted around the stone base, his throat green as Ayarazi's meadow in the baking sun.

"What has happened between you and the Old Farm?" she asked, her brown eyes seeing right through me.

I glanced toward Calev. His smile made me smile. "Nothing. We had an argument. He wants to protect me. And I want to lead."

"Ah. You love one another."

"Well, yes. But not like that. We can't…"

"Oh, yes you do. And him too. And you can. You just have to make decisions. There is always a choice to make. If you choose to live outside your land's caste rules, so be it. I think you two do not care to avoid difficulty anyway. It is not too much to think this attitude will carry you through to loving one another, to mating."

The sun seared my cheeks. "I didn't say anything about mating. We don't talk like that in Jakobden," I mumbled, my tongue not working quite right.

Aunt laughed and steered me back toward the group. "But there are children enough in Jakobden. Talk or not, there is mating going on."

I shushed her as we neared the group and Calev gave me a look with a question in it. My cheeks were definitely getting too much sun.

Aunt leaned toward my ear. "Don't let Calev go, my Kinneret. You are brave. You take him and you make beautiful babies. Do not allow something as simple as caste deny a real love. It comes once, sometimes twice, in a lifetime. I should know."

I couldn't take my eyes off Calev. Once in a lifetime. I believed Aunt. There was no one like him. He was my luck, my heart, the blood in my veins, but I couldn't have him. With everything he already had stacked against him, our union would lead to his destruction. Unless we left Jakobden for good.

CHAPTER THIRTY-FOUR

I cupped my hand at my mouth and called to Oron. "You're certain you want to go first?"

From the grass and stick roof, he waved a hand. "Yes."

He lifted the sideways sail of red silk and bamboo over his head, his body looking tight with the effort. The wind noticed the glider and gave a tug. One of Oron's feet jerked forward and he caught himself before toppling off the roof.

"Go!" I punched a hand in the air.

Calev shouted suggestions about reaching arms as far out as possible and the fighters cheered. Aunt covered her face with her hands.

The wind took the glider as Oron's feet lifted from the roof. He began to fall the five stories down to the straw we'd gathered into a massive pile that covered most of the courtyard. He was going fast. Very fast. Then the silk cupped the air and seemed to slow Oron's descent a fraction.

Oron swore. Loudly.

Then he began kicking and thrashing. "I don't want to die. I'm rethinking this. Save me!"

His leg movement lurched the glider sharply down on one end and his graceful descent became a typical fall. Fast and ending in pain.

We ran to him.

The glider flipped over his head and landed bottom up. Oron was face down.

I turned him gingerly and his face was coated in dust. A long piece of yellow straw stuck to his cheek.

"Am I alive?" he asked.

"Yes, you fool. You're alive. If you hadn't lost your nerve, you'd have been fine."

Calev leaned over and pushed Oron's hair out of his eyes. "I'm going next."

I whipped around. "You are?"

"Yes." Calev and the fighters lifted the glider and headed toward the ladder we'd set against the outside of the house.

I pressed my lips together. Today was not going to be dull.

As it turned out, Calev was the best on the glider.

"Go!" I called up to him from his perch atop Aunt's roof.

There was something in the way he leaped forward and into the air without hesitation, the way he kept his body light and still as the silk eased his descent to the earth. As the straw-strewn ground came up to meet his feet, he went into a run, holding the glider aloft and steady with his lean, strong arms. When his momentum was gone, he lowered the glider to the ground behind him.

The fighters and Oron stomped their feet in praise for his skill. Aunt missed the excitement. She'd gone to the market to gather some dried beef and root vegetables for our journey.

"That will never grow tiresome." Calev ran a hand over his wind-tossed hair and did his stretching thing again, moving his torso around to ease the discomfort in his healed wound.

I didn't smile like he did when I took my turn with the glider. I liked my feet on a boat deck, the water shifting and familiar under me. To have nothing but the sea beneath me.

Calev laughed as we leaned both the gliders we'd created against the courtyard's mud wall, near the gate.

"You look a little green," he said.

"I feel a little green." My stomach rolled like a sea swell. "You think the gliders will hold two riders?"

"I do. But we shouldn't over-test this fabric. It's all we have."

"Agreed."

The others washed and drank at the well in the middle of the yard. We had to go now.

I swallowed and crossed my arms over my stomach, the cutting scent of soap rising over the miasma of cow dung and chicken feed. Aunt had kindly washed our clothes after our first set of practice flights and allowed us to dirty her extra robes and tunics. I inhaled the clean smell and Avi's face floated through my mind's eye.

She'd helped me with washing every sundown as long as I could remember.

Splashing. Smiles. The way she pinched up the side of her mouth when a dab of tar sealant wouldn't come off her skirt. I remembered her putting her underclothes on her head once and doing her version of a trader's jig. Father had snapped at her, but she'd giggled with me when he finished lecturing. His fussing made her cry when she actually deserved it.

My Avigail. My sister. My only family.

The sudden hot burn of tears pressed behind my eyes and I turned to face the Topa trees beyond the gate and wall.

"Ah, Kinneret," Calev said. He put a hand gently on my back. "That oramiral…" His voice went low and menacing. "We will take her back."

Suddenly, strangely, the courtyard blurred and I couldn't breathe, I couldn't take it anymore. I needed all of Calev or none of him and I was tired of worrying about what would happen if I did get him, of what would happen under the threat of being Outcasted. My skin itched and my heart thunked erratically.

I spun to face him and my emotions exploded into a jumble of anger and fear. "Don't make promises you can't keep."

Calev's eyes widened like I'd slapped him, and no wonder. I was acting like a maniac, but I couldn't seem to stop myself.

"All right," he said. "But we—"

My hands rested on his chest. His tunic was both soft and rough beneath my fingers. "I know." I took a heavy breath. My lungs didn't want to expand. "But don't lie to me. And don't try to touch or kiss me again. I won't make you an Outcast. You'll have enough to overcome without an unconventional union."

The words spilled out of me without my direction.

"I…I don't think I can take the beauty of your attention, only to have it ripped away from me when, or if, we return to Jakobden." I was shaking all over then. My hands. My heart. Voice.

Calev blinked quickly and leaned a hand's width away. "What do you mean, if we go back to Jakobden?"

"You will be tried for killing the amir. I hope we can convince them that you were Infused. Your father will help I'm sure, and the amir's fighters we have on our side, but the kyros will be involved." I grasped his tunic and stared up at him, willing him to understand the danger. "You may have strong luck, Calev ben Y'hoshua, but this. This could mean your death."

He put his hands over mine, then his mouth tensed and he dropped them to his sides again. "You're the only one who believes I'm lucky." His grin was sour-sweet with sadness. "I only believe in the Fire's will for my life. Well, that and the arrogance of my father." He laughed quietly.

"Don't make this a joke. I'm tired of joking." I released him, my thoughts flying like wild birds. I'd never wanted to move from Jakobden, but now it was the only way. As long as I could work the sea, it would be fine. "I want to rescue Avi, then take you and her and Oron and whoever else wants to come and go to a place where no one knows us. We'll sail far, far away. To the Great Expanse. To a new land."

Calev's head swept to the side and he clenched his fists at his sides. "I can't leave my family, my people, Kinneret. I am Old Farm. I will always be. It's who I am. Like the sea is for you."

A chill poured over my skull and back. He would never leave Jakobden. I'd known it already. I'd only been denying it the last few days. He would remain at Old Farm. Even if it killed him. Even if it kept us apart, in a way we could never be joined as husband and wife. The cold seeped into my chest and shook me hard. No matter what I did, I would lose him.

If he returned and was killed for slaying the amir, I'd lose him. If he was pardoned, he'd have to marry his Intended. It wasn't really his fault. But after all this, if he wanted to remain Old Farm, he'd have to do as they wished in marriage. He said he was Old Farm and would always be. His first loyalty was to his people. Not to me. Not to the love sprouting between us.

I would never wake up to find Calev sleeping beside me in our own home. I would never carry his dark-haired babies in my belly. I would never feel the length of his body against my own. He would keep secrets with another woman. I would be outside their world. Another type of outcast. Like I'd always been. Kinneret. Scrapper. Low-caste. Witch. I'd lost all chance at kaptan when I'd crossed Berker.

Even if we were considered innocent of conspiring to kill the amir— which most definitely was not a certainty—I'd never kaptan the Old Farm ship. Of course, Calev wouldn't have to pay with his throat's blood for that promise he'd made to the amir because she was dead. But I would pay instead. I would never lead a crew and run a full ship across the Pass. Honestly, I didn't so much care about that part anymore. I wanted my own small craft, a business so I could purchase food and supplies for Avi and me and Oron. I longed for Avi's safety, our freedom, and Calev. But I would never, ever have him because he refused to leave Jakobden and its caste system.

Feeling numb, I pushed past Calev. "Oron. Ready?"

Oron tucked his dagger into his sash. "Yes." He gestured toward the fighters at his side.

Ekrem took a drink from the well cup and set it on the stones. Serhat nodded at me. "We are prepared, my kaptan."

Calev came up beside me as I gathered a bedroll and opened the gate for the fighters who'd lifted the gliders.

"Kinneret. What is it? What did I say? We'll be fine at home. Father will speak for me. These sailors will speak. You had nothing to do with it. You only fled to protect me. Kinneret. Stop. Look at me."

But I didn't, and the others were wise enough to simply follow us in silence. I left Calev standing, open-mouthed, at the first turn of the path leading away from Aunt's estate. She'd agreed to meet us with the food on the beach where the boat waited, under watch of a boy she'd paid to do the job.

When we were far enough from Aunt's place that Calev was a dark smudge on the horizon, Oron tugged my rolled sleeve.

"Is he not coming with us?" he asked.

Ekrem grunted as he adjusted the glider on his shoulders. Although we would definitely need to find a way to fold the creations to make for easier running and climbing on the island, I don't think the sailor's grunt resulted from carrying the thing. He was upset Calev wasn't with us. I knew enough of military operations to realize missing an operative was not the best.

"He'll come." I set my gaze firmly on the slim path pointing toward the sea's shushing tide. "He loves Avi enough to risk his life for her."

"Then why are you mad as a squashed bee?"

I glanced at Oron. "He likes to risk his life. It's pleasurable for someone as lucky as him. It's the drudgery of sun-to-sun sacrifice he won't be a part of. Not for anyone."

Oron's mouth became a tiny circle as he lifted his eyebrows. "Oh. I see. Doesn't care to run off into nowhere with a lowly non-Old Farm girl who just happens to hold both his heart and his—"

"Oron." I glared at him. "I have not mated with him. Not that it's your business."

"Doesn't matter. You hold all the balls in this game." He snickered at his own stupid joke. "The boy won't be able to leave you alone."

"I disagree, Master of Love Experience." I walked a little faster.

"Point taken," Oron grumbled.

Guilt niggled at me, but I didn't apologize. No one asked Oron to get involved in this. But he was wrong. Very wrong. I didn't hold any power between Calev and me. Calev held all of it. In the way his smile made me shine. His caste, allowing him all kinds of choices and respect from everyone. And in the potential mates he probably had clamoring around his father at Old Farm. Miriam, for one. A bitter taste slicked over my tongue. I wondered if she had taken that trade trip north yet with her mother and father. Too bad there hadn't been many reports of wolves.

I shook my head to clear it. We were headed to Quarry Isle to break Avi free. All my focus had to pinpoint on that. If I wasn't my best, and the rest along with me, today's sun would be the last one we'd see.

CHAPTER THIRTY-FIVE

The sun whitened the undulating road of the Pass. The heat rolled over our heads as we neared the oramiral's island. We'd opted for an afternoon escape because the slaves were forced to work from the middle of the night until the sun was directly overhead. The slaves would then rest and eat.

Oron tugged at his tangled, thick locks of hair. "I still think this is madness. They'll see us coming a mile away."

In taut silence, Calev helped me tighten the rope that curled the largest of the triangular lateen sails, adjusting our track a bit. He opened his mouth to say something and I shot a glare, closing that pretty mouth of his.

Rocks like tombstones crowded the water to the West. A hazy block of white and brown and green, the island hulked northeast of us.

As the island grew and eventually loomed over us, I threw the anchor overboard into the shallow water. The anchor's splash was unheard over the crash of the Pass against the island's rocky crust. There was no movement in the watch tower directly over us.

"Just because we don't see them, doesn't mean they don't see us." Oron knotted a rope, making a circle at one end. He threw it over the nearest tall rock at the base of the island.

Calev strapped one of the gliders to Ekrem's back with some extra rope. We'd undone the lashed strips of bark and coconut rope that held the two main bamboo supports together on each of the gliders and folded them for easier maneuvering while on the island.

"I'm borrowing this," I said to Oron as I turned him around and untied his broad sash.

"Hey." He slapped my hand. As the sash came free, he grabbed his dagger before it hit the deck. "Where am I supposed to keep my blade?"

"Up your nose."

Oron snorted. "That wouldn't do at all, kaptan. My nostrils are far too small for such an endeavor." He tsked and looked to the fighters and Calev. "I'm worried our kaptan has had too much sun. Perhaps we should put this mission off until moonrise?"

"Oron." Calev put his arms out and I, with Serhat's help, ran Oron's sash over the glider on Calev's back and knotted the ends of the stained, green fabric on his chest.

"Kinneret." Calev's words stirred my hair. He smelled warm and spicy. "Look at me."

I would not.

"Please." The word was filled with such longing, my gaze flew to his before I could stop myself. He tilted his head and spoke softly as the others steadied the boat against the rocks with bumpers. "Don't shut me out. We need to—"

"We should disembark, kaptan," Ekrem said.

Before Calev could say anything else to make my heart beat too quickly, I leaped from the boat and onto the tiny black rocks and clear seawater of the island's coast. The stones crunched under my feet as I put a hand to my warm dagger hilt and eyed the ascent we were about to attempt. The sun lay on my exposed forearms like a blanket of flame. I turned to see Calev directly behind me. He knotted his headtie. The glider on his back made him look like he had red wings, like he was some creature sent to torment me with his unattainable beauty. But he couldn't have been sent from any hell. He was too good.

Well, he was until he decided we had no future. I gritted my teeth and ripped my gaze away from him.

Behind Calev, Ekrem stared at the cusp of the cliffs above our heads. A sea bird soared out of a messy cliff face nest and dove into the Pass.

From the look I'd snagged when we were close to the island searching for the map, I knew a spindly path was around here somewhere. It led to the main path that stretched between the slaves' open-air quarters, the quarry, and Oramiral Urmirian's fine shelter made of the same rock he quarried.

"Where's the path?" Ekrem's broad shoulders blocked most of the glider on his back from view. Only one red and brown-green edge stuck up behind his ear.

Lichen-covered rocks rose like discarded stone doors at the base of the cliff.

I climbed over a fallen boulder. "Maybe it's farther east than I'd guessed." A tide pool of hand-sized, lime-colored seastingers floated below. "Watch your step," I called over my shoulder.

Rounding another collection of head-high rocks and stepping onto a smaller boulder, I searched the sea for Oron and Serhat. They'd raised the anchor and sails and were working to break free of the crash near the island's base. They had to. Staying close for too long would allow the tide and the rocks to puncture the hull. So we had no way out now.

As we climbed over a natural wall of seaweed and stone, a broad stroke of dirt appeared. My pulse jumped. It rose like a rescue rope until it disappeared into the clefts of the island's side.

"The path. Here." I waved a hand.

A shout punched out from the watch tower far, far above us. "They've spotted our boat," Ekrem said. "They'll fire on them."

Calev hurried to catch up to me, eyes black with fear. "Go, Kinneret. We'll use the boat as a distraction."

Agreeing, I stormed up the path. The sandy dirt ribboned through crevices and past alcoves where sea birds nested. If one flew out, I'd fall to my death on the rocky beach below.

"Don't look, Kinneret," Calev said, his voice breathy as we rushed higher and higher and higher.

"Don't pretend to care," I shouted over my shoulder. It was mean. Mean felt a whole lot better than scared.

"Quiet, you two," Ekrem said from the back. "We should be nearing the top."

He was right. The cliff only reached a jump above us. When we doubled back on the path again, the rocks that had surrounded us dropped away and exposed a valley of extremes.

The quarry was a dip and a crescent of white in the green hill directly across the valley. The oramiral's house coiled at the base of a black rock outcropping, snug and formidable. It was made of the same stone as the amir's abode, but this house lacked the columns, mosaic portico, and treed courtyard. To our left, far above the rest of the island's structures, watchtowers included, the slaves' turreted castle tower rose into the blue sky.

I could smell it from here.

Avigail.

My feet pounded the path, and we neared the slaves' quarters without anyone stopping us. But two guards stood sentry at the entrance. Ten foot tall spears stood at their sides and bells hung on the oramiral's well-known contraptions above their heads. Their shoulders looked every bit as broad as Ekrem's.

I spun, grabbed Calev and Ekrem by the sleeves, and dragged them into the brush off the path. At the island's edge, a man with a bell jangling over his head, raised his arms.

"He's shooting a crossbow at Oron!"

Calev's face was fingers from mine. "We have to get into the quarters now. Oron knows how to evade crossbow bolts."

"And how exactly does one do that?"

"They're well out of range, kaptan," Ekrem said. "He'll go farther out. If you don't mind my suggestions, kaptan, you should cross the path and head, hidden in the brush, up that side of the path. Calev and I will sneak up this way. When you are near the guard, throw a rock and distract the guards. I will take them down with Calev's help."

Calev frowned. "But I'm not a fighter."

I could tell he hadn't wanted to say that. And really, the way he'd moved in his dagger dance had shown he was at least capable of the action.

Ekrem put a hand on his shoulder. "I saw you with your dagger onboard the amir's full ship. You know your way around a blade. Simply strike flesh instead of air."

"Oh, simply strike flesh." Calev shrugged dramatically and rolled his eyes. "No problem then."

I gave Ekrem a nod and squeezed Calev's hand tightly. Too tightly.

"He's right, Calev," I said. "You can do this. You haven't cowered once during this…"

"Hells," Calev said quietly. "Because it definitely hasn't been paradise."

The mention of our ongoing game with Avi hit me in the throat and I had to look up to keep from releasing a sob.

This was a hell. And if we died here, well, I had to tell Calev how I felt before then. If the guards caught me or him and he never knew about my love for him, that would be a tragedy I couldn't stand. Though I was still so painfully disappointed in him and burned raw with his rejection, I had to make certain he knew.

"Calev. I love you. I always have."

I didn't give him a second to respond.

I took off, running across the path like a lizard and diving into the spindly bamboo trees, crunchy grass, and sandy dirt. Rolling, I came up into a crouch. The growth on this side of the path didn't provide nearly as much cover as Calev's side, but the guards remained standing, eyes glazed in fatigue until I was close enough to see the sweat around the metal straps that held their bell bars in place. The bells hanging from the bars over their heads clanked in a gust of wind. An insect buzzed past my ear and I swatted it as I searched the other side of the path for any sign that Calev and Ekrem were in place. Then I caught a flash of red. Gliders. And if I spotted them, the guards would too. Soon.

I had nothing to use as a distraction. The ground at my feet was nothing but grainy earth. Not a rock to be seen anywhere. Not a fallen tree limb. Nothing. Not even a lizard to throw. I took a deep breath of the searingly hot island wind. I felt like I was being slow roasted in this heat.

That was it. Fire.

The perfect distraction.

It would keep the guards far more busy than the easy-to-scout-out rock noise. They'd have to deal with finding water in this dry place. If the fire spread, it could eat this entire island before nightfall. Their oramiral would not be pleased.

I smiled.

Pulling my nub of silvery quartzite and my dagger from my sash, I eyed the bushes and ground for kindling. A flaky length of fallen bark from a eucalyptus shading me was ideal for the job. I struck my dagger along the quartzite rock until a spark fell onto the bark. And died. Only a thin line of gray smoke curled out of the bark. Not enough to start a fire.

Groaning, I lifted the tiny stones and leaf debris around my feet. If I could find some fungus…

A man shouted and another grunted. I jumped up to see Calev holding one of the guards from behind with his dagger on the larger man's throat. Blood trickled down the man's front. My stomach churned. Ekrem stood over the other guard, holding the man's hair. Ekrem kneed the man in the face and the man collapsed to the ground. I went hot and cold all over as I ran to them. My heart thwacked my ribs like a sail cut loose of the gaff.

"Did you kill him?" Calev asked, his voice rising.

"Who cares if he did?" I was already kicking at the slave quarters' entrance.

Ekrem took over and blasted a boot through the wood. The odor of urine and fear and desperation raked nails over my face.

We ran into the round, open room and were immediately surrounded by men, women, and children with shaved heads, white-dusted faces, and dead eyes. Their slave bells clanged in a mournful chorus.

"Avi?" Where was she? My heart leaped high, dropped, and exploded. "Avigail?"

Calev and I pushed through the seemingly frozen crowd. They were probably too shocked and in too poor of health to even react to our surprise entrance.

"Avigail." My throat was raw and my nose burned.

And there she was. Slumped and staring up from the bottom of the stone walls.

They hadn't shaved her head yet. Her sunlight hair still gilded her skull like a crown and veil, but her ragged tunic hung loose. She was skin. Bones. A living wraith.

Not meeting her gaze, I grabbed her and tucked her under my chin. My body shook so hard I was afraid I might hurt her. She was mumbling, but there was no sun for this. They'd be here any second.

"Did you hit your guard on the head?" I asked Calev.

Calev ran a gentle hand over Avi's head and down her cheek. Tears were silver in his eyes and hers. My heart contracted and exploded again.

"Did you put your guard to sleep?" I asked him. "We need to fly. Now." Another smell rose, sharp and lurking, over the odor of the slave quarters.

Ekrem worked his way to us, holding his hands out to keep the slaves from his path. He stopped at Calev's shoulder and lifted his nose to the air. "Smoke." He looked at me and my stomach fell into my knees.

My fire had caught.

"Fly. Now." I set Avi a step away, turned Calev, and began tugging the glider from his back. Ekrem did the same with his own.

"Are you going to take her away?" A woman not much older than me leaned toward me as Calev and I worked to lash the glider supports back together. She had bright blue eyes.

Avi whimpered and put a hand of bones on my arm. I touched her skin briefly, keeping my feelings shoved deep down so I could work. I could not look at her now. I'd lose my every thought, every plan.

My hands were worthless as I tried to tie the lashes. "I can't get it."

Ekrem already had his assembled and was climbing the wall with one good hand and his feet in nooks in the stone.

Calev touched my cheek and edged my shaking hands away. He tied the lashes neatly, his wiry hands quick and sure. We stood. Avi kept a handful of my shirt and Calev's tunic as I hoisted the glider up. The scent of smoke grew stronger. The slaves began yelling and rushing toward the door we'd broken through.

I climbed the wall; it wasn't so high. Ekrem and I helped Calev lift Avi up to join us. We took the glider from Calev then and he climbed up after. The view from the top of the castle wall was chaos. On the path leading to the quarters, a jumble of guards in gray and the oramiral's retinue in yellow fought one another. Fire licked at the trees and grass, spreading down the valley like a river of light.

"They turned on the oramiral's men. Some of the slave guards turned on the retinue!" I shouted and took up the glider.

Now I finally looked Avi in the face. And I shattered into pieces.

My ears buzzed like an impossible amount of insects had crawled inside to fight and die.

Calev and Ekrem readied the gliders and held them aloft. An arrow zipped past the glider he held. He ducked his head and dipped the silken creation outside the wall.

I cupped Avi's face in my shaking hands. "No matter what, hold on to Calev. Hold on with everything you have left, Avi." I was crying. My face felt cold and wet in the wind.

Smoke like acrid wraiths drifted through the air, choking me as I climbed onto Ekrem's back. Avi did the same with Calev, her foot slipping once behind his bent knee and jerking his tunic. Her elbows were sharp as yatagans at his shoulders. She lay her head between his shoulder blades.

The world dropped away from my feet as Ekrem and Calev jumped from the wall. My stomach floated into my throat. My arm muscles spasmed as I held on and lifted myself up to look over Ekrem's shoulder. Below us, another clutch of yellow-garbed slaves ran up the path toward the slaves' quarters. Slave guards in gray tunics raised crossbows at their former comrades and fired. Some came together with yatagans and spears. The sun flashed off their weapons and the bells ringing above their heads.

"What if the slaves burn in the fire?" I said into Ekrem's ear as he slid his right hand down a bit on the glider's handle bar. "We can't leave them there. Those people…"

I shuddered. Their shaved heads. The empty eyes and bones so sharp under their ashen skin. It was wrong to help Avi and leave the rest.

"But what can we do?" Ekrem's beard scratched against his leather vest as he turned his head to talk to me.

A crowd of slaves—skeletal quarry workers and guards in gray— surrounded the flames and beat on the fire with boots and shed tunics.

"They're working together to put it out," I said, pointing back and down.

Calev and Avi soared above my view of that end of the island. Calev's hair flew behind him like a small cloak over Avi's head. A shiver of hope danced over me. She might make it out of this alive. But the others like her…

"Maybe the oramiral won't regain control of the island," I said. "Maybe—"

"He has weapons," Ekrem said. "And food. The slaves will not win out. Not unless his retinue goes against him."

"Why don't they?"

"They are his children."

My stomach clenched. "What?"

"The yellow tunics are his children from bedding other slaves. He keeps them in his housing. Feeds them. Clothes them. Warps their minds into believing he is a god."

The tattered clouds blurred, and I searched the sky for Calev and Avi.

So much evil existed in the world, driven by greed and a thirst for power. Was I like that? Is that why I'd wanted the silver badly enough to risk all my loved ones' safety?

Looking past us and up, I saw Calev's red glider and the ends of his tunic flickering behind him like blue flame. As we lifted in the wind, then drifted down, down, down, past the island's green growth and sand and black rock toward the speck of Oron in the Pass, I was detached from the earth in body and mind. Like arrows, my pains hit me one by one and lodged deep in my heart.

The look in Avi's eyes, her innocence burned away. Calev's rejection.

The slaves we were leaving behind.

The fire I started that might kill hundreds.

The rough landing on the water we were about to experience.

Fear for Avi in that crash.

Where we might go when or if we made it onto the boat with Oron.

It was too much. I squeezed my eyes shut and let the sea sing in my ears. Whispering. Rushing. Questioning. What would my mother have said to do? My father?

They would've said the same thing they always did when we had a decision. Stealing the sentence from one another, picking up where the other left off, they would've repeated what felt now like the only thing I could remember about their wisdom

"When you don't see where to go," Mother would say.

"Put a hand to your stomach." Father would grin and wiggle his black eyebrows.

"Fingers over your heart." Mother always gently pressed her own to my chest and smiled.

"Think of your choices. The one that makes both heart and gut hurt, that is the true path." Father liked to rub his knuckles on the crown of my head and make a funny clucking noise before pulling me into his arms.

I set one hand on my head now, remembering the feeling. The sea waters were flying up to us and the drift over the white caps should've been thrilling. We had escaped after all. We had saved Avi, unless they shot us down with arrows, crossbow bolts, or spears. But as we plunged, feet first, into the chill water, I was far away, in my own boat, beside my parents and a tinier Avi, smelling the orange Mother had bought as a treat at the market. She was listening to my parents' wisdom while I rubbed a hand over my young heart. Calev hadn't been a problem then. He'd been a surety. Like my family, the sunset, the tides.

My hands released Ekrem as our bodies sunk into the Pass. Above us, both gliders stayed afloat, a red slash against the blue-green sky of water. Blowing air from my nose, I pushed my hands through the sea and twisted. Where was Avi? She wouldn't be able to swim in her condition.

Ekrem turned, a dark shape against the inconsistent yellow light, and held out a hand. I waved him on and he kicked, bubbles racing from his sandals, rising to the surface. Spinning again in the water, I saw another shape, this one leaner, lithe and familiar as my own hand. Calev. He jetted diagonally down through the blue-green.

Below him, a ghost drifted deeper, deeper. My heart stopped in my chest. It was Avi.

Driving my feet back and forth, I propelled myself toward Avi, not caring that Calev was already well on his way to her, because her arms unfurled from her sides like a banner dropped from a cliff. My body went numb and everything moved too slowly. I drove toward her, but she was disappearing into the dark, Calev her shadow.

Bringing my arms forward, then thrusting them back, I sped forward. Below and beyond me, Calev stopped. His tunic billowed around him like a storm cloud. I couldn't see Avi anymore. Then Calev whipped around and Avi was in his arms. I opened my mouth, forgetting I was in the water and salt puckered my tongue. With a look at me, Calev—his mouth a line and his eyes furious—kicked his feet and swam toward the surface. He was too slow. She'd be taking in water. She was weak. She would drown.

I swam up beside him and put my hands under his elbow and his thigh, pushing him with every one of my surges upward. We broke the surface, Calev and I gasping, Avi still limp.

Oron and Serhat's faces appeared over the side of the boat. Shouts bounced into my ears. Behind us, the island's rock walls curled lukewarm air off the water and threw it back at us along with threats from the oramiral and his men above.

Our sails weren't up. We were unmoving targets.

Oron reached his arms down. "Hand her up. I have your salt here, Kinneret. You can help her." Calev and I lifted Avi as best we could, the boat bumping against us. "Get our kaptan onboard quickly," Oron said to the sailors and Calev. "She has healing to do."

"I can't heal," I mumbled as Oron tugged Avi over the side and I began climbing the small rope ladder.

Calev put a hand under my thigh to heft me up. "You can. You will."

Something thudded into the boat by my hand. A short, wooden shaft. Feathers. A crossbow bolt.

Calev blasted up the ladder behind me, scooping me into the boat with him. We tumbled to the deck as another two bolts banged into the boat's mast and side.

"That's why the sails are down," Oron said, widening his eyes.

"Well get them up!" I scrambled to my feet and rushed to where Avi lay chest-down near Serhat.

The fair-haired sailor struck Avi's back and water poured from my sister's mouth. On her knees, she coughed and fell forward into my arms. She was light as a bird. Cold as ice.

"Avi? Can you hear me? You need to stay awake. I'm going to sit you up." With Serhat's help, I raised her into a sitting position.

Avi's face was a puzzle of white, purple, and pale greenish. She wasn't breathing.

Calev and Oron shouted instructions at one another as they raised the jib and halyard. The wind shouldered into the sails and we pushed westward.

"Avigail," I whispered into her face. My hand searched blindly for the salt pouch Oron had kept for me. "Breathe. Please breathe. We have you now. You have to live to help me deal with Oron." I searched the deck. "Where is the salt?" I shouted at Serhat and everyone who would listen. Leaning back down to Avi, I said, "And Calev needs someone to help him irritate me."

"Here," Calev was suddenly kneeling beside me and holding the bag of salt. He lifted my hand to his mouth and said a prayer against my skin. "May the One who blessed our foreparents, mothers, fathers, bless and heal the one who is sickened, Avigail, sister of Kinneret. May the Shining Pure

One overflow with empathy and love upon her, to refresh her, to raise her up, to make her strong, to heal her."

I swallowed. "Thank you."

My soul was turning itself inside out. I drew a handful of salt from my pouch. What words had Aunt said over Calev?

It didn't matter. I just had to try. I'd already done things I never thought I could.

Father's long, bedtime lectures about thinking on my magic before taking up the salt made so much more sense now. I could still see the worry in my father's brown-green eyes and the way he tucked my and Avi's sleeping blankets so carefully like he could protect us with mere bedding.

With his caution in my heart and my mother's magic in my veins, I prayed.

"Salt, blood of the oceans, heal.
Wake this one's lifefluid.
Feed your strength to her.
Enliven, spark, breathe!"

My arms shook. I pressed my salty hands against Avi's bony chest. A rasping sound came from her mouth and my heart lurched.

"Please, Avi. Breathe. Cough. Live."

Her cheek, her ear, were warming. Her chest rose in another breath.

And she opened her eyes. Tears ran into my mouth as I laughed.

"Drink?" she rasped. I could barely hear her.

Before I could scramble around for fresh water, Calev's hand appeared at her mouth with a water skin. His hand was steady, holding the drink to her chapped and bleeding lips. I cupped her head and helped her position herself better to swallow. After coughing up the first sip, she worked a few swallows down. I put my hand on Calev's, moving the container away, and he looked at me.

"But she's still thirsty." Water droplets shone on his lashes, confusion in his eyes.

"She has to drink slowly. Or it will make her sick."

He nodded, plugging the skin with its cork. "I'm so glad they hadn't yet fitted her with a bell."

I nodded. It would've made our escape and her landing that much more difficult.

"Kinneret." Avi twisted. Her eyes seemed so much larger than before. Before. It was like an age ago. "Are we going home?"

Icy fingers walked down my back. We couldn't. "We're going to visit Aunt."

"And then home?"

"Close your eyes and rest, Avi." I ran a hand over her head.

She nodded and settled against me, her body shuddering in a deep breath. Waves rose around our boat like blue-green hills, blocking most of our view to the island. No more arrows came our way. No more shouting. We'd made it.

Avi was here in my arms and we were headed to safety in Kurakia, where they wouldn't question us about our past. We could start new there, maybe wait until Berker and the rest of the fighters managed to get off Ayarazi and sneak back there ourselves.

"Kaptan!" Oron stood at the bow, one foot on the side of the boat, his hand up to shield his eyes from the white-hot sun.

"I'll be right back," I said to Avi.

"I'll take her." Calev gathered her into his arms. His smile would be an unguent for her pain.

When I ducked past the rigging, I saw it.

The oramiral's ship.

CHAPTER THIRTY-SIX

"**N**o."

"Yes." Oron swallowed loudly. "We should arm ourselves."

I laughed hysterically. "Oh yes. With our four weapons. That'll work perfectly."

Calev came up behind me and put his hands on my shoulders. Past him, Serhat now sat with Avi, who peered over port, her eyes trained on the oramiral's yellow sails.

"Kinneret," Calev said. "Do you have any ideas?"

I breathed out of my nose, my head spinning with worry for Avi. She didn't even seem like the same sister. Wisdom earned through pain had lurked in her eyes as I'd held her. She could not go through imprisonment again.

What power did we have? What advantage?

The oramiral's boat could outrun ours. He had slaves aplenty that were obviously still on his side, both gray-tunic and yellow. The struggle on the island must've switched track and gone his way. As usual, the world did no favors for those in slavery. It was why some respected those who'd been through it and risen to a higher caste with strong business skills or a stroke of luck. Slavery stripped you down and turned you into a lean, fierce version of your former self. The transformation bled into the generations that came after, into children, grandchildren, making them stronger and smarter. But slaves had to earn their way out. Serve consistently, convince visiting merchants and tradesmen to buy their freedom, or impress their owners to such a degree that they emancipated them. And breaking Avi out of the quarry hadn't impressed the oramiral. What would?

Oron held his dagger sideways in the air, surrendering as the ship approached. Ekrem dropped the sails.

"Kinneret, what's in your head?" Calev still stood in front of me now, eyes questioning.

I bit my lip. I had an idea. It turned my stomach, but it was the best one buzzing around my mind. "You tell him Old Farm sent you to retrieve Avi."

"He'll need a reason. A strong reason."

"Tell them she's your Intended."

Calev rubbed the back of his neck, eyeing Oron as he came near. "A good plan. I don't like it." Calev's gaze flashed to me, a question and an answer in those eyes that I didn't have the sun for now. "But it might work."

Our fighters surrounded Avi, their uniforms making a wall of red leather.

"You have your father's ring?" I asked.

"What are you two planning?" Oron frowned and kept his face turned to the approaching ship.

Calev lifted a hand. A gold band, brushed by age and wear, circled his thumb. The Old Farm sigil, a sun rising behind a smooth leaf, was barely visible on the flattened top. His dark eyes glowed and he clenched his jaw. My heart skipped. He looked more like his Old Farm ancestors than ever. The colors that made up his skin, hair, and clothing echoed the brown sand, black soil, and blue seas. His people had survived the Quest knights' takeover, then the line of the Empire's kyros rulers thus far.

I ran a finger over his ring. My own veins held a tiny bit of Old Farm's blood. My twice great-grandmother had been Old Farm—pushed from the community and made an Outcast because of her affair with my twice great-grandfather, one of the amir's house slaves. I was a jumble of every kind of people that had lived in Jakobden.

A bang, then another, broke us apart. Two grappling hooks housed themselves in the boat. The full ship rose beside us, sails like clouds of tawny poison. Slaves in the same yellow as the sails boarded the ship in a silence that set my teeth on edge. The only sounds were the waves against the hulls and the sour clangs of bells.

The monkey-faced slave that attacked the day they took Avi sauntered up to Calev, Oron, and me. He took Oron's offered dagger and tucked it next to his undecorated steel yatagan. "The oramiral is eager to see you."

My skin burned. "You and your oramiral have sinned and you will pay."

The slave put a finger against my lips. The heat under my flesh shook me. Calev moved to grab the man's arm, but I beat him to it.

My fingers laced around the slave's wrist. "Why are you even loyal to that beast? You enjoy cleaning up his piss and cooking his meals?" I spit at his feet. "Pathetic."

He laughed. "You know nothing, girl. I am Rukn, master of slaves. You are the one with no future. Well, you do have something keeping you alive for the next few days."

"What is that?" Oron asked quietly.

Rukn's black eyes turned. The slave sniffed down at Oron and grinned at me. "The oramiral has two great talents."

A heaviness draped over me like a sail had fallen from its ties and landed on my back and shoulders.

"One is shaping slaves into weapons," Rukn said. "The second..."

"Bone and shell game strategy?" Calev asked, nudging his way between us.

"A fine hand with the oud?" Oron blinked and strummed an imaginary instrument.

Rukn's grin fell into a grimace.

Where was my sister?

I couldn't stand the space there was between us. I wanted her in my arms as if I could protect her from all this. A stupid thought. Across the wet decking, a wan-faced slave held her quill-thin arm. Serhat and Ekrem were restrained beside her.

"Joke all you want, prisoners," Rukn said. "You're dead men. But only after the oramiral has enjoyed pulling every form of scream from your trespassing throats."

"The young girl." Calev jerked his chin at Avi, who shivered. "She is my Intended."

Oron made a noise, then covered it with a cough.

Calev raised his hand and his Old Farm ring flashed in the sun. "I am Old Farm. Calev ben Y'hoshua, son of Y'hoshua ben Aharon. I am under the amir's protection, therefore so is the girl. You had no right to take her."

I thanked the Fire for the strength and confidence in his voice.

The slave's face fell, then he narrowed his eyes. The longer hairs in his eyebrows moved in the sea wind. "Why was she not wearing Old Farm henna if she was so recently Intended?"

"She was sick," I lied. "Unable to participate in the henna ritual."

The slave leered. "Why was an Old Farm, and a sick one at that, on a worthless little boat? Why are you here?" he asked Calev. "She's no full ship kaptan." He pointed. "What is your business with these scrappers, Old Farm?"

So Rukn did believe Calev. At least the part about him being Old Farm.

"We were headed to her aunt's home in Kurakia," Calev said. "She's known for her healing abilities."

It was another good lie. Truth made deception easier to swallow. Something about the liar's eyes.

Straightening, one hand on his yatagan, the slave called out to the men at his sides. "Lies. All lies. Take them on board. All of them. And drag their craft." He spun and leaped deftly to the ship, flying over the netted float skins and the slapping waters between the boats. "They won't be needing it."

Rukn's men swamped the deck and grabbed Calev with quarry-strong hands. Calev went pale. I reached out and put a hand on his back and tried to piece him and myself back together.

"They believe you," I mouthed. Untruth on top of untruth.

As they wrestled Calev onto the full-ship, Oron whispered up at me. "What are you doing?"

The men tore Avi from Ekrem, whose lips went white in his beard. My heart flapped in useless ragged beats between my ribs. Serhat pushed another slave off her arm and climbed aboard the oramiral's ship on her own.

I pushed away from Oron and around another slave as they dragged Avi across the deck. The slave next to me whipped around and hit me across the mouth.

Wincing, I dipped low and rammed my shoulder into his side, moving forward. "Avigail!"

She shouted my name too, and her eyes fluttered like dying nightwingers.

Hands latched onto my arms. "If you injure an Old Farm Intended, you suffer drawing and quartering."

Oron glanced at me in question.

"It's true and you know it, Rukn." I jerked my arms free, but didn't run. There was nowhere to go. "Remember that."

It was an old law, one the first kyros enacted as proof of good intention toward Old Farm in exchange for the brightest lemons, the best barley, and the silver that came with their trade.

The slave holding me ripped my dagger from my sash, tucked it into his own, and hauled me onto the full-ship. He threw me on the bigger ship's deck next to Calev. Blood trickled from Calev's brow and he held a hand against his arrow wound. I licked my lip and tasted blood. I wished it mattered that I was bleeding. That he was. But it would only be the first of our blood spilled.

Oron landed beside us as Rukn called out orders for the lines and sails.

Around a cough, Oron mumbled, "That law doesn't come up very often."

Calev titled his head. "Not too many Old Farm head out to sea with wild, mixed-blood sailors." He smiled sadly at me. He hadn't meant to insult. Humor was his coping strategy.

My hands shook as I pressed them against the worn deck. "Not many Old Farm are exciting enough for wild, mixed-blood sailors."

"I'm beginning to think excitement is overpraised." Oron pulled himself to standing.

Rukn stood at the top of a set of stairs as his crewmen rushed around the ship, working lines and watching the waters. "The Intended and Calev ben Y'hoshua will enjoy a cup of wine in the oramiral's quarters below. Tirin, please escort them out of the sun."

"Yes, Rukn," said a gray-shirted slave with a wide brow and deep-set eyes. He lifted Avi with a care that surprised me.

"Sailor," Rukn said to me. "You and your crew will wait below until the oramiral sees fit to judge your future."

Calev's eyes widened at the black mouth of the full-ship's hull. The odor of unwashed flesh and stale water curled between the bars of the opening. Oron, the fighting sailors, and I walked, with yatagans' points digging into our spines, toward the place that would be our temporary prison.

"This is not the day I thought it'd be," Oron grumbled.

My gaze darted to him as the slaves raised the barred entrance and gestured for us to climb down the ladder into the near dark.

"You thought we'd die in the escape," I said. "So this is better than your hopes."

Oron gave me a withering look before I started down the ladder. "Save your determined optimism for the rats, Kinneret. Their minds might be soft enough to soak it in. Mine is not, although agreeing to this entire endeavor speaks strongly against my argument." He touched his head sharply, then held a hand to Ekrem and Serhat. "Please, go ahead. I wouldn't want the amir's own fighters to wait on measly little me."

The ladder rungs were greasy. When I made it to the bottom, I wiped my hands on my skirt. Ekrem and Serhat climbed down to join me. Above, sunlight ringed Oron's head. He turned to Rukn.

"Speaking of," Oron said, "won't the amir be a trifle ruffled if she hears you threw two of her best fighting sailors into a hull filled with despair and possible infection?"

An invisible hand curled around my throat and I put a hand against the ladder as it shook under Oron's weight. It made sense to bring up the amir, to try and use what we had to gain an advantage, but the mention of her title, the fear that the oramiral and all of Jakobden might know we had a hand in her death…

"Enough," Rukn snapped.

The slave near Oron shoved him with his foot, knocking Oron from the ladder.

Serhat managed to catch him and he hugged her neck, breathing loudly.

"My savior!" he said into her chest.

She scowled and dropped him.

"That was unnecessary. We could've been lovers, Serhat, my sun-haired beauty."

"I'll admit a strong admiration for your knowledge of the sails and the sea, but you are too little for me," she said.

Oron stood, dusting his tunic. "Don't be so quick to judge by size, you lovely beast. I am more than sufficiently sized. Efficient, that's what I like to say. Nothing wasted."

I hit his shoulder. "We need to think about what we're going to do when we get to the island."

Rukn and his fellow slaves replaced the grating over our makeshift prison. The bars from above made striped shadows across Ekrem's crooked nose and reached over Oron's tangled, long hair.

Blinking, Serhat stepped away from the light, her vest creaking as she crossed her arms. "If they take us to the oramiral, and he does not know the amir is dead, we can play confident and possibly secure our release." She studied me. "I don't know what we can do for you, though." Oron received a look too. "Or you."

Ekrem scratched at his beard. Calev and Oron had shaved at Aunt's because of the heat, but Ekrem had kept his scruffy growth.

"It's possible they won't hear of the amir's death," he said. "Not ever. After all, if our crew mates were all sickened by the silver fog on Ayarazi, they may be stranded still."

"You two got over it quickly enough. And the rest seemed fresh as lemons when they shot our handsome Calev," Oron said.

I chewed my lip. "I think they were getting over the sickness. There was a marked difference in their balance and color when we left."

"How long do you think we have before the oramiral hears from Berker?" Ekrem asked.

It was the most important question. We were doomed the moment he got word of the amir's death. "The journey to Ayarazi took us over three days. But that was with a full ship with a kaptan who knew the Pass better than anyone," I said.

"Very humble, this one is." Oron mumbled.

I shrugged. "It's the truth. We don't have the sun for humility." Ekrem and Serhat nodded. "Berker will have half, maybe less of his crew, if my guess on the death toll is right. Many were unmoving when Calev and I woke Oron at camp. And he can't use Salt Magic like me."

The deck was quiet above now, only the sounds of slaves' bells, water, and sail rigging mixed with an occasional shout from Rukn. Was Calev cleaning the filth from Avi's face right now, cuddling her and bringing her back to who she was? I squeezed my eyes shut. I hoped he was, but I wished my hands were caring for Avi. I knew how to help her without injuring her pride. How to joke and tease to take the sting out of needing someone. She was so much like me that way, the pride and independence.

Oron tugged my sleeve. "Or Berker could already be in Jakobden."

"What is the process once they return?" I asked. "How will they inform the kyros of our offenses?"

Serhat looked as though she could bore a hole in the side of the boat with her eyes. The move to my and Calev's side still niggled at her. Strangely, I respected her for it.

"They will have sent a rock dove with the message to the kyros," Ekrem said. "Then the bird most likely returned two days later with orders. Berker will be given control of the proceedings as he was the highest ranked when the amir was murdered."

"How will Berker and the other fighters know we are even here?" I asked.

"Because of the fight on Quarry Isle, I'd guess the oramiral's master of doves already sent a bird to the amir's court with a full report," Ekrem said.

"So if we have Calev's luck," Oron said with a wry smile, "we might have a day until the oramiral knows for certain he isn't the one that's allowed to kill us. That it'll be Berker's duty to punish us."

Serhat stepped forward. "Yes."

"Berker will punish all of us as far as he is permitted." I blew out a breath, my shoulders heavy. "It will be death, and not in a way I'd choose."

"You have a way you prefer?" Oron's eyebrows lifted.

"I'd take a heart collapse while sleeping, or maybe by the yatagan," I said.

Oron nodded. "As opposed to drawing and quartering."

"Exactly," I said. "Or being burned alive."

"Hmm. Yes." Oron tapped his chin. "That is not one of my favorites. I'd like an exotic poison."

"Do you have a plan, kaptan?" Ekrem popped his knuckles.

I smiled grimly. The thought that he still considered me a kaptan of anything was no less than a miracle.

"Actually, I do. If Calev and my sister are treated as equals, they may not be as closely guarded. If the oramiral imprisons us near his own compound —I'm hoping for this because he won't be certain what to do once he's heard who Calev is—then maybe Calev can break us out. We can steal a boat."

"And then?" Ekrem leaned toward me.

I met his eyes. "We go to Ayarazi. Mine silver. Buy our way out of trouble. Shove some of it up Berker's tail."

The ship lurched, and I bent my knees to keep my footing. Oron and Serhat grabbed the same rung of the ladder. He winked at her, and she pulled her hand away as the slaves lifted the grating over our heads.

"Up, prisoners," Rukn said. "It is time to meet Death."

CHAPTER THIRTY-SEVEN

With pushes and yatagan tips, they ushered us onto the island. Avi slipped. Calev caught her and my world shriveled around me. The only thing keeping me from screaming until I went mad was the chance that Calev and Avi would be sent home to safety. Calev would figure out what to do about the lie concerning Avi. Somehow he would charm his father into protecting her. They would be safe. I could get through this with that knowledge.

As the slave guards turned us down the path's right fork, toward the oramiral's housing, I peered up at the castle fortress where we'd found my sister. Guards stood at the door, calm and armed, as if the entire fight hadn't even happened, but the earth showed the effects of our struggle. Blackened ground, crisped grass, and trees like a corpse's dead fingers surrounded the path that led to the fortress and stretched up to the quarry.

Plumes of white dust floated from that far-off area. A handful of slaves, small from the distance, pushed metal carts up the hill away from the quarry, bringing the valuable stone toward us, toward the docks, where it would be shipped to the highest bidder.

The sun was a brand on my exposed arms and nose. The oramiral had set the slaves to work during the heat of the day as punishment for the uprising. A shudder made me lose my step and Serhat grabbed my elbow. This was all my fault.

Now instead of Ekrem and Serhat living to serve and fight and be rewarded, they would be killed. Tortured and killed.

Oron too.

I squeezed my eyes shut and opened them, searching for his stocky silhouette in the messy line of slaves behind us. He walked between two large men, eyes scanning the island. Oron wasn't a very brave person, compared to Ekrem, Serhat, and Calev, but he'd stood by us the whole way just like every day since I'd met him.

The day Oron came into our lives, I'd been eleven years. The fever had dragged Mother and Father away the week before. It hadn't touched Avi. It had hounded me. I remembered a hearty knock on the door of our hut. Avi had cracked it open, then turned to me.

"It's a tiny man, Kinneret."

Oron had edged his way in, taking a moment to touch the shamar yam Calev had tied to our lintel. "I heard you have a boat."

I'd thought he was there to steal from us. Head pounding, I'd pushed off my grass mat, grabbed Father's dagger, and pointed it at Oron. "So what if we do?"

He held up his thick hands. "I'm an excellent first mate. I heard you might need one."

"You'd work for a young girl?"

"Oh, yes." His voice had a flat tone to it. It reminded me of the traders from the North. A filthy bunch of people, Father had always said.

"I find the female mind far sharper than any male's," Oron said. "And you tend to smell much better."

He was teasing me. I raised the dagger.

"Plus, a woman will oftentimes pity a poor soul such as myself. Seeing as I've been cheated on height."

"So you'll work for me, but only because no one else will hire you."

Oron smiled. "You see, the female mind. There it is again, being sharp."

"Father said northerners were dirty. Will you keep the boat clean as I direct you?"

He'd laughed then, a big laugh that made him hold his gut and put tears in his eyes. "I don't think your good father was speaking of mud or offal. He meant something entirely different."

I hadn't understood him then, but after years spent watching him drink and give ladies coppers for time spent in tavern corners, I'd learned.

Oron was roguish, but he was also quick with the sail's lines like no one. He worked hard when he worked. Best sailor I'd ever met. He had saved my life and Avi's.

Blinking the memories away, I put a hand over my heart. I realized I loved Oron nearly as much as I'd loved my parents and aunt.

Before we entered the oramiral's house, I glanced at Oron again. He clucked his tongue loudly and held up one finger, two, then three. Count, he mouthed.

He wanted to keep a count of the slave guards we saw. He hadn't given up hope then.

Had I?

Four yellow tunics walked in front of Serhat, Ekrem, and me. In front of them, two escorted Avi and Calev. Ten—no, twelve—ambled up the path near Oron. I'd seen two at the castle fortress. None stood at the oramiral's wide door, but surely there would be a few inside. I didn't know how many were up at the quarry. It was hopeless. We could never fight off that many. If they could find weapons, Ekrem and Serhat could cut through five each, but aside from them, only Calev was good with a dagger. Avi, Oron, and I were near to pointless. Obstacles, really, for Ekrem, Serhat, and Calev.

They rounded us into an entry room with a flat stone floor and a low ceiling. My sister gave me a brave smile, her sunken cheeks making it a mockery of what it normally looked like. I smiled back, bile rising in my throat. I couldn't wish or pray any harder that she could leave this place with Calev and never set one foot on its horrible shores again.

Near Avi, the biggest of the slave guards had hands on Ekrem and Serhat. Oron stood beside me still and I craned my neck to find Calev's face in the assemblage. He met my gaze immediately and my blood pulsed hard through my body.

He glanced at the slave nearest him. The short-haired woman stared ahead, not noticing us. Calev looked back and mouthed, *I will get you out.*

I nodded tersely, my blood shuddering through my arms, making me want to strike out at these people who thought they could take our freedom at will. What gave them the right to take anyone they wanted and do as they pleased? Just because the oramiral was the kyros's cousin didn't mean he should be able to mistreat slaves, take orphans from Kurakia's mussel shoals to slave outside their own culture, and do pretty much whatever he wanted?

My breath came too quickly. This room was too small. Too filled with sweating people and hate and desperation. How could beautiful stone or silver be worth a ruined innocent's life?

I never thought I'd think it, but now, now I hated silver. Hated what it made people do. Good people and bad.

"You gave a good fight," the well-muscled slave beside me whispered, eyes trained on the oramiral. "We wish you would've won."

My mouth fell open. I spun to whisper back, to find out what exactly he meant and how that might help our situation, but he was raised to his full height now and gave no indication that he'd even said anything to me. His hands shook at his sides as he looked toward the dark corridor at the back of the room.

I turned to Oron. The slave on Oron's far side glanced at me, then gave me a terse nod, something that spoke of respect.

A shrill voice came out of a dark corridor in the back of the room. The slave near Oron whipped his head around and a muscle in the man's jaw tensed.

The oramiral's head brushed the ceiling as he walked out of the corridor. What did he do to these strong slaves to make them fear him so much?

The oramiral's chin was shaved smooth, his cheeks sharp and proud. With his slanted eyes and straight nose, I had to admit that, while he had none of Calev's breathtaking presence and his hair had grayed at the edges, the oramiral was a very handsome man. Strange looking, but not in an off-putting way. His odd features made him exotic.

He took a porcelain cup of tea from a skinny little slave walking behind him and slurped its cinnamon-scented contents. His one pearl earring flashed as he returned the cup to the slave's tray and clapped his hands together.

"Ah, the incredibly ignorant fools are here. Perfect."

The ends of his yellow silk tunic billowed as he crossed the room to Rukn, whose deferential bow only made him look even more like an oversized monkey.

Rukn rose and held a hand toward Calev.

My heart punched through a beat and seized up. Please, don't hurt him. Please, believe him.

"This one is Old Farm," Rukn said. "He claims the scrap of a girl—taken as punishment for her sister's trespassing in your waters—is his recent Intended."

The oramiral's eyes narrowed as he clasped his hands behind his back and stepped toward Calev. "I suppose you have your sigil ring?"

Calev lifted his thumb so the oramiral could examine the slip of gold. "I am Calev ben Y'hoshua. Son of Y'hoshua ben Aharon."

The oramiral clicked his tongue. "Old Farm. I know this sigil."

The oramiral may've been one of the amir's favorites, but he certainly didn't live by her formal manners. She would've always used his full name. It wasn't a good sign. He wasn't showing proper respect.

"And it's true," he said. "A true sigil." He raised himself up and extended his arms. "I welcome you to stay here the night and my slaves will sail you to Old Farm in the morning."

What about Avi?

Calev's face whitened. "I accept. Do you admit to your mistake with my Intended? Such action is punishable by drawing and quartering by the first law of the first kyros."

"Oh ho. Someone knows their laws, do they?" He smiled. "Does the law consider a different recourse when said Old Farm mounts a full attack on my island without attempting to speak to me first?" He tapped two fingers on Calev's chest. "Would've saved the both of us a great deal of trouble, yes?"

My gut went cold. Calev held his chin high.

"I will honor your claim on the girl," the oramiral said quietly. He spun as a chunk of my heart stitched itself back together.

At least Calev and Avi would be safe. Maybe this afternoon, or tonight when they were busy with the night work at the quarry, Calev could free the rest of us.

"But," the oramiral said, "the rest will die. Now."

My head seemed to float above my body. Not yet. "What about torture?" I asked.

All eyes turned to me. Oron smacked his forehead.

But I had a plan. If we could stall our deaths, maybe Calev could get us free somehow. He might figure out a way to get us out if night fell and he had some cover. I just had to stall for time, had to drag this out, or we'd be dead before anyone had a chance to do anything.

"I heard you are fantastic at torturing people." I wondered a bit how mad I'd gone. My voice wasn't shaking nearly as much as my knees. I blinked to clear my light head. "Now you're going to kill us without any excitement at all? Dull."

A small laugh came from the back of the oramiral's throat. "Well now. This one is quite the surprise." He put a finger under my chin. His skin smelled like women's perfume. "But you are only stalling. Are you worth a wait, I wonder?"

I breathed in and out, the sound loud, too loud. "Fine." He nodded.

Strong hands pushed me from behind, and I fell to the floor, my palms striking the stone and sending pain jolting up my arms.

"Stop." Calev's voice only made this worse. I didn't want him to suffer too.

"My apologies, Old Farm, but aside from the archaic law that I will not break because of my relationship with the amir, you have no power here," the oramiral said.

The oramiral grabbed my hair. I clenched my jaw to keep from shouting.

"I think I'll give you my mark. Though I'll most likely throw you into the sea and your wraith form won't show it later, I'd like to claim you somehow. You are so very exciting."

I heard Calev's shouting and struggle as if it was happening far away, in another world.

A chill scratched through me. The oramiral was going to throw me into the Pass. I'd become a Salt Wraith. I opened and closed my hands, imagining salt sharpening my fingers and vengeance as my only drive.

The oramiral didn't give me time to pity myself. He flashed a dagger from his sash.

"Stop!" Calev called out again, and I heard the smack of knuckles to flesh. Calev grunted and brought down every Old Farm curse known to mankind.

Avi's crying grew louder.

Oron tried to grab me and was dragged away to the side of the room.

I had to drown them out. To focus and keep the oramiral's mind on me.

Between the oramiral's fingers, an emerald the size of a bumblebee blinked from his dagger's hilt. The oramiral glanced at the slave holding me.

"He doesn't need to keep me down," I said. "I'll take your punishment. I'm not afraid of you."

I jerked my arm free of the slave's grasp.

The oramiral smiled wide. The steel blade's tip made a small line down my forearm. The pain was bright like the sun at midday. Shocking and loud and never faltering.

"My sigil is simple. Just a cut stone atop a silver coin." His eyes looked into mine. They were as lovely as a snake's when it tries to charm you before striking. "Fitting, don't you think?"

He turned the tip slowly, pressing it into my flesh, to make one corner of the quarried rock, another, and another, until the shape was complete.

Calev exploded from the back of the room. The oramiral stood and shouted as Calev raged through the crowd. Slaves reached for him with slow hands, almost half-hearted in their attempts. Calev's eyes were storms and his blue tunic whipped around him like wind-churned clouds. He snagged a yatagan from the nearest slave's sash and hurled it at the oramiral.

The man dove right and his laugh echoed off the low ceiling. He caught Calev by the throat as the yatagan clanged to the floor.

My heart jumped and strained as I struggled to my feet.

Oron slipped to my side and pulled me back as I eyed the fallen weapon. "No, Kinneret. It won't work."

Backing Calev against the wall, the oramiral's fingers tensed on Calev's throat. Calev's eyes were unblinking. He kicked at the older man, who deftly bumped the strike to the side. The oramiral pressed his body against Calev's, keeping Calev's legs from moving. The oramiral pinned one of Calev's arms to the wall and secured the other with his elbow.

"Stay out of this Old Farm. I don't want your community or the amir's wrath set on me for injuring you, but if you interfere with my work, I'm within my rights to strike you down, or at least, ruin that face of yours. It's nearly as fine as mine. It would be a shame, really."

His gaze slid over Calev's headtie, down his cheeks, and I struggled against Oron. I could strike him now and he would be dead. If I could make my move before his slaves caught me.

"Impossible odds, Kin," Oron hissed.

The oramiral pulled back and knocked Calev across the temple with the dagger's hilt. Calev dropped to the floor, eyes shut.

Returning to me, the oramiral sighed. "That was delightful. Now to finish this torture you are so insistent upon, my sweet."

Blood was ink on my skin, showing the lines of my pain, the strokes of the man who had started me down this path to death.

But really, this was my fault.

So I forced myself to take the pain of the oramiral's dagger. I ignored Avi's cries and Oron's swearing. I didn't dwell on Ekrem's shouts of mercy or Serhat's sucked breaths and murmurs of my accomplishments to the slaves. I didn't even look at Calev on the floor.

I lived in the pain.

The dagger cut the circular shape of a silver coin into my arm as sweat drained from my hairline, down my temples, dripping onto my chest.

"You should smile, sailor." The oramiral's voice was a caress in the red dark of the pain. "You have demons and I'm cutting them out of you."

My eyes flashed open.

He nodded sagely. "I, too, have demons. I know the look of one who knows she deserves the pain. So smile about it. Smile."

"I won't do anything for you. I'm nothing like you."

"Oh, no? You caused all this trouble for these people, these innocents."

"But I've learned from it. I won't repeat my cruelties."

"Smile."

"No."

His eyes glittered and he lifted the blade to my mouth. "Yes." He slipped the tip into the side of my mouth and nipped the dagger up.

I pulled back, and he grabbed my wrist, the one he'd cut. My head swam. It was a small slit, the one where my lips met, but the pain was so much, too much.

"Now you have a jaunty grin, at least." He jerked me into his face. "I always get my way."

At least Calev and Avi might live. It was the only thing keeping me from crumbling in on myself.

It was the light shining through the pain.

An agonizingly familiar voice came from the door behind us.

The oramiral found his feet and looked over me and the rest of the crowd.

"The message was accurate," the slippery voice said. "My sources said the traitors were here and here you are. Greetings, oramiral."

The voice hung in the air as my ears buzzed and my cuts flamed.

Berker.

CHAPTER THIRTY-EIGHT

The oramiral pushed through us to meet Berker. On shaking legs, I stood to see them hold palms up to one another.

"Welcome to my island," the oramiral said.

As they traded formal greetings, Calev rose from the floor, rubbing his head. His face was flushed, but when he was standing, he went pale. He started toward me. Swallowing roughly, he heaved a heavy breath and gritted his teeth. His gaze was on my arm, then my mouth.

I turned toward our enemies.

Berker smiled darkly and his gaze slid to me. "That one, Kinneret Raza, low-caste sailor, she killed the amir."

"What?" Oron struggled against his captors.

The oramiral's face dropped and his lips parted. The shock changed his features. For once, he looked weak, unsure. He swallowed. "Truly?"

Crossing the room to me, Berker tapped my leg with his shoe. "Did you think you would get away with this, scrapper?"

I wasn't about to tell them it was Calev's hand who struck the amir down. If I could convince Berker and the oramiral that I took Calev against his will, at dagger-point, I could get him out. He could still get away and take Avi with him. If Berker didn't recognize my sister. I didn't think he'd ever had the chance to see her. I'd try to get Ekrem and Serhat out of it too, and Oron. I had always been fantastic with lies.

"I almost escaped," I said proudly.

He sniffed. "I don't think so."

"Oh no? I coerced my first mate, an Old Farm, and two fighters into thinking the amir had gone mad and attacked me first and that you wouldn't believe me. That if I could get away to the oramiral and tell my story, we would set things right. I'm a good liar. It was only the tangle of the oramiral mistakingly taking the Old Farm's Intended as a slave that tripped me up."

Hopefully, Berker and the oramiral wouldn't begin figuring the days or order in which the events happened.

Narrowing his eyes, Berker leaned closer. His breath smelled like fish and tatlilav left in the sun. "Where is that sister you were so determined to rescue?"

This was the hitch. He knew why I'd set out with the amir to the lost island of silver.

"She's dead. We came for both her and Calev's Intended. We infiltrated this horrible island, set a fire as distraction, and broke into the old castle fortress. We saw my sister…" I shuddered for effect and nudged the gash on my lip to increase my pain and wash the color from my face. I stared at Berker. "She was dead in a corner. We took up Calev's Intended and used wings of cloth to glide to the sea."

"Is this a child's sleeping mat? Am I to believe this outrageous nighttime story?" He turned to the oramiral.

"It is true, Kaptan Berker. Parts of it, at the least." The oramiral's lip twitched, and he touched the jeweled dagger that sat once again in his sash. "They sailed through the air on framed cloth supports. It was a wonder. Too bad she will die for it. She is rather clever. And quirky."

Berker raised his eyebrows.

"She asked for torture." The oramiral grinned, turning my stomach.

I swallowed bile, and cold sweat washed over my back and face. My arm throbbed, but I focused on Berker's face, on the oramiral's. They had to believe this.

"And Ekrem and Serhat." I nodded at the fighters. "They were persuaded to help me because of their duty to the kyros's law. To the agreement between the Empire and Old Farm. In the face of the amir going mad, they felt they had to help Calev. That he was their duty. And the tiny man…" Oron flinched, but I kept on, guilt gutting me. "The dwarf is a fool. He believes anything anyone tells him."

"Why bring him along at all?" the oramiral snapped.

Maybe if I spun this well, Oron could find a life here. It wouldn't be one he liked, but a bad life is still better than none at all. "Because he works the lines like he was born to it. You'd take him too if you knew his skills. He's the one who designed the gliders. He is dull as a training blade when it comes to people, facts, and lies, but with mechanics, he's a genius."

Oron squeezed his eyes shut. Tears ran from under his lids and his chest heaved.

The oramiral clapped his hands, his face grave. "In light of the developments then, I hand this criminal to you." He pointed at me. "Slaves ten and twenty-three, take the Old Farm and his Intended to Jakobden."

The slaves shuffled Calev and Avi toward the door. Avi sobbed. "Kinneret!"

Keep your tongue, Sister. Keep quiet. Don't give yourself away.

The prayer went around and around in my thoughts like a miller's wheel. I stood and looked at her, tears burning the cut at my mouth. I nodded once curtly, not wanting to ruin my lie. Her mouth opened and she went limp, fainting in the slave's grip. He scooped her up and took her through the door, into the light.

Calev twisted in the slaves' clutches, his eyes a lightning bolt into mine. It was as if he was saying *No. I won't let you do this.*

I knew his thoughts as well as I knew my own. He'd get Avi home, even if it meant my death. He knew what that meant to me, to both of us. But he would do everything in his power, to his last breath, to get back to this island before they killed me, and pull me out of the flames.

I know, I mouthed. A sad smile pulled at my cut. Blood, hot and salty, poured over my lips and down my chin. Our gazes locked and flames washed through my skin, my muscles tensing. His eyes were brighter, darker, more alive than anyone else's. *I love you.*

While Berker and the oramiral convened, the slaves tried to jerk Calev out of the door, but he turned quick and freed one arm, enough to give him a second to mouth back.

I will come for you. I will return.

They pulled him away and he was gone.

I fell to my knees, relief a sweet taste on my tongue. I could withstand anything if I could see them safe, as well as Oron and the fighters.

Ekrem and Serhat could handle themselves in the trial. Because that's surely what Berker would do. He would have to take them back to Jakobden. There was no avoiding it, but after all this, they could handle it with the story I'd given them. Serhat wouldn't want to lie, but Ekrem would lead her where she needed to go. He would slip them both past death, at least. They'd be tortured, but not killed. Ekrem would see to it. He was a survivor. I knew when I saw one, because I was one too.

Until now.

Now I was a sacrifice.

My heart settled into the role. Someone had to take the blame for the amir's death. And if Calev had spoken up, we'd all have suffered the worst of what Berker and the oramiral could think up. It had to be me. It made sense.

"Little man," the oramiral said. "I will take you myself, as payment for my trouble. I could use a fine sailor on my full ship. And I want a set of gliders. They would be rather diverting, I think. Berker, I assume you must take the two fighters who aided in this with you to face trial in Jakobden."

Berker was rubbing his chin, one arm tucked under the other. He hadn't yet fully swallowed the hook. "Yes," he said quietly. "I suppose so."

His gaze flicked to Oron, who'd gone white around the mouth. Oron stared at the flat stones beneath the oramiral's curved-toe slippers.

Berker's eyes widened. "It's all settled then. I won't need to take this girl back. She killed the amir. Coerced the amir's fighters and an Old Farm into breaking the law. She will die now. But first, first I think, she should prove her dagger skills to us. There should be a test of her ability."

The oramiral frowned. "Why do we care how she is with a dagger?"

But I knew. My heart iced over. If they saw how weak I was with the weapon, they'd know there was no way I could've surprised and murdered the amir. The amir had been the sharpest of fighters in her youth. Though she'd been older when Calev killed her, she was still fast. She'd still had her fighter's sense. If I couldn't prove myself with a dagger, this entire rescue mission would very quickly spin into the abyss like a sucking whirlpool, taking all my loved ones with it.

Maybe if I simply showed confidence now, they would leave off the test.

I stood, my head spinning and my wounds growling and burning.

"I'll do it." I smiled and let the cut rip open wider. Blood spilled down my chin and I knew I looked as evil as I needed to look. "I love to show off in front of high-caste weaklings."

Berker's gasp was a nice little gift even though my stomach tried to crawl out of my mouth.

The oramiral shook his head. "She is wonderful. Now let us find a suitable spot for this test."

Berker nodded and started out the door with the oramiral at his side.

THE WHITE WALLS of the quarry blinded me, the dust coating my throat and my teeth. The sun poured onto my head like molten gold, all the beauty taken and replaced with scorching heat. Sweat ran along my temples and rose from the crooks in my arms as I followed Berker and the oramiral. Their men marched behind us. Their faces didn't give away whether they believed I'd killed the amir or not. They might not have cared. The amir never did anything for them. She allowed the oramiral to take whomever he chose as a slave.

Like someone needed burning after death, we were a double-line of grim-faced mourners headed into the very belly of the place that had been my sister's nightmare.

I twisted to find her in the crowd. Two large, gray-shirted slaves stood at her sides. One held her arm with spindly fingers. She leaned toward him like he was a friend rather than a captor. Made sense. She was probably still so weak. Bile rose in my throat. Monsters. All of them. My poor little Avi. I gave her a sad smile and she blinked like a sweet, tiny owl with wings that had been plucked naked.

I breathed out my nose, trying to keep my rage in check, to keep my story believable. She was my friend's Intended. Not my sister. It was the only way she'd get out of here alive.

Berker's gaze scanned the faces around me. I wished he'd get on with this. I was either going to pass the test or not. Freedom for Avi and Calev or the end for us all.

Standing around frying to death wasn't going to change the situation.

"I'm here. You have the dagger. What else do you need?" My arm thumped with the rhythm of my heart. "Should I put on a new skirt and do a little twirl?"

Berker's eyes went dead. "I'm looking for your target." Despite the heat, a chill gnawed at my bones.

Calev stepped up and put himself between Berker and her. "I'll be the target."

I couldn't move.

But it was probably good I was frozen. Berker's dead eyes and oddly quiet voice told me his mood was like the first kyros's fireblooms, a technology lost in time. The old stories said when Quest knights rode over the silent explosives waiting under the road's dust, they didn't have time to scream before the sudden flash ate them whole. Berker was waiting like that, biding time to explode.

"Fine." Berker pointed to the far wall of the quarry. "Stand there, if you would, Calev ben Y'hoshua."

He said Calev's full name like it was a curse. Stupid man. If he knew anything, he'd make sure not to say the name, the name that brought all kinds of luck down on us. A cruel grin tugged at my lips.

"Old Farms are so brave!" the oramiral shouted, and clapped his hands like an idiot. "I hope your aim is good, sailor."

Because Calev volunteered himself, they had to go along with it.

"Now." Berker offered me a dagger, the amir's jeweled dagger. In his other hand, he held a fig.

"Kind of you to offer refreshment, but I can't say I'm overly hungry."

"You will place the fig," he came close, "on your lover's head," he whispered. His breath smelled like old butter and sour wine. "You will spear it with the blade from thirty paces."

I couldn't do it. I didn't have the skill. I would kill Calev right here, right now. "If I don't?" If I can't?

"You'll all be put to death. I think you may be protecting the Old Farm."

I forced my voice not to shake. "Why would he kill the amir?"

"That I don't know. But she was a trained fighter. Seasoned. You are a dock rat. The Old Farm and the two fighting sailors with you are the only ones who could've done it. Since you're lying about your sister, you're doing all of this to protect them both. It has convinced the oramiral. But not me. Failing in this test will convince the oramiral of the truth."

One old question bumped against my lips, forcing its way out. "Why do you say my mother was a liar?"

"Your parents and I tested for release on the same day. Your witch of a mother lied to the masters, claiming your father solved our group's assigned problem instead of me. The apprentice masters gave your father and mother the last two spots, and I slaved here for three more years." He spat at my feet.

I tried to hold myself calm, to still my trembling bones, but my teeth chattered. Was he lying? It felt true, though my heart fought the story. My mother had betrayed him and saved my father. After seeing the slave island with my own eyes, I understood some of his venom. But even if it was true, this wasn't justice.

"I am not my mother."

"No. But when I hurt you, I am closer to feeling satisfied. This is your penance. Your family wronged me."

Shoving past Berker, I stormed toward Calev. My throat caught at the courage in his eyes.

"You can do this, Kinneret," he whispered, no idea that my world had tipped into madness. "I'll save Avi. I'll come back. Old Farm will not stand for this. I won't let them."

He'd need a boatload of silver to talk anyone into saving anyone from the oramiral, especially if Berker ended up in a power position. Which, as the amir's kaptan, he would. He might even secure the position of amir himself. I shuddered.

My hand shook as I placed the tiny fig on Calev's head. It took every shred of my willpower not to touch his face as my hand lowered. One last touch. One last lightning bolt of joy.

"Berker knows," I said.

"He'll be paid. I'll make certain Old Farm deals well with him. If he remembers that someday I will most likely take the chairman position, he will enjoy having this to hold over me."

I swallowed. It wouldn't be a happy life for Calev. Especially if Berker bought his way to being the amir. He'd have the silver from Ayarazi, and buying people and power was the Jakobden way.

"I will see you soon, then."

Calev blinked. A tear ran from his eye. "Soon, my fire."

I grew taller, stronger. I flexed my hand, fisted it, and pressed it against my thigh instead of my heart so no one else would see my declaration of love for Calev. *My fire.*

His lips tucked into a quick grin. My mouth longed to kiss his, to press into the feel and smell and strength of him. I took a heavy, deep breath of the dusty air.

"Sailor," Berker called out behind me. "Now."

The cuts on my arm and mouth throbbed as I put steel around my heart, walked thirty paces back, and threw the knife.

CHAPTER THIRTY-NINE

The clouds hung in the sky. Though the sea cliffs were close by, the waves didn't crash, and the birds froze, suspended above us. The dagger rushed through the space between Calev and me. It was a tear in the colors of the world. A flash. An opening to the white, hot torture of knowing I'd killed my best friend, my love.

The weapon's arc bent. I'd missed.

It was going to hit him directly in the eye. Immediate death.

In that moment of a frozen world, when nothing but the dagger moved, I aged one thousand years. I was an old woman. My body was thin and insubstantial as chaff. Crevices marred my smooth skin, a line for every pain, every crime, every tragedy of my life. Mother. Father. Avi. Oron. Calev. The lines went on and on, from my eyes, along my cheek, to my neck and knobbed hands. But my eyes remained clear. It was my penance in that eternity of a moment—to see Calev's red-brown eyes and the trust glowing from them the moment before I killed him.

"I'm sorry."

His thick eyelashes lowered slowly, so slowly, then lifted again as the dagger landed.

My heart screamed. He wasn't dead. I'd missed wide, but only by a hand. It was enough to prove my lie. Maybe.

Calev's eyes widened. Scooping the fig from his head, he turned to look where the dagger had landed, far to the left.

All my energy poured out of me and I fought to stay standing. Calev was alive. I hadn't killed him.

Giving me a solemn nod, Calev started toward the crowd like all was settled. Hopefully, he'd find Avi and stay with her. I wanted them off this disgusting island now. Yesterday. My head buzzed.

"Well done," Berker said, face void of any emotion. He glanced at two fighting sailors—one stocky, the other with hair like a cactus. "Tie her. Neck to wrists. Wrists to ankles. She has a meeting with the sea."

An invisible battle axe chopped at my temples and the base of my skull. The buzzing grew louder.

It was time to die.

Please, I prayed. *If I must become a Salt Wraith, make me a weak one, unable to harm.*

I had to let go of my vengeance. If my heart clenched the hot anger for Tuz Golge for Infusing Calev, the oramiral for taking my sister, Berker for…everything, I'd have the power to Infuse masses and cause the death of countless innocents.

The spiky-haired fighter wrapped coconut rope around my wrists, making a slipknot. Had he realized how easy it would be for me to get out of that? Of course, where would I go?

The fighter glanced over his shoulder at Berker as he gave the ends of the rope to the other fighter, who wove them around my neck. The men tied my ankles. Another slipknot. The rope scratched at my skin as I turned to search for Avi and Calev.

Calev was looking left and right. The wind lifted his hair as he scowled at Berker.

"Where is my Intended?" Calev asked.

My skin itched with worry and the rough texture of the fibers. The man holding onto Oron's arm pushed him through the other belled slaves and the large group of leather-clothed fighting sailors.

Oron stood in front of the oramiral and Berker, and I frowned.

My first mate gave me an odd look, then faced our captors. "Kinneret Raza did not kill the amir. Calev ben Y'hoshua did."

A spear of ice gored me. "No."

I lunged toward Oron, but the fighters held me. I had to stop him, shake sense into him.

"What?" The oramiral bent toward Oron, but Berker put a hand on his chest.

"What are you saying, dwarf?" Berker's eyes narrowed.

"Don't worry, Kinneret," Oron said. "Avigail is off the island."

"He's lying." I struggled against the men's grip. "I killed her. I did."

Oron swallowed loudly, his eyes watery. "I can't allow you to die for Calev, Kinneret. You're too important, too bright, to die for a crime you didn't commit."

My mind wouldn't soak in his words. This had to be a nightmare. I was asleep. This wasn't happening.

"Silence." Berker waved a hand toward the ground and the slave shoved Oron to his knees.

The men holding me did the same and I hit the ground hard.

"Avigail left with Ekrem and Serhat," Oron said.

Berker smacked him and spit flew from Oron's mouth.

The oramiral straightened and put hands on his hips. "Are you saying the two disloyal fighting sailors escaped? They took the Old Farm's Intended?" He looked to Berker. "Someone please tell me what is happening here."

Berker grabbed Oron by the hair. "Explain."

Oron's throat moved and lines of moisture ran down his face. "They escaped. So they wouldn't suffer when I told you the truth. The Old Farm," he said it with spite, like he'd never cared for Calev at all, like Calev was a stranger, not a friend, "he was Infused when he stabbed the amir. He did it. Not Kinneret. Kinneret is innocent. Calev ben Y'hoshua coerced us all to help him. With his high position, none of us dared oppose the man."

"No…" I realized then I was sobbing. Avi, Ekrem, and Serhat were safe. But Oron? Calev? They were doomed. Their deaths showed in Berker's shining black eyes.

Berker grew very, very still. "What should we do?" he hissed.

The oramiral raised his eyebrows and touched his head, lost.

With a single clap of hands that jolted me, Berker said, "I'm finished here. Throw them all into the sea. And catch the fugitives." He scanned the crowd. "Or I'll throw you all in the sea along with them."

Bells clanking, slaves and fighters grabbed Calev. They dragged us toward the opening in the quarry.

In the crush of sweating bodies, confused murmurs, and the oramiral's shouted commands to make for the cliffs, I found myself within arm's length of Calev, though bound as I was I couldn't reach for him.

A wrinkle appeared between his eyes under his blue headtie. "I'm sorry. I should've told them right away, but Avigail—"

"You were saving her." My throat tried to close around my sobs. "Don't apologize. But…but they'll catch Avi. They haven't had enough sun to escape far enough away yet. Do you think…think maybe your father has sent ships out to look for you yet? Maybe if they find them first...maybe... this is all my fault. All of it. My recklessness and going after the silver and—"

Calev's jaw worked, and his eyes bored into mine. "None of this is your fault. You wanted the silver to change your caste, to improve your life, Oron's, and Avigail's. That's noble. That's a dream worth every risk. If anything, this is all my fault. If only I'd moved faster the night Tuz Golge..."

I stumbled on a rock and the fighter holding me pulled me up before I could fall, my wounds stinging.

"I..." Calev was the picture of misery. "I love you, Kinneret." My heart blazed.

Oron appeared at my side. "As touching as that was, the whole death-confession-moment is entirely unnecessary."

"What?" I choked and coughed dust out of my throat.

Oron shrugged, one slave still holding his arm. The slave grinned.

"We just needed another moment. And a nice distraction. The slaves and the fighting sailors," Oron said, "are going to rise up against Berker."

I froze. My captors pulled me onward.

Calev's mouth dropped open. "When?"

"What do we need to do?" I searched the faces of the men and women around us, but none gave up the game.

Oron licked his chapped lips. "When they take you to the cliff's edge, call up some of your fine Salt Magic, my kaptan." He grinned.

Nothing was funny.

"Don't scowl at me, sweet," he said. "I do think you're too special to die."

"That's not why—"

"I think if you're going to die, it should be for one of the many fantastic crimes you actually have committed. It's a shame to take the handsome one's single chance at infamy."

Calev looked offended. "Single chance? I've committed as many crimes as Kinneret. What about falling for a low-caste?"

"Oh, that's not worthy of infamy really," Oron said. "You've missed the good crimes. Kinneret never takes you along for the truly spectacular infractions."

Calev's gaze went to me. "What have you done without me?"

I threw my head back. How could they be joking right now? "Fire and Sea, give me patience. Just a few pre-harvest opening runs up the northern coast. Nothing that should be illegal. Now where exactly is my sister?"

Before Oron could answer, we were at the cliffs.

The wind, salty and carrying grit, buffeted my body. The slaves and fighters pushed us toward the edge. My foot kicked a clump of sandy dirt from its grassy perch. The earth fell until it disappeared into the roiling waves and angry rocks below. If the men and women around us were making a show of this, they were certainly convincing.

Calev and Oron tugged and jerked as slaves tied their wrists, ankles, and necks, as mine were. Berker and the oramiral slithered around the right side of the group. The oramiral crossed his arms and smiled like this was all a fantastic bit of entertainment. Both his and Berker's tunics waved in the wind—yellow, black, and red.

"I, Kaptan Berker Deniz, declare you, Calev ben Y'hoshua, as killer of Amir Mamluk of Jakobden of the Broken Coast. I declare you, Oron No Name, and you, Kinneret Raza, as conspirators in this man's terrible plan. I give you to the sea."

I didn't have salt for magic and if I did, I couldn't grab it. My wrists were still bound. Why hadn't they untied me on our walk here? Too risky? So I was meant to be the final distraction. If I created a spectacle, the slaves and fighting sailors could hit Berker, the oramiral, and those loyal to him as they looked on.

The tallest of the slaves eyed me and held Calev over the cliff's edge. Calev simply closed his eyes. The muscles in his arms were relaxed, and his lips moved in what I guessed was a silent prayer. I couldn't believe how calm he was.

Then he looked at me, and I knew.

He was calm, because he believed I could pull this off. That I could make magic happen and save us all. Respect. He respected me. I wasn't just the one he joked or played pranks with, the person he kissed for fun. He was following my lead.

I laughed.

The people around me frowned like I'd gone mad. But I was happy, not crazed.

Calev had been following my lead this entire journey. I'd only now seen it. He did love me. And he respected me, believed in me. I wasn't about to disappoint him.

I chanted under my breath, fast and sharp, as I dug salt from under my fingernails.

The Fire and the sea listen.
Listen, please to me.
Your chosen prays along with me."

My eyes flicked to Calev, whose beautiful lips whispered as I spoke to the sea.

Shaking, I slowly raised my voice.

"Lift the winds.

Bring them from the waves.

Bring them high to shield us.

With your power, crash.

Arise. Blast across this field.

Remind all who made this sea and the magic in it."

A spot on the horizon, far out into the Pass, flattened into a watery sheen, like an air-filled sail. It grew toward us, spreading out and on until the sea below the cliff didn't hold a single wrinkle.

It was wind. Sheering across the water. Rising.

The massive gust roared up the cliff and threw Calev and me back, showering everyone in sea spray.

I laughed as Berker shouted, "Salt Witch!" and the oramiral's tunic tangled him, a fancy net around a surprised fish.

The slaves and fighters rose to standing. They'd been prepared, prepped, for this distraction. Their yatagans, axes, and daggers flashed as they turned on their masters, and those few still loyal to them, with wild howls.

Calev had somehow snagged a dagger and, already freed by a stranger, was running toward me with a face of grim determination.

A fighter cut Oron loose, and he turned to see the oramiral's yatagan slicing down. Oron spun.

Before I could shuffle to Calev to shorten his spring, a hand grabbed the rope connecting my neck to my wrists and ankles.

Berker's face leaned into mine.

"Kinneret!" Calev was almost to me when a yellow-tunic wearing slave flung a hand at him. Calev blocked the strike and moved to hit the man.

Berker twisted the rope holding me. My neck burned. Pressure built in my head.

I was choking.

"Your magic won't save you today, witch," he said.

I fumbled with the rope, trying to breathe, to get even a second of air. I brought my knee up like Calev had at the oramiral's house. It connected with Berker's groin and he growled.

He shoved me off the cliff.

CHAPTER FORTY

The air tore at my cheeks, eyelashes, clothing, and hands as I tumbled through nothing. I was headed for rocks or water. I couldn't tell which. If I submerged tied, it wouldn't matter. I would drown. I would still become a wraith.

Fevered, I tucked my thumbs and tried to work my hands free of their ties. The rope bit into my skin as I squeezed, pulled, and fell. One hand slipped free from the rope. I pried the other loose, pain lashing over my cut flesh. Straightening and in a panic, I threw both hands over my head and arched my back to find blue, to find the water, to aim.

The cool blanket of the sea swaddled me.

My head thudded, the deeper water pressing painfully against my eardrums. Green-blue surrounded me. Where was the surface? My lungs screamed for air.

Then luminescence like melted butter slid into view to my left. My ankles still tied, I drove both legs through the water like a fish would, kicking toward the light. I rolled my torso and let a wave of movement course down my body, to my legs. My feet were a tail, a fin.

The light grew.

My lungs sparked and shivered.

I broke the surface with a gasp and swallowed in air, perfect, wonderful air.

Swimming as best I could, I used the movement of the current to drive toward a large rock at the shore. I heard so many noises, broken by the water's sloshing around me. This was taking too long.

Still, I swam. And swam.

I pushed toward the rock, the current helping for a breath, then hauling me out again.

It'd been so long since I fell. My limbs shook with fatigue. If I didn't get to the rock soon and out of the water, I'd miss it all. The battle would already be won or lost.

A heavy swell rose and I went with it, grasping, reaching until my fingers found the nearest rock. The wave crashed and I tucked my head to my shoulder to avoid being bashed senseless against the unforgiving island. Grasping the mussel littered rock, I pulled myself up and scrambled onto the sand. Finally.

Calev. Avi. Oron.

Sheltered by man-sized rocks, I used an emptied oyster shell to cut the rest of my ties. Navigating the rough shore along the cliff's base, I searched the beach for the way back up. The sun had moved. I'd wasted so much light.

"Kinneret!"

I whipped around to face the sea and there, among some wide, flat rocks, under the graying sky, sat a boat with yellow, slack sails. One of the oramiral's, half beached, a hole in its side. Avi huddled near the boat's rope ladder. Her arms shook as she tried to pull back the string on a crossbow. Tears streamed down her cheeks.

On the black and gold sand near the boat, Ekrem, Serhat, Calev, and Oron fought men and women in yellow tunics. The oramiral's personal slaves. Ekrem's yatagan and Serhat's battle axe lashed through the air at their attackers. Calev's dagger was a minnow again. The knife cut the yellow-garbed slave here and there and there again as the slave barely managed glancing blows to Calev's shoulder and arm.

Another fighter—no, it was the oramiral himself—raged down the hill toward Avi. His silken clothing billowed and his mouth leaked blood as he grinned at Avi. His yatagan flashed in the sun.

Ekrem had his opponent on his knees at the prow of the craft.

Soon, he'd be free to fight, but not soon enough to save Avi.

I ran as fast as my shaking legs would carry me. The oramiral would get to Avi before me.

There was no way I could save her.

Avi screamed. "Calev! Kinneret!" Her foot pushed at the base of the crossbow and her fingers strained against the draw weight.

I climbed over the rocks, dodged two dead men.

Oron tried to get to her and suffered a slash from the man fighting him, forcing him back into that life or death fight.

An idea shone in my head. Calev's dagger. It would only work if he acted fast with no questions and only if my guess was right.

"Calev!" I shouted, running. "Your dagger! Northwest, now!"

Without a blink, his hand uncurled in the direction of the approaching fighter. The blade zipped past Avi and speared the oramiral's yellow-swathed chest, right over the heart, with a thick sound. He fell forward into the sand.

Blood poured through his fine clothing as fast as it did any slave's. Caste meant nothing when it came to death. The oramiral was no more.

I smiled grimly. We had done it.

But we didn't have the sun to enjoy the victory.

Calev's attacker grinned at his lack of a weapon as I caught Avi in my arms and threw her to relative safety around the craft's prow. The slave's yatagan arched toward Calev. Just when I thought I'd planned wrong, that my recklessness had once again shadowed a loved one's life, Ekrem finished the man he'd been fighting with one slice across the throat. Ekrem leaped between Calev and the other slave and drove his yatagan into the man's belly.

With a shout of victory, Serhat finished off the man coming at her and Oron scrambled around the back of the man fighting him and stabbed him through the liver. Oron kicked the man into the incoming waves. With that, all our attackers were down and it seemed the gray-clothed slaves had swamped the oramiral's yellow-garbed men on the rise above us.

There was a shout and a cluster of fighting sailors—three large men—scrambled down the slope toward us.

Oron swore. "It's Berker."

My body went numb. My anger was steel and ready to work.

He'd stolen someone's red leather vest. With a yatagan extended and blood running from a deep cut along his face, he and the fighters who remained loyal to him closed in on us.

"Try to edge them around so our backs are to the cliffside," I whispered as Ekrem, Serhat, Oron, Calev, and Avi gathered near.

Berker and his men came in with knees bent and weapons ready.

"You've already lost." I stepped at an angle and silently encouraging Berker toward the sea.

His weasel smile turned my stomach. "No, no. This isn't over. If I capture you, I could convince the rest that you and your little party here must at least go to trial in Jakobden. Isn't it sad? After all you've accomplished, it might still come down to me being high and you low."

Out of the corner of my eye, I saw Calev and Oron helping Avi onto the higher rocks on the cliffside. Ekrem and Serhat stayed close, their blades wonderfully menacing at my sides.

"See?" Berker gestured toward Avi. "Even your most loyal are jumping ship, so to speak. How much easier will it be to persuade the rest of those still alive to follow the laws that have been in place for ages?"

I laughed and rubbed my salty hands together. "I'm pretty convinced I've witched up all the laws now."

His grin faltered.

Reaching my salty fingers toward the shore's rumbling waves, I prayed.

"Waters, meet me, higher, deeper.

I need your cold, your power rushing."

Berker launched his yatagan at me, but the waves were already growling and swamping him and his men. The shush of the sea muffled their shouting. I let myself float below the surface, hoping the others were safe on the cliffside.

In the water, under the rolling wave, I spotted Berker's flailing legs and his men as they fought to swim. The sea was only listening to me and my prayers now. Their strong swimming did nothing. The current sucked the fighters farther and farther until they were only smudges in the blue-gray. Berker's head dipped under the surface as the water pulled him down. He refused to give up his heavy weapon. He met my eyes, jerked once, then sank and sank and sank.

WHEN THE SEA edged away from the shore, Calev retrieved his knife from the oramiral's body, which was lodged between two large rocks.

Soaking wet, I pulled Avi into my arms. I held her tightly, my injuries thumping and complaining. But they were less deep now, still cuts but not bleeding. The sea must've begun to heal them.

"My little lion." I cupped Avi's face as we sat beside the others at the base of the path leading up the cliffs.

Perched on a boulder, Calev and Ekrem were slicking seawater off their heads and laughing. Near them, Oron and Serhat grumbled to one another, but Oron worked a smile out of Serhat.

"I'm so sorry for all of this," I said to Avi. "I'll never put you at risk for something as ridiculous as silver ever, ever again."

She hugged me back, then stared at me. "It wasn't for silver. It was for us. For Calev. Old Zayn. Oron. I know that."

I pressed her sweet head against my shoulder, watching the faint moving shapes above the cliff tops, where the fighting went on. "Promise you'll stop me if I ever try to do something mad again."

"I promise no such thing, Sister." She pulled away and smiled with all her crooked teeth. "We made it through this, didn't we? If we kept to safe things forever, we'd have no kind of life at all."

Oron held a scarf against one of his many cuts. "She'll be insufferable now that she's become so wise."

Over Avi's head, I smiled shakily at him. "I can't believe it. We're alive." I laughed and my throat felt raw.

Calev held out his hands. "Seems we are." He looked at the rest of the island that rose into the sky. "Unless I'm having the strangest dream ever."

Oron rolled his eyes. "In that case, you'd still be alive, Calev. One cannot dream whilst dead." Oron shook his head, then said to me, "Do you truly want to spend large amounts of sunlight with this dolt?"

Calev's dagger whooshed past Oron's shoulder and lodged in a grassy mound.

Calev raised an eyebrow. "This dolt could cut your tongue out if you're not careful."

"Ooo," Oron said.

The sounds of cheering erupted from the top of the island.

Oron pulled Calev's dagger free. "Kinneret always had a penchant for flashy things."

Ekrem, Avi, and Serhat laughed at that, following Oron as he started up the incline.

"We need to find a boat," I said.

"We'll have to get to the dock. It means going back up. Into that." Oron pointed toward the movement on the cliff tops. The goat path we'd used dangled down the rock and growth like a fraying thread.

Agreeing, we started up the incline.

Before we reached the top, a group of slaves in gray and fighting sailors in red danced down toward us, arms around shoulders and chanting something into the salty wind.

"Kinneret Raza, warrior and witch!"

They were smiling, not judging or threatening. I stopped, trying to soak in this new reality.

"We saw the sea obey you and kill Kaptan Berker!"

"And the Old Farm who struck the oramiral on your command!"

My stomach turned, but I took the praise and grinned with all my teeth. My enemies were dead. I felt a hollow sort of triumph, nothing like what I thought I'd feel. The slaves and fighters gave us another nod and hurried past us to the beach, maybe to get a better look at the carnage.

"That's that, then," Oron said. "But I still want off this dirty piece of rock."

Avi grinned, then flashed her lion look. "An island of silver only my sister can find, enemies dead, and freedom for everyone."

I laughed. "Paradise!"

Oron and Calev echoed me and an invisible weight slid off my shoulders. Avi would use what she'd suffered. Not to become someone else, haunted and anxious, but to grow into a stronger version of herself.

As we walked, Calev elbowed me. A question rose in his eyes, a question that made my heart turn over and my head spin. I smiled.

"You go on ahead," he said to the others. "We will meet you at the western dock."

On the path ahead of us, Ekrem and Serhat rounded a rock that grew grass like a fur coat. Oron and Avi followed them, Oron shouting sailing advice that sounded very much like thinly veiled instructions for the bedroom.

Calev looked at me through his dark lashes and heat flashed under my skin. "I know we don't have the sun for this. But…"

My heart thundered and I put a hand over my chest. I had our lives safely in hand. Was I pushing luck to ask that I have him too?

I reached and touched the skin that met the edge of his tunic. "How will we explain all this?"

"When Oron planned this uprising, he told everyone to hold their tongues until we could talk to them. He has a story to spread. And I think I know—"

I pulled him into a kiss.

He laughed against my mouth, warm and sweet and sour.

"I don't know what's going to happen when we return to Jakobden," I said, "but I refuse to miss out on this."

He leaned into me and dragged his lips over mine. A delightful shudder poured through my tired, injured limbs, making me feel nothing but pleasure. He must have felt the change in me because he made a noise like a murmur and the kiss burned from sweet into spicy. His hands tore into my loose hair. His lips and tongue moved smoothly, roughly, and everything in between over my mouth. I was his fire and he was my luck. Fire help the person who tried to stop us.

"Calev ben Y'hoshua," a deep voice said. Calev's eyes went wide and he jerked back.

As I turned to see who had said his name, I realized the Fire must possess a strong streak of humor. I wasn't amused.

Because there, on the path, was Calev's father.

Aside from a slight narrowing of his eyes, his face was blank of emotion. His hair, as black as Calev's but with a streak of gray down the middle, fell to his shoulders and his beard was longer than I'd remembered it ever being. A group of Old Farm men and women walked with him, their sashes embroidered with pomegranates and lemons. They were disturbingly quiet.

"Father?" Calev wiped a hand across his slightly swollen mouth.

I crossed my arms and raised my chin. "We are glad to see you, Y'hoshua ben Aharon."

Regardless of the red in Calev's cheeks and the way he had to turn away from his father and his brother as they approached, I wasn't about to cower after all we'd been through.

"We heard word of the amir's missing vessel. I knew you'd end up here, going after this one's sister," Y'hoshua said in his rocky voice.

We needed a story and we needed it now.

Calev blew out a breath, strode to his father, and moved like he was about to embrace him.

Y'hoshua stopped him. "You have some explaining to do, my son. I see there's been a rebellion. Chaos reigns at the quarry—the oramiral and his men are dead—and we've heard some disturbing reports as to the amir and her kaptan, Berker Deniz."

Calev ran a hand over his head. "It is a very long story."

"Very," I added as we trailed Y'hoshua down to the shoreline, where the ruined boat floated beside the bodies.

Moving to a stretch of rocky shoreline away from the gore, Y'hoshua told Calev to make a fire and wait as he explained to Eleazar how to organize the gathering of the highest ranking slaves still alive for questioning. He found someone to send rock doves to Jakobden to inform Old Farm they would be gone another day.

A woman with a coiled brown braid noticed my arm. "Let me help you with that." She pulled a cloth and a small jar from her shoulder bag. With fresh water from a skin, she rinsed the cuts the oramiral had made in my skin. Her quick fingers told me she was used to this work.

Beyond her, Calev bent to pick up two long sticks of bleached driftwood.

She glanced at him, then at me, her mouth tightening. "I'm Miriam's sister."

The name was an arrow in me. I'd almost forgotten she existed.

My cheeks went hot. "Um. I don't..."

She made a noise of dismissal. "Don't bore me with lies."

I pulled my arm away and pain shot up my arm. I finished the knot she'd started in the wrapping. "I wasn't going to lie. It's none of my business."

The girl put a hand on her hip. Her seal ring reflected the lowering sun. "Ha. You don't look at a man that way unless you already made him your business."

"Thank you for tending to my injury," I snapped and walked toward Calev, who'd made a spark with his dagger and a flint. A moon-hued blaze flickered in the driftwood bones.

Out of the corner of my eye, I watched Miriam's sister glare at me before heading off the way the others had gone.

Calev and I were alone.

"You're not going to tell your father the truth, are you?" I found a seat on the massive piece of driftwood next to Calev, who prodded the flames with his dagger.

He sat and pushed his hair behind his ear. The fire sparkled in his eyes as he glanced at me. "Of course not."

I squeezed my knees. "Good."

"Have any ideas on what I should tell him?"

I did actually. And if I could stop thinking about that girl's comment, I could fill Calev in.

Calev touched my bandaged arm. "I...oh." His eyes flicked to mine. "That was Miriam's sister, wasn't it? The healer?"

He could probably hear the blood boiling in my veins.

"So?" I demanded.

He trailed one finger up my good arm, raising unseen flames under my skin. A grin tweaked his mouth as he leaned toward my ear.

"Miriam is the meanest little snake I've ever known. Just like that sister of hers. I am not going to marry Miriam," he whispered.

My heart crashed like a wave into my throat. "You're not."

I tried to make it not sound like a question. I was not going to ask him to do anything for me. I would not beg. He might break my heart, but no one would ever again tear down my spirit. No matter what caste I was in.

His lips drifted over my ear, and gooseflesh spread over my back and thighs. "No. If you'll have me, I will marry you."

"You will marry me."

He laughed quietly, the air ruffling the small hairs around my temples and neck. "Yes. And I will enjoy everything that comes with it. You, too, if you're up for it."

Heat cascaded down my throat, chest, belly, and lower until I thought I might start my own fire and all the work he'd done to make the sea-colored flames in front of us would be an enormous waste of sunlight.

"Oh, I'm up for it," I whispered back, turning to face him. His dark eyes promised a storm I'd happily die in, lightning and all.

"Calev."

We both jumped. It was his father.

The man had the timing of Oron at the tiller after two flasks of stolen ice wine.

AROUND THE BLUE FLAMES, we wove a story that people would talk about for ages. Calev picked up my line of thought, and we spun that tale like when we'd been in trouble as children together.

Y'hoshua shook his head and tugged at his beard. "So Kaptan Berker found out you had chased off the oramiral when the other fighting sailors were ill."

"Yes. The oramiral killed the amir right in front of our eyes." I let my fatigue play as sadness in my words.

"Turns out, the oramiral was obsessed with the amir." Calev pursed his lips. I was pretty sure he was holding back a laugh.

Y'hoshua nodded. "Many men were. Tragic."

Eleazar came scrambling down the path and spoke into Y'hoshua's ear. The older man looked at me, the wrinkles around his eyes deepening. Then he gestured for Eleazar to sit beside Calev.

"I'm glad you're alive, Brother," Eleazar said.

"Me too." Calev clasped Eleazar's shoulder kindly. "I have some amazing things to tell you about."

"There's sun enough for that later, boys," Y'hoshua said.

"Yes, sir," they answered in unison, their eyes wide and submissive.

I bit my lip to stifle a laugh. Calev looked downright adorable. For some reason, it made me want to smother him with kisses.

"You know," his father said to me, "despite your age, as the last appointed kaptan, you have a strong influence on who the kyros will name as the next amir of Jakobden."

I did know that. And I knew exactly who I'd suggest. "Ekrem will be my choice."

"The fighting sailor?" Y'hoshua said.

"Yes. The man is an expert at strategy. He has a cool head. He would be perfect."

Y'hoshua stood, indicating this meeting was over. "Well then. Eleazar has informed me that none of the fighting sailors or slaves will speak about the events that occurred this day or earlier. They wait for their leader, they say. And that," he pointed at me, "is you, Kaptan Kinneret Raza. Never did I think I'd say that to the sweet-faced dock rat that dragged my son into all sorts of trouble."

Calev's face had darkened at *rat*. "Father. I plan to wed Kaptan Kinneret, if she will have me. Please show respect to my Intended."

Y'hoshua's face hardened. "You would risk your place, your place as my son to have a low-caste sailor?"

Calev grasped my hands, his face was all hope as he looked at his father. "I would."

His father turned to me. "And you would risk his well-being simply to have him as your Intended? Your sister will suffer too."

I swallowed. "I am a kaptan now. And if that isn't enough, along with the silver we found at Ayarazi, we will manage as best we can."

"You are set on this." The vein above his right eye twitched as he looked at Calev. "Even if everyone at Old Farm and in Jakobden proper refuses to speak to you, work with you, or acknowledge your union?"

"Father, will you really turn away from me for this? Because I'm serious. Don't test me."

A vicious grin flickered over Y'hoshua's face. "If I never tested you, you'd never have become the man that stands here now. How would your voice grow loud enough to be heard at the council table? Without struggle, the body grows weak. With plenty of fights, the body develops muscle. Today, you've shown me you finally have the strength to lead." He smiled, warmly this time.

Calev's fingers gripped mine.

I wasn't sure when she had walked up, but Miriam's sister appeared beside Y'hoshua.

"I can't believe what I'm hearing, Y'hoshua."

The poison in her voice put my hand on the dagger at Calev's sash. I was ready if that snake decided to bite.

Y'hoshua turned toward her. "Miriam never hennaed her hands. She was never officially Intended."

I broke away from Calev. "I thought—"

Calev jerked my good arm gently. "Hold your tongue for once, Kinneret."

Y'hoshua inclined his head toward Miriam's sister. "I'm sorry for any pain this causes you or your family, but it was Miriam's choice to make me wait for her official answer to my suggestion of becoming betrothed to my son. She pays for that hesitation. Kinneret Raza has earned her way to high-caste in my eyes and she has also earned my son's heart, it seems." He nodded curtly toward Calev's hands on my arm.

I pressed my cheek into Calev's shoulder.

"He listened to me. For once. He really listened," Calev whispered to me.

The girl's face collapsed, but before a cry came out, she smoothed her features and ducked her head respectfully to Y'hoshua. "As you judge, Chairman."

I opened my mouth, and Calev clamped a hand over my lips. "No, no, fire. Behave."

I scowled at him. The girl deserved a little *haha* from me at least.

"She deserves it," Calev agreed, "but Father won't like it. And things will be much easier with him on our side."

"Fine," I said behind his fingers.

Then I nipped his thumb with my teeth playfully. His eyes widened, and he looked from my face to his father's. I grinned.

We followed Y'hoshua and Eleazar up the path and I spoke with the fighters and former slaves. With Y'hoshua's help, I detailed a plan to get them all off the island for good. The bulk of us left that very day for Jakobden.

We only had one more obstacle to our happiness. The remainder of the amir's court.

CHAPTER FORTY-ONE

At last, the moon reigned in the sky above Old Farm's low, stone buildings, stubbled barley fields, and neat rows of dark-leaved lemon trees. I leaned out of the betrothal room's one window and inhaled the night air. All of Calev's people, along with Avi and Oron, were drinking and eating under the stars, around the corner.

Calev would be here soon. I tapped fingers against the smooth, wood ledge. It seemed today the sun had stayed high for far longer than it should've. Of course, every day since Old Zayn told me about Ayarazi had seemed filled to the edge of the bucket. Especially the day we'd returned to Jakobden minus one amir.

After hearing the fighting sailors account matched mine perfectly—a fine bit of work Oron had done there—and Y'hoshua's own affirmation of everything, the court and the kyros's representative agreed to Ekrem's appointment, Berker's falsified martyrdom, and the oramiral's imagined crime of murdering the amir. Yes, on Age Day, I'd not only turned eighteen, but turned Jakobden upside down.

Now, in the betrothal room, Calev and I would begin the process of promising ourselves to one another.

"Pondering an escape?" Calev said.

I turned away from the window as he shut the room's side door, setting the many candles to flickering. Two bronze incense burners released white clouds of scented air that swirled around Calev as he approached. He wore the same thing as me—a plain white tunic. He looked better in the angel uniform, as Oron had deemed it, than me. His hair was so perfectly black against the fabric and the outline of his trim waist and strong, long legs showed through the tunic, outlined by the burners' inconsistent light.

He sat on a low stool and pointed to another across from him. "Should we begin?"

His voice sounded deeper than normal and his gaze traveled up and down, from the exposed red-brown curls of my head, to my face, along my body, all the way to my dusty, bare toes.

I nodded, strangely shy, and gathered the parchment cone the servants had left for us. It was filled with deep brown henna dye.

Calev put his hand in my lap, and I began to draw the symbols of his family on his palm and fingers.

I took a breath to steady my heart and dragged the pierced tip of the parchment cone down his first finger. A flourish snaked into existence, eventually growing into a lemon, a leaf, and a sun that sat in his palm, a palm I knew as well as my own. I started another design, working around his sigil ring and adding curls like palm fronds along his fingertip.

He shivered and his eyes flashed. They looked larger than usual, maybe because he wasn't wearing a headtie. "You're doing that on purpose," he said.

"Doing what?"

"Tickling me. Driving me mad."

Laughing quietly, I dotted the lemon with tiny circles. "I am not. Now quit fidgeting. Everyone is waiting for us outside for the formal announcement. And you still have work to do on me."

A sly smile drew his lips to the side. "I certainly do."

I felt like a host of violet nightwingers had been loosed in my belly. "That's not what I meant."

I looked away from his mouth and focused on the barley stalk I was creating on the heel of his hand. His skin was gold in the light of the candles and burners. The scent of beeswax mixed with the earthy, spicy odor of the henna. The Old Farm grandmothers, including Calev's own Savta, had added ginger and clove.

"Kinneret." Calev's breath moved over my hair, warming my scalp.

I kept my eyes down, drawing now on his other hand. "I'm almost finished. See?" His palm and fingers were covered in leaves, swirls, dots, hatched lines, lemons, barley, and even a tiny pomegranate. "Hold still for it to dry, then you can start on mine."

He made a little laughing noise, and I looked up. He gave me that thief's grin of his. "What do you suggest we do to pass the sun as we wait?" he asked with all the innocence of a pirate.

He held my gaze, unblinking. A cool breeze drifted through the window and stirred his tunic, pressing it lightly against the lines of his chest and arms.

My body began to feel very, very warm. His pulse moved in the hollow of his throat.

"We can't…" I started. "I mean, you have to let the dye dry."

"I suppose we'll have to make do with *your* hands then."

My heart bumped around in my chest, a clatter of noisy thumps in my ears. Everyone was outside the double doors, waiting for us.

"Kinneret, relax." He smiled. "We can just talk." My heart cracked like a whip.

I was being a coward, fretting over pleasing his father and his people, who waited outside. Since when had I let others get in the way of what I wanted? Since never.

I smiled, enjoying the feel of my blood rising. "There she is," Calev said.

Leaning close, I ran a finger over his sharp chin. I touched the pale strip of skin that was usually hidden by his headtie. I ran both palms down the column of his neck, feeling the tendons and muscles and the flow of blood through his veins. His Adam's apple moved under my fingers.

A knock sounded at the heavy, wooden doors. Calev made a noise, and I spun, dizzier than I'd ever been.

Avi peered in, her eyes happy and her sun-colored braid hanging over a shoulder. The embroidered seashells on her skirt and the five high-caste bells on her sash reflected the candlelight.

"Sorry." She grinned, her cheeks going rosy above the blue of her clothing. "Just wanted to see how much longer I had to listen to Oron trying to goad Y'hoshua into an argument."

Calev and I laughed.

"We'll be finished soon. Promise," I said.

She shut the door, and I eased back onto my stool, giving Calev my hand. "As much as I was enjoying myself…"

Calev's chest moved faster, his eyes a bit wild. "Kiss me, Kinneret."

"Not yet," I said, quirking an eyebrow. "You have work to do first."

Closing his eyes for a breath, he scooted forward and took up the dye cone I'd tossed to the floor. "Back to being kaptan again, are we?" He made a face.

"We are."

"Such a challenging little beast, aren't you?"

I pointed to my thumb. "I'd like the shape of a sail here." I opened my hand to show my palm. "And a combined shell and lemon design here, if you can manage it."

"Of course, kaptan." He drew the cone's tip across my skin slowly. Goosebumps rose along my arms, echoing the touch.

Calev's black hair hid his face. His hands moved smoothly, his knuckles like knobs and his henna designs twisting to life with his fingers' movements.

Every sweep of new lines and curves drawn on my skin brought another rush of heat, and eventually, my breathing matched his. Slowly, he raised his head, his eyes glittering and ebony. He met my gaze, then said my name without a sound, dropping the henna.

Standing, we crashed together like waves.

With only the lightest of clothing between us, my hips pressed into his. He kissed me and I tasted honey and lemons. As his mouth moved to my neck, I breathed him in. His hair smelled like sun-warmed earth. My hands couldn't touch him enough. His chest heaving and strong and hot under my fingers, he breathed my name into my shoulder, and I shuddered as sparks danced down my legs.

A cough broke us apart and I felt like I'd been hit by lightning. Oron coughed once more. "Please excuse the interruption, but Y'hoshua ben Aharon is about as happy as a beached seastinger out there and if you make him wait much longer, it'll be a curse rather than a blessing he bestows upon you."

"Did you stir him up?" I snapped, wanting him to leave. I wanted Calev all over me again.

"That's like asking if it's my fault that Asag fellow was such a grouch. His attitude is a permanent condition, my dear."

Calev studied the floor and ran a hand through his hair. "Come." Oron grabbed our sleeves and pulled us out the doors.

We stepped into the moonlight, our appearance prompting the foot-stomping and smiles of Avi, Y'hoshua, and the rest of Old Farm. They'd set up tall, brass candleholders along the dirt and stone pathway leading from the betrothal room to the main farmhouse. Violet nightwingers flitted through the honey light, one resting on Avi's shoulder. She tried to kiss it before it flew off again.

Oron released us, and found his bowl of drink, raised it, and drank it down.

Old Zayn stood in the dark shadow of a cedar, his smile white. I gasped, and with a nod to Calev to wait, I ran to him and hugged him tightly.

"Easy, young thing," he rasped, patting me lightly on the back.

His hand felt like a sack of tiny bones.

I pulled away and stared. "I lost the compass you gave me."

He grinned. "Ah. Well. It went down during an adventure and I'd say that's more than any compass could pray for, could pray for."

"Did you receive my message?" I asked.

"And the silver too." He pointed to his thick, brown tunic and wide green sash. "I thank you. You are as kind as your parents were."

My eyes burned and I turned, imagining Mother and Father standing beside Y'hoshua, still and solemn. Mother winked. The wish-picture dissipated and Zayn patted my back.

"They are here. In you and your sister. And you make them so proud, so proud. Me too, if you care to know," he said.

I hugged him, a tear escaping despite my best efforts.

"Now go," Zayn said. "Visit me during the winter months, yes?"

"Yes." I smiled at him, then returned to Calev.

Calev took my hand, the henna caking off and scenting the air with cloves and ginger as we walked toward his father.

"Thank you for saving me again," Calev said.

"Saving you?"

"Once, from the sea. Next, from the…everything during our journeys. And of course, now."

"Now."

"Now."

I squeezed his fingers. "You never really needed saving. You're too lucky."

"Haven't you figured it out yet, Kinneret? You are my luck. Not the other way around."

Then Y'hoshua was holding one of our hands each in his larger ones, and saying the blessing. He took up the painted glass container of holy oil.

"I think now, that there's no such thing as simply being born with good fortune," I whispered to Calev. "We make our luck."

"You do it well," he said.

I smiled. The night sky's blue moonlight coalesced into the gold illumination of the candles, making everyone look like dreams among the night insects.

"What do you think?" I asked. "Hells or paradise?"

"I think you know the answer to that one," he said under his breath as his father raised an oiled hand and prayed in a ringing tone.

"Paradise. With the promise of hells to come." Calev's eyes widened.

I laughed. "Life would be dull without any flames to challenge us."

He ran a finger down my palm and kissed my forehead, earning a reproachful frown from his father.

"My thoughts exactly, my fire," he said.

As Y'hoshua rubbed oil into our hands and readied to chant the Old Farm betrothal, I knew I was ready for this. I'd fought hard for this life, an existence stretched between two cultures, and a fantastical blend of exquisite joy and soul-waking pain. There was no greater magic than life itself.

FEVER

UNCOMMON WORLD

1

CALEV

Readying to meet the ruler of the most powerful Empire in the world wasn't a simple task. Especially when he held my dreams in his very spoiled and reportedly vicious hands.

Although my home, Old Farm, sat inside the Empire, we were nothing like the kyros's court. Where we had democratic meetings and long days in the sun, they had a tight-fisted tyrant and deeply dyed tent walls of the finest fabrics to keep them cool on even the hottest months.

Seven horses and more colored packs than I could tally crowded the beaten earth in front of our Old Farm community building. I tied my own pack onto my mount and ran a hand down the mare's neck.

"This is going to be a long ride," I whispered into the coarse, braids of her mane. "At least compared to our usual jaunts around the fields and hills. I'll make sure you have plenty of water and I just happened to nab three of the finest apples on the Broken Coast for you."

Despite my misgivings about the new kyros and his lack of respect for human life, I couldn't wait to see the capitol again. It was a city of tents supported by tall towers and surrounded by a huge wall of stone. There would be sights and sounds there we never saw in Jakobden or Old Farm.

It'd been years since I'd visited, and I buzzed with excitement, thinking of how they would receive me at the fine court there. I was finally of age and they would treat me properly. I might even find the courage to suggest even more changes in the caste system in order to aid those who had once been low-caste like Kinneret and her sister Avigail. Politics and social situations were my strength and I would prove it even more with this quest.

My horse snuffled against my chest as my father walked up behind me.

"Son, are you quite certain you know how to behave in the kyros's court? Full names are required. You can't just think up some wild idea and present it while you're there. Focus on gaining Kyros Meric's mark on the agreement between us and our new amir, Ekrem. Nothing else matters."

"I know." I fought the urge to roll my eyes skyward. He'd only told me the requirements about two thousand times.

Eleazar kicked his horse gently and walked him over. "Brother, I think you should consider asking Ezra to come with us. He has had three audiences with this new kyros. He says the man is…less than kind."

I put my foot in my stirrup and threw a leg over my mare, frustration making my movements a bit more forceful than was absolutely necessary.

"Ezra has work here," I said. "I can handle this. And we have all the protection we need with Serhat and the others coming along." I smiled at the tall, fair-haired fighter.

Serhat nodded as she attempted to steer her horse toward us. She was better on a boat than on a steed. But at least she knew her way around a yatagan. The road to the Empire's capitol was teeming with thieves and the city itself was known to have its rough spots.

Thinking of boats brought Kinneret to mind. Not that she was ever far from my thoughts these days.

"Kinneret said she'd see us off." I held up a hand to block the sun's increasing light, hoping to catch her strolling toward me with those hips of hers.

A group of men and women walked down the road that led to the docks, but none of them had Kinneret's wild hair or the bounce in their step like her. I hoped everything was all right. I'd heard of several people in town who'd come down with a fever. Surely she wouldn't get it. Sicknesses never touched her.

"You don't have the sun to wait on her. If you are going, you must go now." Father handed me a rolled parchment. "This is the agreement. It is the most important item you've ever held, son. If you lose it, if it falls into the wrong hands, our entire culture may cease to exist. Amir Ekrem is a patient man and a kind ruler for our region, but his actions are influenced by Kyros Meric, who seems to never have heard of the word kindness. Do not fail Old Farm, my son. If you do, there is no way the council will permit you to become the next chairman. And I would have to agree."

My tunic rode up against my neck, and I tugged it loose. "I know, Father.

You've told me this again and again." He frowned, so I touched his shoulder as I leaned down from my mount. "I promise I will make you proud."

A rare smile beamed from Father's bearded face. He patted my hand with his calloused fingers. "You already have. I am blessed with two sons who are very fine indeed."

Eleazar mumbled something from his saddle.

Father spun. "What was that?"

"Nothing," Eleazar said. "Shouldn't we go now? Or do you need ten more minutes with your beloved Calev?"

Father glared, eliciting a murmured apology from Eleazar. My brother was going to be a real treat on this ride to Akhayma.

With the agreement safely in my pouch, I rode up to Serhat. She was looking a bit paler than normal. "You feeling all right?"

She swallowed and straightened her back. "Yes, Calev ben Y'hoshua. I am perfectly fit for this mission."

Her red leather vest was immaculate except for one deep cut on her left shoulder. She'd nearly lost her head during the battle at Quarry Isle when we'd fought to free Avi from that awful place. I wondered if she kept the damaged vest to remind herself that she'd bested Death. It seemed like something she would do. The amir's fighters were such an interesting blend of pride and humility, and Serhat was a prime example, though right now she looked in need of another night's sleep. She wiped her eye and pressed her hand against her mouth.

"Don't get sick on me now. I need you on that mount and ready to fight." Several townsfolk had fallen ill with a bad fever.

Serhat untied her water from her saddlebags and drank down three, big swallows. "Just thirsty. I am well. Don't worry." Her thin lips lifted at one side.

"Good. I don't think I'd enjoy hoisting you back onto that elephant you're calling a horse."

Her quiet laugh followed me as I trotted closer to the road. I looked longingly toward Kinneret's new home near the docks, wishing I had the sun to wait on her. But she would understand my leaving, and I'd be back quickly.

Tucking my worries away, I kicked my mare into a gallop and led the party toward the hills that rolled inland.

WE CROSSED the mercurial river that ran through the Empire, past Silvania's deep forests, and onward to the Great Expanse that led to the far West. We were making good progress, but by the time we reined in our mounts at an inn, Serhat looked like a corpse. And the rest of my party didn't look much better.

An inn worker—a tall girl in thick braids—took my mare and held a hand out for the others' reins.

Serhat listed left, then fell from her saddle.

I hurried to her side, Eleazar on my heels.

She was clearly disoriented, blinking and gasping. I put a hand on her head. Heat blazed from her clammy skin.

I sat back. This was awful. "She has the fever."

Eleazar sighed. "I do too."

"What?"

My brother nodded sadly and swallowed. I hit my thigh with a fist as the inn's front door swung open. Why did this sickness have to hit now? A man wearing the dirtiest apron ever strolled out.

"What's this?"

Eleazar and I helped Serhat to her feet as the others dismounted and handed their horses to the girl with the braids. Eleazar panted with the effort to keep Serhat standing.

I adjusted my pack, making sure the agreement was still there and safe. "We need lodging for the night, please. And I think most of my party here is ill."

Kinneret would've lied a tiny bit just to be sure the man wasn't afraid of contracting our illness. I hated lying. I was terrible at it. But I had to make certain everyone was safe. We couldn't sit out here in the street all night, open to thieves and cutpurses.

Swallowing my values, I lied to the best of my ability. "The rest of these men and women ate some bad meat. I had abstained for purity reasons."

Eleazar eyed me, but kept quiet.

The innkeeper wiped his massive hands on his apron. "All right then. Let's get them all inside to puke and be done with it. I am a merciful man, but I will insist on a twenty percent increase on my usual fees."

Eleazar's mouth fell open. Sweat beaded along his red-bronze headtie. "That is not good business."

I touched his sleeve and looked the innkeeper in the eye. "We will pay fifteen more than the last time our people stayed here."

Ezra had told me how much to pay. He'd been up this way to speak with a group of Silvanians that claimed they'd spotted a group of Invader scouts not far from the capitol.

The innkeeper scowled, then stuck out a hand for me to shake.

The inside of the establishment was nothing to crow about. A sad fire on the far side cooked a large bird and four dented tables held a crowd of Silvanian merchants, Empire fighters on patrol, and two families with more children than I could count.

Once Eleazar and I were settled in the best room, Serhat being just one door down, my brother collapsed onto the bedding.

"I'm going to have to leave without you all in the morning," I said.

I didn't want to. It would be dangerous traveling alone to the capitol and even inside the city walls, but this agreement couldn't wait. If we allowed too much sun between the conclusion of the last agreement and the new one, Kyros Meric might think of all sorts of additions that would hurt Old Farm. Amir Ekrem, a friend, would fight them, but he could only do so much without risking his position and his life.

"I know." Eleazar wheezed.

I gave him a cup of questionable water before sending off a letter to Father about the illness. The inn's rock dove took off with the message securely bound to its leg before the sun set.

"He'll want you to wait for him." Eleazar's hand drifted toward the side table, but the cup fell from his hand.

My throat tightened. He was truly sick. This wasn't like him at all. I cleaned the water with a folded rag, then did my best to get a night's sleep. I had to rise before anyone and ride on. I couldn't let my father stop me due to this fever. He'd never give me this opportunity again and I couldn't stand the thought of failing him and disappointing Kinneret with my lack of political skills.

Tomorrow, I would ride like the wind.

2

AVI

The door to my new house was the brightest blue. We'd bought the place right after our bell removal and our rise to high-caste, and Kinneret had let me choose the azure color. I'd picked the hue to match Oron's glass gaming pieces although Kinneret thought I'd selected the shade to echo her beloved sea.

I pushed the lovely blue door open and saw my sister at the table. She stared at a map of the Pass, the new ports she'd marked dotting the jagged coastline.

"Aren't you supposed to be seeing Calev off before his trip to court?" I set my shipping schedule beside her elbow. "Eh. Kinneret. What is wrong?"

She shook her head, then looked up at me with glazed eyes. "Oh. I'm not feeling well." Her fingers dragged over the map, smearing a row of black circles.

"Kin?"

She slid from her chair and tumbled to the stone floor, her head knocking the wooden flooring.

My heart seized.

Tossing the chair aside, I took her by the arms and cradled her head in my lap. Her forehead was hot as the decking at midday.

She blinked and moved her chin as if she was recovering from being hit in the jaw. "I'm fine. I just forgot about Calev's trip. I'll go now."

"Oh no you don't."

I heaved her up and walked her to the bed. Easing her down, my skin pressed against hers. She was absolutely burning up. My mind whirled. This couldn't be the fever that had killed the sailmaker's son, could it? He was a horrible person, but no one deserved to die like that. There were more who had the same type of illness in the merchant's quarter in town.

"I'll be fine," Kinneret croaked.

Then a memory crashed through my mind. My parents side by side on the bed, their cheeks bright red. I could still smell the sickness.

"I'll be fine," my mother had said.

And she'd died the very next morning.

Now, I dabbed a wet cloth over Kinneret's flushed face. She didn't seem to notice the attention.

Panic climbed my chest and choked me. "I'll be right back, sister. Don't get up."

I rushed out of the door, sprinting past the sailors on their way to their ships and weaving between women and children on the path into town. Old Farm wasn't far. Maybe I could catch Calev before he left for Akhayma, and he could come and pray for Kinneret and be her luck and get her well again. He had a special link with Kinneret. He would save her, and I wouldn't lose her like I'd lost Mother and Father.

The Old Farm courtyard was empty except for a few men talking over a list of some kind.

"Where is Calev ben Y'hoshua? Did he already leave? It's an emergency."

"Avigail Raza." The closest man smiled. "I'm sorry, but yes, you missed him. Is there anything we can do?"

"My sister. She has a fever."

They traded glances. "We have a healer here. Would you like us to call him?"

"Please." I smiled in thanks for their offer, but I had no real hope for this. The sailmaker's son had seen a healer, and he'd died all the same. "Have you heard about anyone else that has this sickness?"

The man frowned. "Sadly, yes. Five more fell sick in town. None here yet. Two of the townsfolk have moved into the next life."

I made the sign of the Fire on my forehead as a ringing sounded in my ears.

Kinneret was not allowed to die.

I needed her here. I wasn't ready to be on my own and the world was a better place with her in it. She'd worked hard to end much of the low-castes' suffering. It was her that petitioned to end Outcasting. None had been subjected to it since. She had more to do in this life.

"Are you all right? You aren't becoming ill, too, are you?" the man asked.

"No. Please send your healer to Kinneret Raza's house at the docks."

"We will do it immediately."

I didn't wait for their bows and kind words. Maybe Oron knew which route Calev was taking to the capitol. Maybe I could follow him and get him back here before it was too late.

Oron was on our old boat, rolling up the sail. On his free days, he always went out on his own. He said he had ghosts to conquer, whatever that meant.

When I told him about Kinneret, he dropped the sail and raced to our house.

BY THE TIME the sun was down and the Old Farm healer had left, Oron was as panicked as me. He paced the floor at Kinneret's feet, the sound of his soft steps mixing with the shushing of the Pass beyond the docks.

I knelt beside the bed and brushed my older sister's hair away from her sticky cheeks. "I'm going after Calev," I said quietly so I wouldn't disturb her rest. "He can heal her."

Oron set his hand on the back of my head. "Avi." The oil lamp hanging from the ceiling cast flickers of light across his face. "Calev isn't a healer. Our girl will heal on her own or she won't. That's that."

I shoved his hand away and stood. Studying his eyes, I could see he would keep repeating this if I pushed my plan to go after Calev. The healer, Ekrem, and Calev's father had thought I was delusional when they heard my idea to bring Calev back to heal her.

Well, I wasn't about to just sit here and do nothing.

I was Kinneret Raza's sister and we didn't understand the words *give up*.

Ekrem, Oron, Calev's father, and the healer were all wrong. Calev could give Kinneret strength enough to heal. And I would prove it and save my sister. She'd risked her life for me not long ago, and by the Fire, I would do the exact same for her.

When deep night poured over Jakobden, I leaned close to Kinneret's ear. Her chest moved slowly, too slowly, up and down.

"I will bring him back for you, Sister."

I wanted to cry over her, to beg her to wake up and heal herself, but I was too old for that now. I knew it would do no good.

So after a gentle squeeze of her limp hand, I slipped past Oron's sleeping form in the other bed and ghosted out the door.

I didn't care what dangers lurked in the Empire's capitol. I would go there and find Calev before Death could grip my family again.

3

CALEV

Night dropped like an axe as I galloped across the desert plains. At home on Old Farm, the sun danced toward the horizon and gave us time to tuck our scythes away in the barns and wash our hands for the blessing. But here, just outside the Empire's capitol city of Akhayma, the arid plateaus to the West cut off the sun's brutal heat, leaving only cold and shadows as I rode up to the city gates.

I smiled into the darkness, almost wanting to laugh. I'd made it, even though there'd been so many problems. I was here and nearly finished with my duty. Kinneret and Father were going to be so proud. This would prove I was ready to become Chairman of Old Farm. Soon, I'd have the position to take care of Kinneret, not that she needed me, and to hold my head high.

Hopefully, Eleazar, Serhat, and the rest would join me soon. I'd made sure a healer was paid to visit them while I was gone. They were strong. They'd get through this illness.

At the gate, guards armed with poles and sheathed yatagans gave me a once-over, then waved me through the stone arch and into the moonlit city.

Covering the bubbling canals, tents tied to tall, skinny towers rippled like sails between masts. Cinnamon, wine, peppers, heated metal—the air here held nothing of home. The last time I'd been here—years ago—I'd ridden behind Father on his mount, my fingers digging into his sash to keep from toppling from the saddle as I strained to see it all.

I reined my horse in and patted my pack gently, reassuring myself. The edges of Amir Ekrem and my father's agreement—a delicate promise between two very different cultures—pressed into the soft leather. All I had to do was get a good night's rest, then present the document to the kyros in the morning for his approval. Old Farm needed this agreement with Jakobden's amir to remain secure. Without it, the Empire could do as they liked with my people and their lands.

I swallowed. I only hoped Kyros Meric would continue to support the treaty. Amir Ekrem did, but I would have to remind the kyros that we grew valuable barley and rare lemons like no other farm could.

Laughter tumbled out from a path leading south through the maze of streets. I followed the sound of rolling dice and the smell of minted, roasted lamb. The path between the tents that ran along the waterways wound its way under a row of signs hanging over doorways. I knew enough desert tongue to read the word *inn* below a painting of an egret. Out front, a boy—too old to be missing teeth but missing them all the same—took my horse and one of my silver coins.

"I'll need her back at dawn," I said.

Normally at this time of the evening, I'd be chasing after Kinneret. My face heated at the thought of the night before I'd left. We needed to marry before I died of want for her. She was so busy during the day working on Amir Ekrem's full ship and retooling Jakobden's fleet that we didn't see one another nearly often enough.

Just inside the inn's open door, a woman, wearing a dark kaftan, smiled from where she sat on a tall stool. She stood and reached for my pack.

"You need a place to stay, my lord? Why are you on your own? Where's your fine retinue?" Her accent opened the trade tongue vowel sounds as she commented on my embroidered clothing.

"I'm from Jakobden. Old Farm. There's a bad fever. Some of my retinue are sick at home and the rest are now recovering at inns along the route."

The last person I'd checked on before leaving was Serhat. The innkeeper's daughter had been mopping her blond hair with a wet cloth.

"I do need a room, please," I said. "But I'll keep my things, thank you."

One of the men seated around a green and red gaming table mumbled a slur about Old Farm men and virility that pinched at my good mood.

I eyed the man, grabbed the hem of my tunic, and shook it, lifting it just a little. "It's not true, good man, but if you'd like to check yourself…"

Being around Oron had definitely changed me. Kinneret's first mate, a wine-loving man from the Northern Isles, never missed an opportunity to shock people with jokes you laughed at but probably shouldn't. Before I knew him, I would've ignored the stranger's bawdy slur and probably blushed like a fool. Oron's influence had washed some of the innocence off me and made me bold.

The insulter said something that was surely swearing, but his friends laughed good-naturedly as the woman led me through the crowded room.

The room for rent was a slice of space and a hammock between two walls of striped wool. Not the best accommodations. But my legs ached and my stomach roared with hunger. This would be good enough. I started to set my pack in the corner, then turned to the woman.

"What do people here do about stealing?"

"Thieves lose a hand. No exceptions. Not a lot of stealing going on."

"Well, all right then." I'd still keep the agreement in my sash. I wasn't going to be separated from it any second of any day.

The parchment was smooth under my fingertips as I unrolled it a fraction. My father's name, inked in dramatic calligraphy, tossed a smile over my lips. The entire top third of the agreement lay blank and ready for the kyros's sigil and name. I wondered what type of brush or quill his scribe would use to create the colorful rendering of *Kyros Meric, the Eternally Victorious*.

With the agreement tucked away behind the silk and linen pomegranates embroidered on my sash, I sat at an empty table in the main room.

"I am Samira, not that you asked." The innkeeper's smile held a touch of mockery. "What can I get you?"

I ignored her less-then-respectful tone and soon my stomach was full of lamb, flatbread, and honeyed dates speckled with some herb that was familiar, but I couldn't place. The room blurred, and my sore muscles eased a little bit. I decided to play some cards.

I COULDN'T UNDERSTAND the first punch. What it was. What it meant for me.

I'd just come out of the inn to catch my breath, to try to clear my head of the wine I'd stupidly gulped too much of during the card game. The lotus tower holding up the tents in the area cooled my palm, then my cheek as I leaned into it and tried to stop the world from spinning. I couldn't remember how long I'd walked. Why had I done this to myself? I was smarter than this.

But was this just from wine?

My thoughts were foggy. My head was going to hurt badly during my audience with the kyros tomorrow. I pressed my back into the tower and the moon eyed me disdainfully.

"You're right, moon. Wine is never worth the headache."

Some men walked out of the inn, laughing, and started down the road, their arms thrown over one another's shoulders. It was late. Maybe they could walk back with me, make sure I didn't further ruin my reputation.

I took a step toward them. The wooden signs, marking each establishment, blurred in my hazy eyes, white paint looking wet and dripping. Then they disappeared into the night.

A stranger came up on me fast.

When knuckles crashed against my skull and my headtie slipped over one eye, I was equally as surprised as the chicken who took the brunt of my collapse into her nesting spot beside the tower. The part of my mind that didn't seem to care about my possible death begged the question: Why was it always chickens? Chickens in Kurakia last time. Chickens here now. They dogged me like awkward ghosts, haunting my every misadventure.

I shook my foggy head, ignoring a disgruntled *squawk* coming from behind me, and—hoping to hide the agreement from my attacker—I rolled, keeping it under my back, but still in my sash.

A man with a ragged beard laughed. The same man that had been playing cards with me earlier? Another? He kicked me in the stomach.

My breath blasted out of me. My lungs couldn't grab any air. I was going to vomit.

Gasping, I held up my hands and lifted a foot to push him away. But he had friends. Two of them. One had definitely been at the inn. I recognized him. Another kick came, this time to my knee. Pain spidered up my leg.

A fist launched into my face. As heat that would eventually become pain seared my nose, I grabbed for a sleeve of one of the men and missed.

"What's in your sash there, *bather?*" The man slipped fingers under the knot and tugged. "I knew one of you rich Old Farm's once. Think you're better than the rest of us."

Bather. A slur that mocked my people's holy cleansing ritual.

I forced my fingers to stay away from the agreement. It pressed against my spine. "No, we don't. And I have no money. Spent it all on food and wine."

"Sounds like our plan, Behir," the second man said.

"Yeah, but the *bather* still has something in that fancy sash of his."

"I told you I spent it all on dinner."

"And all that gray plant too." The bearded man elbowed the man next to him.

277

"Gray plant?" I mumbled through the pain. They weren't making sense. I hadn't bought any of that.

Then I realized what had happened. The bits of herb sprinkled over my honeyed dates—it had been gray plant. A full leaf of that foul plant could put a horse to dreaming. I looked up at my attackers realizing they'd planned this robbery. Had the innkeeper known about it too? Had she been in on it?

They laughed as I tried to get to my knees. Maybe I could run off. Find a dark alley to hide in. Blood streamed from my nose, hot and deserved for all my foolish actions.

"You have something in there, don't you? Tell us the truth, Old Farm," the first attacker spat.

I couldn't lose the parchment. Father would banish me. Well, maybe not banish me, but close to it. I'd be humiliated in front of everyone. Before Ekrem became the amir, it would've meant war. Now it meant tense negotiations that would set back the harvest. Without the agreement, the peace between Old Farm and the kyros and amir could be ruined.

I had to think. I had to think quickly like Kinneret.

I tried to smile even though my face felt like a road at midday—trampled and far too hot.

"Fine," I said. "I lied."

They traded a look. The third man popped his knuckles.

Swallowing, I slid my coin purse out of my sash and opened it up, showing the coin I had for the trip home.

Would the kyros help me get back if I didn't have a silver piece to my name? If he didn't, I'd be stuck here until I could work my way to affording water and food for the return journey. I'd be late, far, far behind schedule. Father and Ekrem would send messengers. There'd be misunderstandings. Dangerous misunderstandings if I went missing.

"I have a little left." I closed the bag and held it out. "Take it. Enjoy a meal on me." I turned to spit blood out of my mouth, the sudden movement making my nose flame.

The ragged-bearded man clapped his skinny hands. "This one is pretty funny." He snatched the purse and tucked it into his sash.

His friend kicked my leg out from under me. I fell again, the night still spinning like the string toy Kinneret's sister, Avi, loved when she was little.

"I still want what you're hiding in your sash. That parchment." He looked at his friend. "He's funny and funny means clever. That writing could be the deed to a fine horse. Or a note on silver owed. Could be worth a lot. He wants us to leave and there has to be a reason he'd give up that coin so quick."

Quick? They'd all but beaten my nose in. I fought panic, wrestled it into the back of my mind. "Only because I have an Intended at home who'd prefer my face intact enough to shower her with praise."

The last punch was a surprise too.

It hit like a horse's hoof to my head.

I woke up lying on my side, head pounding, with the sun stretching over the sandy earth to shoot me in the eye.

Sitting up, I touched my shoulder, my back, and the gritty road under me.

They'd stolen the agreement. A cold sweat rolled down my neck. My reputation would be ruined before it had a chance to be born. I'd never get the chairman position. Kinneret would be a fool to wed me and she was no fool. I couldn't stop imagining the furrow between her eyebrows and the sound of Father scolding me.

4
AVI

B linking tears away, I smacked the horse's flank and she sped up, hooves roaring over the clumps of scrub and dusty earth. My legs quivered. I'd never ridden so far. At least I was better at it than Kinneret. My sister ruled on the water, but on a horse's back, she wasn't worth much. I'd taken right to riding when Calev first let me try at Old Farm.

I swallowed. I had to get them together again before Kinneret burned away like Mother and Father.

Tears blurred the sight of a family with a loaded down camel. Grain traders led a massive six-wheeled cart pulled by braying ox-lions. A band of colorfully dressed entertainers looked more likely to pick the coins from my sash than make me laugh. I wiped the wetness from my cheeks.

Crying wouldn't keep Kinneret from dying. Calev's love might. I had to get to him. Now.

The Empire's capitol loomed in the distance like a rogue wave ready to crash over all of us down here on the wide and sandy road.

Calev would believe me. He'd believe Kinneret would get better if he came home to her. All the rest of them thought I was a madwoman. But Oron, Ekrem, and Chairman Y'hoshua would wake to find Calev's second best horse and me gone, and know I was a *smart* madwoman.

Inside Akhayma's walls, I ignored the bizarre tents and wild smells— both pleasant and rank—of the city as I pushed through the crowd.

"Come on, Arrow."

Sweat matted the mare's sinuous neck. I moved toward one of the waterways that streamed under the tented pathways. She lowered her head to drink and the dawn's light skirted over her dusty mane. She and I both would need nine baths after this horrible trip.

A man shouted at me in some foreign language, then switched to my own—what they called the trade or common tongue. "Stop." He shook a fist at me and jerked Arrow's reins out of my hand.

I ripped them out of his fingers. "Back off."

"The signs." He pointed at a tiny, wooden square covered in five languages. *No drinking from the canals. Cups only, please.*

"I don't have a cup. This is ridiculous."

The man kept jabbering on at me in his language and mine. There weren't any bowls anywhere. How did they expect travelers to water their horses? There had to be containers to use somewhere—

Crockery crowded a booth set up beside the main thoroughfare. I dragged Arrow away from her drink and pointed to a tiny bowl in front of the merchant. "Could I use this? Just for a second? I'll bring it right back."

The thin-faced woman shook her head. "No. Buy only."

I looked to the sky. "Fine." I gave her the coins and finally my poor mount had a good drink and me along with her.

I eyed the man who'd shouted at me. His long-sleeved, coat-tunic bore an emblem with a thick, blue line and a sun. "Are you in charge of the water?"

Crossing his arms proudly, the man smiled.

I had to grin at his transformation. "You really should have a larger sign at the front gate. One that details exactly what visitors are supposed to do. It would keep the shouting down."

His face fell, and his arms dropped to his sides. "You, a little girl, offer me advice?"

I splashed some water on Arrow's neck. "I'm fifteen and then some." Since the horrors of Quarry Isle, I felt like I was more like ninety-years-old. "Now, where do I go to see someone who has a meeting with the kyros and his scribe?"

Blinking, the man stuttered, "You'd go to the Kyros Walls and present yourself." He waved toward a narrower path cobbled in reddish stone.

"Thank you," I said, heading off. I'd wasted enough time.

If Kinneret's condition worsened...no, I wouldn't think about it. It didn't do any good to thrash around and cry. I had to focus on finding Calev. His calm head and his heart for my sister—that was what would fix everything. Kinneret was right; Calev was luck made real.

~

AT THE KYROS WALLS, a guard with a dark red beard stopped me.

"Appointment with the lower bench?" he said in accented trade tongue.

"No. But my friend has an appointment with the kyros and—"

He snorted. "Move on, girl."

It was all I could do not to ram my heels into my mare and trample the idiot. I breathed out my nose and nudged my horse forward, just a step.

"You misunderstand, good man. My friend is Calev ben Y'hoshua, son of the chairman of Old Farm in Jakobden and sent here by Amir Ekrem to approve an agreement."

The guard across the way tugged his helmet off and his sweat-slicked black hair held the shape of the metal. He took hold of my reins. "Like he said, move on. Before you get into trouble with your stories."

"It's not a story. It is the truth. And you will be punished if the kyros learns you were the reason his new amir in Jakobden failed to uphold a truce lasting centuries!"

I wasn't totally sure all of that was true, but it sounded good.

Suddenly, my horse jerked, twisted, and shied away. The red-bearded guard had done something to her.

As I faced him, the other guard slapped the mare's hind and she shot toward a walled pool. I moved her to the right to miss running headlong into the water, fury igniting my insides.

"You will be sorry!" I shouted over a shoulder as I trotted into the market.

I'd have to find Calev another way. I fisted my hands around the reins. Being nearly an adult was the worst. No one gave you leeway like they did with children. No one gave you respect like they would if I was a year or two older.

Nearby, a merchant called out, selling painted shoes. She had a nice smile so I slid off my horse and approached her. "May I ask you a question?"

She nodded and picked up another pair of shoes to show me. Yellow phoenixes flew over the toes.

"I'm sorry. I don't have coin for new shoes, but I wondered if you could tell me where most of the inns are here?" Maybe Calev had stopped to rest on his way to the kyros.

She shrugged and held out a palm. "Maybe. For two smalls."

Two smalls wasn't much, but it would cost me a meal. "Never mind."

I turned to mount, but a hand on my arm stopped me.

282

A boy about my age looked down at me. He had nice, dark eyes and his lips lifted at one corner. "The inns are on that side of the city."

As the woman—maybe his mother?—left us to talk, the boy's gaze wandered over my face and clothing. Not many here wore a simple, short shirt and long skirt like I did. I guessed I wore a Pass sort of style, suited to ranging around a boat and dealing with sails.

"But be careful." His tongue danced inside his mouth and made his words sound really beautiful. "Some are not good places for a pretty girl."

Warmth rose along my neck. "Thank you for telling me." I tried to pronounce everything slowly so he'd understand.

A wide smile flashed over his mouth. It was a nice smile. "You don't have to talk like that. I'm fluent in the trade tongue. Despite the accent of my birth language."

I swallowed. "I didn't mean to insult you."

"You didn't. We see many, many visitors here in Akhayma."

Part of me wanted to stay to hear stories about these visitors and his run-ins with them. But most of me pushed to leave, to get to Calev, to help my sister. There really wasn't any sun to spare.

"Thank you," I said. He gave me a quick bow and his jet-black hair shifted over his forehead. "I wish I could stay and talk to you." My cheeks were probably going the color of my poppy-red sash. "But there's an emergency, and I must go."

"Of course." He looked back at his table and tent where stacks of tattered books, small leather pouches, and lengths of rough wool vied for space. "I could come with you?" His eyes widened, hopeful.

My heart beat twice in a breath. "Oh. Yes. That would be...good." It wasn't only because I wanted to hear his voice some more or watch his half smile appear again. It was because he knew the way. This would be faster. Smarter.

WE WALKED Calev's mare through the tangled roads.

"Are we really getting anywhere? It doesn't feel like it. Don't take me through the scenery." I gave him a pointed look. "I don't have the sun for that."

"I wouldn't dream of wasting your day...what is your name?"

"Avigail Raza. Avi. Avi, for short. You can call me Avi." I rolled my eyes at myself.

"I am Radi." He placed a hand on his chest. His fingers were a bit knobby and a strong vein lined his skin, showing he worked hard like I did. "Please call me Radi."

"I'm looking for a friend. My sister's Intended. Do you use that term here?" It was an Old Farm word and I had no idea how to translate it.

"No, but I think I know what you mean." He eased around two men arguing next to a goat freed from its pen. "The one she will marry? Yes?"

I nodded and took a deep breath. The air smelled like animals, tangy spices, and clean water. "His father is the chairman of Old Farm, the native community next to Jakobden, and he has a renewed agreement between Old Farm and Amir Ekrem. He has to get the kyros's sigil applied to it for the agreement to be official. To keep peace in Jakobden."

Radi's eyebrows lifted. "That is important. But you said emergency. What turns this job into something dire? And how are you involved? And please, if you don't care for my questions, feel free not to reply."

The mare tripped on the edge of a stationary cart of rolled rugs, and I urged her left, her feet thudding on the sandy ground.

"I'm only a very curious person," Radi said. "My father says I got it from him."

The thought of family pierced my determination like the tip of a knife to thin skin. "My sister is like that. And our mother was too."

I gripped the reins between thumb and forefinger and set my palm against the mare's neck to feel her familiar coat. I hated being so far from my family, from Kinneret when she was so sick.

"I can tell you. It's nothing that needs to be secret. My sister..." The words didn't want to crawl up my throat. I grabbed each one and threw it out of my mouth. Sweat gathered on my upper lip. "She has a deadly fever."

Radi's black eyes fluttered close for a moment and he briefly touched my hand. His skin was very smooth. "May the Holy Fire help her."

With my thumb, I made the Holy Fire circle on my forehead. "If I can urge her Intended to hurry up with his duty and get home, I think he can save her."

"How?" he asked, hurrying more now.

I liked that my story had prompted him to pick up speed. Around carts of date palms and green vegetables, people with reed baskets on their heads, and well-dressed men and women, we zigzagged through the crowded streets like fish with the current at our backs.

"It's hard to explain," I said. "They need one another. It's like my mother and father were. If Calev comes home, if he is there for her," I tried to swallow around my tight throat, "I really think she'll heal. She's so sick, I..."

Tears rolled out before I could stop them. I sucked my trembling, lower lip into my mouth, knowing I looked like an out-of-control child but unable to stop.

Radi paused and faced me. My pulse ticked more quickly. Fear for Kinneret dwarfed the fact that this fine-faced stranger was being so kind. The crowd streamed around us, bumping gently. A dubious thought wriggled into my head. Why was he helping me so much?

"I'll do what I can," he said. "We'll find the inn and all will be well."

I wanted so much to believe him. I pushed him and nodded to move on. "Talk while we walk. Why *are* you doing this?"

Radi bit his lip, and his throat moved in a swallow as we rounded a group of women holding one large jug each. "Two reasons." His chest moved with a rough breath. "One. I wanted to leave my family's stall before my cousin came."

"Why?"

"He likes to fight."

"You don't? Or are you not good at it? Or both?" We rounded a corner and split to the right.

"I thought you said your sister was the curious one."

"This isn't curiosity. This is *being aware.*"

He grinned. "Ah. I'm very good at fighting. I'm quick."

He flashed a look that was both fierce and dangerous. An odd feeling stirred around my heart. When he turned his head, I wished he'd look at me like that again.

"But I'm not very good at fighting with someone I don't really want to hurt," he said. "I tend to respond with the most vicious attack. My father taught us both. To be safe in the city at night. But my cousin is good at pulling punches and holding back. I get excited and end up hurting him every time."

"It must not be too bad if he comes back for more."

"I still don't like hurting him." Radi frowned.

"And your second reason for helping me?"

"You're rather pretty."

I held my breath, suddenly afraid of doing something to ruin those wonderful words.

"And smart," he said. Well, those words were even better.

Forcing myself to breathe and quit acting like what he said mattered, I tugged the horse to move faster and said, "Fine." I had no idea what else to say.

"Yes. Fine." There was a little laugh in his tone and I wasn't sure I liked that. No, I couldn't lie to myself. I did. I liked it too much.

The water in the canals rushed by the side of the road, protected by small walls marked with painted calligraphy. "Do those words say what section of the city we're in?"

"No. That's the name of the kyros. *Kyros Meric, the Eternally Victorious.* And there and there spell out the name of his wife. *Seren, Pearl of the Desert.*"

"Are we getting any closer?" This was taking too long. Calev would have had to get to the kyros today, finish his duty, and get home. Or just go home and come back later to see the kyros.

"We're here."

Around a bend, a row of tents showed similar wooden signs painted in white pictures and letters, hanging from high posts above the doors.

"Here are the inns. Most of them anyway. See that one?" His first two fingers sent my gaze to a sign with a flower. Wide, open petals hovered above a bunch of words I couldn't read. "That is the Lotus Inn. A nice establishment."

The next one showed a ship and a cupped hand. "And...the Harbor Inn, maybe?"

"Yes. That's it exactly," Radi said. "We can speak to the innkeepers together if you like."

Gratitude loosened my choking grip on the reins. "Please." Who knew if they'd speak the trade tongue? I didn't know a lick of the desert language.

I described Calev to Radi and he did the same, in the desert tongue, to four different innkeepers.

None had seen him.

Radi jerked his chin at the fifth inn's sign. "The Egret's Regret."

Ignoring the name and Radi's wince at the worn-down look of the place, I rushed to the woman at the front door. "Please. I'm looking for a man. In a headtie." I tried to repeat the phrases Radi had used.

The woman's brow wrinkled.

"We are looking for an Old Farm man with a blue headtie and a handsome face," Radi said. He said some more that I couldn't untangle.

The woman's mouth popped open, and she let out a stream of sounds that overwhelmed me.

Radi nodded then spoke again.

I gripped his sleeve. "Well?"

"She saw him. He was here. Paid to stay last night," he said. "Played cards. Had too much gray plant. Left and never returned."

The air went cold. "No."

"I'm afraid so."

I hefted myself onto the mare's back and held out a hand so Radi could mount up behind me. He was basically a stranger, but I thought I might need him later. Plus, he said nice things. And in a time like this, I needed some nice things.

"He wouldn't have gone far," I said.

The tents butted up to one another for the most part, but a few left alleys between. Flies buzzed over a pile of something smelly in the nearest one. The next held two men slumped against a lotus tower's base. Neither had Calev's hair or silhouette.

"This isn't a lovely part of the city," Radi mumbled beside my ear.

"I noticed."

"If he fell asleep out here, at night…"

"There are bad places in Jakobden too. I used to live in one. You don't have to tell me the risks. I know them. I lived them."

"How old are you?"

"Fifteen and a little more."

"You act older."

"Being poor makes you grow up sometimes." I didn't want to talk about what I'd been through. I had enough on my mind.

Radi squeezed my shoulder gently. "You're well-dressed now. How did that happen?"

"That's a long story. Keep looking for Calev. Please."

"Of course."

If I didn't find him, Kinneret would die like the others in town had. Her fever had come on so fast. Just like Mother and Father's had. I could feel the truth of it like burning metal inside me, like an arrowhead lodged and searing under my ribs.

5

CALEV

An aching pain groaned from more parts than I cared to count. Putting hands on the sandy dirt, I sat up and my head boomed like a tiny cannon had fired between my ears.

"Ugh." I wiped my hand down my face. Dry flakes of blood came off my mouth. My tongue found the split in my lip.

"Old Farm," a voice over me said.

The sun shot over the tents and made it impossible to see who was talking. I held up a hand to shield my eyes. Dark kaftan. Delicate nose.

"What are you doing?" It was the woman who owned the inn. She helped me up and touched my cheek gently, though it still hurt. "Got yourself robbed, eh?"

"I suppose so." Then a shiver rushed through my throbbing head. The agreement.

"What is it? You're alive. It could've been worse."

"No. Not that." I palmed my waist, where my sash used to be. "They stole the parchment. The agreement. It's gone."

She ran a hand down my chest and her mouth tucked up at one side. "You probably lost your money too. I can help you. You can work for me for a few days. Make back what you owe. Get more to travel home?"

I shook my head and untangled her fingers from my tunic. "I have an appointment with the kyros today. He has to apply his sigil to the agreement…the peace might not hold and my father and Amir Ekrem will have to calm the advisors and…"

The cannon in my head blasted more pain that echoed through my scalp. I rubbed at my head, then saw that my smallest finger was bare. They'd taken my sigil ring. My throat went drier than it'd already been.

"They'll never know I'm who I say I am. They'll never know."

"You're Old Farm. Someone in a place of power? You talk of an amir and the kyros."

"My father is Old Farm's chairman. I was sent here to show the kyros the agreement of peace and trade between the Empire and my people. To gain his approval. And his signature. His sigil."

"I know very well what a sigil is," she said quietly, more to herself. One hand hitched onto her hip. She clicked her tongue. "What to do. What to do."

I rammed my fingers through my hair. My headtie was gone too. Those men had stolen everything of value after knocking me out. Without a headtie or an Old Farm sigil ring, the kyros would never believe I was who I was.

"I need to wash. I have to at least try to meet with the kyros."

"Let Samira handle it." She set a finger against her chest. "I know what to do." She hooked her arm through mine.

"Wait. Did you put gray plant on my food? Those men were laughing about it. My head…"

"I did no such thing." She was clearly insulted.

"Fine. But you did tell me stealing didn't happen around here. The whole thing about losing a hand and all that?"

"That's what I tell nervous customers."

"Nice."

Her shrug said it all. "You wandered into the night with an entire stalk of gray plant in your belly."

"They put it on my food. When you weren't looking or something. I didn't—"

"If you'd listened to me last night, Old Farm, you'd be happy and on your way now."

"You didn't tell me anything, Samira."

"I did. You just don't remember."

I took a heavy breath. She was probably right.

What was I going to do? I had no coin, no sigil ring to prove my blood, no parchment to show the kyros. My clothes were ripped in places and a string of blackened blood ran down the front from where my lip had opened up. I was in no condition to present myself to the ruler of most of the known world. A man who, if the stories were true, had a touch of madness that gave his immature nature a jagged edge. I couldn't enter his court looking like a desperate, lying beggar with rocks at the bottom of his grain sack.

Samira led me into the dark glow of the tented inn where she closeted me into a back room with a bowl of clean water and a cloth. She wiped my fingers clean, and because of the world being blurry still and the pain pulsing over my body, I let her finish every knuckle and nail. After a large cup of water soothed my parched throat, the world cleared a little.

"I can clean myself up."

She raised an eyebrow. "You look ready to vomit. Let me help you." The cloth was soft on my cheek and she dragged it down my neck, a new attentive gleam rising in her eyes.

Taking her hand gently—thinking of Kinneret's fierce laugh, the one that squeezed my heart and lifted it—I moved Samira's fingers away. "I can do it. Thank you for all your help."

Pursing her lips, she cocked her head. "All right then. But if you change your mind, handsome and desperate lord, you call out. I'll be at the front." Her hips swayed as she moved toward the door's flap. "Oh wait. I should maybe call you *servant*, eh? You'll need to pay me eventually."

She was enjoying this far too much. And I had the uneasy feeling she was keeping something from me. "Samira, if you think you can force me into a tumble…"

"No, no, lord servant. I'm no criminal. It's a simple matter of working off your time in this room and the food I'm about to give you. Simple business. You'll owe me. Whether or not we tumble." She winked and glided out of the room.

A grumble rose to my lips, but I closed it off. She was right. Father had taught me enough about business outside of Old Farm. Cities like this, even a smaller town like Jakobden, didn't function like my home and my people, giving and taking as needed. *They aren't family,* he'd said. *Only true family can give up food for one another when times are lean.*

Blood came off my chin easily with the wet cloth. Not so from my clothing. I washed my dusty feet. My right shoulder pinched as I stripped my tunic off over my head and I swallowed a squeak of pain. Taking up the needle and thread Samira had left beside the bowl, I turned my tunic inside out and began stitching the two rips along the sides.

I was such a complete and utter fool. I'd be lucky if Kinneret would even look at me after all this, let alone marry me. I'd be lucky if Amir Ekrem didn't take my head. He wouldn't want to, but Serhat would. She'd press him. In the years I'd known her, I'd only seen her not get her way twice.

Samira returned with a steaming plate of flatbread and some sauced vegetable I didn't recognize. I reached for the cup of watered wine she held, but she jerked it away.

"Eat first."

The vegetable tasted green and fresh, the sauce spicy and cinnamon-like. As I drained the weak wine, I realized why Samira had insisted I finish my meal first. The simple bed in the corner blurred. My knees trembled, and I braced myself on the lotus tower that held the establishment upright. Samira's hands felt prickly as she helped me to lie down.

"Sleep, lord servant. You need it."

"What did you...you gave me something...I have to leave now. Can't wait." I tried to argue, but darkness wrapped me up and stole my mind. I'd been drugged. Again.

Fevered dreams bit into my sleep.

In my nightmare, my father and the elders glared at my empty, open hands. Sweat soaked my tunic and blood ran from my lip. Kinneret pushed a curl away from her face and refused to look me in the eye. Explanations sifted from my mouth like useless chaff.

I had to wake up.

Wake up.

But I couldn't. My eyelids wouldn't open.

Can't.

Darkness swamped me.

AN ANIMAL'S bray shook me out of my stupor. There was some commotion in the street beyond the inn's thick, woven walls. I had to clear my head. Water. Water will clear the drug away.

The room was nearly black with only a strip of light coming in between the cut in the door's flap. Nearby, someone was humming. My head pounded.

The water, I reminded myself. On the table.

I pushed off the bed and my knees hit the floor. How had that happened? I lowered onto my elbows and pressed my forehead into the thin rug, desperate to ease the throbbing. Fighting a rush of clinging heat and nauseating dizziness, I eased myself to standing and put a hand against my stomach.

Where was my tunic? I only had my small clothes on. Had the woman undressed me? How long had I been out?

The table rocked under my palm and water lipped over the edge of the bowl. I plunged the cup into the cool liquid and drank all I could before I thought my stomach would burst.

Maybe Samira meant to keep me here for some strange purpose. Maybe she just thought she was being helpful. Regardless, I had to leave and I had to leave now.

6

AVI

The street beside the row of inns bustled with men who seemed to be late for important things. Two donkeys and a camel, loaded up with sacks and bedrolls, brayed their opinion on being tied together.

Radi and I had talked to someone at every inn—the owner at all but one whose employee said she was out on an errand. Worry pinched clawed fingers into my shoulders and neck and I couldn't believe it was this hard to find a person. Radi, arms crossed and leaning against a lotus tower's white stone, tapped an elbow, thinking.

"You probably need to get back to your parents' stall in the market," I said.

He yawned wide despite his obvious effort to fight it. His white teeth were straight except for one tooth on top, on the side. "I do. But what's your next idea for finding your brother-in-law to be? I hate to just leave you."

I'd had no luck at the Kyros Walls, but it was really the only place to go. Nothing else stuck out in my mind. "I'll try to get past the kyros's front guards and try to see the kyros himself, or maybe a representative."

Radi held out a hand to lead me back through the maze of tents and people of all colors speaking in three different languages. I took it and gave him the best smile I had in me. I could've figured out a way back on my own. I really just liked the feel of his fingers on mine.

I felt strangely lonely.

I'd only been gone four days, but it felt like so much longer. It was silly.

293

But the foreign tents, languages, and scents were waves crashing over my head. I couldn't seem to get a good breath.

At the market, merchants had set out their tables in front of tents that appeared to serve as both home and goods storage. Beside Radi's family's stall, a woman and a man in rich black clothing haggled with a short man. Their hands moved nearly as fast as their lips.

"Radi!" A young man—a little older than Radi and me—burst from behind the table and knocked a roll of blue wool to the ground. He hugged Radi. "Where've you been? I wanted to try the sweep Nuh showed me."

"That fighter has more patience than my wonderful mother," Radi said. "Are you paying him or something?"

The man I guessed was his cousin laughed and punched Radi in the arm, well, tried to punch him. Radi slipped his shoulder back and the cousin missed.

"No, cousin. He said I remind him of the brother he lost during the Invader attack. Before you were born."

Radi spun and held a hand out toward me. "Bash, this is Avi. She's looking for her brother-in-law. He's needed back at home. They're from Jakobden."

Bash's eyes went wide. "Ooo. Near the Pass. Have you seen a Salt Wraith?"

"I have. It's not something to be happy and excited about."

"Of course. Sorry."

"It's all right. I guess if I hadn't had seen them myself, I might think they're interesting too."

"Her sister is sick," Radi said, "and needs her husband-to-be."

I ran a hand down Arrow's warm nose and let her lip my palm, savoring the feel of her soft horsey lips. "Kinneret has a deadly fever and—"

"Wait." Bash put out a hand. "Your sister is the great Kinneret Raza? Mistress of the Pass?"

"Mistress of the what?"

"The Pass! The one who did all the amazing things that the traders are all talking about." He put his clasped hands over his heart and blinked. "Kinneret Raza."

"Um. Yes. She is. Is everyone really talking about her?" I turned to Radi, who shrugged.

Bash waved Radi off. "Don't ask him. He doesn't talk to anyone who knows anything."

"Except that he happened to spend all morning with Kinneret Raza's sister." I couldn't help but smirk.

"Except for that, yes." Bash smiled. "Why are you here? Oh wait. You said she had a fever?"

Radi cleared his throat. "If you'd shut up for a minute, she could tell you."

I did.

"But," Bash stammered, "but why can't she heal herself? She's amazing!"

"She's not a healer. My aunt is. She's on her way from Kurakia, but I don't know if she'll get to Jakobden in time."

"Aren't there other healers?"

"Yes. And the amir has called them in. No one has been able to heal her. A lot of people have this fever." I turned to Radi. "Thank you, for all you've done to help. I need to go now."

"I'll be here if you need a place to stay tonight."

"I'll find him today. I have to. I have to get back home."

He nodded, and his cousin smiled sadly. I left them explaining everything to Radi's parents, who were curious about where he'd been all morning. Radi gave me one last look and I tried to memorize his features. I didn't want to forget the boy who'd been so kind to me or the way his fingers had felt on mine.

"YOU CANNOT PASS," the guards at the Kyros Walls said. "Public supplications take place tomorrow. Today is only for those with appointments to see the kyros or his retinue."

"I just need to see if my brother-in-law is here. He does have an appointment with the kyros, for the amir in Jakobden." I wasn't sure exactly how that worked, but I wasn't going to tell this guard. "He's probably inside, waiting for a meeting right now." Since he hadn't been at any of the inns, this was the only answer.

"Right."

"Why don't you believe me? Do you really hear stories like this all the time? This is because I'm not from Akhayma." I looked to the skies as another group of people—blessed appointment holders, I had to assume—sidled past me and walked happy as you please into the kyros's courtyard.

"No," the first guard said. "We have many visitors."

"Then it's my age. I'm a little girl so you can't let me in to see the big important kyros."

"Say it again, and you become our prisoner. No one is to speak ill of the

ALISHA KLAPHEKE

kyros." He eyed the five bells on my sash. "Even if you are high-caste. You can wait until the supplicant's day."

"When is that again?" My mind was flying from one idea to another, all of them worthless.

"Tomorrow."

"I can't wait. This is important." My vision blurred, and I wiped my hand across my eyelashes. "Please. Isn't there someone else I can ask?" Kinneret could be dying right now. Or what if I waited one night, then she died on our way home? "There has to be a system for this sort of thing, for emergencies, right? Help me, please." I palmed my eyes again, angry that I couldn't seem to stop crying.

"That's enough," the second guard said.

A man in a rippling black kaftan and a well-dressed party rode up to the gates, blocking my view. I swallowed and nudged my horse away from the entrance, veering left and following a stream of men and women with steel at their belts and shiny, pointed helmets. I pounded a fist against the saddle in front of me. Arrow snorted.

"Sorry" I sighed. I was apologizing to a horse. I needed some sleep.

As I let Arrow stop to snuffle a patch of green near the canals, a skinny little boy with wild hair threw a stick into the air. My thoughts shifted and surfaced, one by one, in my head. None of my ideas would work. I couldn't pretend to have an appointment now. The guards had seen me. I didn't have enough money with me to bribe someone with an appointment to bring me in with them. Everyone gaining entrance had looked like clan chieftains anyway. They weren't going to care about one kaptan in a faraway township. My gaze followed the spin of the boy's stick as he tossed it up again.

I had to think like Kinneret. She never let anything get in the way of what she wanted.

The little boy caught the stick neatly between his teeth. Amazing. Especially considering flames flickered at the ends of the stick. A crowd gathered around him, stomping their feet in praise and tossing him small coins. A girl and a boy, siblings from the look of their similar noses, ran past.

"I'm going to tell Mother about that new boy!" the girl said.

Her brother nodded. "Su will want to see too. I'll get him."

I searched the crowd for Calev. "Calev ben Y'hoshua! Where are you?"

The noise of merchants calling out, hooves on the ground, and the rush of everyday life in this big city trampled my shouts

296

If only I could toss fire and catch it in my mouth. Then maybe I could get everyone's attention. Or at least Calev's.

I huffed a breath. What would Kinneret do?

Wait. That's it. I tugged Arrow to a stop beside a man selling ponies. If I did something that got everyone's attention, surely Calev would find me.

But what could I do?

"You want to sell your fine mount?" The pony merchant set a gentle hand on my horse's neck.

"No. Thank you." I had an idea. A foolish plan. "I think I'm going to need her for a ladder."

This was the stupidest idea I'd ever had. But it was just the sort of thing Kinneret would do and somehow get away with.

"What?" The merchant scratched his head.

I dug my heels into Arrow's sides and drove through the crowded street toward the Kyros Walls, a good length from where the guards stood so if they came after me, I could get back on Arrow and ride away, into the crowd. I edged Arrow sideways against the pale stone, took my feet from the stirrups, and went to a crouch on the saddle. Arrow huffed and sidestepped.

"Easy now. Be still."

Using the balance I'd learned on boats, I stood on her back and reached as high as I could. I needed handholds to climb. Arrow shifted her weight onto one back hoof and I caught myself against the wall, heart drumming.

"Girl, what are you doing?" The pony merchant had followed me. He stood below, taking Arrow's reins.

"Don't worry about it."

"Can I have your horse when you fall and crack your head open?" Seeing my scowl, he let go of the reins. "Such a face on such a young person."

"Mind your own business." I was going to fall and this was so stupid. But I couldn't wait another night to get to Calev. Kinneret was dying. Every minute here was a minute wasted.

He held out his hands. "All right. Don't say I didn't warn you."

Finally, my fingers dug into a space between the stones. I jammed a sandal into another uneven place in the Kyros Walls and pushed, leaving the saddle's surface. My other foot dangled as I shuffled it around and searched for a little ledge, a flaw in the quarried white rock, some mortar that could be crumbled away. Sweat gathered under my shirt. My caste bells jingled as if they worried I was going to fall.

A woman below gasped and said something in the desert tongue. Another voice replied. They were almost right under me.

"Just some…entertainment. For the kyros. That's all. No problem here," I panted, knowing full well I looked completely mad climbing up the wall.

I shifted to another set of handholds. The top of the wall was only an arm's length away. I reached and reached, my one lodged foot shaking, and grasped the high, toothed edge of the walls. A sad grin split my dry lips. Kinneret would've loved to be here doing this with me. Normally, I would've told her to stop being a crazy person. But I had to risk this for her. If I could get Calev's attention, get him home, she'd be all right. I was sure of it. My heart thrummed with the truth of it.

I waved my arms. "Calev ben Y'hoshua!"

The crowd—a clutter of black and red and orange kaftans—teemed on both sides of the walls. A huge black-blue tent with star-shaped panels of silvery material commanded the kyros's courtyard. Smaller tents, with people going in and out, surrounded it. Some paths were lined with smooth rock and a simple stable at the far end revealed swishing animal tails and servants with large bells suspended over their heads and attached to metal belts. A few faces peered up at me. I had to be louder.

"Calev ben Y'hoshua! I'm looking for Calev! An Old Farm with black hair and an agreement from Jakobden's amir!"

Only a few more people looked up. I was going to have to be like the boy with the fire stick. I tied my skirt between my legs so I wouldn't give *that* kind of show, placed my hands on the wide surface of the top of the wall, and lifted myself into a handstand.

"Avi!" Radi's voice bounced up to me.

My elbow buckled.

Someone else shouted.

I caught myself. My lungs were about to burst.

"Avi, you have to get down! You'll be arrested!" Radi's words were strained, high-pitched in his stress.

"Is everyone paying attention?"

"Yes, for Holy Fire's sake, yes. Get down! I have a cousin—very, very distant but still— who works for the kyros's wife. Her name is Meekra. Mother said she thinks she is her handmaiden. Mother said we might be able to get a message to her and some information if we're lucky. Get down, please!"

I lowered my feet and stood upright, looking not at Radi's side of the wall, but toward the courtyard. High castes and nobles stared, their servants gawking beside them.

"If you meet a Calev ben Y'hoshua," I called out, cupping my hand to my mouth, "tell him to find his sister at…" I couldn't name somewhere everyone knew in case the guards decided to come after me. "...at the place he would feel most comfortable!" I repeated the message, then noticed a shift in the crowd by the gates. I spun to see the guards, on the other side of the wall, pushing through the people and toward Radi.

"Run!" I called to him.

"No! I'll help you down. Start climbing. I'll help you!"

"Just go!" The guards were already closing in. "Go!"

Radi positioned Arrow below me. "Hurry!"

My thundering pulse choked me. I rubbed my palms on my skirt, untied the knot, and lowered myself onto my stomach. I found a foothold and pretty soon Radi's guiding whispers were nearer. With my feet on the saddle again, I took Radi's hand.

"Come on!" I jerked on his fingers to get him to jump up onto Arrow behind me.

He huffed, then mounted easily, his muscled calf showing as his kaftan billowed.

"Go!" I shouted into Arrow's ear. She lurched forward. We were going to get away.

Large hands thrust through the crowd and grabbed the reins, jerking us to a stop.

Radi and I slid from Arrow's back. The ground jarred my body and my teeth banged together.

The first guard clamped down on my wrist and hefted me up. "Don't even believe you are high-caste."

"This one definitely isn't," the second guard said.

Radi set his jaw as the man put a yatagan's long, steel edge to his throat.

My skin felt too thin and my heart beat in my ears. "Please. You must let me speak to the kyros. Or his advisor. I'm not lying."

The guards led us—along with Arrow who certainly didn't deserve to be a part of all this—to the back of the city.

"This boy's cousin is the kyros's handmaiden. We need to speak to her. Where are you taking us?" I asked. "To see the kyros?"

The guards laughed and Radi shook his head. "They're taking us to the cells."

My bones were hollow. My heartbeat echoed through them.

"Radi. I'm so sorry. You should've run. I'm so, so sorry."

"You didn't force me to do anything. I'm here because I want to be. Well, I don't want to be here exactly. But, you know."

"Shut your mouths," the first guard spat as we crossed under a huge arch and into a sloped area filled with archery targets, a long row of what looked like stables, low buildings crowded with armed fighters, and a line of barred cells. The sun burned the image into my eyes and a shiver tugged at my limbs.

They were going to cage us like animals.

A stable boy ran up, and with direction from the guards, took Arrow to the stables. As her shiny coat and silky tail disappeared, my stomach worked its way toward my throat. She was my only way home. I couldn't make it back to Jakobden on foot. Not on my own.

The guards pushed Radi and me into the same cell.

"Wait, please," Radi said. "My cousin Meekra works for Pearl of the Desert. Can you at least send a message to her? She won't know my name but—"

The guard ignored Radi.

The clang of the bolt sliding shut blasted through me, turning my legs to pudding. I curled a hand around the bars to keep from falling.

Radi winced, his face a mask of pity. Two men and a woman crouched in the back corners, their clothing in rags and their faces thin. They looked at us like we might eat them for breakfast.

"Avi." Radi grasped the bars and looked into the training field. "What are we going to do now?"

I dropped to my knees and stared at the lock, with no idea how to escape. We were trapped. Maybe for the rest of our lives. Worrying for Kinneret, I'd acted like her. Reckless. Not at all like myself. I should have planned and taken my time. Figured out something smart instead of climbing walls like a fool. And now Kinneret was going to die without Calev to save her and without her only family at her side.

I put my head in my hands and cried.

7
CALEV

M y stomach growled as I dried my hands on the cloth near a pile of clean platters. I'd spent an entire day, a night, and most of this day too working off what I owed Samira, picking up after idiots who acted like I had my first night here. Now I had to leave. To get to the kyros.

Today was an open supplication day for people who didn't have formal appointments, messages from foreign rulers or any of the Empire's amirs. Today, even as a ragged nobody, I could get into the Kyros Walls. What I would do once I had the kyros's attention, I wasn't sure, but the sun hung low in the sky and there was no time left for wondering. The last rays pierced the tent and gave Samira's inn the glow of blood.

"Leaving so soon?" Checking that none of the patrons peered over her countertop, Samira set two bags of coin in a hole under a wooden carving of a desert lion.

"Yes. You said the kyros sees anyone today, right?"

She nodded. "And in five days, he will again."

"In five days, I'll be at home."

"What are you going to show the kyros to prove your story?"

"He'll believe me."

The slant of her eyebrow told me she didn't think so, but I didn't care. I had to try.

"Thank you for all the help. I won't forget what you did for me."

Samira's eyebrow lifted mockingly. "Ah, it was nothing. If you want to work again tonight and get a meal out of it, come back to me, lord servant."

"*Lord servant* isn't a title I relish. I think my time wearing it is over."

"So haughty is the lord servant! We'll see how you feel when the kyros throws you out on your handsome bum."

"Goodbye, Samira."

"May the Holy Fire bless you."

"But not so much that I won't work out an indenture to you for the rest of my days, hm?"

She smiled wide. "That's about right."

THE LINE GOING through the Kyros Walls snaked around the oasis pool and through the market. It was nearly nightfall, and I was close enough to study the hilt of a guard's yatagan. Small pomegranates decorated the length of it and made me miss home.

Or did I?

Father was going to explode when he heard all of this. He'd publicly punish me at best and Kinneret would never have me as her husband. At worst, I'd be cast out of Old Farm.

My empty stomach rolled.

Father and the amir were expecting me by nightfall in two days. My failure would shame Ekrem as the new amir. The agreement between the Empire—with Jakobden's amir as representative—and Old Farm had been continuous and peaceful for two hundred years.

My knuckles pressed into my forehead where my headtie had been until the robbery.

Had I already started problems between the people at home? Had I already lost my people's chance to remain as we were, with our own traditions and commerce, separate from the Empire?

Surely, Amir Ekrem would be merciful. He was a good man. But even if he and his advisors didn't begin tougher negotiations or accuse Old Farm of not taking his rule seriously, I would still be seen as a failure and a fool. How would I provide for Kinneret without my position?

I blew out a breath, staring at the people in front of me. Why was this taking so long?

I nudged the man in front of me. "Sorry, but do you think we'll get in today?"

The man bunched his lips. "Hmm. Maybe?" He shrugged and crossed his arms in a strange way with both hands on top of his forearms.

Closing my eyes, I prayed very, very hard.

"You," a deep voice said.

It was a new man. He wore a warrior's kaftan and pants, but with detailed embroidery around the collar and down the sleeves. He had a bright blue sash devoid of bells, which spoke of his pure desert bloodline. His gaze went from my own clothing to my face like he was looking for clues.

"Come. Why are you here?" he asked.

Hope soared inside my chest. Hope mixed with the fear of falling into even worse trouble. Following him through the Kyros Walls, I explained everything. By the time I stopped talking, we'd arrived at the finest tent, the one with stars along its top.

"I don't believe this wild story." The man didn't look at me as he said those terrible words. Instead, he peered inside the kyros's tent and pulled something green from his sash. "But I do know the kyros was set to meet with an Old Farm representative. Yesterday."

So even if I did gain entrance and did everything right, I'd still be on his bad side for missing the appointment. My stomach rolled. Kyros Meric was known to be mercurial. One wrong word and your life was forfeit. I swallowed. I had to keep my wits about me and do the best I could.

"It's the truth," I said to the warrior. "I swear it. Ask me anything about Old Farm."

"There have been strange tales coming out of Jakobden. No one quite understands what happened to dispose Amir Mamluk. And the talk about that girl and her abilities with the cursed waters there..."

"Kinneret. She is my Intended."

"Your Intended?"

"She will be my wife."

"And tomorrow you'll be the kyros, yes?"

"No. I'm serious. I was with her during the discovery of hidden Ayarazi. The deaths...the—"

"Enough. Your story is interesting. The kyros won't want to hear all of it, but his wife, Seren, Pearl of the Desert, will. And I, Erol, one of her personal guards, do everything I can to please her."

His black eyes shone as he guided me into the tent and pressed the green something from his sash into my hand. "Chew this mint so you'll be presentable to the royals."

I did as I was told, thinking of what Oron would say. He would've made some comment now about better places to stick that mint. I wished I could laugh.

My guide Erol walked over to the copper Holy Fire bowl and passed a hand over the flames, praying silently. He gave me a look. Though I wasn't wearing my sigil ring or my Old Farm headtie, I had to show them I was who I said I was.

I shook my head, politely refraining from worshipping like the rest of the Empire. The guide's eyebrows rose, but he dipped his chin in acknowledgment and led me up a long rug where I bowed to the royal couple and their general.

The kyros leaned on the arm of his silver gilt chair, looking bored. His wife, Seren, Pearl of the Desert, stood tall in a dark blue kaftan, a yellow sash and—like the old amir had in Jakobden—she wore a slim length of leather around her head. A single, high-caste bell hung from the tie, touching a spot between the eyebrows.

After the guide spoke to them, Seren smiled kindly, but her eyes were tired. Being a kyros's wife probably wasn't the easiest of roles and she'd only been married a few weeks. Despite the tired eyes, she looked as young as Kinneret.

The kyros himself was a weasel of a man. Just the way he sat, angled away from his wife and with that sulky posture told me everything I needed to know.

He looked me up and down. "You claim to be Amir Ekrem and Chairman Y'hoshua ben Aharon's emissary?"

"Yes, my kyros." My words shook a little, but I managed not to sound like the idiot I was.

"Where is the agreement? Am I to apply my symbol, my royal sigil, to your forehead?"

Some of the courtiers around laughed, but most narrowed their eyes like I'm sure I did. His wife, Seren, breathed out through her nose, irritated.

"It would be an honor, my kyros, but I doubt the ink would hold under the weight of three days of hot travel."

Kyros Meric smiled. "Perhaps you're right. Can you tell the details of the agreement?"

He'd need them to create a new copy to sign and seal. He also probably wanted them so he could check my story.

"Of course, my kyros."

As I started detailing the bushels of lemons and olives and the amount of barley and wheat we'd produced on average the last ten years, my tongue moved slowly and my mind whirred facts out too quickly. I stumbled over percentages of profit through trade.

Erol said something quietly in the desert tongue. The kyros nodded and shifted in his chair.

I smoothed my wrinkled, sashless tunic and tried not to worry about what he'd said. "So the amir will keep thirty percent of the late harvest trade profit and an eighth of the actual products."

The kyros waved impatiently. "Fine. Fine. But what happened to you? Why are you presenting yourself to me like a pauper?"

"I was robbed, my kyros."

He sat up, a hand on the hilt of his personal dagger. An emerald winked at me. "In my city? No."

"Yes."

Every sound in the room blinked out of existence.

All I could hear was my own heart beating the consequence of what I'd done. I'd publicly disagreed with Kyros Meric. My life was forfeit.

Pressing my lips together, I bowed low, pressing my forehead into the rug. My heart pounded erratically.

Shaking, I lifted my gaze and saw Erol speaking with the kyros. Seren put a hand on Kyros Meric's arm, her eyes imploring.

"You should die for your disrespect," the kyros said.

My stomach clenched. I forced myself to keep breathing. I had so many more things to do in life. I didn't want it to be over yet. I wanted to become chairman of Old Farm, to enjoy my engagement to Kinneret, to be Avi's brother and Oron's confidant.

"But I won't have you killed just yet," he said. "If you are who you say you are...well, I won't put the Old Farm chairman's son to death so quickly." The kyros nodded to two guards. "Take him to the cells. I'll have to think on what to do."

The cells? As in, prison?

I held up my hands. "Perhaps, my kyros, if you sent a rock dove to Old Farm and asked them to verify my story—"

The guards grabbed my arms. Their fingers dug into the bruises from the robbery, but the pain lancing through me had nothing to do with flesh and bone. My pain was the agony of knowing I had failed, miserably, utterly, and totally failed.

I imagined Father's angry eyes, the dejected set to his mouth when he learned his eldest son was rotting in a cell in Akhayma. In my mind, I saw confusion twist Kinneret's beautiful face and could almost hear her arguing that the story couldn't be true, that her Calev wouldn't do something so stupid, that I'd never risk staying at a low inn or fall to thieves during such an important mission.

Before I closed my eyes and let the guards drag me from the tent, I saw Seren whispering in Kyros Meric's ear. Probably yet another person shocked at my behavior, at my lack of propriety, at what they believed were lies.

As they walked me to a row of barred rooms near the military training facilities, I hated myself more and more. Because I'd been in a hurry to rest and eat, I'd spend my life wasting away in the kyros's prison.

8

AVI

Radi elbowed me and jerked his chin toward the other cells. "A new prisoner."

"We have to focus on how we can get out of here."

The man they threw into a cell two down from ours had shoulder-length black hair. I squinted. Something about him plucked a string in me.

I hurried to the far side of the cell and looked again. Dirty tunic. Definitely not from here. From Jakobden. But the fabric. The little red spots—

"Pomegranates!"

The noise of the training field—yatagans banging together and horses galloping—covered my outburst.

Radi eyed me like I'd gone as mad as the man humming in the corner. I grabbed the front of Radi's kaftan and shook him.

"That's my brother-in-law!"

I pushed away from him to go see again, to make sure. It was impossible. But I was almost sure.

Radi came up beside me. "Don't yell to him until those guards leave. You'll draw the wrong kind of attention."

"But that guard is here all the time. What about him?"

"He's a middle-caste guard. He won't care as much as the high-caste ones."

I did notice the bells on the permanent guard's shoulders. But a shout built up behind my lips regardless. I had to call out to Calev, to get him to

307

turn around, to see if it really was him. The high-caste guards traded words with the middle-caste guard, and they grumbled. One made some sort of joke and they all laughed before the high-caste ones stalked away, heading toward the city's back gate.

"Calev!" I hissed. My bones pressed into my skin, into the bars, like I could squeeze through if I only tried hard enough. "It's Avi!"

Radi kept an eye on the guard, who scraped something off the bottom of his boot and spit into the dirt.

The cell between us and the man I thought might be Calev was crowded. Eleven people milled about the space, blocking my view.

"Move!" I waved an arm at them.

One woman glared at me and chewed her thumbnail. Everyone else completely ignored me.

I growled and bumped the bars with the bottom of my fist.

Radi began speaking to the people in the next cell. The foreign words sounded so beautiful, though I didn't have time for beauty right now. Several faces looked up at him. Most shifted to the front of the cell.

The man I hoped was Calev had his arms crossed and his back to me. His body was coiled with anger, probably frustration.

"Calev!"

He spun. Familiar eyes widened. Inside me, joy opened her arms and threw happy tears down my cheeks.

Calev flung himself against the bars, his face pale. "What are you doing here?" His words were a shaking sail in an undecided wind.

"Me? What are *you* doing here? You should be honored. You're doing the amir's work. And the chairman's. Why did they lock you up?"

Calev's gaze flicked between me and Radi. "Because I'm an idiot."

"I'm going to need more than that." I pressed my forehead against the metal.

As he ran hands through his hair, a purple bruise showed along his forearm. And another under his cheek. His headtie was gone. It was obvious something terrible had happened to him.

I sighed and introduced Radi. "He helped me look for you. The guards here wouldn't let me into the courtyard. When we failed, I climbed the Kyros Walls and went a little mad trying to get everyone's attention, to see if you were around."

Calev bent at the middle, shoulders moving in a heavy breath, then straightened. "I was careless. I stayed at a low-fare inn and drank too much. Let down my guard. Stayed in an inn I shouldn't have. Some men laced my food with gray plant, then robbed me. They took the agreement between

Jakobden and Old Farm. They took my ring." He held up a hand, his lips tipped low at the edges.

I scratched my head and blinked.

Calev nodded and looked away.

"You *are* an idiot," I said.

Radi made a noise that said he disagreed.

"Well? He is. How could you, Calev? You have everything. Why would you risk it by being careless in a city you don't know?"

"Says the girl who was arrested for climbing the Kyros Walls," Radi said quietly, raising an eyebrow.

I flashed him a glare.

"There's no excuse," Calev said. "I was careless. Arrogant." He breathed out heavily. "Then I presented myself to the kyros. I told him everything. But he didn't believe I'd been robbed and my mouth moved before I could stop it and I disagreed with him. Out loud."

Radi sucked in a startled breath. A few of the people in the other cell turned their heads to stare at Calev.

"I'm guessing that isn't a good thing," I said.

"No," Radi said. "He should already be dead. I'm surprised he's not. The kyros is…" He eyed the guards and let the words fall into silence.

"I only wanted to assure him that I was telling the truth," Calev said. "I've made a mess of everything I've done since I entered this city. The kyros said he wanted to think about what to do with me."

My news, news of home, thrashed around in my chest like a screaming rabbit ripped open by a fox. I had to tell him. Even though he looked ready to break into a thousand pieces already, shame cracking his features and movements. He needed to know about the fever.

"I came here to get you," I said. "To bring you back fast."

Calev cocked his head, listening.

My throat burned, and my happy tears from earlier began to sting my skin. "Kinneret is dying."

He went still, his hands frozen at his sides. It looked like he'd stopped breathing.

"She has a fever." The truth scraped claws against my heart. "Many have already died from it. It's the same one that killed our parents. But if you go to her, if you're with her, she'll find the strength to heal. She'll fight it and win."

"Did your aunt come over from Kurakia?"

"We sent a rock dove, asking her to come and try to heal Kinneret and the others. But it takes time for word to get across the Pass this time of year."

Nodding, Calev paced a small circle, his hands in his hair again. "She can't heal herself."

I shook my head. "She tried. She's too weak. She keeps thinking she hears Mother and Father. Then she wakes and is crushed by their loss all over again. The fever has her mind." I squeezed the bars until the pain of it stopped my tears.

Calev's gaze snapped to my face. He didn't have to say a word. I knew exactly what his eyes were saying.

We have to get out of here now.

"Enough talk," the guard barked in trade tongue. He knocked the hilt of his dagger on our cell door. "More noise means less food."

The people in the cell between Calev and us shifted apart and Calev disappeared from view.

I breathed out and looked at the ceiling. "Radi. What can we do?" I whispered.

"I don't know. He won't listen to us. None of them will."

We tucked ourselves into the far corner, away from the humming madman and the guard who walked the strip of dirt in front of the cells.

"If I could get word to my family," Radi said, "maybe my cousin Bash could bribe the guards. Such a slight offense as yours…I don't think they'd come after you. More important worries on their minds. But your brother-in-law, well, his offense is great. I don't know, Avi. I don't know what we could do even if we weren't trapped alongside him." Radi's eyes were serious, burning.

Shaking, I took his hand, held it to my chest. "Thank you for caring. I'm so, so sorry you're here because of me, because of us."

He gripped my fingers and his mouth tried to smile, but only managed a lift on one side. "I made my choices. This isn't your fault. Or your brother's."

He set his forehead against mine and we shared a breath. He was still a stranger, but a stranger I was glad to have on my side.

9

CALEV

The moon hid behind billowing clouds, leaving us prisoners in the gray night. The floor of the cell was nothing but cold dirt, and though all I wanted was to rage my way out of this place and back to Kinneret, exhaustion dragged me into a fevered dream.

We were on Kinneret's boat.

The small dhow dipped in the water and the one triangular sail snapped in a burst of sudden wind. In my dream, the hull was just big enough for us to lie down beside one another.

"What are we going to dream about, Calev?" Kinneret's voice was low and teasing in my ear.

In my mind, her breath flowed over my temple as she pressed the length of her strong legs, stomach, and chest against me.

I shivered.

She smelled like sea salt and the night flowers that lined the path away from town. Her eyes were almost the same light color, contrasting with her dark skin. She thought Miriam's dark eyes were prettier, and maybe they were, but Kinneret was Kinneret. Her coloring meant little. She could've had purple spotted eyes and I'd still think she was perfect. Perfect for me, anyway.

"Tell me," she whispered in my dream.

I decided to show her instead of wasting time talking.

Her lips parted slightly as I kissed her. A warmth stirred deep inside me, and I smiled into her jaw, then the long column of her neck, pulling her closer. She was so soft and had so many angles and curves.

I was lost. I was found.

Still dreaming, my hand drifted over her stomach and my thumb passed over the arch of a rib, the smooth skin. She made a noise, a gentle exhale, and I couldn't stay still. I moved onto my elbows and cradled her beneath me, her head in my hands.

"This could prove an embarrassing kind of dream to have in a prison cell, my love." Her laugh made her body buzz against my hips and chest.

I planted a kiss under her earlobe where her pulse beat, then slid a hand to her lower back, her shirt crumpling under my palm. She wrapped her arms around my neck and tangled her fingers in my hair, grabbing a little roughly. A grin tugged at my lips.

"I don't care," I said into her soft, soft skin.

"Yes, you do."

"No. I really don't." I aligned our bodies and inhaled, my stomach smoothing across hers. "And I think we need less clothing on. Now."

She put hands on my chest, her eyes widening. "Something's wrong."

I sat up. The boat melted away.

Everything in the dream was black except for us.

Kinneret's face paled and she looked at her hands. Her fingers curled into skeletal claws.

She gasped. Or I did.

"What's happening?" I patted her head and came away with strands of her hair. My stomach twisted. "Are you sick?"

When I met her eyes again, her pupils dilated. She fell back. I caught her. Bones pressed through her skin and a scream built inside my throat.

"No!"

The nightmare shattered and I was awake again.

And then I saw the cell door, the rising sun over Akhayma's military training field, and Avi's worried face peering through the bars two cells down from mine.

I turned, kneeled in the corner, and vomited.

"Bring him some water, please!" Avi called out to the guard.

The man grumbled but opened my cell door and handed me a sloshing bowl of cool liquid. Surprised that he cared, I drank a sip, but couldn't manage the rest, instead setting it on the ground. I wiped my mouth with my sleeve and stood on shaking legs, hoping the guard's behavior meant something positive.

Radi and Avi stood staring through the bars.

"You all right?" Radi asked, kindness in his eyes.

I nodded, my skin throwing off the scent of fear and my mind shoving out images of Kinneret's skeletal hands in the dream.

The guard was sharpening his dagger on a whetstone, and the brass studs on his leather vest reflected the Holy Fire in the bowl beside a plate of chicken.

"Do you know my story?" I asked him quietly. I had to get out of here.

He stopped and glanced my way. "Old Farm. Or maybe not." A shrug lifted his shoulders.

"My father is the chairman."

"Rich boy."

"Yes, I am." The words left a bitter taste on my tongue. "And I could make you richer."

"How is that exactly? From what I can tell, you are trapped in a cell and have nothing but the ratty tunic on your *blessed* back."

"For now. But when I leave here—"

"No sign of that happening anytime soon."

Avi and Radi came forward, listening from their cell.

"It could happen right now," I said. "There could be men on their way here to release me, to apologize, to send me on my way to do Old Farm business."

The guard went back to sharpening. I raised my voice, just a little.

"Then you'd be the same. Stuck in this lowly position. Guarding filth. No glory here, hm? Unless you count the redistribution of waste materials." I wiggled my eyebrows at the chamber pot by the door.

Standing, the guard narrowed his eyes. "Do you want to be beaten? Because I can arrange that. Even from my *lowly position*."

"Or," I whispered as he came close, "you could leave my door and that one over there open before you leave and find yourself the lucky recipient of a rich, unnamed uncle's gift in five days when I've had time to return home unscathed and put things in order. No one would need to know if you used the silver wisely, slowly."

I almost sounded like Oron. He would've sworn or made it all seem even dirtier than this bribery attempt really was.

Dagger in hand, the guard rubbed his chin with a knuckle. "It's tempting. We'll see, blessed, rich boy. We'll see."

Every bit of me wanted to beg, to tell my story, to paint a picture of Kinneret and her suffering and try to play on his sympathy. But my time with Oron had taught me that some men had no sympathy. Maybe this stone-faced guard was one of those sad souls. I retreated before I ruined my chance at success.

A new guard jogged up to the older guard. They traded some words and the old guard started toward the city. He looked over his shoulder and pursed his lips, shaking his head a fraction. My heart fell. I held tight to the bars to keep from sliding to the ground. Avi and Radi whispered together, Avi's frown making everything worse.

I'd failed. We were stuck.

The new guard opened Avi's cell and jerked her arm, holding out shackles. Radi stepped forward, but the guard shouldered him back expertly. With Avi in chains, the guard welcomed another guard into the cell and they grabbed Radi, ringing his wrists in metal too.

I slammed a hand on the door as the new guards shackled Radi and Avi.

"Where are you taking them?"

The guards' silence flooded my mind with the nightmare about Kinneret—her hair falling from her head, the grip fear had on her voice.

Avi looked at me with big eyes.

A shudder wrapped around me.

The shorter of the two guards led them away—To their punishments? To their deaths?—and it was as if Kinneret's life drained step by step, heartbeat to heartbeat.

A shout built in my lungs, and I unleashed it, seeing red.

The taller guard kicked the door. "You should behave. I'm to take you to the kyros for your sentencing."

My hands fell to my sides.

Avi and Radi's silhouettes blended into the walls' shadow as the city took them.

I stepped back, trying to keep my frustration in check as the guard opened my door. He linked my hands with thick, steel shackles engraved with the Kyros Meric's title. I was marked as his property. No better than a cow, fit to be used or slain as he saw fit.

THE KYROS WASN'T SITTING at the high table in the main tent this time. Instead his general and his wife Seren regarded supplicants with serious eyes, explaining the kyros wasn't well today.

While a middle-caste woman detailed who she believed had murdered her husband and a high-caste man my age explained a bad trade with one of the steppe's noble clans, my heart jumped from erratic, jolting beats to sluggish rolls that left me dizzy.

Kinneret, I will get back to you. Be strong. Be strong.

Finally, it was my turn.

My knees hit the carpet.

The general's aged voice rumbled through my spinning head. "Stand. Give your name."

Putting a hand on my knee, I managed to straighten. I raised my chin and did my best to give him the look my father would've. "I am Calev ben Y'hoshua, son of Old Farm's chairman, Y'hoshua ben Aharon."

"You spoke out against the kyros, Calev ben Y'hoshua."

"I am sorry, General, and Pearl of the Desert." I knelt again. "It was an accident born of frustration."

Seren waved a hand so I would rise up. "Tell us your story, Calev ben Y'hoshua. Not about the agreement and the robbery. Tell us about your connection to the girl and boy who threatened the kyros's peaceful home with a dangerous and disrespectful stunt on the top of the Kyros Walls."

"Please, will you tell me where they are? Where they've been taken? She is my Intended's sister. The man, the boy, he is a friend of hers. The girl, Avigail, came here to bring me home. My Intended, Kinneret, is dying of a fever."

"The girl and boy are being questioned by the lower bench. As a favor to my new husband. Are you a healer of some sort?"

"No."

"Then this is all a story to waste our time," the general snapped.

"Avi believes that if I go to Kinneret, she'll heal. She'll be able to fight the fever until her aunt, who is a healer, arrives."

"Why?" Seren's look intensified.

"Because we love one another."

The general made a noise and crossed his arms, but Seren's eyes narrowed and she asked me to tell her more.

"I don't know if Avi is right," I said. "I've seen plenty in the last year to let me know there is much in the world that is…difficult to understand. Maybe she's right. Maybe my love for Kinneret can save her. I'll do anything to try it. It's all I have to give."

"Love is all you have to give," Seren said in a whisper.

I nodded. "Yes, Pearl of the Desert."

The general jerked a hand at some men. "Take him back to the cells."

Seren opened her mouth to say something, but no words came out. Her silence took my breath and made the world seem too heavy to bear. Was she going to save me? I would likely never know.

10

AVI

Rain trampled down from black clouds and onto my head where I stood, back in our cell. I'd thought it hardly ever rained in Akhayma. My heart chilled.

Had Calev's luck run out?

With shaking fingers, I rung out my hair, then braided it again. Radi stared into the training fields, unblinking. I put a hand on his arm, feeling like I'd known him for so much longer than I had.

"What are you thinking?"

"About Meekra. About how we might drive the guards crazy until they decide to send a message."

Leaning against the bars, I searched the cells for Calev. He stood at the front, near the door, his forehead pressed into the metal and rain dripping off his chin and the scant beard growing there.

"Calev."

He didn't move. I eyed the guards, not wanting to push our luck. Some more important looking people had questioned us while Calev spoke to the kyros. They'd frowned and murmured to themselves, then sent us back here. At least we weren't dead yet. I supposed Calev had nothing to share since he'd been silent as stone when we got back, only gasping in relief to see us alive.

"Calev!" His head turned and one hand slid down the bars. "Did you see Pearl of the Desert's handmaiden?"

His eyebrows drew together as Radi came up beside me. I stood closer, enjoying his warmth in the wet, chilly rain.

"Maybe. There were several there serving…"

Radi pushed into the front corner to get closer to Calev. "Was there a girl named Meekra? Or something like that?"

Calev shook his head. "I didn't hear any names. Why?"

"She's my cousin," Radi said. "Distant cousin. I don't think she knows. I thought maybe if she was told we were related, maybe Pearl of the Desert would be more apt to listen to our story."

The man at the back of our cell hummed more loudly. He sounded like angry bees. I hoped he wasn't going to strangle us in our sleep. Not that I could sleep.

"Ask to send a message to her," Calev said.

I rubbed my temples. "We did. They won't. But I'm going to try again. Guard!" I called out, heading to the door. "He has a message for Pearl of the Desert's handmaiden, Meekra. This is her cousin, Radi."

Radi put a hand over his heart and smiled tentatively. He blinked silver raindrops from his thick, black eyelashes.

The middle-caste guard ambled over. "Fine. Fine. What is this message? You better not be wasting my time. The others will never let me hear the end of it."

"We're telling the truth. This is important."

"He really is Meekra's cousin?" Respect and not a little awe flavored the guard's question. That would work to our advantage.

"She is very close to his branch of the family." I was lying almost as well as Oron. "If she finds out Radi is here, she'll definitely want to talk to him."

"Why are you just now mentioning this?"

I gave him my best glare. "We told the other guards."

The guard looked at his boots, kicked the bottom of the door.

"What can I tell you to persuade you to send the message?" Radi cocked his head.

The guard's puffy eyes flicked up. "Where was she born?"

Radi winced, then smoothed his face with a hand. "Akhmim."

The guard lowered his head and stared at Radi like he could somehow see through him. "I'll send a boy with a word. You better be telling the truth. What do you want the message to say?"

"That her cousin Radi has been wrongfully imprisoned and he knows something that will help her lady ease the kyros's worry about Jakobden."

"I doubt the boy will even get through, but fine, fine. I'll send it." With a nod, the guard ambled away, waving a hand to a stablehand wandering through the training fields.

I squeezed Radi tightly. "Thank you."

His smile warmed me even more than his body.

The guard waved a boy over and bent to speak into the messenger's cherubic face. The boy took off at a run.

Calev and I traded a look. It wasn't much to hang our hopes on, but it was something.

HOURS PASSED and the rain finally let up. Radi and I sat in the back of the cell, in the corner opposite that humming madman.

"Is this all right?" I set my head on Radi's shoulder.

My right eye kept twitching. I was so tired. Too tired to sleep. I couldn't stop staring at the far gates leading to the city, straining to see that messenger boy or a woman who looked well-dressed enough to be a handmaiden in the royal household.

"Of course, it's all right." Radi's voice rumbled in his chest. His knobby hands rested on his thighs and his breathing was a little uneven.

"Are you feeling sick?" It wouldn't have surprised me. This wasn't exactly a kyros's tent out here in the chill and wet and knowing we could be put to death at any second.

"No. I feel great. Considering."

I sat up, the ground wet under my palm, and looked into his face, at his crooked tooth and lopsided grin. "You're not breathing right."

He pinched his lips together. "I have a beautiful girl practically in my lap. How do boys usually breathe in these situations?"

The skin over my collarbone prickled. "I…I don't know."

I froze, not wanting to move. Scared to move and do something wrong. Something to make him stop thinking I was beautiful or I don't know… I felt like a sail tie that had been unwound and left to fly in the wind. I might break free of the knot and soar into the clouds. I might lash someone in the face. I might fall into the sea and drown.

A final drop of rain rolled down my cheek. Radi touched it, too rough at first, then easing. He dragged it across my face, then cupped my chin.

"May I kiss you?"

"Now? In prison? When my sister is dying?"

"It's terrible. I'm sorry. I'm terrible."

The world wasn't storming anymore, but my heart and mind were still being thrashed by worry and fear and anger and frustration. I suddenly wanted the heat of his lips on mine and the tiny, brief relief of knowing someone was right there beside me in this storm.

"Please do," I said.

"Please kiss you?"

"Yes." Tears welled in my eyes, hot and blurring Radi's face.

Gently, he set his peaked upper lip against mine, then his slightly chapped lower one. The chill went out of me and left me so, so warm. He pressed lightly, just once, then pulled back.

I wanted to say *Thank you* for being here for me, for helping me and risking everything for a person you just met. But I could only manage to say, "Now *my* breathing is uneven."

"Radi." Calev's voice rode across the air.

Radi shot to his feet, leaving me in a heap on the ground. "Calev ben Y'hoshua."

I got up, anger warring with curiosity.

Calev stood in his cell, arms crossed and face cloudy. "If we escape this, we will need to talk."

"Yes. Of course," Radi said, his cheeks going dark.

I smiled sadly. I was blessed to have a brother in Calev. He wouldn't be too harsh with Radi. He was only protecting me. As long as he didn't get too carried away...

A bright shape came over the hill from the city. A woman. The messenger boy trotted by her elbow.

"Calev. Look!"

The guard approached a woman—*Meekra, maybe?*—and he gave the woman a small bow. She was older than Kinneret, but not by much, and she wore a fine, black kaftan and a pink sash. Black hair flowed over a shoulder, hair like Radi's. When the guard pointed to our cell, her smile—lopsided like Radi's—slid off her face. She slipped a small bag to the guard, a coin to the boy, then turned right back around and left.

"Wait!" I called out.

The guard hurried over and banged his dagger's hilt against the bar. "Hush, girl. You'll get your food portion soon enough."

"I'm not hungry. I—"

The guard leaned so close that I could smell the spiced chicken he'd eaten earlier. "Trust me. Hush."

Radi and I gave Calev a loaded look and we settled back into our corner.

"Did she pay him off? What's going to happen?" I asked Radi like somehow he would know.

His lips came close to my ear, sending a shiver over my neck. "She definitely paid him some coin. But I don't know what for."

I squeezed my hands, pulling my skirt into my fists. "I guess we'll have to wait. I'm not good at waiting."

"No one is, are they?" Radi's gaze drifted over my face like he was trying to figure me out.

"I guess not."

THREE GUARDS BROUGHT flatbread into the cells. I took one, knowing I'd need my strength no matter what happened, and worked my mouth around it, trying to soften it enough to take a bite.

Radi frowned at his piece and turned it over. He must've been lucky enough to avoid stale food until now. I hated I was the reason he was eating it now.

The madman stopped humming. I turned, thinking he'd be eating, but he was staring at the door.

"Little birdies may fly," he whispered in a rasping voice. "Little birdies. Little birdies."

I choked on my bread. "Radi. The door. The guard left it unlocked."

"Come on." He dropped his portion, heading to the front of the cell.

I picked up the bread, tucked it in my sash for later, and followed.

The guards both had their backs to us, eating a much better meal.

Calev stood by his own door. He reached out a hand and pushed it open with a slight creaking noise. His was unlocked too. Flinching at the sound, he eased out of his cell. The people in with him just stared at the guards.

I opened our door and we took two steps. Shutting my eyes for a second, I prayed no one would say anything. My sandal caught on the cell door's frame. Heart tripping, I grabbed the bars, my breath leaving me in a gasp. Radi touched my back in support.

The middle-caste guard who'd taken the coin from the woman laughed loud and smacked the other one on the shoulder. He met my gaze with those puffy eyes of his, and my lungs froze. With a word, he could have us killed for trying to escape. But he gave a nod no one would notice except us and went back to his joking and eating and keeping his friend from turning.

We joined Calev and hurried into the shadows cast by the walls and highlighted by the moon. I swore he'd aged a year in a day.

"Ideas on what to do now, sister?"

I set my forehead on his shoulder for a second. "Act like we're supposed to be walking through these training fields and into the city instead of escaping?"

We walked as fast as we could without being noticed, thankful for the dark and dripping weather that camouflaged our shapes and our noise.

"So that was Meekra?" I asked as we passed through the back gates. Every guard gave us a questioning look. One started to call out a question, but we slipped into the city's darkness before he could sound the alert to our presence.

"I guess," Radi said.

"You knew she was born in Akhmim?"

"No. I guessed. It's a town near here."

"I doubt you guessed right," Calev said, not unkindly. "I'd bet she was only helping us out despite your error. Her mistress seems very open-hearted. It wouldn't surprise me if the woman at her side was the same."

I didn't care who helped or why. I just wanted to get out of this city and back to Kinneret with Calev and maybe Radi too since I doubted he could return to his family's cart. With every quick step, I glanced over my shoulder, just knowing there'd be fighters coming at us, ready to lock us back up or kill us on sight.

11

CALEV

O n this side of the city, things were quiet. So different from the opposite side of Akhayma, where I'd lost the agreement and my only chance to show Father I could be the man he hoped I could be. I gritted my teeth, wishing more than anything that I could go back and do everything over again, the right way.

Canals gurgled as we passed through an area of dark, quiet tents. A man snored like a congested camel and a child called for his mother. In the market, tables were all folded up and put away. The sounds and smells of earlier had been washed away by the night's chill air, the sage and dust smell of the desert not so far away. We stopped near one of the booths that served as a home too, its striped walls gently lit from within.

Radi eyed the front door—slats of wood in a frame set over fabric lengths matching the walls. "I have to tell my cousin what's going on."

"But you're going to come with us, right?" Avi's admiration of this Radi colored her voice. "They'll find you here."

"I...guess I do have to come with you. Unless we hear something from Meekra."

"Could she manage to have you pardoned?" I asked.

"Anything is possible, I suppose." Radi slipped through the door.

We waited in the near dark. My ears strained to hear soldiers shouting that we'd escaped or dogs braying and on our scent. But so far there was nothing but the normal city sounds.

"Do you hear anything?" Avi grabbed the front of my tunic, her eyes bright and scared.

I cupped her hands with mine. "No, but—"

Noise exploded from the back of the city.

I ripped Radi's door open, sending the interior woven flaps fluttering. "They know. We need to go. Now!"

His family blinked and spoke rapidly in the desert tongue, handing him a bundle and shoving him toward us.

We took off down the street, Radi leading. Horses' hooves pounded the ground behind us.

"We'll never outrun them," I said.

"This way." Radi jerked my arm and I pulled Avi along as we sidled into an alleyway.

It was dark as the pitch Kinneret used to seal her boat. "What now?"

"Hopefully, they'll go past us," Radi whispered.

Avi bunched her hands and pressed them to her mouth. I put an arm around her and kissed her head, hoping to settle her down so they wouldn't hear the caste bells shaking on her clothing. Thankfully, Radi wasn't wearing any. He must've been purely of the desert blood.

The sounds grew louder. We huddled farther into the tight space between the tents. No noise came from the tents, so these must've been used as shops only during the day hours. The scent of oiled wood and a damped fire told me the one to our backs was a carpenter's place.

"No one's in there." I jerked my head at the tent. "Can't we slip under the wall and hide?"

"That's a big offense," Radi said. "If we're found in someone else's place, we will definitely be hanged. They take crime seriously here."

"It didn't seem to keep my attackers from stealing my things."

"Crime has increased. Because of the kyros. He raised taxes. Some of the low-castes and even a few middle are feeling the squeeze, so to speak."

The horses' pounding and the soldiers' voices rolled closer still. Then they were passing us, slowing, talking. One horse knocked against the carpenter's shop and shook the tent's posts and lines, pushing us.

Avi gasped.

The soldiers went quiet.

My heart beat against my temples, and I held Avi's fingers tight. Heat poured down my chest. Radi swallowed loud enough for me to hear.

Feet crashed to the ground. Someone had dismounted. Footsteps approached, grit crunching under boots.

Radi waved to us. He wanted Avi to wiggle deep into the alley of cloth walls, but there wasn't any room. The carpenter's place came together with the neighboring tent. Was there a passageway between the walls of striped wool?

I lifted a foot, trying not to scrape the ground, and nodded to Avi. She held my wrist with her cold fingers, clutching to me like her life depended on it. As if I could save her. But I couldn't. I could only follow Radi and hope we weren't heard.

At the spot where the tents came together, Radi pressed a hand out. It was so dark. I could only just now see more than the white stripes of the walls and the rough shape of Avi and Radi. There was the pale yellow of Radi's sash and the light streaming from the street where they were searching for us.

A man shouted and rushed into our hiding place. Avi pushed against me. Radi heaved himself through the tiny opening between the tents.

I spun and tried to help Avi through, but large fingers hooked my shoulder and arm and yanked me backward. Avi came with me and we landed in a pile at the soldier's feet, my hip hitting the ground sharply and Avi swearing and sounding like her sister. Radi hadn't been found.

The warriors hauled us out of the alley, not saying a word, features hard under their shining helmets. The middle-caste guard who'd left our cell doors open was nowhere to be seen. He probably fled with that money as soon as he could get away from the others.

An Empire fighter with a long face tugged my arms behind me and lashed them together with twine. The rope bit into my skin as he looped a knot over the saddle and began trailing me along like I was a prisoner of war. An enormous, bearded warrior bound Avi up, tying her to another mount.

Would this be it? After all we'd been through?

Kinneret would die without us there to say goodbye. Avi and I would hang or be whipped until dead, whatever horror the unpredictable kyros decided we deserved.

My legs were filled with lead weights and if I hadn't been tied to a horse, I would've crumbled to the ground.

They herded us back toward the Kyros Walls. At least Radi had escaped. I didn't know where he'd go. They'd probably know him by sight. Maybe they wouldn't bother going after him for such a minor infraction. It seemed Avi had been the one to really break the rules.

Avi tried to walk closer, but the fighters edged their horses between us, hooves inches away from our sandaled feet.

I couldn't stop thinking about Kinneret. Worry ate at me, biting here, gnawing there. I'd be nothing by the time I escaped again, if I ever had the chance. They wouldn't have to kill me. I'd die from fear for her.

They brought us to the main tent even though it was full night and no one seemed to be around. Inside, Avi and the warriors passed hands over the Holy Fire bowl while I went to my knees to wait, showing respect in advance.

Seren, Pearl of the Desert, slipped from a back room and into view. I should've studied her gaze for some kind of hint as to what she planned to do to us, but I couldn't stop imagining Kinneret and the sickness chewing at her bones.

Hands pushed my head down to bow lower, like Avi already had.

When we were allowed at last to stand, Seren frowned, studying me. The woman I believed to be Meekra, her handmaiden, came up beside her.

"The Holy Fire gave me an idea about your Kinneret tonight," Seren said. "So I couldn't let you leave. Not yet."

Invisible arrows pierced my heart. My breath stuck in my throat. I glanced at the Holy Fire bowl near the door. Its blue-orange Flame shimmered as if it knew we were talking about inspiration, all the blessings given to those the Fire chose.

"Is she..." My tongue couldn't create the horrible word—*dead*.

Her eyes seemed to tip downward at the edges, her lips going into a frown. "She may be soon."

Snakes slithered over my heart and I fisted my hands. "Can I save her?"

"I don't know. But I know you won't make it if I don't help you."

"So you believe my story about the agreement and Old Farm and the thieves?"

"I do. The Fire told me I need to send you home with a new agreement marked with Kyros Meric's personal sigil. I'm not sure how to make that happen though."

"The kyros still doesn't believe me." I didn't think it was a good idea to point out the fact that he obviously didn't believe the Fire had told her anything either. Or she hadn't told him for some reason.

"He may listen to me if I...put the idea in his head properly," she said.

I nodded.

She began to twirl a piece of green wool she had tucked into her sash. It looked like a piece of the clothing people wore in the mountains beyond the desert and I wondered what it meant to her.

"Take them back to the cells," she said, her gaze faraway. Meekra's mouth opened like she wanted to argue, but Seren held up a hand. "I have a plan."

~

THE CELL DOOR clanked shut and we were imprisoned again. Seren's guards sent the rest away and took up positions to watch us through the night.

We were left in the dark to wonder if tomorrow would mean Seren's success and our freedom, or her failure and our death.

1 2

AVI

The sun rose as I wiped tears off my face.

Sister, I'm trying to get him home to you. We're trying.

I still didn't regret coming. I couldn't have stayed there and watched her waste away. But nothing had gone as planned.

Seren's guards—the big man with the beard, the one with a face like a horse, and the thin one who'd captured us in the city—took us from our cell and brought us to a tent near the stables.

Bows, yatagans, and axes lined one wall. Two long tables crowded the front of the room. The man who'd been at the kyros's side when I'd seen him earlier stood near two other soldiers.

He crossed his arms and his gray eyebrows drew tightly together. "The Holy Fire gave my kyros an idea last night."

My knees shook. I tried to take a deep breath to keep from falling over. Meekra wasn't here. No Seren either. We were doomed.

"He said," the general continued, "the Fire told him it was in the Empire's best interest to believe your story and send you on your way with your agreement approved."

I was a drowning girl suddenly pulled out of the waves. Air whooshed into my lungs, bringing me to life. We had a chance! A chance to save Kinneret!

Calev rushed to hug me, his hands sticky with nervous sweat.

"If you'll give my scribe the details," the general said, "all will be put in order. You're welcome to send your words of thanks to my kyros. Only one as strong in the royal blood could be so blessed as to hear so much from the Fire."

It had been Seren's blessing though, not Kyros Meric's. Well, it wasn't our secret to tell. I didn't much care who had done what, as long as we got out of here fast.

"Further, my generous kyros has decided to give your new amir two fine horses as a gift for his new appointment. You may return quickly to his service on these mounts." He nodded toward the door where the opening showed a yellow horse with a black mane and a full ebony mare with a beautiful star on her nose. Beside them, Arrow stomped her front hoof to get some attention. The chairman's horse, the one Calev had ridden here, nuzzled Arrow familiarly.

I pressed my hands into my face. I'd never been so relieved.

"Please thank Kyros Meric for his outstanding generosity," Calev said. "Please let him know we are in awe of his blessed ideas, and though I am Old Farm, I hold the highest respect for his path in life."

His blessed ideas? Humph. He'd taken credit for Seren's gift from the Fire. Then again, maybe that's how she'd wanted it. I wondered how she'd managed the trick.

As we mounted and thanked Seren's men for loading our packs with water, blankets, dried figs, and barley cakes, Meekra walked up.

"I see our kyros decided to let you go." There was a little spark to her eyes.

I leaned over in my saddle to speak close to her ear. "How did Pearl of the Desert do it?"

"How she always does. By waiting until he prays over the Fire and making suggestions as to what he, as the most blessed and rich in royal blood, must be hearing from the Fire."

Her lips turned down. I could tell she wanted to say more, to say the kyros was an arrogant fool who ate up praise before he tasted it for truth, but of course, that would be treason.

"Have you seen my cousin Radi since last night?" she whispered.

My heart cinched. "No. He escaped. I think."

Meekra looked over her shoulder. "If you see him on your way out of Akhayma…"

"I'll send you a rock dove as soon as I can."

"With…indirect language?"

Ah. She needed me to speak in code. He must not have been pardoned as of yet. "Can't Pearl of the Desert do something for him?"

"If we can find him, we'll protect him. But if the kyros's men find him first, we may not have a lot of options."

The gray-haired general stalked out of the tent and handed the new agreement to Calev, who bowed from his saddle.

I cupped my hand at Meekra's ear. "I'm glad we have Pearl of the Desert to help the Empire."

"Yes. Not all our leaders are merciful. We are indeed blessed to have Pearl of the Desert. Without her as kyros's wife, our city would be a different place." Meekra touched a letter tucked into her sash and smiled sadly. "She gives everything for her people."

"Tell her we love her for it."

"I will, Avigail Raza." Meekra pressed my hand between hers and gave Arrow's hind end a slap to send me off behind Calev.

"Come, Avi!" Calev's face was hopeful as he wrapped the two new horses' leads around one hand and tightened his legs around his father's mount. All I wanted in the world was for that hope to be fulfilled. All I wanted was to see Kinneret and him, smiling on their wedding day. All I wanted was home.

13

CALEV

The horses couldn't go fast enough. I'd have slowed a little for Avi if she showed signs of needing it. So far, she was as driven to get to Kinneret as I was, shouting at Arrow, cheering the mare on. Prayers flowed from my mouth, a constant stream of *please please please.*

Hold on, love, I said in my mind, hoping somehow Kinneret would hear me. *I'm coming, love.*

I squeezed the reins, remembering the musky scent of the henna on my hands, the henna she'd painted on my skin. Shivers rolled over my arms and back. Her light touch. The tease in her eyes. The shift of her hips under the ivory cloth of the Intended ceremony clothing. I called memories up to make her strong in my mind. The courage in her face when she commanded the Tuz Golge. The moment she moved the very sea itself.

You're strong, love. Stay strong, love.

What was I going to do when I arrived? I couldn't save her. I didn't know anything about healing.

Avi glared at me over Arrow's head, determination blazing out of her eyes. She believed my presence would help Kinneret. I had no choice but to latch onto that faith.

The sandy plains and high, flat reaches of the hammadas gave way to the Greening's grasses and rolling hills. Stopping only when we couldn't stay on our horses without toppling over, we raced past the huddled villages, zipped between spice traders' caravans, and rounded clutches of pilgrims on their way to visit the heart of the Empire and the silver basin where the Holy Fire was lit every quarter.

~

AT KINNERET'S new home by the docks, Oron sat, head in his hands. I slid off my horse, legs aching, to help Avi down. She slapped my hands away and pushed her hair out of her sweating face.

"Go. Go!" She waved at the blue door.

Oron looked up. A smear of dirt marred his chin. Red, puffy skin circled his big eyes.

I didn't wait to hear news. I pushed the entrance open, not knowing if I would find my life or death. Hers and my own.

Sunlight fell through the square window and onto Kinneret's ashen face.

Her lips were slightly parted and chapped. Her hair lay across her striped pillow, thin, and without its usual curl. I kneeled by her simple bed and swept her hand into mine. Her fingers were hot.

My heart jumped. *Alive.* She was blessedly alive.

Her eyes opened. "Having an adventure without me, hm?" she croaked. "Is this revenge for the time I went port-hunting and left you at home?" A smile bent her mouth.

I lay my head on her chest, keeping my weight back. She was on fire with fever. Her skin seared though her clothing. I breathed in the smell of stale linens, sweat, and green herbs used for healing teas.

"How are you?" I turned my head to look into her face, my fingers unsteadily holding hers.

"I've been better."

I tried to laugh. "I imagine."

She winced like something pained her, so I sat up, easing away.

"Don't go," she whispered, closing her eyes. She reached a hand around the back of my neck and let it sit there. Her chest moved in a deep breath. "I want to enjoy you as long as I can."

Tears blurred my vision. "You're not going to die."

"If I do, don't let anyone kaptan Ekrem's full ship but Avi or Oron. Swear to me." Her fingers tightened on my neck.

I shrugged. "I heard that new fighting sailor was pretty good. What's his name?"

She moved like she was about to sit up. "That idiot?"

"Settle down. I'm only teasing."

"Evil."

"It's your fault. I used to be a good boy."

Her eyes were slits, watching me. "What fun is being good?"

Oron walked up, hands clasped in front of him. His chin brushed my elbow as he leaned in to lift, then kiss Kinneret's free hand. "I claim at least some of Calev's moral ruin. You must admit I've had a part to play in the drama."

Kinneret laughed weakly as we helped her sip some tea Oron took from the side table. The steam circled her head and made her look like a spirit.

Someone knocked.

Avi opened the door, biting her lip. "Your father's here, Calev."

The muscles around my jaw tensed. Of course he couldn't wait to hear about my duty. He'd think it was every bit as important as Kinneret. Maybe even more so.

Like he'd read my mind, he leaned in and said, "Talking to me won't change her condition, my son."

Giving Kinneret a pained look, I squeezed her hand, then joined my father in the blazing sun.

He unrolled the new agreement, brow furrowing. "This isn't the original." His eyes threw darts at me.

"No. I was robbed. In Akhayma. But this one has the kyros's sigil. It's legitimate."

Reading it over, he mumbled to himself, long beard shivering as he said the words under his breath. He rolled it back up. "It's fine. But tell me, what did you do wrong to be attacked wearing an Old Farm sigil ring and with the funds to stay in a safely located establishment at every stop? I did speak to Serhat."

I swallowed as Oron came out of the house.

"Is Serhat well again then?" I asked.

"Yes." Father's gaze held me down. "Now answer my question."

"I stayed in a terrible place because I was an idiot. Some men put gray plant in my food and robbed me."

Father stiffened. "Calev ben Y'hoshua. What were you thinking?"

Oron barked a laugh, though the sound didn't hold half his normal enthusiasm. "Most likely he was thinking it'd be nice to forget you and yours for a while."

Father's look could've competed with the desert heat. He glanced at my hand and his mouth dropped open. "Where is your ring?"

"They took that too," I said.

His temper was going to get the best of him and mean the worst for me. He was going to deny my request to be the next chairman, take me completely out of the council's vote. Then what would I be for Kinneret? If she survived.

Father's face softened. "She is strong. She may live."

I glanced over my shoulder, not wanting Avi to hear Father's brutal honesty.

Oron touched my arm. "Avi's inside still. She can't hear us."

I nodded. "Can you wait to be angry with me?" I asked Father quietly, feeling like a child but knowing I had to ask it of him. I needed mercy.

His large hands covered my shoulders. "Yes. There will be consequences, but…"

Oron pushed his way into the conversation. "But you have a soul so you won't annihilate his future while his Intended sits on Death's door?"

Father's arms dropped to his sides. "Exactly so, Oron No Name."

There was a shout from the docks. It was Serhat, tall and blonde and pointing at an approaching dhow. The boat's triangular sail dipped in the wind as it came into the harbor.

A Kurakian woman in bright blue stepped onto the dock as Avi roared out of the house.

A light filled my chest and lifted the weight from my aching legs. I ran toward the water. It was Kania Turay, Kinneret's wise aunt.

"Aunt Kania!" Avi ran down the slope and crashed into her mother's sister.

"Ah, ah. Dear one." Kania stroked her niece's braid. "I will do what I can."

A DAY PASSED in a whirl of bruising herbs Kania brought from the red dirt of Kurakia. The house smelled green and sticky.

"She isn't soaking it in," Kinneret's aunt whispered in my ear. "You must warm her up and get her to take the healing. To accept it."

I felt cold even though the room was stifling. "I don't know how."

Kania patted my hand, then ushered Oron and Avi from the room. "You will," she said over her shoulder. "You have a certain magic of your own, a magic between you."

She seemed so sure, yet doubt plagued my mind.

I sat on the very edge of the bed and rubbed Kinneret's arm. She did feel stronger now. The muscles under her brown skin weren't just wasted strings like yesterday. They'd plumped back up and there was a healthy warmth emanating from them. But it wasn't enough. Death breathed down her face, robbing it of color. I was going to lose her.

"Kinneret." I said her name like a prayer. "Kinneret." The sounds whisked over my lips, soft and sure. My love for her was the only thing I was truly sure of. "Kinneret."

Her eyes stayed closed as they had for hours. She breathed shallowly, like she'd stop at any second.

"Please wake up. Do you feel the good medicine in your blood? Your aunt put it there. You have to…let it in." I touched her collarbone, her neck. The skin there was too cold. It made me shiver.

With no idea what I was doing, just following the powerful tug I always felt to get nearer to her, I climbed onto the bed and lay directly on top of her. It was probably stupid. I was probably hurting her, but the pull—this was what my heart was telling me to do.

"Am I hurting you? Is this helping?" I propped myself on my elbows, my hands in her hair, my thumbs on the pulse in her temples. Smoothing my palms once down the sides of her head, I breathed warm air over her mouth.

She inhaled, moving me upward.

"Kinneret? Relax. Let the herbs do their work. Let your aunt's magic beat this. You can let her medicine fight. You don't have to fight. Let down your guard." I would be here always and I'd never act like such a careless idiot again, risking those I loved.

And stars, how I loved her.

She was so strong. She'd never once stopped fighting in life. Asking her to give in to the medicine and her aunt's magic, asking her to stop fighting —this was an impossible thing to ask. She'd fought her way from what others called a low-caste salt witch to being one of the most respected kaptans on the Broken Coast. Nothing had ever been given to her. Fighting was as natural to her as breathing.

"Calev." My name was nothing more than a whisper on her peeling lips. Invisible blades cut my heart at the longing in the sound.

"I'm here. I won't leave again."

She made a humming noise and shifted her body under me. Was it my imagination or was her skin warming, her temperature becoming more even?

Please let her live. She has so much more to do. I need her. Please, I prayed silently.

Her pale, blue eyes fluttered open. "Calev?" She blinked and her eyes widened. "You're really here?"

"I am."

"I thought I was dreaming." Her chest rose in a deep breath, a good breath.

"I dreamed of you while I was in Akhayma." My face flushed at the memory, and I hated myself for thinking like *that* while she was so sick.

"Tell me. About the dream." Her eyes drooped shut.

I swallowed. "I think the night of our Intended ceremony inspired it."

One eye opened, just a little. A smile curved her right cheek. "Tell me everything."

"You're too ill for...all of that."

"All of that."

"Yes."

She breathed deeply again and the color of her forehead, cheeks, and neck warmed to a nice flush. She looked at me. "I think I'm feeling better."

"It's your aunt's herbs. Her magic."

"It's yours too."

"I don't have any of that."

She moved and I slid to the side so she could lift herself to her elbows. She coughed, and I leaned to get her cup of water. With a small shiver, she took the drink and finished it all. With the edge of the cup, she drew a line down my neck, then my chest.

"Oh, yes you do," she said, her voice hoarse.

I kissed her smooth forehead, my muscles easing. "Please tell me you're finished trying to die." She really was feeling better. Hope rushed through me like wind through a field of ripe barley, pushing me, tugging me along its path.

"For now." She smiled up at me. "I need a bath."

I sat up and she did too, hanging her legs over the side of the bed as if she'd not just been at death's door.

I couldn't seem to stop smiling. Was this really happening? I was afraid to be happy. I ran a hand over her thin forearm. Her skin was oily and smelled like her aunt's house in Kurakia, green and biting and spicy.

She lifted a lock of her hair and sniffed. "Definitely a bath."

"I could help," I choked out, trying hard to contain myself.

Avi knocked and swung the door open. Her top teeth held her lip. "Aunt says you're feeling better."

I looked at the shuttered window, then at Kinneret, who shrugged. Kania just knew things.

"I am," Kinneret said, and a laugh bellowed out of me, happiness joining hope and throwing me right into pure joy.

Kinneret opened her arms and Avi ran into them, tears silvering her cheeks.

Oron and Kania came in laughing as Oron finished telling her something about his northern tastes in women.

"You have a powerful magic, Calev ben Y'hoshua," Kania said.

Avi moved away from Kinneret and put her hands on her hips. "I told you so."

I felt stronger than I ever had as I took Kinneret in my arms.

Maybe they were right. Maybe love was a magic all its own.

Never, ever again would I risk the magical life I had here with Avi, Oron, and Kinneret. I would live up to Father's expectations, and if I didn't, these amazing souls would still love me. I knew it as sure as I knew the beat of my own heart.

EPILOGUE

Kinneret

AMIR EKREM'S full ship dipped over a wave and my stomach thrilled to feel the drop. The wheel moved under my hands, the wood polished and as ebony as Calev's eyes. The sea stretched out beyond us, purple and black and bursting with possibilities.

I shouted directions to a dozen fighting sailors who scurried to do as told. Lines were tied. Sails trimmed or angled. Ropes knotted to hold crates of Old Farm lemons that scented the deck and the salty sea air. The ship creaked as we rolled over another swell and I shook out my hair, letting it fly behind me like my own pennant.

Avi peered into the compass box, her movements light and quick.

Yesterday, a trader from Akhayma had brought her a message from the boy she met there. A boy named Radi. His family had told the trader that Radi was gone from the capitol. He was safe. For now. This Radi fellow asked if she would go to the next Gathering. There, he would try to find her among the representatives from every noble clan, from every town and city, in the Empire.

Avi hadn't stopped smiling since.

But she hadn't heard the whole message. There were reports of Invaders attacking border towns again. Some said a drought had hit their western lands again and that war was on the horizon. I wondered if Kyros Meric could manage a war against those wild Invaders. From what Y'hoshua said, Meric wasn't wise like his father had been. Although so far Invaders didn't have the cannon us easterners had, they'd still give Akhayma and her people a load of nasty trouble. Deadly trouble for the new kyros and his new wife. I swallowed. Calev had told me about her. Under different circumstances, we could've been friends, he claimed.

Well, Avi didn't need to know the dark news about the Invaders. If it did come to war, Jakobden would be the last to feel it. There was plenty of sun to worry about that later.

"Are we on course?" I asked Avi.

"We are directly on course, Kaptan Kinneret. We'll be in Silvania in no time."

Silvania. Land of the proud, and too often, Jakobden and Old Farm's competition for port control.

"I don't like that smile, love," Calev said into my ear. His breath flew over my skin.

A pleasant warmth trickled down my neck and arm. "I'm only excited to trade with our neighboring country."

"You're excited about having the best ship in their port."

"It's a nice bonus."

The wind blew over my cheeks and fluffed the sails above us until they matched the blossoming clouds over head.

Avi watched the blue-gray sky's petals of mist open and close. "Is it going to storm?"

Oron took a bite of a plum. "I hope so. Watching Kinneret silently boast about her accomplishments is getting boring. When do I get a turn at the wheel, great kaptan?"

"Maybe right now." I turned to look into Calev's eyes and nodded toward the kaptan's quarters, my quarters.

Serhat ran a hand over her blond hair and waved to Avi, getting her to help teach a new sailor how to read the wind.

Calev met my gaze, his eyes hot. "There's definitely going to be a storm."

I gave Calev a teasing grin. "You're terrible at judging the weather."

He just glared and raised one eyebrow. "Am I wrong?" He wasn't talking about the weather.

Desire zinged down my body. "Oron can handle it," I said. "Can't you, Oron?"

Oron raised his chin and straightened his new tunic. The shapes were too tiny to be sure, but I guessed they were naked women. How he'd persuaded a fabric worker to create something like that…

"I'm insulted you'd even question it," he said.

I left him with the wheel and led Calev down the stairs and under the deck to my door. I remembered knocking on this door when Amir Mamluk was behind it. With Berker.

With a kick, the heavy oak door gave way. Calev slid hands around my middle and followed me inside. His fingers tripped over my sash and found skin where my shirt met my skirt.

I shivered and used a foot to slam the door shut on the old, sour memories of Berker and Mamluk, very ready to make new ones with the black-eyed, soul-lifting, luck-made-flesh love of my life.

PLAINS OF SAND AND STEEL

UNCOMMON WORLD

1

SEREN

A hot, desert wind swirled around the dais, tugging at Seren's beaded kaftan and combing fingers through her jet hair as she stared down at the city. Her chest ached remembering her mother, who'd died when Seren was a baby, her father and sister—gone too —lost to Invader steel. But this city, it was her new home, and it eased that ache as she gazed at its people. Her people.

Akhayma looked a lot like a hand. Fingers of water slipped from the oasis and through the many canals. Stone walls cupped everyone in a dusty palm. The scene pulled a smile out of Seren. The grin would topple soon— Meric would see to that—but for now, the turned-up edges of her mouth held.

She savored the touch of happiness like a rare fruit as the pool's mosaics scattered moonlight between conversations.

"...and your grandfather shaped the steel that fought back the Invaders..."

"Your ancestors found this oasis and built Akhayma with their own hands."

Tonight, on this most special of nights, there wasn't any talk of business. Lovers didn't argue, and co-workers kept their talk for another time. Tonight, Seren's people laughed, wove stories, passed down details about *family*. That was what this was about.

Seren's smile broadened, lifting her cheeks and helping her stand beside the man she was too young to be married to and would never, ever have

343

chosen for herself. Her father—the former High-General—had tried to keep her from this marriage, but the former kyros had ordered it. And not even generals said *No* to a kyros.

She stepped closer to Meric, hoping it wasn't too close. Sometimes he wanted to show her affection in public, but other times, no. Only ninety odd days into a marriage at seventeen, and she had little idea how to be a wife. Her smile wavered. She forced her lips up, afraid the light, easy feeling would be impossible to find if she lost it now.

"We should do this more often," she said, keeping that smile in place and ignoring Meric's narrowing eyes.

He coughed. "The Fire Ceremony?"

"Just rolling back the tents to open the city to the sky. It makes everyone more...talkative."

The varied languages floated through the night air like music. Coming back here, to the city of her birth, hadn't taken away the pain of losing her father, mother, and little sisters of course, but it lessened the ache in her soul. Akhayma had always been home.

Meric scowled at the Holy Fire bowl. Inside the large, silver basin, Flames danced in the lahabshjara leaves.

Beside them on the dais, the head of Clan Azjorr smoothed his black-striped kaftan. "Do you need another basket, Kyros Meric?" He gestured toward a servant clutching a hefty load of the emerald leaves.

Another cough tore through Meric. "What I need is to get on with this so I can rest."

The clan leader's cheeks darkened.

Seren apologized to the nobleman, using her black eyes to show her empathy, then spun to face Meric. "Let me call the physician."

"He never heals me."

Seren nearly pulled a muscle trying not to roll her eyes. Barir did help. When Meric let him. Her husband was older than her, but he was such a child.

"None of them fix anything." Meric glared in the general direction of the physician's home. Then, taking his position over the silver basin, he raised his high-pitched voice. "We gather here to honor the Holy Fire," he called out over the crowd.

He sounded like a bleating goat. Seren would've taken a goat over him any day. Goats didn't yell at anyone or insult good people. She imagined a goat's head in Meric's finely embroidered kaftan and had to stifle a laugh with her sleeve.

Despite Meric's distinctly lackluster delivery of the ceremony's opening words, the city quieted for their kyros.

"Giver of knowledge and wisdom," Meric continued, "weapon of our people, blessed and unrelenting. Holy Fire, grant us the Flame of your strength and invention. May ideas flicker from dreams into reality."

A warrior wearing a sweat-darkened military kaftan stepped out of the line. He was a scout.

A chill slid through Seren's bones.

The scout paused at the dais steps, his helmeted head bowed reverently.

Seren hurried over. "What's wrong?" she whispered as Meric went on bleating.

Standing on Meric's other side, General Adem eyed Seren. His gaze lashed out and she flinched a little. His eyes drew a line from her to Meric, who was still praying. He wanted her to wait until Meric finished speaking to talk. But this scout wouldn't be standing out of military line if everything was fine. Something was wrong and the Holy Fire would understand if there was an emergency. Seren clutched the scrap of mountain wool she kept in her sash, a bit of the skirt she'd been wearing when Invaders cut her family down.

"What is it, scout?" Meric snapped at the younger man.

The scout hurried up the stairs and approached Meric.

The wind rose, sand giving it little teeth. Seren raised the thin scarf hanging at her neck to protect her face and to mask any response she might have to the scout's report. An old trick of her father's.

Adem removed his silver helmet, his hair a close match, and inclined his head to listen.

"We spotted Invaders on the horizon," the scout whispered between Meric's continued coughing.

Seren shook her head. Surely she'd heard wrong.

"An army of them, my kyros," he said quietly to Meric. "Some on horseback."

Adem's mouth tightened. He kept an eye on those around them. "I was afraid of this, my kyros. When we first heard of their movement, I thought they were headed another direction, to invade lower Silvania instead. But… well, they will most likely strike Kenar for supplies after their journey from the West. They could conceivably cross our borders in two days. Kyros, you must tell me what you wish to do." He stared at the Holy Fire bowl. "But please, finish the ceremony first."

Adem's face seemed to blur, his gray beard and sun-browned skin hazy.

Seren blinked, the chill deepening, seeping into her blood, her heart. Meekra rushed to her side, and Seren took the handmaiden's slim fingers in her own. Despite her friend's kind touch, Seren's mind threw out memories of the Invaders' sharp eyes, their wide, steel weapons, the way they shouted when they killed like it hurt them to shed blood, but they loved it anyway. She'd known they'd return. It was why she prayed for ideas from the Fire, kept up her studies of Father's military scrolls, and trained in horse and bow daily.

"I must…" Meric's coughing doubled him over.

Chilled blood racing through her, Seren took Meric's arm and started him toward the stairs.

"But you must finish…" Adem started.

"What should we do, my kyros?" The scout twisted a hand around the hilt of his yatagan.

"He'll answer you as soon as the physician treats him," Seren said, hoping Meric *had* an answer.

General Adem addressed the city, and Seren watched over her shoulder as dark and light eyes both turned up to focus on him. "There is a military issue we must deal with immediately. Your kyros has blessed the basin, and you may come, one family at a time, to light your homefire sticks. May the Fire bless us all."

As Seren hurried Meric away, with their guards and servants around them, she said, "Call for your father, Meekra."

She didn't care that Meric thought the physician never helped. Meric was wrong. Barir knew several ways to calm this cough he struggled with day-to-day.

The Kyros Walls rose up beside them as they entered the courtyard and headed toward the main tent. Another gust of sand grated across Seren's bare forearms and the single bell tied around her head to hang between her eyebrows.

"And Cansu," she said to the long-faced guard who'd been kind since the day he was assigned to Seren, "you will go with Meekra. I don't like this weather."

The two rushed into the night while her other two guards and a handful of Meric's fighters followed Seren and Meric inside.

In the main tent, the moon bled through the ceiling's patterned weave. Light in the shape of blurry stars dotted the room. At the door dividing the main tent from Seren and Meric's personal chambers, the guards took up positions, relieving the men that had been there during the ceremony.

"Erol," Seren said, "Protect the back entrance to my chamber along with the others serving there now. Tell them nothing. I don't want anyone worrying."

Hossam, black hair more wild than normal, pushed the door back, the woven flaps too, and helped Seren get Meric inside. Erol sped past them, heading out the rear door of the bed chamber. Hossam gave Seren a quick bow, then left to join the other armed men and women in the main tent.

Another tight cough shook Meric. Seren worked the knot in his ceremonial phoenix sash, then threw it to the ground, trying anything to make him more comfortable. White skin ringed his mouth. He dropped to sit on the bed, chin down, hands splayed and covering the bedcover's calligraphy that spelled out his name and title. *Kyros Meric, the Eternally Victorious.*

Lying back on a tasseled pillow, he shut his eyes, gasping like a fish without water.

Where was Barir?

Meric needed the physician now. Maybe Meekra and Cansu were having trouble getting to his quarters in the weather. What if a sandstorm hit right now?

Tears burned at the corners of Seren's eyes. Invaders. Sandstorms.

Meric *had* to be all right.

She didn't know how to take care of an Empire. Images of maps and lists of agreements—from Father's time as the old kyros's general—flickered through her head. Father had taught her a lot. But talking about leading was different from actually doing it. She wasn't the heir anyway. She didn't have any royal blood.

The whistling in Meric's lungs kept on, and he gasped more violently, his back arching at a painful angle. Seren couldn't stop shivering.

Barir walked into the room, tugging at his long, gray beard, his dark eyes worried. Meekra and Cansu trailed the physician like shadows.

Seren heaved a breath. "Please. Help him."

Meric's color was all wrong.

"I need to dose him with ka'ud," Barir said as he approached the bed.

Meekra tucked a curl of dark hair behind her ear, took her father's medicine satchel, and set it on the side table.

Cansu's throat moved in a swallow. His hand brushed the five high-caste bells on his sash as he joined the other guards outside the door.

Seren heard Adem's low grumble of a voice outside the door, probably asking for a report on the kyros's state.

"I'll tell him he's being treated," Meekra said.

Seren couldn't look away from Meric. The sudden hollowness to his

347

cheeks. The hair hanging over his left eye. His kaftan rumpled under his arms and how he did nothing to fix it.

"Thank you," she said to Meekra.

Barir pulled a length of the rare, resinous wood from his bag and set a shallow dish on the bedside table. Praying quickly over the Holy Fire bowl in the corner, he lit the ka'ud with the Flames and arranged the smoking wood in the dish. Blue clouds billowed over the kyros. Barir listened to Meric's lungs, his head on his chest.

Meric's shifting legs stilled.

Something sharp and cold cut into Seren's heart and she reached for his hand. His fingers were too limp.

"Meric?" Her heart beat in her ears.

He didn't move. Didn't speak. His lips had gone blue.

Barir rose. "Pearl of the Desert, I don't want to tell you this."

She held her breath.

"Please forgive the bearer of bad news." His voice dropped to a hush. "The kyros is dead."

The buzz in her ears was deafening.

Meric, the man whose father saved her from the Invaders who'd killed her little sisters and father, the man who acted like a spoiled child one minute and a violent storm the next, Meric the Eternally Victorious, was dead.

Shaking so badly she could hardly stand, Seren positioned Meric's hands on his chest as was custom. He looked so much like his father had. Her own father's closest friend. Sweat bloomed across her forehead and chest.

No. It can't be.

Barir stared at her and moved his lips like he was about to say something.

"What should I do?" An invisible sandstorm tore at her thoughts, her heart. She gripped the edges of the bed to stay upright. In the corner, the Holy Fire's orange-blue fingers spread over emerald leaves.

"You should pray, general's daughter," Barir whispered.

"Now?"

"I've seen you pray, my lady." His mouth relaxed into a solemn line.

Seren was shaking all over. "Don't call me *my lady*. You've known me since I was a baby."

"You are the highest in the land as of now." Face grave, he nodded toward the Fire.

She went to the bowl and passed her hands over the flickering light. Bright heat tickled her palms. Her eyes fluttered shut, then open again. A familiar peace slid over her like a warm breeze on a chilly night, and her shaking eased. The small basin's copper surface reflected the orange-blue Flames. Barir stayed quiet.

Please, I need help, she prayed silently.

Holding both palms at an angle over the Fire, she took a deep breath. The skin between her eyebrows twinged and a warmth rushed through her heart, all the way to her fingertips.

A curl of Flame appeared in front of her face, hovering high over the bowl.

She gasped.

Barir said something quick and quiet under his breath.

Many prayed to the Holy Fire. Only a few in history were blessed with the Hovering Flame, the true light of invention and purpose.

The flesh in Seren's hands glowed with the intense shine of the Holy Fire. Illuminated from within, bones showed under red skin as a vision burned into her mind.

The corners of the Empire shimmered into view. Places she'd traveled to with Father when he was still the High General. Far off towns and seas. Markets and boats. Laughing children. Men and women talking, some singing, some arguing. Light skin, darker skin, people from every clan in the plains and the border towns in the mountains where Father had taken the family when he retired.

Then Akhayma came into view.

A shadowy cloud churned in the sky beyond the walls. Above it all, a length of pure white linen wrapped itself around Meric's body. The storm near the walls shimmered, became men with wide weapons of steel, screaming and weeping as they swamped the city, more deadly than any storm. In the vision, Seren waved a hand and hid Meric's corpse in the night clouds. She took up his best kaftan—a kyros's kaftan, hemmed in silver phoenixes—and raised it above her head. The invading men blew into dust. *Kyros Seren!* the people shouted, suddenly smiling and holding their homefire branches. Their lights became the stars above the desert, and a calm covered Seren's panicking heart like a great, invisible hand.

The vision faded.

The thread of Holy Fire in front of her face unspooled and fell into its brother and sister Flames.

She faced Barir. The real world—along with its very real trouble—intruded as suddenly as an arrow from the darkness, piercing Seren's calm and bleeding it dry until she trembled again. All in the time it took to breathe in.

The things she'd seen…it had only been her imagination. She hadn't seen a vision. It was impossible. Wasn't it? The Fire had given her ideas before, but they'd been simple words and thoughts in her head, small things like the idea to free that kind-eyed young man from Old Farm and to hire the famed mercenaries of Silvania. It was odd enough to gain those ideas without royal blood, but actual visions? It just could not be. But…

"I saw something." It was like a stranger said the words. She felt detached from her own body.

Barir took a shuddering breath, the ka'ud smoke clouded around his black hair. "A vision. You had a vision." His hand went to his mouth.

She swallowed. "Maybe. I…" She was coming apart, her ears buzzing, the world spinning.

Suddenly she was in Barir's wiry arms, his graying beard brushing against her head and his shushing sounds in her ears like she was still a child.

"Do you want to tell me what you saw? It may help us all in this terrible moment. No one has seen a vision in the Fire in, one, maybe two, centuries." He held her away from him enough to look into her eyes. "You are blessed. Chosen."

Focusing on his face, the face she'd known as long as her own, Seren told him what she'd seen.

Barir's eyes sharpened. "The Invaders approach. Kyros Meric is dead, so General Adem will send for Varol, Meric's brother and heir of the royal blood. But you can't let that happen."

She'd only really heard one word. A name. Varol. She swallowed a bitter taste rising in her throat. "What?"

"General Adem will send the city into mourning. Invaders or not. He will. He is arrogant. That shroud you saw? That was the city mourning. The Invaders triumphed while we mourned."

The traditional mourning song slithered through Seren's head.

The soul is heavy,
Three days, three days,
Your shoulders are free,
Take up the weight of Death.
The soul is tired,
Three days, three days,
You slept through the night,
Give your sleep to the Dead.
The soul is starving,

Three days, three days,
Your table is full,
Give your food to the Dead.
The soul is heavy,
Three days, three days,
Your shoulders are free,
Take up the weight of Death.

Her people would be weakened. Her warriors weakened. Her adopted family weakened, and at the mercy of the merciless.

"But he can't force everyone to mourn," she said. "If everyone stops eating and sleeping, we'll be easy to defeat. He would know that."

"You saw yourself pushing the mourning away. Then you saw our city at peace. Seren. Pearl of the Desert." He used the title given to her when she was married to the kyros. "You must claim leadership of the Empire. You have been chosen."

"No. That's not…"

"Then how do you see it?"

"We must announce the death and tell everyone to wait until after the attack to mourn."

"And if we survive, which we won't, General Adem will call for Varol and he will become kyros."

She hugged herself. Meric's younger brother was so much worse than even Meric had been. The way he used people…

Father had saved a slave working for Varol. Because of the woman's skill with the horses, Father had paid for her apprenticeship with the stables here in Akhayma. She'd been raised to middle-caste before he retired. But she still carried Varol's scars. Thick, clawed fingers of raised skin striping her back and shoulders. Seren's stomach clenched.

General Adem's voice came through the door. "May I enter to see the kyros, Pearl of the Desert?"

"I…"

Barir whispered in Seren's ear. "I will claim the kyros has something that may be contagious. I will keep everyone away. That will give you time."

"Time for what?"

"Pearl of the Desert." Adem rapped on the door.

Barir put his hands on Seren's shoulders. "It will give you time to fight off the Invaders. Then, you can decide whether or not to embrace your fate."

"My fate? No. That can't be what I'm supposed to do."

"Why not? You are a general's daughter. You traveled with him. You learned from him."

"I'm not of royal blood. I'm not even fully desert blood. General Adem would never support me."

"He isn't fully desert either. Not many are."

"That doesn't matter," she whispered. "He's ruled by tradition. You've seen him. He worships the royal blood nearly as much as the Fire. And if he finds out I hid Meric's…condition, he'll have me beaten to death."

"The Fire showed you what to do. You know you trust in it."

"About this though…this is madness."

Adem knocked again. "I must insist to see my kyros."

Seren hugged Barir again. He kissed her forehead like she was Meekra's sister, another daughter.

"I'll keep everyone out," Barir said. "We can talk about the rest later. And my dear Seren." His eyes softened but were no less unblinking, his stare no less steady. "Fate rarely waits until we're ready. How many times would we say *No* in preparation for something great? Every time. We would never feel fully armed. You are more ready than most and you must believe you are enough."

Wisdom glinted in his eyes. But he wasn't right about this. There was no way he could be right about this. Mind humming, she followed him out of the room.

Shutting the door behind them, Barir bowed to Adem. "General, our kyros has contracted what I believe to be a contagious disease of the respiratory system. We must keep everyone out, except Pearl of the Desert, Meekra, Cansu, and myself since we have been in close contact already. We've all taken a ka'ud potion, so we may come and go without danger to others, but no one else should be risked. It could lead to an epidemic."

Seren bit her lip. They were lying to the highest ranking military man in the city. To Meric's right hand. Cansu looked confused, but he held his tongue.

"It is…for safety," Seren said. "We must be very careful. Especially now that we're under attack. I will tell the rotating guards to keep all of this to themselves, and to make certain no one, including them, may enter the chamber."

Adem looked to the door, blinked. "Can you heal him?"

"I can't say yet. It is…" Barir glanced at Seren. "Too soon to tell."

Adem's body tensed beneath his armor, and his jaw sharpened—a warrior trained to absorb a strike when he had to. Though this blow had nothing to do with fists or steel. It was Adem's loyal heart taking the news that his beloved royal was seriously ill. Seren had never been close to Adem, but sympathy flooded her nonetheless.

"Fine," Adem said. "I will pray for our kyros and lead the troops as best I can until tomorrow when, Fire make it so, I may speak with our kyros for his final decision on what action to take."

With a curt bow to Seren, he spun on his heel and headed for the Holy Fire bowl at the main tent's door.

Meekra's eyes couldn't get any wider. "Should I go in with you, my lady?"

The guards and fighters standing watch shifted their weight, looking like lost children instead of people trained to kill.

"Yes, Meekra. We'll tend to the kyros." She waved, indicating Meekra should join her inside.

"I'll announce the quarantine to the criers so everyone will know to keep their daily supplications to themselves for the time being," Barir said before they left.

Seren turned, knowing the tears at the corners of her eyes made her look too young to give orders. "Tell the scribe too. He must take hold of the business side of things while we...until the kyros is well."

"My lady." Barir bowed and held Seren's gaze for a heartbeat. "Remember, you are blessed."

Seren rushed into her personal chambers, wanting nothing more than to run away from the burden Barir's beliefs and her vision had stacked onto her shoulders.

2

ONA

The kyros's famous capitol wasn't what Ona expected. The city's name itself meant *tents*. Last she checked, tents were not made of rock. Slowing their horses, Ona and Lucca reached out—his hand rough with one broken finger; hers smaller and scarred at the knuckles—and touched the nearest section of the wall. Smoky, white stone lay in between layers of rock the color of dead leaves.

Lucca's sudden *hm* made Ona jump in her saddle. "Never seen anything like this. Even in the most decadent villas." He looked back. "Did I startle you? Excited about meeting a kyros? Nervous you'll want more than he can give?" He wiggled his thick eyebrows.

The kyros and his kin were known to be the most handsome men in the world. "The kyros and I want the same thing," Ona said. "Dead Invaders."

A memory of her aunt's eyes going glassy iced her. She remembered the palette knife, gripped in her own hand, dripping Invader blood, the blood of the man who'd slit her aunt's throat. Ona could still feel her innocence flying away like a frightened bird.

She flexed her hand around her sword's hilt. The promise of revenge warmed her belly.

Someday. Somehow.

Lucca's normally cool gaze held an edge of worry. He ran a hand over his curly, dark hair. "I wonder what they'll think of us."

Ona's saddle creaked as she leaned back. "We might have to prove ourselves." One young man and a nineteen-year-old didn't look like much.

Until they started fighting.

The city's walls went up, up, up, and the child artist hiding inside Ona wanted nothing more than to study the honeycomb design above the city's bronze doors. Shoving that part of her down, she bumped the horse's sides with her heels.

At the doors, guards stopped them with spears to the face. They wore helmets shaped like upside down acorns and vests Lucca called *jerkins*. Once Lucca and Ona explained—well, Lucca explained more because he spoke the trade tongue a lot better—that they were mercenaries here to serve Kyros Meric, the guards hurried them through, one man coming along as escort into the city proper.

And when Ona saw it, she gasped.

Now *this* was what she'd had in mind.

Impossibly high towers shaped like lotus flowers sprung up between swathes of suspended fabric that protected canals of rushing water from the sun. The tents, lightly rolling like waves, were every color in the world. Gray as a goose's feathers. Yellow like lemons. The greens of olives, spring grass, and the lakes near home at midday. Some were the bright red of an enemy's blood and others the purple of old wounds.

Black goat fur striped and framed all the tents, even the ones inside another ring of walls. The tents reached higher than any in the rest of the city. The colors used in the dye looked darker too. Richer. Ona bet the kyros lived there somewhere.

"When it rains, that fur swells and seals the stitching," Lucca said, switching back to their own tongue. "Everyone stays nice and dry, and the rainwater drains into rigged barrels. Ingenious. I assume you need to *soak* this in."

"Ha. Ha." Ona slapped her knee dramatically, ignoring the bite of how well he knew she still wished to enjoy art and be a part of that world.

The life she'd imagined—working as a fresco artist with her aunt—was barred to her now. To take pleasure in colors and lines, shapes and creation would be an insult to her aunt. Revenge had to come first. It'd always come first. Life was no longer paints and charcoal. It was blood and bone, pain to answer the pain.

"Please tell me you're not comparing all this fine color to something violent." Lucca loved to fight, but he appreciated the technique, not the blood. He justified every battle, whispering their enemy's crimes under his breath before every battle.

"Only the red and purple," Ona said, shaking off her stillness to joke.

"You mean the pretty rose and the nice eggplant?" Lucca said in a nasal voice.

She gave him a look.

As they trotted along behind the guard, Lucca pulled out a skin of watered wine to drink. "It wouldn't ruin everything to ease off the killing mindset a hair. We are more than mercenaries." He patted his saddlebag where he kept two small books of history and numbers. "You should look to the peaceful side of yourself once in a while." He handed Ona the drink.

The wine tingled over her dry mouth. "You should stop being such a dainty little mushroom."

"Mushrooms can kill."

"Only the poisonous ones."

"And they do it so well, residing peacefully in the forest until someone bothers them. Then," he snapped his fingers, "death as needed."

Ona pretended to shiver. "Is that your plan for a new chant? *We will ruin you! But only as needed!*" She punched a fist into the air.

Lucca laughed then, loudly. She grinned, proud to pull it out of him. "Yes, I suppose that could be my motto."

Ona snorted. Grinning, Lucca slapped his gathered reins lightly against his gray-spotted gelding, and the horse trotted on. Ona's chestnut mare hurried to catch up.

Blacksmith forges lined the road, emitting sparks and blistering heat. Ona and Lucca leaned from side to side, surveying the making of the finest swords in the world.

"I have to get my hands on one of their swords."

"*Yatagans.*" Lucca nodded at two of the skinny, slightly curved versions of a sword sitting on a table at the back of the forge.

"Right."

"They mine the iron ore over that way." He pointed to another walled area attached to the southwest side of the capitol.

A group of men and women walked by, laughing and talking really fast in the desert tongue. Some were light-skinned like Lucca and Ona; others had darker skin. Most had black hair and eyes, but some had brown braids and green or blue eyes. A blend of the people originally from this desert, fighters from border towns brought in young to defend the Empire, and others from the borders whose families had served as slaves before rising through the castes. They all wore sweeping kaftans or military leather vests. Jeweled daggers hung from their sashes, fighter or not.

Two in the approaching group had bells jingling at their sashes, but the rest appeared to be purely of the desert blood and not required to wear the caste bells. Bells or no bells, there were some seriously beautiful people in this varied city.

At an open market, the canals' gurgling and the bang of blacksmiths' hammers competed with camel grunts, tea hawkers shouting, and the tempting call of the baker with his mound of cookies topped with pistachios. Ona bought one with a silver piece that had to be foreign to the seller, but didn't make the man blink an eye. Seemed Akhayma had plenty of visitors from far away.

Ona waved her cookie at all the gorgeous tents, the food, the children playing in well-stitched clothing. "See all this? They have wealth. Power. Smarts. With the kyros and his army, the Invaders will be crushed into nothing. Now, if we can just get them to attack."

"Your wishes are my wishes, Onaratta Paints with Blood," Lucca said wryly, prompting their old joke and using their mercenary titles.

Ona bit into her treat. The pistachios' salt argued happily with the dough's sweetness. "As long as yours don't war with mine, Lucca Hand of Ruination."

The two canals bordering the marketplace flowed into a huge pool lined in yellow and blue mosaics. A silver gilt bowl that could easily hold three fat men stood on a pedestal above the water. The kyros's graceful language poured over the sides. Ona wished she could read it.

She touched the guard on the shoulder. "What's the bowl for?"

"The Fire Ceremony. We held one last night, small girl."

Ona flexed her sword hand. "You mean *scary woman*."

Lucca urged his horse between them. "At the end of every quarter, *tiny face*," he said with a teasing smirk that she determinedly ignored. "They pull back the tents, build a bonfire in the bowl, then after the kyros blesses it, they use the branches to light the family fires in town. The Holy Fire keeps the city's inhabitants close to true wisdom."

Whatever that meant.

"This past ceremony was…difficult," the guard said as they walked into the inner ring of stone walls. Two more guards raised their palms to him as they passed. "Normally, it is the most beautiful night. Once the fires are lit, all sit quietly and pray and reflect."

They just sat? Boring. "It sounds—"

Lucca jabbed Ona's arm with a fist. "It sounds perfect," he said.

At an enormous black and blue tent, the guard stopped, his face holding some quiet sadness. "Please wait here, Silvanians," he said before disappearing inside.

Silver stars dotted the outside of the tent and a red rug ran under the entrance flap to where the horses' hooves sunk slightly into the gritty earth. Lucca and Ona dismounted and waited under the sun.

"How long will we have to wait?" Ona asked.

Before Lucca could answer, two women and a man—each with seven bells on their tunics' sashes—gave them a mint leaf, then took the horses.

"What is the story?" Ona held up the leaf, then tucked it behind her ear and did a makeshift dance, swiveling her hips and rolling a shoulder.

"Maybe it's for our breath?" Lucca shrugged and ate his.

Ona snorted and popped hers into her mouth as the guard appeared to lead them through the flap.

The tent was even more beautiful inside. It was like being inside a structure made wholly out of the colored glass Silvanian priests used in the cathedrals. The sun glowed through the blue, turning it lighter, but richer. The red of the rug sparkled with silver threads and the fabric stars twinkled in the muted light.

Their guard-guide fellow gestured to a copper bowl of green leaves that burned a deep orange.

Lucca spoke in Ona's ear. "Fire is their way to connect with a higher power, remember?"

"And?"

Slinging his most withering look, Lucca stepped toward the fire bowl and passed a hand over the flame. "Do what I do, Ona."

She tried to appear serious as she did the same movements, but the heat did nothing to inspire her to prayer.

At the end of the room, a tall, weathered soldier, five bells on his sash, stood at attention, holding his helmet. Beside the soldier, a woman with black eyes ringed in green cosmetics wore one bell tied to a ribbon across her forehead. As she tilted her chin, studying Ona and Lucca, it rolled along her smooth skin. She worried a little scrap of wool at her sash like she was nervous. But she shouldn't have been. This had to be Seren, Pearl of the Desert, wife to Kyros Meric.

The guard introducing the mercenaries bowed deeply and held up a palm, calling himself Erol. A thick, blue smoke that smelled like night flowers streamed out of a heavily guarded back room as he spoke in the desert language, adding in Ona's name and Lucca's.

Ona mimicked the guard's respectful movements, with a side-glance at Lucca. He wasn't bowing. Or raising his hand. He stood there with his mouth hanging open.

"Lucca," she hissed.

He swallowed and dropped to one knee. "Pearl of the Desert."

Ona muffled a laugh against her arm. Even the impossible was possible. The infamously unshakeable Lucca, finally flustered by a pretty lady. He'd better watch himself. Surely, they wouldn't be too keen on a foreign mercenary making eyes at the kyros's lady.

Ona cleared her throat, running a translation through her mind. "Akhayma is so beautiful, we have trouble…telling a story…no…speaking. Yes, speaking!"

Everyone grinned.

Lucca shook his head once and seemed to come back to his senses.

The kyros's wife stepped forward and gestured to a bronze and blue enameled tray of small, cylindrical glasses. "Of course. You must be very weary after your long trip. Please sit and have some tea. Please forgive the ka'ud smoke. Kyros Meric is very ill." Her gaze fell on Ona—her eyes were so sad—before falling away to focus on the servant pouring the tea. "The smoke helps his lungs."

~

AFTER A PAINFULLY LONG stream of pleasantries—during which Ona thought Seren was going to either nibble her lip off or tear that odd piece of cloth she kept—Ona pushed her untouched tea to the side.

She looked at the man they called General Adem, an old fellow whose glare she admired. "Your kyros told one of the Silvanian kings that you all were willing to pay good silver if we train your warriors, right?"

General Adem leaned forward, focusing the blaze in his eyes on her. "We don't need training, Silvanian. We are the best fighters in the world."

Ona had to smile. "I have heard you're the best with the steel. Making it *and* wielding it. But we have something you don't. A way to improve the amazing skills you already have."

"So we can help one another," Adem said. "We teach you our fighting techniques, bow and yatagan, and you teach us yours. We've heard stories about your successes. I've read the reports. I'd like to know specifics from your own mouths. Tell us about your abilities."

"Tell us more about yours first," she said.

Lucca kicked her under the table. She ignored it. The Empire had some way they used fire, some sort of blessing Lucca had mentioned. Refusing to blink, she held herself calm as the general weighed the force of her stare. He wouldn't be finding her will lacking.

Seren opened her mouth, probably to break the stand-off, but Adem's lips slanted into a clever grin. "All right then, Onaratta Paints with Blood. If

359

we summon Holy Fire, some of us receive ideas, strategies. Those with royal blood have been known to hear ideas from the Fire."

Seren looked at her hands, turning them over and running a finger over the veins. Why did she look guilty?

Ona focused on the topic at hand. Getting ideas from fire, that was pretty impressive. "And your people still nearly lost all to the Invaders last generation?"

Adem went very still. Seren paled, her mouth a line above her pointed chin, as Lucca's eyes closed and he breathed out through his nose.

"The Holy Fire gave…Kyros Meric the idea to hire you," Seren said.

Ona grinned. "Then it can be useful."

"Yes. Very." The general looked ready to relieve Ona of her tongue. He took a breath, then sipped some tea. "When my kyros is well again, he will decide for certain whether or not to use your services."

Anger bubbled in Ona's middle. The leader of their mercenary band would definitely do his best to kill her and Lucca if they failed to bring back a load of silver. She didn't think she could give up Silvania's forests for good and hide away. Her fist landed hard on the table. "Dom said it was all set!"

Seren's mouth fell open. Adem tensed like he wanted to strike Ona.

Lucca smiled too wide at Adem and Seren. "How about I explain a little about our abilities, the power that seems to run in some Silvanians' blood."

Adem's gaze was flat. "That would be good."

"Our people pass down the talent of warrior chants," Lucca said.

"Like the magical symbols of the northern witches?" Seren asked.

Ona grinned. "It's slightly different. We don't use *lykill*—symbols—in our work. Just the words. We, as you may know, have a fighting blood. There isn't a day goes by that we don't argue."

Seren's smile lit her face like the sun had walked into the room to shine on her pretty features. "You are a passionate people. Much like us. We come from many places, but here, we come together with a love for family, honor, fine weapons we make with our iron, and…food." She laughed, a quiet and unpracticed sound, like she hadn't relaxed in a long while. "I've read about your struggles to hold the various sections of your lands, the fights between cousins, and your love of fine fabrics."

"Not that you can tell from *our* sad clothing." Ona nodded at her plain long shirt, ripped short pants, and dust-covered tall boots.

Lucca grimaced at his own outfit. Though he topped the ensemble off with that oddly attractive face of his, Lucca's clothing was no better than Ona's.

"Mercenaries don't dress as typical Silvanians," Ona said. "We favor the freedom of living in the wild." At least she thought she said that. She really needed to work on her foreign languages.

"You still manage to look striking." Seren's curious gaze slid over Lucca's mouth, then to the white streak in Ona's reddish mess of hair.

The slaves' bells clanged as they dished out what smelled like lemon and cardamom meatballs, lamb-stuffed and roasted onions, and an eggplant and pine nut salad of some sort. Ona's mouth watered like she hadn't had a meal in days. She'd eaten a lot of Empire foods—sold at markets in each Silvanian town—lured by their spices. The dishes were as gorgeous as they tasted. Green and white nuts, red sauces, browned meats, and glistening honey. She licked her lips as the servants scooped a tiny amount of each dish onto her plate.

The contrast between the large slave bell and the tiny, high-caste bell Seren wore wasn't lost on Ona.

There were slaves in Silvania too. Also in the northern isles—Ona had seen plenty of sad folks go to that snowy place where they'd probably never escape a life of hard, unrewarding work. She'd seen them on trading days at the ports. There wasn't any caste system in Silvania or in the northern isles, so the poor souls couldn't move out of their low position. At least here they had a chance to move up.

The guard, Erol, who'd led Lucca and Ona into this tent hadn't worn any bells. So, slavery and caste definition were for those with mixed heritage, like Seren and Adem, who didn't look like they were only of the desert blood, their noses were a little different, less pronounced.

"How do you use these chants you speak of?" Adem asked, plucking an eggplant from his platter. "My kyros will need to know the details."

Lucca took over and Ona let him. He spoke more clearly. "We say the words we've learned from those before us. The chant...its intent bleeds into us." He curled his fingers into a fist and held it to his chest. "If it is a chant about strength and speed, we hit harder with our swords and fists and run faster. When we chant of agility, we can leap over opponents or twist in ways that wouldn't normally be possible."

Seren pulled her hands together and edged forward. "To have a voice that holds so much power..."

Adem glanced at her, but spoke to Lucca. "The kyros will be very interested to watch your training."

Seren put her hands in her lap, the light in her face going dull.

Ona made a mental note to go ahead and hate this Adem fellow.

"Yes, Pearl of the Desert," Ona said. "Our throats hold more power than any sword or bow. Our words are our strongest weapon. We'll be happy to give you a nice taste of it on your training fields later if you like."

Seren smiled. "I'd like that, Onaratta Paints with Blood." She looked about ready to burst into tears suddenly. What was going on here?

Adem stood and took up his helmet, bowing to Seren, then to Lucca and Ona. "I hope the chants serve as well as one thousand weapons. If the Invader wolves do come, we could be but dust on the plains by next moon. Now, if you'll excuse me, Pearl of the Desert?"

Lucca's face clouded as he studied Adem.

Ona knew that look. Lucca was guessing the general had a secret.

"Do you know if there are any Invaders in the area?" Lucca asked, dangerously quiet.

His own brother had run away at thirteen and had been taken by Invaders. She didn't know the details. Lucca refused to talk about it and she didn't want to push him.

"You'll receive military reports as we see fit, mercenary," Adem said.

Lucca pushed away from the table and bowed to the general even though Ona was fairly sure he wanted to make an obscene gesture instead.

With Adem gone, Seren cleared her throat. "I...you're welcome to rest in a guest tent closer to the rear gates, near the entrance to the training areas. I hope you'll be comfortable there. If you're not too tired, I'd love to see your techniques later this morning. At the hour of ten?"

Lucca smiled. "That'll be fine. Should we tell the general?"

"Nah," Ona said. "She's the kyros's wife. Right, Pearl of the Desert?"

Seren frowned and her eyes filled again. "You're right, Onaratta."

"Call me Ona, please, Pearl of the Desert."

"Only if you call me Seren." She glanced at Lucca. "And you as well. But only in private, please."

Lucca put a fist to his chest and bowed deeply before the mercenaries turned to go.

Back in the sunlight, Ona smacked Lucca's shoulder with the back of her fist. "You and I need to chat," she said in Silvanian.

He stared straight ahead as Erol led them to the guest tent. "I don't know what you're talking about."

"Oh yes, you do," Ona said.

"Fine. The lamb was a little dry," he said. "But I still think this job is going to be fun."

Ona crossed her arms. "I'm not talking about the lamb."

"The tea wasn't my favorite." He pretended to study a merchant's table of crockery as they passed through the last of the market.

"Not discussing tea either, Master Lusty Eyes," Ona said.

"That is not my name and you know this."

"It is now."

Erol scowled and waved a hand to hurry them along.

"No," Lucca spat.

Ona nodded. "Yep."

He glanced at Erol, the usual wariness wrinkling his forehead. "Seriously, Ona. Stop."

The man couldn't understand Silvanian. "Fine, Master L.E. But don't think I didn't see how...*that situation*—" Ona fluttered her lashes "—affected you."

"Noted," Lucca said quietly.

"Good."

"Good."

3

SEREN

Thoughts and emotions tumbled through Seren, pricking and striking, as she stared at Meric's body. With Meekra's help, Seren had rolled him up in bed linens and she knew very well she was some kind of terrible soul to be able to do that without sobbing or passing out cold. She relit the ka'ud wood. The clouds' resinous scent covered the odor she didn't want to think about—the smell of Meric's body longing to return to the air and earth. It was a small mercy that no one was permitted to enter the kyros's personal quarters because of Barir's quarantine. Not that Adem wouldn't necessarily barge in anyway. And if he did, well, Seren wasn't sure what would happen. She could picture him dragging her into the courtyard and…

"I am ready with your clothing, Pearl of the Desert." Meekra's voice was light and steady through the thick, woven doorflaps that led to Meekra's smaller chamber. Seren had slept in the smaller bed in that separate chamber last night with Meekra at her feet on a cot.

Pulling her shoulders back, Seren went to her and let Meekra dress her in a pair of sky blue pantaloons since she was headed to the training fields to see Ona and Lucca in action. Over the pantaloons, Seren slipped on a thin, dark blue kaftan with a bright orange hem and sash. Meekra held up several silver bangles that clinked lightly.

"You'll have to unclasp your fist, my lady."

"Oh." Seren placed the tiny slip of parchment Adem had sent after the early morning meeting on her cosmetics table. The words glared at her in black ink. He'd thought Meric would read them.

I will view the Silvanian mercenaries at their work, my kyros. No need to send Pearl of the Desert, my kyros.

Seren set her jaw. He'd never liked her. Not since Father argued with the old kyros about her someday marriage to Meric. Father had seen the cruel streak in Meric. But Adem had called her and her family unfit.

"Not respectful of the royal blood," he'd said. "They have a burden to bear. The Fire sometimes speaks to them, tells them things... It is a burden of that blood, to know what will happen, to know what you must do despite your own fears and limitations."

He'd been so rude to Father. She'd been surprised Father stood there and took the verbal abuse. Now she understood. Father had retired at that point and Adem had taken his place beside the kyros. Adem held the power and Father had held none.

But despite her non-royal blood, she'd seen a vision. She hadn't simply heard something—that in itself hardly ever happened for a non-royal—but images of possibilities and ideas had poured through her mind almost as real as the world around her.

If only Adem would believe her, that she was what Barir thought she was...blessed. But what if it was a one-time thing and she wasn't truly blessed and would lead the Empire into ruin? Why would Adem ever believe she was blessed when she didn't believe it herself? She knew the answer already. Adem never would.

Well, she was going to the training fields to see the mercenaries. No matter what Adem thought about it. And she would ask him what he would do if Meric died. Maybe Barir was wrong. Adem might choose to wait to mourn and properly protect the city.

That would mean your vision was false, a voice inside Seren whispered.

As Meekra applied sparkling green cosmetics to Seren's eyelids, Seren pushed the worry away. She'd question Adem. Carefully. One thing at a time.

"Do you want to talk about all of this, my lady?" With a click of metal on lacquered wood, Meekra slid the cosmetics box closed and looked at Seren with patient eyes.

"Can we think about something else? Is that horrible? It's horrible. I know it. But I have so many things to figure out. And I have to watch the mercenaries' demonstration to see if their efforts are worth our warriors' time right now."

Meekra ran a hand gently over Seren's hair and Seren couldn't help but let out a sigh.

"You're human," Meekra said. "It's all right to need a change in focus for a breath or two." She brushed Seren's hair as she talked, her words and movements soothing. Seren was so lucky to have such a devoted friend. "My sister's coming-of-age ritual is today."

Seren took a deep breath and let her mind wander from Meric and the Empire. "The blanket looked beautiful after Izzet and Najwa added that ring of bright green for fertility."

Meekra smiled sadly. "She loves it. If I may say so, my lady, you're a rare rose among the flowers of the royal household."

"I don't know about that. I do have fewer thorns than Qadira though." Qadira never failed to mention her clan's bloodlines in every conversation. She was a relentless snob, but her father, chieftain of their powerful clan, helped Akhayma's economy stay strong with his keen business sense. Needless to say, Qadira soundly refused to join in on the inter-caste weaving.

Meekra's hands went to her hips. "A *shawakk* plant has less spikes than that girl."

Seren almost grinned, then reality tore at her chest. She fought a sob. Meekra rested a hand on her shoulder.

"Did your father tell you anything else about last night?" Seren asked.

Meekra chewed the inside of her cheek. "No. Just...about the kyros. And how we must keep it a secret."

"Not why?" Seren asked, standing and going to the back door to check that the rotating guards were in place. "No one is to enter. No matter what happens. Do you understand?"

The guards nodded and bowed quickly. "Yes, Pearl of the Desert," they said in unison, worry tightening their eyes.

"Even if there is an emergency. I will handle that. As will my personal guards. One of you go now to the men and women positioned at the front of my chamber and at the main tent's entrance. Give them my instructions."

"Yes, Pearl of the Desert."

Seren ducked back inside and looked at Meekra. "So your father didn't say why we must keep this tragedy a secret?"

Meekra's gaze drifted to the wrapped body. "No, my lady. If you want me to know, I'm here to listen. But I trust you. As does my father."

Meekra's loyalty glowed inside Seren, warm and steady. "Thank you."

Seren would've asked her to stop with the *my lady*, but she'd given that up the first week. Meekra said General Adem would have her head if he heard her using anything less. He might not have been Seren's ally, but tradition ruled all for that unbendable man.

~

WHEN SEREN ARRIVED at the training field with her guards, three military units were practicing with yatagans, steel flashing in the red, morning sun.

"Do you see General Adem?" she asked Cansu.

The guard ran a hand down his long face as he studied the men dodging and swinging among plumes of dust and the servants coming in and out of the stables to the far right near the entrance to the archery course. "I don't, Pearl of the Desert."

A gust of wind lifted his hair off his forehead, and she felt a little lighter seeing the calm obedience in his face. She wondered if maybe her father had looked like Cansu when he was a young man before age tinged his hair with white and silver.

Erol scowled like he always scowled and squinted his brown eyes, pointing at the sun dial. A sliver of shadow approached the hour mark as a young hawk screeched overhead. "Perhaps he will be here at the hour, my lady."

Heat pricked at Seren's cheeks. She'd forgotten that she'd set the tenth hour of the morning as the time for Ona and Lucca's demonstration. "Of course."

"Did the kyros not receive my message, Pearl of the Desert?" Adem said behind her.

Jumping, Seren turned to see him bow and hold his palm up. His tone of voice didn't match his respectful movements.

"He-he did, General," Seren said, hating herself for stuttering.

Adem made a noise under his breath. "It's quite warm, my lady. Wouldn't you be more comfortable in the shade of your tent? Or perhaps you haven't had the chance to practice your archery in a while, what with the ceremony preparations. I can easily oversee the demonstration and organize the strategy if you wish to leave."

"I don't wish to leave." Her legs were shaking again. She rolled the end of the wool piece tucked into her sash and tried to steady her voice. "Two ideas came to me concerning the Invaders," she said quietly. They hadn't announced the scouts' report yet so not even her guard knew the danger riding toward them.

"Surely your ideas can wait until later, Pearl of the Desert."

She took a breath. "We don't need to wait until some later meeting time.

It's only us here, with my men and yours. A perfect moment for discussing strategy." She spoke as quickly as she could. If she stopped, her voice might refuse to work altogether. Adem was just so intimidating. "The sun dial says we have ten minutes before the mercenaries arrive. Firstly, I'll ride into Kenar with the force you select for the attack. We will—"

"You must not, Pearl of the Desert. The kyros would never want you in that kind of danger."

"I rode with him when we faced the Invaders at the last clan Gathering."

"That was a small contingent of brigands, broken from their brethren. Not an organized force like this will be, my lady."

"Nonetheless, I killed a man," Seren said.

"With an arrow. From a distance," Adem argued. "We will be head on this time with the clash coming on in a small area. It will be very different, my lady."

"Yes. It will. And I have another idea concerning that."

"Leave the strategy to me and my kaptans, Pearl of the Desert."

Her body tensed. He'd given her an order. Without Meric at her side, he would run right over her.

Hossam must've noticed her sudden stillness, her uncomfortable stance, because he put a hand on the hilt of his yatagan. She shook her head slightly. What if he'd pulled his weapon? Adem would've killed him or maimed him at least. Seren swallowed. It was nerve-wrecking to be in charge of so many lives.

Adem bowed shallowly. "If it pleases you, Pearl of the Desert," he said, correcting his tone.

Heat burning her cheeks, she glanced at the gate leading to the city. Her feet tingled, wanting to hurry away to safety. But there wasn't any safety. Not anywhere. But before she talked strategy, she needed to at least give this boar of a man a chance to prove Barir wrong. Surely he would agree the mourning must wait until after they'd dealt with the Invaders.

Clearing her throat, she tried to meet Adem's eyes. She settled for his forehead. "Kyros Meric is no better this morning."

Adem's head dropped and he rubbed his chin.

"What if," she whispered, "he doesn't pull through this?"

Adem's head snapped up. He stared into the distance. "It would be a horrible tragedy. We would of course mourn." He looked at her, eyes narrowing. "You know the custom…"

"But we're about to be attacked. Wouldn't mourning put us at further risk? No eating or sleeping? Doesn't seem like the way to prepare for an enemy."

"We won't allow them to frighten us into giving up the very traditions that have given us this life. Do you think you know better than centuries of leaders? Than those with the oasis blood, the Fire-blessed, royal blood?"

A drop of spittle marred his tidy beard. He looked over her face and took a breath.

"My lady. I apologize. But surely you must see you are in the wrong."

She definitely saw something. But it wasn't that she was wrong. It was that Barir was right. Adem would never hold up the mourning ritual. Unless…

"Have you ever had a vision in the Fire, General?"

"Of course not. I have no royal blood. Or not enough anyway. None but the kyros's direct line does. The sun is too much for you, Pearl of the Desert. Your mind is suffering."

She pushed the insult aside. "I'm fine. So no one outside the royal blood has ever had a vision?"

"Of course not." He paused. "I would like to see the kyros today. Regardless of what the physician says."

Seren's heart knocked around inside her chest. What could she say? "If you contract the illness, we could lose both of you and then where would the Empire be against the Invaders?"

Adem crossed his arms and watched a woman and a man spar with their bows, fine quivers set to the side. "True. I'll give it another day and we will see what the physician says, my lady."

Seren did her best not to pass out with relief as she nodded. The feeling was brief though. She was still in the same awful place. Meric was dead. She'd seen the horror Akhayma would experience if Adem was allowed to lead the city in mourning. Adem would never believe she'd had a vision.

For now, she would keep Meric's death a secret. As for taking control, no. She couldn't. She wasn't of the royal blood. No one would support her. It'd never been done. At least to her knowledge. All she could do right now was give her ideas to Adem and hope she was doing what was best for Akhayma, the Empire, and the people she loved more than anything.

She'd start with an idea she'd had over the Fire after reading a scroll about a battle in the mountain region eighty-five years ago.

"I-I think we should evacuate Kenar," she whispered.

"We've already done that, my lady."

Oh. She locked her knees to stop their trembling. This whole situation was a nightmare. What would Father have done? *Keep on. Push through your obstacles. Eyes open. Heart ready.* She could almost hear his voice soaking through the hot air.

"We can hide in the buildings before moonrise tomorrow night," she said. "In the homes and shops. When the Invaders arrive, we'll surprise them."

"Your timing is spot on," Adem said quietly, "but with that strategy, we'll be separated from one another, my lady. Our archers won't be able to see their flag go up. They won't know when to attack. The foot soldiers won't be united when it comes time for a shield wall, Pearl of the Desert."

"The surprise will be worth it, General. I think." She rubbed sweating palms on her kaftan. "Especially if our warriors do benefit from the mercenaries' training," she said, trying to turn the conversation and avoid his arguments. The sun glared down on them as she tried to imagine what Ona and Lucca's chanting would look like.

They walked closer to see the fighters and the guards came up beside them.

"You truly believe they'll learn anything in such a short time, my lady?" Adem's tone mocked her.

"What good is it to believe they won't?" Seren said.

Hossam snorted a laugh and quickly covered his mouth. Adem whipped around. Hossam stilled, looking as though he'd never moved in his life. It should've been entertaining, but everything was too much, too heavy, too hot for Seren and the air filled with black spots.

Her head swam in the heat waves.

Hossam shouted for Meekra, who was several steps back, talking to the stable keep about Seren's horse, Fig.

Meekra appeared at Seren's side and held out her arm. "Are you all right, Pearl of the Desert?"

Seren leaned against her until the spots faded and she could breathe again.

"It's very hot," Meekra said. "Hossam, would you mind getting a damp cloth for our lady?"

"Of course not," he said, his eyes sincere.

"You locked your knees, didn't you, Pearl of the Desert?" Adem's tone reminded Seren of her old history tutor.

She wanted to argue, but he was right. Her cheeks grew warm again. "Yes, I think so, General."

Hossam handed Meekra the damp cloth, and she arranged it at the back of Seren's neck. The cool wet fabric on her skin cleared her vision, and she straightened up.

Ona and Lucca broke from the wall's shade and marched into the growing sunlight. Though they were far away, it was easy to tell them apart from anyone else. Ona's walk was springy, but also predatory, like a falcon on the ground, like she hunted an animal no one else could see. Lucca loped like a desert lion, his head shifting this way and that, always on the watch.

Adem took off and Seren hurried to follow, their path colliding with the mercenaries. Lucca and Ona stopped and bowed.

"Good day, Pearl of the Desert, General Adem," Lucca said. Ona just grinned.

The sun shone off Lucca's high cheekbones. He looked different from anyone she'd ever seen.

"We're ready to see what you can do," Seren said.

Ona rubbed her hands together. "And we're ready to show you."

Adem's hands fisted. He started toward the units, motioning to a warrior carrying something in his hand. The man strode over to a stand holding six small flags. He withdrew one and replaced it with the one he'd been carrying. Seren was fairly sure each unit and training activity had their own color. The units on the far left, nearest the slope that led to the prisons, sheathed their swords and gathered in front of them like rows of silver coins. The men stood straight and still, their helmets blinding in the sun.

The sound of the iron ore mines floated over the walls. Donkeys' brays, picks' cracking, and machinery's squeaks trickled into the air.

Adem introduced Lucca and Ona to the other soldiers, using their vicious mercenary titles.

To Seren's side, Ona and Lucca whispered in Silvanian. Ona pointed at Erol's yatagan and raised her eyebrows hopefully.

"You want a yatagan?" Seren asked.

"Um, yes. Yes, I do," Ona said.

Seren nodded. "We can arrange that. If you are all you say you are."

Lucca's gaze snapped to Seren's face. Dark hair swept over his forehead and his eyes burned with truth. He looked completely different. So foreign. Why did she feel like she could trust him already? Like that mouth could never lie? That was a foolish thought. All people lied. The real question, Father would've said, was whether or not he would lie for her or against her. Wait. That wasn't right. That sounded…suddenly Seren imagined this Silvanian mercenary pressing her against a lotus tower, his lips on her jawline. *Lie against her.* She was an idiot! She wiped the fantasy away with a quick swipe of the wet cloth across her neck. Father would've said the real question was *would he lie to bring her goal to light or to drag it into the sand?*

"We are exactly what we say we are, Pearl of the Desert," he said. "I'll show you."

Her heart bumped oddly in her chest. "I hope so."

The general stepped back and held a hand toward Lucca as an invitation to begin.

Ona stepped forward instead. A smile pulled at Seren's mouth and almost turned the corners of her lips up. The mercenary pulled her wide yatagan—her *sword*—from her belt, along with a stone. A flint, maybe? Lucca said something to her. She looked to the skies in irritation but stepped back, allowing him to take the warriors' attention.

Spreading his arms wide, Lucca addressed the units. He obviously thought the troops could do with an explanation before Ona's demonstration. Lucca's features were dark slants of purpose and drive as he paced the dirt in his tall boots.

"We're so pleased you're open to learning what we have to teach." Under the rims of helmets, eyes narrowed. Meric had ordered it; being open had nothing to do with it. "And we look forward to learning from you as well. That overhand sweep to a two-step strike especially." He wiggled his eyebrows. "Plus, we'd love to work on your style of using the bow on horseback. I've heard you can shoot at the wildest angles."

The fighters grinned and murmured, elbowing one another.

"We may be from vastly different places, but we have one thing in common. We all want to be prepared when the Invaders strike. The small bands of them never stay away for long and all of us have lost someone we know. Who knows when they might come in full force." He paused, his face darkening like a coming storm.

Seren's chest tightened. The Invaders' land was ravaged by drought off and on, so they kept coming. Why didn't they try to negotiate? Why didn't anyone try to negotiate with them? And the way they killed...that haunting shriek. It was almost like they'd been possessed by some evil spirit. Like they were tortured and had to take their pain out on the world.

A hidden memory suddenly surfaced in Seren's mind.

She was closing the shutters of the house in the mountains, right before the attack. An Invader at the front of a group had spotted Cyren, a neighbor boy, and pushed him into a haystack before the rest of the unit made it to the top of the rise. To hide him. To keep him alive.

So the Invaders did have hearts. They'd spared Cyren.

Why then did they kill when they could simply injure? Why did they annihilate when they could negotiate? Seren pushed the puzzle out of her mind and focused on Lucca's words.

"As Silvanian fighters," Lucca said, "we learn to chant." His voice was deep, strong, as he walked a line in front of the warriors, not a drop of sweat on him. "Not all can do it. Seems it's like most skills—some are born to it, others can pick it up with practice, others never do learn. A chant is a phrase spoken loudly. While said chant is being shouted, the fighter strikes their steel with a flint to make a spark."

There was a flash of movement, then Ona was dragging a flint over her weapon. Sparks danced away from her hands.

"Desperta Ferro!"

Her voice echoed across the plain, against the stables, along the city walls. She drew a spark again and yelled foreign words into the air. Her arms moved like lightning, blurred in their speed. The steel she wielded was an arc of silver, a spray of shining power in her hands. No one would be able to touch her.

Seren's throat knotted. Seren had trouble speaking up to her own general, but this woman, this Onaratta Paints with Blood, had Seren's father's confidence, Mother's too.

"Pearl of the Desert, are you all right?" Meekra asked.

Below, Ona called out, "Nuh! Haris!" She held her sword poised and ready.

Two warriors sprang past the rest, Adem urging them on.

"Draw your steel and face me!" Ona said in heavily accented trade tongue.

The warriors stalked, then struck, one high, one low. She slipped three steps back, her boots a blur of darkness, until she had them stacked. They swung at her, but Ona's sword flipped and cut the air twice as quickly as the men's. Nuh almost sliced through her thigh, but she spun, flicked the tip of her steel toward their hands, and had them unarmed and on their knees before Seren's heart beat ten times.

The unit remained silent as they stared at Ona and their fellows on their knees, defeated. The only sounds came from the iron mines, everyone's breathing, and the grit under Lucca's boots as he faced Seren, watching for a response.

Seren's breath rushed out like she'd been hit in the stomach. "Amazing. It's...amazing."

Adem began stomping his feet in praise.

The unit joined in, raising shouts of "Victory! Victory!" It was Meric's war cry.

Erol took two steps forward. "I can't believe what I just saw." He turned, remembered Seren was there, and added, "Pearl of the Desert. I'm sorry. It's..."

"It's something we need to learn," Hossam said to Seren and Erol, "that's what it is, Pearl of the Desert, war brother." He nodded politely to each in turn.

Ona sheathed her sword and spoke to the units, including the two warriors it seemed she'd already befriended. "You have to feel the words inside you."

Lucca interrupted, "Most chants begin with *Wake iron, wake!*" The men nodded at the translation of what Ona had shouted.

Nodding, Ona continued, "You must believe the words. Know they work to make you faster, stronger, and they turn your weapon into another limb. Everything gets...the world falls behind and away from you when a chant is working. You move like, like the lightning before the thunder."

"It's a miracle." Adem studied her and Lucca. "We may actually benefit from this."

Seren wanted to praise them, but a hand had closed around her stomach. She wasn't sure what she felt. Having these mercenaries on their side, training her warriors, was a true blessing. But something scratched at her, under her skin.

She wanted their power.

Not necessarily the physical ability, but the raw confidence they oozed. The people fed on it, drawn to these two, already their disciples. To help her people defeat the Invaders, she needed that confidence. Confidence that her own father and mother had possessed, but she failed to exhibit.

Seren swallowed, her throat still tight. Barir was mad. There was no way Seren was chosen. She had none of Ona's type of leadership skills or power.

Lucca and Ona divided the unit into two groups and they separated on the field, the mercenaries explaining and laughing and looking generally very hopeful.

"We should return to the city," Seren said to Meekra.

Meekra took the damp cloth from Seren's neck as they made their way toward the back gate. "The Silvanian woman is a force, that is for sure, my lady."

Seren pressed a hand to her chest, wishing, wishing, wishing. "A force. Yes. Exactly that."

She'd never been so jealous in all her life. She wanted so badly to be as confident as Ona and Lucca were, to have the power Ona displayed with such ease.

They passed under the arch of the back gate and headed toward the Kyros Walls. Seren's ears buzzed with the sound of Ona's voice and the power that had flamed through her words.

"Will we get to see the other mercenary chant, Pearl of the Desert?"

Meekra asked as they passed through a clutch of nobles dressed in black, yellow, and red.

Qadira raised a palm to Seren, her kaftan's wide sleeves fluttering like a nightwinger. Najwa grinned as she bowed, the three high-caste bells on her black sash catching the sunlight. Seren gave the group a nod, her thoughts pushing her toward her tent, toward an empty place to think.

What would Lucca look like chanting and fighting like Ona? Inside the main tent, Seren removed her outer kaftan, suddenly too hot. Cansu, Erol, and Hossam stayed by the main tent's entrance, giving Seren and Meekra some space and privacy.

The door to Seren and Meric's personal chamber hung still and dead between the rotating guards on duty. The ka'ud wood smoked lightly, the blue puffs ghosting through the tent's seams. Seren inhaled. Under the heavy, nectar-like scent of the wood, the odor of death stirred.

He had to be buried. Now.

Meekra took Seren's kaftan and opened the chamber's thick, inner flap. Seren flexed her hands which were lightly calloused from archery, but smooth and lacking the muscle in Meekra's. Meekra, with her strong hands, could help her dig, but then Meekra would be that much more involved in this dangerous scheme. She studied her friend's face, the small scar beside her chin. Meekra had told Seren about that scar, about her younger sister accidentally kicking her during one of their friendly wrestling matches when they were little. Their family was intact and Seren wouldn't do anything to threaten that. Seren couldn't ask Meekra to help bury Meric. She had to keep her safe. Well, safe as possible.

She could bury him herself. Maybe.

Following Meekra—neither looked toward Meric's body on the bed— through the room and into the side chamber, Seren wondered how long it would take to dig an almost six foot long hole, at least two feet deep. She honestly didn't know. What if Adem came to the door and Meekra had to cover for her? If Adem pushed his way in and saw everything, Meekra's deceit would mean death.

While Meekra prepared a bowl of clean water, Seren, stomach in knots, went back to the door and peered through the flaps at her guards. The men talked quietly with the others stationed at the main tent's door. The sun cut through the pinned flaps and illuminated one side of Cansu's, Erol's, and Hossam's faces, leaving the other side dark. If she trusted them with her secret, they'd help her with this terrible task. They probably already knew Meric was dead. Cansu had seen him right before Barir confirmed it.

Erol muttered a word to Cansu and Cansu's face broke into a boyish grin. The old kyros—Meric's father and Seren's father's closest friend—had chosen him because he noticed details most did not. The way one warrior frowned when a certain kaptan entered the room. How a foreign emissary failed to bow properly or how many times the ore masters visited the training fields to watch their steel used. He never drew conclusions, but he grabbed all the elements so she could. But his face was as easy to read as a scroll written yesterday. He'd never keep a secret with that face. And it wasn't as if she could trust Hossam and Erol with this and not expect Cansu to find out.

No, her guards were good men, but they weren't the people she needed right now. If they knew, fine. But she wouldn't confirm their suspicions. That way, if anyone questioned them, they'd be safe. They wouldn't be held accountable for what she was doing.

What would Father have done?

Not wanting to lean on loyalty and endanger those closest, he'd have picked out two strong workers and paid them to keep quiet. Workers or soldiers with nerves of steel and no allegiance to Adem or any of the kaptans or ore masters. No secret agendas like so many warriors had.

And then it came to her.

There were two people in Akhayma with no allegiances past silver—which she could provide. Two people with nerves of steel. Yes, if she paid them enough and convinced them of the secret's necessity, they might just be the two people she desperately needed.

"Meekra?"

"Yes, my lady?" Meekra's head poked out of the side chamber's door flap.

"I'll take care of myself. Will you please tell the mercenaries to meet me at their tent at sunset tonight, after the day's training is complete. I need to see them before tomorrow."

Because tomorrow she'd have even more weighing on her. Tonight, she had to face the death sitting in her very chambers.

4

ONA

"No, no. Not like that. What did you chant? *Like the power of my grandmother's little finger?*" Ona grabbed Haris's shoulder and stopped him hacking at the wooden target. "Try this. Let me see if I can translate right...um..." Pushing the sleek man away—he reminded her of a cat—she faced the target herself and pulled out her sword and flint.

She struck it and watched the spark leap and fly. "*Wake iron, wake!*"

Her sword grew lighter, moved easily through the air as she sliced across the target's battered wood. As she drew the weapon back, she struck the flint again. She felt the sparks in her blood, fire singeing veins.

"*Strike like a storm, fast and faster.*

Like the water, unrelenting.

Iron in the hand. Iron in the heart.

A blade unstoppable!"

She leaped into the air, sword in both hands, and slashed down on the target's peak, a blow that would've blasted through any fighter's skull.

Haris hurried to the opposite side of the target, his eyes like slits and his mouth smiling cruelly. "*Wake iron, wake!*"

His flint scraped his yatagan and fire jumped from the contact. Slipping the flint in his sash, he shouted in accented trade tongue,

"*Be the instrument of my passion,*

My drive, my life.

I am a storm they don't see coming.

I am the heat inside a fatal wound.

Wake iron, wake!"

Ona sheathed her own sword, her cheeks hurting from smiling. "You basically just called yourself an infection, but all right. It worked." She stomped her feet in praise. "Much better."

A couple of other warriors came over, patted Haris on the back, began talking in their own desert tongue.

Across from a set of archery targets, Lucca's unit lined up, nearer to the stables. The sun bleached the stable roof, a lone tree's waxy leaves, and the warriors' dark heads. Holding a bow, Lucca sat on his gray-dappled horse in front of the fighters, several arrows tucked between his fingers. His other hand gripped the flint and struck it against the arrowhead. Like he'd stolen and thrown a piece of the powerful sun, a spark jumped from the flint.

"Wake iron, wake!
My body spins with the swiftness of the falcon."

He dropped his flint into his pocket, a movement smooth from loads and loads of practice, and let an arrow fly. It thunked into the center of the first target as his mount jolted toward the second target.

"I dive and my enemy sees my talon, my sword, flashing!"

His chant, one of Ona's favorites, boomed across the field and echoed along the training area's walls. He fired another arrow and hit the second target. And one more arrow, nearly splitting the first.

"My iron consumes his soul!" he shouted.

Lucca drove his horse past the third target, then pushed the animal back in a half turn. He loosed three arrows and each of them found the middle of the last target. His unit erupted in cheers as the first of them stepped forward, black hair waving in the wind.

The warrior repeated what Lucca had done, but at the end instead of turning his own mount around, he arched his back and shot upside down, hitting the target one time more than Lucca. Lucca shouted in smiling surprise and ran to the man, already asking how, his hands lifted in question.

Adem's raspy voice droned through a speaking cone. "Attention."

Ona whipped around to see the old man on the rise where Seren had stood earlier. The soldiers scrambled into lines and faced their general. Adem kept looking over his shoulder like Seren might return, like he was a boy afraid of getting in trouble.

Ona glanced at Lucca. He shrugged. So he didn't know what this was about either. Strange that Adem would interrupt them right after training had started.

Adem spoke too quickly and his voice echoed oddly through the cone.

Ona couldn't catch what he was saying. Something about scouts. Then one word rang clearly across the field.

Saldirgan. Invader.

Ona's blood took the sparks from earlier and ran with the feeling. She could leap over a mountain, slay one thousand without sweating a drop, push the sun back to savor the day.

They were coming. The Invaders from the West, the warriors who had ruined her life, were coming to Akhayma. Her heart soared. She would finally get her revenge.

She grabbed Haris's bony arm. "I can't hear him well enough. What is he saying? When will they arrive? How long do we have to prepare?"

Haris blinked. "Um, he said tomorrow, tomorrow evening. And the kaptans are to meet with him immediately at the weapons tent. Just there." He pointed to a large, oblong shelter beside the stables. The kyros's flag, blue with black calligraphy, snapped over its peak.

The crowd was already moving back into training with Lucca lost in the mass of men and women.

"I'll walk with you, if you like," Haris said.

Ona barely heard him. In her mind, her enemy stomped toward them, their weapons stained with her aunt's blood, their hands—too pale, too cold—ready to rip someone else's innocence away like they had Ona's. Their shriek, pained and howling, echoed in her ears.

Clouds like fists gathered around the afternoon sun, squeezed the orb's pale light, then let it go in watery lines that made Ona squint. Movements smooth, Haris led her past the busy training field and toward the weapons tents. Everything had a sharp edge to it. The ends of Haris's black hair, the white stripes of the tent, the curve of her boot's toe in the gritty earth.

Inside the weapons tent's dim light, Haris said goodbye and slipped out the door. The room was filled with men and a few women talking with one another, serious looks on serious faces. A man in front of Ona straightened his dark blue kaftan and adjusted the black sash at his waist. His yatagan hung from a shiny, silver chain.

"Have you seen Lucca Hand of Ruination, the other mercenary?" Ona asked, trying to smooth her trade tongue.

He inclined his head politely. Stars, he was pretty. War and want both sent that rush through Ona's blood. The more, the better.

"No, Kaptan Onaratta Paints with Blood," he said. "I have not, but may I say I am particularly impressed by your abilities and those of your associate."

"Oh. Thank you. Kaptan..."

"Rashiel Ozan."

"Thank you, Kaptan Rashiel Ozan. Will I see you at the evening meal?" He'd be great to question for military details and also great for some after dinner activities.

"Yes," Rashiel said. "I'll look for you and perhaps we can talk more about your skills."

"I'd like that very much." Ona angled herself toward him, wondering if he was as good at kissing as he was at good manners. "Maybe I could even show you a thing or two."

She could take over the world. Her enemies were coming and they would be destroyed. The world was new, and she was ready to celebrate it already.

One side of his mouth quirked into a grin. "You are very young."

"I'm a kaptan."

"And so you are. I'll see you at the evening meal then." He smiled and lightning zipped down her spine.

Lucca's mouth was suddenly at her ear. "You're flirting and death is riding at us." He nodded politely at Rashiel as the man turned. Adem entered the tent from a side door.

"This surprises you?" Ona said.

"Not really." The muscles around his jaw tensed and he stared ahead. "If the Invaders are coming, we should leave immediately."

Ona's stomach twisted, but hope surged over the sick feeling and drowned it. "I want my chance at them."

Lucca's eyes pressed shut for a beat. Then his shoulders straightened and he opened them, protectiveness practically shooting out of them like arrows. "What will happen if you do kill a bunch of Invaders? What then?"

"Then I'll live out my life as a mercenary, content in knowing the ones who murdered my aunt and made me become a killer are dead."

"What good will that do?"

"It's called vengeance, Lucca. Look it up in one of your books."

"If *you* looked it up, you'd find out vengeance has a pretty bitter aftertaste."

Ona felt like someone had tightened a horse's girth around her middle. Why didn't he understand?

She grabbed Lucca's sleeve and jerked him closer. "They ruined my world. They took my aunt's life like it was their right to do it." Her fingers shook. Heat seared the corners of her eyes. "I won't let them get away with it. I want to shove them into the ground and drive my sword into their hearts. All their hearts. I want to—"

Lucca put his hand over her shaking one and began plucking at her grip on his shirt. "All right. All right. But listen to this argument."

Adem was talking to a group of other kaptans and two of those ore masters, the men and women in the long, sweeping, black cloaks who ran the iron mine operations, Akhayma's main source of wealth.

"I don't want to risk my life for someone else's war," Lucca said. His breath smelled like mint. "If someone attacks Silvania, I'm all in. But this?"

"Someone else's war?" Ona's hand curled around the hilt of her sword. "It's not someone else's. It's yours! It's mine!"

A few heads turned their way, but they didn't speak Silvanian, so they couldn't know what Lucca and Ona were arguing about.

Lucca's pinched mouth fell and his eyes went shiny. She knew he wasn't going to argue anymore. Not today anyhow. She could almost see their friendship in his look. The rawness of the violence they'd committed together in the shadows under his lower lashes. The way no one else's life mattered as much as one another's during battles between the people who paid them hiding in an early wrinkle between his eyebrows. She knew he saw a lot in her eyes too. Her desperate hope flickered back at her, a gut-wrenching plea for him to understand her need to kill every Invader she could get her hands on.

Her hope won out and the heat of her anger cooled. She wanted him to want this revenge too, to really want it, not go along with her because he loved her and their friendship. This could mean his life, and she didn't want him to stay and fight if he didn't truly feel it.

"It's...ours," she said. "They hurt Silvania too. Not recently. But in the past. They ravaged my village and a dozen more past that. They tried to take yours too." She wouldn't mention his brother's abduction. Not until it was really necessary. "Don't act like that was a once in history occurrence. They could strike Silvania again if they take this territory. It would be even easier."

Twisting away, he raked hands through his hair. "I don't know how we'd leave anyway. One does not break a deal with a kyros if one wishes to keep one's head." His voice went quiet. "So I guess we're staying."

"We can do it, Lucca. We could lead our units against the Invaders." She could almost feel her sword driving into an Invader's throat.

"I seriously do not like that look in your eye." Lucca moved to get closer to Adem and his cohorts.

"You're not even looking at me," Ona said to his broad back.

"Oh I can see it. I can see it better than you."

"That doesn't make sense."

"Just…keep your head, Ona. That's all I ask. This isn't a mercenary fight, a battle for silver or respect. This will be true war. Mind your tongue, keep your options open, and stay close to me."

"You're awfully bossy, you know," she said.

"Just now noticing that?"

"Guess when we don't have the rest of the crew around, there's no buffer," she said as Adem's associates stepped back and let the older man take control of the room.

Meekra appeared at Lucca's side, dipping a small bow. She looked very out of place in here. "Pearl of the Desert requests you two receive her at your guest tent at sundown."

Lucca's mouth popped open. He shut it firmly and swallowed. "Of course." He lowered his chin and watched Meekra leave.

"What is that about?" Ona asked. She took Lucca's dimpled chin in her fingers and turned his head toward her face. "Hey. Pearl of the Desert isn't going to suddenly show up here so you can stop staring at the door."

"What?" He looked so shocked that she'd noticed his painfully obvious longing. "No."

"Hm."

Adem clapped once to gain everyone's attention. "A middle-sized unit, some 8,000 fighters will pass our borders by tomorrow afternoon. We ride to Kenar to meet them, to surprise them tomorrow night." He detailed a plan.

"If I may, sir," a warrior said, "where is our kyros?"

Adem stilled. "Unfortunately, our kyros is unwell."

"Shouldn't Pearl of the Desert be here? Her father taught her well." A few of the other fighters murmured assent.

Adem's voice was calm. Too calm. "I assure you, I know Kyros Meric's will in military matters and have hopes that his condition will improve when we crush the Invaders before they have time to take a full breath of our air!"

The warriors around Ona and Lucca raised their fists and shouted as one. A smile cracked Ona's dry lips as Lucca sighed resignedly and nodded. They were staying. And Ona was finally going to get the revenge she'd always wanted.

"WHAT DO you think about how it went?" Lucca asked Ona as they cleaned the day of training off their necks and faces. The fires in the copper bowl by the door, and the ones hanging from chains, scattered rays of orange over the purple, black, and white weave of the guest tent.

"They're no mercenaries, but they'll do." Ona gave up on simply washing her face and dumped her entire bowl of clean water over her head.

"They're better than mercenaries," Lucca said. "More talented with bow and sword. And they'd fall on a sword for the kyros."

"Or for Seren."

Lucca nodded. "I think so."

"And so would you."

"Ona."

"You wish she'd fall on your *sword.*" She winked.

Lucca's eyes flashed toward the door. "Be careful."

"No one around here knows Silvanian."

"Willing to risk my life on that?" He gave her such an older brother look before leaning over his washbowl to finish scrubbing.

"Oh, don't get your trousers in a bunch." Ona passed him on her way to the door and kicked the back of a knee, almost making him fall.

He growled. "So our long journey didn't change you much."

"You worried it would?"

"Hopeful," Lucca said.

"That stings."

He laughed.

"Wait." Ona turned from her view of the city. Night was already growing into corners between tents and along the lotus towers' eastern sides as the sun's light shimmered pink and readied for its exit. "Are you serious?"

That Lucca shrug said so much.

Something like a dagger's prick hurt her heart. "What exactly are you hoping I'll change?"

"Uncross your arms, Ona. I adore you. I want you to be happy."

"I am happy."

Lucca rubbed his bottom lip with a knuckle. "So I'm pretty certain the kyros's wife coming to call isn't normal behavior," he said, abruptly changing the subject.

"Since when has our life ever been filled with *normal behavior?*"

Maybe if Ona killed every Invader she could get her hands on, life would have the chance to become normal. Maybe she could even think about art again. Ona stared into the night, the comforting dark spreading like the hope inside her.

5

SEREN

"Geneal Adem did what?" Seren stared at Hossam, who stammered and ran a hand over his hair outside the main tent's door.

"He announced the invasion and held a meeting with the kaptans after you left the training field, Pearl of the Desert."

Adem had told the troops about the Invaders! He never would've done that to Meric. She didn't know whether to storm into his tent and demand an apology in Meric's name or pretend she was fine with it and had possibly even planned it herself.

"My lady," Cansu started, "didn't the kyros order the announcement and the meeting? I would've thought…"

So they really didn't know he was dead. She'd thought maybe they'd figured it out. She'd almost hoped they had. Almost. But it was best they didn't.

"Yes. Yes, of course the kyros ordered the meeting. I was…confused about the timing."

"Ah," Hossam said. Cansu and Erol nodded, looking relieved.

Seren breathed out in a rush. One problem down, another very terrible and very big one to go. "I need to see the mercenaries."

THATCHED mats crunched under Seren's slippered feet as she followed

Hossam, Cansu, and Erol toward a discreet, mostly unknown exit from the Kyros Walls. Her mind whirled around the day's events. She hated leaving Meric's body under the rotating guards' watch. Would they adhere to her instructions and stay out of the chamber? What if Adem came and ordered them away? She should've left one of her own men there.

A simple door was hidden by a false waterworker's station that passed through the stone barrier and posed as an outbuilding with all the usual calligraphy. *Danger. Waterworker managerial staff only.* Erol creaked the door open quickly, entered the dark, empty room inside the walls, and they all passed through, into the streets.

The city was quiet during the hour before sunset. Most were inside, preparing to eat with their families and talk about their days. Street sweepers made use of the empty pathways. They worked their wide, fan-like brooms, pushing waste into neat piles for proper distribution. Canal purifiers cleaned the water with sieves and powders that disappeared when diluted. Rock doves cooed from the few places on the tops of the stone walls that weren't spiked with iron.

But even in the quiet, the city wasn't peaceful. News of the approaching Invaders had spread. The voices past the walls were tense, snipping. A child was shushed harshly. Fear shook the air like the tremble of a bowstring before the arrow flies.

Seren gripped the piece of her old skirt and said a silent prayer for the family she still had—the people of Akhayma. Her hands shook, barely capable of tucking the green wool back into her sash let alone raising a bow or sword to defend her people. Her body longed to curl up on itself, to give in, but Seren forced her bones into a proud, confident posture. A lie she didn't think she could morph into truth.

A baby cried far off, near the outer walls. Water trickled and jumped down the canals, a splash cooling Seren's foot as she maneuvered around the tents, her guards around her like older brothers. A woman started down the street beside them, then entered a shop with a wooden sign showing a painted shoe. Seren's own slippers were green, white, and red, but not from any paints. Emeralds, pearls, and rare rosestones adorned her feet. Further blessed, her shoes had more heat protection in the sole than most in the Empire. Somehow, she had earned these luxuries simply by being the general's daughter. How could she ever be enough? Barir was wrong. She wasn't chosen or blessed any more than they were. If she was, she'd be confident, wouldn't she? She wouldn't feel like she didn't deserve any of this.

The guest tent, not too far off, where Lucca and Onaratta stayed, glowed amethyst in the twilight. Seren's stomach jumped.

Lucca's voice rumbled under Ona's beyond the woven fabric.

"Goat milk," he said to her in the trade tongue. "Remember, trade is a blend of Luk and the desert tongue."

"Since I know neither, that's completely helpful," Ona shot back, her words correct, but her inflection off. The sarcasm was very clear though.

Erol's face bunched in confusion as Ona mimicked Lucca's earlier words. "Goat milk."

A smile touched Seren's lips. "They're having a lesson." The simplicity of it, the humility and humor, gave her the push to go on inside.

Ona dropped a wooden bowl to the carpeted floor. She muttered something about goats, dancing, and death that was maybe an attempt at a curse.

Lucca bowed, then offered his low, pillowed stool.

Light flickered in the Holy Fire bowl near the door. Seren added three lahabshjara leaves from the bowl's supporting dish to boost the flame, passed hands over the heat, and whispered a prayer. Her muscles relaxed around her neck and shoulders. She was calm, but no visions shimmered into her mind.

Facing Lucca and Ona, she took a breath. "I need you to promise you won't tell anyone what I'm about to tell you. I'll give you another payment of silver equal to the amount given for the training."

Ona's eyes widened with greed, but there was a cinder of anger in them too. Now that she thought about it, that cinder had been there all the time.

"What's bothering you, Pearl of the Desert?" Lucca said in absolutely flawless trade tongue. "If I may ask? Please remember, we're yours to command."

Ona rolled her big eyes and tucked a lock of red hair back into one of the two knots of thick waves on her head. "Quit showing off, Lucca. If you'll forgive me for saying it, Seren, your language cuts the ear like a bad piercing."

Seren had to smile. "Many foreigners say so."

A large, metal oil lamp hanging from the highest point in the tent cast star patterns on the aubergine walls, red and blue carpets, and Ona's back as she bent to clean up her spilled food.

A spicy scent tweaked Seren's nose and her stomach growled. "That's Kurakian chicken."

Ona wiggled orange-stained fingers. "It is." She handed Seren a morsel.

The chicken's flavor roared across Seren's tongue, and before she could ask for another bite, Lucca handed her a bowl.

His hand nearly brushed hers. A pleasant rush sped up her arm. A slow smile spread over Lucca's mouth, but he looked down, not meeting her eyes.

Ona cleared her throat. "You do remember I'm sitting right here."

The room was suddenly far too small for all three of them.

Lucca's gaze snapped to his friend. "Ona."

Seren hadn't intended to flirt with the man. Her husband was dead and the enemy was coming and she...

Ona broke through her panic. "Do you like a lot of spicy foods?"

"I do," Seren said. "I request the hottest dishes from around the world. It drives our cooks mad, but the people love it when I offered samples at the seeding festival. But Meric never wants me to mingle with them and I wish he'd—"

Her stomach dropped. Just like that, she'd forgotten he was dead. She'd been annoyed by him again, frustrated again.

Lucca sat back against a metal-tooled trunk and looked up at her through his thick, black eyelashes. "Why are you really here?"

Veins and tendons stuck out over the back of his hand. He had a warrior's fingers, scarred and rough. His face showed none of the ever-brewing anger of his friend's. His eyes were soft. He'd removed the green-blue brigantine from earlier. An ivory shirt stretched across his broad chest and well-muscled arms. Fine leather pants covered his shapely legs and a sword rested beside his feet, where he sat cross-legged on the floor. He was so foreign, so strange. Unlike Meric or his brother Varol. They never would've sat on the floor or comforted anyone with the idea of simply listening.

"I need to know how deep your loyalty goes," she said.

"We signed our agreement," Ona said. "You were there. Plus, if you're offering more silver, that much more, you can bet we'll do pretty much whatever you want. Especially if it has to do with smashing Invader skulls into the earth."

Seren's heart raced like Fig on the track. "I have a problem. Something terrible. But I have an idea to fix it."

Ona's grin sharpened. "It was your idea to hire us, not Kyros Meric's, wasn't it?"

Seren nodded.

Lucca smiled wryly. "I would've said *thank you* before the Invaders were spotted heading this way."

A fist squeezed Seren's heart. "I'm sorry you'll be tangled up in another person's war."

"There's that phrase again!" Ona punched her thigh. "It's not *someone else's war*. It's our war. The Invaders are our enemies too. Believe me. Whatever it is you want us to help you with, know that we are yours to command."

She seemed passionate enough. There was truth in her voice. If Seren could convince her this plan was the best move in the situation, maybe she could be a strong ally. Well, there was only one way to know...

"Kyros Meric is dead." The words fell from Seren's mouth like a curse. "If I don't hide that fact, General Adem will send the city into mourning. Three days of fasting. Three days when no one, except the very young and very old, will be permitted to sleep."

Ona held up her hands. "Right when you have a bunch of bloodthirsty maniacs driving toward your door?"

"It won't matter to Adem. He's overconfident. And he strictly adheres to all traditions. It was torture getting him to agree to hire you two. That he accepts you and your training speaks highly of his fear."

"Then why wouldn't this same fear lead him to forgo the mourning?" Lucca asked.

"He won't. That's different. There's nothing in our books about not receiving foreign aid in military training. There is, however, plenty about proper mourning. Especially for those of the royal line. He'd say Meric's soul won't reach the Heavens without his people taking up the weight of his death. It's about balance. It's...difficult to explain to foreigners."

"You don't believe it?" Ona asked.

"Whether I do or don't, it doesn't matter. If we all starve and refuse the rest we need, we'll fall under the Invaders' steel. I won't allow my people to be taken as slaves or cut down. Somehow, after the battle, after we've survived, I'll tell Adem...I'll pretend Meric has just died."

Lucca pushed a curl of his black hair out of his eyes. "That sounds difficult. At best. What if the fighting takes longer than a day or two? Adem will be able to tell the kyros has been dead for a while."

"Not if I have Barir—he's a physician and father to my handmaiden— coat Meric's skin in ka'ud oil. The smell will overpower anything else. And it's colored. It should..." A shiver raked fingers down her back. "...mask the look of his flesh."

They all stared at the ground for a breath.

"Have you told your guards?" Lucca eyed the door.

"No."

"Why not?" Ona frowned.

"I don't want Meric's death to show on their faces." Such a frightening half-truth. "In front of Adem and the other fighters. They know them all too well. I don't think it would remain secret."

"Plus, it's dangerous for them to know. If the general finds out they helped you cover this up, they'll die, yes?" Lucca asked.

Seren had been stupid to think she'd keep the true nature of her choosing them over her guards. Lucca and Ona were anything but stupid. "Yes."

Ona stopped pacing and crossed her arms. "Oh. So the real reason you're asking us is because we're expendable."

Seren winced. "It's because you'll be able to hide the truth. No one knows you or your mannerisms. They won't spot your deceit." She was spinning around the truth, her words slicing and cutting like an Old Farm blade in the dagger dance. They *were* expendable. But there was no way she was going to say that aloud. Even if they already knew it.

Ona and Lucca traded a look, then both nodded as one.

"Fine," Lucca said. "We'll help you hide the body."

"Wait." Ona held up a hand. "Why don't you take control of the Empire since Meric is gone?"

Barir's very similar advice floated through Seren's mind. She rubbed her eyes and her fingers came away green and sparkling. "Because I'm not the royal heir. Meric's brother, Varol, is. Adem wouldn't support me. No one would."

"I doubt that," Lucca said. "I've seen how the fighters respect you. And your own guards, too. They said your father was a high ranking general before he retired?"

"Yes."

"Did he teach you?" Ona leaned closer, eyes bright.

"Yes, but—"

"Then what's the problem? You can become kyros," Ona said.

"No. That's not how it's done."

"This isn't a normal day in the Empire. The kyros is dead and you have a giant army headed right for you. Take the reins, Seren." Ona smiled.

Another shiver cut Seren through the middle. "General Adem would never allow it. He'd have me put to death as a traitor to the royal bloodline."

"What's so important about having royal blood?" Ona asked.

"Supposedly, the Fire only truly communicates wisdom to those with a lot of royal blood."

"Supposedly?" Lucca rubbed his lower lip.

Seren swallowed, both cold and hot spinning through her chest. Emotions, good and bad and in between, buzzed inside her head. She couldn't tell them about the vision. Then they'd keep on about her taking over. They didn't understand. Adem would never let it happen. And she was just...Seren. Not a kyros.

"If you are still willing to help me, we should go. Now."

Lucca stared for a minute longer like he could see inside her mind. Then he gathered up his weapons and he and Ona followed Seren to the door.

THE STREETS WERE STILL quiet when they all reached the secret door into the Kyros Walls. Inside the courtyard, it was a quick walk to the back entrance of the tent.

Meekra appeared at the door. "May I help you, Pearl of the Desert?"

"Can you keep a look out for General Adem or any others who may wish to...see the kyros?" Seren whispered, glancing at Cansu, who stood closest, then at the rotating guards who stared straight ahead. "He wants to have a private discussion with the mercenaries."

A knowing look crossed Meekra's face. "Whatever you need, my lady."

Cansu and Hossam took positions outside the back door. Erol went around the front to take a place beside the rotating guards there.

Seren led Lucca and Ona past the bed and lit the lantern. It flickered like it didn't truly want to give light to the blue-black weave of the tent's walls. The ka'ud wood smoked strongly, but as Seren said a prayer over the Holy Fire bowl, a hint of death greeted them, a quiet, sneaking sweetness.

Ona stood beside Meric's wrapped body on the bed. Her lips parted to speak, but Seren pressed a finger to her own lips and pointed toward the door.

Lucca's hand covered his mouth as he looked at the kyros's corpse. "Sun and stars," he whispered.

Folding her hands in front of her, Seren stared instead at the gold phoenixes on the carpet under her slippers, wishing none of this was happening.

Normally, Meekra and Seren would be writing a letter to Meekra's cousin who lived in Jakobden, near the eastern coast. Normally, they'd giggle over the drawings Seren added to the bottom, sadly untalented sketches of the city's tents and ridiculous recreations of Qadira's latest dramatic fit about her royal bloodline. Seren had thought marriage would end the youth that she should've had for at least three or more years, but Meekra had helped her retain some lighthearted bits of it.

Now, *now* her youth was truly finished. Gone.

As Ona and Lucca whispered about what to do, Seren fought a heaviness that wanted to press her into the ground. She and Ona looked about the same age. They should've been planning betrothals and learning trades or raising nieces and nephews, not orchestrating the hiding of a body. Not holding an entire empire's fate in their hands.

But then, Seren's little sisters were dead. They'd had no chance at anything. She had to make her life worth something.

She wound Meric's music box. Tinny minor notes crept from the ornate box delivered as a gift from the powerful Clan Azjorr their wedding day. Meric played the music when he couldn't sleep, so the guards wouldn't think anything of the sounds.

Seren coated Meric's cheeks, neck, and every other exposed area of skin with fragrant oil.

Lucca crossed his arms over his wide chest. He tapped a slow rhythm on his shoulder, thinking. "Please don't think I'm being disrespectful but…"

"Considering what we're about to do, I won't ever label you anything but most loyal associate. Or even dear friend."

"We need something for the digging."

"How about this?" Ona held up a water bowl and touched the black calligraphy along the lip. "Its edge is pretty sharp."

Seren grabbed her recently cleaned chamber pot that sat by the door to the smaller chamber. Her stomach turned and sweat rose along her back and forehead.

"This could work too. And let's use that yatagan to loosen the dirt," she said, pointing to one of Meric's many weapons. "Then we can dig out the soil with the two containers and hide the dirt under my bed."

Ona and Seren took turns listening for anyone approaching and helping Lucca dig a shallow grave. Sweat poured off Seren's chin and down her back as they finished. Ona artfully arranged a few pillow seats so nothing was obvious. For one so martially inclined, she had an eye for appearances.

"My kyros," Erol said through the door.

Seren's pulse drummed. "He is resting. He is unwell still." Earth and sand blackened her nails and she tried to dig it out, making her nail beds burn. "What is it?"

"General Adem wishes an audience," one of the other guards said.

Lucca's mouth opened and Seren's head went light.

"Is he here now?" she asked.

"I am," Adem said. That unmovable attitude of his painted his words. If she demanded he leave, it'd grow into an argument and only draw attention to her lies.

Seren closed her eyes and thought of the Holy Fire.

6

SEREN

The imagined Flame shook, then Seren saw an image of Ona on the bed, swathed in coverings with the oil lamps doused. Seren opened her eyes.

It might work.

"Good," she shot back through the thick weave of the door. She raised her voice so he could hear her clearly over the music box. "Your visit will surely help Kyros Meric. Give us ten minutes to ready ourselves, please, General Adem."

"Of course, Pearl of the Desert. I'll wait in the main room with my kaptans."

Ona came close. "We're his kaptans now too. Should we say we're meeting with the kyros? Maybe then he'd go away?"

"That won't make him leave. Those kaptans he favors, they're snakes slithering after power. Too smart, all of them." A thought hit Seren's head. "Surely they won't all demand entrance to my chambers?"

Lucca hefted Meric's body onto his shoulder, then maneuvered him into the hole. "What are we going to do?" he whispered, sweat glistening along his brow and sticking his hair to his forehead.

"Ona. I have an idea." Seren touched the wool at her sash, mind whirring.

Ona crossed her arms. "I don't like the sound of this."

"You don't even know what it is yet," Lucca said.

"Still don't like the sound of it."

"Let's finish this...then I'll explain."

They covered Meric with earth, leaving a good bit still under Seren's bed, before spreading both of the carpets out over the makeshift grave.

"I must insist," Adem said, startling them, "that I see you *now*, my kyros. I apologize for disturbing you, but I need to know if you approve of the plan Pearl of the Desert wishes to enact."

Lucca and Ona gathered around Seren. "Ona, you are going to pose as Meric," she said.

Ona tilted her head. "You aren't serious."

"I am. Trust me. Lie on the bed. We'll wrap you up so Adem can't see any of you. You're smaller than Meric, but I certainly can't play the role and Lucca is too big. Turn onto your side and let Adem speak to you. You don't need to answer."

"And if he finds her out?" Lucca's lips became a tight line.

Seren clasped her shaking hands. "She dies. I die. You die."

"An average evening," Lucca said, his tone cutting.

Ona chewed her lip and put a hand on the hilt of her sword. "I really don't like it."

Lucca's eyebrow lifted. "If it doesn't involve her sword, she doesn't like it."

"I don't either, but there is no other way. He," Seren jabbed a finger toward the door where Adem waited, "won't leave. That's why I didn't argue with him. Believe me. When he has that tightness to his voice, he'll dig his heels in. There will be no moving him on the issue."

Seren locked eyes with Ona. "I will destroy the Invaders. I will help you gain the revenge I see in your eyes. I will even take their king if I can, and spill his blood and end the suffering he causes with every new attack. Are you with me?"

Ona's shoulders moved with a deep breath. She nodded.

ON THE BED, Ona looked like a cocooned moth. Nothing of her showed.

With Lucca at Seren's back, Seren leaned close to Ona. "Remember my promise. You will have your revenge. And I will have mine."

Seren turned to Lucca. "You should go. If you're found here, Adem will wonder why Meric would be trying to hide a meeting with you."

"Agreed," he said in his oddly beautiful accent. "I'll stay nearby."

If she wasn't so shaken up, his words would've been comforting. He seemed so sincere. *Fire, please let him be. And Ona too.* She sent him out the back where Meekra stood talking quietly with Hossam and Cansu.

The wooden door opened and General Adem's hand appeared at the woven flap, the second part of the entrance. "Pearl of the Desert, may I enter?"

"Yes, but I'll go to my small chamber and give you both a moment. Know that the kyros is not awake and seems unwilling to talk."

Through a crack in the door between Seren's room and the small chamber she now shared with Meekra, she watched Adem walk slowly to where Ona lay. As she picked dirt from her nails nervously, Ona shifted in the bed.

Adem stopped. "My kyros. My deepest apologies for disturbing you, but we launch what I can only assume is *your* plan at Kenar tomorrow night. I wondered if you had any last minute tweaks for our strategy."

Ona made a small noise and rolled over.

Seren stepped closer but didn't show herself. "General Adem," she said, "I'll notify you if the kyros makes any changes to the plan."

He scratched his beard and kept looking at Ona's wrapped form. "How long has he been like this, Pearl of the Desert? How long has he been...unresponsive?"

She swallowed. "I told you he was very sick."

"If he is not alert to give the order to move at sunset—"

"We'll move anyway." She tried to sound confident. She definitely didn't feel that way. "He ordered it when he was alert. With me."

Adem breathed in through his nose and ran a hand over his beard. "With you alone."

"Yes."

His gaze slid under her skin like a newly sharpened yatagan. She waited for the pain, her mouth working. She needed to say something to get him out of here.

"This isn't going to work," he said quietly.

Did he mean he knew what was really happening here? Or something else?

"I..." Sweat rolled down her back.

"You cannot simply pass orders on to me, Pearl of the Desert. You have no experience. If you were older, wiser...if you had royal blood perhaps, but..." He tugged at his short beard. "I will send two more physicians to see to our kyros in an hour, after he's had some rest. If they deem him unfit to rule, if his body is determined too weak to carry out his duties, we will proceed from there."

"What does that mean?" Seren whispered.

"We will see." He wasn't even really talking to her. Deep in thought, he stared at the kyros—at Ona.

"Barir is his physician," she said. "I'll call for him. Meekra!"

Meekra slipped inside, her gaze going immediately to Ona.

"Get your father," Seren said. "The general wants another examination."

Adem shook his head. "No. I will send the two that help me and my kaptans. It's wise to get more than one opinion on something so important. No offense to your father, Meekra, or to you, Pearl of the Desert."

Meekra paled and bowed under Adem's heavy gaze.

Seren forced her eyes to stay fixed on Adem. She demanded that her body stop shaking.

Adem turned to Seren. She didn't even want to blink, to give him any indication that she was at all nervous or that anything was wrong. Her eyes dried and burned. Adem stared, distrust coating every feature, every movement.

"Any-anything else?" Seren asked, willing her voice not to shake.

The general tapped his yatagan's hilt. Once, twice, very slowly. "I think we are finished here, Pearl of the Desert."

He swept out of the room.

Seren could barely hear over her own heartbeat. "I need the Fire," she whispered to Meekra.

Seren held her hands over the flickering Light as Lucca's low voice mixed with Ona and Meekra's whispering. They were telling him what had happened. She'd made such a mess of everything. Adem's physicians would of course realize Meric was dead. Adem would know she lied. The best case scenario was that Ona, Lucca, Meekra, and Seren's guards would escape punishment and only Seren would die a brutal death for the deceit. Her stomach rolled.

The Fire touched her palms lightly as she whispered her fears. The others came closer, watching a glow blossom inside her flesh, between her fingers, turning her skin the color of the dying sun.

Ona swore and Meekra sucked a breath.

The Hovering Flame appeared in front of Seren's face, blocking everything else from view. The striped weave of the tent walls faded away. The ka'ud smoke dissolved. She closed her eyes and let a vision take her.

Akhayma's outer walls stretched toward the afternoon sun where it held court in its blue empire. But a dark substance stuck to the tops of the walls, to the parapet. The substance moved like shadows. Her heart shuddered.

Invaders.

There was no dark substance. They were men.

They crawled over the walls with ropes and slid into the city, steel drawn. The people screamed and fled. Blood ran over the jeweled tips of Seren's shoes.

The vision dissipated and Seren's eyes flew open.

She faced Ona, Lucca, and Meekra, who was on her knees.

"They're already here. The Invaders."

Ona unsheathed her sword.

"You're blessed, my lady," Meekra whispered. "Chosen. Father was right."

"What?" Lucca looked from Meekra to Seren.

Seren flew out the back. "Hossam. Cansu. Come with me. We're going to gather the army. We are being attacked."

"We are?" Hossam's eyes were big as moons.

The vision flashed through Seren's head. "They're climbing the walls. You and you," she said to the rotating guards, "stay here and do not, for any reason, leave this spot. You are not to enter my chamber. You are not to allow any others—besides myself, Meekra, Barir, or my personal guards— into the room. Do you understand? This is a matter of life and death."

The tallest man of the two swallowed loudly. "Of course, Pearl of the Desert."

She turned to Cansu. "Tell Erol to keep a watch on that front entrance. To stay there with the other guards. They must keep order here and protect the kyros and keep everyone out of my chamber."

Cansu ran into the night.

Seren twisted the wool at her sash. Just sending the army into that space wouldn't be enough. The people wouldn't have time to flee. They needed a way to defend themselves. This was all going to happen too quickly. She remembered a military scroll her father had shown her. Of a war against a larger force. The queen of this foreign country had armed the people.

"Let's go to the training field. Gather a force to meet them."

The others nodded and they took off. Not caring even a little how non-high-caste she looked, Seren ran with Hossam, Meekra, Ona, and Lucca through the streets until the back gates gave way to the torch-lit training field.

At the faintly lit training field, Hossam waved to a boy with a trumpeting horn. At the boy's expert blare, all eyes were on Seren, who stood beside him on the hill.

"Assemble. Now!" Hossam bellowed.

Lucca and Ona rounded up a few more fighters from the stables, then ran back up to join Seren on the hill.

Would the warriors listen? Akhayma had no time to waste.

As Cansu joined Seren, the fighters traded glances, but then the men and women, some armed, some coming from their rest time, lined up.

Seren didn't know where Adem was. She was just glad he didn't seem to be around here.

The units assembled in the near dark. Light blinked off armor and yatagans. Mouths whispered and eyes widened at the unusual command. These fighters needed Seren to be strong and confident.

She swallowed, then raised her voice, hoping with everything that she hadn't misunderstood the Fire's information. "The Invaders are attacking now. Arm yourselves. Take an extra weapon or two. Head to the front gates. Hand out the extra weapons to anyone who will take them. We will need all the hands we can get."

The lines of fighters shifted their weight, their faces puzzled. Two actually laughed and elbowed one another. A nearby unit hissed insults at the ones laughing.

Meekra stepped forward, gaze on Seren, asking for permission. Seren nodded. If Meekra had an idea what to say, Seren would take it.

"Our Seren, Pearl of the Desert," Meekra said, "saw a vision. I witnessed the Hovering Flame myself."

The fighters began murmuring excitedly. No one was laughing now.

Lucca shouted, "I too saw the Flame!"

"And I!" Ona said as she ran toward the stables. "Now get your tails on it, warriors!"

The two men that had fought Ona during her demonstration held up their hands. The rounder one pounded his shield with his yatagan's hilt.

"She is chosen! Blessed!"

Seren didn't know what to feel. There was no time to feel. So she just gave her people what they probably needed. An inspiring leader.

Cansu had Fig and was handing Seren a bow and quiver. Slinging her quiver over her shoulder, she pressed a hand against Fig's warm body, then let the horse nuzzle her hand with a petal-soft nose. Seren mounted and raised her bow over her head.

"We won't let them take our home. We will never stop fighting."

Both foot soldiers gathered around Fig's stomping hooves. Mounted fighters rallied, faces turned to Seren. Her warriors were a river of metal and leather, gaining momentum, and she longed to unleash their power on the enemy.

Gripping her bow, feeling familiar carvings against her skin, she raised her voice and tried so, so hard to sound confident, to feel the Fire's faith inside her. "They will regret this day until their last breath!"

With a great shout, the troops rode with her, galloping into the city, their voices giving the command to all: Fight.

7

ONA

T he world was a blur of movement.

Ona's horse snorted as they dodged tables of spices and fruit in the market, women and men with scrolls tucked under their arms or children on their hips. The people stopped to stare as the Empire's army flooded the streets and raged toward the front gates. Dust coated Ona's tongue, sweat poured down her face, but she smiled. This was the day. She'd waited years for this day.

Her mount's hoof slid on the dirt and cut into a canal, jarring her. Muscles clenching, she adjusted her weight and kept her seat. Lucca looked over his shoulder to see if she was keeping up. She was.

At the tall, bronze gates, the crowd was quiet.

A chill rippled Ona's flesh.

Haris handed a blade and a shield to a man in a ragged kaftan and a sash weighed down with loads of shoddy, little bells. The man nodded, then turned to what Ona assumed was his eight or nine-year-old son.

"Hide in the agriculture district. Stay until all is quiet."

"All is quiet now." Tears pooled under his big eyes and anger like a coal burned in Ona's chest. The little fellow didn't deserve this. She hadn't either.

Lucca was talking to the barrel-chested Nuh. "Anyone up top spot anything yet?" He jerked his chin toward the archers on the parapet.

The fighters and the people who probably never thought they'd need to fight lined up to form a wall of shields, steel, and nocked arrows.

Nuh nodded. "The earth has been moved around the base of the walls but I haven't heard why they think—"

A howl tore the quiet. Ona shuddered, nearly losing her sword. Ropes soared over the walls. A flash of metal. The five, blood-red lines down the surcoats.

Invaders.

She knew them well. After all, they'd been in every nightmare since the day they killed her aunt.

They oozed over the walls, jumping from the ropes amid Empire arrows.

"Stay by me, please, Ona!" Lucca loosed three arrows of his own.

Ona fumbled for her flint and struck it across her sword. *"Wake iron!"*

Lucca threw a spark from an arrow's head with his own flint, chanting at the top of his lungs as they split the crowd of unhorsed people and came up side-by-side with mounted Empire fighters.

"Wake, iron! Wake!
Rise for me in battle!
Let your unshakable strength
Bleed power into my limbs!"

Little spears of orange and red shot from Ona's blade as she chanted too.

"Wake, iron! Wake!
Rise for me in battle!
It is the dawn of their destruction,
And the first fruits of our day!"

Ona's blood was filled with horses chomping at the bit and ready to charge. She felt her lip curling. She was ready to rip sword, tooth, and shield into the enemy. Ona could smell her own fear and rage like vinegar and blood. Her hands had never vibrated with this kind of power.

She was going to kill so many people today.

As Invaders flowed around Ona and Lucca, clashing with other warriors' yatagans, Ona blocked a downward strike with her shield, her movements foggy to even her own eyes, her body rushing like a storm-tortured river. She pushed the attacker's sword-hand back, and sliced low, taking out his leg before he could even think about defending himself.

"My iron is the end of my enemy
The beginning of his next life," she chanted.
"A last cold kiss before the soul break
His sword is a branch against my blade
A weak will and his blood is mine

I am the power he cannot fight,
The force he cannot halt,
The strike they do not see."

Out of the corner of her eye, she saw Lucca raise his sword, circling his left shoulder at a dizzying speed. His blade opened the Invader where neck met body. A spray of blood marked Lucca's brigandine, a visible shout. The scent of war swirled through the air: iron, blood, sweat, spark, and foreign oils.

The Invaders' skin smelled like disaster. Ona pushed and fought a memory of men in the doorway of her aunt's villa. *Not now.* They wore the same five slashed sigil on their surcoats, the identical faces of want and desperation and that sick mixture of loving and hating the horrors they committed. She couldn't weaken now.

Use it, she told herself. *Use the fear, the anger, the need.*

Two hulking men bore down on her. Her horse was actually slowing her, trapping her in the thick of things. Slipping off, the men blinked at her speed. The chants were working. She scooted left and right, stacking the Invaders, so only one could come at her in turns. The first hesitated, shieldless, but with sword ready. She raised her shield to distract him, lifted her knee, jumped, then kicked him in the chest with her other foot, knocking him into the next man. She soared high and drove her steel into the man's throat. Pulling her weapon free before the other man realized what was happening, she drew the blade across his cheeks.

A foul way to die for a foul way to live. The blood was black and beautiful in this light, and if there hadn't been a crowd of Invaders fighting four paces away, she'd have been tempted to use it to paint the walls.

Laughing like a demon, she hurdled the bodies, pushing back into the fray. Five men surrounded Lucca, who'd jumped onto an overturned ox cart.

She began shouting.

"My body spins with the swiftness of the falcon,
I dive and my enemy sees my talon, my sword, flashing
My iron consumes his soul."

Lucca echoed the chant and leaped into the air like a stag, making soldiers stop and gawk. He flashed down in a quick twist and drove an Invader's sword to the army's feet. Then Ona had no more time to watch her friend spread ruination, because a woman like a tower swung a sword at her face.

"Wake iron!" she spat.

Her sword sparked, raining orange and white and green, and began moving with her thoughts, asking only for a fraction of the power of Ona's muscles. Ona had the woman at her feet, bleeding from three wounds before she could squeal like the Invader pig she was.

A sun-colored head appeared beyond a knot of Invaders. Though he didn't have a crown or even a fine helmet, Ona knew who he was. Her heart knew who he was. Its shivering rage told her.

The king.

Sweat ran down his bearded cheeks. The moisture darkened his ugly surcoat as he lifted a large sword with both hands. It banged onto an Empire fighter's shield.

Ona turned to find Seren in the chaos.

She rode into the fight, firing arrow after arrow and taking Invaders' lives like she was Death itself—relentless, shocking, and cold.

"For our city!" Seren shouted, her earlier fear washed away.

The people echoed her and surged toward the gates.

Seren could certainly keep that title of hers if she wanted to. This was proof enough.

Ona struck another man at the neck, two more at the thigh, crushed one's nose with the edge of her shield, and spun to find Adem.

Blood covered half his face and dripped from his beard. He fought well, no wasted flourishes, no fancy moves. Just clean cuts and practiced precision. No surprise there.

She and Lucca cut through the enemies until Ona dropped her shield, reached out a hand, and grabbed the king by the hair. The strands of his sunny mane cut off the circulation in her fingers as she put her sword to his throat. Victory surged through her heart, beating like drums in her chest. This was the best day of her life.

"Back off!" she shouted to the other Invaders, knowing the steel at the king's neck would make her meaning plenty clear.

"Ona!" Lucca's face was pale. His lips made a line and he gave her a nod.

The rest of the Invaders did indeed back away, fear glazing their eyes. Those strong enough retreated to their ropes, climbing away. The injured leaned against the walls, sadness making their eyes large and hatred twisting their mouths. They were so much larger than any Empire fighter or Silvanian. But their cheeks were hollow and their skin parched as they watched her drag their king to his knees.

She held the ruler tight. He laughed under his breath and she let the sword nip him, loving the red trickling from his neck. This man was like the sun to them. She wanted to end him. Now. Now. Now. She could taste his death on her tongue like wine.

Adem found Ona's side. "Congratulations, Onaratta Paints with Blood." Though his words were pretty, he didn't seem so pleased in saying them. He had to be jealous.

Adem addressed the retreating Invaders in their own tongue. "We will send word for a ransom and terms."

Ona looked to Lucca, who seemed as surprised as her that Adem knew the language.

"Ransom, hm?" the king said in perfect trade tongue.

She nearly dropped her hold on him. "Shut it." She leaned her sword into his neck again.

Surely Adem was only talking ransom to ward them off. Ona met Seren's gaze. Seren's eyes were on fire. They shared a vicious smile and Ona knew they were of the same mind.

This king was going to die, hopefully by Seren's own blessed hands.

SEREN

Barir and the other physicians had settled the injured on cots near the back gates, to the Northeast, and as the sun rose over the day Seren had feared would never come, she walked among them. Even beside her loyal Meekra, the steadfast Cansu and Hossam, her insides felt cold, so cold. A part of her had truly believed Akhayma would fall under Invader swords last night. Thankfully, her body had been so tired that despite the nightmares clawing at her on the bed in Meekra's chamber, she'd slept a good handful of hours.

A fighter on a cot near a table covered in clean cloth and shining surgery instruments bit a strip of leather to keep from crying out. A physician with small, steady hands tugged a thread and needle through his wound. Seren set a hand on the man's forehead. Sand and sweat lay on his skin. She dipped a cloth in the clean water, drops falling quietly into the bowl amidst the fighter's muffled grunts of pain. He squeezed his eyes shut. Singing a mountain song, Seren wiped his brow and cheeks like her mother had when she was little and sick.

As the physician tied up the stitches with precise movement, the warrior's eyes flicked open. Seren took the leather from between his teeth.

"Our Blessed Pearl." His thick fingers curled around her hand gently. "Thank you for warning us."

The physician glanced up, gaze watchful, careful. Unlike the warrior, this physician wasn't in a haze of pain. He could see the danger in the situation. If Adem spoke out against Seren, all who supported her would be imprisoned. And that was a best case scenario. She hadn't seen the general since the battle.

"Shh. Rest now, warrior. Thank you for your courage." She offered a smile that wasn't easy to give and walked on.

Fighters lifted their palms when they could. They called out thanks and blessings, telling her she'd saved them all with her vision, that she was their leader now, deserving and righteous. The formality of chewing mint and bowing was absent and Seren wished it could always be like that. Battle stripped life to what was truly important.

But she didn't like them calling her righteous. She had a body buried under her bed. The body of their kyros, the body of her husband. She was far, far from righteous. Meric had to be properly cared for. Today. She put aside her planning to pay attention to another fighter.

An angry gash marred the woman's muscular throat and the blood flow had slowed to a trickle. Her eyes stilled. Seren's chest ached. The familiar feeling was a lot like hunger, a gnawing want, but one that would never be satisfied. She closed the fighter's lids with her fingertips and whispered a prayer. Feeling the dead woman's sweat on her own skin helped her take some of the weight of the warrior's death.

"Thank you. You've done what I haven't yet been able to. You gave *all* for those you love. Drift to that next place, fighter, and know you died with the ultimate honor."

Meekra appeared with a bowl of water and Seren washed her face and hands.

With one last prayer said above the wounded, she and her retinue walked along the smooth city walls, toward the back gates and the training area.

On the hill above the archery range, slaves—hoping to earn their way into the caste system—rubbed yatagans with cloths, scrubbed bloodied shields, and sewed new fletching onto new arrows, ignoring purpling bruises and blood-soaked wraps on their arms and legs. The large bells over their heads rang lightly.

A group of warriors brought another load of arrowheads. The differences between the men and women were suddenly shocking. Seren had never really noticed the lack of muscle in the slaves and their hollowed cheeks. The thin hair and downcast eyes. She hated herself.

Her own ancestors had been slaves. Being partially mountain blood, they'd had to serve until someone apprenticed them. Then, the next generation had worked their short, rough lives trying to earn enough silver to remove caste bells and move up to middle. They'd failed. She remembered what Father had told her long, long ago. It'd taken her family four generations to become high caste and that was partially luck. Father had impressed the kyros during a feigned training battle during his time as a base-level fighter and he'd been moved up quickly. Father had always claimed it had less to do with himself than the fact that the kyros had been in a good mood that day because he had just learned his wife was pregnant with Meric's younger brother, Varol.

Some of these slaves and low-castes had fought for Akhayma when she'd ordered the warriors to give out weapons to anyone who would fight. And now, here they were, in the same poor position as before. Given little to no respect. The cost to remove a bell didn't seem high to her, but she'd always been high-caste, through her father's work as a high ranking general. Maybe the cost was more significant than she'd thought. And if it was, that wasn't right. If a person was willing to fight, willing to work, they should be treated the same as anyone else.

Anger surged through Seren, hot and unforgiving. Anger at herself and everyone else who'd participated in this for so long. She knew the Empire treated people better than the Northern Isle folk, but it still wasn't right.

Tonight, she'd demand the removal of every slave's metal belt-and-bell contraption.

She'd heard that Jakobden's new amir had done the same, with Meric's reluctant permission, made only because Jakobden was an odd, but highly profitable little corner of the Empire.

And war or no war, Adem or no Adem, she couldn't stomach that part of the Empire's traditions any longer. The metal bell belts were leaving. Tonight. And the cost of removing a caste bell, the price of moving up in the Empire would be lowered. She could call up the scribe. Have it announced at the feast. Maybe it would go over since everyone was simply relieved at having lived through the attack.

9

ONA

"Not so kingly now, are you?"

Ona sneered through the bars at the Invaders' king as Lucca walked down the slope separating the training field from the line of cells to join them. Mud caked the king's once shining hair and the new day's heat pulled his stink into the air.

"Muddy as the pig you are." Maybe he wouldn't understand what with her Silvanian accent and all. She gave him a very specific gesture to ensure he picked up her meaning.

Lucca knocked a knuckle against the king's bars. "Ona. That isn't polite."

"I didn't intend politeness," she said, switching to their own language.

"I suppose as long as you don't run him through before Seren and Adem do what they want, you can have your fun." He looked at Ona. "He'll probably need to keep most of his limbs for now."

She plucked her knife from her sash and reached an arm through the bars. The king's dark eyes moved, but aside from that he remained utterly still, sitting in the mud with his hands and feet bound like a Silvanian slave. She'd done the binding herself after the battle late last night. She ran the tip of the blade up his cheek and pressed lightly into the soft flesh beneath his eye.

"Eyes aren't limbs. He doesn't really need two of these, does he, Lucca?"

"I'd say one works well enough for the dirty work his kind do. But Seren might not like you damaging the hard-earned loot."

Ona's knife bit into him and a speck of blood appeared. He didn't flinch. She pressed a little harder. "They're ugly eyes anyway."

"You think so?" Lucca crossed his arms. "I think he's rather good looking. Different from us. Different from the many kinds of people here. But yes. Definitely a fine looking man."

"Are you going to fall for every foreigner you meet now?"

Lucca's eyes widened and his nostrils flared.

Ona shrugged. "He doesn't know what we're saying."

Lucca's jaw tensed. He spun and walked away. Ona sighed and returned her dagger to her belt.

"A Silvanian, hm?" The king said perfectly. In Silvanian.

Her heart tripled its pace. Maybe he hadn't fully understood her comment about Lucca and loving foreigners. And even if he did, he could never guess it was Seren Lucca seemed to be interested in.

The king closed his eyes. "I appreciate your people's talent with paint."

Everything in Ona's view, except the man's face, went white.

"I saw a young man who could craft a fresco so true to life that I would've sworn the birds he made could take flight right off the wall," he said.

Ona threw herself against the bars, sword out. Hands pulled her back. Shaking, she turned to see two of Seren's guards—Erol and his never-ending scowl and Hossam with that mop of hair. Cansu must've been injured or somewhere resting.

Seren adjusted the tie at her forehead and the bell there shot the sun back at Ona.

"Come, friend," Seren said quietly, gaze flashing to the king and back. "We should celebrate our success."

"But he—"

She looked directly into Ona's eyes. "I know. Believe me. I know. But we can't do anything about it yet. We have to be wise." One of her hands went to the wool on her sash. "Let's go to the feast."

The king laughed and they both turned.

Seren frowned. "What is so amusing? I don't think, in your position, you'd have much to laugh about."

He shook his head, looking down at his bound feet, and said something in his own language.

Seren stiffened. She turned and started off, her feet moving fast. Erol and Hossam trailed her.

"What did he say?" Ona said as she caught up.

"Merely a slur. I won't repeat it. It's some sort of cultural insult."

Ona gave her a look.

"Fine. He spoke metaphorically, but I think the intent had to do with a squirrel instigating the act of love with a lion," she whispered, making sure the guards couldn't hear.

Ona snorted. "That sounds difficult."

The wrinkles between Seren's eyes smoothed. "It would have to be. At least for the squirrel."

"She'd end up as dinner rather than lover."

"But now that I think on it, he used the female term for lion. He said *lioness*."

"She won't be bothered much then. Doubt she'd even notice his tiny intentions."

Seren pressed a hand over her eyes.

"Are you really going to ask for a ransom? Or was that only a ploy to get his men to back down? Or was that just Sweet Bean having some fun with the pigs?"

"Sweet Bean?"

"That's what I call General Adem."

Seren's face was priceless. "No, you don't."

"I do. Just in private."

Behind us, Erol and Hossam laughed quietly.

Seren cleared her throat. "General Adem already sent a message concerning the ransom. It includes a demand for silver and that all Invaders return to their own borders."

"I suppose it makes sense. Might as well get the silver coin to go with all the trouble." The Empire wouldn't have to actually release him. They could just get the silver and then kill everyone in sight, including the king. It was a smart plan.

"These raiders have sent us so many refugees," Seren said. "We need to build onto the city."

"You shouldn't have to. The bastards should leave people to their homes."

Ona's jaw pinched as she ground her teeth together. Her bones pressed against the leather and metal of her sword as she gripped it tight, wishing that foul king's warm blood covered her hand. Like a Northern witch's healing symbol, it'd dull the pain in her body and heart, she was sure of it.

"But they haven't," Seren said. "So we have to move forward."

"I'll move forward when every last one of them is bleeding at our feet."

"Even their children?" Seren's pretty, green-dusted eyes grew sad.

"They didn't spare me any horror and I was still hanging on to childhood when they came."

"And they didn't spare my two sisters."

"Is that why you keep that piece of wool? To remember them?"

Seren's eyes filled, but she fought off the tears. "This is from the skirt I wore when the...attack happened. It's the last thing my little sisters touched."

Ona let her feet lead her toward the guest tent. She felt detached. "I'm sorry for what you lost, Seren." But she wasn't sorry about young Invaders. They'd only grow up to be the same kind who'd killed Ona's aunt.

Maybe Seren needed to hear another story about the Invaders. Taking a breath, she began.

"My parents died when I was a baby. I lived with my aunt. She was a fresco artist." Ona's gaze softened. "Her fingers were always so cold...but her heart... Her villa was filled with the goats no one wanted. And the runts from every dog's litter in town. The place reeked of piss, but it was home."

Seren grew very quiet. Ona's cheeks burned and her words came fast and quiet.

"I was working with her when they came," Ona said, almost whispering. "The warning—the town bell—it wasn't nearly early enough to do anything. I still had my palette knife in my hand when they burst through the door. They bashed the animals' heads. They cut my aunt down like a beast at market."

Seren glanced at her, face quiet. Ona searched for pity. There was only a shared sadness and anger. Ona swallowed and continued.

"My cousin had taught me about knife-fighting. The back streets of our town were not as nice as yours here. Without a thought, without even knowing what I was doing, I rammed my painting knife up and under one of the Invader's ribs when his back was turned."

Her weapon hand coiled up, ready to strike.

"Before the other man could kill me, their leader called them back. I watched the man I'd stabbed bleed to death from his mouth. His foul blood mixed with my aunt's on the stone floor. I swore that day I'd see them all dead. All of them."

Seren stopped. She touched Ona's elbow. "We will end this. Together."

"You have to tell everyone about the Fire. About how you saw them coming. Adem needs to do what you say." It was amazing what she could do. She needed to be in charge here. Not Sweet Bean and his moods and dangerous traditions.

Hossam and Erol didn't say a word, but they had to have heard Ona. If

Seren wouldn't accept her role, her very obvious calling to rise up and use the special talents she had to fight the Invaders, maybe their gossip could force her into it. It couldn't hurt. It could only help. If she was considered blessed or whatever, Adem wouldn't be able to get mad at her for hiding Meric's death either, would he? Ona doubted it.

They walked in silence, the city's colors blending into the blue and red of early evening. Men in blue-striped kaftans led a line of camels. Three boys pulled a cartload of newly forged swords, their iron black and silver and promising. This city controlled the best iron ore in the world. Under the sands and arid plains, the makings of so many weapons waited to be molded. Ona took a deep, cleansing breath. It was good to stand atop such a place of power with the woman who would soon be in control of it all.

Seren wasn't really going to give the king back. She wouldn't. Not after the talk they'd just had. That was key. She was only faking to get the silver to build up the city for all the refugees. That was fine. It was smart.

The main tent, where every noble and their brother seemed to be laughing away, rose up in front of Ona and Seren, blacking most of the sunset sky.

Ona smiled as Seren took a breath.

It was time for her to claim her place. *Only hope Sweet Bean won't get in the way,* Ona thought as they pushed into the tent to join the celebration.

SEREN

Seren's breath stuck in her throat. A double line of nobles, ore masters, advisors, and fighters created a corridor inside the main tent, under the flickering oil lamps and moonlit star shapes fitted into the ceiling. Seeing her, they stomped their feet on the thick rugs and shouted for her.

Her heart stood still.

"Blessed!"

"Pearl of the Desert has saved us!"

"Chosen! The Fire has chosen you!"

"Kyros Seren!"

The tent glowed all the more. The woven walls Seren knew so well were both brighter and darker—the black, white, red, and blue contrasting brilliantly. The patchouli and ginger Meekra had added to Seren's hair wash rose into the air. She smelled like a kyros. Her kaftan was the darkest black and embroidered with silver phoenixes, a kyros's kaftan. But though the cheers and beauty of it all warmed Seren, she still didn't feel like a kyros. She was an imposter, like a girl wearing her mother's shoes and trying not to trip.

"I'm not k—" she started, but Ona grabbed her arm gently.

"Take the title, my lady." Ona's grin sharpened. "You can do so much more with it and Sweet Bean won't be able to touch you. No matter what he finds out."

Seren's face grew too hot then. "He could still do much," she whispered before raising her hands to the gathering. Barir was there, next to Meekra. His face was bright as a star as he nodded.

"Thank you," Seren said, trying to sound calm and sure.

She did want to be who she was supposed to be. But this wasn't going to be simple. It was dangerous. She was breaking all sorts of traditions. According to her sources, Adem was finishing up injured warrior counts with the kaptan charged with overseeing the medical procedures. He would be here soon if he wasn't already. She craned her neck, trying to see further into the crowd.

"Thank you all," she said, pushing her worry away for the moment. At the Holy Fire bowl, she said a quick, but fervent prayer, then turned to face her people. "You saved us. All of Akhayma joined together to save ourselves. I'm just blessed to be a part of it."

Like her thoughts had called him up, Adem stepped out of gathering, face grim. Seren swallowed.

"So. You saw a vision in the Fire."

It didn't sound like a question. It was an accusation. He thought she was lying. No surprise there.

"I-I did."

"Even though you have no royal blood. You are the first to see a vision in centuries."

Seren swallowed.

"And you believe you should hold the title of *kyros* in Kyros Meric's absence?"

"I think I have to." She clasped her shaking hands. "The Fire showed me taking up his royal kaftan."

Qadira and a few other nobles murmured things like "See?" and "It's a miracle."

Adem's left eyebrow twitched. His lips parted, but he didn't say a word. With a bow, he disappeared into the crowd.

Seren stared at the spot where he'd been as the tent filled with conversation.

Lucca appeared, smiling at Ona and Seren. His face still glowed from battle. He seemed more alive. "May I escort you to your table, Kyros Seren?"

"I will never get used to that title."

She looked into Lucca's face, glad that the person who had her arm was someone who knew all her secrets and still respected her. His hair was wild and his eyes, too. It was like she was really seeing him for the first time. He was different from other men. Rough-edged but lovely. Strong, patient, humble—thrown together in a wonderful mix. All his movements spoke of strength and grace and a restrained wildness. There was a flutter in her stomach and it was a wonderful departure from what she'd been feeling lately.

"Thank you for everything you've done for me so far and I truly hope this horrible set of events have ended and we will be at peace and you and Ona can finish training with our fighters because the way you moved today in battle was breath-taking and you practically glowed. Did you know you lit up like that? Can you feel that?" She sucked a breath, face flaming. She was a babbling idiot.

But Lucca simply smiled. A dimple appeared in his cheek. "You impressed me today too, Kyros Seren. Congratulations on the triumph." He kissed her hand and his hair brushed her wrist.

Her skin tingled. Heat spread down her arm and into her body.

Adem walked up to the high table and took his seat like he hadn't challenged her in front of everyone.

Seren gave him a tight smile as the musicians took up their instruments.

Lucca gave Seren a look that said *Do you want me to stay?* and Seren shook her head.

"Go enjoy some time with Ona and the other kaptans," she said.

With a low bow, Lucca walked away. At the other table, he said something to Ona and she threw her head back to laugh, the oil lamps lighting her cheeks.

They'd made this horror less of one. Seren didn't know what she would've done without Meekra, her guards, and them. She was grateful for their courage, loyalty, their ability to shift and move with what had to be done. She could never be Chosen without them, she thought, smiling sadly to herself.

Barir waved to Meekra and slipped away, probably going back to his patients. He was a good, good man.

Seren relaxed into her chair, determined to ignore Adem—Sweet Bean, she thought, grinning—and his scowling. This was where she belonged, in the middle of her friends and those she considered family. At last, Seren felt...complete.

The white-haired *riqq* player stood and held the goat-skin drum with both hands, his fingers starting a rolling rhythm like a fast heartbeat. The metal discs along the riqq's sides clinked together like dropped coins. A man with a large nose lifted a polished oud to his chest and plucked the strings as only an expert could. All around, feet tapped under kaftans and tunics.

Soon as the music lessened, Seren would thank everyone for their courage today, and she'd make the announcement about the slaves and the caste bells.

A raucous group of warriors beside Lucca burst into a traditional song, drumming their fists against the wood in a double and triple sort of beat.

"The water rose and called them,
To the plains they came,
For yellow fruits and sun-warmed skin
Days without war and wanting."

Their voices, male and female, twisted together in a clashing set of notes that painted the scene inside Seren's mind. A mountain accent and several Akhayma natives' lilts blended beautifully.

"So spin your wife and daughter,
Twirl your husband and your son,
Bring your spark and feel your heart
Beat and sing for the promise of the plains!"

Loving the chaos of the instruments and the professional musicians mixed with the impromptu singing, Seren closed her eyes. The happy sounds spilled over her and cleaned out the thoughts of battle, of blood, and the horrible things she'd done, at least for a moment.

A soft voice startled her. "Sorry," Lucca said. "If you want me to leave you alone, I will." She opened her eyes to see him bent at the waist, mouth quirked into a smile that made her heart tumble.

She straightened, hands suddenly sweaty on the chair's arms. "Of course not. What is it?"

"I know it's risky. I know we're in the middle of a war. But I wondered if you'd like to participate in the musical mess happening there?" He shrugged toward the tent's center where nobles and merchants, advisors and kaptans, lifted hands and feet to the beat of the music.

On the outskirts of the jumble, Ona twisted like a column of smoke, her hips drawing a good bit of attention from the fighters nearby.

"I can't dance with you." Everyone would see and as far as they knew, she was still married.

"No, I'm a terrible dancer. I do however play the ocarina." He produced an odd, almost oval-shaped...thing with holes. A green glaze shone along its sloped edges. "It's a folk flute from Silvania. And I could teach you how to play."

Dancing wouldn't work, but learning an instrument? Surely none would take offense to that. Not in the middle of this wild feast.

Smiling, she moved away from the table, checking quickly to see that Adem was busy talking to an ore master. The master's black hood was pulled away from his face. Both men wore serious faces, but they weren't looking at her.

She trailed Lucca to his table, stopping here and there to greet people.

Izzet came up to her, big eyes glistening. "I want to thank you again, Kyros Seren." She grinned wide at the new title. "For everything."

"Did you finish weaving that green fertility ring for the blanket?" Seren asked.

Meekra's sister was about to come of age and Seren had pulled together a group of girls—all around the same age as Seren—to weave the ritual blanket. It'd been difficult to say the least, convincing the high and middle castes to work with the low. The low-castes, like Izzet, had been scared as kittens at first, jumping at every one of Qadira's snooty commands. But with a little coaxing from Seren, a few jokes from Meekra, and some well-placed comments from high-caste Najwa, the group had settled into a rhythm.

"We did!" Izzet's smile was contagious. "It looks beautiful. I hope she likes it, my kyros."

"She will. You're truly skilled at weaving. If I can talk the Azjorr's weaver into taking you on as an apprentice, would you like that?"

Izzet clapped her hands, then looked nervously at Erol, who'd come closer to make sure all was well with Seren. "That would be perfect," Izzet said, reining her excitement in.

Lucca turned to see what had kept Seren. She waved to Izzet, then hurried to catch up with him.

Greeting Ona with a nod, Lucca sat on a high stool and cupped the ocarina between his large hands. The instrument was a bright green, a lot like the weaving Izzet had worked on. It caught the light and shone like Lucca held an emerald. He blew softly. Mellow, low notes floated from the instrument and turned a few heads nearby. Lucca's eyes shuttered as his song spun toward the draped ceiling, high and straining and lovely. The notes plunged into something deep and dangerous and quite fast. Seren's heart matched the rhythm and she allowed herself to imagine dancing with Lucca.

He'd give the ocarina to Ona and begin circling Seren with slow steps like a hunter. Seren would lift her hands and bend them at the wrists, back and forth and back again, sharp and quick, as she looked Lucca in the eye. She would be the symbol of Fire. As the music grew more complicated, he would move his arms down and out in smooth motions, simulating the rhythm of a hunter's horse galloping. Normally, one would need to be solemn, but Lucca would definitely grin slyly as his circle around her tightened. Soon, he'd be so close that she'd have to raise her arms over her head to keep her movements correct. His hand would brush her side and she'd shiver. Her arm would graze his shoulder and they'd bump together a little, laughing.

Seren put a hand to her cheek, feeling warm.

Ona leaned in, whispering. "Seren, Seren, Seren. If you ogle him like that, don't expect him not to come after you when everyone's gone to bed."

Heart pounding, Seren's mouth popped open. Lucca lingered on a discordant sound that was oddly pleasant and goosebumps flickered over Seren's arms.

Lowering the ocarina, Lucca looked up, eyes warm. "Want to give it a try, Kyros Seren?"

"She definitely does," Ona said quietly, smirking.

Seren reached out a hand. She copied the way he'd held it, positioning the first four fingers of each hand over the larger holes on the top.

He hissed a little and grimaced. "Not so rough, my lady. It's an instrument, not a weapon."

Ona laughed and elbowed Seren. "That's my girl." She laughed again.

Seren grinned, not entirely sure what Ona meant but glad to make her smile.

"Like this." Lucca was suddenly very close, his mouth mere inches from Seren's and his breath sweet from the mint he'd chewed. Black stubble lined his strong chin and darkened the dip below his nose. His lips looked soft and she wondered how they would—

He took her fingers in his and goosebumps rose, tingling and warm, along her arms again. His gaze wandered from their hands to her arms, then back again, some emotion she couldn't name moving his mouth into a half-grin. Gently, he posed her fingertips on the ocarina.

"Keep your fingers curled," he said, his dark amber eyes glowing, "sitting just heavy enough to close the opening." Seren couldn't stop looking at Lucca's mouth. Her whole face went hot. He smelled so good. "Keep them ready to leap away to form new notes." Thankfully, he didn't seem to notice how bizarre she felt around him.

Seren nodded at his directions, not trusting herself to talk. She felt like a young girl around a first crush instead of a widow and a kyros. Another miracle.

When her hands were in place, Lucca continued. "Now blow out with a sound like *too*. And lift a finger one by one, starting from here, on your right."

Her notes were nothing like his, but they were simple and pretty and she found herself pulling the instrument away and smiling like a fool.

"You did well!" Lucca nudged Ona with his foot and set her to stomping in praise, an indulgent look on Ona's heart-shaped face. "You can be more gentle with the mouthpiece too. You don't need to bite it."

Ona erupted into laughter, and Seren had the distinct feeling she was missing something. Lucca glared, and Ona threw an arm over her mouth. Once again, Seren was a little lost, but it wasn't so bad. Being lost with Lucca was actually very pleasant.

Meekra appeared at Seren's shoulder.

"Kyros Seren," Meekra whispered, her pensive gaze on Ona. "General Adem left the tent."

"Did he tell anyone where he was going?"

"He headed toward his tent. With those two ore masters that hang on his every word."

Ona had taken the ocarina from Lucca and had it on her head and was swiveling her hips. "Queen of the Squawking Horn Pipe," she sang.

"You look seriously intelligent right now, Ona," Lucca said dryly. "Gentle folk," he held out a hand, "look upon my proud war sister, Onaratta Sings like Dying Dog."

Seren almost laughed, but Meekra was wringing her hands and was right to worry. "If you see him, tell me. If you hear anything, let me know right away. Please double check the guards are in place at the back entrance to my chamber."

Meekra nodded and slipped back into the dancing and joking, disappearing into colored kaftans, flushed faces, and the smoke billowing from Seren's chambers.

Lucca grabbed the ocarina from Ona, an indulgent look on his face, then began to play. Ona grinned at Seren—Seren had never known smiles could be aggressive but Ona managed it—and linked their arms, pulling Seren into a dance.

Ona sang in Silvanian, something about daggers and eyes, and Seren lifted her hem and moved her feet in time, trying to keep up until Erol walked up with Seren's bow in hand.

"I think we should have a contest, my lady." Erol scowled, but it was his happy scowl. Seren was fairly certain his face didn't really know how to not scowl.

"Archery here? In the tent?"

Erol nodded and gestured toward a barca set up in the corner beside

Hossam and Cansu. The leather target's decorative bells twinkled in the lamps' light.

Ona rubbed her hands together. "This'll be fun. Eh, Lucca, you need to be a part of this."

Lucca lowered the ocarina and eyed the target. "If you insist, Onaratta. And if it pleases you, Kyros Seren."

He dipped his head at Seren and her body felt lighter, like she was made of light and shadow instead of flesh, like a breeze might lift her and take her away. Her worries and fears couldn't settle on her shoulders. They slipped right through her and she let herself enjoy the feel of it.

"Definitely. Just know that I'm going to beat you, Lucca Hand of Ruination."

"He is pretty good, Kyros," Ona muttered.

"And so am I." Seren took her bow from Erol as he raised his voice.

"Nobles, war brothers and sisters, friends and respected guests, please clear the aisle. Kyros Seren, the Blessed, the Chosen One, is about to start an archery contest!"

"What is the prize, Blessed One?" Qadira called out, her perfect eyebrows lifting. She smirked at Seren, most likely hoping she'd make a fool of herself.

Seren spotted Kaptan Rashiel in the audience. He'd helped Meric with the contest on her wedding day and was the type that got along with everyone.

"Kaptan Rashiel!" The man turned his head, then quickly put his cup down and stood, smoothing his military kaftan. "What should be the prize for this impromptu archery contest? I'm entering so it's not right that I choose the winner's gift."

Ona whispered to Lucca and wiggled her hips as she eyed Rashiel. Lucca's fingers drifted over his sly smile and Seren had to drag her attention back to Rashiel.

Rashiel cocked his head, thinking. "Noshu's colt?"

Seren smiled at the mention of Fig's mother, Noshu. She'd given birth to a lovely ebony colt with a fine head just eight days ago. "Perfect, Kaptan Rashiel. But whoever earns this prize must promise never to sell him. Fig will want her half-brother nearby."

Lucca grinned as servants brought in several bows and a lashed bundle of arrows. Blue and black fletching brightened the ends of each one and new steel heads gleamed from the tips.

Ona's eyes shone and she mumbled something about the horse and

Seren's demand. "You are kind, Chosen One," she said, louder now. "Too kind."

"Why don't you go first, Erol?" Seren lifted a hand toward him.

With what passed as a pleased look for Erol, he took three arrows from a servant's hand, raised a bow to aim and spread his feet. One, two, and three flashed across the tent. Two near the bull's eye and one a little right. The room stomped feet in praise.

Erol nodded his head and stepped aside. Three more fighters and a scribe lined up to give the contest a try.

Lucca handed Seren a stick of minted lamb, which she took and gobbled up quickly, happy to have her appetite back.

"The scribe's not bad." Lucca's eyebrows lifted.

"But not as good as you."

The corner of his mouth moved. He shrugged in what Seren was learning was a very Lucca-like movement. It meant *yes, but I'd rather not say it aloud and seem prideful.* He held his three arrows, his thumb smoothing the first one's fletching as he leaned against the lotus pillar. She pressed her back against the pillar too, her arm brushing his. Warmth from his olive-toned skin rushed through the point of contact and suddenly her heart was beating too quickly.

"Think you can beat me?" Seren swallowed and stared at the phoenix on the tip of her shoe. Its rosestone eyes seemed to blink in the flickering light. Lucca wasn't answering, so she raised her head.

He'd turned to face her, his deep, reddish-brown eyes hot. "I won't insult you by not trying my best, my kyros."

Shivers rode down her back though she wasn't sure why. She wanted to say thank you or make some clever quip, but her mouth didn't want to work.

He leaned closer. The collar of his green brigantine vest rucked up a little. It rubbed the side of his neck and trapped a strand of his thick, shoulder-length hair. Without thinking, she reached toward him, slipped her thumb under his collar and straightened it. His nostrils flared in surprise, his lips just inches away and his gaze burning into her eyes as she pulled away. She could still feel the softness of his brigantine, the heat in his skin, the strength simmering under his restraint.

"If you want…" she said, his breath mingling with hers. "We could maybe…"

His fingers danced over her closest hand, glancing to see if anyone was watching, then moved back the slightest step. His throat bobbed once, from the hollow at the base all the way to the slope under his jawline. Chest moving up and down, he whispered, "If this is your strategy to make me lose the contest, it's a good one."

"I wouldn't—"

He interrupted with a teasing smile. "I know. I was joking. But we should laugh. I should walk away. This archery contest is about to turn into a display of my longing for you, and I don't think that would be beneficial to either of us—past the point of pleasure, anyway."

Joy spread arms wide inside Seren and she felt like she was falling, but in a good way. Breathless. Free. Untethered.

She was about to argue for him to stay, but Meekra appeared beside Rashiel, her face drawn and pale as she approached, a warning in the coiled tension of her clasped hands and tight jaw.

"Kyros Seren," she started.

Adem walked up behind Seren and Lucca made a noise like a growl.

"Pearl of the Desert," Adem said quietly, the fires' light cutting across his eyes.

Seren nearly dropped her bow.

Turning, she saw Adem had brought two men, black bags in hand. Not ore masters this time. These were physicians.

Seren's heart clenched and stopped. This was the end.

SEREN

Adem had brought physicians to evaluate Meric's condition. Seren was going to be sick.

Extending a palm to the physicians, Adem addressed the room, "In my great concern for Kyros Meric, I've brought two physicians, fresh from a long rest. Thank you for the opportunity, Pearl of the Desert. Welcome, good men. This way, please."

Completely ignoring Seren's open mouth and the permission she definitely, absolutely had not given him, he led the physicians toward Seren's chamber. Hossam and Cansu stood guard. They seemed petrified, completely unable to move, their gazes cutting to Seren. The brightly painted archery target beside them looked completely cheerful and completely out of place.

Seren's hands shook. "What is this?" Heading toward Adem, she bumped a table sharply with her knee. Pain leeched up her leg and she wished for what felt like the thousandth time that she was graceful and confident like Ona, like Lucca, like Meekra, like Barir, like everyone around her but herself. She fisted her hands around her scrap of green wool, frustrated that she couldn't seem to raise her voice and take hold of the situation. She would die. Meekra would be implicated. Barir would definitely die. They would be beaten to death. Probably tonight. And left in a ditch outside the city walls, rubbish to fall under Invader boots.

"Go on in, physicians." Adem wasn't even paying attention to her. Like he hadn't heard her.

"No." Her voice wasn't nearly loud enough.

The first physician stepped away from the door, but the second put a hand to the wood. They hadn't heard her. Lucca was at her elbow, Ona too. She could feel their hot rage on her behalf. Meekra joined them and whispered a prayer under her breath.

They gave Seren the strength to speak up.

"I said *stop!*"

The second physician shoved the door open.

Hossam drew his dagger. He thrust the weapon into the man's side.

Adem had his own blade to Hossam's throat before Seren could say a word.

She grabbed Ona to keep from falling.

"Stop," Seren whispered, everything moving too quickly. "All of you. Stop!"

Adem's physician dropped to his knees and clutched at his side. Blood pooled around his slim fingers.

Hossam looked from Adem to Seren, panic stinting his words. "The physician disobeyed you, Kyros Seren. It isn't a fatal wound. At least...I didn't intend to kill him. I—he disobeyed, my kyros."

The injured physician slumped all the way to the carpets where he lay with arms outstretched and face white, his bag by his side. His associate, lips pulled back in a grimace, kneeled beside his limp body.

The physician was dead.

Seren's order had killed an innocent man. Not an Invader. Not an enemy or a criminal. A physician who probably had a family, children, a life. Bile rose in Seren's throat and she fought to stay standing, her legs trembling.

At Hossam's throat, Adem's arm twitched.

It wouldn't take but one small move to end Hossam's life. His broad smile would be gone. His fierce loyalty.

"This is not how tradition mandates," Adem snapped. "No matter how ill the kyros is. This is not how we run the Empire."

She had to be strong. To be the kyros. If not, Hossam was going to die right now. *Holy Fire, help me.*

She drew herself up and let go of Ona, who gave her arm an encouraging squeeze.

"General Adem. My husband's health is my business first." Her voice didn't sound like her own. It wasn't nearly strong enough. Confidence didn't glow from the tone like Ona or Lucca's words always did. But maybe pretending to feel it would fix some of this horror. "This is how *I* run this Empire. You had better get used to it."

Adem stared into Hossam's chest, not meeting Seren's eyes.

He would order her arrest. There was no way this would work. He had history behind him, years and years of only strong royal blood ruling like she was trying to do. He'd never swallow her sad attempt at authority.

But slowly, slowly he lowered his weapon.

Hossam took a breath, his bushy beard moving as he worked to keep his face from showing anything. What did he feel? Anger at Seren for putting him in that position? She wouldn't blame him. This was a mess. A tragic mess.

Still not meeting her eyes, Adem barked commands to remove the poor man's body, bowed to Seren, then left the feast with two ore masters whose draping cloaks followed them like spilled ink.

It had worked. She'd done it. She'd taken command over Adem. She was kyros. A shiver rocked her, but she held her chin high. Now if she could just feel right about it. If she could be confident in this…

Ona's grin could've swallowed a world. Lucca relaxed against a pillar, arms crossed, nodding like he'd expected her to succeed all along. Meekra's eyes shone with tears and she touched her family ring, probably thinking of her father, Barir, and how he was the first to tell Seren she was blessed.

"Meekra," Seren whispered. "Please quietly let Lucca and Ona know that I need them to come to my personal chambers after the feast. If they're willing."

"What about the quarantine? Won't someone question them coming in?"

"I'll simply bring them in and do what must be done. We don't have time to worry about someone reporting it to Adem. I've jumped past the line of what is dangerous anyway. I have to smooth out the mess I've made. We'll keep Erol, Cansu, and Hossam only at the doors. I'll send the rest of the guards on errands. Oh, please get more ka'ud ointment from your father. We'll need a lot of cloths that we can burn…after we finish what we need to do. And a burial shroud. Can you get your sisters to help you gather everything? Am I asking too much?"

"I know what we must do. You don't have to explain anything. And no, you could never ask too much of me, Blessed Pearl, my kyros. I would give my life for you. For Akhayma. For the Empire."

Meekra bent her head and looked up at Seren through thick, black lashes. Seren knew very well she'd be lost without her.

Seren rubbed a palm over her friend's silver rings. No words would be enough, but she needed to say them anyway. "Thank you for your courage.

I'd be lost without you." She squeezed Meekra's hand and Meekra squeezed back. The corner of Meekra's lips lifted despite the fear flickering through her eyes. "If at any point, you can't do this," Seren said, "you don't want to be a part of this, you go. Go back to your family's tent."

"I will never, ever leave you, my lady." Meekra's voice was almost a growl. Seren imagined her as a mother desert lion, watching over her cubs. "Never."

Seren hugged her, breathing in her comforting scent of olive oil and soaps, and went back to the high table.

The table of district heads turned, faces lined with worry. Clan Azjorr's chieftain sat very still beside the waterworks district's head. They had paused their seemingly deep conversation. The man she was looking for huddled with the records keepers, every one of them squinting to see, their eyes weak from years spent pouring over scrolls.

"Scribe?"

The man scurried over, back hunched a little, but face bright and intelligent. "My lady? I, I mean, my kyros?"

"As of this day, the Empire will no longer enslave those captured in battle or foreigners who wish to live in the Empire. The Empire will no longer take a *volunteer*," Seren sneered at the word because they were no such thing, "from every border town so said town may rule with their own local customs. We will take true volunteers into our army and reward them so that they will come of their own free will. Foreigners will be low-caste, but the cost of bell removal will be halved."

The district heads erupted into questions, polite but demanding. No one dared disagree openly but their unhappiness with her decree showed in their faces. Seren held up her palms and they quieted.

"The only reason we eat here today instead of bleeding to death under Invader boots, the only reason we hold the Invader king and are about to accept a sizable sum of silver and the surrender of our enemies is because every caste gave blood—slave, low-caste, all—to fight. Together, we protected our city and our Empire. And now, we will respect one another and live to fight another day."

Almost everyone in the tent stood and most stomped their feet in praise, drowning the district heads' questions. Meekra ordered household staff around the tent to help slaves remove bells outside and called in the criers to spread the word to the city. The scribe went to his pedestal in the corner to record her pronouncement.

There were pockets of those who narrowed their eyes at Seren and whispered behind heavily ringed hands. The head of the waterworks district raised his voice, but Clan Azjorr's chieftain shoved him back into his chair, shutting the man up.

"She saw a vision, fool. She is blessed!" The chieftain turned and bowed deeply. "May we all learn to be as merciful as you, Blessed Pearl."

Seren's hand went to her chest, swallowing. She felt like she was at the edge of a cliff, toes barely hanging on. The music started up again, and she slipped into her smoke-filled chambers to wait for the others to arrive so they could take Meric from his temporary resting place under the ground beneath the rugs, and pretend that he had just died. Ka'ud had thoroughly soaked the air and every fabric in the chamber. Hopefully, it would hold when the body was unburied.

At the archery target, bows, and arrows were swept out of the tent by those wise enough to know the contest wasn't going to happen now. Seren leaned against the lotus tower's cool stone and sighed. Her bones were too tired for somebody so young.

AFTER THE FEAST, when the main tent emptied, Seren sent all the guards except her own to see to the release of the slaves and be sure their names were recorded in the books and their new low-caste bells attached to their sashes.

Meekra still hadn't returned with the ka'ud ointment when Lucca appeared at the back door, his slightly curly, black hair shining in the sunlight and his dark eyes serious. He put his hands on his wide, leather belt, then crossed them, then clasped them.

"I'm here to help. In any way you need, Kyros Seren."

Despite his obvious worry and nervousness—which was completely understandable—something about his presence made her feel like she'd taken a step back from that imagined cliff's edge.

"Thank you. You…know what we have to do?"

"Yes." His voice was dark.

"Then let's do it quickly and never talk about it again." Her stomach knotted as she removed her outer kaftan, rolling her shirt sleeves up. "Is Ona coming?"

Ona herself answered as she slipped in. "Yes, she is." She smiled sadly and patted Seren on the back roughly. Seren didn't think she meant to be rough. It was just Ona's way.

They used the same two bowls as before to dig up Meric's body.

Death's scent ghosted from the wrappings as they brought him up. The subtle odor clung to their damp skin as they brushed the dirt away from the fabric. With the ka'ud smoking, they peeled back the wrappings, and with wet cloths, cleaned Seren's former husband's face, hands, and feet. Not too much of the sandy earth dirtied his clothing, but it had sneaked into his ears and around his hairline. Touching him, even through the cloth, sent shudders rippling through her. She'd never forget the feel of his dead flesh, the stillness of his chest and eyes.

Lucca helped to lift him onto the bed and clear away the last of the dirt.

"Kyros?" Meekra's voice streamed through the door.

Seren's heart jerked like an arrow had struck her back. "Come in. No one saw you? Followed you?"

"I don't think so." Meekra held a stack of cut cloth, a shroud, and a crockery tub tied with twine. "Everyone is too worried about themselves right now. And all anyone wants to talk about is you freeing the slaves. Some of the nobles are angry. They'll have to pay their workers now. All of them, Blessed Pearl."

"I'll meet with the district heads soon. We'll figure out some solutions together. Maybe by then Adem will have accepted things the way they are."

Seren took the crock from her with careful hands and a whispered prayer, like this was a part of Meric's funeral. She hadn't loved him. But he had been her husband. And everyone, no matter how they acted, deserved at least a little respect in death. She dipped fingers into the translucent mixture and smoothed it over Meric's eyelids, cheeks, hooked nose, thin lips.

With a look that asked permission, Ona reached for the crock and Seren nodded. Ona took a portion and ran it along Meric's forearms and hands.

Meekra, showing her skills as the daughter of a physician, expertly wrapped Meric from his feet to the crown of his head, securing the strips of linen with more ointment.

Seren scrubbed her hands in a bowl of cold water. Lucca stood with his arms crossed over his chest, staring at Meric's body.

"What was he like?" he asked quietly.

Goosebumps drifted over Seren's arms. "He was…" She didn't want to speak ill of the dead.

Ona laughed without any humor and put her feet on the floor. "Your face says it all."

"Meric didn't respect me. He ignored almost all of the ideas the Holy Fire gave me and he shouted often. Even though nothing he was angry about was ever my fault. He was mercurial."

"He was a horse's back end," Ona said.

Lucca made an indeterminate noise.

Erol cracked the door open, but kept his gaze on Seren. He had to know everything that was going on. All of her guards did. Thankfully, they were steady as rock, unwavering in their position. "Kyros Seren. We have news. The Invaders are here. A small party with a cart and what appears to be a trunk of silver."

Closing her eyes, Seren breathed deeply. "The ransom." Then she looked at Lucca, who held himself silent as a memory, his eyes giving her that same feeling, that illusion of safety in this dangerous, dangerous world.

Ona clapped a hand on Seren's shoulder. "We better get our units ready. Just in case." With a wink, she was out the door.

On his way out, Lucca touched Seren's arm. A tingling warmth pooled under his fingertips, heating Seren's skin like his touch was another kind of healing balm.

"I will be by your side. I will keep eyes on Adem."

"Why are you so loyal to me?" A touch of guilt twinged inside her, but she needed to understand. She knew Ona's motivation. Revenge. Ona believed Seren was the key to getting it. But what did Lucca see in Seren?

"I've followed three people in my life." His hand fell away from her arm. "One. My father." His lip twisted as some past event cut him. "Two. A Silvanian king." He looked to the tent's striped ceiling in exasperation at this king. "Three. The leader of our mercenary group, Dom. All of them are cunning as foxes. None hold others higher than themselves though. You do. You truly care. I never realized it, but I think I've been looking for a leader like you all my life."

Seren took his hands in hers, soaking in his presence as best she could before she had to leave and deal with complicated enemies she was sure were far wiser than her.

Lucca's gaze dropped, his cheeks going a little darker.

"I will do everything, everything in my power to deserve your loyalty," she whispered.

The Holy Fire in the bowl behind them flickered and snapped.

Lucca kissed Seren's hand and left.

Please, Holy Fire, she prayed, *give me the ability to live up to that man's hope.*

12

ONA

L ucca's snores woke Ona. At least he was finally asleep. Now if only she could do the same. It'd been the longest couple of days in the history of the world.

Moonlight from the edges of the door lit Lucca's upturned face. Ona pulled an overly tasseled pillow from under her head and threw it at him without any real force. He grunted and rolled onto his side, one hand resting on his shoulder, fingers twitching in a pattern she knew as well as the hilt of her sword. Ring finger, pointer, pointer, small and ring together. The first tune he played on the ocarina every time he picked the silly thing up. He had hands like her aunt's—muscled but graceful. Memories fevered Ona like a sickness. Her aunt's face floated to the surface of her mind, then shattered into sharp pieces that stung and pressed against her head. Losing someone never got easier, no matter what stupid people said.

Lucca's blanket slipped to the floor.

Ona crossed the room and put the ridiculously ornate blanket back on him. "Filthy wild man." She smirked. "You've come a long way from the forest floor."

Shaking her head, she lay down and remembered the day they met.

She wasn't sure when she'd started running that day, the blood covered palette knife still in her hand, but she'd ended up in the forest beyond her town, across the river. A very confused group of strangers had faced her. They had weapons. Loads of them.

Lucca wasn't the first one she'd seen. It was Dom. Tall, fair, bearded, and possessing a scar the length of her favorite paintbrush. The badly stitched line ran from hairline to nose, and diagonally to his ear, where a silver bob dangled.

"You don't look like much either, if you don't mind my saying." Dom's voice was strong, but had a watery quality like thinned paint.

If she opened her mouth, she'd start screaming for her aunt again, so she settled for the most obscene gesture she knew to combat his tone and make him think twice about using the club at his belt.

"Oh!" Dom laughed and the others with him.

Their fire ring—stones hastily stacked—was cold and black. They knew better than to light a fire that might alert the still-roaming Invaders.

"I suppose you've met the nasty Western pigs, then?" He motioned to a girl about Ona's age and she brought her a cup and a cloth.

Ona didn't know what to do with that either. Horror had stuffed her head full to bursting.

"So you can abrade me with your fingers but can't seem to figure out what to do with a generous offer of wine? Hm."

And that's when Lucca appeared. He'd been stretched out by the fire ring, one knee up. A position Ona now knew he took every time he sat on the ground. He'd stood, and pushed his black curls out of his face. His eyes matched his hair and he had a mouth her cousins would've swooned over. Ona preferred boys with sharper features, like the trader's oldest son, Cesco.

Cesco was dead too. She'd seen his body on her flight out of town.

They were all dead.

Dead. Dead. Dead.

Lucca frowned at Dom and waved at Ona's hands. "After that..." She wasn't sure if he was talking about her palette knife or her obscene gesture. "...yes, I think she's a born fighter."

He looked into her face like he was reading a map of some far off place. He took the cloth from the girl and wiped her free hand clean. "I'm going to take this palette knife now."

"What? Oh. Good." Her voice was a stranger. She was so cold.

He uncurled Ona's fingers from the metal and wood. Her muscles and tendons quaked. She'd been gripping the thing like it was the key to unlocking the door holding her in this nightmare.

Dom snorted as Lucca rubbed the blood from Ona's nails. "Planning to keep her, Lucca?"

Lucca's gaze seared the other man, then he turned back to her and his eyes gentled. "You're welcome to stay with us until you feel like yourself again." He must've read the road she'd been down on her paint and blood-stained face. "Or, at least until you make a decision about who to be now."

"Wh-what are you?" A few new faces peered at her as she shivered. None of them looked like her aunt or herself or anyone in town. Their features were straight, strong, and confidence beamed from their every move. One cleaned a sword with a dirty rag. Another held up a jeweled necklace and made some joke about it with their friend. Shiny-coated horses and two ponies tore greenery from the base of a tree where another man used his hands to explain the layout of the next town down the river.

The smell of her aunt's villa burning pushed her out of the now for a beat, and the ice in her gut spread. She put her palms on her knees.

Lucca's fingers gripped her arm. "Eh, you're all right. It's over."

She opened her eyes. "You never answered my question." Her voice sounded more familiar. She willed her heart to stop quaking.

"We're mercenaries, military for hire. I am Lucca Hand of Ruination. I'm a condottieri, along with Dom. We lead this band and fight for the families that hire us."

"I know what mercenaries are. I'm seventeen, not stupid."

Lucca barked a laugh. "I think she's going to be fine, Dom. And we're going to want to train her." He looked at her palette knife where it rested beside the cup of wine. "You could wield a better weapon against those who'd like to take things from you."

A surge of some unknown emotion heated Ona's freezing insides. She felt alive again. "A better weapon." Her smile cracked the cut on her mouth. She licked the new, salty blood. "I'd like that."

A year later, Ona was the youngest ever to become a condottieri, a leader like Lucca. That cold helplessness would never hold her again. She refused to let anyone or anything make her feel like that. She would get her revenge. She would see the Invader king dead. Nothing, absolutely nothing, would stand in her way.

The now-familiar sensation of heat rolled down her body, just under her skin, starting at her head and searing its way to the tips of her toes and scarred fingers. She didn't need any Holy Fire to justify her actions or lead her into this war. She was a living, burning, scorching flame made into flesh, armed to protect the only loved one she had left and to exact justice for the loved ones brutally stolen from her.

1 3

SEREN

A river of calming, comforting sounds poured from the stables' open double doors and into the cool night. Seren knew she shouldn't be here. She should be planning and plotting. But she needed space and quiet. Just for a little while. Horses shuffled their heavy hooves in the dusty straw, the tips of their shoes clipping and knocking the wood floors. Fig's half door squeaked lightly on its curlicue hinges as Seren slipped inside, laying a hand on the mare's suede nose. The horse snuffled against Seren's fingers and found the sugar lump she'd brought. Fig's proud, black head rose, and twisting her swan neck, the mare nuzzled against her owner.

Seren's mind loosened as she smoothed Fig's sun-hued mane. She truly wished she could sleep here in the barn. So much had happened, but the stables remained quiet and comforting. But so much had happened. Meric's death, for one. She didn't really miss him. Not in the way she should've. He hadn't been kind. Or respectful. And they hadn't had that fever that Father used to talk about when he remembered Mother. He'd claimed he felt a rush of heat when he looked at her. Said there were moments when the fever was less, but it was always there.

But Meric and his father had saved Seren from a horrible fate and given her Akhayma again, a new family that couldn't replace hers, but that she loved nonetheless. Meekra, Barir, Cansu, Hossam, Erol—all the people of the city. She couldn't mourn Meric as a wife should, but she'd honor him by doing everything within her power to save their people from what her first family went through. She didn't want another Empire girl to lose her sisters and father right in front of her eyes. Ever.

The fever had Seren thinking too.

Really, the only instance she'd felt something like that fever Father had taught her about was when she looked at the city, the faces, and heard their voices, their varied languages. She was in love with them. Holding Fig close, she savored the feel of the mare's pulse near her own beating heart. Fig snorted lightly into Seren's hair. She smiled, tension leaking away.

Fig knocked a hoof against the door, her foreleg a bright white against the black of the rest of her. Grinning at the demand for more stroking, Seren began to fashion a tiny braid between Fig's ears. She used to braid her little sisters' hair like this. Her heart surged in her chest. She swallowed. There were days when she'd coiled her sisters' light brown locks in a way similar to Ona's. Maybe that's why she felt so close to Ona already. It wasn't just Ona's hairstyle. It was the way she plunged into life like her sisters, Beti and Cati, had. Ona definitely would've approved of how they used to sneak pastries from Mother's tin and point to Father in blame. Beti and Cati would've grown up to be a lot like Ona if Seren had to guess.

Seren smiled, sadness a familiar song in her heart. Ona was so strong. A blessing to have on her side. And Lucca. Seren's heart reared its head again, but in a completely different way. A warmth traveled up her chest and into her face. Hm. It felt much like a fever.

She shook off the feeling. "I know it's late, Fig. But are you up for a ride?"

Fig snorted approval and pushed to leave the calm of her stall.

WARRIORS ON PATROL watched Seren as she wedged arrows between her fingers. When she nudged Fig into a gallop, the mare tossed her yellow mane. Her black body shot forward past a line of flickering torches.

Despite the fact that, tomorrow, Seren would face men set on tearing her world apart, she smiled wide enough to hurt her cheeks. Maybe because of it. She wouldn't let them destroy those she loved. She'd enjoy her horse, her archery, her people, her city. Their threats wouldn't stop her from living her life. The ransom would work. Or it wouldn't. Nothing could keep Seren from feeling gratitude, such fantastic, beautiful gratitude.

The first barca's painted circles and stars dared her to hit them. She raised her arm, aimed, fired. One to the center, a second to the right. The next target proved wilier. It lay on the ground, and she had to point her elbow to the stars as Fig blasted past, hooves raising dust that clouded

Seren's already dulled night vision. Her shot went right and she snarled in frustration. One more barca. She twisted in the creaking saddle to launch a last arrow behind her, at a target positioned opposite of the first. The shot thudded into the thick leather, but too far right. Again.

Finished, she tossed her bow gently on a haystack. She pressed a heel into Fig's side to turn her. "Run, girl. Run."

The horse snorted in agreement and her sides heaved as her hooves pounded the earth. Fig wasn't the most expensive mount in the stables, but she was fast and she was Seren's friend.

Cool wind rushed over Seren's head, unspooling the ribbons of her hair, and she urged Fig to go even faster. They tore around the training field. The stables, the watching soldiers, and the surrounding walls blurred, leaving only sound. The tightness in Seren's shoulders fell off her and she wasn't the Pearl of the Desert or kyros. She was just Seren.

Fig threw her head and snuffled. Seren let her slow down and rubbed the dip below her left ear, her favorite spot. Her warmth was better than any blanket. Fig trotted up to a thick-framed boy recently taken on to man the horses at night.

The boy gave Fig a gentle rub. "Kyros Seren. Our Fig might be in a different stall while they put in the new feeder systems, if it pleases you, my lady."

Seren dismounted and picked up her bow. "Ah. Yes. Because she doesn't care for the hammering."

"Of course, we may not be putting the system in now that…that we are…" The boy's throat moved and he stared at the walls as if he could see the Invaders beyond them, readying for the ransom that would hopefully come tomorrow and end all of this.

Seren touched his arm. "It will be fine. Replace the feeders. Start on it tonight if you think it won't wake everyone." *Staying busy sometimes means staying sane,* Mother had always said.

"I'll be happy to fetch your arrows, my lady."

Thanking him, she headed back to where Cansu and Erol waited on the path toward the city gate. Sleep wasn't going to come tonight. She knew that. But Meekra wouldn't rest until she returned, so Seren hurried back to her quarters, praying every step along the way that the next day would go as planned.

SEREN

Six men worked to open the city gates. Four tugged at the wooden posts of the cranks, and the other two swept sand and rock from the doors' path with wide metal flats like fans. With a shudder, the gates thudded against the city walls and a plume of dust clouded into the air. Seren drew her shoulder blades down toward her spine and lengthened her neck, as Meekra had shown her. *A long neck can do wonders for the will,* she said. Seren had sent Meekra to stay with her family, to help her parents protect her sisters. Just in case.

Ten Invaders in red and white surcoats and metal boots surrounded a large cart that transported wooden trunks through the towering doors. Coins clinked inside the chests, and the jointed metal on the enemies' feet grated together, sounding remarkably similar to a venomous dune beetle's warning.

Seren wished she could hold a weapon at the ready. Wished she could've worn the leather, bronze-studded vest Meekra had ordered to be made for her. But she had to appear peaceful and trusting. This was a delicate thing. Her foot bounced. She flexed her hands, her palms damp and sticky. It was nearly impossible to stand there and just watch the people who'd killed Father, Cati, and Beti traipse right into her home.

One man stopped at Cansu and bent at the waist toward Seren. It was an ugly bow and his upturned face showed little respect. Meric would've said something. He would've quipped and thrown out a smirk and kicked sand in the man's eyes. Then, the warriors with the lead Invader would've traded trunks for swords, and Meric would've ruined it all only for his vanity.

Seren knew better. *One fool shouldn't ruin peace,* Father had always said.

"Good sun to you, warrior." Seren took her time with the unfamiliar language.

Her fighters on the walls tensed. Was it something she'd done or had they noticed something that she missed?

She scanned the Invaders and the trunks they set at her feet. Red, irritated skin surrounded the Invaders' eyes. Was the arid climate hampering them? Their country was in full drought, so she'd heard. But drought didn't mean they'd be accustomed to the dry wind across the flat rises of the hammadas or the acidic breeze through the lahabshjara trees clustered in areas where groundwater hid under the sandy earth.

The chests they brought were far too small to hold a warrior. So no surprise attacks there. The Invaders' weapons sat at their belts, untouched by twitching fingers or curling hands. Their gazes didn't waver from the back of their leader's dark blond head. They were focused on him, as expected. Seasoned warriors took note of exits and armed soldiers with quick side looks instead of gaping. She'd learned that much from watching Father in new situations when they'd traveled the Empire.

She turned to Erol and Hossam. "Present our prisoner."

They took up the ropes on the silver-gilt Empire cart, the one that held the king in his wooden cage, and brought him forward. The king's beard hung limply, all of its curl gone. A cut on his cheek still showed red, and one along his neck, but no blood leaked from the wound. He held his shoulders straight and nodded once to his general. A darkness flashed over the Invader general's eyes and he opened his mouth to say something.

"He has been our prisoner," Seren said. "I wouldn't present him to you in some false way, in a false show of some imagined respect. You'll receive honesty from me, if not in battle, then when we are face-to-face."

Their general gave a curt bow, but didn't look at her as Adem worked the fist-sized bronze lock on the cage. Adem swung the door open and stood at the back of the cart, offering his shoulder to the king, so the man could step to the ground with some dignity. Disgust poured off Adem, waves of fury she could almost see.

The king ignored Adem and hopped to the ground. His gaze shifted to Seren. "May I please have my sword? It's a family heirloom."

Seren waved to Cansu, who brought the shining weapon forward and presented it to the king.

An unsteady, fearful warmth traveled the length of her. This was the peace the Empire needed. The only way to keep it would be to help these terrible people. Without relief from their drought, they'd come back again and again, desperation whipping them on like a vicious master. Akhayma was just lucky they'd only brought a middle-sized force and not their entire army.

A shudder wrapped cold arms around her.

Father had told her about the Invaders' full-scale siege of the formerly rich trade city of Vadi. He'd narrowly escaped. His story painted a clear picture of the Invaders' colored tents that indicated who would live and who would die if the city surrendered. Each day they put up a new tent, a new color. Each day the threat grew worse and worse. Now, Vadi was nothing more than a wraith of a town, twisting in the sandy wind. A victim to the white tent, then the red, then at last, the black—the worst of them all. The air howled through the empty mouths of tumbled towers and moaned about the horrors seen there.

Beside Lucca, Ona's face twisted. She stood still, too still, murder in her eyes.

Seren was fairly certain Ona mouthed the words *Bad idea* as she nodded at the king's sword.

But Ona wasn't the leader here. Ona didn't know what it took to keep two peoples, so vastly different, at peace with one another.

Seren had watched Father and the old kyros sign a contract with a violent group from the North who had magic in their blood. With trade agreements, the Empire had no further trouble from them. If both sides gained what they saw as fair and good for their people, there was no need for bloodshed.

"I propose one more agreement," Seren said.

The king stood beside his general and cocked his head. His hair was nearly as bright as his weapon, despite the dust.

"What is that, Kyros Seren?" he asked in the trade tongue.

"We'll help you dig wells along our border," she said. "For your use. We know you attack out of desperation."

The king's eyes chilled. "We are to come begging at your wells to keep us alive?"

Adem stepped to Seren's side. "It's a generous offer."

"It must seem so to you," the king said. "You'd much rather separate my head from my body. But for me, one who knows what my armies can do, well, let us say it's not an offer I take with a smiling face and open heart." He looked at the single bell hanging from the tie at Seren's forehead and frowned.

Out of the corner of her eye, Seren saw Ona move. Lucca put a hand on Ona's stomach to stop her. His lips moved as he whispered to her.

"But we've made peace here," Seren said. "I don't think you understand. This is an offer made out of goodwill. No other silver need exchange hands. No further allowances made."

The king's upper lip lifted. His hands became fists. "My people were in stone castles the size of mountains before yours learned to milk goats. We will not bow to your tented *city* of puddles and ignorant fire."

He drew his sword.

A dozen Invaders dropped from the underbelly of their cart, rolled free of the wheels, and stood, armed and seething, before anyone else realized what was happening.

There was a shout. A mass of red and white poured through the gates.

Shock pulled any word Seren could've said right out of her mind. They'd tied themselves to the bottom of the cart. She'd been tricked.

The world exploded into a storm of steel, wood, and sound.

Before she could get her mouth to work, Cansu, Hossam, and Erol were in front of her. All she could see was a wall of vest and helmet and muscle.

She shoved Hossam, but he didn't move. "I need—"

Lucca handed her a bow and quiver over the guards. "I'm into the fray!" he shouted before taking off toward the gates.

Pushing through Cansu and Erol, she climbed onto the Empire cart and crouched near the silver-painted planks of the far side for protection. She nocked an arrow and aimed at an Invader who was picking off Empire archers on the parapet like plums from a tree. She took him down with a shot above his metal plating. Seren fired again and again until she had no more arrows. She froze, lost on how to move on, the world spinning around her, attacking her with metallic smells and screams that clawed at her heart.

Her Akhayma would be lost—Meekra, Cansu, Erol, Hossam, Adem, Barir, Qadira, Najwa, Izzet, Lucca, Ona. She'd lose this family like she had Mother years ago, then Father and her sisters.

Ona shouted above the chaos, her sword in the air. She was vengeance come to life. Her words, though intelligible, were sharp as her blade. Every move was an artistic stroke, throwing death like a color onto the canvas of the city.

Onaratta Paints with Blood.

The title fit too well. As violent and horrible as she was, a fierce love showed in the way she fought. In each determined move, Ona's devotion to her aunt's memory shone.

Seren had to shake herself out of this daze. She'd only escaped the last few Invaders' swords because of the thickness of the fight. But her limbs were made of stone, her heart suspended and silent.

"Kyros! Fight! We fight with you!" Lucca began his own chanting, his arrows hitting fast and true.

Lucca's face held none of the gentleness she'd seen before. His dark eyes were cold like he'd turned his heart off. His movements were exact as a mathematician's work. Measuring distance with a glance, he threw his bow aside and drew his sword. Fighting fit the weave of him, of who he was. This wasn't personal, or, he didn't allow it to touch him the way Ona did.

Either way, they were supporting her, risking all for her people.

A brightness poured over Seren, waking her up. She grabbed her dagger and dove into the fray, heading for Lucca and Ona.

Together, the two mercenaries burst through a handful of sword-wielding Invaders like knives of lightning. Their limbs glowed. Their speed numbed the mind.

Ona leaped over an attacker, and as she did, slit the man's throat. Chanting in Silvanian, sounding like an ancient warrior goddess, she dropped behind another. One swift strike to the side of the neck, and he was gone.

Lucca threw foreign words like daggers and spun as an Invader made to run him through. He was faster than wind, vicious as a desert lion, with bared teeth and feral eyes.

Seren grabbed a fallen quiver. She fired one, two, three more arrows into the roiling mass of men and women. She hit the first two—heavy-bodied Invaders raging toward Erol—but missed the third, who cut down one of her warriors.

Seren draped a steel plate over her heart. Battle was no place for feelings, she reminded herself as the odor of blood and sweat poured through the rising dust and swirls of sand disturbed by feet and falling bodies.

A group of Invaders broke through their contingent and ran west. They'd go after her people, the innocents, with the strategy to break the city's spirit. Seren thought about the little boy who'd offered Meric his incense stick during the Fire Ceremony, about Meekra and her sisters at their loom. An Invader's broad sword would cut clean through the boy's neck and his parents would see it all. An Invader's shield would bash Meekra and her family's heads, destroying their world in a flash.

The metal Seren had imagined over her heart shivered, tried to crack. "Stop them!" she shouted. "Cansu! Hossam! Stop those men!"

Cansu turned. His mop of hair flapped across his bleeding cheek. Hossam grabbed Cansu's jerkin and pulled him away from the fighting.

Fire, let them be fast enough.

Two more of Seren's men surrounded her as she stood to shoot from the cart. An Invader's arrow peeled past her ear and knocked into the wooden floor behind her.

"If you're going to fight, do it better!" a familiar, grainy voice said. Adem.

Seren jerked the arrow from the cart and lodged it, and two others from her quiver, between her fingers. With the first shot, she moved the next into place and let loose, and then again and again.

"Better!" Adem grunted and drew his yatagan up and at an angle to slice an Invader's thigh. The man fell. "Why did that contingent go west?"

Seren didn't know if he was truly asking her or if he was thinking out loud.

A huge Invader with silver hair and a ruddy face pushed Adem to the side with an oval shield and climbed onto the cart. The wagon lurched forward. She almost fell, grabbing hold of the side. The Invader, weaponless, struck out with his shield. She tried to move to the side, but the heavy wood still banged her jaw.

A tiny bloom of white marred her vision. A strange tightness broke across her head and neck. But no pain. It'd come later.

She swiped her dagger at the red-faced fighter. Gasping, heart skipping, she missed. One of her own fighters came at the man from the back. She angled herself and slashed across the bridge of the Invader's nose. He growled. His hands flew to his bleeding face. Adem aimed for him and swung his yatagan. Seren ducked behind his fallen shield—which had caught on the side of the cart—to catch her breath. The man fell under Adem's blade.

With her pulse beating in her tongue and temples, Seren rose and jumped over the side. Her dagger bit into an Invader's exposed forearm. He finished off an Empire fighter and faced Seren. Blood ran into his smile. He spit out a phrase in his language. Sword poised, he lunged right, then cut left, striking toward her legs.

Spinning, she dodged behind a panicked horse and shouted, "Onaratta Paints with Blood! Lucca Hand of Ruination! Get the king!"

She stretched to see their weapons blazing through the crowd, laying enemies low. The glint of the king's hair shone just past Ona's glowing reach.

Seren's fighters moved like the point of a huge arrow and pushed the Invaders closer and closer to the gates, away from Akhayma's heart.

Ona drove her sword against the king's. His dropped to the ground. Seren rounded the horse and ran. Ona's arm shot out—too fast to see—and wrapped around the king's shoulder and neck. Ona's sword tipped toward the tender spot below the king's chin and worked her way back to the bulk of the Empire's warriors.

Seren shouted something; she didn't even know what she'd said. They had the king in hand. All was not lost.

Then, with another swathe of men downed, the Empire had ten or so Invaders surrounded and the rest in retreat.

Akhayma's warriors shut the city gates and let up a shout of victory.

"Take the rest as prisoners." Seren climbed back onto the cart. "Give up your weapons." She made a sweeping motion to ensure they knew what she meant. "We won't harm you."

Ona's head swiveled and she glared directly at Seren. The rage of battle still heated her. Surely, that was the only plausible reason for her to look at Seren like that.

Hossam ran from behind a clutch of black tenting. Blood spatter dotted his cheeks. "Kyros! They are attacking from the West. A full scale attack!"

Adem took the king from Ona and threw the man at another Empire warrior. "Go!" he shouted at the Empire fighters.

Seren waved her dagger. "Ona, Lucca, go!"

Ona handed the king off to three other fighters, an ugly sneer marring her face. She and Lucca mounted two unmanned horses and galloped away alongside Adem and the rest of the warriors not currently holding prisoners.

Fire, help them, Seren prayed.

15

ONA

How many times would Ona have to capture the king before Seren ended him? Rage sliced at Ona as she rode beside Lucca, wind slapping her hot cheeks.

Ladders of rope hung over the walls' striped stone, lank as corpse hair and crawling with hundreds of Invaders. Ona's new mount reared. She tightened her legs around the horse's middle. The sneak attack by the front gates had been a feint. Where had they hidden from the watchers on the parapet? It was those trees. They'd hidden in those thick-trunked trees. Clever pigs.

Lucca chanted beside her, eyes wild.

"Wake iron, wake!
I am the blade and the blade is me.
I move like wind, invisible, untouchable.
Death is my storm
My enemy is grass
Bent beneath my steel!"

Shield on his forearm, he struck his flint across his weapon. Red and yellow sparks leaped joyously over the incoming army.

Ona drew her own sparks, screaming a chant, her skin feeling like it was on fire.

"Wake iron, wake!
Deliver those who've shed the blood of my kin,
Throw their bodies at my feet,

Their heads rolling at my heel,
Let the blood in me rise to avenge my loves!"

Sparks burned her hands, but no pain bit her as she swung steel and sliced through an Invader's throat. Blood painted Ona's blade, brought it to life as it lit up to match the light under her skin, the fire in her heart.

Her aunt's round face flashed through her mind, stopping her heart. In the memory, her aunt turned away. The image faded.

Ona sucked a breath of sandy, copper-and-horse-and-sweat scented air and kicked heels into her mount, driving the gelding toward Lucca. He struggled against a group of three huge men. He was keeping them at bay, his horse's hooves dancing, his blade clanging off one sword, then another, a shield, then another.

"Wake iron!
Help me leap like the sparks from your flint!
I fly like fire in the wind!"

She drew her feet under her as the horse kept on, then she jumped.

The world seemed to still as she rolled her left shoulder back and drew an invisible arch with her blade, using her legs to shift her weight, and slashed steel across the neck of one of Lucca's attackers.

The man beside him roared, leaving Lucca, and thrust his sword at Ona. He screamed and moaned in that sick combination of sound only Invaders could make, like they hated war but loved it too. Ona dodged his strike and cut his leg, her arm jarring as steel hit bone. The pale man fell, face twisted, and she thought of those addicted to the gray plant. That's what it was. Invaders were addicted to bloodshed, to killing.

Ona stepped back, pausing in the chaos.

Was she being merciful by ending their lives? She wanted nothing to do with mercy.

Shoving her battle-fevered questions away, shutting out any thought that led to not killing Invaders, she drove into the fight. But there were so many of them. As she took down three more, the wave of attackers pushed forward. More swamped the walls, falling into the battle with fresh arms and steel begging to be wetted with Empire blood.

She found Lucca and he glanced at her, his sword still working.

We're going to fall.

The Invaders would win. They'd take all. They'd live on to laugh and have families and breathe fresh air. They'd live on while Ona's aunt stayed dead. They'd live on while Ona died under their boots.

A guttural scream clawed its way out of her mouth. Lucca's lips parted.

Shaking overtook her sword arm and she dropped her weapon. Her scream matched the Invaders.

No. No. No.

She couldn't *understand* them, their love-hate feeling for battle. Never. She couldn't be *like* them. Ona had thought she'd seen her worst day in this uncommon world already. But this, this was the worst.

"To me!" a bright voice called out in the desert tongue. "Rise, Akhayma, and fight!"

Ona grabbed her sword. As she fought a bear of a man, she strained to see who was shouting.

The Empire warriors called out and surged forward, renewed by whomever this was.

A tall figure in simple trader's clothing rode a stomping, black stallion and sliced his way through Invaders on the edge of the battle. That was no trader. Power practically poured out of the man's vicious gaze. Whoever it was, she wanted to meet him. If they lived through this.

Arms aching, Ona brought another enemy to his knees, then looked around. All the Invaders were either dead, scrambling back over the walls amid arrows flying, or held by Empire fighters.

The Empire, Lucca and Ona too, had won.

It was over.

The tall figure who'd rallied everyone raised his yatagan high. "I salute you, Akhayma warriors. And I, High General Varol, invite you to feast with me tonight!"

Varol. Meric's younger brother.

Lucca turned to face her, blood coloring his chin. He didn't need to look at Ona like that. She already knew this was going to make announcing Meric's death and claiming it'd just happened a lot more dangerous. But Varol had saved them. The Invaders would've won if he hadn't showed up. How had he snuck into the city?

Bumped by other injured, battered fighters, Ona found herself following Varol's steed out of the carnage and toward Seren's force at the front gates. Varol gestured widely, taking up space. He was tall, but it wasn't his height that made him *larger* than everyone else. It was the way he moved. How he commanded. Questioned. Demanded. She stared as he doled out orders about prisoners and securing the front gates and sending warriors out of the city to follow the retreat and make certain it was genuine.

Lucca trotted up. "Seren has her work cut out for her now," he whispered, keeping an eye on Varol who had maneuvered his horse back a little to speak with Adem.

Ona tried to concentrate on his words, but she was still buzzing from the battle. He'd cleaned his face. She hadn't. She wore Invader blood like a testament to how much she'd loved her aunt and how much she hated the Invaders. Part of an old Silvanian poem flitted through her mind. *With battle, with blood, she painted her love for the lost.*

"Ona? Are you listening?" Lucca leaned into her face. "You all right?"

"I'm fine. So Varol is here. That might be a problem."

Annoyance flickered over his face. "She has to announce the death before Varol even gets back to the main tent. It'll look suspicious regardless, but if he finds his brother's body, it's all over."

Seren's force streamed away from the front gates. Kaftan sleeves billowing around her, she shouted an order to give the prisoners water, then take them to the cells.

"Water," Ona scoffed. "She should kill them all." A bitter taste sat on her tongue. "Why is she keeping them? Does she enjoy torture? I could try that idea on, but she doesn't seem the type."

Lucca crouched and drew his sword across a little mound of sand gathered against a lotus tower. Some of the blood came off the glinting metal. He sheathed it and glanced behind them. "I guess she has a strategy."

"They'll turn on her the second they get the chance."

"She won't give them the chance."

"Won't she? I've seen the bleeding heart inside her. I like her—don't give me that look—but she seems the type to forgive too easily."

"You think anyone who forgives at all does it too easily," Lucca said.

"No, I don't."

"You do."

Ona gritted her teeth. "You're wrong."

"All right. Maybe, *maybe*, you'd forgive someone on your deathbed. Never a moment before."

"What's the problem with that? You can't forgive them when they still have the opportunity to hurt you again."

Lucca squeezed his eyes shut and shook his head. "We need to find you a tutor."

She nudged her horse into his, nearly bumping him from his seat and knocking him into Nuh, who walked beside them. Lucca nodded toward Ona to show Nuh who to blame. Nuh gave a tired smile.

"I don't need a tutor, idiot," Ona snapped.

"You don't understand the meanings of some words," Lucca said, using his older brother voice. "Like forgiveness."

"Do you grip the meaning of this?" She flared her fingers at her forehead, making Nuh suck a breath.

He cupped her hand, ruining her beautifully rendered obscene gesture.

"Give Seren a chance," he whispered. He said her name like a strange chant made stronger through whispering.

"She was actually going to ransom the king." Ona hadn't realized how mad she was until now. Fighting had pushed all that away for the last three hours.

"For peace. To avoid a siege. Don't pretend you knew what they were up to."

Ona's normally loud and perfectly functioning mouth jumbled into a mess of anger and tight lips.

Seren had lost her pretty head if she thought Ona would sit idly by while she actually ransomed the king. Ona had thought it was Seren's ruse to gain silver. A ruse gone bad when the Invaders showed how much they valued an agreement with the Empire. Ona bumped her fist against her thigh as she stormed away from Nuh and Lucca. Seren had tried to release the king! Seren making deals with Invaders was like watching a mouse fight a rattlesnake. Bad idea, mouse. If Seren wanted to win against snakes, she had to become a snake. Ruthless. Unforgiving. Striking first, not waiting for peace.

Ona had to talk to Seren, to make her see sense. The king had to die. He was the head of that army and the head had to be severed. There was no making peace with Invaders. How could she even think it? She'd come so far—getting over that dead husband of hers, claiming the title of *kyros*, showing Adem what she'd put up with and what she wouldn't. Why give all that up and go soft? She'd end up as a meal and the rest of Akhayma as a side dish.

16

SEREN

Varol was here. Chilled to her core, Seren drove Fig back toward the Kyros Walls. She needed to meet with the kaptans, but before that, she had to do something about Meric. Varol's sharp silhouette rode ahead of her, dark and slim. With Hossam at her side, astride a black gelding, she set a hand on Fig's neck, soaking in the familiar warmth. If Varol made it back to the main tent and found Meric's body, it would be difficult indeed to explain everything—*to lie* about everything— before he ordered her death. She couldn't imagine him listening patiently. Definitely not.

Ahead, warriors on horseback and on foot, kaftans torn and voices rough, moved through the city, following Varol like he was the star in the sky that could lead them home. One man handed Varol a skin of water. Varol tipped it high, drinking all without a thought to the thirsty, dust-coated fighter he'd taken it from.

"Kyros Seren, I congratulate you on your win." Kaptan Rashiel bowed from his saddle, his hair falling over a bruised cheek.

"Thank you, Kaptan Rashiel."

"I can't wait to hear how High-General Varol managed to sneak into the city."

"Me either." Seren tried and failed to keep the worry out of her words.

Hossam made a noise that said he felt a similar distrust of Varol.

Rashiel gently kicked his horse to get closer. "I am your ears and eyes when you need me, Kyros Seren."

Lucca's voice rode over the crowd, his accent punching through the chaos. "Kyros Seren! I will make sure no one disturbs this hard-won reprieve." Skin subtly glowing from the fight, from his chanting, he cut his eyes right, over the crowd and toward the tent where Meric lay. Reluctantly, she followed his gaze, then nodded.

"Hossam, a little help?" she said.

"Clear the way for your kyros, please!" Hossam raised his fist and urged his mount onward.

Slowly, too slowly, Seren and Rashiel took up Hossam's wake and sailed through the merchants injured in the fighting they hadn't been trained for, the mothers who'd taken the strike of an Invaders' shield to defend their families, and the exhausted warriors.

Inside the Kyros Walls, Lucca disappeared into the main tent with Nuh at his side to check on the rotating guards, to see that nothing was amiss. Lucca knew as well as she did that something must be done now. This very moment. Seren hurried to dismount, handing Fig off to a stable boy. Rashiel held the heavy doorflap open for Seren. Varol wasn't beside the high table. He wasn't standing at the Holy Fire bowl. He wasn't here at all. Good.

Seren stopped to pray at the Holy Fire bowl as Nuh spoke to Lucca at the door to Seren's chambers.

She needed help with two things.

Spinning the tale of Meric's death and thinking up a way to finally defeat the Invaders. They would set up a siege. It was only a matter of hours before that horrible white tent went up in the plains beyond the city walls. There'd been so many of them. There would be more.

The Holy Fire bowl burned bright and promising. Flames brushed Seren's palm as she prayed silently about Meric, about everything.

I need a strategy to fight the Invaders, to defeat them without losing all of my army. I can't sacrifice every warrior. Then, I'd only rule a city of the dead.

There'd be no Fire Ceremony with hope and happy faces, no Age Day rituals, no weaving in groups as people told stories and sang songs. It would be a city of mourning. A city without enough hands to keep it from disappearing into the unforgiving sands of the Emptiness.

Pale shapes flickered in Seren's mind.

Clouds?

She squeezed her eyes tight and focused on them, trying to *see* them more clearly. They disappeared into darkness. Seren stepped away from the bowl and put her head in her hands, her fingers still warm from the Fire. Why couldn't she see anything that made sense?

She'd have to come back later. Varol could arrive any second.

449

Leaving Rashiel to his own prayers, she hurried toward Lucca and Nuh.

The men bowed and held up their palms. Nuh hefted a spear from the corner and took up his stance on the opposite side of the doorframe. Lucca's skin was its normal olive tone again. Seren fought the urge to touch the blood on his chin, to make sure it wasn't his. She put her hand on her dagger's hilt instead.

"Is Ona all right?"

His mouth pinched a little, but he said, "She's fine. Now, what can we do?"

"Just be here."

"Always."

His dark eyes, the piney scent he carried, his devotion—Seren suddenly felt empty. The muscles in her legs, stomach, and arms tensed, like they were ready to close the distance between Lucca and her. She wanted to enjoy the fullness she knew she'd feel in his arms.

Blinking the ridiculous feeling away, she pushed into her chambers. Her mind buzzed with the horror of battle, Varol's arrival, Adem's mercurial support, the pull she'd felt toward Lucca, the pained look that crossed his face when she asked about Ona, and this—Meric's body on the bed. Ka'ud smoke swirling around her head, she turned quickly and simply stood at the closed door, staring into the stripes of wool instead of at the wrapped corpse in the room. She took a deep, slow breath, tasting sweet-dark ka'ud.

I can do this. For my people, because I've been called, I can do this.

At the back entrance, she spoke to the other guards. "I need rest. See that no one disturbs me, please."

Both men nodded. "Of course, Kyros Seren."

Varol wouldn't barge in. She had given herself a little time. Hopefully.

The door opened and Seren's heart reared. But it was only Meekra. "Let's clean you up, my lady."

Seren trailed her into the side chamber, both of them knowing they didn't want to remain in the same room as Meric's body. Meekra poured a bowl of water, dipped a cloth, and motioned for Seren to sit on her stool. Seren closed her eyes as Meekra wiped blood from her cheeks and neck. She brushed her hair out, humming a melancholy tune that made Seren want to cry. But she was too overwhelmed to cry. Worries and dark images of the long, long day flitted through her mind like bats. She lay on the bed in Meekra's chamber for a while, not sleeping, as all that had happened washed over her. Varol wouldn't stay away forever. He'd be here soon and she had to figure out how to handle it.

~

DRESSED in an emerald kaftan decorated with silver buttons the shape of phoenix eyes, a pair of lime green pantaloons tied tight at the ankle, and an orange sash—clothing she hardly remembered putting on—Seren pushed her chamber door open and returned to the main tent.

Lucca was there, talking quietly to Nuh. Both had cleaned themselves of blood and dirt, but dark circles under their eyes said neither had rested. Lucca's gaze found her and her heart jolted at the concern in them. He blinked and a wrinkle flashed between his thick eyebrows as he touched his full, bottom lip with a knuckle like he was thinking. Cansu and Hossam had returned, and everyone bowed to Seren. The atmosphere in the tent was like the brief time between thunder and lightning as Seren stood beside the high table and tried to think of what to say, what to do, how to act like the leader the Empire needed.

The main tent's door opened. The bleeding dawn brought in Varol and Adem, who walked side-by-side toward the high table—lithe Varol, in his prime, with smooth skin and a cobra's stare, and weathered Adem with his cold, calculating gaze that measured Seren, sizing her up. Seren's bones felt brittle and weak. She had to be strong, to believe she was strong. Imagining the Holy Fire, she called up the memory of that first vision. Her mind showed her Meric in the pale ivory death shroud and the storm churning beyond the city walls. Her hands fisted, nails cutting into her sweating palms.

She had to do this. It couldn't wait any longer.

One more breath as the two men in her way stared her down, advancing, nearing, closer, closer.

"Kyros Meric is dead," she said.

Varol took three decisive steps, raised a hand like he was going to hit her, then froze. "How?"

Her guards put hands to their hilts, but she stayed them with a look.

Adem simmered behind Varol, the early sun oozing through the tent and over his studded vest and graying hair. If he didn't suspect anything, he wouldn't have looked so angry. He would've been shocked, saddened. But she had to plow through, keep to the plan.

The ka'ud burned her nose, the scent like fingers scratching at her eyes. "The cough that always bothered Kyros Meric grew worse." She focused on Varol. "He developed a fever. I'm sure you've heard this from General Adem."

Mixing truth with a lie helped it soak into its audience. Seren hated herself for knowing that, for using what she'd learned at Father's side as he dealt with politicians and back-stabbers. Father had never been dishonest. It was one of the reasons he'd been practically forced into early retirement.

"He has been very ill since then," she said. Lucca's gaze warmed Seren like a touch. She wished Ona was there too, ferocity shining in her face. Seren needed more of that fierce demeanor to rule here. "His life flickered to dark just as we had word of the Invaders arriving. Then there was the attack...I wrapped him myself so his body would be clean for his funeral."

Hands shaking, her gaze flicked to Adem. If she could talk him into believing her version of the timing of Meric's death, he would lead Varol her way. But only anger colored Adem's features. Was he really so sure she was lying or was she misinterpreting all of this?

Varol inhaled sharply, tugging her attention to him. Rage tore at his sharp features, distorting them so she couldn't tell what made him angry. Did he know she was lying? Or was he furious that he'd been denied saying farewell to his brother? Or was he grieving?

As one, Varol and Adem practically pushed past Seren—not touching, but oh so close—beyond the rotating guards, and into the sleeping quarters. Seren began to follow, heart clicking like a beetle on its back.

Lucca caught her arm. His fingers dropped away quickly, but his gaze stayed on her. "Should we come in with you?" He glanced at her guards.

Seren had to handle this without looking guilty. "No. But thank you."

Lucca's mouth tucked into a grim half-smile as she pushed the chamber's flaps open, riding Adem's heels.

Meekra, quiet and steady, slipped in too, and stood at the back entrance of the inner chamber. The lotus pillar partially shadowed her face from the flickering oil lamps.

Ka'ud smoke billowed around Varol and Adem as they bent to examine Meric's wrapped body. Meric looked like a grotesquely large doll, nothing like a person. No humming presence came from him anymore. His spirit was tightly bound inside that shell of a man. He had to be burned soon so his essence could rise to the heavens.

Varol hovered over his brother's covered face and tensed. His hand went to the bed's edge, long fingers clutching at the silver-tasseled hem. Seren thought Varol might fall to his knees, grief shoving him down, but he straightened and turned. Chewing the inside of his cheek, he dragged his gaze over Seren's face. The unspoken accusation was there, visible as the hooked nose on his face.

Seren found she was suddenly very angry. She wanted to snap at him, to tell him that he had no right to look at her like that. She'd supported Meric. His death wasn't her fault. Sure, she'd woven lies around the tragedy, altered outcomes to suit her goal. But her goal was only to insure the safety of the Empire, to rise to the Holy Fire's call. She needed to say all of this, but the words wouldn't wake up. They slept inside her, quiet as the dead. Again, she wished for Ona's fiery determination, blazing courage, powerful voice. The same courage Seren's parents had both possessed in bulk.

As her heart hammered away, chiseling at her ability to stand there and act as the person the Fire had called her to be, Adem pressed a finger to Meric's throat, feeling for a pulse. He jerked his hand back, his fingers splayed. "He is gone, High General Varol. He has been for a long while."

Had he thought she'd wrap a sick man and bury him alive while his mind slept? Fire, no one could be that horrible. She swallowed, her stomach twisting. "Perhaps the funeral should take place—"

Varol lifted a hand and curled his fingers into a fist. "The funeral will be as I order it."

Adem stepped away from the bed and raised his fist to Varol. "May the Holy Fire welcome your brother." He turned to Seren, his eyes cold as the black ice that lined the roads to the ports of the north. "May the Holy Fire welcome your husband."

Varol was trembling. Sweat shone on his face. He picked up a glass pitcher from the side table. He threw it at Meekra. It burst against the pillar beside her. She screamed, covering her face.

Mouth dropping open, all nerves forgotten, Seren ran to Meekra.

Varol and Adem strode out of the tent, not a thought given to Varol's behavior.

A shard had stuck in Meekra's cheek and Seren gently plucked it free, fingers trembling in the hot anger running through her. Blood welled and trickled down Meekra's face.

"It'll be all right," Meekra whispered, taking a slip of dark cloth from her sash and pressing it against the cut. "I'm all right. But…" Her wise, brown eyes pleaded with Seren. "He is as awful as he's always been."

And Seren knew what Meekra meant. That Seren had to keep hold of her reign here and drive Varol out of the Empire.

"He is no good for our people," Seren hissed, ears ringing from the crash and from her own anger.

She helped Meekra gather the broken pieces, ignoring her tuts of disapproval.

Rage-filled tears leaked out of Seren's eyes. She rubbed the hot flecks of salty water away and set the last of the shattered pitcher on the table. These weren't tears for Meric, but they'd give her story the look of truth. These tears were for her people and the tangled leadership they'd have to deal with. And all of this during a siege.

Seren had no idea what to do.

17

SEREN

At the funeral on the training field, Seren's people gathered into an enormous circle and hummed, a pulsing noise deep in their throats. Adem, Cansu, Erol, and Hossam lifted Meric's wrapped body up the ladder set against the pyre's thick stilts and settled it on the lahabshjara leaves and striped pillows. Tongues of Flame glittered like amber in sunlight around the ivory linen encasing Meric's thin arms and legs. Tails of silk, a different color for each of the Empire's noble clans, flickered in the breeze beneath the pyre, slowly beginning to smoke. Chieftains removed their yatagans from their sashes and set them, hilt first, on the ground around the pyre tower. Though Meric had never set foot on a battleground, as kyros and leader of the army, he would receive a warrior's funeral.

The women of the high-caste—many who'd never accepted Seren because of how she talked to the low and middle-caste as equals—gathered into a smaller circle within the larger one. They took up the prepared buckets of oasis water. A few gave Seren kind, sad looks. Perhaps Seren's part in defending the city had won them over.

"May the Fire bless you, Chosen," one of snobby Qadira's friends whispered, her face clean of any judgment. She seemed sincere.

Seren dipped her head in thanks and clutched the handle of her own bucket.

The water sloshed as the women took the traditional three steps, nine, three, pausing appropriately to say a quiet prayer as they continued toward the pyre's base. They joined in on the humming with the rest of the city's inhabitants.

Seren raised the proper notes in the back of her throat, enjoying the feel of being a part of her people's ritual. The humming filled her, calmed her, and strengthened her legs so she could keep on. As one, the women stopped. They poured the clean water into the dusty ground, watering the tiny purple flowers that grew there, and protecting the city from fire.

Varol, as a blood relative, received the lit torch of lahabshjara branches and began his brother's ascent to the next life. More ka'ud burned around Meric's body. Only a kyros's funeral could demand such a rare sacrifice. The flames leaped and strained toward the sun, the blue smoke like a great hand raising Meric up and up and up.

Seren had never loved him, but the thought of never seeing him again strangely cut her heart. She was glad for the moment when the rest of the city came close, tucking in together.

Ona came up, her hands clasped in front of her. Seren couldn't tell whether Ona was ready to embrace her or run her through.

Meekra approached too, but she gave Seren and Ona space to whisper, her own eyes on the pyre and a chaotic look of anger and sadness on her face.

"Death is a thief," Ona said very quietly. "It doesn't ask permission. It always makes me feel cheated." Her nostrils flared as she stared at the ground.

Seren set her bucket at her feet and linked an arm around Ona's, nervous about the gesture of closeness, but wanting it enough to risk making an idiot of herself. Seren hoped this new friend's courage would burn into her own flesh. "I hope you weren't injured badly during the battle."

"I'm fine. But...we should talk." Ona toyed with the hilt of her sword. Seren had never seen her nervous.

Varol blew the ram's horn, sounding his grief to the world and making Seren's soul shiver. With Adem at his side, Varol then tucked the horn under his arm and began to climb the earthen stairs to the hill that sat above the field, on eye-level with the pyre itself. Seren's heart stilled. His pale brown mourning kaftan, a match to everyone's clothing, whipped in the wind and made him look like a simple nomad, heading to his flock of goats.

"What's he doing?" Ona followed as Seren and Meekra walked toward the hill.

That was exactly the question battering Seren's mind. She shrugged, and Ona broke away to join Lucca at the base of the small slope.

Varol cut a proud shape on the rise as he lifted his hands. His voice carried and an ugly feeling crawled through Seren, like he was infecting her people.

"People of Akhayma," he shouted. "I feel your grief along with my own. Our dear kyros has left this world."

Smoothing her hair, Seren took a place beside Varol while Ona and Lucca joined Rashiel, Adem, and the other kaptans to the right.

"Kyros Meric has been taken too soon." Varol turned his head slowly and looked at Seren. He wanted to see if she would fight him for a place here, for the right to speak during this holy time. And she must. She didn't necessarily need to outdo him right now, not at this solemn moment, but she did have to keep him from announcing a full mourning. She had to hold on to her title, her rank.

Shaking, she stepped forward. "We'll continue our mourning, as is tradition, for two more days. But we'll only dress in our earth-colored clothing and say our prayers over our Fires." To Varol's right, Adem stiffened. "We must be ready to fight again. Kyros Meric would've wanted us to protect ourselves, not weaken our bodies with lack of water and sustenance."

That was a lie. Meric would've wanted all to die along with him. He would've seen it as unfair that anyone live past his death.

Varol looked at the ground and nodded. Relief cooled Seren like a breeze.

Whispering and comforting one another with touches and hugs that Seren was painfully jealous of, the people went to the pyre and began their group prayers. Their voices rose with the smoke. It was sad, but also lovely.

Adem seemed to shake himself. He slipped behind Varol and ripped his helmet off, his hair rumpled. "Pearl of the Desert. We must observe the proper mourning duties or Meric won't be accepted into the Fire's afterlife." His eyes were fire, and she was very afraid of being the next to burn.

But Varol joined her as she stared Adem down. For once, she and Varol were on the same side.

Seren opened her mouth, but Varol talked over her. "My brother's soul is beyond reproach. Nothing we do could keep his soul from crossing over."

"General Adem," Seren said, "we can't let our people fast and grow weak staying up all hours to hum and mourn."

She touched the green wool, her fingers shaking as Varol's eyes pierced her resolve and left her bleeding doubt. Did he support her in this or not? The man was as unpredictable as a storm in the Emptiness.

"The general and I will handle this, Pearl of the Desert," Varol said.

They weren't calling her *kyros*. The Holy Fire's vision had shown her the city's only chance at defeating the Invaders was with her at the lead. It seemed arrogant. The role was too big. But the Fire had called and she had to answer.

Down the way, Ona argued with a man twice her size. Beside her, Lucca shook his head and his lips moved, saying something that was probably wry and wise in equal measure. Barir whispered with Meekra, their steady gaze on Seren. Meekra's cut was visible from here.

Seren straightened her back. "You mean *Kyros Seren*, don't you?"

"You should join the others." Varol smiled, sickeningly sweet. "Soon enough, you may return to the Green Mountains to retire like your father."

Her throat burned, words pushing at her tongue but too weak to rise. She couldn't leave here. The Holy Fire had blessed her with ideas. She was meant to care for the Empire, not to molder in a far-away town.

"You'll have a quiet life as a former kyros's wife should." He turned away, dismissing her, and addressed the people, breaking their mourning sounds apart.

"As next in line," he shouted, spreading his arms wide, "I humbly accept the role of kyros and will do everything in my power to protect you, to honor my brother's memory."

Meekra and Barir's mouths dropped open. Down the line of kaptans, Ona frowned at Seren. Lucca cocked his head and took a step like he wanted to join Seren. She didn't know whether to ask them to come forward or not.

Small groups, who managed to hear over the pyre and the distance, wore confused looks. Several fell to their knees to show respect. The rest realized what was happening and kneeled alongside their neighbors. Questions showed in the way they moved and leaned close to whisper. This wasn't the way things were done. None of it.

Seren's guards were still and too quiet at her sides. Cansu's eyebrows had shot together, pensive and seemingly frustrated, but not really surprised. Did they know this was going to happen? Surely not. They were loyal. She was awful for even thinking it. Cansu looked at Erol. Erol's eyes were angry. Hossam's chest rose and fell too quickly. So they hadn't known. They were still loyal.

One couple in the crowd below the rise noticed Seren and held up their palms distinctly turned toward her instead of Varol. He didn't seem to notice.

Another family held their palms toward Seren, and another, another. Their concern tugged at her heart. She grabbed the front of her mourning kaftan, a deep pain slugging through her chest. Her people were supporting her, asking for her support in return. She couldn't let Varol take them from her. They were all she had left. They were her family.

Varol and Adem started back toward the city and the crowd dispersed as she and her guards, Meekra too, left the pyre. Lucca and Ona quickly found her side.

"What are you going to do?" Lucca whispered. "Shouldn't you speak out against him?"

Ona bumped him out of the way. Her foreign eyes were wide and she almost looked fevered. "You aren't going to keep that king alive, are you?" Her sheath clicked against her belt's buckle. She was a ball of energy. Dangerous energy. "Will Varol put him to death? You know the Invaders will begin a siege any minute, right?"

Seren had to think of a smart way—not some tantrum-throwing or power-hungry way—to remind her people that she was kyros here and she cared for them first. Unlike Varol. Akhayma was tired. And hungry. Emotionally exhausted. What did she want right now? What did her body need? Food. Simple food and the knowledge that someone cared.

Seren stopped and Hossam nearly ran her over, mumbling embarrassed apologies through his beard.

"Wait," she said. "Cansu, Erol, Hossam, spread word that Kyros Seren will host a simple meal for the people inside the Kyros Walls. When the sun is high."

Lucca grinned, taking some of the chill out of Seren. "This is a great idea."

"But what about the prisoners? The king?" Ona snapped.

"I'll deal with all that later. First, I must gain control again and comfort my people."

"There's no sun for comfort, my kyros." An ugly tone tarnished Ona's pronunciation of Seren's title. She stormed away. Seren reluctantly let her go.

Lucca touched Seren's arm briefly. "I'll talk to her."

"Thank you."

A smile surprised Seren as it crossed her mouth. This was good. This might work. She gave details to Meekra and messages for Erol to deliver to the high-castes, organizing, not a feast, but a coming-together, a humble way for the people to draw together under her wings.

∼

SEREN SETTLED at the head table the house servants had placed in front of the main tent. The sun glinted off platters of chicken kabobs and bowls of flatbread and nuts.

Lucca walked over and refreshed Seren's hot tea even though a gruff house servant argued against him doing that sort of work.

"May the Holy Fire continue to bless you, Chosen One," a tiny woman wearing a striped, brown mourning kaftan said.

Seren handed the woman a piece of flatbread piled with meat for the little ones jumping at her elbows. "May the Fire bless us all. We're going to need it."

The crowd split and Adem marched through, a circle of kaptans and two ore masters around him.

Father once gave Seren some advice when a group of girls were being particularly mean during their small group tutoring: Treat your enemy as your friend and watch them fall into the role. When Seren had invited the girl who told lies about her to a special Age Day party, she'd ended up telling Seren she was only jealous of her looks. They'd never become friends exactly—Seren couldn't trust her—but at least the gossip had stopped.

"Another shout for our brave General Adem, who helped defend our city at our most desperate hour," she said over the multitude of conversations.

Everyone turned toward Adem. Watching Seren curiously, they stomped their feet and raised their fists. "Our general!"

He bowed his head respectfully to Seren, but he didn't stay. He moved quickly into the main tent, his circle trailing him. Through the open flaps of the tent's door, Seren watched him sit at his usual spot at the high table inside. A red silk scarf hanging from a lantern fluttered between them, so only half his face—furrowed brow, angry eyes—showed.

She had to get a read on the man, to manage a guess on what he and Varol were planning.

"Meekra."

Her friend came forward and offered a plate to Seren, who took it and whispered, "I want to send a bowl of clean water to the general. And another portion of this meat." Seren leaned closer. "Have you heard anything about Varol?"

"He was seen going into his tent with two women. I think he is…taking some time for himself." Meekra rolled her eyes.

"I'm thankful for it. His absence allows me to gain a hold on the city again." Seren glanced over her shoulder toward Adem. "When you take the provisions to Adem, see if you can hear anything his friends there are saying."

Nodding, Meekra hurried off and pasted a humble smile onto her pretty face. Seren had a guess that simple beauty could glean more than any unit of armed torturers, but she knew she'd have to play the latter role soon with the prisoners.

Seren would have to find out troop counts. Mounted versus on foot. Information on the Invaders' food supplies and their wounded.

Facing the crowd, Seren raised her voice. "From the Fire that burns within my heart and around my thoughts, I thank you all for your sacrifice and dedication. We've suffered a terrible loss, losing our Kyros Meric, but at least we have a victory to temper our grief. Lucca Hand of Ruination and Onaratta Paints with Blood, we owe you a heavy debt. You fought as if your own people hung in the balance, and you spearheaded the last push that drove the Invaders from our city!"

Ona wasn't in the crowd, though Seren pretended she was. She was most likely sleeping somewhere. A well-deserved rest.

Lucca, showing nothing more than a ripped sleeve and a swollen sword hand, grinned and tilted his chin down humbly, raising one fist to his chest in acknowledgment of the cheers and well wishes.

With happy shouts ringing, she closed her eyes to think of Meric. She didn't miss him, but this should've been his moment. And that was a tragedy.

"Erol, Cansu, Hossam." The men turned to face her. "I need to go to the parapet and see what the Invaders are doing."

She should've had reports from the scouts already. Maybe they were reporting to Varol.

Would Varol openly rise up against her as she fought for her title? Or would he continue to be absent like he was now?

"Lucca, would you go with me? I'd like a mercenary's view on this. You've seen fighting styles that my father probably never experienced."

"I doubt I'll be much help, but of course, I'll go. So," he whispered, "what are you going to do about Varol?"

"Ignore him and carry on."

"You think that's safe?"

"Nothing is safe. He probably believes I had a hand in Meric's death. He'll be furious when he hears of the food I gave out and my speech, the way I'm clinging to my role here. But he has yet to show his face, so perhaps he only wanted a title and not the trouble that goes with it."

"From your mouth to the sky's ears."

"Where is Ona?"

"I'm guessing she is in our tent, fuming."

"Fuming? What is she angry about?" Seren kept her voice down as they passed two converging canals. Water splashed under the cover of the tents, sounding like a crowd whispering.

"That you didn't kill the king. That you're keeping prisoners alive. You shouldn't trouble yourself with what one mercenary thinks but—"

"But there could be more who share her anger. And now Varol is here to happily take on disgruntled warriors to fight me."

"Exactly."

"I'll have to execute the king eventually. I can't say I'll be very mournful about it. But I have to wait and see what makes the most sense strategically. There could be uses for him that we haven't yet thought of. Kaptan Rashiel agrees."

"Maybe you could listen to what Ona has to say? Maybe it'll give you some insight on possible outcomes?"

"I agree."

Lucca watched the road, eyes wary, his body close to hers. Nothing in his face said he judged her incompetent. He simply stood by her and helped when she seemed to need it most. Her heart glowed warmer and warmer as they walked on.

"I thank the Holy Fire I met you, Lucca."

He blinked, then smiled. "I hope you don't regret that after all this is through. I should probably stay away from you completely, considering."

"Don't you dare. Anyone who tries to take you from my side will suffer severe consequences."

Lucca's eyes shone. "Your wishes are my wishes, Kyros Seren."

"Is that a Silvanian saying?"

"It's a Lucca and Ona saying. Ona always follows it with *As long as yours don't war with mine.*"

"Yes. That sounds like her."

Seren hoped she could help Ona understand the need to be careful with their prisoners and not act rashly. Ona would be the worst kind of enemy. Seren would have to make time to listen to her, to explain too. But that would have to wait until she had a firm grip on what this siege looked like. Seren wanted to see the battlefield with her own eyes.

Qadira's father, leader of Clan Azjorr stopped near Seren, bowed low, and raised a palm—more than necessary for a casual public appearance. "Kyros Seren, we support you in full."

Qadira herself, and her younger sister and mother, joined him. They bowed too, but Qadira sneered, giving Seren a pretty clear picture of what she really thought about this unplanned display of support.

"I appreciate your words, Azjorr," Seren said to the chieftain, nodding to both husband and wife.

The wife smiled sadly. "Kyros Seren, we are your people."

"Please," the chieftain said. "Please claim your place."

An ore master, possibly one Adem had been whispering with lately, came around the corner. He walked behind them, not even noticing Seren's presence.

Lucca tensed.

Seren turned to the family. "Please be careful."

Qadira twisted to see who Seren was looking at before Seren and her retinue continued on.

So Azjorr would support her against Varol. But to keep her place, she'd have to think up a way to win against the coming siege to prove she was meant to be the Empire's kyros, its protector and caretaker, its leader blessed by the Fire. If only she could figure out what the Fire had shown her. What had those cloud-like objects been? She needed to talk to some engineers or inventors. She needed fresh ideas from afar.

Something Seren couldn't name gnawed at her as they started through the market and toward the front gates. Something was wrong. Very wrong.

The merchants weren't shouting about their spices, bags, or shoes. A snaggletoothed boy and twin girls each carried a ball around the bubbling shallows of the canals that branched away from the sacred bowl and pool. Normally, they'd be kicking them, racing to see who could get their ball to the city walls first. Even with the mourning, children were children. The animals were acting strangely too. Camels, donkeys, and goats munched and shuffled too quietly, subdued.

She stopped. Turning to Erol, a cold sweat rose along her back. "The tent is raised, isn't it?"

A weathered scout coated in dirt and wrinkles ran up and bowed hurriedly. "My kyros. You must see this." Three more scouts, young like Seren, came up behind the more experienced man. They looked like they'd seen ghosts. Or thought they'd soon be ghosts themselves.

Rushing toward the front gates, Lucca nimble beside her, passing wide-eyed faces and too-quiet rows of black-striped tents, Seren said one prayer, a thousand prayers.

Two large men, steel blinking at their sashes, appeared on the path. Dust rose around them like dark wings.

Seren stopped, turned, then rounded a corner, her men with her and the scouts trailing.

"Are they following us?" she asked Hossam. Her heart stuttered, then began to beat too quickly.

Cansu looked over his shoulder as they hurried on, heading down a different route. "I think so, my lady. Do you want me to go after them?"

"No. Just…stay alert."

Hossam nodded and said something quiet to the scouts.

Those two…they had to be Varol's men. Or Adem's. Only the Fire knew what their plans were. To watch her? Or to do something more sinister? This was her life now. Dodging attacks and telling lies.

AT THE TOP of the walls, Seren stared out at the plains and the hammadas behind them. The ground spreading from the city outward weren't dusty and brown anymore. The earth was silver and white and red and gold with more Invaders than sand in the Emptiness.

She gripped the smooth stone to keep from falling. Lucca, the scouts, and her guards grew very still.

In the midst of the warriors, a white tent displayed the Invaders' silent message loud and clear.

"What does the tent mean, Kyros?" Cansu asked.

Seren was fairly certain he knew. He just didn't want to believe the tales. He was hoping she had a better answer than what he feared. What they all feared.

"If Akhayma surrenders today, all will be spared. Tomorrow, the tent will be red, and next, black. The stakes will rise with each day. They have committed to this siege. There's no scaring them off now."

Groups of Invaders pounded their shields with fists, the low thumping echoing up and over the stone barrier. The sound echoed the panicked beating of Seren's heart.

"But you won't surrender, will you, Kyros?" Erol's voice was sharp as a dagger's edge.

"No. And I'll be thrown into the vast sands of the Emptiness before I let

Varol or Adem do it either." She knew what came with surrender. Father had told her those stories too. Mother had never made any songs about those terrible, serious talks. "I'd rather us all die fighting than live to become Invader playthings. Surrendering to an Invader is far, far worse than any death."

18

SEREN

After sending Erol and Cansu to look around and listen for information about Varol and Adem's movements or public statements, Seren, Lucca, and Hossam headed to the guest tent. "It'll be quiet there," she said. "I need to pray."

Inside, Seren paused at the Fire and passed her palm over the orange and blue light, Lucca standing beside her with hands clasped in front of him and Hossam near the door. Seren tried to let go of her worry and stress, to trust in the Flame and the calm solidness of Lucca nearby. She'd hoped to have some space, away from the main tent and everyone else, and this was perfect. The Fire had shown her something earlier and she needed to know what it was and how it could help. The Flames wouldn't have bothered with a vision if it wasn't important. Besides, she didn't have any other ideas on how to deal with the siege and Varol and all.

Spreading her palms wide over the flickering tongues, she pushed that urge to flee or scream or crumble aside firmly. She closed her eyes and eased into the feel of the Holy Fire, the heat running fingertips over her skin. A gray night washed over the darkness behind her eyelids. There were those clouds again. The odd shapes faded, then she saw tiny black puffs of smoke, then a blink of white light in the vision.

Her eyes flashed open. "Black powder?"

Lucca frowned. "Like the easterners use in their cannon?"

Seren twirled her wool scrap around her finger. "We've never used it here because the Invaders don't have access to it. I suppose Akhayma's never needed it."

"How would we use black powder anyway? You don't have any cannon, do you?"

"No. But I don't think the Fire was showing me that anyway." She pressed her fingers against her temples. "Why can't I see it clearly?"

"Would it help to tell me what you think you see?"

His kind eyes warmed her middle. "There are these ivory...clouds. But I'm not sure they're clouds. They're rounded, floating. I...I don't know. Somehow they're connected to the powder. The black puffs came from the bottoms of them, or were around them. I can't see it. I can't." She pressed the heels of her hands against her eyes, an itch building inside her chest. "I can't."

"Don't knock yourself over the head about it. You can only do what you can do. Maybe if you try not to think about it, it'll become clear. That happens with me sometimes. When I focus on something else, the problem untangles in my head. Ignore me if I sound like an idiot. I don't know anything about your Fire or running a war."

She couldn't help but smile. "I'd never ignore you. Even if you weren't a trained mercenary who does indeed know a lot about war, about fighting."

"War isn't simply fighting and you know it."

"But some of the elements are the same."

"How did you learn so much about war, Kyros?" Lucca asked as they walked out of the guest tent and into the last of the day. The orange-red orb bled into strips of clouds like bandages.

"I read all of the military scrolls and books I could get my hands on. My father, the former High-General, encouraged it. We used to talk until late at night, boring Mother to death. When she'd had enough, she poked fun at our serious talk with little songs she made up." A smile drifted over Seren's mouth. If only they were here... "But I still have so much to learn. I don't know why the Fire has chosen me."

"Because of your humility. You're willing to learn and try new things, risking your reputation. I've seen nobles whose egos hogged all the acreage in their big heads."

"I probably need more confidence."

"You have enough to get the job done, Kyros. Listen, if it pleases you, I'll find Ona and try to talk to her again."

"That would be helpful, thank you. I need to question prisoners."

A shudder jarred her, shaking off the warm feeling of talking with

Lucca. Somehow fighting in a battle was less horrible than doing damage to captured enemies.

Lucca almost took her arm to steady her, then he glanced at Hossam and stopped himself. She wished he wouldn't hold himself back. "I can come with you, my lady," he said quietly, words full of respect.

"No. I'll be…" She couldn't say fine. Killing and torture and questioning was the furthest thing from *fine*. "I can handle it."

He gave her a nod before heading away.

She started toward the back gate, under black-winged swallows that dove and spun to catch their prey. Seren's feet knew the way to go and it was a good thing because her mind was occupied with strange pale shapes and blasts of black powder. Someday, she hoped, there wouldn't be as many terrible duties and frightening visions. But today was full of them. She found that invisible armor for her heart and set out to bleed information from her enemies.

"THE KING—HAS he been placed in the larger cell away from his men?" Seren walked under the back gate's arch, Hossam at her right, adjusting his sash and brushing dirt from his uniform.

Erol and Cansu came out of the gate's shadow and into the moonlight. They'd been listening and learning all they could about Varol's movements, his orders, and how Adem was playing into them.

Seren paused, a hand going to her chest. When had she gone from doing everything she could to protect them and keep them out of danger to using them to spy on the men who could have them killed with a word?

"Yes, Kyros Seren," Hossam said, worry etched in the wrinkles around his big eyes.

Seren started walking again. She had to keep going. There was no way to keep these wonderful, loyal guards safe anymore. No one was safe anymore.

"What did you learn, Cansu, Erol?" she asked. "I'm fine, Hossam." She smiled at him to soften her curt words.

Erol and Cansu bowed their heads as they worked to keep up with her increasing pace moving into the training area.

"An ore master and several guildmasters met with High General Varol in his tent, my lady." Erol's jaw tensed. "Two scouts reported to him as well. Not the men who came to us. Those two are in the barracks, resting. They are loyal, it seems. Also, those loyal scouts told us High General Varol entered Akhayma through an abandoned mine. Hearing about the newly accessible mine, the scouts used it to watch the Invaders fall into their siege camp. Looking through an opening in the shaft, the scouts counted the Invader troops."

"Adem cleared the mine for Varol." Seren rubbed her lip, talking to herself.

Cansu looked at the sandy path in front of them, his voice taut. "The Invaders number at 40,000."

An invisible knife touched Seren's throat and she halted again, just for a breath, before continuing on. She'd seen them. She'd known there were a great many. But 40,000. How could they fight that many without losing every man, woman, and child in the city?

Overhead, darkening clouds hovered over the training field, the walls housing the iron ore mines beyond, and the hammadas in the far distance. 40,000 warriors. Akhayma was boxed in, trapped, surrounded and Seren couldn't see a way out.

Cells lined the slope leading away from the training fields. Torches flickered like dying stars, lighting the grounds unevenly and throwing yellow and white beams against the shadows. Seren waved the prison guard forward and the man slipped a mint leaf from his pocket into his mouth, bowing as he hurried. His plum-shaped face was familiar. Ah. Meric had used the man twice to interpret for captured Invader scouts during her first days as his wife. That felt like lifetimes ago.

Hossam took a prisoner from the crowded cells. Perspiration wet the captured man's light brown hair. It clung to his face as Hossam shoved the man's cheek against a stone block. One visible eye turned to look from Seren to Hossam to the interpreter.

"Give me your best guess on what your army will do next." Seren gave the interpreter a minute to do his job. "And we can kill you and be done with it. I've no desire to cause you additional pain."

The prisoner spat at her slippers.

Sick with this duty, Seren stepped back, holding her kaftan away, and shook her head.

"Take another finger then," she said quietly.

Erol raised his yatagan over the stone block as Hossam forced the prisoner's hand into position. Seren's stomach clenched. But this was war, and she'd cut a thousand fingers to save her people from what her family had endured.

The finger came off with a horrid thunk and a soul-ripping shriek not unlike the screams the Invaders released when they killed—full of pain and drive both. Cold sweat beaded on Seren's forehead and upper lip. She bent to look the prisoner in the face.

"Now, will you talk to me?"

He spat on her cheek.

Raising herself up and taking Cansu's offered square of linen, she pronounced the man's sentence. "Run him through, quickly for his courage, but properly for his crimes against our people."

Hossam laid the body in the growing pile they'd haul outside the walls tonight.

The guards brought a new prisoner to the block. An unseen hand pushed Seren closer. This Invader was wiry like Haris—one of the fighters who'd taken to trailing Lucca and Ona—but a much fairer version, with pale eyes and unusually short hair. His fellows called out what sounded like encouragement in their language from behind the cell bars. This one was liked. Could that be what was drawing her to him?

"Will we see the same fate come to you, soldier?" Seren asked. She quieted to let the interpreter do his job.

On his knees, the wiry Invader stared ahead at nothing.

"What job did you do for your king?" she asked and the interpreter spoke quickly.

The Invader turned to the interpreter, then to Seren, surprise and caution twisting his mouth and eyes. "Sword. Shield. Like most."

His eyes said something entirely different. "No." She pointed to his face. "I see intelligence there. A man like your king would see it too. Surely he had more use for you than merely raw fighting. Do you really want to continue supporting that dog of a king only to lose your life?"

"Could I ever have a full life here?" the Invader asked.

When the interpreter finished speaking, Hossam almost dropped his hold on the man.

"Yes…you could," Seren said.

Cansu and Erol traded a look. She gave them one that snapped them back to attention, almost confident for once.

"If you can give me a solid idea about your army's probable next move and aid me with fresh strategies to counter," she said, "you could live in the tented city as a rich man for as long as the Holy Fire wills it."

"I'm an engineer."

"One who makes gears?"

"Yes. And systems. Mechanisms. I don't know if that translates…"

"I understand. Like ways to move water or waste."

"Exactly."

Seren wound the green wool at her sash around a finger and paced. The prisoners behind the engineer had gone quiet.

"What about...black powder?" she asked quietly.

The interpreter stopped, his face wrinkled in confusion. Seren cupped her hands together, then quickly fanned her fingers and spread her arms wide. The engineer's eyes opened wider.

He nodded slowly, swallowing. "But," he said through the interpreter, "you must promise I stay here after. If we create something together."

A dark hope bloomed inside Seren. She leaned in close enough to see the dirt in the pores on his nose. "Before I promise," she whispered, the interpreter at her knee, "tell me why you're willing to do this horrible thing to your people."

"It's this or die, yes?"

"Yes. But you could die...honorably, or so your people would say."

"You know what we do. You've heard the stories?"

Seren fisted her sweating hands. Her sisters' screams seared her memory, so perfectly recalled that her eardrums burned like coals. "I've lived the stories."

The engineer's face tightened. "So you know there is no honor for me to claim. I don't care to suffer for my people. I'm not like them."

The sadness in his voice tugged at Seren's heart. *But he could be lying.* She swallowed her fear. "It is agreed then. I swear on the Holy Fire to protect you for as long as you care to live in Akhayma if you help me win this war."

"I swear on the only one I trust. Myself," the engineer said.

Seren nodded. It was sad, but it seemed an honest oath. "Hossam, bring this prisoner to the mercenaries' tent." She didn't want this plan flashed in front of Adem or Varol. Not yet. Employing an enemy didn't seem like the best way to garner support for her position as kyros. But if this worked...

"Yes, my lady."

"And call for a kaptans' meeting right now. I'll meet with them before Adem can realize I've called them together. I'm surprised he hasn't called another of his own." Too busy meeting secretly in his own tent or Varol's. "Send out the messengers to let everyone know. Lucca too. And Ona." Her cheeks heated, realizing how casually she'd mentioned them, with no titles, in front of her fighters. But she wasn't going to take it back or correct herself. Formality wasn't important in this case. These men knew her well.

"Of course, my lady," they all replied.

Hossam helped the engineer up and started toward Lucca and Ona's lodgings, the place it seemed Seren would always come back to.

19

ONA

G rit clouded each of Ona's steps and coated her scuffed boots and threadbare leggings as she paced from the agricultural section of the city and through another merchant area where a little whip of a boy flung himself at her.

"Kaptans meeting now, Onaratta Paints with Blood!" He tugged at her sleeve and went on in heavily accented trade tongue she could hardly understand. "Kyros Seren has called you there. You must go now."

"Ergh." Ona feared she wouldn't be able to hold her tongue with Seren right now. She was too frustrated with the fact that the king was still alive.

"Now." The boy bounced on his toes, the twelve tin bells on his sash jangling. "You have to go now. Please."

"What are you, ten? Maybe nine years old? What happens if I don't go because I'm kind of irritated, and they find out you told me and failed to get me there?"

He cocked his head as he worked out what she'd said. "No food tonight. Maybe a beating."

"Skies. A beating?" Ona sighed heavily. "I'll go." She shooed him away and he left reluctantly.

She stormed past tables folded against tent posts and half-walls. Families blabbered behind the thick fabric of their homes and shops, some cried over the dead, although not so many had been cut down. Others mourned their worthless, former kyros. Why? Ona couldn't figure it out. Meric had been pretty pointless from what she'd heard.

472

Honestly, she couldn't figure anyone out.

Where was Varol? He was all *I'm here to take over!* then he promptly disappeared. Ona wanted to see him again, to watch the people around him react to his naturally powerful presence. It was intriguing. The man didn't need chants. Must've been that royal blood. She couldn't help but be impressed. So why wasn't he using this power to get this war over with?

And Seren, why was she not murdering the king and dancing on his disgusting body? What reason could there ever be to hold on to a monster like that? The Invaders' white tent said they would only stop their siege with full surrender. There was no turning back now.

"Why doesn't she understand? I thought she understood!" Ona shouted, shattering the night's quiet sounds.

"Kaptan Onaratta!"

The moon did its level best to cut through the suffocating clouds. Light glinted across a smooth brow. A warrior Ona didn't know waved, a helmet on her knee as she scooped a handful of water from the canal with a wooden cup and splashed her neck. "Did you hear the kyros is questioning prisoners? Someone said she is keeping one alive, maybe giving him freedom, to work on strategy. She is wise, isn't she? Is your leader as wise?"

Ona's chest caved in. First, the king. Now this? That was it. She had to talk to Seren in private. She could explain everything in terms she'd understand.

"Well, Kaptan, what do you think?" the fighter asked.

"What do *you* think I think about it? And what business is it of yours?"

"Our Kyros Seren certainly weaves a different pattern than Kyros Meric ever did. Fine work during the attack," she said, droning on and on—utterly blind to Ona's glare.

Ona started down the main roadway to the market, her ribs strangling her heart. Seren was freeing the very people who took Ona's and Seren's own loved ones. The people who destroyed both of their childhoods. And she wasn't just letting them go. That would be bad enough, but she was employing them!

Her sword was drawn before she knew what she was doing. She dashed it across a cart's wheel. That big, fancy sacred bowl at the oasis would be an even better thing to smash. Ona took a rough breath, then coughed with all the stupid sand in the air. She let out a swear. She needed a good cup of wine five minutes ago. Ten minutes ago. Yesterday. Her throat was a wasteland.

"Ona," a voice growled near the oasis' pool of gurgling water. Nuh's belly hung over his belt as he bent to fill a skin, drank a mouthful, and wiped his mouth with the back of his hand. "That's the goat farmer's cart you damaged. He's one of the middle-castes Kyros Seren asked to advise her. He'll be one of her favorites. Better watch your actions, friend."

"Better watch yourself."

"So sorry, Kaptan Ona!" He grinned. "Hey, aren't you supposed to be at a kaptans' meeting? Might be over by now."

Ona seriously considered slicing the smile off his stupid face. It took a lot for her to turn away and keep on.

In a narrow lane, a girl no bigger than a desert tree sapling offered Ona a green scarf—an imitation of the strip of wool Seren wore on her sash.

"I will give you a good price," she said in a cracked version of the trade tongue. "Maybe you can earn Holy Fire with the kyros's kind of clothings." She pushed the fabric into Ona's free hand, then saw the sword and drew back.

Ona sheathed the weapon and gave her a quick smile. It wasn't easy. "No. Thank you."

The little girl grinned back weakly, tears in her eyes. "Thank you for the fight. For helping us stay safe."

Throat even drier, Ona stared at the Invader blood under her own nails —crescent moons of black-red blood carried from the birthplace of those who stole the life from her birthplace.

"I'll always fight for you." Her aunt's nimble hands flashed through her memory. "I'll never rest until all the Invaders are dead."

The girl made a circle on her forehead with her thumb and dipped her chin.

"Learn to use this." Ona pointed at her sheathed sword. "It'll do a lot more for you than Holy Fire or those tears of yours."

The girl nodded and hurried into her family's tent, jabbering about something, Ona maybe. Ona turned a corner, and the child's finch-like voice faded beneath the night noise of the market, camels snorting, water rushing, the sounds of cooking, and the occasional groans of the injured assembled near the holy place.

Ona had to convince Seren that every single one of these Invaders was capable of making children like that little girl cry.

Seren would make a great leader. She was decisive, her looks gave her an air of power, and she had great ideas. Surely, she'd come around and see sense. Releasing an enemy into her own city was only a slip. A mistake born out of her good heart. She'd wise up. And Ona was the one to help her do it before it was too late and they had a wolf loose in their own woods.

Ona suddenly wished she wasn't spending the day alone. She wasn't going to grab another random soldier to talk to or kiss. Those moments never added up to satisfaction.

For the thousandth time, she longed for a match. A true match.

Lucca was the closest, but he was like a brother. She huffed. And other boys, well, they were too easy to figure out, and also, to intimidate. The only person who'd come close to really capturing Ona's whole self was that duke's son from the raid when she'd almost died and Lucca saved her. The lordling had been curt, cutthroat, and very close to perfect. A good challenge.

Voices sneaked from the closed flap of the guest tent. All thoughts of boys spilled away as Ona pushed in and found a challenge she wasn't expecting.

20

SEREN

S eren blinked as Ona walked in and froze, looking like a very surprised and very angry statue. Where had she been all this time?

"Kyros Seren," the engineer said through the interpreter, "what is the idea trying to hatch in your thoughts?"

Giving Ona a nod—if she wanted to watch this, maybe that was good as it might change her mind—Seren explained what she'd seen in her vision.

"This sounds like a balloon," the foreign man said, his angled eyes focused. "Maybe a square of fabric filled with air and set into the wind. Our people make them for Children's Day."

The celebration's name pinched Seren's heart. The enemies had families. Of course they did. But it was so much easier to fight them without being reminded of the fact that every time an arrow landed, it was taking away someone's mother or father, brother or sister. She tried hard to imagine Invader families participating in an event named for their children. All that light-colored hair waving in a breeze, smiles on their broad faces instead of grimaces, fingers wrapped around colorful crafts instead of gripping the hilt of a sword.

"But the...balloons I saw rose on their own," she said, trying to focus. "Steadily, not simply with the wind."

The engineer snapped his fingers, looking less and less like a prisoner of war as his passion overtook his fear. "I talked to a friend of mine about the possibility of this." The interpreter scrambled to keep up. "I thought maybe if we used hot air, the balloons could do just that."

"How do we make hot air?" Seren asked.

"With fire?" Cansu said, looking sheepish.

"That fire." The engineer pointed to the Holy Fire bowl near the door.

Ona unfroze slowly and looked at the Flames, her lips parted.

Seren rubbed her lip, thinking. "A bowl attached to the square of fabric, open only to catch the hot air?"

"The fabric would need to be painted with rubber. Rubberized," the engineer said.

This actually made sense. "And it floats over the enemy..."

The engineer looked at the ground. "Yes," he said mournfully. "It is filled with black powder that..." He made the explosive movements with his ivory hands.

"But how do we keep the powder from going off before it is where it needs to be?"

Drawing an invisible line in the air, the engineer said, "Long fuse."

"Your king's army will lay siege to the city if they gain reinforcements," she said.

"And they do."

Ona's face flushed, her teeth gritted and showing. "Why. Are. You. Trusting. Him."

She drew her sword.

Before Cansu, Erol, or Hossam could move, she had the blade at the engineer's neck from behind. "Let me end him for you, my lady. I'll help you with your idea and no information will be leaked to our enemies."

Hossam moved toward her, but Seren held up a hand. "Ona, I—"

"Please." Agony wrinkled Ona's brow and pulled at the corners of her mouth.

She'd been through so much. Seren knew how it felt, the need to do something about the hollowing, cutting, burning pain of not having your family any more, of someone taking them from you violently. Seren's arms ached to grab Ona, to hold her close and grieve with her. Ona needed to cry, to release that dark pain. It wouldn't stop the agony, but it'd do her so much good to allow tears to clean the vengeance from her blood.

"Ona. Listen. What if this man," she pointed at the engineer who to his credit stood erect and still, "is the key to finally defeating the rest of them?"

"Will you..." Ona glared daggers at the interpreter so he wouldn't translate, "...kill this one after we have the deed done?"

The engineer's gaze moved from Seren's face to the hand and blade at his throat. He didn't know the words, but he understood Ona's meaning well enough.

"Of course not." Seren stepped forward and touched Ona's dusty sleeve. "What if he isn't like the ones who hurt us? What if he was simply born to this violence and knows nothing different?" Seren looked into the engineer's eyes, willing him to say something that might help his case.

Ona's fingers shook against the hilt of her sword. Seren could've ordered her off the man, but Ona was lit up like a fuse, ready to spark a fight Seren didn't want to win or lose. The lantern's light touched the white streak in her red-brown hair. Seren had seen others with a streak like that. It sometimes resulted from a terrible shock. Ona had risked more pain pretending to be Meric. For Seren. For her people. After all Ona had been through, she deserved Kurakian chicken and laughs with friends, not…this. Seren's heart strained against its own beating.

"This man, he is different from the others," she said.

"No, he is not." Ona's voice was tight and low. "It's in his blood. They're all…pigs. Vermin. Filth."

A line of red leaked from the spot where her blade kissed the engineer's skin. If she killed him, the idea could be lost. This was Akhayma and the Empire's only chance against a siege. Seren felt it in her skin. This could mean Meekra's life, and her younger sisters' lives, the wise as an owl noble Najwa, her cousin Qadira, and the giggly low-caste Izzet. Lucca and his warm smile would be wiped from the earth alongside Ona, her fierce energy snuffed out like a northern candle's flame. Seren clutched at her stomach. Everyone she knew and loved would die.

"You're my friend," Seren whispered. "Don't force me to use my rank against you or—"

"Or what? Come now, Ser—Kyros Seren. I don't understand where your head is. We're on the same side. Why can't you see they *all* have to be eliminated?"

Seren closed her eyes against the raw pain in Ona's face. "Enough." Seren gestured to her guards. Cansu and Hossam grabbed Ona.

Ona swore. "Get off me." Jerking free, she raged out of the tent, not sparing one look for Seren.

With a word, Seren held her men back from going after Ona. Meric would've had her killed for this disrespect. Seren said a prayer that her friendship with Ona would last through the fight.

Erol tended the engineer's bleeding neck with a cloth.

"My apologies, prisoner," Seren said to the engineer. "My friend has suffered a great deal at the hands of your countrymen and she…well, it won't happen again."

478

The engineer gave Erol a nod of thanks and held a second cloth against his wound. "Am I still 'prisoner' then?"

"I...I don't want to..." It was such a difficult situation. Seren had never faced something like this. She thought of what her mother would've done. *Honesty, that's the only way through things,* she'd always said.

"Am I?" the engineer asked again.

Seren looked the man in the eye. "You are if you know what is good for you. A free man would be dead by sunrise. Onaratta would take you, or another of my own warriors would. Probably Erol right there. Don't give me that look, Erol. I can see how you look at him. Either way, you," she said to the foreigner, "wouldn't walk on two legs for long. This venture of ours...won't be popular."

The black lacquered tray Seren had ordered Cansu to bring sat propped against a stool. She took it, sat, and emptied a pouch of sand across its surface. "This is how I'm seeing this new weapon."

The sand curled around her finger and the emptied lines formed a rounded shape connected to a firepot instead of a bowl.

"The fire would need more cover to stay lit in the open like that. Plus, we'll need space for more ingredients below. A sealed spot underneath the flames."

The engineer leaned over to draw and Hossam moved closer, hand on his hilt. The engineer added a long fuse coming out of the side of the bowl, then a deeper well to the container. "The ingredients that explode will go here," he said through the interpreter.

"So the cloth is rubberized silk," Seren said. "The fabric will hold the hot air, the contraption will lift off and float above the enemy as they sleep."

He swallowed. "So this will fly above your enemies, then blast apart, setting fire to tents and men. Throwing shards of pottery like arrowheads."

This had to be terrible for him, betraying his people.

"It's this or you die," she said quietly. "I'm sorry you're in this situation. But you are. And don't think for a second that I'll change my mind." She spoke with far more confidence than she had. "Remember: it wasn't us who began this war. If this works and we humble them further, perhaps we can negotiate a lasting peace. I have no desire for violence, but they have to be humbled. You all displayed the fact rather plainly, don't you agree?"

He nodded. "I did not choose this war." He focused again on the sand drawing on the tray in Seren's lap.

"The problem is how to keep the fire from sparking the powder too soon," she said, trying not to think how many like him were out there, simply doing what they had to do to survive. "Also how to stop the fire at the right moment so the balloon will float down or at least explode in the air. Could we simply shoot them down with arrows?"

"Might disturb the contents before the proper moment," he said.

They both made a thinking, humming noise.

"What if we made small, clay firepots with only enough oil to take them so far. We could try different amounts and see how far they go," she said.

He hummed again. "And how high. I've never worked with the powders and explosive ingredients so there will be...tries."

The interpreter frowned, knowing the word was off.

Seren smiled. "Experiment. He means experiments."

"Yes. Experiment," the interpreter agreed.

"You might end up dead," Seren said, watching for his fear. It was there, but his eyes also showed the will to do this horrible thing and live to see another day.

"I escaped death twice this day. Why not try for three?" he said, his tone dry as the Emptiness.

"Silvanians claim third time's the charm." Seren smoothed the sand in the tray to hide the weapon from anyone who might tell Adem what she was up to. She needed the first time to be the charm, so to speak. This one and only try was stolen, snatched between the threat of damning secrets and wavering loyalties. If this went badly, not only would she be killed, but she might end up killing her own army inside their own walls.

It simply had to work.

21

ONA

Ona threw the tent flap out of her face, the pinch of Hossam's strong fingers lingering on her arms and shoulders as she wove through the moon-bleached city. The striped tents were skeletal beasts that murmured in jumbled languages.

Seren was a fool. Well, maybe not a fool. But too soft. Much too soft. Gah! The look on her face when that pig mentioned some special day for children. As if they truly celebrated anything but killing. No way. Ona couldn't imagine that in one million years.

And the Invaders would use Seren's weakness to find another, larger crack in the Empire's defenses. Offering the king for a ransom had been the first break. This engineer was the second. If he didn't slit her throat while they worked side-by-side, he'd find a way to get the gates open at the training field, the mines, or the main entrance to the city. Maybe he'd smuggle counts of weapons and fighters out by way of another traitor in their midst. Thousands of possibilities spread through the situation, spidering like mold from a leak in plaster.

The scent of hot iron, fire, and a banging that just about fit the force of Ona's anger poured from one of the many blacksmith forges. They were running non-stop now that war had arrived on their pretty doorstep. One of those spooky ore masters in their too-long black cloaks accepted a new yatagan from a smith in a soot-smudged apron.

The ore master turned the blade and moon and fire light washed over the man's face. He'd been beside Sweet Bean at the feast. They'd whispered like old pals.

"That's a beauty," Ona said in the trade tongue.

"It is, friend of our Pearl."

Not using her title, hm? "I need to speak with General Adem. In private. Do you know where I can find him?"

The man's gaze was as sharp as the yatagan.

Ona stared back. "Are you going to help me or stand there with your sword in your hand all night?"

He sniffed a laugh, paid the smith with a suede pouch of noisy coins, and led Ona away from the city center and to a towering blue tent where the general himself stood outside, pulling at his beard and chewing his cheek. Seemed Ona wasn't the only one plotting.

She reminded herself to be careful with this. She cared for Seren. She didn't want her punished or shamed overmuch. Just because Seren was wrong in this, didn't mean Ona wanted her dead.

Adem stopped, frowned. "To what do I owe the honor?"

"We need to talk." Ona nodded toward the tent.

His eyebrows lifted, but he pushed the flap aside and stopped to pass his hand respectfully over the bowl of Holy Fire. The inside of this tent was very different from the sunset purple light of the guest one. The deep blue gave the illusion of being underwater. Slits, cut around the tent's peaks let in moonlight and made Ona think of the sun on the tips of the ocean waves near home. She put a hand to her head, suddenly in pain about what she was doing.

But she'd be careful. Seren didn't have to suffer in this. Not if Ona handled it like Lucca would. Smooth. Calm. Level-headed.

For a second, Ona wished he was here to smooth the situation and pet Sweet Bean's ego properly. Too bad he wouldn't have helped her with this. He was all for Seren, no matter what she did. She'd claimed his heart. He'd never judge her actions objectively. No, Ona was all on her own.

She thought of her aunt. The way the side of her mouth used to tuck up when Ona spilled the vase of priceless brushes or decided she had to paint a goat's horns in green and yellow stripes. It was a smile that said No and Yes. Ona had to go behind Seren and Lucca's back this time for her aunt. The Invaders had to be stopped. Seren and Lucca would understand once this was over and they were safe.

She squeezed her hands into fists, feeling every knuckle and nail. *For you, Aunt. I won't let them live. I will see every last one of them dead.*

Adem gestured to a three-legged stool near a low table that held scrolls of parchment, ink, quills, and groups of dark stones positioned in what Ona had to guess was where he believed the Invaders had retreated to beyond the hammadas.

"I'm not sure how to start." Ona ignored the stool and kept a hand on her sword. She chanted *Wake iron! Wake.* to herself silently in case he decided what she said called for a quick death.

"With the most immediate need." His voice had fangs.

"Kyros Seren—"

"You mean Pearl of the Desert. High General Varol is kyros now."

"Whatever."

Adem's mouth twisted.

"She spared the life of an Invader prisoner and is working with him to develop a weapon she wants to use against the Invaders."

His mouth turned down, moving his trim beard. "And?"

"And? And he is with her, by her side, capable of killing her, spying on us —any number of crimes."

"It doesn't matter."

"How can you say that? You hate them as much as I do. Am I the only person who hasn't been hit on the head too hard? He is the enemy. They all must die for what they've done over and over again to your people, to mine, to the Empire. The kyros offered peace and they tried to slay us all again. Doesn't that prove the color of their souls?"

He held a hand out like Ona was a snorting horse that needed to be gentled. "You'd already know everything if you'd cease your rambling." He pointed to the stool.

Ona still didn't sit. "Fine. Spill it then. What are you up to, Sweet Bean?"

The look in his eye could've split her head in two. "First, you must swear by the Holy Fire and reaffirm your role as a warrior for the Empire. For the true heir to our lands, Kyros Varol."

She looked to the ceiling. "Oh, please. Like an unannounced meeting or chatting about politics with a Silvanian mercenary keeps with tradition. You break what traditions you choose to break. Haven't you noticed this about yourself? When are you going to ease up?"

He spun, took up his Holy Fire bowl, and held it out to her. Blue flames licked deep green leaves. "Swear. Or this meeting is adjourned."

"In the name of all the…"

"Mercenary!"

"Fine. Fine! I swear by the Holy Fire to fight on the side of the Empire, for the true heir of the power of the Empire, now and forevermore, may my soul be wiped from time if I break this hallowed oath. Will that do it for you?" It didn't mean anything so who cared who she promised to support. These were just words Adem needed to hear.

With one more steely look, he turned, set the fire on a long desk beside a chest of drawers, and said quietly, "I am going to take Pearl of the Desert...away."

Ona suddenly wished for the fire's heat. Her insides had gone cold. "Away?"

"You don't need to know the details. She will not be harmed, but she will be removed from the situation here so her ridiculous tactics and lies about being Blessed don't get in the way of Kyros Varol's strategy to win against the Invaders. Will you help me smooth the transition to a leader who won't spare a single Invader, no matter what they offer?"

Ona's heart pounded in her ears. If she said the wrong thing now, Seren could be sentenced to death. Maybe Lucca too. This felt surprisingly similar to the day she'd walked onto the iced up lake near Aunt's villa. The glassy surface knocked and echoed under her boots. A crack cut across the blue-black and she raced to the shore before she could lose her life to the cold, winter water.

Now, Ona's sweaty fingers flexed on her hilt. "I could talk to the fighters who might lean toward supporting him."

"Good."

Ona's heart gave a kick as she pictured Seren's trusting grin. "The Pearl of the Desert should be protected. In every way. No matter what Varol thinks she has done, or is doing." She sounded like a simple child. But she didn't want to say anything that could be directly related to the crimes Seren had already committed. Vague seemed the way to go.

"Of course," Adem replied, his voice slicker than Ona liked.

She could talk to Haris, maybe, then let him nurture the others' desire for a ruler of the royal blood and someone with a stronger policy against the Invaders.

Ona's first two fingers popped as she flexed her sword hand. An errant question flittered through her mind: *would my hand look different if I'd been able to wield paint brushes and charcoal instead of steel?*

She met Adem's cold gaze. "Lucca and I are with the Empire. No matter who reigns as its head."

A muscle at Adem's jaw twitched. "Lucca." He was no Lucca supporter. That was pretty obvious. "Very well," he said. "But don't think you're not being watched. I have eyes. Everywhere."

Ona shooed his warning away. "Varol has experience in battle?"

"More than the Pearl of the Desert."

"He should listen to her though. To her ideas. Well, some of them. She is a smart one."

He looked away, shifting his weight.

Ona didn't like where this was going. She could already see Seren beaten and bloodied at Adem's feet. "We also nabbed the king, don't forget."

He wouldn't look at her. "You must keep this from the other mercenary."

Could he tell that Lucca had feelings for Seren?

"You will not tell him anything or I'll have your head. I'll know who told and I'll have you surrounded and beaten before you can utter a word."

"I get it. I get it. I won't tell him." It was as if someone else had said the words. How could she so easily throw off Lucca? But Adem was right. He wouldn't see the situation clearly.

Ona offered her forearm in agreement. Adem wrapped his wiry fingers around her sleeve and squeezed, a copy of her own movement.

"It is agreed." He cast a glance over his shoulder at the door.

Ona studied his face. Was he hiding the fact that he'd go right now to Seren and order her death? It wouldn't be impossible. Ona swallowed, her head pounding suddenly. Ona cared about Seren, even if she didn't agree with her. She didn't want the woman killed.

"I love her too, mercenary," he said softly and Ona moved away, shocked that he'd been able to tell what she was thinking, that her own emotions were so plainly written on her face. "I didn't care for her family, but...Varol is simply the proper ruler. He has the royal blood. And I truly hope she stops lying about the Holy Fire and these..." His gaze sharpened. "Are you certain you know nothing about the kyros's death?"

Ona's skin prickled like lightning was about to strike. "He was sick. Now he's dead. Not much to that story." She cleared her face of the lie. Wiped her fear and deceit away like she had so many times while training under Dom. One couldn't survive that man without some well-told lies. When Lucca wasn't watching, he stripped weaklings clean of silver and dignity both.

Adem stared, weighing her words.

"Listen, this isn't my world here," Ona said. "It's yours. Don't ask me to untangle the mess you and yours have made. I'll play my part."

With one last look, Sweet Bean turned. "Fine. Just so you know, you're a gifted liar. And Kyros Meric's brother is a gifted leader. You'll see." He began pacing. "As for your part, talk to those with only desert blood and feed their fear that Pearl and those with her blood might wrest the Empire from the royal family. As for the rest, with mixed blood like mine and hers, we'll rely on their training. High General Varol outranks Pearl." He crossed his arms over his chest. "Kyros Varol will make all of this worth the trouble. You'll see. He is a force unto himself. A born ruler."

A quiet shiver spread under Ona's skin.

Adem raised an eyebrow. "That smile alone tells me you're equal to this delicate mission."

"I live to destroy the Invader pigs and do whatever I must to make that happen. Never doubt that fact."

22

SEREN

That night, Seren slept—and the city with her—everyone lost in sheer exhaustion. Lying on the bed in Meekra's section of the chamber, Seren pushed the thought of Meric and Adem and blood and lies out of her mind and savored the memory of Lucca smelling like pine and leather, his large hands on her waist. She forced herself to dream about what she'd accomplished. She'd driven off the Invaders—they even held their king—and she'd done it without Meric, and without Adem finding out about Meric. She had success, but it didn't...it didn't feel like she'd thought it would.

She woke before dawn, thinking about the engineer, a man who'd been her enemy, but who was currently working toward bringing her idea to life. A square of the rubberized silk he'd given her before she met with the scouts sat on the side table.

"Meekra, I'm alert enough for a report on anything else you've heard."

Meekra stretched and yawned, her eyes tired. "I haven't gathered any information that will really help I don't think. I walked past them in a crowd of merchants and heard something about the rumors of catapults in the siege."

It was nothing Seren didn't already know.

"There was one thing that seemed odd. My father said Adem and an ore master were talking as he walked through the injured troops. It doesn't make sense. The ore master said something about putting the jewel in its box."

Jewel? The city? It was the jewel of the Empire. Or maybe something about the ransom chests they still held? Seren's mind churned with images, snippets of conversation, voices. But nothing materialized into an explanation.

Meekra shrugged and brushed out Seren's hair. "I'm sorry I wasn't more help to you, my kyros."

"Just having you at my side is a great help." Seren touched Meekra's hand. "Sometimes I feel like all I have around me are vultures waiting to pick my bones clean."

"But everything is going well. Considering."

Seren rubbed her head, feeling less like she'd slept and more like she'd gone into battle again. "Considering, yes."

"What is that, Kyros Seren?" The one lamp they'd kept lit danced in what was left of the night's darkness and made the square of rubberized silk glow.

"It's a treated fabric we're going to try to use in a special weapon."

Meekra smiled, her white teeth bright in the dim tent. "The Holy Fire gave you this idea."

"Yes. Please keep it to yourself though. I don't want General Adem to know what I'm up to. Not yet."

Meekra nodded and scooped a cup of water from an enameled bowl. She handed it to Seren. "I worry about him, my lady."

Seren sipped the cool water, then handed the cup back to Meekra before removing the shift she'd slept in. "I do too, Meekra. I do too."

Meekra handed Seren a fresh mourning kaftan, pants, and sash, and after they'd dressed, they walked into the main part of the bed chamber.

Seren stared at the bed, where Meric's body had once been.

"Lucca Hand of Ruination to see you, my kyros," Erol said from the door into the main tent.

Blinking, Seren looked away. "Please let him pass, Erol."

Lucca appeared, holding a thick door flap up, and she waved him in.

He smiled sadly and leaned toward her ear. "Your engineer nearly blew his hands off near the mine wall."

Meekra had told Seren as much when she'd sent her for an update last night. "He'll figure it out. Don't look at me like that, Lucca Hand of Ruination. He will figure it out. He is quick as lightning."

"I'd say I'm jealous of the admiration you bestow on this pale hero," Lucca whispered as they walked into the main tent. "But quickness isn't always enviable."

The mischievous tilt to his eyebrow explained the innuendo. Heat seared Seren from chest to forehead. The bell hanging on her forehead was a coal against her skin.

Meekra smiled shyly behind them and pretended to be busy with her sash.

Seren looked back at the mercenary. "Lucca."

He shrugged and walked with her, Erol, Cansu, and Hossam into the purple light. No one but them was awake yet, it seemed.

"You did get some sleep before coming back to my door?" Seren eyed her guards one at a time.

"We did. For four good hours. We are fine, my lady." Hossam grinned.

They headed out of the Kyros Walls and into the sleeping city.

A hand flashed from the dark and grabbed Seren's neck.

Not even thinking, she drove a palm upward to break the hold as Lucca shouted for help. Steel blinked from Cansu's hand as he spun. Meekra put herself between Seren and the attacker—attackers. There were six now. All cloaked in thick headscarves that hid everything but their shining eyes. Hossam engaged two with his yatagan, shifting left so Erol and Lucca could fight the others swarming in the fading night.

One attacker held small daggers in each hand. Tapered fingers fanned out and heat jabbed Seren's thigh. Seren looked down, whirling to get behind a lotus tower. A line of blood streamed down her leg. A tiny knife lay on the ground beside her slipper. She dipped to pick up the weapon, a slight pain curling around her shallow wound. She cursed herself for not carrying a good weapon.

Erol watched Lucca fight. Why wasn't Erol moving? Was he too shocked? But he was a trained warrior. "Erol!" She threw the dagger that had been in her leg at the slim attacker.

Erol rolled a shoulder and drove an elbow into an attacker's face, dropping her to her knees as Hossam stepped back. His attackers were faster than him.

"Scatter!" Seren shouted.

Her guards and Meekra split down the alleys and streets, disappearing into the night. Seren's wound screamed as she pounded down the stony road, heading back toward the Kyros Walls. If she could get to the enclosure, someone would defend her, hand her a weapon, something. She was a fool for not carrying her own yatagan. All she had was her jeweled dagger, which was near to worthless against a well-armed fighter. Her lungs burned as she pulled in as much air as she could. The road went right in a quick curve and as her foot landed in the turn, the pressure in her cut threw stars into her view of the Kyros Walls gate.

"I am your kyros and I need your protection!"

Guards stepped away from the gate and drew their yatagans, their movements too slow. Were they confused? Or bought? One jolted away from the walls and ran at an attacker following Seren. The man attempted a chant. The two clashed together as Seren passed through the gate. The second guard dashed after her, slowing as she did, alarm written in his features.

"I didn't realize what was happening, my lady. Forgive how slow I am!" His gaze went to the blood on her kaftan.

"It's fine." Her breath wouldn't come. Her heart was trampling through her chest. "Leave. Find Meekra, my handmaiden. You know her?"

"Yes, yes. Of course. Where do you think—"

"Somewhere between here and the physician's tent. Barir. Her family. To the East. Go! Go!"

Nodding, he sped off, his boot scooping out the dusty earth near the edge of the cobblestone pathway and his yatagan drawn and ready.

A crowd was already gathering around Seren in the dawning light. She straightened. Was it Varol or Adem? Or both? The attackers had their faces covered so they didn't want to be seen coming after her. The plot had failed to kill her. So far. She spun and the faces around her blurred. A financial advisor. A clutch of ore masters. Two clan chieftains with hot tea still in their ringed fingers. And Kaptan Rashiel.

"Kaptan."

He bowed deeply.

"Please escort me to my chambers." Her leg hurt, but it wasn't serious. "I need to wrap this cut."

"Of course, Pearl—kyros." The poor man didn't know how to address her.

"I am still your kyros," she said, her declaration sounding too much like a sad little plea.

Rashiel bowed again, holding a fist to his chest. "Of course, my kyros. May I ask what happened to your guard? And are you certain I shouldn't call for your physician? And just so you know, there is talk about Varol. He is planning something," he whispered as he came close, keeping the others at bay.

"I think he was planning this." She gestured to her leg, then to the city beyond the walls where only the Fire knew was happening to Lucca, Erol, Cansu, Meekra, and Hossam.

Then there was a shout and Seren turned to see Hossam, Erol, and Cansu hurry through the gate. Her heart relaxed a little. Erol was bleeding from the eyebrow. Cansu held one arm against his side and Hossam had a large gash down his arm, the fabric of his shirt lying open like dead skin.

If she admitted to being attacked, it might only encourage others to side against her. Since she'd stopped the practice of slaves wearing the tall waist-to-head contraptions, there had been talk against her.

"I arranged a practice attack to prepare my guards for assassins in case the Invaders try to kill me or take me to trade for their king," she said loud enough for all to hear. *Please, Holy Fire, let Meekra be safe. Please let Lucca be safe.*

"Very wise, my kyros," Rashiel said. "And brave."

"My lady!" Hossam's booming voice echoed off the pale stone walls. His eyes were round and worried.

"I'm fine. I trust you did well during our practice attack?"

He looked to Erol, who of course frowned, and then to Cansu whose lips parted. "Ah," Cansu said, realization of what she was doing dawning on his face. "Yes. We drove all of the sparring partners away."

"And Meekra? Did you escort her to my chambers or maybe to her home?"

They exchanged tight glances. "No," Hossam said. "She ran away from the action. Seeing as she isn't trained, that was wise, yes, my lady?"

"Very. And the mercenary?" Seren twisted her wool piece and swallowed the bitter taste at the back of her throat.

"I haven't seen him yet, my lady."

Seren tried to swallow, coughed, and tried again. "You three go tend to your wounds. Kaptan Rashiel will escort me to my chambers."

"You're sure, Kyros Seren?" Cansu's voice was an oud string about to snap.

"Yes." She was far from sure about anything, but cowering beside her wounded guards wasn't going to fix anything.

The older scout from yesterday appeared at Rashiel's side. "My kyros, Varol called a pre-dawn meeting with the kaptans. He did not include Lucca Hand of Ruination."

Everything was falling apart. Seren couldn't help but imagine Meekra and Lucca bleeding to death in the street and the Invaders readying to change the color of their tent and sharpening their blades.

Holy Fire, help me.

23

ONA

Varol stood at the front of the room looking exactly like what Ona wanted in her life. No one whispered while his dark gaze swept through the room like a storm. Every kaptan here straightened sash and weapon and back under his eye, his natural command whipping them into their best. What had he done to them—what kind of reputation did he have—to get this kind of response out of such a varied group? Ona grinned. He was absolutely terrifying. Most of the kaptans were here, or so it seemed. But Lucca was nowhere. Rashiel wasn't here either. Hadn't Lucca heard the horn? Hadn't Adem or Varol sent him a messenger boy? Maybe not. Maybe they knew Lucca was too infatuated with Seren to get any real work done.

"Kaptans." Every head turned to watch Varol. "We come up against the beast we hoped never to see again. The beast is vicious. Unwavering. But we have made it bleed already." He grinned and Ona was pretty sure it matched her own smile. "We insulted it with our victory. We made it whimper and run."

Murmurs floated up. Some might've been questioning—maybe Seren's supporters—but Varol was what was important here and now. He was the solution. He was the key to revenge.

"We have a plan to deal with this little siege." Varol cocked his head and glanced at Adem, who stood silent in the tent's shadowed corner.

Little siege? Well, that wasn't Varol's best comment. Although Ona hadn't seen a siege herself, there didn't seem like there was anything little about it. But he was just being delightfully arrogant, right?

"Yes we do, Kyros Varol." Adem stomped his feet, and with a look, encouraged the rest of the room to join in. Some did. Some didn't. Varol didn't seem to notice either way as he spread a map on the table and began to talk strategy.

A man next with a thin beard leaned closer, interrupting Ona's conversation with herself. "What do you think of this, Kaptan Onaratta Paints with Blood?"

"Varol is the one to follow."

"You truly believe that?"

"You don't?"

The man cast a look at Adem, then the door. "I know what Kyros Seren says about him. That he is ruthless. As spoiled and rash as his brother was. More cruel and selfish."

"When did she say this?"

The man cleared his throat and coughed. "Um, well, I overheard her at Kyros Meric's Age Day feast."

Ona painted Varol in her mind. Dark slashes of that strong, hawk nose. The slant of his cunning eyes. She unwound the scarf from her neck and tied it to her belt, suddenly really warm. "He's a take-charge kind of person and that's what we need. Seren shows too much mercy when it comes to prisoners."

The kaptan grinned. "You'd kill them all."

"Wouldn't you?"

"Probably."

"Then we're agreed."

BACK AT THE GUEST TENT, Lucca paced a line in front of the brazier. Fresh blood marred the shoulder of his brigantine.

"What happened to you? Why weren't you at the kaptans' meeting?"

"Because I was busy being attacked by Adem and Varol's fighters."

"What?"

"They tried to kill Seren."

"How do you know it was Adem and Varol?"

Lucca stopped, lifted his chin. "Ona. Really."

"I bet there are a bunch of people who want to take her down. She keeps the Invader king like a pet, frees slaves—which I'm fine with of course but still it'll anger the people who used to benefit from it—and now she's taking an Invader's advice on weapons to fight his own siege! She's being an idiot!"

"They cut her leg up, Ona. They tried to kill me. And Meekra. They were this close to slicing Seren's throat open."

Ona's stomach turned. She knew what that looked like and didn't want to imagine it on a person like Seren, a good person like her aunt had been. Suddenly, a weight sat on Ona's shoulders. "She doesn't deserve that. I, I'm sorry."

"Well you didn't do it. Don't apologize."

Ona rubbed her stomach and stretched her neck. "Maybe they weren't going to kill her. Maybe they were just going to lock her up or something."

Lucca's knuckle pressed into his mouth and his eyes shut in thought.

Ona grabbed a skin of water and drank down the contents. The liquid cooled her throat, but it didn't taste like water should. She missed Silvania.

"You aren't going to like what I have to say." She threw the empty skin on her bedding.

Lucca turned, his big brown eyes looking right into her. She pushed on.

"Seren should be restrained. For her own good."

Lucca's eyes flashed, quick and mean as lightning. "Ona."

Ona fought the discomfort of disagreeing openly with Lucca for the millionth time lately. She didn't want them to be at odds. But... "She is at risk. You said it yourself. Varol could decide her actions with this foreign engineer constitute treason or—"

"What are you really worried about?"

"I'm worried about Seren."

"And?"

"She wants to undermine Varol's authority. She said she wanted to get Adem alone and talk to him. If she disrupts what Varol is trying to do, if she asserts her claim as kyros—there are a lot of those with the same blood as her, and they'll support her—we'll be mired in an internal fight while we lose the real war."

A ragged sigh slipped out of Lucca. His fingers tore into his thick head of hair. He had to know Ona was right. "She deserves to rule," he said. "Just because she isn't of royal blood...I can't believe I have to argue this with you."

"It's not an argument."

"It's feels like one."

"Well, it's not. I don't even think she wants to rule. She should. But she doesn't. She's too fearful. Stop shaking your head. I'm right, and you need to shut your mouth and listen. Varol has the steel to finish the Invaders—

you've seen how he commands—and he has the right to rule. We don't have time to let Seren get in the way. This war is only beginning and you know it."

She knew full well he was picturing exactly the same thing as her.

The tent the Invaders had probably already put up today. The red tent. Even if Akhayma surrendered now, they would cut down every man in the city. Tomorrow would see the black…No city survived an Invader siege. If Akhayma did surrender, which they never would if Ona had any breath left in her body, the city's population would be turned into slaves, beaten, tortured. They'd be lower than the Invaders' underfed camp dogs.

Ona grabbed Lucca's arm. "Our only advantage is that we have their king. And Seren wants to risk losing him and use this new weapon she developed with one of the enemy!"

"You supported her—"

"Before she began trusting an Invader. How can you not see this is madness? Stupidity. The division she could cause, it will cost us the win!"

His face hardened. "I am loyal to Kyros Seren. I pledged my sword to her. As you did."

On her toes, Ona leaned into his face, heart shuddering, fingers pulsing against the hilt of her blade. "No. You pledged your prick and it's ruined us."

Spinning, she blasted out of the tent, ignoring Lucca's calls and half-hearted attempt to catch up.

ONA WAS BACK IN THE KAPTANS' tent before anyone could stop her.

Two guards she didn't know leaped inside after her, their big hands grasping her shoulders and a hunk of her hair.

She glared at Varol, who stood over a table, a map laid out before him. The lantern hanging from the ceiling nearly touched his head. He met her gaze with his amber, snake-sharp eyes. Fire lashed through her body, and she swallowed, fingers twitching, longing to draw the lines of him. For a second, she thought maybe he'd order her cut into pieces and hung from the walls. But by all the sand in the Empire, she wasn't about to tremble.

"I need to speak to you." It probably would've been better if she'd waited to talk.

He did nothing more than give the guards a glance, but they scurried out, leaving them alone.

His breath was steady, quiet. He straightened, graceful and lean, walked around the table, and stood not a hand's width away, his chest moving slowly, surely. His cheeks, above his trim beard, had to be soft as the finest sand. Charcoal could sweep across the surface, easy and smooth. She could draw his kingdom there beneath those flickering eyes. The dramatic rise and flats of the hammadas. The long stretches of peaked dunes beyond the city. Hawks circling. And the bodies of his enemies like wheat broken by the scythe. Varol was more than a man. He was a Place, the Power of that Place, and the Strength to beat back those who'd ruined Ona's life.

"The Pearl of the Desert means well," Ona said in the trade tongue. Her voice was quieter than normal, but she didn't hate it as she would've guessed. "But she plans to undermine your authority." She stumbled a little over the words, hoping he wasn't behind the attack on Seren. "You need to restrain her or some of your warriors will rise up. We'll lose the siege before it's begun."

"You know a great deal, mercenary," he said.

"Yes, I do."

"There is a steep punishment for barging into my presence uninvited."

Ona grinned, sparks punching under the skin of her neck, back, and thighs. "Try it."

He had his emerald-heavy dagger unsheathed before she finished her whispered chant, but she still drove him back and onto the ground. Her knee pinned his wrist before he could draw blood.

"You are fast," he breathed, his throat moving, his eyes like death. His gaze touched on her chin, on her palm raised to strike, on her eyelashes. "Why do you look at me like you do?"

This was the strangest, most exciting conversation she'd ever had. No pleasantries. No polite talk easing into an understanding. It cut to the quick.

"Because I wish I could draw you."

"You are an artist?"

"I used to be." Ona spat the words, wanting them out of her mouth before they could soften her. "Before the Invaders ripped my life apart."

"Why do you want to draw me?"

"I like powerful people. Especially handsome ones."

His smile was the strongest sword, a storm in the desert. So even though she seriously enjoyed the feel of his body under her, she let him up.

"Does that mean you'll tell me everything you know, mercenary?" He brushed himself off and sheathed his curved dagger. "Do you know anything about what happened to my brother?"

A chill brushed over Ona's skin.

A guard pushed into the tent, his freckled face pinched as he passed his hands quickly over the Holy Fire bowl. "Kyros," he said, bowing. "The Invaders replaced the white tent with the red."

Varol rolled up his map and tucked it into his sash. "How many now? Any more troops?"

"We don't have an updated count yet, my kyros."

"Get the others." Varol downed a cup of something and slammed it back onto the table. "Meet me at the parapet. Send for Adem."

The guard dipped his head and hurried out of the tent.

Ona's hands curled into fists. "Are you going to hang their king from the walls?"

A shadow flitted over Varol's eyes. "What is your name, mercenary?"

"Onaratta Paints with Blood."

He smiled again. A shiver flashed through her body, all the way to her toes.

"I'd bet that is a fitting name for you, little falcon."

Ona bristled. "Little?"

He lifted a finger and traced his lower lip, thinking. "All the better to surprise and cut deeply."

"I'll take it." Ona owned the night, owned her life a bit more, as he swept out of the tent to begin the destruction of her enemies. She'd never felt so satisfied.

24

SEREN

Hossam, Erol, Cansu, and Meekra flanked Seren as she sat in Meric's chair and listened. A line of supplicants, all in mourning brown, waited to speak to her inside the main tent's shade. Varol and Adem had turned them away. She understood reducing supplicants' pleas during this war, but pushing them all away with no explanation? That wasn't the way to keep the city calm and cared for.

A wooler with a respected name told Seren how he'd been urged to raise his prices. Meekra quickly scrawled down amounts and other information into her report.

"I don't think anyone will be able to pay that much. I'm afraid my... contributors," he said, meaning the noble family who'd invested in his wool trade, "will find a way to show their displeasure."

It was Qadira's clan, Seren just knew it. Meekra traded a look with her that only solidified her thought. "But you haven't been forced to alter contracts you already established?"

"No, Pearl of the Desert—ah!—I mean, Kyros Seren." He winced. The people didn't know whom to call what and she didn't blame them. The power struggle wasn't their doing. She was simply grateful Varol hadn't contradicted her title in the open since the funeral. It was coming though. Like pressure in the air, it pressed against her skin and spoke of high winds and rough skies.

"Let it be known," she looked to Meekra to make certain this decree made it to the scribe for official recording, "no prices will be raised during a time of war. We do not profit from problems we experience together. We must remain united."

She needed to organize a system. The people had to share necessary goods to survive. She had to take the noble families out of the equation. She could already imagine Qadira's sneer at her judgment call here.

"Nidal." His eyes widened as she said his name. She knew many of their names. She and Meekra used to sit up at night and recall names, something Meric scoffed at and Varol would too, if he knew of it. "I'll announce a city-wide gathering of basic goods and I myself will pay those who contribute."

She removed all the rings from her fingers and tucked the emeralds, pearls, and rubies into Hossam's large hand.

"We can collect food stuffs, milk, blankets, bandages, and medicines at the economic advisory tent beside the back gates. That way, if the customers can't pay, your family will still eat."

She motioned for Hossam to hand the rings over to Nidal.

"I place you in charge of this endeavor and you may employ anyone else willing to help."

Hope smoothed Nidal's wrinkles. "Thank you, Chosen One."

Erol arrived wearing the mean-eyed look that meant he had a message. Seren waved him forward as he fussed with his mourning kaftan.

"I have a message from the engineer. He hasn't been able to make the weapon work yet, but he is hopeful that a new arrangement on the fuse line will help. And, Kyros Seren? I want you to know, we, all of us, your guard, want you to know that if you challenge Varol openly, we're with you."

A sunny light filled her and she pressed a hand over her heart. She hadn't asked them, not wanting them to risk their lives for her. It'd been silly really because they'd risk it anyway, had already risked it. It was all too much to bear but she had to bear it. She'd let the Flames burn through her and find courage for this moment, to make it to the next.

"Thank you," she said.

Erol nodded, meeting her eyes. Beside him, Hossam and Cansu inclined their heads too.

AT THE ARCHERY RANGE, clouds interrupted the moonlight and turned it into strands like spider webs. The ends of Seren's hair lifted lightly in the breeze. The engineer waved as she walked to where he stood alongside the training field, bare except for three archery targets. Leaping from foot to foot like a boy, he gestured to ten contraptions. They were lined up opposite the leather and sand-stuffed targets.

He rambled until the harried interpreter grabbed his arm. "Slow down!"

Each of the contraptions included a shiny, silk pocket and a two-sectioned clay pot attached to the silk by way of thin wires. Seren squatted by the closest one to examine the contraption.

"Lahabshjara Fires." The engineer pointed to the top section. It looked like a deep bowl.

"And here is where the powder sits, yes?" She tapped the head-sized ball at the base. One wire, attached to one that ran up to the silk pocket, hung near the ball's side. "This will take the static—built up by the pocket going through the air—and bring it down through this." She touched a tiny hole in the ball's wall, through which the wire would eventually be threaded. "And it will spark the powder blend."

He frowned until the interpreter finished his work. After a little backtracking, the engineer nodded, giving her the rest of the conversation through the interpreter.

"So," she said, "the wire isn't quite ready." She pointed to where it would go. "But you have an idea on how to fix that."

Nodding, the engineer grinned and pressed his palms together. "Never seen woman with," he made a flourishing kind of motion with his hands, "these...type ideas."

"It's the Holy Fire that gives me these ideas. And perhaps if you asked more women about their thoughts, you'd hear more good ideas."

He bowed in that awkward way the Invaders had. "Should we get to work now?"

"Yes."

With careful fingers, they inserted the magnesium fuse wires into the small holes in the sides of the clay pots. The containers held rust, saltpeter, and another ingredient with a name as difficult as the engineer's, which she didn't bother trying to say. The complicatedly named ingredient provided oxidation to improve the weapon's performance. She understood that much.

"What about the wind?" she asked, using the interpreter's services.

The engineer glanced at her, then the sky. The interpreter gave her his words. "No wind, Kyros."

"There is a little," she said. "The winds are unpredictable here, engineer. Tell me the weight will be enough to keep the pockets of hot air from drifting too far."

"I'm certain. We aim for the targets. Just there. Fuses should spark by then and…"

She imagined the puffs and sparks she'd seen in her vision. "Inferno."

"Yes."

"The warriors and stable hands have been warned?" Fig's stall window was open, but Seren was too far away to see her.

"Yes," the interpreter answered for the engineer.

"All right then. But only try the three first." She stood, dusting her kaftan and going to stand behind Erol, Hossam, and Cansu.

Cansu smiled, approving her choice of safe vantage point. But honestly, if the wind blew wrong, it wouldn't matter how many big men or women she stood behind.

The wind had died and there weren't any reports of sandstorms or otherwise. It wasn't the rainy season, so they had no fronts of cold wet to worry about. Seren's hands shook anyway.

Holding the pockets of rubberized silk up, the engineer and two other warriors lit the small exterior fire bowls. One man dropped his flint and had to be replaced with someone less nervous around this new technology.

Seren leaned around Erol to see better. It was taking an eternity. If they couldn't get the fire going properly, the silk pockets would never fill and rise. The whole thing could catch fire. She twisted her green wool around her fingers, pulled, and released it, the soft fabric, the memory of them, helping her breathe.

Please don't let the flames get too near the fuse strips.

Slowly, the heat from the small flames filled the silk bladders with hot air. The first lifted into the sky. Then another. She clapped her hands together. The Holy Fire's idea had come to fruition. Adem may not have witnessed its success, but he'd hear of it. From more than her. He'd present the idea to Varol. It would work out. This weapon, set off next time from the parapet to descend and ignite the Invaders, would end the war.

Two of the weapons—one refused to light—floated toward the archery targets like silent ships on invisible water.

She pushed past Cansu and found the engineer's side. "When will the static be enough to ignite the magnesium strip?"

He crossed his arms and tapped a lip. "I do not know."

"If they don't explode within the training field walls, the Invaders might see them. They would know…"

"Many variable in this experiment."

"Yes." Sweat pooled at the base of her neck, between her collar and skin. Her heart strained to keep beating regularly.

A flash of white and orange blinded her.

She rubbed at her eyes and looked again. Two weapons blazed with flame and ate the targets in great washes of light. A cheer went up from the fighters behind them.

"Somehow, I'll make you safe here in the city," she said to the engineer. "Or anywhere you chose to go in the Empire."

"How?"

"I don't know. But I will do it. I promise you."

"Thank you, Kyros."

Another of the flying weapons sizzled, but a sudden rush of air lifted it. Seren's hair blew against her cheek and pressed her toward the gate to the city.

"No." Cansu was at her side then, his mouth open.

The weapon danced and twirled in the sudden wind like a demon. It reached the top of the wall that divided the training fields from the market, the shops, and everyone's homes.

She had to shoot it down. Her bow was in the stables.

Horses snorted and stamped, smelling the black powder. Seren grabbed her quiver and bow and ran back outside. In the center of the fields, she spied the swollen silk and fire heading over the wall. She loosed an arrow. Her shot pushed the weapon over the wall. It dropped out of sight.

No.

Everyone was running now. Calling for water. For people to back away. Shouting for the gate guards to clear the area nearest the wall. The residential area.

A sudden shift threw another weapon at the stable roof. A flash of light and the hay outside the main entrance went up in flames.

Seren called out to the men staring. "Don't just stand there, my warriors! Go to the city and help the people. Stop the fire from spreading! And you, you, and you, come help me put out the one there." She ran for the stables.

Hands shaking, Seren tried to slide the bolt on Fig's stall door open as others worked to smother the spreading fire surrounding the entrance and inching up the wooden walls. Panicked whinnies sounded beyond the thick wood slats of Fig's stall. Sweat slicked Seren's palms. The bolt didn't want to move. Ironically, rust—the same thing as what was currently causing the thatch and mud roof to smoke into angry arms of fire—blocked the latch's mechanism.

Screams tore out of the city, beyond the wall, and Seren's heart lurched, tears pooling in her eyes.

Lucca ran into the stables, his face marked with ash and his mouth pinched. "Step back." With one boot, he smashed the stall's bolt loose.

Seren leaned past him and slid the bolt free. Fig shot from the stall, not that Seren could see her. Smoke clouded the world and clawed at her lungs.

"Free the other horses," she coughed.

"They're already—" He pointed to the small herd galloping and stomping around the fields, indistinguishable in the dark and chaos.

In the city, smoke rose into the night sky. No one was left in the training field except them. And Seren knew she should've been the one to rush into the city. A warrior rushed down the hill from the back gates and toward the stable, Lucca shouting at him. This was entirely Seren's fault. Turning from Lucca and the other man, she threw herself further into the stables, rushing, stumbling in the smoke and dodging frightening snorting horses, to reach one more latched stall.

"One more!" she called back to Lucca.

His head turned. His hair whipped against his face. "Seren! No! Get out of there!"

She ran into a wall of gray. Acrid smoke burned her throat and eyes as the fire ate at the stables. A thud rocked a closed stall door. A hoof hitting the wood.

"I'm coming!" She worked the bolt. Three tries. Four. Finally, it came free. The stall was full of smoke. But no horse. She clicked her tongue. "Where are you?"

Eyes watering, she looked down. One white sock showed near a hoof, like Fig's foreleg, but this wasn't Fig's stall. Thank the Holy Fire this wasn't her stall. It was a horrible, selfish thought, but at that second, she didn't care.

Her heart in her burning throat, she tugged at the animal's leg to try and wake it.

"Wake!" She clapped her hands, coughing and spitting ash. Heat roared above her head and there was a crack. A beam crashed through the roof and into the stall. Smoke blocked the view of where it landed. "Wake up!"

She clambered over the animal's body. To its muzzle. The horse's lips were still and soft. Every curve and dip of the animal's mouth was as familiar as her own and her heart stopped beating, hanging in her chest as her mind screamed the truth. It was Fig.

She sucked a breath, choking, and a shout crawled out of her throat somewhere between a cry and a scream. Lucca split the clouds of smoke and grabbed her arm. He dragged her from the stables as the roof caved in.

Fig was lost in the monster of smoke and fire and broken beams.

Not caring about the possible consequences, Seren let him hold her tight against his chest. She couldn't breathe. Grief and guilt joined the smoke in clogging her lungs and squeezing her heart. Lucca covered her mouth and nose with a wet cloth. Finally, she could take one breath, two.

The smoke cleared and let the moonlight coat the awful scene. Coughs tore from Seren's chest, horribly reminding her of the night Meric died.

"They controlled the fire in the city," he said. "None are dead."

Thank the Fire. Her stomach twisted. Fig. Her poor, poor Fig. "Injuries?"

"A few," he whispered into her hair.

Tears ripped down her face. Her eyes felt like coals and her heart sank and sank. The ground under her feet threatened to break, or maybe it was her legs that didn't want to hold her anymore.

"If the wind hadn't turned, if we'd had more weight..." Her tongue grew too dry. Words failed her.

Lucca took the wet cloth as she pulled away and started toward the city gate.

"What are you going to do?" he asked.

"I'm not sure," she said. "But I can't hide from this."

Four fighters brought out a cart filled with smoking debris. Ruined tent sections. Charred stools, shields, and baskets. She gritted her teeth, and they walked around the cart, to the gate, meeting Erol, Hossam, and Cansu, as well as a group of fighters she didn't know as well—a grim welcome party.

Cansu came forward. Gray ringed his normally perky eyes and he stammered as he greeted her formally. His throat moved in a slow swallow and he looked at the ground.

"Pearl of the Desert, Kyros Varol ordered we take you to him for questioning. Do you...do you want us to..." He threw a look at the fighters behind him.

She was numb. They had to be Varol and Adem's men. Not loyal to her. Should she ask her loyal fighters to call her kyros? Was this the time to make a stand? Cansu's eyes moved like a bird's. No. She couldn't order them to their death. Not if she wasn't certain this meant the end of her and the beginning of Varol. She had to be sure.

Lucca was asking Hossam and Erol something, but she couldn't hear what he said. Her feet were somehow already moving past the damage her weapon had done, the smoking shops that lined the wall between the city and the training fields.

She whirled to see Lucca and her guard on her heels. "Lucca Hand of Ruination, I command you to reinstate order at the training fields and secure temporary lodging for the warriors who lost their tents."

"Are you—"

"Go." Her demand came out like a plea. *Please, go, Lucca. Go and hide among the fighters, find some way to disappear.*

"But I can come with you," he said quietly.

"No. Do as I order." Seren fought her desperate need to get him to safety and burned her words with an authority she didn't feel.

His lips parted. He searched her face, then nodded curtly and spun on his heel. Seren memorized his broad, round shoulders, the blood-red belt at his trim waist, and the lilt to his walk. Lucca. He knew she was trying to protect him, didn't he? She scratched at her hot skin and pressed fingers against the pounding pulse in her neck.

She had no sun now to think of the fever of love.

Her world was crumbling.

25

ONA

The moon began to show through the last of the daylight. Seren was off seeing supplicants right now. Just more proof she couldn't run this war. She should've been here, plotting. Well, nothing was stopping Ona from forcing her way into the planning now that the red tent was up and the black was close on its heels. She'd see Varol and she'd be a part of this strategy if it killed her. Varol's guards—both could've been the dead kyros's twin brothers—stopped her at the door to Varol's tent on the western side of the Kyros Walls courtyard.

"Kyros Varol requested my attendance." She had to get in. She couldn't live with herself if she ended up having to go along with some stupid plan against the Invaders. But surely Varol's plan was magnificent. If anything, she just wanted to know about it.

"You have a message you can show us?" the first asked.

"No."

"Then you may not enter."

"I'm Kaptan Onaratta Paints with Blood."

"We know, Kaptan Onaratta. And please forgive us. But we're not permitted to allow anyone entry unless there is a proper reason."

Mentioning Seren might work. But what title to use? These were obviously Varol supporters if they were guarding his meeting.

"Pearl of the Desert sent me with a message." The guards straightened. "It's urgent." They shifted their weight foot to foot and Ona could hear Varol's distinctive voice calling a meeting to order. "If you don't let me in,

I'll put one of my favorite chants to work and your best parts will drop right off your worthless bodies."

The guards practically jumped away from the door. "Please, yes. Kyros Varol will want to hear your message."

"You bet he will." As she passed, she glanced over her shoulder and waved a feigned farewell to their groins. They winced in unison and Ona barked a laugh, sauntering into the meeting.

Varol's men barely looked at her as she walked the plush rug path to their table. None made a move, only shifting their gaze back to their leader.

"This meeting is short one Silvanian mercenary," she said.

Varol's mouth lifted a fraction at one side. He stood and his men copied the gesture. "Indeed?"

"I'm sure you want to hear how the chanting units are evolving. Adem told you about this, yes? Also, you especially need info from someone who traveled through the Empire, listening to tales of past sieges like the one that is about to start up at our front door."

He ran a finger over a dirtied sword that looked familiar with its twisted hilt. "You served a fine helping of information already."

"That was only about what I could do. It wasn't the sum of what I know." The back of her neck prickled. She was pushing her luck. Varol could order these men to kill her with one word—a word she might not even understand. If she chanted, she could most likely best six men, but getting out of the city, that would be a feat. And if she did, an ocean of Invaders could be waiting outside the pale stone walls.

"So tell me what you know." Varol's words were quiet as a well-sharpened blade slicing through skin.

His men's eyes were cool, appraising. They were nothing compared to their leader though. Mere stars beside the sun. Every one of them would've already had her taken away. They had closed little minds. No new ideas. Their Holy Fire probably did nothing more than warm their hands when they passed their palms over its flame.

"My unit is coming along. There are five men who can chant and improve their speed on foot. It won't be long until they'll be better in battle."

"I already know all of this," Varol said. "Anything else?"

She cleared her throat. "The Invaders are blind with arrogance. If you slay their king as you plan to, then attack from the opening to the mines behind them, they'll be confused twice over. They won't believe their king could die or that we could surprise them. We'll come at them from the back on horses, with those small bows you all have, the ones shaped like a calligrapher's stroke."

"We don't have enough horses."

"You don't need too many. Just enough to appear serious about the attack. They will rage at us with their proud chins high and we'll pretend to retreat. Instead, the warriors will shoot backward and cut them down. I've seen what your fighters can do with the bow. It'll be easy for them and it'll muddle the Invaders' minds. We'll paint the plains red as a field of poppies."

Varol rubbed his hands together. "So we split our forces. Fighters on foot at the gates and on the parapet. Horseback archers at the back in a false retreat. I like it." His gaze went to her mouth. "I like you."

Smiling a little, he dismissed his men with a flick of a hand.

They were alone. She was alone with the man who was going to humiliate, then annihilate the ones who'd ruined her life.

He walked toward her. "Tell me your story. Why are you like you are?" He raised one sharp, black eyebrow.

Stars burst under her flesh, waking her up. She was so alive with this man. His amber eyes glowed, invited her to lay her soul in his hands.

And so she did.

When she'd told him about her aunt and the palette knife, she stepped closer. Light from the tent's ornate ceiling spun a web over Varol's swept-back hair, his wide shoulders.

"For the first time, I truly believe the Invaders have enjoyed their last victory. You, Varol." His gaze cut her for using his name. "You will restore my ruined life. Not the innocence, but the beauty. Seren can't do it. She is too weak. Right now, she's developing a weapon with an Invader engineer. No one who thinks *they* can be trusted is good for our cause. You, Kyros Varol, are our savior."

"You don't know me."

"I know enough."

"I doubt that."

"Then tell me your story," Ona said.

"I shouldn't waste my time."

She shrugged. "Your choice." He could whistle the tune of *Old Goat, New Hen* for all she cared. Just being this close to a person so powerful was heaven itself.

His gaze went to the door. She couldn't let this talk end now. She'd go back to the guest tent and Lucca would be gone, going after Seren. She wanted something of her own. Not just something. She wanted Varol.

She took another step. Varol's breath touched her cheek and neck. Her heart kicked like a spirited horse. "Tell me about the worst moment of your life."

"Aside from my brother's funeral."

"That wasn't the worst. I saw your face. You're angry it was out of your control, but you don't miss him."

"You really don't care if I kill you, do you?" Varol smiled. He untied and retied a second sash at his waist. Odd he wore one creased with dirt over the fine brown he already had on. Must've been part of the mourning.

"You won't."

"You're a bit of a fool."

Ona shrugged. "Or courageous. It's a fine line."

"I think you crossed that line long ago."

"I'm here, aren't I? Talking alone with the most powerful person in the Empire?"

"You should work on the art of conversation."

"My own style has gotten me pretty far," Ona snapped.

He laughed. It was a pointed sound that would always be aimed at someone. She had to lean her head back to look him in the eye, but she was all right with it. After all, she could gut him if he became a problem.

"I was a second son," he said, "in a family who only had need of one. I was more cunning than my brother. Smarter. But none of it mattered. My brother's smallest feat was echoed through the world. My greatest accomplishments were lost in the noise of my father ordering me around."

"That's what gives you your will though. Your strong will."

He smirked. "A blade sharpened in the fire, hm?" His tone bit the air.

"Trite, but true."

"You're so young."

"I've seen more than most old women. And you're only twenty? Twenty-one?"

He nodded. "How would you draw me?" He took her hand and put it against his cheek. A shiver rolled down her back and stomach.

She traced the fine bones around his snake eyes, the hook of his proud nose. "I'd concentrate here and here and here. This is the center of your power."

"It's where I feel the Holy Fire's ideas when they come." A sheen of sarcasm pooled around his words. Ona didn't think he held too tightly to the almighty fire.

He closed his eyes as her palm slid over his cheek, to his trim beard, and down his sinuous neck. He was so warm.

"I'd show the world the lines of you," she said. "How your Will holds the Empire up toward the heavens."

His hands gripped hers and heat flooded her body. He cupped her skull and dragged his thumbs over her shivering lips. His mouth found hers, and she dissolved into a wash of red, black, blue, and green, the world a buzz around them. His lips forged a path down her neck, and she blinked, catching a glimpse of an elegant jawline, a peek of tendons wrapped around a strong shoulder under the edge of his fine, harvest-brown kaftan. Head moving down, Varol found her collarbone. She tried to say something saucy, but gasped instead.

If he thought she'd tell him to stop, he was wrong. Minutes or hours passed, Ona wasn't sure about the time. All she knew was Varol's power and the way it made her mouth feel, her body feel, her heart feel. This was how it was supposed to be. A man powerful enough to challenge her, to frighten her a little. In his strong arms, his cobra eyes on her, she was the person she'd longed to be for what felt like forever. She was steel and he was flint, and together they burned the hurt out of her soul.

A VOICE SHOUTED beyond the tent walls. Whoever it was called out in the desert tongue, then finally in the trade language.

"Fire! In the city! The training fields! Fire!"

They pushed away from one another, and Varol tucked his kaftan into place. He pulled the door open to trade words with his guard in his quick native tongue.

He turned to her, eyes still hot, and Ona said, "Go."

In the quiet of the tent, Ona's mind returned to the sword on the table.

2 6

SEREN

Throwing worried glances over his shoulder, Cansu led Seren to the sacred bowl. Varol and Adem waited. They stood beside a row of Adem's loyal followers, three lines of warriors behind them. The moon bleached their faces into the white of picked bones.

Seren's heart fell into her stomach.

Adem's eyes, ringed in purple, held defeat instead of triumph. Maybe he agreed that the planned flaying of the king was the wrong move. Maybe he'd support her.

Cansu, Hossam, Erol, and Seren stopped at the edge of the pool. Water lapped against the sides, a drop splashing Seren's sandal, cooling her heated skin. Before Varol could say a word, she bent, dipped both sets of fingers, and stood to draw the water over her forehead and down her cheeks. A blessing from her city, her water, her people.

"Pearl of the Desert," Varol said, his voice like a heavy bell. "You're charged with the murder of Kyros Meric."

Varol held out the water bowl that they'd used to dig Meric's shallow grave. Varol tipped it over. Sandy dirt and a tassel from Meric's favorite sash ghosted into the air.

Seren's body turned to water. She stumbled, Hossam and Erol catching her. She was no longer kyros, or the kyros's wife, no longer untouchable.

They must've left the bowl and tassel under the bed, with the extra dirt. That—along with the information Varol had probably gained from Adem and whoever else supported him—would be plenty to sentence her for murder.

This was it. This was her end. *I'm sorry, sisters, Father.*

Ona walked out from behind Varol, her face washed of any emotion. She stopped for a breath, eyes on Seren, and started toward her. To speak up for Seren? To further crush her? To stand by her side? But before Ona could move away, Varol put a hand to Ona's waist, keeping her there, by his side. Her body almost seemed to melt into his.

Seren gripped her guards' arms, heart hammering. Every conversation with Ona—since Varol's arrival—unraveled, then wove itself into a new pattern. The people gasped at the break in tradition, at the touching between Kyros Varol and a woman who wasn't his wife.

This was Ona's secret. She and Varol had been lovers.

A crack cut through Seren's heart and a shudder ripped through her limbs.

Her friend had lied. She cared for her enemy, taken into her arms the man who would take Seren's people from her and endanger their lives. When Adem had sent for Varol, Seren had felt a sting, but he'd done it because tradition was in his bones. He'd done it because that was what was expected of him. Ona had sided with Varol because she believed he was the better ruler. She believed he could save them from the Invaders, not Seren.

It was a bleeding, burning rendering of Seren's heart.

True betrayal.

Varol raised his hands. "As your kyros, I'm here to comfort and protect you in this trying time. I promise today will see our victory against the Invaders. I'll kill their king before their very eyes. And to avenge your former kyros and my brother's death, I condemn Seren, Pearl of the Desert to death."

Seren couldn't breathe, let alone beg Varol to listen to reason. Or ask for help.

He turned to her. "Take her to her cell. She, along with that Invader pig, hangs from the walls at dawn."

The moon bled silver into her eyes, blinding her as strong arms dragged her away from her people. "You can't hang their king from the walls. It'll only anger them and make them fight harder!"

But Varol wasn't listening. Adem glanced her way, face unreadable.

27

ONA

"You aren't going to kill her, are you? She didn't kill your brother." Ona followed Varol into Adem's tent. The walls were darker than Varol's quarters or Seren's. The place was like a cave and Ona swallowed, suddenly feeling like she was being buried alive.

Varol spun. His eyes blazed. "She hid my brother's death from General Adem. From me. She never sent word. Adem did. After the fire that she started, the general told me the whole story. I believe it because, although he never approved of Seren, he didn't want to see her dead."

But Adem couldn't have told him everything. If he had, Lucca would already be dead.

Varol stormed toward Ona, step by thunderous step, and she backed up, a little bit enjoying his venom.

"Adem told me she hired some unknown person to pose as Meric in my brother's own bed," he spat. "Seren is a devil." Varol's hips pinned hers to the lotus pillar that supported the tent's heavy fabric walls. The stone chilled Ona's bones. "I will not permit her to live on after making a mockery of my family and our line of rule. She will die and she will die in pain."

She shivered, and this time it had nothing to do with attraction. She decided she only liked his venom aimed at her enemies. Seren wasn't quite an enemy. She didn't want to see her die either. She only wanted her…out of the way. Out of the way of revenge. If she proved to be a barrier again, well, that'd be her fault. Nothing mattered more than making the Invaders bleed.

"Fine. All right. I understand." Ona ran a hand up Varol's chest. "But kill their king first. Not at the same time. He doesn't deserve to die beside one of yours."

"She is not one of mine."

"The people don't see it that way. Neither would the Invaders. They'll see one of ours dying and think it's chaos within our ranks."

Adem walked through the door. "It's time, my kyros."

"What do you think of Seren dying beside the Invader king?" Varol kept to the trade tongue.

Adem's lip curled for a second. It was so quick, Ona thought she might've imagined it. "You meant to say *Pearl of the Desert*, my kyros," he said, giving Seren his version of a proper title. "And your will is ours, my lord."

"Onaratta Paints with Blood says if I kill her beside him, the Invaders will think there is chaos within our ranks."

Adem shrugged, but his eyes didn't match the carefree statement of his body language. "So what if they do? They'll only become more arrogant, or more confused. Either way, it won't be true. You are the kyros and no one will speak against you."

"They won't speak against me, but will they act against me, General Adem? Have you heard rumors?"

He swallowed. "Those born in the Green Mountains like...her, they may wish she was given more honors."

"You are of her blood."

"But I never lived there. I was born to middle-caste soldiers who raised me to fight for the Empire, not for one of its tiny borderlands."

"I've seen your loyalty. Don't fear me."

Adem gave a small bow. "As you wish, my kyros."

"We'll take Onaratta's advice. Now, let's go kill a king."

His words thrilled Ona's blood. She flexed her hand on her sword hilt, ready to see her enemy die.

VAROL, Adem, and two fighters had the Invaders' king on the parapet right above the main city gates. The heavy wood doors were shut tight against the enemy army. It was something of a risk for Varol to be up there. If an Invader could slip past their archers, he could let an arrow loose and bring their kyros down. But she guessed risk was part of the show. They wanted to confuse, enrage, stir up the pigs.

Men, women, and children jostled around the ranks, bumping the lines into disarray with their pointing and shouting, their kabobs of peppered, green-herbed goat, and their caste bells jingling everywhere. The atmosphere was celebration with a bright stripe of fear.

Ona had bought Seren some time with the whole *not proper to die beside the king* thing. Ona wanted to get her out and persuade her to flee. The plan for success was in place—trick the Invaders and outmaneuver them. They didn't need Seren's unpredictable weapons. Her instability. And Ona needed Lucca focused too.

Speak of the devil. Some ridiculous half cloak and hood shadowed Lucca's face. Nuh walked beside him, eyes on the parapet.

"What are we doing about Seren?" Lucca said into her ear.

"What is this?" Ona picked at the half cloak's ratty edges.

"Who cares? Focus, Ona. No one knows where they took Seren. He hid her somewhere. By sundown, she'll be dead."

"He'll wait until we destroy the Invaders." He was the one who needed to focus.

"What if he doesn't?" Lucca's eyes were wild. "Or what if we lose and she is trapped?"

"I don't know where her cell is," she said. "How can we get her out if we don't even know where to look?"

Lucca growled and leaned left and right, like he might burst right out of his skin.

"It can't be that hard to find," she said, giving Nuh a look. "Try the farming district. It's the only area that isn't stuffed with people. I'd hide someone there and set a guard. You can ask around. Someone will talk. A wife who likes your eyes. A child you can bribe…"

"Well then, let's get to it," Lucca said.

"I'm watching the king die."

"Ona. Please." He pushed fists against the front of his brigantine like he was trying to keep his heart in his chest.

But Ona's empathy only glowed so bright. Inside her, revenge blazed like a beacon fire. "Absolutely not."

A woman with green eye cosmetics like Seren wore bumped into Lucca and Ona. The lady craned her neck to see Adem's men fitting the king with a noose.

"This is the meaning of my life," Ona said. "To watch Invaders suffer and die. I wouldn't miss this for her, for me, for you. You must understand that. You're the one who introduced me to the idea."

She didn't know when Lucca had backed away a step, but he had, and his lips had paled. "I shouldn't have," he said. "You don't even know what you're so upset about losing anymore."

"I lost my life." Heads turned. Ona lowered her voice. "Now I'm going to watch him lose his."

Varol spat words into the king's face, words in the desert race's tongue, lovely, complicated, hate-filled words. Ona loved the shape of them on Varol's deadly mouth.

When she turned back, Lucca was gone.

Varol faced the Invaders and shouted something at them in the Invaders' beast-like language. He grabbed the king by the back of the collar and showed him to his army. The king barked out words and the kyros slammed him against the parapet. Adem lashed the king to the stone and Varol began his bloody work.

Everyone went silent.

Each time the whip's metal tips flashed in the sun, Ona smiled.

The steel had to be some of the best. They didn't make anything less in this iron ore city. Despite the amazing cut of the weapon currently ripping him to shreds, the king had been impressively stoic, holding fairly still and not crying out. At the fifth stroke, he lurched and shouted.

Ona cupped a hand to her mouth to help her words fly. "Is it strange to see your own blood pooled at your feet?" she shouted in the trade tongue, and laughed, loud, though none near her joined in. She stared at the warriors and merchants and wives and brothers. "What's wrong with you? He is our enemy. He has taken our loved ones and poured their blood on the ground. Why don't you enjoy his suffering? It's cleansing." She laughed again. "I love it."

The whip cracked again. Snapped. Whooshed through the silence.

Varol stopped, handed the whip to Adem, then took a long dagger from his sash. He said something in the king's ear, pulled the man up by the hair and sliced the golden locks away, dropping them outside the walls.

The crowd did shout then, and the fighters banged fists on chests and shields.

Ona rubbed her hands together. It was time for the pig king to die.

The warriors near Adem and Varol lifted the king and his arms reached out. They pushed him over the wall, and the rope was the only thing left to see from inside the capitol city.

Varol looked down. His gaze latched onto Ona. She raised her sword, hilt first, and touched it to her forehead, swearing fealty the way Silvanian mercenaries did. She lowered her weapon to see him smiling, and he was the most vicious, gorgeous thing in the world. Heat flooded her stomach and tingled in her thighs and the tips of her fingers. She'd never wanted a man so much.

A rumbling rose from the Invaders, but she didn't wait around to see what would happen next. She still loved Lucca, and he needed Seren to live through this. Ona didn't want Seren to die either, so she had to find the woman and free her before the battle began.

∾

WHEN SHE FINALLY FOUND LUCCA, he and Nuh were questioning a reed-thin man in the farming district. Lucca grabbed the man by the arms, shook him. From this distance, Lucca looked like a crazy person.

"Tell him, Nuh," Lucca shouted. "Tell him his kyros has been tricked and needs him to tell us every single detail." A curl dropped over Lucca's face and a dot of spittle appeared on his lower lip. "We don't have time for this. We have no time!"

The man let out a string of foreign words, and Nuh released him. Nuh rubbed a hand over the back of his neck and explained. "He doesn't know anything. No one here has seen her. Or any of the high general—the kyros's —guards."

Lucca let out a loud, gritty breath toward the sun. He pulled out his sword and slashed through a sapling with a shout.

Ona came up behind him. Carefully. He was her friend. But he was a dangerous man. Especially when he was like this.

Once, right after Ona was promoted to condotierri, Dom had enjoyed enough wine for four people and had jumped onto Lucca's horse bareback.

"Let's race, Ona!" Dom's words had slurred together like a smeared painting. "I want to see how Lucca's two ripe fillies perform." He'd smacked the horse's side hard and taken off into the black night of the forest.

Lucca had moved fast, not needing a chant. Mounting the nearest horse, he'd taken off, then returned later with a laughing Dom. Foam ringed the horses' mouths. Lucca tied them up and spun to face Dom.

Lucca struck Dom twice with a fist across the jaw, dropping the taller man. His foot on Dom's throat, Lucca took Dom's sword and threw it to Ona.

"Do what you want to him for speaking to you like that. Just don't kill him. You know what he's worth in a fight."

Ona had cut her initials into Dom's thigh, a permanent reminder that she'd get her vengeance no matter who wronged her.

Now, Ona put an easy hand on Lucca's back.

"Let's look somewhere else," she said, wondering what he'd do if he'd seen her with Varol during Seren's arrest. "We have time. We aren't attacking until nightfall, when the moon will show the Invaders' stupid, overly shiny breastplates, but won't give them the light to see exactly what we're up to."

He nodded too quickly. His color was high.

She glanced at his sword and he seemed surprised to see it unsheathed. He tucked it away and followed her and Nuh away from the farm district.

"I'll find out where they're keeping her," she said. "From Varol."

"Why would he tell you?"

"Even in the middle of a siege a man is a man." Ona raised her eyebrows. "Bet on it."

Lucca's grin lacked any sort of good humor. "I'd never bet against you."

28

ONA

"When do we send the first wave through the front gates?" In Adem's tent, Ona paced a line in front of Varol and his men. Adem ran a hand over his chin, glancing up every now and then from his war map. Nuh and Haris stood beside Ona like her own retinue. "We should wait until we have the group who'll perform the false retreat at the mouth of the mine."

Varol nodded. His finger drew a line down Adem's map. "Agreed. How many should make up the front division, General Adem?"

Sweet Bean's eyes narrowed like he could see the warriors moving along the parchment's markers. "Three units, I think. I'll lead them."

Nuh made a noise that almost sounded like "No."

Ona knew why. Adem was basically offering himself as a sacrifice for the city. The front force would take the heaviest hit as the false retreat unit performed their little act.

Varol glided past the table and came up close to Ona. The men around them stiffened at the second breach in tradition with regard to him and her and their glaringly obvious physical attraction.

Sweet Bean looked ready to pop out of his hard shell. "Kyros Varol, please. This is not proper behavior from one such as illustrious as you. The royal line must uphold our—"

Varol's fingers started at Ona's temples, ran down the two sides of her face, and came together at her chin. Ona was clay for him to mold. She sighed. He was cruel, but just. Finally, at long, long last, she'd found a leader

519

worthy of her purpose. She allowed him to tilt her mouth to his where he paused.

"General Adem, are you my father?" he asked.

"No, Kyros, of course not."

"Then why—"

"Your father is dead," Adem said.

"Exactly so. And so is my brother. You know all the secrets about that."

Adem breathed out through his nose. Ona's stomach tightened. Varol's mouth touched her ear, made her shiver. Neither man knew everything.

"Would you agree then, General, that I am the embodiment of our Empire?" Varol asked. "That I am the pinnacle of what it means to be of the Holy Fire's home?"

"That's why you must act with reserve until you are wed to a woman who equals your beauty and who shows patience and calm."

"*Must act.* Hm. That doesn't sound like something you should say to a kyros, does it, mercenary?"

His eyes made Ona dizzy with want. He could order anyone he wanted to fall on their sword.

"No, it doesn't," she whispered.

"See? Even this lowly, foreign mercenary knows. She'd lead the charge at the front gates if I asked it."

"I would," Ona said, "but I'll fight beside you, my kyros."

"Beside me? I don't think so."

"I thought—"

"That we were equals?"

"We…" The room's heat closed in. Ona searched for the right word. He understood her, didn't he? "We connected."

"We certainly did."

"I thought up this plan. You can't throw me into the fray as a distraction. My unit will be more useful in the second wave, after the false retreat depletes their numbers."

"I *can't?*" Varol's voice raised the hairs on the back of her neck. "Kneel, mercenary."

She swallowed. "Varol."

Adem stepped closer. "You will address him properly, Silvanian."

Ona gave in. A rock under the rugs jabbed her knee. She wiped her palms on her brigantine as Varol looked down, his cobra eyes were trained on her, instead of aimed at her enemy. Where had she gone wrong?

"You will lead the distraction attack," he said. "At the front. With that unit you and the other mercenary supposedly trained."

She would die. She might cut through twenty, thirty Invaders, but there'd be a thousand more and she'd be a sacrifice for this city. Her unit couldn't chant well enough. Only a few showed true promise. They'd all die.

"And if I refuse?" she asked, almost whispering.

A light in his eyes struck out. "Then you'll lose your pretty hands. Or your head, depending on my mood."

"I betrayed my friend for you," she said, thinking of Lucca's wild eyes. "And Seren. I kept her under control while you plotted." Ona thought of the look on Seren's face when she stood beside Varol.

Adem pressed two fingers into the bridge of his nose.

Varol glanced at him, then back at Ona. "Yes, but you didn't tell me their secrets. General Adem did. And you…" He moved a hand over her head, pressing harder and harder until her neck cramped. "You were a part of their deceit."

"Kyros Meric died of a cough and a fever."

"You, a filthy, low mercenary posed as my own royal brother in his very bed. You attempted to fool my general."

Icy fingers tore at her confidence. She gritted her teeth against the chill. "I was good enough for you and your wandering hands. And I *did* fool him."

His hand struck her cheek hard. Blood heated her lip and dripped off her chin. "Or perhaps my general was biding his time," he said.

Adem studied the ground. He'd been tricked by Seren, Lucca, and Ona. But she'd been fooled, too. By Varol.

Her veins shouted, but her words refused to rise. She stood, pushing against Varol's hand, rebelling against her own weakness, her mistake, those icy fingers. "I'll lead the first strike, the distraction. And I'll slay more Invaders than anyone in history." For the first time in her life, her voice shook and her words thinned.

"Of course you will. Because I have ordered it so," he said. She was choking, suffocating, his words—instead of hers—held all the strength of a chant as they smothered her. "It is truly sad the Invader king told me one truth that none of you could," Varol continued. "That pig told me a story about a rodent and a lioness."

Ona grabbed the front of her vest. Choking. Smothering. She remembered the slur the king had spat at Seren. She hadn't understood it then, but now…

"Ah, I see you know what I'm talking about. Are you ever telling the whole truth, mercenary? Forget it. I don't care. Lucca Hand of Ruination has designed his own ruin." Varol snapped at two of his personal guards.

"Find the male mercenary. Don't wait to run him through. Do it fast and let it be done. I have better things to worry me."

Before Ona could fall to her knees, defeated, Nuh and Haris dragged her from the spinning tent and away from the man she'd thought was the answer to everything.

29

SEREN

Varol's men moved Seren quickly through the streets, presumably so no one could follow without being noticed. She'd seen Cansu's face when Varol announced her arrest. He would try to free her. Erol and Hossam, maybe not. They'd merely looked at the ground like they were afraid to meet her eyes.

And Ona.

Her friend. Or she'd thought she was.

Varol's men walked Seren into the main tent, tugged a hooded cloak over her, and steered her out the servants' door. The only sound this far from the gathered crowd was the water trickling through the shallow canals as it slipped from tent shadow to tent shadow, hiding from the sun.

"Where are you taking me?"

The men stared ahead, their silence as loud as any shout. They passed out of the Kyros Walls, through the back gates, and into the training field. The clay pot weapons made a border between the archery range and the stables. What a waste. Where was the engineer now? Had he escaped? He was probably dead. Another waste.

Seren could hardly put one foot in front of the other. The sun bleached the sky and scorched her head, turning her high-caste bell into a branding iron. She may've been the highest ranked woman in the Empire, but now she was nothing more than a prisoner.

There wasn't a soul in the training fields. If the Invaders managed to scale the walls here, they'd enter without a yatagan drawn or an Invader's sword unsheathed. The idea of steel brought Ona punching into her thoughts.

Had she been lying this whole time? Had she told Adem Seren had hidden Meric's death? But why had Ona helped her only to turn on her?

Varol couldn't know she was the one who'd posed as Meric. He'd never stomach kissing a woman who'd been involved in that. Not that he'd loved Meric. Well, perhaps he had a little. But his jealousy had been the main player in that drama. The foremost affront to Varol was what he'd see as a humiliation, the dragging down of his royal family. He could verbally attack Meric, but Holy Fire help anyone else who did so.

How deeply was Ona involved? When had Ona given up on Seren?

One of the men looked back toward the city as they entered the scorched stables. Seren's throat closed and she forced a sob down. Her Fig. Someone had dragged the bodies of the horses that had been lost past the stables and covered them in sackcloth. They'd be burned soon. Seren would never run a thumb over Fig's scarred ear again. Fig wouldn't nuzzle against her shoulder and make her feel like no matter what problems she had, mistakes she made, that she was enough. At least Fig's half-brother, the young colt, had survived. She strained to hear his high whinny, but there was only the wind and the men beside her.

Gray-green scrub grew in tight fists on the hill behind the stables.

"There is nothing here. You've made some mistake," Seren said.

They urged her on with the butt of their yatagans, closer to the hill and the empty, dry space stretching to the outer walls. They stopped at the incline's base and one guard shifted dusty earth from a spot in the ground below a lone tree that had stubbornly sprouted and boasted a handful of leaves. As the guard cleared more sandy dirt, a line appeared, then two.

Someone had set a wooden frame into the dirt. No. It was a door. A secret door lying against the slight rise in the ground.

The guards lifted the door and led her down a set of sunken steps. Lamps hung from posts that jutted out of the rough, wooden walls. It was like a mine but without the noise, carts, and tools. Newer slats ran along an opening to the right. This had been a mine a very long time ago. At the end of the passage, they veered left. Bars extended from ceiling to floor, broken by a latched door of shorter cylinders of iron.

This was to be her prison.

The cell shrank and she was miles away. Only habit kept her from grabbing the guards to stay standing. She fisted her hands and her nails branded her palms. Clearing her throat, she ignored the sweat pooling on her lip and along her back.

"This will be satisfactory." She lifted the cell door herself and climbed inside before they could force her. "I'll be very safe here." A bed of grasses lay against the wall. "Maybe the Holy Fire—oh!—there isn't a Fire bowl." If she couldn't pray, she'd never last an hour. She needed something to focus on.

The guards traded a look. One nodded. "I'll bring you one, Pearl of the Desert. It'd be wrong for you to go without in your position."

Her position. Was that as a person who'd ruled the Empire for a matter of hours, or as a person who was about to die?

The lock on the latch door clicked as the guard turned the key. They walked away and left her in the cell. Alone.

The lamps burned steadily. Silence weighted her ears. Her heart beat, urging her to panic, scream, shout out for help that would never, could never hear. A shush-shush sounded all around and reverberated off the walls like drums. It wasn't someone coming for her. It wasn't the pound of hooves or boots. It was only her pulse.

No one was coming.

Would the horses—those still alive—startle if she screamed? Would they hear her at all?

Lucca would've searched for her, but she'd sent him away. She pictured his easy smile, his confident gait, and the way his eyes widened as he listened, really listened. *Lucca.* She pressed her palms together, remembering the feel of his hand, the promise of support. Had he understood why she ordered him to go? The hurt in his eyes had looked so real. He had to know he wasn't below her, no matter their respective ranks. She'd only wanted to protect him.

She hoped he was long gone, escaping before the Invaders grew comfortable in their siege and had time to watch for single riders. She imagined him galloping away, his mount kicking up the dust as he drove toward his home full of dark green trees.

But that was optimistic. More likely, the Invaders would catch and question him.

Her stomach dropped.

Their questioning involved fists, blades. He wouldn't tell them a thing. Her heart knew that. At least there, if he survived, he had a chance at a life. If he'd stayed here, Varol would've had him put to death alongside her. It was only a matter of time.

Cansu would look for her. She knew it. But Adem would know it, too. He'd assign Cansu to a position where he'd have no opportunity to attempt freeing her. Could Cansu break away and gather people loyal to her? What then? She didn't want a war within a war.

If she stayed here, kept quiet and accepted her punishment—part of which she surely deserved—her warriors would be led by a pompous, self-serving kyros. He was no good for them. Adem would advise him well, but Varol wouldn't listen. He never had. Not when Meric and Varol's father gave him direction during the first trade attempts with Silvania and the negotiations with Jakobden's amir. It was why they'd had to send another group to Silvania. He'd insulted their reigning families so much that they'd refused to meet with representatives for three years. Why did Adem have such faith in him?

Seren pressed her fingers against her temples. Her head pounded. She could reach through the bars, but even if she had something she could work into the locking mechanism, she'd never have the angle to dislodge the spring.

Footsteps sounded. Seren leaned into the iron rods. Before whoever it was came around the corner, she straightened and smoothed her hair.

One of the guards who'd brought her there held out a Fire bowl. "For you, Pearl of the Desert."

She bit her lip, hiding the hope she shouldn't even have. It was *good* Lucca was gone, that he wasn't here to try in vain to save her, that he was far, far away from Varol.

The guard set the bowl of lahabshjara leaves and little flames on a collapsible pedestal beyond the door. He lit it, and with a nod, turned to leave. It was a poor setup for the Holy Fire, the bowl precariously perched on the wobbly pedestal.

Working her arms through the bars, she stretched hands over the flame. "Holy Fire, I…"

No prayer came to her. No visions or comforting ideas. It was over.

Varol held her people in his cruel hands. The red tent would be gone by sundown and that meant no one would survive this siege. Tonight they would raise the black tent and all would be cut down when the Invaders won.

She fisted her hands, the Fire licking her knuckles. Why wouldn't Varol at least try her weapon? It would decrease their numbers. There were probably more ideas, too. From their fighters, from Lucca and Ona. She'd ruined everything. She pulled her hands back and accidentally knocked the Fire. The bowl tipped and slid to the ground. The Fire thinned, then went dark, its potential snuffed as surely as her own.

30

ONA

T he noise stirred and lifted the dust as Ona's unit gathered behind the towering doors to Akhayma. The doors' carved and molded flames reflected the moonlight and formed eyes that watched them assemble for a battle people were probably going to make wild tales about for eons. Ona was sick to her stomach. The tales were probably going to be true. And not good. Not good at all. Warriors of all sizes, ages, breathed the same desert air as her. They held their weapons ready, hers straight and familiar—theirs slightly curved, thin, more wicked. How did she end up here? It felt so very wrong to be away from Lucca and going into a fight. Like she was missing a leg or something.

Archers fired from the walls far above. There was no way to tell if they were having an effect on the Invaders' massive army beyond the layers of stone and wood. Her ears couldn't pick out the sound of arrow tips hitting metal or flesh. It was only the noise like a storm of shouting, pleading, feet on the ground, hooves against the earth, steel, and her own heart's fierce thrust to win, win, win.

And then she had no room left in her to worry about Lucca, Seren, or herself.

The men on the opposite side of these walls had shaped her into a creature who only saw beauty in shattered bones and ripe blood. She had no room for friendship. Certainly not for love. Seren was a fool for not focusing on her purpose. Lucca, a fool with her.

Varol might've tricked Ona, but she'd win. She'd survive this and her revenge would shine bright all over his city, so bright he couldn't ignore or blame her. She'd be the instrument of victory. Nothing could push her off course.

Her body thrummed as Varol's warriors began to pull the doors open. The archers let thousands of arrows fly into the dusty air. She dragged her flint across her blade, sparks flying around her unit as they began chanting and striking their own flints. Power sang through her muscle and bone, buzzing, howling, shrieking. Sound blasted through the open doors, so many voices and shields and swords, and Ona ran straight into her enemy.

"Wake iron! Wake!
Take my enemy's breath
Steal from him
As he has stolen from me!"

Her sword clanged against another. The man spit at her and shouted in his ugly language. She swung their linked weapons down and jerked back.

"Wake iron!"

She drove her sword under his plated chest. He fell forward. Spinning, the steel and horses a blur, she met another. Dragged her sword across his throat. Varol's fighters cut and hit around her, a river of movement and death. Nuh flipped his yatagan and drove the tip into a shorter man's eye. Ona ended three more Invaders, her hands so much faster than theirs, wrapping them in death like an invisible shroud.

Stepping onto bodies, she drove toward a man wearing a finer surcoat over his armor. He shouldn't have been here. This was a place for grunts. Ona's rage shrieked from her mouth and she ran her blade straight through his neck before he could raise a hand. Beyond his shoulder, the Invaders were grains of sand. So many. So, so many. Gooseflesh rippled over her arms.

A shape up on the city walls jerked her out of the moment.

He still wore his hood, but she knew the set of those shoulders, the lift of that chin.

"Lucca."

He waved for her to retreat, a quick movement, singular and loaded with panic.

"No!" As if he could hear her.

He gripped the parapet.

A force knocked against Ona's spine. Cold and heat both fizzed up her skin. She whispered a chant and kicked the attacker away before spinning to bring her sword down on the exposed flesh at the back of his neck.

Her body sagged. Lucca was still there, but now he fired his bow along with the others, the dark arms of his sleeves moving in rhythm with the warriors around him.

Ona brought her aunt's face to mind as she leaped over a pair of Invaders. She pulled out her dagger, and in one move, drove steel into the base of their necks and through their worthless spines. Her aunt's face flickered. Changed. Ona's stomach lurched.

She cut down another enemy, and three more, chanting as she painted the ground red.

The familiar horror in her aunt's face shifted to sadness. Her imagined eyes met Ona's. Her lips turned down at the edges, a smear of blue paint marring her olive skin.

Pushing the image away, Ona sheathed her dagger, drew her flint again. Atop an overturned cart, she tore the flint across the steel. Light flashed in the dark. This was her path.

"Wake! Wake! Wake!"

Something burned down her cheeks as she twisted and struck, severing an Invader's arm. Her sword ate into an enemy's leg. Blood's metal scent swallowed everything except the image of her aunt, the haunting exactness of every pore and wrinkle and color.

Ona blinked as Nuh tripped, crashed against a dead man, and was stabbed.

Her aunt looked at her from her memory. Looked. At. Her.

Shoving her thoughts back into the fray, she saw Varol's men—her unit —surrounded by silver, red, and white. The enemy coiled around them and her, and opened its mouth to swallow. Beyond them, there were so many more, an endless nightmare made of sword fangs, moon-washed faces, and shining carapaces of armor.

In Ona's head, her aunt stared. She mouthed one word. It rushed through Ona like a cold wind. *Wake.*

"No!" she shouted at her memory, refusing her.

Blind with the need to paint the world with blood, Ona ran directly into the tip of a sword.

The world blurred, stilled.

The Invader smiled.

Ona looked up to find Lucca, but he was gone.

Pain launched itself from the wound and screamed its way into her heart. Her aunt—the memory of her aunt—lowered her chin, looked at her clean hands, lifted them for Ona to see.

"Your wishes are my wishes," Ona whispered to Lucca, to wherever he was. "As long as yours don't war with mine."

Enemies faded to gray, her revenge bled out of her, and she knew no more.

31

SEREN

Anoise from the tunnel, beyond the bars, had Seren on her feet.

"Guard?" Her hands shook, so she clasped them behind her back.

But it wasn't the guard.

A figure with dark brown curls and parted lips came around the corner, bow and arrow at the ready.

"Lucca." Her shoulders fell away from her ears where they'd been strung up tight. A warmth slid over her bones. Her trembling hands slid through the bars.

Two vicious, foreign words broke from his mouth. He threw his weapon to the ground and rushed to her, banging one palm against the iron. "How do I get you out?" His hair stuck to his sweating face as he turned right and left.

"I don't know." She hated how defeated she sounded, but she couldn't pretend with Lucca. He'd see through it.

"How did you find me?"

"Erol. He saw them take you into the stables. Cansu guessed there was a place here. Some rumor the men heard."

Her soul swelled. "They're loyal after all." But dark circles had formed under Lucca's eyes and an invisible weight pulled on him.

He dropped to the ground, the bars a wall between them. "She's gone, Seren."

She grabbed his hand. "What? Who?"

He coughed and pulled away, covering his face with his fingers. "Ona… he killed her."

She gripped the bars to stay standing. "Varol?"

"Yes."

She knew he'd turn on Ona. Seren should've warned her about his ability to manipulate and the black place where his soul should've been. "How?"

"He put her at the front. Her whole unit. She was the distraction for the false retreat unit going out through the mines now."

"Did you…did you watch her fall?" The trade language didn't translate this the way Seren wanted it to. She wanted to ask if he experienced her end—a respect for doomed loved ones—but she didn't know the words.

Finding her hand, Lucca's fingers curled around hers. His words were ghosts. "I couldn't. I walked away. I left her."

He kept glancing over his shoulder as if Ona would appear. Like a fighter who'd lost a limb, Seren could tell he felt her phantom presence.

"She betrayed you," Lucca said. "Us. I'm sorry. I should've known he'd be too tempting for her."

"What turned her?" Seren asked quietly.

"It wasn't anything you did. At least, I don't think so. She saw Varol as more powerful. Capable of bringing down the Invaders. It's all she cared about. Revenge. And his presence had to tempt her physically. She loved beauty. In her strange way, she still loved beauty."

His tears wet her fingertips as she pushed his hair out of his eyes. "Lucca. We will honor her."

"You have to hate her."

"I don't. I think I understand why she did what she did. We will honor her. After all of this…"

But she knew it was impossible. He had to flee. Seren had to die. Varol wouldn't honor a Silvanian.

"I should've warned her about him," Seren said. "How he flips easy as a coin. How he hates anyone not of the desert race." She squeezed Lucca's fingers.

He shrugged, but it was a stiff movement, a show, an act. "I suppose someone had to lead the unit. She dropped more than most before her end." He breathed in through his nose. "She looked up at me before…she saw me on the walls in my hood."

"You shouldn't have been there. What if Varol saw you?"

It was as if he didn't hear her. His mind was there, with Ona in the battle. Seren ran a finger over his thumb and a scar on the back of his hand.

"There was no injustice in her being chosen," he said. "Not really. I know Varol did it to get rid of her, but someone had to go. Nuh fell beside her. I should've been there."

Seren swallowed and tasted salt. No one should have to die. But this was war. "But it wasn't her war," she said.

Lucca's eyes flashed. "It was her war. Every battle with the Invaders would always have been *her war*. That's why she's dead. She wouldn't let go of the blood. She clutched at her past like a talisman. A foul token. It didn't protect her. It didn't move her to greatness. It...it killed her."

He shuddered, and his words shone a flickering light into Seren's mind, though she couldn't see what they illuminated. She touched the green wool tucked into her sash as he straightened himself and stood.

Such power in his face. Would it be enough to survive grief and a kyros who wanted him dead?

"You need to escape the city, Lucca. Before Varol or Adem finds you. They won't hesitate to kill you now. Please. I can't lose someone else." The shape of him had become such a comfort. So quickly, he'd soaked into her doomed heart.

"I'm not leaving without you," he said.

She hit the bars with a palm, surprising him with the force of it. "There's nothing I can do. I deceived everyone. I pushed myself into things I shouldn't have. I wasn't careful."

"You are the kyros."

"No. I'm not."

"You are. I've seen you lead. This is your fate. This is your purpose. Why are you letting it fall between your fingers?"

"I'm in a cell, Lucca. You don't have the key. Varol and Adem have an army behind them. Another army lies beyond the walls. This is impossible. It's over."

"Capturing the Invaders' king seemed impossible, but you did it. Leading a city that's never seen a woman at its helm seemed impossible. You did it." He gripped the bars and stared into her face. His tears had left lines on his strong cheekbones, in the stubble on his jawline. "What is holding you back from at least trying to get out of here?"

She touched his face, then stepped back, her fingers lighting on the scrap of her wool skirt.

"I just don't know what to do. It's not like I've been here before! What do you expect from me? I'm only a girl from a little village with grief I can't lay down and—"

He didn't say a word. He didn't have to. Her words echoed in her mind, spinning into an image of Ona's rage and need for revenge. Heat reared up behind her eyes. She wasn't letting the past go and moving forward. Ona hadn't either, and she'd died because of it.

For a second, Seren could almost see her sisters' small fingers bunched in her green, woolen skirts. She remembered her father's black boot, the sound of his heel against the wood floor as he stepped between them and the small band of Invaders who'd kicked their way into their home in the mountains.

"Ona wouldn't let go of what happened to her," Seren said, mostly to herself. "She was a slave to revenge. And where has it thrown her? Varol didn't repay her betrayal of us. Revenge isn't a just master. She wouldn't release her past, and now she is gone. Dead on the field."

Her throat closed on the words. They both fought tears, their breath mingling in the dank cell. Seren gripped Lucca's fingers around the bars.

"Our Ona died at the hands of the ones she hated," she said.

The ones she hated. Seren's chest collapsed as she relived the sound of her family dying. Her heart stuttered. The feel of foreign fingers on her arm as she was dragged into the sun. The shout of Meric and his father as they fought off the Invaders.

Her soul quaked with the sensations of the past.

She remembered riding in a cart, jostling away from the Green Mountains.

The first sight of Akhayma.

Her new life.

Then it was as if the Holy Fire itself burned inside Seren. She could see everything inside her soul. And she hid from what she saw.

"No." She pushed away from the bars and crossed her arms over herself, the muscles in her throat strangling her. "But what if I fail and die? My sisters, they didn't even have the chance to live. They should be here. My sisters. My sweet sisters. Their soft cheeks. Their sharp, little minds. They could've been so much, lived so much."

She wasn't making sense. The room spun around her, and she ripped the wool from her sash and pressed it into her skin, remembering every laugh, touch of a hand, joke by the fire, their little wishes and hopes and wild dreams.

"It isn't fair. It isn't right that I'm here. I'm nothing to them. They were so colorful, Lucca. You should've seen them. If you could only see them."

She ended up slumped against the bars with Lucca's body warming one arm, one leg, both hands. She pressed her wet face into his sleeve, into the bars, until she only saw black and the stars behind her eyes.

Lucca's finger lifted her chin—an awkward angle through the iron—and he took her green wool, tucked it back into her sash.

"Keep the sour-sweet memories. I'll do the same." His gaze drifted over his belt where a shape had been scratched into the leather—a remnant from some memory with Ona, probably. He met Seren's eyes. "But don't let the tragedy hold you back. Let it move you forward."

Seren set her palm against her sash and the hidden spot of green inside.

Squeezing her eyes shut, she tried to ignore Lucca's words and the Holy Fire's clarity, the light of them. But they wouldn't let her shift them away.

Lucca was right. The Fire was right.

Ona died holding on to her pain. If Seren clutched at her own horror and held it and acted with it always judging her every word, not only would she die too, but her people would bleed under Invaders' swords. That couldn't be the path the Holy Fire wanted for her. Not after thrusting her to the highest position in the Empire.

She breathed once, slow and shaking, and let the light wash over her. They sat there for long time. Breathing. Grieving.

Then Seren opened her blurry eyes.

Blinking, she settled her past into her heart to keep it, to use it.

Ona's mistake may've betrayed Seren, but it had also saved Seren. Seren would not make Ona's mistake.

When Seren's vision cleared, she was someone different.

Lucca's lips made a line and he nodded once. "Time to move forward?"

She wiped her face and rose. "Too bad there is a wall of iron in my way."

He did a little half laugh, half smile, and her heart tripped even though she was stuck in a cell with only a handful of hours left to her on this earth and death all around them both.

"What's so funny?" she asked.

"They didn't think a chanter would find you," he said.

Stepping back, he pulled out his sword and flint. He slashed the flint across the steel and a spark danced into the air. He chanted in Silvanian, then grinned again and switched to the trade tongue.

"Don't change it so I can understand," she said. "Just do what you need to do."

"I think it'll help if your will is behind it too."

"I wish I had a Fire bowl."

The lines around his intense eyes smoothed. "Can you use the spark I create?"

Seren stepped back, thrown by the idea. "Maybe. The improbable sometimes happens. After all, I never would've predicted I'd fall for a Silvanian mercenary."

His eyes burned. "Seren."

Her insides melted, and she wanted out of this cell for yet another reason altogether.

He began to chant, his trade tongue strong and direct.

"Wake iron!
Be stronger than your kin here,
Force your will through your lessers!
Part what has been joined!
Join what has been parted!"

The fire leaped from his sword. Seren opened her hands to aim her palms at the tumultuous light.

"Holy Fire," she whispered under his chanting. "Tell me what to do. Lead us. Help us."

He struck the flint. Two arms of orange unfurled into the near dark. She kept praying.

"Shout it, Seren!"

"I can't...I don't know if this is right. I don't want to say something wrong..."

"Feel it, Seren. You are the kyros. This is your Holy Fire. I give it to you. I submit to you. Own your place, Seren. Shout! Shout! Shout!"

The sparks dove out his sword and flint, jumping, twisting, striving, as he chanted his power into the room. Her bones, warmed by his presence, now burned like she was the spark, the flame, the power he was calling forward. She was shaking. Gasping. Her words grew and grew and grew.

"Holy Fire." Her voice reverberated off the ceiling, the walls. "Please give me the spark of ideas. I am the sultana and I will aid my people." The words echoed in her ears.

Lucca slashed at the bars. His sword caught against the iron. He'd bent the bars, not broken them. "Don't hold anything back!" he shouted above his flint-striking.

She splayed her fingers and Lucca's sparks danced toward her flesh. "Holy Fire, I am Kyros Seren and I ask for your guidance, your help. Free me to protect the innocents from the errors of a wayward man."

Her palms lit up like bright candles, and the Fire appeared between her eyebrows, falling to a jagged spot on the door. A flaw in the iron, an opportunity.

A smile like a blade sliced over Lucca's face. *"Wake iron, wake!"*

He drew his sword back and slammed its edge into the Fire's chosen place.

32

SEREN

Outside the cell, Seren crashed into Lucca. His hands drove up her neck and into her hair. Her mouth found his and she could never get enough. The taste of him, the scent of Silvanian pines in his skin, the feel of his jaw under her fingertips, the beat of his heart against hers.

She pulled away. "We need cloaks."

Lucca was panting. "Wh-what?"

"Ore master cloaks. They wear better hoods than this." As he picked up his sword and sheathed it, she held up the end of the hooded clothing he'd found.

She grabbed his hand and started to run.

The tunnel gave way to the moonlit night and the distant sound of battle. The stables had been emptied and the archery field was an ocean of stillness.

"Oh, I've seen the cloaks," he said. "Those long, black ones."

"Yes. I need Meekra. She'll know where to find some. The royal household has a few for guests Meric didn't want others to know about. I sent Meekra to help with some things near the western side of the city. But do you know if Meekra was imprisoned or..."

Seren clutched at her stomach. She hadn't thought of her until now, thinking Meekra was safe because she hadn't been around during the arrest. Seren and Lucca scanned the cells at the far end of the training field but only saw prisoners in homespun, filthy wools, darker clothing too, but none of Meekra's finer clothing. The moon was a blank-eyed skull, a reflection of the death suffocating her city.

"I don't think so," Lucca said of Meekra. "I haven't seen her. Not since you ordered me away."

"You know why I did." Seren pulled him through the inner gates and toward Barir's home. Surely she'd go there when she learned Seren had been arrested. "If you die too, if I lose you too…"

Lucca's mouth found Seren's disheveled hair and he breathed, "Shhh. We'll come through this. Somehow. Now, where are you taking me?"

"To the physician's. He is Meekra's father."

Thankfully, people were either hiding with their children in their tents or the adults were out there, in the fighting. No faces appeared at windows. No curious families manned the tables in the market. All the merchandise had been locked away and only a bat swooped over the oasis pool. Something small rummaged through a dropped sack of grain.

Meekra herself opened the door when we arrived. "Come in, Kyros. Thank the Holy Fire you're alive."

Seren crushed Meekra in a hug. "I'm so glad you're all right," Seren said, looking at Barir's whole family. "I'm so glad all of you are all right."

Meekra smiled gravely as Seren moved to the Holy Fire bowl. Seren passed hands over the bowl, and her eyes shuttered closed as she murmured a prayer from childhood, a blend of old beliefs and new. She wasn't going to ignore any parts of herself anymore. She was from the Green Mountains. But she was in love with the desert. She was a woman and a leader. She was kind, but she was fierce. She needed new ways to pray, and the combination suited her soul.

Lucca's large fingers uncurled over the Holy Fire after hers. He spoke in his language, his lips puckering and his tongue dancing.

She gave him a sad smile. He'd have to learn new ways to live too. Ona had been his family and she was gone. His smile answered hers, he nodded once to leave that conversation until later. She agreed. It wouldn't be a good thing for both of them to end up on the floor crying. They had to hold the rest of their grief until they either won this or lost it.

Barir and the rest of his family stared at Seren's torn kaftan sleeve, her smudged cosmetics, and swollen eyes. Coming close, Meekra's little brother lifted a woven blanket worn to threadbare spots along one side. They didn't have time for this, but she *had* to make time for this.

Seren kneeled and reached out a hand to touch the blanket. It was soft as a spring lamb and obviously well-loved. It was probably his mother's coming-of-age ceremonial blanket, given to her youngest and last child to mark the end of her childbearing years.

"I can't take this from you, good man," she said to him.

His big eyes shone. "Oh no, Kyros." His S slipped through the place where two front teeth should've been. "I only mean you can borrow it. 'Til you're happy again."

Meekra gasped and took his shoulders, but Seren smiled, tears threatening her, and brushed a hand over the faded fabric.

"Of course." Seren pressed the blanket once against her heart, then handed it back. "I feel happier already."

The boy grinned and hid his head in his mother's kaftan. She patted his jet hair, and Seren's chest ached for a mother and father she'd lost too soon.

Standing, she spread her hands. "I hope I don't endanger you further with my visit," she said, then explained what she needed with as few details as possible.

With a solemn nod, Barir left to find the ore master cloaks while his wife served mint tea, her younger children heading to the sleeping mat to shut their tired eyes.

"What happens next?" Meekra asked quietly.

"I have to see what's happening beyond the walls," Seren said. "I can't make any decisions until I know how many warriors both sides have left. Have you been to look? Have you heard anything?"

"No. The front gate unit assembled, then I left." Her face told me she knew no one in that force would live past tonight.

Lucca's eyes fluttered shut and his fist pressed into his stomach.

"Though I have, I see, um, Onaratta Paints with Blood in…error," she said to him in broken trade tongue, "I honor her courage."

He must've understood enough of it. His sad eyes flicked to her face and he bowed his head.

"I need to speak plainly, Kyros," Meekra said.

"Of course." Did she worry they weren't friends? "We've been through enough to shed this formality."

A small smile tried to bend Meekra's mouth. "But we need you to keep some of it. We need you to be a leader, not merely another person. Will you finally stand up to General Adem and High General Varol?" Seren loved that she refused to call Varol anything but his original rank. "We need you," Meekra said. "We need you to be strong. Not only smart or kind. Akhayma must have your power."

Lucca's hand warmed Seren's back, not touching, but hovering just above. She could feel the Holy Fire inside her too, driving her to embrace her calling. "I swear by the Fire I'll do everything in my power to save this city."

"If you don't," Meekra said, "we won't be the only ones to fall under the Invaders' yatagans. The entire Empire will be open to attack." Moisture gathered on her thick lashes and she made a noise like a sob.

Seren squeezed her hands. "I'll do my best. That's all I can promise."

Meekra nodded and wiped her eyes.

"Will you find Cansu, another fighter named Haris, and maybe Hossam and Erol?" Seren asked. "Be careful, but will you see if they'll help us? It's very risky. But..."

"But we're all going to die if we don't all take some risks."

"Well said."

Barir came to the door, arms were heavy with black cloth. "I have three ore master cloaks. Here." He handed them out.

"Where should we meet you?" Meekra asked as she pulled one over her head.

Seren slipped hers on. Lucca did the same. They'd be nearly invisible in the night and beyond question in the day. Hopefully. At least until Varol realized Seren wasn't waiting for her death in that awful hole in the ground anymore.

"Meet us at the archery range," Seren whispered to Meekra, watching the younger siblings huddle together in bed. "If the men know where any of the clay pot explosives are, tell them to bring them."

"What if they're afraid to join you?" Barir asked.

Meekra raised her chin and tilted her head. Seren knew she was waiting for her to rise up like she'd promised she would.

Lucca pursed his lips and gave Seren an encouraging nod.

"Tell them their kyros asks them only to do as much as they would for their own families. That is to say, I am their mother. Their sister. Daughter. Aunt. They have to join me now or die in shame tomorrow."

Meekra smiled and everyone raised a palm and bent at the waist.

"May the Holy Fire bless our kyros," everyone said in unison.

And with one last prayer over the Fire, Seren, Lucca, and Meekra bid the family farewell and launched into the deep night.

⌒

Warriors rushed past Seren and Lucca to mount a group of stomping horses held by low-castes. Fig's soft nose moved in Seren's memory and she shook it away to focus. The group gathered at the ring road that led to the old mine exit. Most never knew the dusty path had been smoothed and kept free of tents originally for that purpose. Now, it was only a way to move more quickly to the part of the city where people gambled at all hours and if you didn't watch yourself, skilled fingers would pluck you clean of every coin, ring, and bit of treasure.

Behind a group of archers—newly stocked quivers boasting arrows with fletching in the Empire's blue and black—Lucca and Seren climbed the stairs to the top of the walls.

"We'll need more tips soon, master," one fighter said, seeing Seren's ore master cloak. He nocked an arrow and let it fly into the teeming mass below.

The moon exposed the Invaders' glinting armor and brushed lightly over our warriors' peaked helmets. The clash of steel on steel punctuated the rough, lower sounds of human effort.

The white tent was gone. In its place, a red tent commanded the plains and the army swarming in its dust and around our walls.

"No mercy for any man. Isn't that what it means?" Seren asked Lucca quietly.

His hands clutched the parapet as he scanned the horizon. He held on like he was afraid he might lose his mind and jump off. Seren shivered. This was probably where he watched Ona die.

"The red tent." Pain tied his voice in knots. "Yes, if they take us, they'll kill every man in the city."

A shiver quaked through Seren's chest. She pulled her cloak more tightly around herself. "You should've tried to escape."

"I made my choice."

Seren thrilled to hear it, but his decision also gutted her. Gutted her as well as any yatagan's edge.

At the front, near the gates, the Invaders set ladders against the city walls. When one fell from our warriors' arrows, another took his place. Seren's eyes couldn't help but search for Ona's body. But it was so dark. Even in that green brigantine, so different from all the other soldiers' blood red jerkins and the Invaders's white, silver, and red, Seren still couldn't spot her. She didn't want to ask Lucca. He wore his grief on his shoulders, the weight unhinging his usual grace.

"Look. Here they come," Lucca whispered at her ear. He pointed to the old mine, on a hill a half hour's ride away when the plains were clear.

A dark river of shapes—horses and their riders—poured from the spot where the flat land gave way to a ridge surrounded by the thick-leaved lahabshjara trees.

"I can hardly see them. Are they firing now?" She tugged Lucca close. "Wait. They must be. The Invaders there are turning to face them. Do you see?"

The enemies moved like the sand stirred by a wind, swirling back, then around. The Invaders had no archers that far back, so the Empire warriors shot arrows into them and advanced quickly. But the Invaders were no cowards. They rushed to close the distance, their numbers far exceeding the mounted unit. Two went down under the western swords, then a handful more. A shape at the back waved a hand three times and the movement was echoed through the unit, and they turned their horses back the way they'd come. A swathe of fifty or so Invaders pursued them on foot. Seren was sure Adem had wanted more to chase them, so the unit could circle a good hundred or two and take them out with the false retreat.

"It's not enough," she said.

An enemy's arrow sliced the air beside Lucca. Both of them dropped to a crouch, the archers nearby firing shot after shot.

Lucca's face was shadowed by his hood. "You're right. That's not going to win us this battle. What do we do?"

The wind tugged at Seren's hood and she grabbed the edge to keep hidden. She looked past the parapet, the night air tangy with the scent of blood. The mounted unit fell one by one to the dark, to the wide swords of the Invaders.

They were all going to die.

"We have to get the clay weapons released," Seren said. "Now."

THEY RACED to the prison cells.

The first row of cells held Invaders captured during the battle. Most were bandaged from being forcefully questioned. All wore a unique blend of fear and defiance in their light eyes. The engineer was nowhere.

"He has to be here. If not, he's gone and we're finished."

"There!" Lucca pointed at a small cell, too short to hold a man really, at the end of the row.

Cold bars held her engineer with the unpronounceable name. Fists curled into his lap, he sat at the very back. Sweat rolled down his pale face.

"Broken," he said in terrible trade tongue. He held up a shaking mess of what used to be his hands.

Seren's stomach lurched, and Lucca butted his head against the framing with a shout of disgust.

"We're going to free you. I'll get medicine for you. For the pain. We need to make more weapons and release them now. Lucca, should we try our magic on these bars, too?" She had to smile and laugh and cry at the same time. Life was full, bursting, pushing the real Seren out of the fertile soil of horror and joy.

Lucca dipped his chin respectfully and drew flint and sword. As quickly as they could, they chanted together, the Holy Fire from his spark leaping at her palms. Heat twinged at her forehead, and in her hands, and a column of orange and blue twisted from the air in front of her eyes before trailing onto a bar near the base of the cell door.

In two strokes, Lucca had the engineer free.

The man couldn't seem to stop talking, but they had no idea what he was saying. The other Invaders answered him, their talk awed, afraid. The engineer only seemed excited as he gave Seren a quick bow.

Meekra's voice came out of the dark behind us. "I know you said not to bow and give you away, but what you did...that wasn't exactly discreet."

Seren turned to a group of warriors, five or so untrained men and women from the city, and Izzet, Qadira, as well as two of the older male cousins from Clan Azjorr. Everyone carried a bag or sack—hopefully supplies to make more weapons—and some held the ready pots uncovered.

Izzet giggled a little hysterically. "Thank you for trusting us to support you, Kyros Seren."

Seren smiled. "Thank you for agreeing to come. And Qadira...I have to say I'm pretty surprised."

The girl huffed. "It's not like I have much of a choice," she replied, sticking with the desert tongue. Seren knew the girl couldn't resist any chance to be exclusive. "My entire clan is behind you. Even if they can't all show their faces here right now."

Cansu's long face wore a grim smile. Hossam walked beside him, his bushy hair like a storm around his wide face. Erol glided through the moonlight, frowning as ever, as he brought up the rear with nine other warriors. Meekra had brought Barir too.

Meekra held out the leather vest she'd ordered for Seren. A phoenix spread silver and copper wings over the black leather. Bronze studs flickered in the moonlight. With reverent movements, careful and solemn, Seren accepted the vest. She temporarily removed her ore master cloak and slid the vest over her head. She tied the side laces up herself, adjusted her sash, and put the cloak on again, keeping the front open for the time being so she could see the phoenix. She looked up and Meekra nodded approvingly.

The vest felt right even though it covered most of her kaftan's fine embroidery. This was her. Kyros and General. A true leader as Meric had never been. A lover of the people as Varol never would be. This was who her people needed and this was who she would be. An image of the Holy Fire blazed in her mind's eye. Warmth flowed through her veins as she smiled gravely at Meekra, Lucca, and the rest. She refused to disappoint them. She would prevail. They would win. The Invaders would be destroyed and Varol would be brought to his knees, thankful for what the Holy Fire had shown her.

Wind tossed her hair around her as she stood tall and held her arms open wide. "The Fire in me burns to see you. We have to keep this secret as long as we can."

Meekra covered her lips to hide a nervous laugh. "Well, perhaps you should stop making such bright sparks with this handsome Silvanian."

"Hush, you." Seren gestured toward the engineer. "Please, Barir, will you look after his hands? We need him at his best. Alert. He is the brains of this operation."

Meekra urged a man in a pale brown kaftan to the front. The interpreter. Seren took a breath, and her engineer smiled despite the pain he was surely in.

Lucca leaned left to see the whole of our small band. "Meekra, did you speak with Haris? I hadn't seen him with Kaptan Ona's unit, so I wondered if he...if he escaped that...duty."

Her face bunched as she translated the trade tongue. "No. In market maybe. But not." She faced me and switched to the desert tongue. "I thought I saw the soldier he is talking about. But when I looked again, he was gone."

Lucca rubbed a hand over his face. Seren wished she could hold his head in her lap and wash his fear away with her fingertips and lips.

"I think he went with Nuh," Lucca said. "To the front. With Ona. He didn't have much of a choice. Like Nuh. They had him and would've killed him."

"No time to worry about it now," Seren said. "The red tent's been raised. There'll be no mercy for any man if they win. And at the end of this awful night, the black will go up." Her throat tightened, and she pushed her grief for Ona off her mind.

Meekra's hands fisted in her kaftan. "What does the black mean?"

"Death to all. Every man, woman, and child, if the Invaders take the city. There's no use in worrying. We have to create more of these terrible weapons and do our best to thwart the enemy. We will not go down so easily."

Cansu clapped a hand on Lucca's back and they set themselves to the dangerous plan.

33

VAROL

The men, slaves and warriors alike, scattered like mice as Varol hurled his helmet through the tent flap and stormed to the bowl of Holy Fire. The distraction of five full units and the false retreat had failed. They'd fought through the night. Only pulled back at sunrise. As Varol waved hands over the Holy Flame, words flashed out of his mouth, almost painful.

"Holy Fire. I need you now. I need ideas. I need more men. What can you do for me? I am your kyros, leader of the only people in the world who properly honor your Flame."

He wiped a hand, two hands, over the licking heat, his heart hammering his bones. It sounded too much like the Invaders' ladders bracing against the walls his forefathers built. But no ideas came, no flame curled from his hands, heart, or mind.

The Invaders would take this city. They'd kill Varol in the worst possible way. Cut limb from limb. Dragged by horses in opposite directions. Crucified upside down. Only their imaginations would limit them.

Why had he even come here? Foolish. This city was a lost cause. He should've regrouped in Jakobden or farther north. Now these pigs would grind their way through his family's lands, foul the earth, and muddle his people's blood even further.

This was all because of that woman.

Seren, Pearl of the Desert. Ha. She was no pearl. Yes, she had lovely eyes and a body that would make any man's blood rise, but she was no woman of the desert. Her soul lacked the passion of the desert's heat, the voice of the wind across the plains. She was weak. She should've kept to the high-caste women's gossip and made children. She'd done nothing but harm the Empire. She claimed she loved the people, but what did her actions show?

She'd taken that Silvanian, Lucca Hand of Ruination, as a lover. She'd thrown off Varol's own brother, a virile man with royal blood for a green-tinged mercenary. Varol spat onto the rugs and fisted his hands over the Holy Fire. He'd enjoyed the female mercenary's company, but he never, ever would've chosen her over a woman of his own land, his own desert blood.

The Fire wasn't giving him anything. Why? He was worthy. More worthy than anyone alive. The orange tongues flickered and went out. He kicked the pedestal. The holy bowl rolled and crashed to the ground.

"Kyros!" Adem stopped at the entrance to the tent, his mouth dropping open. He held a roll of parchment.

Varol jerked it from his grip. "What's this? More foul news? Can't you give me some strategy? What good are you?"

Adem raised a palm and bowed.

Varol snorted. "A bit late, don't you think? Stick with shocked shouts of my title. It's more in tune with my mood, General."

"My kyros, the missive shows our numbers and theirs. And the last count on arrowheads we have in the city as well as our food supply, which is quickly dwindling."

A red heat rose inside Varol. He launched himself at the General, dagger going to the old man's throat. Varol held it there against his pale, wrinkled skin, Varol's mouth at the general's ear. "I hear the judgment in your tone. Your people always have that sneering edge to their words, even when you speak the proper tongue." Varol moved the blade to Adem's mouth. "Maybe I should cut the sickly attitude from your mouth."

"As you wish, my kyros."

To his credit, the man didn't shake. Not at all.

Varol released him and sheathed his steel. "Good answer. And you are in luck, my friend. I have an idea."

Varol glanced at the Fire bowl, askew at the corner of the red and blue rug. He motioned to a slave, who hurried to pick up the copper basin, refill it with lahabshjara leaves, and relight the Fire.

Pacing helped Varol think. "We'll send out another force with axes. Their aim will be to cut down those ladders, to destroy them beyond repair. A ring of our most skilled warriors will surround them with shields and—"

His guards and two others burst into the tent, panting and sweating. A river of blood poured from the younger man's brow. Dark circles ringed the older warrior's eyes. They both raised palms and bent.

Varol waved a hand, impatient. "Speak. Speak."

Adem jerked his head at the Fire bowl and they each headed over to pay their respects and say a prayer.

"We have no time for that!" Varol motioned to a slave to bring the older one to him. "Tell me what I need to know." The slave grabbed the man by the sleeve and pulled him to the table.

The warrior rubbed one of his puffed, dark eyes with a rough hand. "The Pearl of the Desert has escaped."

"From her cell? Who reported this? Where are Badi and Hanif?" They'd sworn they locked her in the secret cell. No one knew where that was.

The younger fighter stepped forward. "This is more important, my kyros. There is a breach. In the south wall. The Invaders, they're driving through the break we repaired last season!"

Varol's heart burned black. "Send the blue and gold units to the breach. The general and I are right behind you." The older of the reporting warriors started out of the tent. "You. Find Seren. If she is still in the city, find her and report back to me. Do not act. Do you understand?"

"Of course, my kyros."

"What is your name?"

"Haris, my kyros."

With a nod, Varol left his new spy and headed into the new day to mount his steed and see how long he had to live.

THE CITY WAS EERILY quiet as Varol and his guard wove through the tents and over the canals to the south wall. The sun soared, already clearing the walls. That damned black tent was out there. Sitting in Varol's plains like a blight about to spread plague. He could not let them win. If he did, he'd forever be the kyros who lost the Empire. For all the ages, he'd be the beaten snake, the husk of what used to be a proud line of rulers.

Digging heels into his horse's sides, he spurred them faster toward the first Invaders ever to force their way into Akhayma's walls.

Varol reined in as the group approached the break in the striped stone. Already, twenty or more Invaders had climbed through the formerly plastered crack and were engaged with Empire warriors. They were big men. So much taller, broader than Varol remembered. What had their kind been like before drought took their green lands and turned them to dust? They must've been grotesque. Like giant, pale beasts.

"Larger only means a louder sound when they fall," Varol said to himself, recalling his father's words. "General Adem! You and yours move to the area there by the smaller canal. I'll cut off their leading head."

But Adem wasn't beside him. He didn't ride up next to the warriors to Varol's back either.

"Where is the General?"

A shout spewed from outside the wall's crack and another clutch of enemies broached the barrier, foreign swords flashing in the sun.

Varol leaped from his saddle and drew his steel. Spinning and cutting, they were no match for him and his royal blood. The only reason the Empire was losing to these people was because there were so many of the beasts.

Varol and his men slashed throats and Onaratta would've said, *painted the ground with their blood*. Varol ducked another blow and slid his sword clean through a shin, meat and bone nothing to Akhayma steel. Warmth rushed over him. What a power he had in his hands. The steel born of his blood and his land.

Two more dead. Another. Another. The Empire warriors were beating them back. Only six Invaders still stood on this side of the wall.

Hanif galloped around Varol and ordered a group of men and women to block up the crack. Good man that he was, he set an additional archer on the walls above to keep the enemies at bay while they stuffed the crack with plaster and rock and whatever else they could get their hands on, whatever would make it difficult for the Invaders.

"Yes, Hanif! Very good!" Varol swung his weapon over his left shoulder and arced the metal down, separating a man from his head. "Is Badi at the cell?" he shouted above the din.

"No, my kyros." Hanif took an arrow to the arm, a wayward shot from over the parapet. He grunted, broke the end off, and cut down a man heading for his repair crew.

"Where is he?"

"At the front, my kyros. The Invaders are gaining ground. Our archers are slowing. Fatigue, my kyros."

"The ladders!" one of Varol's shouted from behind. "They've cleared the top of the walls, my kyros!"

"Holy Fire save us!"

With a push kick to the man he fought, Varol freed himself from the fight. His mount stomped beside the nearest canal, smart eyes on Varol. He whistled and the horse flew to his side. Varol was mounted and galloping before he could look again for Adem. Maybe the general heard the report as he rode in the back of the group. Maybe he knew about the ladders.

Varol rose up in his saddle, the tassels whipping his thighs and the wind tearing at his hair. Varol had to get to him, formulate some strategy. If they didn't pull this nightmare together, in hours, they'd all be dead, no matter who supported who as leader.

3 4

SEREN

eren didn't want to sleep. If she did, she might wake up to Lucca in chains. Or everyone in Akhayma dead. But her body was still only a body and it hadn't rested in what felt like years. The scrape of sandals and boots on grit and the muttering of her loyal group working together to create more clay pot explosives filled her ears as she settled onto the straw in Fig's old stall. The black of the scorched roof beams and the sun through the partially burned out wall pressed on her eyes like pointing fingers.

"Just for an hour," Lucca said, throwing a horse blanket over her. It was hot, but she was shivering anyway.

"Wake me if anything..."

WHEN SHE OPENED HER EYES, Lucca was curled up beside her and the sky had gone a vicious red. She scooted closer and made her shape fit Lucca's, pushing wakefulness away, denying what tonight would be. The black tent was up. Had been all day. Death was close enough to hear, taste, smell. Seren breathed against Lucca's back, driving fear away, enjoying the press of his body on her chest. His voice rumbled through them both.

"I wish Death wasn't slithering up our trail," he whispered, his voice raspy. "I'd be doing more than sleeping."

Hot shivers rose along her neck and fell over her shoulders and down her legs. She pressed her cheek against his shirt. "So would I."

He spun. "Ah. Forget Death. We have plenty of time to die." His hands slid around the back of her neck, soft and certain.

"I'm not entirely sure that makes sense," she said.

Lucca's lips moved along her neck. If she stayed here, it'd be a lovely way to die. "I'm very sure I don't care," he whispered, the moisture of his lips warm on her skin.

A little moan escaped her mouth. She pulled away before they forgot things they couldn't forget. With a reluctant nod, Lucca joined her in standing up and brushing the straw away.

Cansu walked in, his face grim. "The black tent, Kyros. I saw it."

Seren touched the wool at her sash. "It's nothing we didn't already know." The rest of the group gathered in the ruined stables. She fought to keep her voice loud enough for them to hear. She wanted to go back to the straw and Lucca and be ignorant of all this, but of course she could never—would never—do such a thing.

"We knew if we lost this war, we'd all be killed. Don't let scare tactics throw your focus. We have our plan. Launch the weapons over the walls. Bring their numbers down so we can strike and have a chance to come out victorious."

"What about wind?" the engineer said through the interpreter. Both men's faces were streaked with dirt and sweat.

"We can't worry about it," Seren said. "We don't have the time to wait for a perfect moment." The loss of Fig tugged at her like the little mare was still here, nuzzling and giving Seren strength. She wished she could feel something of Ona, despite what she'd done. "Are the weapons prepared?"

"Kyros Seren." Her chest seized at the sound of Adem's voice.

Hossam had him by the arm in a flash. Lucca slipped to come up behind him, faster than Seren thought a man could move. Adem's color was high, but he didn't fight Lucca or Hossam's hold on him. He had blood all down the front of his jerkin, black smears on red leather. A blade had sheared a spot so deeply that Seren could see his brown mourning shirt underneath. Blood crusted one long earlobe, but his earth-hued headtie, another tribute to Meric, remained firmly in place across his forehead.

Seren stepped past Cansu, Meekra, Barir, and the engineer. The clay pots lined up like soldiers along the stables. Their silk inflatables lay like long cloaks behind them. They couldn't hide this. Adem would know exactly what they were doing. But he didn't have any warriors with him, none of his usual retinue.

"General." Seren kept her face clear. It was better to let him give some information before he took anything more from her.

He raised a palm and bent low, so low that his knee rasped the ground before he stood again. "Please forgive me. Take me into your confidence. And even if you won't, know that I will no longer support the high general. I accept your decision either way."

"What changed your mind? You were ready to watch me die."

"I must speak bluntly if this is to work," Adem said.

Lucca unsheathed his sword an inch, but Seren held up a hand to hold him back.

"Please do." She clasped her hands and tried to be calm, still, confident.

"I still believe you're a criminal. What you did, hiding Kyros Meric's death, giving orders and telling me, telling us all, they were from him…" His lip curled. "It disgusts me. You dishonored the true kyros, the true royal blood."

"I did what needed to be done."

He opened his mouth to add something, his gaze going to the burned stables behind her, but she cut him off.

"I made mistakes," she said. "I'll make more. That doesn't mean I can't lead my people."

Meekra smiled so brightly Seren could practically hear it. Lucca's fiery eyes made her feel like she could take on the entire world.

"I mourn my husband in my own way." Seren put two fingers on her chest, above her heart. "I didn't love Meric. But he was my husband, and I appreciate the fact that because of him I found my purpose, my people. He is why I have a chance to help our people survive this war."

"I don't doubt your passion for the Empire, Kyros Seren. That, I've never doubted. We can come together on that point. Varol is a fool. He throws our people, and himself, into the fight without a calm head. He is a bright fire that will burn itself out and scorch the rest of us with its heat."

"Sounds like Ona," Lucca whispered.

"Very much so, from what I saw," Adem agreed. "I was wrong to choose Varol over you because of tradition. I don't know how this will turn out, but I'd rather die on the right side. But know this, we will most likely die. Varol has an army loyal to him. The Invaders, well, I don't see how we can win this. My best guess is they will sleep tonight—they don't have much to fear from us and they know it—and after dawn, they'll overcome our walls and lay waste to the city. We won't be able to hold back another concerted effort with the ladders and their numbers."

"We have a plan," Seren said.

"A good one," Lucca said, releasing Adem. "Just as brave as our kyros."

Adem kneeled beside one of the pots. "How exactly are these meant to work?"

Seren rubbed her hands together and joined him as the rest went back to work. "The leaves will burn and fill the silk with hot air. This," she held up the fuse line, "will charge as it lifts into the sky. The charge will ignite the chemicals we have inside the pot." She showed him the tiny hole where the fuse would be set at take off.

"And then?"

Lucca stood over them, arms crossed. "Boom."

Adem stood and dusted his hands. "I hope *they* experience the boom and not us."

"That is the risk." Seren eyed the walls leading into the city. Stars shone like one thousand eyes. "It's time."

WITH THE WEAPONS in wooden crates, they started toward the city.

"We'll have to move quickly," Adem said, "or the high general will hear about what we're doing."

Seren shook her head. "No. Walk strong and calm. Act as though this is our duty and there is no need for secrecy. If the people believe this is all a part of the kyros's plan, they won't think to report anything. They'll talk, yes. But not report. Besides, no one will notice me in this cloak in the night."

"And this is why I should've supported you, ore master," Adem said slyly.

"It's never too late to start a new friendship. One of mutual respect."

"Your mercy is commendable, my kyros."

Seren couldn't help but smile.

NEAR THE MAIN GATES, lines of warriors held shields above their heads to hold off enemy arrows raining over the walls. Their blood flowed into the canal that curved beside the first row of tents, and all had bandaged limbs or heads. Most held their yatagans low, their arms shaking with fatigue.

Varol was there, on his prancing, black steed. He shouted orders and lifted his fist to the stars. The moon was a mere sliver, the edge of a silver blade above the chaos.

"Lucca, take your group past Varol, to the top of the walls. Meekra, show him the best way to go. General Adem, come with me. We'll start this to the right, in the direction of the black tent. If we can get that to go up, the fire may spread more easily."

"It is the mercenary!" A man pointed at Lucca and pulled the hood from his head.

Hossam jerked the man away. "Haris! No!"

Varol swung around and charged up to Lucca.

Seren's stomach dropped and she ripped her hood down. "High General Varol, if you have something to say, you may say it to me."

Something between a laugh and a shout pealed from Varol's mouth. "Good of you all to arrive together. Makes it much easier to dispatch you in the middle of this mess."

"Mess indeed. Let's put away our rivalry for now and focus on protecting our people."

"Rivalry? There is no rivalry." He waved a hand and his army took hold of her much smaller one. A man grabbed Seren and laughed close to her face, his breath foul and hot. "There is only you a criminal and me a kyros," Varol said. He smiled at Haris. "Bring me a very long, very sturdy rope."

Varol unsheathed his yatagan, nearing Lucca.

"Lucca!"

Lucca couldn't move. He was surrounded.

Without a word, like Lucca wasn't worth a moment of his time, Varol sliced his steel along Lucca's leg. He fell hard.

Seren's world went white for a breath.

Varol eyed her, riding closer, stepping through the army and raising a shield one fighter handed him. "I hope all that foreign food hasn't made you too heavy for what I have in mind. Bring her to the top of the walls. And the former general, too."

Fewer and fewer of the enemies' arrows fell over the walls. The Invaders were headed to their tents to sleep. All the better to kill everyone at sunrise.

The warriors holding Seren took the clay pots, then dragged her up the stairs to the parapet, Varol like a shadow behind her.

Haris appeared, a heavy rope circling his body like an enormous snake.

"Tie her hands," Varol ordered the archers, who were wet with sweat. The battlefield beyond them showed campfires flickering to life and that horrible black tent at the heart of the swarming Invaders.

"I don't have..." an archer started, holding out his bow and arrow.

Varol tore the black cloak off Seren, exposing her brown, silken kaftan and the face everyone recognized. Below, warriors whispered her name. They traded her varied titles like coins.

Varol grunted and tugged the sash from her middle. "This will do."

She leaned onto one foot and twisted to see Lucca as Varol bound her hands behind her back. It was dark, she could make out Lucca's shape—a seated man in the middle of a standing army. He reached a hand up. He had to be bleeding heavily. Varol knew how to make a cut that would kill slowly but surely. She squinted, willing her eyes to work like some night creature. Was he telling her something?

Varol's hands were rough as he finished the knot at her wrists. She kept twisting to try and see everything, to see Varol. The whites of his eyes showed too much, like a panicked horse. He knew as well as her that Death was close, very, very close. It was a stench in the air, a finger running along the neck, an ache in the bones.

Freed from her sash, Seren's green wool fluttered from the folds of her clothing, to the ground. It was only a dark spot near her feet. It was her world.

Varol picked it up. His gaze snapped to her mouth. "And this will keep you quiet until I have you where I want you."

Adem ripped his arm away from the soldier who held him. His gray hair fell over one eye. "What will you do?"

Death's nearness had stripped them of titles and rituals.

The warriors at the foot of the walls stared up, faces pale in the night's uneven light. Seren's fingers twitched, longing to wipe their hot cheeks with cool water. They needed comfort, support.

"Pray over the Holy Fire. Don't give up hope!" Some of her words threaded through the horses' hooves shuffling, the sound of thousands moving, coughing, moaning, dying, but most were lost to the night.

Varol gagged her with the green wool. "Keep quiet, Pearl." Disdain oozed off the name.

Then a change washed over his features. His jaw set. His eyes narrowed.

"My brother, my royal blood," he said, "deserved full mourning. *The soul is tired, You slept through the night, Give your sleep to the Dead.*" He quoted the mourning folk song. "You never mourned. You. Rebelled." He flicked his kaftan back and stepped away, lifting a hand toward the battlefield. "Lower her down. Over the walls. You'll spend one night awake, criminal, staring at Death for a true kyros's passing, for mourning. It isn't enough, but it's all you can offer. And offer it, you will."

The men tied the rope to the parapet and pushed Seren over the side.

She didn't fall far.

The rope caught abruptly, and she thought her shoulders would pop out of her skin. Her stomach and ribs screamed as the rope cut into her and her descent continued. The body-strewn ground, the stomped out campfires' ghostly smoke, and the sleeping Invaders crept closer and closer as Varol's men slowly lowered her.

Varol's voice dripped from the walls and into her ears, his words a hissing whisper. "When the sun rises, they will end you in what I would imagine will be a spectacular fashion. But for now, stay awake and bear a portion of what you should've when my brother first left this world."

The descent halted. Her slippered toes dragged along the gritty earth and her stomach lurched with the pain of the rope and the smell of war.

Directly in front of her, close enough to hear a shout if she uttered one, the black tent hulked like a sleeping beast.

The rope had slid up her body. Her sleeves bunched above her elbows. She pushed one arm down, twisted—bumping the wall painfully—and worked her way out of the binding. It moved up and over her head, and she hit the ground on one side, jaw smacking the earth. She sat up and shook her head. Her sash remained tight on her wrists.

Varol had to be watching still, but she couldn't see him. A bank of clouds choked the stars' light and a gentle wind teased the ends of her hair. One thousand thoughts flew through her mind, but one shone clear.

If she was going to die, she wanted to see Ona one more time.

As if the wind read her thoughts, it increased and pushed the strip of clouds into the horizon. The stars once again illuminated the plains and hammadas, the desert to the Southwest, hills and lahabshjara trees to the North and East.

And then she saw the sword.

The broad, steel surface of Ona's weapon reflected a swathe of silver in the middle of three fallen yatagans and more bodies than Seren could count. Her stomach heaved. She vomited into the muck at her feet.

But could she find her?

She squinted into the dark, looking for the bright points of brass on the back of Ona's brigantine. The white streak in her brown hair. It was impossible.

Stumbling over bodies, she kneeled beside the sword. It'd fallen along a smooth boulder where it shone like melted starlight. Seren wanted to touch the hilt and imagine Ona's strong, pale hand, but her own hands were still bound. Blood and dirt caked the sword's edges. But it was sharp enough to work.

Between the bodies of two Invaders Ona had most likely killed, Seren leaned against the propped sword and pressed the sash that held her wrists into the metal.

There was movement on the parapet. *Varol.* She could see his shape, the way he moved.

The blade divided the sash and Seren's hands fell to her sides. The flesh burned, not only because she'd nicked herself, but also because the blood had been inhibited too long by the knot. Feeling pricked its way back into her hands as she took the wool from her mouth. The wool had nearly gagged her. A cough built in her throat. The Invaders would hear her, realize how close she was if she made any noise. But maybe they'd only think it was one of their own? The cough echoed from her mouth. She couldn't stop it.

A pop sounded to the right.

Her pulse jumped. She couldn't see what had made the noise. The smell of the field and the fear in her heart blinded her as much as the dark.

There wasn't a Fire here, but Seren sat by Ona's sword and prayed. Prayed for Ona's soul. Prayed that her dearest friend, her Lucca, was still alive. Prayed Adem had kept the clay pot weapons close by and undamaged.

Even if Seren had to die, maybe they could persuade Varol to use the weapons and they could live. Some of her people could live through this. Tears came then, hot and fast and untamable.

"I understand," she whispered to Ona's sword, Death's perfume overpowering. "You gave me so much. I don't know if it matters, but I...I forgive you. I miss you already. Varol did seem like the strongest voice for our side, but—"

Voice.

Seren had the strongest voice now. She'd used it in the cell, when Lucca helped her escape. She only needed to wield her words now.

A plan formed in her head. She wouldn't know for certain if it worked, the walls blocked her view of her loyal warriors and the fuses, but...the truth of what she might accomplish sang through her like a song. The notes had always lived inside her, but she'd never known the words. Until now.

She looked at Ona's steel, the filthy ground, the dead warriors and their open eyes and swollen limbs. Just beyond the sword's hilt lay Ona's flint. Seren gathered the piece of cool stone and took up the familiar weapon. A sound built in her chest.

With one last silent prayer to bless her defeated friend, Seren marched to the front gate, speared her green wool on the tip of Ona's sword, and struck the flint to raise a spark like a falling star.

"*Wake iron!*" she called out.

Varol appeared on the parapet, his face in darkness.

"*Wake soul and Holy Fire!*" She switched to the desert tongue, then repeated the words in the trade language. She wanted all to understand. All who would listen. The flint drew out another spear of blinding light. The

559

Invaders would hear. She didn't care. "Light the fuses of our weapons. Beg our people to show the Invaders Death!"

"You do not rule here, Seren!" Varol called out, his words erratic and pitching up and down.

"I am your kyros!" She shouted. She raised the sword as the sun rose over the hills and lit the green of her talisman. "This ends on my word!" Striking the flint, power tugged at her heart and burned between her eyebrows.

Shouts erupted behind Akhayma's gates.

New, strange clouds filled the morning sky.

The creations the Holy Fire had shown her soared through the gentle wind on silk. In the glowing light of dawn, they fluttered, their metal fuses like silver tails.

Seren spun to see Invaders emerging from tents and bedrolls to stare at the lone madwoman on the battlefield in her silken slippers.

One of the clay pots sparked. The silk incinerated. There was a bang.

The weapon blasted into a thousand pieces.

Seren's ears rang. An Invader gripped his leg, his mouth open to yell as blood poured between his fingers. Another weapon exploded in a flash of light. Shards tore through a small tent. A third broke apart and fell onto a group of pikemen. They covered their faces, shouting, as the bits of clay embedded into their exposed arms and scalps. They screamed and fell, never to raise a sword against her people again. Two weapons exploded, not far away. A chip of clay hurled through the air and snapped at her back. Heat seared through her skin.

She ran for the walls.

Archers fought with Hossam on the parapet, with Cansu, too. Their hands flew at one another. Cansu called out.

Ona's sword thudded to the ground as Seren grabbed the rope they'd lowered her down on. She put her feet on the wall to begin a climb. Something knocked the pale rock beside her head. She looked down to see an arrow with bright red fletching. The Invaders were firing at her. Hand over hand, foot by foot, she ascended. Her arms shook and another arrow landed above her head.

Booms and crashes sounded in the Invaders' camp. Orders. Gasps. Shouted commands.

Sudden screams eroded her focus. Gasping, she slipped to the earth. She covered her ears. More explosions. More. More.

She spun and shouted, "It's only because you wouldn't stop! You left me no choice! I have to protect my people!"

Only because of the men running from the last of the weapons drifting down and the skull-splitting shrieks was she still alive.

She looked up and took the rope again.

Varol appeared on the parapet. His hair stuck out at all angles and his kaftan lay in shreds over his chest as if he'd torn it with his own hands. "Go ahead, try to climb, little kyros!"

This was the end. She was bleeding. Trapped, an enemy before and behind.

An arm and a yatagan snaked around Varol's throat. Adem.

She cupped her hands at her mouth. "Kill him!"

Adem's blade slid like a minnow, flashing and quick, and Varol tipped over the wall and fell. He was a blur of silk as he passed Seren and slammed into the ground.

Victory poured strength into Seren's limbs. She tried to climb again. Slid down. Arrows were coming fast and she was cut again, on the arm, then along her calf. Quickly, she tied a knot in the rope and shoved her foot inside.

Adem leaned over the wall.

"Pull me up!" she shouted. The howls of pain behind her squeezed her chest. She could hardly breathe.

At the top, strong hands helped her over and she fell into a familiar chest.

Dirt and blood lined Lucca's strong-boned face. Two lengths of cloth wrapped around his injured leg and he'd slung his bow over a shoulder.

"How did it happen?" she asked. "How did you light and release the explosives?" She wanted to think it was her, but that was impossible, wasn't it?

He smiled and pressed his mouth to hers. She tasted salt and him and knew if he hadn't been here, she'd have been at Adem's feet weeping. Lucca's power gave her power.

"When you called up the Holy Fire," he said, "the fuses…a spark bloomed over each one. The loyal soldiers, and some high-castes hiding in the crowd, grabbed the devices and lifted them into the air before Varol's men could shake off their surprise."

Seren closed her eyes and whispered gratitude into Lucca's arms. The terrible sounds of the final victory clambered over the walls and shot into her ears.

It wasn't beautiful. It was war. But her voice had proved strong enough to protect the city that had become her home, and for that, she'd never stop being grateful.

35

SEREN

Meekra draped a deep purple kaftan over Seren's shoulders and looked toward the door, smile widening. "I'd tell you that you shouldn't be here, but I believe I'd be outvoted."

Seren turned to see who she was talking to. Lucca ducked inside.

Sadness hung on his shoulders like a thick, unwanted cloak he couldn't seem to shed. She still saw Ona every time she looked at him. She was sure he still saw his friend everywhere. In his sword. The scars he'd made when they fought side by side. Under the trees, though the ones here were nothing like the green giants they'd lived under back in Silvania.

"Ah, my noble mercenary," Seren said, working to raise the corners of his frown.

His gaze drifted to the ground and he sighed, pulling himself up as best he could these days. Then humor lit his eyes and he smiled, setting his grief aside for a little while.

With his chin tilted down like that she could almost see what he'd rather be doing than letting her have time to prepare for the Fire Ceremony.

Meekra left through the back. "I know when I'm not wanted." A laugh hid in her words.

Lucca took Seren's fingertips in his but glanced Meekra's way. "If your mistress is late for her appointment, rest assured it'll be for a good reason. A great reason."

"Stop bragging, Silvanian," Meekra muttered, her voice fading beyond the tent walls.

Seren kissed him. "You've been into the spicy tabouli I ordered for the feast."

"I thought it might improve my chances. Increase your attraction to me."

"Like you need help with that."

A sly grin pulled at his mouth. "Now that you have undisputed control of half the globe, I wondered..." He shrugged.

She grabbed his face and enjoyed the widening of his eyes. "Slave or kyros, I am yours and you are mine. Besides, you're the reason I have the role I do. You and Ona."

She pressed lips to his palms. Though it'd been months, losing Ona still burned. It was so much worse for Lucca. He looked to the floor, studying the blue star shapes and black calligraphy woven into the rug. She wished she could take a measure of his hurt and help him carry the weight of it.

He shook a little, then blinked. "Don't frown for too long. There will always be losses." His silver ring caught the firelight as he put a finger to her chin. "Life is a battle."

"If that's true, I think all in all, we are winning." She set her forehead against his and the next half hour was pleasure and healing, breath and hearts beating, the joy of being alive.

~

THE STRIPED TENTS of the city sat in rolled bundles along the lotus towers. The canals glittered and showed all the constellations of the plains. The Basket, the Stallion's Neck, the Old Man's Hand. Women holding family Fire bowls and smiling men wearing their darkest black gathered with children around the oasis pool.

And there was Fig's half-brother, the colt she'd named Flame, held gently by Meekra's sisters. He danced a little sideways as they braided pink blossoms into his mane and tail. He'd never, ever replace Fig, but he would ease the hurt in Seren's heart as he grew and became her primary mount, a new friend.

Volunteers from every merchant group had scrubbed the mosaic tiles holding the water and the pieces shone like rings. The moon was a pearl in the sky and again in the water. Everything was rich, beautiful, and so very dear to Seren.

Akhayma was not her birthplace, but it was home.

Nobles and successful merchants filled the silver basin with more lahabshjara leaves, then lit the emerald heap. The Holy Fire danced into the night and painted children's cheeks yellow. The workers pulled the ladders clear of the basin, and stepped aside for Adem, who was walking tall and straight around the pool. His reflection moved across the silver bowl as he approached.

In his shining helmet, he bowed deeply and came close. "My kyros, I would like to again offer my apologies for—"

"Stop."

He looked up.

She came closer, waited for him to rise. "We've been through this. You only did what you thought was best for the Empire, for our people. For that, I can't fault you. I consider you my most valued general and advisor. As long as you stay in line anyway."

He sighed and bowed again. He'd changed in good ways so far. Reducing punishments for lesser crimes. He himself had put forward the idea to reduce the silver required for lower castes to move into higher castes. General Adem was becoming a veritable leader on the trail into the future.

"I will forever be your old steed, stubborn and true, Kyros," he said.

"May the Fire hear your will." Seren couldn't seem to stop smiling as he maneuvered the blue steps into place below the Holy Fire's bowl.

With Lucca standing beside Adem, and the city gathered and kneeling, she climbed the three steps to come face-to-face with the holiest of Flames. Her hand found Ona's sword at her sash, the metal cool and sure.

I wish you were here, Seren whispered to Ona, wherever she was. They'd never found her body. Lucca had led a Silvanian funeral for her anyway.

Seren lifted her palms and raised her voice. "Holy Fire, grant us the Flame of your strength and invention. May we see ideas flicker from dreams and into reality."

A red glow illuminated the center of her outstretched hands and turned her fingers to sunlight. Heat touched her forehead, gathered in front of her eyes, then drew power from her palms and spun into a visible flame, floating. The small curl of Fire turned inward at the top and bottom, rose up, then cascaded into the roaring Holy Fire. The sacred Flames reached toward the moon and her people sighed, her name on their lips.

"Kyros Seren, our Pearl."

EPILOGUE

Cold seeped into Ona's pores and came out through her shaking teeth. She clamped her mouth shut and hoped that might make it easier to see where she was. A big white striped something loomed in the distance, bouncing as she flew away.

Flew? No. She tried to move her hands. Only her left responded. Splintered wood supported her cold, cold, cold body. She was in a cart. But she still had no idea what that big white striped something was.

She'd been hit hard over the head before. During a raid on the ocean-facing villas near Holy Iacopo's Piazza when she first began her mercenary work.

She thought maybe she'd been hit hard again.

But she'd never been this frozen. That was new. She closed her eyes and began to thaw a little. The shaking in her teeth moved as she warmed. The trembling faded into a larger feeling she hadn't been warm enough to notice until now. A heat, aching and wrong, pulsed out of her chest, right above her heart.

A face appeared above her. Though he had brown hair laced with a copper hue, his chest was covered in the blood red and ghostly white uniform of the enemy.

Invader.

She tried to sit up, and both the cold and the heat swallowed her whole. Before the black took her again, words—first in the Invaders' tongue, intelligible, then in Silvanian—crept over her ears.

"You're alive." The Invader's gray eyes flickered with something that might've been hope, but Ona was too dizzy to know for sure. "You might soon wish you aren't. Don't tell the others I speak this tongue. It's not difficult to kill someone who is already mostly dead."

FOREST OF SILVER AND SECRETS

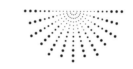

UNCOMMON WORLD

1

KINNERET

"You're grouchier than normal, Oron." The full-ship rose on a swell, and Kinneret barked at one of her fighting sailors, leaving Oron to continue his determined stewing. "Trim that sail like you've been told twice already," she said to a different sailor. "No, not like that. Move. Let me do it."

Kinneret pulled the lines herself, back straining against her fine new clothing, until the sail was set to match the wind.

"I'm not grouchy." Oron handed her the spyglass and scratched at the mass of tangled braids on his head. "I'm pensive. There is a difference."

"It's not fun. No matter what you call it."

"And that's all I'm here for, Kaptan Kinneret? Your fun?"

"Oh shut up. You know I love you." She dropped a quick kiss on his forehead. He tasted like salt and smelled like the wine she was missing from her quarters. "Despite your thievery."

"My what?"

"And your grouchy pensiveness."

Oron's brow unwrinkled for a heartbeat, and he scanned the horizon, one hand lifted against the sun. "You'll want to take us two knocks southwest before that current up there kicks hard north."

Kinneret hurried to the woman currently in charge of the wheel and passed the information on. Oron could be a fool, but never about sailing. He'd proved that many times over, and Kinneret knew enough to listen to him right away when he offered advice at sea. At sea. Not on land. Especially not on land in taverns.

The coastline was a strip of bare, pale rock in the distance, but the raucous country of Silvania wasn't all that far off.

South of here, her own home of Jakobden—ruled by her friend Amir Ekrem—sat beside Calev's home of Old Farm on the Broken Coast.

Though the waters of the Broken Coast—often called the Pass—held dangerous currents that loved to drag ships into its warm depths, she was well accustomed to them. She knew them, and the city and towns there, like the back of her hand. Yes, Jakobden was a cutthroat port city similar to the place they were headed now. But Jakobden's and Old Farm's ways were second nature to Kinneret. She knew when to steer southward, when to creatively lie to a client—for mutual benefit they didn't understand, of course—when to watch for wraiths.

But Silvania was almost entirely foreign to her.

Wealthy merchants, warring nobility, cursed forests, and sparkling cities of the finest materials combined to create a country no one could help but be curious about. And wary. Of course, being cautious wasn't exactly Kinneret's style.

She had no idea how she was going to help Amir Ekrem form an alliance between his corner of the Empire—Jakobden—and this foreign land of Silvania. Even if they did share a common enemy—the Invaders had barely lost a siege attack against the Empire's capitol recently. Though Kinneret's soon-to-be-husband Calev might be up to the job, Kinneret was no peace-making delegate. She was far more likely to start a war than develop an ally.

Perhaps that was why Oron was less than happy. Or maybe it was because he had to teach her and Calev Silvanian as well as his native tongue from the Northern Isles for the purpose of rubbing elbows with the foreign traders so they might gain some rare bluehare cloaks and amber beads.

"Let's go over my verbs again."

"Let's not and say we did." Oron produced that stolen bottle of wine, drank, and offered it to her.

"Kind of you to offer me my own wine."

Oron grinned and fluttered his eyelashes.

"That was a gift from Amir Ekrem. For my upcoming wedding."

"And it has been sitting mournfully in your quarters since the day the amir gave it to you."

Kinneret and Calev had yet to set a wedding date. She wasn't putting it off, but life was just so busy right now with all the new and exciting work on the full-ship for Amir Ekrem. Calev wasn't going anywhere. They would marry soon. Just…not yet.

"Can a bottle of wine mourn?" she asked, pushing away from Oron's implication that she was stalling the wedding.

"Oh yes, my dear. Oh yes. I heard its woeful bawling from my humble hammock in this great ship's belly. *I'm all alone, dear Oron. Great master of the drink, please save me from this wretchedness.*" He took another swig, then lifted the bottle toward someone behind them.

Calev walked up, wearing a long, emerald green tunic, a blood-red sash, and his jeweled dagger. He waved off Oron's wine offering. Kinneret's spirits rose like she was the ship and Calev was the sea. His eyes flickered over her face and his smile turned sly. A blush filled his cheeks and Kinneret's stomach and neck warmed as she remembered what they'd been doing in her quarters not an hour ago. His lemon and earth scent haunted her skin. Her lips were still sore. She touched them.

Oron groaned. "Please leave off all the gooey eyes. I've never been sick at sea, but you two make quite an effort at ruining my stolid reputation."

As if he ever would be deemed stolid.

Calev ignored Oron and ran a hand down Kinneret's back, over the strip of bare skin between her short shirt and long skirt. His warm fingers danced down her spine, then drifted along the curve of her backside. Sparks of pleasure flashed over her, and she pressed closer, feeling the strength of his thigh against her middle.

Oron lost the fight not to smile at them and stalked away, shaking his head. "Young people."

"We should practice our new languages." Calev's mouth brushed Kinneret's ear and she nearly melted into the decking.

Kinneret tried the *to go* conjugation in both Silvanian and Northern Isle. "I don't think my Silvanian accent is too bad. But the other…"

Calev laughed. "That Northern Isle tongue is a rough one. How they do that *R* sound—I don't think I'll ever get it."

"It's all right. We'll have Oron." She moved to shout to her first mate across the deck. "Why do we need to bother learning the Northern Isle tongue if you're there to speak it, Oron?"

Oron looked up from the compass box, face going dark. "I will not speak it. Not with those people."

Kinneret and Calev both joined him at the box. The wind threw a handful of water into the air and dampened Kinneret's chin and hair. "What do you mean you won't speak it? Of course you will. That's the main reason you're here. Amir Ekrem asked you to help me talk to the Northern Isle folk who will be there for their yearly trade. In addition to trading for bluehare and amber, we might join up with them, as well as the Silvanians. Because I really don't think the Invaders are finished trying to kill everyone."

"I left the Northern Isles for a good reason," Oron said, "and I don't care to spend a single moment in my blessed life breathing the same air as those people ever again."

"Why do you hate them so much?"

"Let's just say there isn't anyone like me—a dwarf—in that upper-caste merchant crew you'll be meeting at Silvania's finest port."

Kinneret and Calev traded a look.

"Yes," Oron said slowly. "I see you have it now. They left me to die on the breakers as a child of ten. Thought I'd never be able to work the land because of my short stature. And they knew I had no magic in my blood to perform greater works around the island." Northern Isle folk had magic stronger than any people, but it faded as they drew away from their islands. "I didn't understand all of that when it happened, but later, I figured it out through stories traded around the sea."

It made no sense. "You're stronger than most of the amir's handpicked guard. Why would they think you couldn't work as hard as anyone else?"

"Superstition, really. That is what rules the people of the Northern Isles, the people of Snowfallen specifically. It's the largest, most remote of the Isles. And superstition is their weakness. Their crime. If anyone doesn't fit into the all-powerful Fellriki's idea of what Snowfallen should be, then it's the breakers for you."

"Who is Fellriki?" Kinneret asked.

"The strongest *seithr* in their reclusive world." Seeing their looks, he explained further. "A seithr is a person who can carve symbols and make things happen. There is something in the blood up there. Some carry the ability. Others don't."

"Seithr are like…witches?" Kinneret smiled wryly. The slur that was usually aimed at Salt Witches such as herself didn't hold any power over her any more.

"Exactly."

"Snowfallen is the richest of the isles, isn't it?" Calev frowned at the sky as if he could tell what the weather would bring. He definitely couldn't. The poor thing was still terrible at reading the sky's hints. She'd feel worse for him if he weren't so intelligent in other ways.

Oron nodded and wound the end of a sail's tie around a post.

"What is a bluehare anyway?" Kinneret imagined blue bunnies and snorted. Why would that be considered a high-caste sort of thing to wear?

"It's exactly what you think it is. But the animals are very rare and only found on Snowfallen, along with some other very strange creatures. The air on that island…" Oron studied the horizon, a deep line between his thick eyebrows. "The place is stuffed with magic. They'd take over the world if their magic didn't slowly evaporate on long trips."

Kinneret took another look at the compass, then held four fingers above the horizon to measure the sun's height. "Well, we don't have to *like* them, Oron. But we do have to talk to them. It's Amir Ekrem's order, and it's an order that will help us keep our homes safe from Invaders."

"I don't see how people that far north can help, honestly." Calev tilted his handsome head.

She loved how he freely admitted when he didn't understand something. So many believed if they admitted ignorance, they'd be thought of as fools. Calev knew better. Information fed his smarts and Kinneret loved him for that wise humility.

Too bad she was terrible at being humble.

"If the Northerners offer Jakobden a good deal on fine things such as furs and beads," Oron said, "the Invaders may be bribed into leaving us alone. They can take those things from us, then sell them along the Empire's routes for food and water. That is Amir Ekrem's angle. To have items on hand that we can offer to the Invaders if they come by sea to Jakobden."

"It's a long shot," Kinneret said, "but I've heard of things like that happening in Kurakia and beyond."

"Avi has you reading history again, doesn't she?" Calev grinned.

Oron chuckled. "Like trying to teach a cat to enjoy water."

Kinneret's younger sister did have a seriously ridiculous addiction to the amir's library. But it wasn't as if Kinneret didn't read.

"I like books fine, too," she snapped.

"You like them as much as a desert lion would like being shoved into a saddlebag." Calev laughed and Oron joined him.

They were probably right, but they didn't have to be so annoying about it. "Watch yourselves, or this feline might decide to test her claws."

A sailor shouted for attention from the sky cup. "Rough weather ahead."

Sure enough, dark clouds shifted in the distance between the full-ship and Silvania's shore. Several fighting sailors left their posts briefly to pray over the Holy Fire bowl.

Kinneret had thought this trip would be smooth. But with Oron's past and this coming storm, the mission had suddenly grown very, very rough.

Lightning flashed, blinding Kinneret for a moment.

Would her Salt Magic work on the water this far from home?

2

ONA

Wait. *You speak Silvanian. But you're an Invader. And also, am I dead?*

This was what Ona wished she could say, but her mouth wasn't currently working. Her lips were nothing more than sand and dry, little canyons. The rest of her body wasn't operating either. She moved her eyes—the only parts that would move—to see that she rode flat, on a wooden cart. The wheels creaked over the rocky ground. Every once in a while, a patch of deep, emerald green showed somewhere in the blurred, watercolor distance. The man closest, the one who'd spoken to her, the one with the brown and copper hair, glared. Three other men rode in the cart. They all wore Invader white and red and a few pieces of metal armor. So yes. She'd been captured. She wasn't dead. She wished she was. But her heart was definitely working too. It was doing its level best to beat its way out of her chest. Not dead. But the battle at Akhayma…

Ona remembered seeing Lucca up on the parapet, his arrows driving into the enemy, his dark head turning to see her. Then her aunt had appeared in her head like a vision. A memory, yes, but more than that. She had looked at Ona, had told her something. What was it?

Wake, her aunt had said. A hallucination born from blood and pain.

Ona squeezed her eyes shut, not wanting to think about what *Wake* meant, what that vision meant. Ona wasn't Seren. She couldn't see true visions like Akhayma's ruler. Ona wasn't blessed. Nor did she deserve any kind of blessing. Seren had a heart of gold. Ona's heart was most likely a sad shade of gray.

"Yes, that's very good," the Invader who spoke Silvanian whispered. "You look nice and dead again. Keep that up, and maybe we'll both stay alive." The edge of his lips tipped up and he lifted one eyebrow, eyes trained on wherever they were headed.

Acting dead wouldn't be a problem.

Ona's eyes and heart might've been working, but she was as hollow as old bone. Vengeance was the only thing that had kept her going since the massacre at her aunt's villa. And recently, during the battle at Akhayma, Ona had taken down many Invaders like the ones who'd killed her aunt and the one who'd slayed so many in her Silvanian town. But vengeance hadn't satisfied. It'd left Ona empty, shelled, cored.

She had no idea who to be now.

The sky faded from blue to pink, then finally to black, and still the cart bumped along. Pain lay on her body, a constant, burning companion. Consciousness floated in and out of her head as her lungs took air without even asking permission. She wasn't so sure she'd have given it.

"Did Akhayma fall?" she whispered, feeling the Silvanian-speaking Invader beside her.

The man's gaze narrowed under his tawny eyebrows. "No. The Invaders lost. We lost."

Ona almost sat up. Lucca. He could still be alive. He surely thought she was dead. A light flickered inside her chest. Lucca. Her only friend left in the world. He had to hate her. She'd sided with Seren's enemy, his beloved Seren's enemy.

The spark inside Ona's hollow body was made of one thing: the need to ask forgiveness.

Wake.

"Have to get back." Her voice was a croak. "Lucca. Seren."

The warrior's face was suddenly in hers, his gaze staying on the rest of the Invaders, watching them like one does a wasp nest. "What did you say?"

"Back to Akhayma. I need to get back."

The man's eyes flattened like he was somehow disappointed in her words. "Well," he said, "that isn't happening. Now, go back to being dead."

She was trapped. In a broken body. Surrounded by the enemy. Heading to an evil place. But that spark inside burned on, quiet and unrelenting, beating out the one thing she cared about: forgiveness, forgiveness, forgiveness.

3

KINNERET

The pewter clouds swung low and balled like fists as Kinneret turned the stubborn wheel, the wood smooth under her calloused hands. She wished to let the ship go where it may, let the storm have them for a bit to keep damage down, but there was no time for that. They had to be at the main Silvanian port before the most powerful merchants went off for their seasonal hunts along the northern coasts and the Northern Isle folk sailed back into their foreboding region. The Silvanian king would leave for his country estate very soon.

Wind whipped Kinneret's hair around her face. Salty water dripped into her mouth. "Sails down. Tie them up. The wind will take them and we'll be headed under."

Calev and five fighting sailors battled the jib sail's tie. Its end cracked across the deck like a great whip, then circled back. Against the ship's side, it snapped and tripped two sailors who landed hard on the planks. That jib sail needed to come down. Now.

The reedy man in the sky cup climbed down the main mast and hurried to help another sailor knot the lines securing the foresail. Thunder echoed across the unending horizon. A school of fish rippled beneath the waters' surface.

From the stern, Oron gave Kinneret a nod. It was time for Salt Magic. Though the magic never worked as well outside the Pass's cursed waters, it was worth a try.

"Take the wheel, Ridhima."

The woman slid into place, long-fingered hands curling over the indents where Kinneret's had just been.

"Watch it, kaptan!" Calev shouted.

The jib sail's line zipped over Kinneret's head. She ducked. Calev leapt and snagged the tie right out of the air.

Water chilled Kinneret's feet through the spaces in her sandals. The soft, leather bag of salt on her sash was full and ready. She drew out a handful and threw it above her head. The storm snarled like an angry desert lion and swallowed her offering whole.

"Wind and rain,
Strength and pain,
Sea, I hear you,
Sea, I see you.
Sail and dodge,
Push and pull,
Sea, hear me,
Sea, hear me."

The wind sounded different here, storm or no storm. They'd left the Pass now and this stretch of water felt like a stranger, one with a familiar face, but a foreign voice.

A wave reached high and crashed against the jib sail. The ship moaned.

Oron shouted through the open door that led below deck. "All hands! On deck now!"

Sailors streamed onto the deck, some half-dressed with just one boot or missing a shirt.

Oron grabbed the two closest. "Forget tying. Just cut the jib loose. Now!"

They rushed across the deck toward the sail at the bow, pulling knives from their sashes. Everyone else clutched onto posts or the masts. Two sailors lashed down the sealed barrels of Old Farm's finest wheat heads—they'd kept that part of the load above deck to watch for mice. Calev and Oron tied themselves and several others to the main mast.

Raindrops thickened into a deluge. Water drummed onto the decking and soaked Kinneret through. The Salt Magic had to work. She was not about to die from a storm at sea after all she'd been through. No. Even if they were out of the main waters of the Pass and far from where her magic thrived.

Lightning flared from above. A crack sounded, and all heads turned toward the sky cup. A jagged line marred the foresail mast, but the support held. If that mast broke, it would come down on the sailors like a giant hammer and most likely punch a mean hole in the ship. Kinneret gripped a post and clung on, her heart hammering. Shouts and prayers rose from most mouths, from Calev, Oron, and the others tied to the neighboring mast. The sea growled and raised a gray-brown hand to strike again.

Clutching the ship like a friend she'd learned to trust with her life, and keeping her gaze on Calev, Kinneret breathed the wet air in. She closed her eyes, reached into her bag for more salt, and shouted another prayer.

"Sea, be with me,

Hear me, see me..."

The wind ripped the grains from her palm and hissed. It felt like a reluctant agreement.

The ship tilted, then evened out as the rain turned into a drizzle on Kinneret's upturned face. Her shoes grated against the decking and someone called for help.

Opening her eyes, she dared to hope. The clouds broke apart to show the sun. The sea smoothed into rolling hills below. The Salt Magic had worked. But barely.

4

ONA

Ona's eyelids fluttered. Bright, white stars winked back. Her mouth was still so, so dry. The Silvanian-speaking Invader reached toward her ruined vest as the cart ambled on.

"Back!" she tried to shout, but it came out like a rasp of dry air.

The man rolled his eyes, spread the fabric apart, and dabbed Ona's wound with a damp cloth. A shudder rocked her.

"I'm sorry," he whispered. "But I only want you to appear dead, not actually be dead. Don't ask me why. I have no idea."

"Because you miss your native tongue?" she whispered.

His mouth tensed. His hair was a blend of so many colors. She could almost see the hues in bright spots on her old palette. Copper. Sunlight. Mushroom brown. His eyes were gray, but more than that. They had green in them too, bright shots of leaf and moss. Ona told herself to focus. A study in colors was no help in this moment. Or any moment. But she couldn't stop studying the angles of his nose and forehead. No, Ona told herself, knowing lines and shape won't help either.

"Nope," he said, answering her earlier question. "That is *not* it. I'm an Invader. I just speak a lot of languages."

Ona was too tired, too parched, and too hollow to wonder at the lie coloring his words.

He pulled out something green and crushed it. A tangy odor spilled into the air. "This'll keep your wound from putrefying."

580

Ona's skin caught fire as he pressed the mashed plant into her wound. She bit her lip, a groan pouring out of her.

From the front of the cart, another Invader looked over his hulking shoulder. He barked at Ona's caretaker. The words were sharp and jumbled and they meant nothing to her. All except one word. Dante.

"Is your name Dante?" she whispered.

He speared her with a look, the whites of his eyes bright. "No."

Jabbering back at the man in front, Dante-not-Dante closed Ona's torn vest as best anyone could and hopped off the cart before she could speak to him again in Silvanian.

The men argued. They weren't calling him Dante. It was D'Anton. An Invader name. It just happened to sound a lot like a Silvanian name. Curious.

But why did she care? Even if he was originally Silvanian and named Dante, there were hundreds of Dantes. What did it matter? She knew she'd heard of three or four. Hadn't there been one that worked the docks by the fishmonger's? And another who ran with the street gangs?

Lucca had mentioned the name once. Had said the name like a swear word, like a curse under his breath. Just the once, during a tangle with another group of mercenaries bought by the nasty man who kept a castle by the southern border of Silvania. Why did she remember that so clearly? He'd only done it once.

She wiped her head. Sweat had soaked her hair and face. Fever. From the wound. That's why she was asking herself one thousand questions. Shut it, Onaratta Paints with Blood, she told herself. You're a mercenary, not a lecturer.

But was she a mercenary anymore?

No. The fight was gone from her. She was simply Ona. No one. A husk. A shell.

The dark claimed her blood and bones, and the day faded into nothing.

Rain woke her.

Before the battle that had given Ona this wound, Seren, leader of the Empire, had said the Invaders attacked because of the drought sucking their land dry. Seren had said the Invaders were desperate for food and water. The water droplets cooled Ona's face. This couldn't be the Invaders' land, not with this rain.

And this rain...it wasn't soft or misty like the occasionally damp mornings in the oasis of Akhayma had been. These were tiny, angry drops that smelled like pine.

Ona's eyes flashed open.

Home.

Her heart surged. She fisted her hands.

If they were traveling the edges of Silvania—where she and her only friend Lucca were from—then the Invaders had decided to use a branch of the Great River to get back to their side of the world. The waterways would bring them to the sea, and from there they could slide back into their drought-ridden and desperate homelands. If she ended up there, she was good as dead.

She wasn't sure she cared.

D'Anton had taken over driving the cart while she slept. He tugged the horses' reins gently, and the cart rolled under the spreading, twisting branches of a Silvanian Lob Pine. The angry man that D'Anton had argued with earlier—Ona decided to mentally deem him *Bull*—hopped from the cart, then grabbed a bucket from a hook on the cart's side. Rainwater sloshed from its edges and ran down his thick beard as he drank it down. A third Invader with narrow, icy eyes jerked the bucket from him and gave it to the horses. Bull shouted and punched the man with the really light eyes. Ona would call him Ice King. The man swayed, but held his ground. Ice King lunged, but D'Anton slipped between them, a hand on each of their chests, rain drizzling down his sharp cheekbones and chin. He spoke in quick sentences, his words like shouts too.

Did they have to yell everything?

Ona's head throbbed like someone clenched it in a big, sweating fist. She imagined Invader mornings at home.

Good morning! I need food! The weather is dry today again! Yes! We need to go kill people and take their land! Pass the butter!

Yeah. She'd rather die than spend another second with these people. If she tried to escape, they'd kill her. She had no strength. She couldn't even move most of the time without feeling like she was going to vomit up every last bit of her innards. But that would be fine. She didn't really care to live anyway. Not if she couldn't get back to Lucca and Seren. Her body began to feel oddly light. She was floating. The pulsing in her wound and head pulled her under.

"Get up," D'Anton said, suddenly at her side with one eye watching Bull and the Ice King. He kept his voice low under the splatter of rain on pine needles. "You must stand. Now."

Ona imagined shoving him away, but of course, her arms were dead tree limbs. "I'm dead. Remember?"

"Nope. It's my job to get you tied to this tree for the night. Now help me get you up."

"Just kill me and get it over with. It's fine. Really. You don't even need to feel guilty for killing one of your own. I'm worthless at this point. I'd rather die than be a slave anyway. We're on our way to the river that will lead us back to Invader lands, right?" She swallowed and looked away from D'Anton's pitying eyes.

"You never know where life will take you."

She rolled and, with his hand on her back, maneuvered her fevered body off the cart. The world listed sideways. D'Anton helped her to the ground, and the pine's bed of fallen needles cushioned her as well as any pillow. She leaned against the sap-sticky trunk as D'Anton cut the twine that bound her wrists. He wound a rope around the tree and his tunic slipped over his collarbone.

A brand showed at the spot where his neck met his shoulder. The pink, shiny flesh was just a simple *X*, but it meant he was an Invader and had been through their initiation into manhood. There was something they did that involved fire and fasting, but she didn't know the details. Even if D'Anton had originally been Silvanian, he was forever marked as an Invader. He knotted the tie, and the rope bit her hipbones. Wasn't much of a knot though.

"I could get out of this in a blink if I wasn't two minutes shy of being a corpse."

"I'm sure."

The old Ona would've snarled and told him exactly how she'd be out of that pathetic tie and have his blood on her hands in a heartbeat. That spark inside her, that need to someday see Lucca and Seren, told her to wait, to smolder, to burn quietly until she saw more options than blind violence and pointless snapping.

Ona closed her mouth and watched D'Anton walk away to join the rest of her enemies. The drips of rain and the scent of pines lulled her into a fevered sleep. She almost had the energy to fear what tomorrow might bring, but not quite, not quite.

5

KINNERET

The main port of Silvania was the stuff of dreams. Tall ships with sails of sunset pink, ruby, sunlight, and midnight blue dotted the bay. Polished skiffs zipped through the crystal water and bobbed beside the ten docks. The center of trade on a worldwide level, Verita saw Northern Isle traders with furs and amber, Kurakian spice merchants, lumber men from the remote Green Mountains, and of course, southern contingents like Kinneret's who brought citrus fruits and specialty grains.

Kinneret, Oron, Calev, and Ridhima left the rest of the sailors in charge of the full-ship. The small group took a smaller vessel into the bay. Kinneret tugged her oar and slid the skiff neatly into a spot beside the second dock. Calev threw their rope over the decorative cleat, which featured two bronze fish facing away from one another, their metal scales green with an aged patina. The port city lay along the lapping water, showing off merchant houses with scalloped columns, paints that cost more than most made in a lifetime, and windows with pointed arches.

"It's too beautiful. My eyes hurt." Kinneret could almost forget she was here on business.

Oron rubbed his hands together, his black mood forgotten in the light of the gorgeous city. "She is a lady in repose, resting near her lover, the sea."

"Poetic."

Calev chuckled. "Can't you appreciate something without relating it to women or wine?"

"Not all of us have the goods in real life." Oron jerked his chin at Kinneret. "*We* poor souls are left with only our imaginations."

They hopped onto the smooth boards of the dock and only a touch of the heat rose up through Kinneret's sandals. Many couldn't afford fine shoes like she now possessed. She promised herself she'd go without once a moon cycle just so she'd never forget that pain.

Her hand strayed to the high-caste silver bells on her sash. A quiet contentedness warmed her as much as the sun because at least *some* of the injustice back in her home of Jakobden had been fixed by Ekrem. They'd helped him into power, into becoming the new amir. It'd been a great victory for the poor of the area because Ekrem actually cared about other human beings, unlike the previous amir.

And now they were here to help Amir Ekrem achieve another success: to gain a strong ally against the Invaders. Though the Invaders hadn't attacked Jakobden, there were rumors about bands of them breaking from the main force that had attacked Akhayma. These bands were said to have been securing boats. If the Invaders ended up with boats, they could possibly move against southern ports like Old Farm's and Jakobden's. Ekrem had told Kinneret, Calev, and Oron that he was willing to provide Silvania food and soldiers if Silvania was attacked. In return, Ekrem suggested the Silvanian king agree to send a number of ships and a military presence toward the Broken Coast to defend Jakobden and Old Farm if Invaders were indeed spotted. It was a good plan. A fair plan. But the king of Silvania was known to be a greedy, cunning man. He wouldn't be easy to deal with and neither would the Northern Isle traders who graced his shores.

When Kinneret, Calev, and Oron were halfway up the dock, another skiff floated up beside them.

Oron stiffened.

The sides of the boat were glacier white and held a party of Northern Isle folk. One woman, about Kinneret's age or maybe a touch younger, stood tall. The wind ruffled her cloak—it was made of the famous bluehare —and tossed the woman's black and silver braids. Her fingers curled around a staff decorated with hundreds of carved runes. Magical *lykill*, they called them. She was a *seithr*, a magic worker from the far north. A blade glimmered at the end of her staff, almost brushing the woman's cheek.

Kinneret put a hand on Oron's shoulder to show him she had his back, but she also faced the party with a smile. They may have come from a terrible culture, but she had business to do with them and she would get it done. All the better if they saw Oron as her high-caste first mate. Success was the best vengeance.

"Greetings," she said in her best Northern Isle tongue.

The woman in the skiff wrinkled her nose.

"Oron," Kinneret said out of the side of her mouth, "greet them for us and show them you're high ranking despite their prejudices. This doesn't have to go their way, but it does have to move forward. For Ekrem. For Jakobden."

"Fine." Oron shook off Kinneret's hand and opened his arms wide. "Welcome to Verita, northern traders." He said more, but Kinneret couldn't follow the garbled language. She traded a shrug with Calev. Oron might not love this, but at least he was doing his job.

The seithr and an older man with a braided beard joined them on the dock. The man said something fast and sharp back to Oron, who bristled.

Kinneret whispered in Calev's ear. "The man won't look at Oron. See?"

Calev's lip curled.

The seithr did make eye contact with Oron, but she was the only one in the party who would. Kinneret gave her a genuine smile.

Oron held out a bag of silver coins, then faced Kinneret. "How much should I offer for twenty bluehare cloaks?"

Kinneret scrambled for the charcoal and paper inside her sash. She wrote out the number Ekrem's scribe had told them to start with, then handed the information to Oron. He glanced at the slip, then spoke again.

The seithr spoke up for the first time. Oron traded a sentence with her, then she looked to Kinneret and Calev and began to speak in the common tongue, also known as the trade tongue. Kinneret didn't realize any of the Northern Isle folk knew that language.

"Do you think us wrong to push such ones as him from our nests?" The seithr pointed at Oron with her bladed staff. Her words were accented strongly and awkwardly timed, but the meaning was clear. She was asking them their opinion on the Northern Isle custom of killing off children who are different from the average person.

Kinneret knew exactly how she felt about that. "I want to trade with you," she managed to say in the woman's tongue. "But this…" She didn't have the language for this. "It is…disgusting what you do." Some of that was in the trade tongue. Would she understand?

The seithr's eyes flashed. "You do not know us. You do not know our ways."

Calev stepped between the woman and Kinneret. "We want no fight with you," he said in the Northern Isle language.

He took the silver from Oron, who looked about ready to burst into flames. If they didn't make a deal quickly, Oron might just start a battle right here on this dock. Kinneret might end up on a spit for taking that battle and turning it into a war. Her rage colored everything around her.

"Let us trade and be done," Calev said. "This for twenty cloaks. Please deliver them to our skiff here and the woman named Ridhima, who will see it to our full-ship. The skiff is marked with a yellow and black flag." He pointed. "Then you are finished with us and us with you."

Kinneret wanted to shake the seithr. "I don't need to know anything more. This man is my friend, my first mate, the best sailor I've ever met in all my years at sea." She turned to point at Oron, but he was gone.

"Oron! Wait." Kinneret ran toward the city. Oron was already disappearing into the crowd beyond the waterside.

Calev came up beside her, nervous sweat rising on his upper lip. "There. I see him."

Oron wove between two market stalls selling bright orange berries and wooden screens carved from good, Silvanian pine.

Kinneret hurried after him.

Oron's hand went up and he shouted over his shoulder. "I just need to clear my head. Leave me be. I'll meet you tonight. At the king's castle." He disappeared around the pink and white brick corner of a merchant's house.

Kinneret kept on, but Calev stayed her with a hand. "Give him some time. He'll be all right."

"Why does he care what those strangers think? They're a bunch of asses. They are all stuck up in their little islands with that madman Fellriki filling their heads with lies. Who cares what they think?"

Calev's big brown eyes softened. His fingers trailed over Kinneret's elbow and down to the sensitive skin on her wrist. "You know as well as I do that we can't always be sensible when it comes to what we care about." A grin turned his mouth.

A tickling feeling danced through Kinneret's middle and she kissed that grin lightly. "True." Oron was well and truly gone now. They'd never find him in this teeming mass of people and donkeys and carts. "But I'm worried. If he isn't at the king's castle by exactly sundown, I say we go after him."

"Agreed." Calev eyed the dock, squinting against the sun. "Should we go back and try to get the goods Amir Ekrem wanted for the kyros's visit? Or has that ship sailed both metaphorically and literally?"

"I really don't want to talk to those people again. Ekrem can send the kyros something else. One of those old books or some of our silver. It'll be fine."

"True. And Old Farm can offer some goods too. I have no desire to speak with the Northern Isle folk again either."

They started toward the western road, which would lead to the king's castle, and hopefully, a happy ending to this stormy quest. Silvania was a dangerous land full of age-old curses and powerful, rich families battling for land. If Oron landed in the wrong place at the wrong time, he could find himself dealing with new wounds instead of old ones.

6

ONA

"Wake up. We have to go. Now."

Ona opened her sore eyes to see D'Anton's shadowed face. A deep blue like the color of rain clouds covered his cheeks and chin. He whispered, kneeling beside her and fiddling with something behind the tree.

Taller than the two closest pines, the Invaders' fire flickered. Ice King laughed as Bull worked with a whetstone to sharpen his short sword. He splashed a handful of water from a bucket onto the stone and ground the blade with quick, expert strokes.

Pain clenched Ona's wound with corpse-cold fingers. "I think I'm trying to die, so can it wait?"

"You are truly going to meet death if you don't shut your mouth and start running."

"But I'm tied…" She lifted her hands to see the remnants of her bindings. She was free.

D'Anton held a knife by his side, his gaze on the other men. "Come on."

He yanked her up. The place where Invader steel had run through Ona's middle roared with agony. It was right below her shoulder and made breathing painful too. She stumbled, but D'Anton pulled her along, over a fallen log that smelled of rot and rain.

"They are drunk on a stash of Silvanian wine they stole from a group of traveling merchants an hour from here. Killed every one of them, down to the young girl with them. Now they've decided you're next. They think it'll be great fun to see how long it'll take you to die either from dicing you up or from a stab wound to the stomach. They haven't decided."

"That's a compliment really," Ona croaked, curious as to why she didn't feel afraid. "They know I'm hard to kill."

"Oh yes. A fine compliment you can take to your grave."

"Why do you care?" She leaned heavily on him as they approached the horse that had earlier been latched to the cart. The horse snorted and stomped the earth.

"I told you that I have no idea why I care about you. But I do. And it's the first time I've cared about anything in a long time."

Ona should've felt warmed, but she felt nothing. Just that nagging need to get back to Lucca and Seren to apologize for all the lies and the treachery.

"I'll mount, then pull you up behind me." Looping the reins over the horse's neck, D'Anton ran a hand down the animal's neck. It snuffled into his shoulder gently. He sprang onto its back with surprising grace, then held a hand down to Ona.

Knowing full well that pain would scream through her with the movement, she gritted her teeth to keep from yelling, grabbed his arm, and swung a leg over. The pain squeezed every bit of energy out of her and she slumped against D'Anton's back. He tugged her hands forward and lashed them at his stomach so she wouldn't fall off.

Why did she trust this Invader? He could be taking her further into the forest to kill her himself. But he spoke Silvanian. And something about his features, his gestures…well, she was too exhausted and hollow to do much but go along with him.

Bull's voice shot through the trees. He shouted something in their language and crashed toward them.

"Hold on with your legs as best you can." D'Anton kicked his heels into the horse and turned its head east.

Shouts trailed them, and moonlight wove through the pines to touch the ground before the horse's hooves. Rain dripped lightly from the needles and washed Ona's hot cheeks. The sweet water ran into her mouth and around the place where her head met D'Anton's back. His bones and muscles moved under his muddied surcoat. The cloth was rough and chafed her skin, but she couldn't bother to move. The horse jumped, avoiding a rock or something of the sort, and she slid sideways.

D'Anton's hand caught her side. He pushed her back into place as easily as if she weighed nothing. "Stay on, please. Remember, you are tied to me. If you fall, I fall. Then we're both dead and I actually care about dying. I've decided I might have some living left in me yet."

She was about to ask him where they were headed, but the sound of more horses snapped through the wood. D'Anton said something in the Invader tongue and kicked the horse.

Ona turned a fraction to see behind them. Bull and Ice King were a bow shot away. She and D'Anton would never make it riding two on one like this.

"Cut the tie. Let me fall. You go on. We won't win this race."

D'Anton simply shook his head once and kept on. She had to persuade him to leave her. He'd been kind. She was a bad person. He shouldn't die for her.

"They're going to shoot me in the back," she said. "They're already within range."

"It'll be tough considering I broke both their bows before I untied you at the big pine."

"What about axes? Or knives?"

"They don't have any. Just their swords and they won't toss them around. They don't have any money except the little amount they stole from the merchant party. It's not enough for them to get home if they have to buy another weapon."

A gloved hand grabbed Ona's shirt and pulled hard. Her body acted without her mind's direction. Pure muscle memory. She slammed the bottom of her fisted hand into Bull's nose and was rewarded with the glimpse of dark blood running from his nostrils before she collapsed against D'Anton. The move had brought the screaming pain back again and she fought the urge to moan like a beaten donkey. Bull had fallen back, but Ice King kept on, his sword out. He wasn't going to make the same mistake and get within Ona's reach. He'd just nip her spine and see where that took them. Smart.

"He's going to stab me, D'Anton," she said, her voice far too calm.

D'Anton threw something over his shoulder. Their attacker shrieked and both he and his horse tumbled to the forest floor. Ona strained to see what had taken the man down. A blade protruded from the Invader's eye. She shuddered.

She actually shivered at the sight of violence.

Not since the time before the Invaders took her aunt's life at the villa had she been sickened by the death or injury of an enemy.

Who was she?

Onaratta Paints with Blood didn't shy away from gore. She unleashed it and used it to rain down vengeance. But now...now she had no desire at all to spill blood. She didn't even want to see it.

"Is Tantor still following?" D'Anton asked.

She assumed he meant Bull. "Yes. He is behind that copse of beech we just passed. How is someone so drunk so fast?" she mumbled.

"We need cover."

"We need Lucca," Ona whispered, barely audible, half in the world of fevered dreams. The forest blurred and she heard a young voice calling out. "Do you hear that voice?" Now the sound of cracking branches drowned the child's voice. A sigh echoed through the trees and she shivered violently. "Or are they animals? Birds?"

"Birds at night?" D'Anton steered the horse down a ravine, his gaze flitting from their makeshift path to Tantor behind them.

The horse crashed through the brush and into a swathe of land that was bare of trees. Stumps remained along the border, but the rest of the area had been plowed in preparation for planting. A sick feeling slithered through Ona's stomach. The place felt...angry and, maybe...sacred? What an odd sense for a place to have. How could a forest be sacred?

A buzz vibrated under her flesh warning her of something unseen.

Then she remembered something from her childhood. She had passed through an area like this once with her older cousin. They were searching for charcoal to buy. The forest she'd gone through with her cousin had air that weighed on your shoulders and sank into your chest. They hadn't found any charcoal burners' huts there, and they'd fled quickly. This place felt similar to that forest, but this place was...more.

The scent of the pines rose to the point that all other smells were drowned out.

This wood felt somehow...deeper, more powerful. The pull and tug of this specific forest grabbed hold of her like a great hand. She and D'Anton didn't belong here. If she listened hard enough, she could almost hear the felled trees screaming in the spirit world beyond, shouting against those who had cut them down.

Squeezing her eyes shut, she moved her swollen hands inside their ties and tried to relieve some of the discomfort there since she couldn't do anything about the pain of her wound. "No cover here. Let's leave. Go around."

D'Anton's head turned as he quickly surveyed the new border of the forest, a good gallop away. "Doom and donkey balls," he swore in Silvanian.

Ona grinned despite her pain, her hollowness, and the fact that she was probably about to be chopped into pieces. It was a specific curse Lucca had used once when they first tangled with the leader of their chanting crew. "Where did you hear that?" The fever took her words and blurred them into nonsense, and her eyes closed against her will.

When she opened them, she saw a hand reaching out of the dark toward her. The world moved too slowly. Like a nightmare. The hand didn't belong to Bull or D'Anton.

Leaved branches tipped the fingers like brown and green claws.

That strange hand snatched her hair. It pulled hard. Still tied to D'Anton, she fell as he did, dropping from their mount. She was tugged away as D'Anton rolled to his feet and the horse bolted into the night with a frightened whinny. The moonlight showed their attacker. Too long and too slender to be human, he had skin like tree bark and eyes black as pitch. Her body rejected the creature and shook hard. A scream pealed from her burning throat.

D'Anton shouted back, but the words were lost in the rustle of leaves as the tree man dragged her into the line of growth she'd seen beyond the logged strip of land. As far as she could tell, another tree creature had D'Anton.

Panic flooded Ona's veins with energy. She was more herself than she'd been since waking to see D'Anton's face the first time. She took hold of the tree man's hand on her head and planted her feet in the musky-scented earth. With a twist, she had the creature on his knees. He grinned and horror washed over Ona. The look was entirely foreign. Thoroughly evil. Not at all what she cared to see in the dark when she was seriously wounded.

Pain lashed through her wound. Her head swam, tangling her thoughts and knotting up her ability to reason. The tree man stood and grinned again. She nearly vomited with fear. Why couldn't it be bunnies? Or goats? Why did it have to be hellish creatures bent on death and torture and who knew what else?

Before she could move a muscle, two vines wrapped around her ankles. The tree man smiled as the vines jerked her upside down and lifted her into a huge oak. The air in her lungs left in a rush. Black spots floated in front of her eyes. The creature leaned in and wrapped its arms around her and the oak at her back.

With her face smashed against the thing's leg, her heart beat like a hummingbird's in her mouth and in her wound. She lashed out with her hands, trying to grab something she could injure—leg, groin, pressure points—but the tree man didn't seem to feel a thing. A rushing sound filled her ears and the world darkened at the edges. A tingling feeling crawled over her feet, inside her boots. She twisted to look, her body shouting against the movement and her vision blurry.

The creature spoke in soft, unintelligible phrases and the forest seemed to echo him in snaps and the rush of wind through leaves. The tree man moved his head of dark, green leaves and finally Ona could see her feet. Over the rugged boots she'd fought in for years, rough bark grew and spread and covered her to the ankles.

A sheen of sweat covered her back and face.

The creature was somehow melding her with his oak.

A feeling like a giant hand crushing her chest stole what little air she could suck in. She thrashed wildly. "D'Anton," she grunted out. "Bull. Anyone. Help!"

Death would be better than this, whatever this was.

But D'Anton was nowhere around. He was probably going through the same thing.

Still upside down, she strained against her ties as sweat dripped from her neck, to her cheeks, then into her mouth. It tasted like fear. Her nail beds were on fire. Splinters had lodged themselves into her fingers when she'd tried to grab and tear the creature's form. A rotten smell mingled with the pine's scent. The foul stench twisted something wonderful and familiar into a disgusting odor she knew she'd never forget if she managed to escape.

The tree creature's soft refrain needled through her panic and into her ears. Her eyes grew heavy. The pulsing, hot pain in her wound, nails, and head faded. A cool breeze dusted her forehead. The sensation of a man's strong but gentle hand floated down her back and cupped the back of her skull. A sigh left her lips. She knew this was a dream, and that she should properly wake up, but she couldn't help wondering whose hand touched her. A sharp voice in the back of her mind urged her to fight, but she couldn't find the desire. She only wanted the sweet touch, the cool air, the ease of pain.

"Woman. Fight." D'Anton's words slashed through the haze of pleasure and blessed darkness.

Ona opened her eyes to see that her vision was partially blocked by bark. She tried to lift her arms, but they wouldn't move. She was upright now, but she was halfway inside…inside the trunk of the oak. Her throat constricted. She struggled to find her awareness, to blink and breathe and wake up from whatever magic the creature had poured into her.

A light flashed outside the tree. Moonlight on steel. D'Anton slashed a sword through the air and came down on what looked like another tree man. Maybe the same one that had caught Ona. The blade bit into the thing's shoulder and brought it down.

"Can you move? Are you alive?" D'Anton's hair was lank with sweat and looked almost black in the ethereal light of the forest. She was suddenly struck with worry for Lucca. She had to get back to him, to make sure he and Seren were alive and well.

"I'm here." Her throat felt swollen.

D'Anton spun to fight off a second tree creature. The tree man towered over D'Anton. It whipped a long, sinewy arm of ivy, bark, and leaves at D'Anton's newfound sword. But when the thing's branchlike fingers curled around the steel, it hissed and fell back.

D'Anton didn't hesitate. He drove the blade into the thing's chest and ended that one's life.

Ona didn't have time to shudder at the violence now. She was entombed and found she did care about her well-being after all. This wasn't how she wanted to die. If she was going down, it would be in blood and glory, not rot and impotence.

The beautiful male voice whispered inside her head. *Sleep. Feel. All is well.*

"I don't think so." She gathered every shred of will she could find inside her broken body and soul, then drove herself forward. The bark around her cracked.

The first tree man stood, leaving the arm D'Anton had cleaved off on the forest floor, and rushed him. D'Anton shouted, feinted right, and went left. The sword cut the creature in two.

D'Anton hurried toward Ona. "I'll cut you out," he called, his voice now so much stronger than the other one in her mind.

Ona shoved herself forward again and a long piece of wood broke away and fell to D'Anton's feet. The space allowed her arms to move and she braced her palms against the trunk. With one hard push, she blasted through the tree's body and tumbled to the ground. D'Anton caught her arm and helped her up.

Blood rushed away from her head. She shuddered. Pain returned in waves, pulsing in her ankles, where the tree had laced ivy to lift her, throbbing inside the wound the Invader had given her during the great battle of Akhayma, beating inside her heart, where she ached over Lucca and Seren and all she'd done to hurt them.

D'Anton went down with her and pulled her into his chest. "Is this...all right?"

It was, but she couldn't seem to talk. Who was she right now? She wasn't Onaratta Paints with Blood. Onaratta never would've been caught so easily, given up so soon. But she had to be glad she wasn't that person anymore. That Onaratta had betrayed her dear friends. She'd done the worst and sided with the enemy against the only two people alive who loved her despite all of her flaws.

She spit leaves and dirt from her mouth. "Those things. They're green men, aren't they?" she whispered.

She'd heard about them in childhood stories and legends shared over watered wine and bonfires. Spirits of cursed forests drew humans in and drained them of life. She never paid much attention to the tales, but she did remember something about a god ruling the green men and how this god created these beings from humans with especially strong souls. The more recently created green man, the more powerful. But she didn't recall a single thing about any sword they didn't like or any way to escape them.

"You should run," she said into D'Anton's shirt. He wasn't wearing his Invader surcoat anymore and the fabric against his skin was simple linen. "I am a terrible person and...you should go. Escape while you can. If you can. Use that sword."

He brushed a tentative hand over her back and patted her lightly. "I'm not going anywhere. Besides," he leaned back and tugged his shirt down at the collar to show his Invader brand, "no one will tolerate my presence with this on my flesh. You are the only one who seems to accept that I'm not an enemy."

She laughed—a harsh sound that had nothing to do with good humor. "Because I tend to side with enemies. I told you. I'm terrible."

D'Anton cocked an eyebrow and put two fingers under her chin. His breath was warm on her cheek. "There is nothing terrible about doing your best to protect yourself."

"Even when you fight on the side of wolves who would consume the ones you love most?"

"I'm guessing it wasn't that simple."

"It was betrayal."

"You're allowed to make mistakes. They don't define you."

She set her spinning head on his shoulder and just let this stranger hold her. He was wrong. Mistakes and victories were the very two things that did define a person. But she was too tired to argue.

A branch snapped behind them and Ona's heart jumped inside her chest. They were up in a blink.

"What was that?" D'Anton put a hand on the hilt of the sword he must've found here in the forest's shadowed depths. Markings in the blade caught the few rays of moonlight that filtered through the oaks and pines. Those were no ordinary maker's marks. They were runes like the ones the Northern Isle folk used. Power ebbed and flowed from them like a heartbeat. She could almost feel it bounce against her skin and eyes.

But she was too exhausted to ask about anything. "I need a nap very badly."

Three tree men walked out of the darkness. The largest of them exhaled and somehow it was terrifying.

"No time for a nap now, I'm afraid." D'Anton hoisted Ona up, and then they were running.

Pines tall enough to scratch the stars blurred as Ona raced, zigzagging, through the cursed forest behind D'Anton. She was limping, but the very clear memory of being encased in that oak drove her on like madness. She was numb again, her mind switching off like it often did in a fight. Her boots crunched over the last year's pine needles and crisp oak leaves until an oval of smooth silver appeared in a small clearing.

She and D'Anton both pulled up short.

"I don't like the look of that," he said.

He'd read her mind.

"Go around." Ona began tugging him east, where more trees lurked, thick and dark.

The green men broke into the clearing. Their bark-covered feet—more like roots—pressed the earth where D'Anton and Ona had stood seconds ago.

The creature in the front spoke. The sounds weren't words. They were noises. Branches breaking. Wind in dry leaves. Water over rocks. The whispers started up again.

Shivering, Ona wiped sweat from her brow, then pressed her hands over her ears as they came up to a spot where the growth was so thick, it would be nearly impossible to get through it. She began tearing at the smaller trees and undergrowth all the same. The scent of rot and pine was overwhelming and she was fairly sure she was about to vomit. Not overly helpful during a fight. They had to get through this and out of here.

The tree men slowly advanced, their sounds and the forest's whispers growing louder and tugging at Ona's consciousness.

"It's just water though right?" D'Anton hacked at the growth with his sword, then glanced at the silver pool beside them. The water was too smooth. Too still. "We'll never outrun those things in here." His words were quiet and true.

Ona swallowed a burning lump in her throat and stopped pulling at branches. She did not want to go through the water, but she did like the look of the meadow and thinner trees beyond that silver pool.

The tree men advanced and suddenly sped up, branch arms reaching and mouths whispering, cracking, hissing.

Heart in her mouth, Ona snatched D'Anton and dragged him into the shining surface of the water.

He shouted, but his voice was lost as Ona fell beneath the silver pool's eerie surface.

The water felt like thousands of feathers brushing over her.

The sensation wasn't horrible, but it was definitely creepy. She'd take a blunt hit to the head over this adventure any day. Her mind whirred as her feet paddled to find the surface. The cloudy, metallic liquid surrounded her completely and blinded her of everything else. Her lungs burned with the need for air. There should've been the sound of bubbles or her own yelling —because she was shouting D'Anton's name—but silence shoved into and through her ears.

The silver water leaked through her clamped-shut lips and into her ears and snaked through her hair. A sound like an army of horses rose in her mind.

Then she was run through with a sword.

In the same place she'd already been wounded.

Eyes slamming shut against the fierce pain, she grabbed at the wound. But there was no sword. No new wound. Only the slightly healed one. But it pulsed like a fresh cut. Her head went light and her stomach flipped.

A hand grabbed her back and she struggled against it, her lungs filling. She was dying. This was death, here to claim her inside this magic pool of horror and pain.

The fingers clutching her clothes yanked hard and pulled her free of the silver water.

D'Anton leaned over her as she turned onto her side and vomited.

He put a hand on her back. His eyes were on the forest beyond.

Were the creatures gone? Was she dead?

Ona coughed and sat up, the new pain the pool had brought faded and only the true pain from her healing wound thudded in time with her panicked heart. She touched that wound, making very sure she was right and that she hadn't been somehow run through again under that water.

The silvery stuff dripped from D'Anton's confused face. His eyebrows knitted and his dimpled chin moved under the beginnings of a beard. "Did the water hurt you?"

The forest was quiet. The meadow was free of any tree men. "Are they really gone?"

"Well, I don't see them, so let's be optimistic."

"That pool." The surface was still. No ripples. She shivered and twisted to vomit again. "It's poison. It...I was wounded again. In the same place. I heard the Invaders' horses..."

"You relived your worst moment."

Ona nodded. She felt like a tiny girl again. Small. Lacking muscles or experience or skills. Gritting her teeth, she stood and jerked her chin at the sword D'Anton had obviously dropped on the forest floor.

"Time to tell me where you found that."

"Are swords no longer a favorite of yours?"

"Nothing that comes from this place is my favorite."

"I feel the same." He retrieved the weapon, and they began walking back the way they'd come.

She hated it, but there really wasn't any other way out of here. She was not going back through that cursed water.

"I found the sword beside the oak that took you." Tucking the sword into his belt, he frowned. The sky beyond the trees was growing lighter. The morning showed a cut below his ear. Blood had crusted in his hair, and he was limping nearly as much as she was. "Blackened growth surrounded the blade, and well, with all those strange symbols—it had to be powerful in some way. I grabbed the thing and hoped for the best."

"It worked pretty well against the green men. I wonder if that's Northern Isle magic in those symbols."

"I don't know. I didn't think their magic worked outside the isles, but I'm no expert. This may be made from a steel I haven't run into yet."

"Let's not say *sword* and *run into* in the same sentence for while, all right?"

The side of D'Anton's mouth lifted, and Ona wondered what it would be like to kiss him. She swallowed, shocked at the fleeting thought. She'd thought she was too beaten down to think of kissing anyone ever again.

D'Anton turned and walked backward to talk to her. He was surprisingly nimble. "The silver pool didn't injure me, thanks for asking."

Guilt tugged at Ona. Despite all her lessons, she was still thoroughly selfish. "I'm sorry. I'm glad you weren't hurt."

As he turned, his shirt moved down, pulled by the sword he'd tucked into his belt.

Ona's mouth fell open. "Your Invader brand. It's gone."

D'Anton froze, then clutched at his shirt. He craned his neck to try and see, then gave that up and moved his fingers over the formerly burned and scarred spot. The skin there was the same olive tone as the rest of him.

His face changed. His eyes had been haunted and dark. Now the light irises brightened and the lines around his mouth faded. "It is. It's gone."

"You're not an Invader anymore. The silver pool cursed me and blessed you. Typical."

D'Anton rushed toward Ona. She tensed but was too fatigued to react as he grabbed her up gently, hugged her, and planted a kiss on her cheek. He lifted his hands in the air and his feet moved in a quick little dance. "I can't believe it!"

Recognition shocked Ona.

She had seen that dance. When? Where? She shook her head. She was thinking about all the wrong things. "What are we going to do if we run into the tree men again?"

"Fight them," D'Anton said.

"That much I had figured out on my own, thanks. I need a weapon."

D'Anton slid a small knife from his boot and handed it over.

They headed into the forest, Ona's body in full revolt. But what could she do? She wasn't so far gone as to simply lie down in the pine needles and let them kill her. She didn't want to live really, but she also didn't truly want to die. And living was obviously going to take some work.

She took the lead and D'Anton nodded, giving her a tentative smile. His fingers floated over his missing brand. She wished she had some of his newly found happiness to get her through this forest of silver and secrets.

"Happiness doesn't end the dung life brings, but it sure helps clear the air."

"What was that?" D'Anton moved his hair behind his ear. His eyes were warm and his limp was already fading. She was glad to have him in this nightmare with her.

"Oh nothing. I was just being wise. Try to listen next time."

7

KINNERET

Kinneret scanned the crowd one more time, looking for Oron's familiar tangled locks and cynical face. Nothing. She touched her salt pouch, feeling powerless.

Night descended on the port town of Verita in shades of violet, ocean blue, and blazing yellow. Musicians in bright tunics and caps crept out of every corner. They played lutes, woodwinds, and small drums to those wealthy enough to throw coins. Men in outlandish Silvanian robes sauntered past merchant stands of iced milk. How much did keeping milk frozen cost? Probably enough to feed one thousand low-castes. It was chilly here, but not cold enough to keep ice. Kinneret rolled her eyes, her worry turning to anger. Lanterns glowed from strings across the courtyards leading up to the roads of water.

"Let's search for him, all right? I can't just stand here."

Calev followed her as she hailed a boat. "But where should we look?"

"I don't know. But I'm not twiddling my thumbs while Oron is robbed and beaten to death in some dank alleyway."

"Oron is no stranger to a city full of thieves and roughs. Shouldn't we give him just one night to himself?" Calev's earnest eyes studied her.

"I don't know. He was really upset."

"How about we search for him after we meet the king? We should at least present ourselves. Amir Ekrem expects it. I'm sure Oron will be fine. He probably went to have a drink and kiss a tavern woman."

Kinneret sighed. "Maybe you're right."

They returned to the skiff, where Ridhima handed over the ancient tomes from Ekrem's library and the crate of fresh lemons—gifts for the king.

THE KING'S city castle boasted high walls with arrow slits and pointed arches. A stable full of stomping black horses stood across the inner courtyard from a dock that was somehow fed through an extensive tunnel system that led to the sea.

Kinneret breathed in the scent of the ocean, letting it fill her with confidence.

At the door to the main housing, a guard appeared. His puffy short pants competed with his silk, striped hat for attention. Kinneret settled on the hat. The feather on top really said *regally employed*. She snorted a laugh and Calev elbowed her.

The guard cleared his throat and spoke in a slightly accented version of their language, the trade, or common, tongue. "The king awaits you."

Kinneret didn't think so. Silvania's pompous king wouldn't know the smallest thing about her. "He awaits me?"

"Are you not Kinneret Raza, Amir Ekrem's full-ship kaptan and the liberator of Quarry Isle?"

Calev wiggled his eyebrows. "She is indeed. And my Intended." He winked at the guard, which Kinneret thought was maybe a little over the top. Had he nipped a bit of Oron's wine earlier? "I'm her assistant."

The guard frowned. "If I'm not mistaken, you are also Calev ben Y'hoshua, next Chairman of Old Farm and legendary dagger dancer."

Kinneret laughed hard at Calev's blush, then clapped him on the back. "Yes. The dancing is actually very attractive."

Calev groaned, fully embarrassed now.

"No, really," Kinneret said to the guard. "You should try a good dance instead of that hat. Might grab a nicer form of attention."

The guard blinked, then turned on a heel and stormed into the castle. Without another word to them, he called for servants. A man with grape vines in his hair took the lemon crate while a woman in a bright purple tunic gently accepted the books. One of the books had silver-edged pages and had to be worth a kyros's sum.

A floor of white and gray marble led them through walls of framed mirrors and long windows set high, near the painted ceiling.

"I'm going to hope that somehow that guard didn't understand your little hat comment," Calev said.

Painted rock doves, intricate crowns, chariots, and wild ocean waves crowded the ceiling.

Kinneret whistled at the interior. "Humble fellow, this king."

Calev laughed, his blush finally fading. "Oh yes. A real man of the people," he whispered.

Kinneret's loud laugh startled the guard who walked primly several steps ahead.

The lustrous hallway brought them to a room with gossamer curtains over open windows. The sound of Verita carried on the breeze—boatmen singing for their customers, men and women trading quick words in three different languages, and the clink of coins changing hands. The curtains whipped inward, chasing a sudden gust, and their movement drew Kinneret's and Calev's eyes to the silver gilt throne at the end of the room.

The king stood and opened his arms. "Welcome!" His head nearly brushed the throne's velvet canopy.

His courtiers quieted and turned. Every set of eyes on Kinneret felt like fire pokers. Like somehow they'd know she came from nothing and was only recently raised out of the muck of poverty. But why should she feel ashamed? Pushing those worries aside, she raised her chin and faced those wealthy nobles down.

"Thank you, your highness," Calev said charmingly.

Kinneret bowed, mimicking his movement. "We bring greetings from Amir Ekrem in Jakobden. He hopes our people can be fast friends in these dangerous times."

"Ah. Yes." He motioned to a servant who brought a tray of low, wide glasses to Calev and Kinneret. She took one filled with a dark, red wine. Oron, once again, crossed her mind. She hoped he was simply drinking somewhere and not lying in a gutter. "Please," the king said, "make yourself at home in my castle. We have rooms prepared in the northern wing."

"Our amir sent gifts for you, your highness." Kinneret gestured to the servants behind them.

The king studied the stack of books, murmuring appreciatively. "Very fine indeed." He turned to read the label on the crate. "Old Farm lemons! My dears, gather round. We will all enjoy a slice of the tartness that only the ancient land of Old Farm can produce. You will think yourselves turned inside out with pleasure!"

Calev beamed with pride. Once the group had gushed over their precious lemon slices and questioned Calev about soil types, harvesting times, seed storage, and planting rituals—which the king snickered through obnoxiously—Kinneret decided it was time to move forward.

"Your highness," she said, "if the Invaders strike your territories, Amir Ekrem promises to send—"

"Ah. Ah. Ah." The king held up a finger, then sucked another lemon slice. He puckered his lips and shook his head. "So deliciously tart. Kaptan Kinneret Raza, we will discuss our new friendship tomorrow. After a feast. And some dancing!" He winked at Calev, who grimaced.

As much as she loved seeing Calev charming the court, she couldn't stop worrying about Oron. "We would really like to complete negotiations now, if you don't mind, your greatness."

Calev squeezed the bridge of his nose.

Your greatness might've been a little over the top.

"We would love to feast with you tomorrow before our talks, your highness," Calev said, bowing deeply to the king.

With one more lemon slicing demonstration, the king dismissed Kinneret and Calev. They found themselves outside the castle walls, staring up at a starry sky and still wondering where Oron had gone.

"I'm finished waiting around." Kinneret headed toward a boatman who had a dark green craft at the nearest dock. "We're going after Oron. All right?"

Nodding, Calev hopped into the boat and handed a coin to its master, a man with a wide, upper body and a lean face. "Where can we go to get a good cup of wine?" Calev asked the man.

Kinneret twisted on the boat's seat and looked across the waterway to where it spilled into a larger convergence of liquid roads. There were boats everywhere. So many people. How in the world were they going to find Oron in this if he didn't want to be found?

The boat master lowered his long, wooden pole into the water and pushed them away from the solid ground. "A stretch of taverns run along the western edge of Verita." His accent was strong, his voice deep and rumbling—like most Silvanians. They seemed to exaggerate parts of words which made their version of the Common Tongue sound like a whole new dialect to Kinneret's ears. "You get all sorts in there though," he said. "I'd be careful, if I were in your shoes."

Calev sat beside Kinneret. She took his hand in hers, reveling in the warmth and the familiar calluses. "What if we can't find him?"

"We will. And we'll be back before the Silvanian king misses us tomorrow." Calev's smile lit his face and drove the slight chill in the air away.

Kinneret leaned forward and pressed her mouth to his. His hands drifted over her cheeks and down the column of her neck. His lips followed the path, then he nibbled on her collarbone and sent rivers of goosebumps along her skin. Her entire body warmed. She tangled her fingers in his hair, not caring a bit if the boat master was looking. Calev's touch was the only thing that could shove the fear from her mind and remind her that they'd been through worse than this and would see the other side of this trouble too.

Calev pulled back and a lock of his jet hair fell over his face. His eyes were hot. "We need to marry. Soon."

Her heart lifted. She wanted nothing more. "As soon as we return."

"What about your second mission to Akhayma?"

"There are others better suited and Ekrem will understand."

Calev ran his lips over hers, and she shivered.

"Here we are," the boat master said in his thick Silvanian accent. Kinneret decided she didn't like the sound of it, but he was a good fellow, bringing them here so she stuffed her prejudice out of her mind and gave the master a smile.

The tiny, silver-haired goddess on the boat's prow bobbed as they hopped out and onto a courtyard. A dozen or so taverns sat side-by-side, the ancient buildings like drunken friends leaning heavily on one another. Kinneret passed the boat master a tip.

"So little from those who have so much?" It was an old Silvanian saying and about the only thing Kinneret really could translate. She raised an eyebrow. These boat masters made more in one night than she and Avi had seen in their lifetime—before recent events. Finding the silver on the island of Ayarazi had turned days of aching stomachs and desperation into a blur of filling meals and satisfaction. But she had no desire to hold out on the man. She certainly had enough to go around these days. After giving the man five more coins, she joined Calev, who was already talking to a musician outside a tavern with three arched windows.

"He plays the eagle bone flute, too," Calev was saying. He must've been describing Oron.

The musician shook his head.

Kinneret took Calev's arm. "How about we go in and check?"

"Are you mentally prepared for a load of drunken Silvanians?"

"As I'll ever be."

Though the sun had only just dropped below the horizon, women with rouged cheeks lounged over rich men in every available spot in the tavern. Pushing past a laughing bunch of Silvanian sailors, Kinneret found her way to the barkeep. Calev asked for a bowl of wine.

Kinneret crossed her arms and leaned back on the polished wood of the keep's counter. "Your Silvanian isn't as limited as you led me to believe, Calev ben Y'hoshua."

He shrugged and took the wine from the keep. "I didn't want to make you feel bad."

"It doesn't really. I mean, it's wonderful that you speak it so well, but honestly these people seem like pigs."

Proving her point, the sailors dared one another to drink a bowl of wine in one go. One man spilled half of the red liquid down his front, then belched loud enough to shake the roof.

"I apologize to pigs everywhere," Kinneret said. "These sailors are far worse than any boar I ever met."

"Meet a lot of swine, do you?" Calev's eyes shone over the lip of the wine bowl. He took a sip, then handed it to her.

She accepted it, wishing she had the optimism to joke right now like Calev did. "We'd have seen him in here by now, don't you think?"

Calev opened his mouth to answer, but the sailors suddenly erupted into a song Kinneret couldn't understand at all. She caught two words she could translate. *Payment* and *Go*.

The group of them sang their way out the tavern door, leaving the place much improved with their absence.

Kinneret finished her portion of the wine and handed it back to Calev. "Let's go to the next tavern. We'll look through all these spots, then we'll head back and double check he didn't return to the king's castle while we were gone."

"As you say, kaptan."

The next tavern was pretty much the same. Women. Sailors. Wine. This one had a quartet of musicians so half the crowd was dancing. After giving Oron's description to countless people and getting nowhere, they headed back toward the king's castle.

Stars glittered overhead, and the air smelled of the sea. Kinneret's feet itched to be back on a boat. Cobblestoned land always felt dead under her feet. She missed the movement of water under her, the way a swell would rise to meet her sandals, forcing her to adjust her stance, to dance to its tune. Like a very determined and bossy friend who demanded respect. That thought brought her back to worrying about Oron.

Where is he? Please be safe, old friend.

A figure swept up beside her. She spun, taking out her dagger.

It was the Northern Isle seithr from earlier—the woman about Kinneret's age with the extremely thick, bluehare cloak she refused to take off despite the mild weather.

"I am no threat." The woman held her staff with its carved runes like she was offering it to Kinneret. "Your friend. Men took him. Drunken men, sailors, took him to a cursed forest. Payment to gods?"

Kinneret gripped Calev's tunic. "Is she talking about Oron? She is, isn't she?"

Calev just nodded, his mouth open.

Should they trust this seithr? What would be her motivation for lying? To send them into a trap for some reason? It was far-fetched. It made so much more sense that a group of wined-up sailors happened on Oron, who was in a rough state of mind, and the Silvanians decided on some entertainment. It might've been that group from the first tavern.

"What do you know about Silvania's cursed forests?" Kinneret asked Calev. Trees covered most of this country and ran through some of Jakobden and Old Farm too, ignoring human borders.

"Not much. One trader told me about tree spirits in humanlike form. They claim victims for energy. Something like that."

Kinneret hugged herself tightly. She'd heard a story about those forests once too, from a merchant in the tavern beside Jakobden's main port. After she'd stolen a coin from his bag, she'd overheard him talking about how the tree spirits delighted in taking victims, man or woman, who wandered into their depths. One man escaped, but was missing every one of his fingers. She could imagine Oron's strong, able sailor hands being pulled apart, finger by finger.

"We have to find that forest. Now."

"Any Silvanian should know where to find it, right?" Calev eyed the seithr's staff warily. "I'd know if there was a cursed forest near my city."

"I've heard of one, but I have no idea if it's the same one or if that was only a story." A wave of gratitude rose inside Kinneret, briefly tamping down the anger. She touched the impressive seithr briefly on the shoulder. "Thank you," she said in probably the worst version of the Northern Isle tongue ever.

The seithr's deep-set, luminous eyes made her seem older than she had to be. "We," she said, still trying the common tongue, "we are not...perfect."

Kinneret fought back a very cynical laugh at the biggest understatement she'd ever heard. Her people had very little respect for life if the life in question didn't fit their idea of strength and talent. "No, you are definitely not." Maybe this woman could someday change that in her island home. "Far from perfect, but tonight, you're a gift of the Fire. And that makes up for it, just a little bit."

The seithr was obviously finished trying to untangle Kinneret's words because she simply spun and walked off like a kyros, head high.

A couple carrying vats painted with olive designs walked past.

Kinneret jumped in front of them. "Is there a cursed wood near here?" She surprised herself, using passable Silvanian.

The couple pointed toward a wooden sign beyond the next turn on the roads of water. A large boat with tall, maroon sides drifted past, blocking what was written there. Kinneret took off toward the water and finally read the chipped, silver paint.

"Does that say Eastern Woodland Road?"

Calev nodded. "I think it's less than two hours walk from here."

Kinneret's stomach clenched, wondering what they might be doing to Oron. But he was no slouch. He was a fighter. Hopefully, he'd get away. Doubtful with the odds, but still, it was a possibility. "*When* we find them, my lucky one."

"What are we going to do if we do catch up to them? We have two knives, and your magic doesn't work on dry land—except maybe for healing, right?"

"Right. But we don't have time to get help. If Oron disappears into some nightmare of a forest, Fire only knows what will happen to him. He has risked his life over and over again for Avi, me, and for you, and I won't let anything get in the way of me saving him."

"Even good sense?"

Kinneret unleashed a glare. "We'll figure it out. We always do."

"True."

8

KINNERET

The city's busy water roads and stone pathways gave way to sparse villages. Manor houses loomed on hills dotted with skinny conifers. The villas and farmlands faded, and the dark lines of forests showed on the horizon.

Kinneret stopped to unbuckle her waterskin from her sash. The liquid cooled her throat. The moon was high and traffic on the roadway had dwindled to nothing.

Calev watched the shadows near the scrub growth lining the road. "We can't travel all night. This is dangerous and you know it."

Something small shuffled in the bushes and Kinneret was proud that she didn't jump. It was a bit scary out here at night. They would have a tough time defending themselves if a group of thieves decided to rob them or worse.

"I see your point. If we end up dead, what help are we to Oron? But there aren't exactly a bevy of inns out here."

Calev pointed at a flicker in the distance. "There are charcoal burners. They might put us up until sunrise."

Kinneret's knee-jerk reaction was to grimace at the idea. Everyone knew charcoal burners were an odd bunch. But then again, she was considered pretty odd herself, so she wiped the ugly look off her face and nodded. "Maybe. Just for a few hours." She fixed the waterskin onto her sash.

Calev brushed a piece of hair behind her ear. "You are so sensible these days."

"I'm so dull now that I've grown a brain."

"Dull as sailing through a typhoon."

She smacked him lightly. "Brat."

The charcoal burners' huts huddled beside a line of oaks that swayed in the moonlight. Three huge piles of dirt belched plumes of smoke like doors to the underworld. Men and a few women stood over the charcoal beds.

"Who is it there?" a man called out in a rough version of the trade tongue.

Calev waved. "Two travelers. We hoped we could spend the hours until dawn in one of your homes if it's not too much trouble."

"In our homes?" A woman stepped forward, arms nearly black with charcoal dust.

"Yes," Kinneret said, "if you allow it."

"Such manners for us burners!" The woman laughed and motioned for them to follow her.

The hut the woman led them into was nothing more than four straw mats, a dirt floor, and a thatched roof. The burner gestured to the two mats closest to the door. "Take these. I washed those blankets just yesterday. Sleep as long as you like, travelers. We don't often enjoy the good manners of those who pass us by."

Kinneret's mat was fine. She was well used to sleeping on straw. But sleep didn't want to come. She gave herself a headache staring out the tiny window above Calev and praying for sunrise to come quickly. The moon rose higher still, but the trees blotted its light.

"Calev. I can't do this. I can't sleep while Oron is out there."

He sat up and yawned. "I know. Me either."

Outside of the hut, the woman who'd taken them in smiled from her perch near the burning wood. "No sleep for you?"

"My friend is in trouble," Kinneret said. "I can't rest. We'll have to risk the road and keep on."

Another burner with a long beard studied them. "Where is your friend? Where are you headed?"

Calev closed the hut door and threw the latch to keep it shut. "We believe some drunken sailors took him into a cursed area of the forest."

The burners went very, very still.

"You can't go after him," the woman said. "You will die. The cursed wood is angry. More angry than it has ever been. The animals have acted strangely for a long time. But now, now it is worse."

The other burner tugged at his beard. "We only take fallen wood for our charcoal now. Even here, beyond the cursed boundary. We know better than to anger the forest. You should heed our warning. We've heard stories from the burners south and north of here."

Calev glanced at Kinneret. "What kind of stories?"

"The curse grows stronger. Something foul brews there."

A chill crawled over Kinneret's scalp. "All the more reason to hurry so we can help our friend."

"Well, good luck to you. You will need it," the woman said.

KINNERET DREW close to Calev as they took up their journey down the road. They stayed silent, listening for approaching hooves that would mean either a group of very successful thieves or a group of armed men and women. Silvania seemed to have a lot of those. Though there were strange night insects that called to one another from the trees framing the rocky pathway through the countryside, nothing else seemed to be awake at this hour.

They stopped at a fork in the road.

"Left or right?" Calev asked.

Kinneret looked at her compass. The trees in front of them, not left or right, grew taller than the ones they'd passed so far. Pine scented the night's breeze. A rumble of thunder sounded over that part of the forest and the light of a far-off storm glowed inside towering clouds. "Straight ahead, I think."

Calev's throat moved in a swallow. "Onward."

Off the road, the trees grew thicker and thicker, but just when Kinneret thought the wood might thicken to become a truly deep forest, a cleared area crowded with tree stumps appeared.

Kinneret suddenly wished she had a cloak.

Calev ran a hand over a stump and whispered a prayer.

A plow peeked out from a tangled mess of ivy. Someone had thought to farm here and been persuaded to give up the idea.

Calev shook his head. "They should not have felled these elders."

He was talking about the larger trees that had been cut down. Old Farms always talked about trees like that. Normally, she would've teased him for it, but right now, she completely understood the sentiment in all its layers. The air was heavy and heady. She felt as though she looked out over a field of corpses instead of merely trees. A shiver flew over her shoulders.

"There is something here," she whispered.

Thunder rolled far, far away. Over the wood, the sky flashed a pale orange.

"I think we found the cursed forest." Calev looked beyond the stumps, into the deep, dark green, awe widening his eyes.

This was all somehow worse because there were no drunken sailors to fight. What was here felt so much more dangerous.

Panic flooding her senses, Kinneret cupped her hands at her mouth. Suddenly, she was desperate to find her friend. "Oron!"

A child's voice called from the darker part of the forest. "Help. Please!"

She wasn't certain she'd really heard it.

Then she heard it again. It sounded like a young boy, his words jumbling from the trade tongue into nonsense.

"Please…"

Kinneret and Calev glanced at one another, of the same mind. They needed to find Oron, but they also couldn't just leave some poor child alone in this awful place. Kinneret took off toward the forest, past the felled trees, where the wood resumed its dark reign, Calev just behind her.

"I suppose we'll rescue him too," she said, talking about the boy.

At the line of dark pines and hulking oaks, something sharp wrapped around Kinneret's wrist.

A burning pain seared her flesh, and a scream built in her throat.

Calev helped her tear at the ivy's strange red leaves. The plant didn't seem to burn him like it did her.

When she was free, boils rose along her forearm, her hands, and all the places the ivy had touched. Tears streamed from her eyes. Calev shoved his hair out of his face and gently held her wounded hands as he looked around frantically. Kinneret focused on controlling the pain. Fainting in a cursed forest probably wasn't the best idea.

"Help!" the boy shouted again.

Kinneret scanned the trees for him, but pain overtook the search as Calev dragged her through more pines and tall oaks to another treeless expanse.

"There." Calev pointed to a silver pond that lay among the fallen leaves and pine needles. "You can rinse off."

Like the moon had poured half itself onto the earth, the water shone brightly, still and eerie in the night.

"Go in. The leaves must hold some oil that your skin doesn't tolerate. I've seen such a thing at Old Farm. Little Kinsey can't touch the greenery around the well. Gets boils like this every time she does."

Almost dizzy with pain, Kinneret stepped into the pool. The water hissed around her wounds as she dipped them beneath the cloudy surface. This water didn't feel like water usually did. But the pain dissipated. She sighed in relief.

A soft voice carried on the wind. It wasn't the boy. This was a male voice. A man. But it wasn't Oron. The words layered on top of other words and other voices. They weren't in any language she'd heard, but somehow Kinneret knew they were asking her to go to them.

Come. Strong one. Rise. I wait.

Kinneret swallowed and fought the pull. "Did you hear that?"

Calev cocked his head, then nodded. "Oron?" he called out, his voice tentative.

He held his hands out to Kinneret and she took them, climbing out of the water. Her skirt clung to her legs, so she shook the fabric out. The welts on her arms had faded completely, but she didn't feel healed. Something in that water...

A crash sounded in the wood and both of them raised their knives.

A big, well-muscled man and a limping woman with a fierce face emerged from the trees. They shouted something in Silvanian and gestured toward the silver pool. Then the woman noticed Kinneret's wet clothing. She pressed her lips together, then touched the man's arm and nodded toward Kinneret. The man let out a rush of Silvanian.

Kinneret finally figured out what he was asking.

"Were you blessed or cursed?"

9

ONA

Ona switched to using the trade language, her arms shaking from the pain in her wound and the fear of the tree men returning. She and D'Anton had tried to escape the forest the way they'd come, but the clearing of tree stumps was nowhere to be found. It was fairly obvious this was a part of the wood's curse. "Were you blessed or cursed by the silver pool?"

The woman with the dark, red-brown hair answered. "Blessed, I think. Some ivy...it burned my skin. The water cleaned it away and healed my wounds." Her voice was strong, but she wouldn't make eye contact so she was either seeing Ona and D'Anton as potential enemies or she was hiding something.

The man with her was obviously an Old Farm. The sash tied around his trim waist boasted embroidered barley and bright lemons. His hair held the imprint of a headtie though he must've lost it somewhere along the way. He was a very fine-looking man with his sleek, jet-colored hair and laughing eyes. The way he angled his body toward the woman showed his strong attraction to her. Ona would've bet every man, and a few women, had glanced her way.

D'Anton clasped forearms with the other man, then with the woman. He told them their names and they did the same.

Ona's mouth popped open. She spoke quickly, knowing the green men could return at any moment. "You're Kinneret Raza, the one who took down the Oramiral?" This Pass Witch had raised the seas to do her dirty

614

work and kill that disgusting slaver on Quarry Isle. How could someone so powerful be stuck here? "Why aren't you on the Pass, working for your new amir?"

"I *am* working for Amir Ekrem." Kinneret raised her chin proudly.

Ona didn't blame her. The sailor should be proud. She'd done something no one in history had accomplished. And she'd taken the formerly low-caste ability to work sea salt and prayers and turned it into a magic everyone in the South wished they possessed. The Salt Witch touched a small bag tied to her sash. That must've been where she kept her salt. Ona was seriously impressed. Too bad they were far from the sea in this place of nightmares.

"Amir Ekrem sent us here to negotiate an agreement with your king." Kinneret eyed D'Anton.

He tugged at his tunic and watched the surrounding branches, the shadows between the pines and the gnarled roots of the hulking oak trees. Without his Invader surcoat, his clothing was plain enough that it could be from anywhere really. Ona wasn't about to divulge D'Anton's secrets. He'd saved her from a fate worse than death, a life inside some cursed tree. Who knew what pain she would've endured in there? Without D'Anton's help, she wouldn't have had the chance to someday find Lucca and Seren, to find a way to make up for what she'd done. But would these two find out that D'Anton was an Invader? If they did, it would come to blows. Ona was positive she didn't have the strength to fight them, then battle more tree men.

A good twist of the truth was in order. "D'Anton here helped me escape from a band of rogue Invaders, who'd also taken him." Oh, but he had an Invader name. How could she explain that? "But he was taken as a child. They raised him there. That's why he has an Invader name. He is actually Silvanian."

D'Anton's gaze flew to Ona, but she kept her eyes focused on Kinneret. He had to be Silvanian. What was he so upset about? Why hide it now? Whatever. At least this hidden truth would help him keep this legendary sailor's ire off his back.

Kinneret studied Ona's face. Ona felt exposed, almost wishing she had her sword. This witch was nothing short of terrifying. The woman cocked her chin in a way that said she knew Ona was twisting the truth. Ona had heard Kinneret grew up on the streets of Jakobden and such a rough upbringing probably taught her to read people better than most. There was something about her, something that made Ona want to fight her best again. The corner of her own mouth lifted, and it surprised her.

She realized then that D'Anton had been watching her. He gave Ona a small smile that unexpectedly flipped Ona's stomach. She blinked, then turned away quickly. At least he didn't seem angry about her story of his past.

Now that she was fairly certain these Jakobden folk weren't going to murder D'Anton, Ona broached the terrible topic that was most important to their survival in this cursed forest.

"Kinneret. Calev. There are men who seem to be part of the forest. Their arms and faces…it's hard to explain. It's like they're part tree."

Her throat thickened. She wasn't ready to tell them about being inside a tree for those brief minutes. The smell of rotting wood. The feel of the bark crawling up her legs. The tightness in her chest.

"They're called green men," she added, "and they're controlled by some sort of god of this dark wood. I've heard about them in stories, but I had no idea they could be real. They attacked me. And D'Anton. You should be on your guard at every second. We tried to escape, but the way we came in isn't there anymore."

D'Anton led the group down another path on this side of the silver pool. "This way seems to go in a similar direction to the way we came in, so maybe it'll lead us out," he suggested. "Where did you two enter the forest?"

Calev spun his dagger, then held it at the ready, his other hand floating near Kinneret's body like he had to be near her all the time. "I've heard tales about the cursed forests of Silvanian." His eyes were wide as he looked up into the arms of an oak as tall as the entrance to Akhayma's walls. The sheer scale of this wood was mind-blowing. "We came in through a field that had been stripped of both elders and young ones."

The Old Farm's face was serious and reverent, full of mourning, but what did he mean by *elders and young ones*?

"He's talking about mature trees and saplings," Kinneret said. "It's an Old Farm thing." She waved off any questions Ona might've had. "Anyway, there was an area where some enterprising farmer had cleared the trees."

"That's where we ran in, too." Ona touched her wound gingerly.

D'Anton pulled three leaves from his pocket and popped them into his mouth. His face bunched a little as he chewed, most likely making a medicinal paste for Ona. The plant must've tasted horrible.

"You don't have to do that for me," she said.

"I know." He glanced her way and pushed his hair behind an ear.

A wave of gratitude swept over her and she hated it. She didn't deserve his kindness. She was a monster. Suddenly Ona found herself on the ground panting. Three faces stared down at her as emotions raged around her heart, weighing her down, drowning her.

The dagger D'Anton had given her lay beside her right leg. She must've dropped it. "I'm fine."

Kinneret knelt and pulled a small amount of salt from her pouch. The salt on her fingers twinkled in the scant moonlight through the leaves. "I might be able to heal you a little. I'm not sure, but I'll try."

Ona moved her clothing away from the scabbed wound and D'Anton pressed the paste gently against the skin there. His thumb brushed her collarbone. Her breath caught in her throat. Kinneret's hands were on her then, very warm and confident. The witch began to whisper about the sea's tie to the earth, about healing and light, about life flowing. It sounded ridiculous and beautiful at the same time.

A cluster of dark leaves snaked over Kinneret's shoulder and pulled her back.

Ona's heart dropped.

Calev shouted and lashed his dagger at the living branch. The darkness cloaked the body and face of the creature.

Ona angled herself at the thing's dead side and jabbed her blade up and in, aiming for the lungs and praying the thing had organs to injure.

D'Anton disappeared into the black forest.

Kinneret's hands hung at her sides as the creature drew her backward. Her eyes glazed over, unseeing.

The green man's face appeared in a column of moonlight, and he nearly looked human. Leaves unfurled at the end of his eyelashes and his voice was soft—

Calev shouted Kinneret's name and the sound shook Ona awake. He lunged to strike. His dagger seemed to hit just under the tree spirit's arm, but the creature didn't even flinch.

D'Anton appeared behind the creature and dragged the runed sword across the thing's neck, just above Kinneret's head. The green man shrieked and that soft, lulling voice shattered into wails crowding Ona's ears.

Kinneret's eyes cleared, and she bit down on the thing's branchlike arm. It didn't let go.

The deafening noise increased.

Ona dropped back and covered her head with her arms, her dagger forgotten. She was no warrior anymore. All her muscle memory was gone. No. Despite the change in her, she would fight for this proud, amazing woman. She wouldn't cower here in fear.

Shaking off the terror as best she could, Ona leapt at Kinneret's foot.

She latched on as the shrieking creature dragged them both into a circle of star shine and oak trees. Kinneret looked down at Ona, but the famed sailor wasn't herself. A darkness blacker than ink, colder than midnight, deeper than any forgotten cave, cloaked the whites of her eyes and the color of her irises. She was lost to the forest.

A memory flowed through Ona's mind as she clutched onto Kinneret's leg, digging in her nails. Calev tried to force the creature down and D'Anton sliced at its legs.

Time slowed. Ona's thoughts slipped away.

Her mind showed an image of the last mural she'd painted with her aunt, before the Invader attack that destroyed her life and turned it all to hate and vengeance. The mural stretched over the western wall of her aunt's villa. On it, women and men in flowing, amethyst robes danced around a sparkling fire of white and blue and orange. Trees grew around the borders—Ona had yet to detail the pines' fine needles—and one special pine showed the faint outline of a slanted smile. That grin had always bothered her. When her aunt had first sketched it and chalked it, she'd asked why it had to be there. There was, of course, a reason, because her aunt did nothing without good reason. She'd been a sensible one despite being an imaginative artist. Ona remembered the sorrow in her aunt's eyes when she explained.

"You know Silvania has its cursed forests here and there," Ona's aunt had said that day so long ago. "They demand sacrifices. We must paint as it is, not as we want it to be."

Her aunt had never again mentioned the curse or anything about tree spirits, but Ona had heard the stories from other children her age.

She shook off the memory to see time speed up again.

The wood's soft, sickly whispers hounded her, though the shrieking had stopped. The spirit still had Kinneret in its arms, but she was fighting, thrashing, her shape and the tree creature's blurring and blending in the dark. It didn't seem to be hurting her though, just holding her and pulling her toward a massive pine. Ona gave one last wrenching twist to Kinneret's leg and the witch shouted something at the same moment.

She broke free.

With a shout from Calev, all four of them were running through the night-cloaked forest. Branches scratched Ona's cheeks. Her wound pulsed in time with her racing heart. Roots and scrub grabbed her feet, and she stumbled time and time again, only to feel Kinneret's hand on her arm, D'Anton's fingers bracing against her back in support, or Calev's head turned to check and make sure she was getting back up. She ran for herself, but she also ran for them. Here were good folk that didn't deserve to die in a cursed wood and she would do her very best not to fail good men and women ever again. Considering her past, it was the least she could do.

The pines and oaks gave way to a stretch of maples and sycamores along a bubbling river. They stopped, everyone panting. The scent of sweat, last year's musky leaves, and clean water filled Ona's nose.

"Back to back." D'Anton made a circle motion with his hand and held his etched sword high. "Ona, you rest in the middle of us. Take a breath. Then we'll move on."

"Agreed," Kinneret and Calev said together.

"So these are tree spirits." Kinneret nodded like she was trying to convince herself.

Ona shared her memory and the awful, and painfully vague, bits about sacrifice.

Kinneret whispered something and stood a little closer to Calev. "We have to find him."

"Our friend, Oron," Calev said, "was taken here by a group of—"

"Mules who'd had more than their share of drink and will definitely wish they'd never been born to this life if I get my hands on them." Kinneret gestured with her dagger.

The woman had been in fights, but she most likely had no formal training. She moved with the knowledge of what strikes could kill and maim, but without the grace of a true warrior.

Ona stood, tired of being the one everyone had to care for. She dusted herself off and joined the circle. "We can get him back. D'Anton's sword works well against them."

He ran a hand over the symbols shining eerily in the steel. "I found it here. In the forest. It's etched with runes."

The sun was rising, throwing pink at tree trunks and along the ripples in the small river flowing beside them. The strands of deep brown and pale yellow shone in D'Anton's hair. Kinneret's skin, light brown and lovely, became paler and rougher toward her hands. Maybe that was from sailing, from the rough work on lines and with the sea water always leeching the moisture from her. Calev's bright green tunic pulled against the muscles in his leg as he leaned to look at the weapon.

Calev took the sword from D'Anton and examined the runes. "I wondered why yours worked and mine didn't. It couldn't just be the size."

"Oron would've made a rough joke about now." Kinneret's eyes looked wet. She cleared her throat and sighed. "What happened right after that tree spirit grabbed me? I have a blank spot in my memory of it, although I guess it could just be the fact that I was being maimed by a tree, for Fire's sake."

Ona tucked her blade into her belt and accepted a small strip of dried meat from D'Anton. "Your eyes went blank. You stopped fighting the creature."

She glanced toward Calev, who nodded and stared at the meat D'Anton had given him like he had no appetite. "I remember feeling the tightness at my throat. Then the whispering. This will sound like madness, but did the loudest, clearest voice sound...pleasant?"

Ona knew exactly what she meant. That was how she felt when the whispers gathered into one voice and spoke directly to her. "Yes. I wanted to follow the voice. That one voice."

Kinneret was a little green around the mouth as she studied her rough hands. She curled her fingers tight and closed her eyes for a breath. "I can still hear it."

She could? "Does anyone else?" Ona asked.

Calev and D'Anton shook their heads. Calev watched Kinneret very, very closely. He ran a thumb over her elbow. His gaze went to her fisted hands and she put them behind her back.

"I don't think they're chasing us right now. Let's look for Oron," Kinneret said.

"I can do some tracking." The edge of D'Anton's mouth lifted and his eyebrows rose.

"Where did you learn?" Ona remembered Lucca's stories of tracking when he was a child. He told her a tale about following a herd of deer and nearly toppling off a waterfall in his excitement to tell his brother when he spotted them.

Kinneret whirled and smiled at D'Anton. "Please. Get on with it with all my blessings. If we find him, you can have a position on my full-ship if you choose."

D'Anton's eyebrows rose to his hairline. "Thank you." He bowed slightly, then faced Ona. "I learned from my father. It's the only thing he ever did for me." Crouching, he ran fingers over a spot on the forest floor.

Exhausted and sharing what little food they had, the group wove through the forest. It seemed like this Oron fellow was Kinneret's right hand man as well as a sort of father figure. The old Ona would've argued to forget about Oron and focus on getting out of here, but this new Ona heard Seren's voice in her ear, felt her kindness in her heart. Seren would've died before she left an innocent man in a forest full of monsters. Although Ona could never be good, she could at least try, at this moment, to do the right thing.

"This is for you, Seren, and you, Lucca," she whispered.

D'Anton stopped. His hands fell to his sides. "What did you say?" He turned slowly.

"Nothing. I was just...nothing." Ona's wound was definitely better, but pain still thrummed through the area as constant as a horse's gait on a long journey.

"You said *Lucca*."

The way he said it—it sounded different from the way she'd always pronounced her best friend's name. Not wildly altered. Just different. This was how that name was meant to be said. She knew it, somehow. A shiver rolled over her.

"Yes. He is my friend. Was my friend."

D'Anton was in her face in a blink. "Who are you?"

"I am, well, I *was* a mercenary. I fought with a group. Although I never met the king or any nobles, we worked for them all at one time or another. You know how it is." D'Anton was from Silvania. He knew about the trouble between the nobles and the king, and how mercenaries hired themselves out to the highest bidder. "I met Lucca in a forest on the other side of Silvania. Near my village. I—"

"Black, curly hair? Lost a brother?"

And then she knew.

Her knees wobbled.

This was Lucca's runaway brother, Dante.

She gripped his arms, digging her fingers into the cloth and flesh, and studied his face for a resemblance to her dearest friend. Her heart cinched tightly with a mix of joy and sadness. The likeness showed in the deep set of the eyes and the slant of the shoulders and the chin. She hugged Dante close and fought the urge to cry.

1 0

KINNERET

Kinneret didn't want to break up this reunion or whatever it was, but Oron wasn't getting any more rescued.

She touched Ona's back. This D'Anton—or Dante—fellow seemed just fine with her all over him, but they needed to move. "If your friend Lucca was trapped in this wood, you wouldn't waste any time. Can we please continue tracking?"

Ona turned, nodding, and wiped her eyes. "I'm being an idiot. Sorry. I just…" She looked at Dante with new eyes. "You're his brother. He *has* to see you."

Dante looked shaken. "So he's alive?"

"I hope so. He was inside the city when you attacked, but you lost the battle. So there is a good chance he lives still. He is close with the new kyros, Seren."

Kinneret held up her hands. "Wait. When *you attacked*? Dante is not an Invader. You can't be an Invader." It wasn't a question. He couldn't be. Invaders were bloodthirsty and insane. Dante was kind and helpful and nothing like the Invaders she'd heard about.

Or maybe he was just very good at acting.

Calev had a knife against Dante's side before Kinneret could suggest it. She loved Calev more every day.

"You better answer well, or you'll find your spleen at your feet," Calev whispered.

Dante nodded. "Just my spleen? No other internal organs will be damaged?"

"I can be merciful."

Dante raised an eyebrow. "You do realize I'm twice your size and have fought professionally for more years than you've been a man?"

Calev spoke through gritted teeth. "I don't have a problem skewering an old man if the old man is an Invader."

"I'm twenty and four."

Ona's hair tumbled out of its ties. "Stop. Ugh." She pushed her fallen hair over her shoulders. "Stop with the pissing contest, you two. Dante was an Invader, but he isn't now."

This made no sense to Kinneret. "But he is Silvanian. I'm so confused."

Dante eyed Calev's blade. "I ran away from home at thirteen. My father was a violent man. He never hurt my mother or brother, but he was an absolute terror to me, his disappointing first born. I made it into the Empire, then a rogue pack of Invaders captured me and took me to the West. I was forced to learn their language, train with them, and was branded as one."

Kinneret grabbed his collar and tugged it down. "I don't see any brand."

"The silver pool erased it," Dante said. "I was blessed."

Hmm. That could've been a lie. "And exactly how did you two meet?"

Ona took over. "His cohorts captured me after I was seriously wounded. When they realized they didn't have any cards to play or wars to fight, they decided to chop me up into bits for the fun of it. Dante helped me escape."

"That does prove some honor." Calev lowered his weapon.

Kinneret studied Ona. She was well-muscled like a fighter, but she didn't defend herself like one. "If you were a mercenary, why aren't you fighting like one?" Kinneret had seen ten-year-olds fight better than Ona had against that tree man.

Ona paled. "I'm not who I was before my injury."

"Fine. Well, it's great you found one another and perhaps you can head on back to wherever this Lucca is once we get out of here, but let's find my innocent friend now, all right?"

In terse agreement, Dante took up tracking again. He halted to touch the ground or a tree branch every now and then. The rest kept their weapons raised, ready to defend themselves against the tree spirits if the creatures decided to attack.

Kinneret stayed behind Dante, eyeing his movements. Was he truly tracking? Was he motivated enough to do this right? "Have you seen anything definitive?"

Dante lifted a broken branch, then tossed it down. "This place is riddled with activity. The green men are everywhere. Their feet...if you can call them that...seem to be more root than anything, and they leave different marks. I've seen no less than five human footprints. One small. An older child. The other is from a heavier adult with unusually rounded feet. How big is this friend of yours?"

Kinneret described Oron.

Dante led them into a grove of thick-bodied pines. A fog that definitely wasn't normal ghosted toward them and cloaked the wide branches and dark leaves.

Everyone froze.

The branches of the pines were so tangled and full of needles that the morning sun failed to break through, casting only a weak glow over the foggy grove.

The air was even heavier here than the rest of the wood. Kinneret had almost grown used to the weighty feel of the cursed place, but this, this was so much more. It pressed on her shoulders and caressed her cheeks with resin-scented moisture.

A tingling pressure slid up Kinneret's fingers and into her arms. She'd tried not to look at her hands during the last hours because the water had done something odd to them and she didn't really want to think about what it meant. The skin had gone moon white and an uneven texture spread along the backs of her hands and along the sides of her forearms up to her elbows. Now, the white was fading into a silvery brown.

Like the skin of a pine.

"Took you long enough," a voice croaked from somewhere to the right.

Kinneret's chest caved in.

A long, wide crack marred an ancient tree, and Oron looked back at her from inside.

She ran to him, the rest on her heels. "Oron! Are you all right?"

"Yes," he whispered hoarsely. Half his face was covered by the tree, like the thing had simply grown up around him. Only his right side remained exposed to the world. "I'm feeling quite grand. Though I am glad you're here. These tree spirits aren't the best company. They don't laugh at any of my jokes, and if you can believe it, they don't have a stitch of wine."

Calev and Kinneret both latched onto the bark near Oron's nose and began trying to break him free.

"Why did you go off on your own? That was truly stupid. I shouldn't even bother rescuing your stubborn tail." Anger made it easier for Kinneret to keep from screaming and being completely worthless with panic. "It was those drunk Silvanian sailors that took you, wasn't it? I knew they were trouble."

"It was them. And yes, I am truly stupid. But one cannot judge matters of the heart with the same law as one does...ah, never mind. Just get me out of here, please."

Calev grimaced and pulled again. Ona and Dante joined them in trying to rip the pine apart.

The wood groaned like a person. Everyone pulled their hands away from the tree.

Oron swallowed with difficulty. "I don't think force is going to work. This escape of mine needs a bit of drama."

Then, as if the forest was waiting for its cue to speak, that soft, honeyed voice slithered into Kinneret's ears.

I await your arrival, strong one. I am Runnos. We will be as one.

A feeling like gentle but strong hands floated over Kinneret's body and up into her hair, along her scalp. She swallowed and rubbed her ears, trying to get the sounds out of her head. Her heart pounded like she'd jumped off Amir Ekrem's full-ship and into a cold ocean.

"Did everyone hear that?" The rest of them looked at her blankly. "Guess not."

Calev's eyes widened. "Kin. What is happening to your hands?" He took them and ran his fingers over the rough skin and oddly colored flesh.

"I think I had some sort of reaction to that water. In the silver pool."

"Cursed." Ona frowned, looking Kinneret up and down.

Oron tried to cough, but didn't seem able to expand his chest enough to do the job. "That voice—that'll be the god of the wood, Runnos, unless I'm mistaken. Real piece of work. I've heard them speak of him. Has big plans. I think you, Kinneret, will have to say hello if I have any chance of shedding this rather uncomfortable new outfit. There is a boy who lives in this forest. Near the spring. I think you should try to find him too if you can. He is a strange one, but he seems to know exactly where the tree spirits gather. He may be able to give us some hints on how to deal with Runnos."

Kinneret ignored the bit about herself. "Fire and sea! I forgot about the boy. Calev and I heard him calling for help before the attack."

"I heard a boy too. When we first entered the forest." Ona swallowed. "I'd decided it was one of the forest's tricks, but maybe not. Maybe he *was* trying to get some help for you, Oron. We'll have to get him out of here too."

Oron groaned a little, then coughed. "Yes. That's probably him. I've only heard snippets about him from the voices in the trees."

Calev's eyes flashed. "What does Runnos want with Kinneret, Oron? You said you think she must say hello to him."

"His green men...that's what they call themselves in my head...anyway, they said he has been waiting for one such as you. Sounds ominous, doesn't it? But maybe you can just have a nice chat about what they're all so worked up about and gain my freedom."

"They're upset about something?" Kinneret tore a strip from the bottom of her skirt, soaked it in water from the pouch attached to her sash, and stretched high to reach Oron. She worked the dripping cloth toward his mouth.

Oron struggled to sip from the fabric. He couldn't move his head much. Kinneret fought tears and gave him the bravest smile she could muster. He closed his one visible eye in thanks, and she climbed back down.

Calev's mouth became a line. "Runnos and his tree men, they must be angry about the trees that were felled. It's an offense against this sacred forest. I knew it."

Dante unsheathed his rune-etched sword. "Should I use this to try to free Oron?"

"That is a fancy piece of steel." Oron's one visible eye moved. "And for the record, I vote *Yes*."

Calev crossed his arms. "I don't know. It might anger the spirits more if you do."

Kinneret squeezed Calev's shoulder. "Let's try to find the boy and see if he can give us some insight on Runnos in exchange for helping him escape this place along with us. Then, we can go to Runnos and I'll bargain for Oron's freedom. Maybe if I promise to punish the Silvanians who cut the trees down in the clearing and make sure it doesn't happen again, the god will release you," she said, touching the bark near Oron's face. "I think Calev is right. If we just cut you out with this sword, the creatures might simply pop out of their trees and take us down. It's not the smart move."

Ona nodded. "I will stay here with Oron if you wish. I can keep the rune-etched sword in case all goes wrong. That way you'll have Dante and Calev to fight at your side if Runnos attacks. If I hear your scream, I'll cut him free, and we'll do our best to get to you with the runed weapon."

Kinneret traded a look with Calev. She didn't love this. Not at all. Neither did he, she could tell. But Ona's plan was a good one. Calev was already nodding.

"Thank you," Kinneret said. "Now Dante, do you think you can find this spring Oron is talking about?"

"I can find water. If it's that certain spring, I don't know. But I can find the water."

"Too bad you can't find a convenient little sea. Then I'd have this Runnos on his knees." It was frustrating that her magic only worked on salt water. She set a hand against Oron's head. "Stay strong, friend. I'll do what I can. If it all fails, I will die trying to get you out of here."

A rumbling echoed through the wood. The ground vibrated under Kinneret's sandals. "What is that?"

Before anyone could answer, a crowd of animals charged into the grove.

Rabbits scurried underfoot. Birds blackened the fog. Deer rushed past, bumping against Kinneret's sides and blocking her view of the others. Ona screamed, and Kinneret glimpsed Dante as he raced to the mercenary's side.

11

ONA

Astag's antlers tore across Ona's side and ripped her undershirt and the flesh underneath. Heat and pain poured through her ribs. She fell against the tree. Dante was there before she knew she'd called out, and his body shielded her from the torrent of fleeing animals. Huddled at the base of the tree trunk, she grabbed the toe of one of Dante's boots like it was an anchor that would keep her safely in place.

Finally, the rush of animals faded into a few foxes and a hawk. Dante knelt and moved her arm gently to see her wound. His fingers touched her lightly here and there as the wounded area pulsed with pain and buzzed with numbness.

His lips drew in. "I don't think your ribs are broken. But they are bruised badly and you have a pretty good cut. Why must you insist on getting hurt every few minutes?" He gave her a wry grin as he scoured the ground, presumably searching for more of his healing plants.

"I like to keep it interesting."

"I thought I had the interesting part covered, thank you very much," Oron snapped from above.

Dante spoke to Kinneret and Calev. "What was that all about? Any ideas?"

Now that Ona knew he was Lucca's brother, she saw it in every move and word. He was so Lucca. But he was also just Dante. Similar, but so, so different. She'd never wanted to study the slope of Lucca's forehead and the way he moved his mouth when he was worried. Not like she studied Dante.

628

Point in fact, she really couldn't stop staring at this runaway with the complicated past.

Ona hissed as Dante pressed something green against her side. "Maybe they're off to say hello to Runnos as well?" she said, gritting her teeth.

Calev shrugged and turned his sun-browned face toward Kinneret. "Did you hear his voice just then?"

"No," Kinneret said, "but their activity must be tied to his presence and his anger at the cleared part of his sacred wood. It makes sense, right?"

"Unless we're about to be consumed by a massive forest fire." Calev sniffed the air like he might suddenly smell the source of such a blaze.

Kinneret eyed Ona. "Well, Dante must stay here now. You can't defend Oron when you're bleeding in not one but two places. I want Oron protected by the best fighter we have here. Right now, that's Dante."

"Plus," Dante said, "I'm the only one familiar enough with the plants here to find something that will help Ona heal further."

Ona hated this weakness in herself. They were right. Dante would have to stay.

Dante nodded. "The spring will be up there somewhere." He pointed through the grove, toward an area that was covered in ridged stone. "Look for heavy moss on the rocks and you should find it. If you don't, come right back here and I'll go out and find it."

Ona was disgusted with herself. Where was her ferocity? Her spirit? Her ability? She was so frail now. Like a spring flower, trampled and not strong enough to face the summer heat.

Kinneret and Calev gave them one last wave, then disappeared into the trees.

Dante settled himself at the base of the tree that held Oron and supported Ona's back. He laid the sword across his lap and kept a keen watch on the trees, his gaze moving with every snap of a branch or coo of a bird. Ona was watching his pulse beat against the skin under his jawline when he spoke quietly.

"What is my brother like?" He turned his gray eyes to her, and she froze.

"He is my best friend."

The edge of Dante's mouth lifted. "I'm glad, but I don't know you well, so the fact tells me little."

"Good point. I'm not who I was."

"And who was that?"

"A ruthless mercenary who wanted only revenge and didn't care what she destroyed on her way to getting that revenge."

"Cheerful," Oron said from above.

629

Ona had thought he was sleeping or whatever one did stuck inside a magic tree. "Right. Well, I did crack some jokes from time to time." She hoped her heavily accented trade tongue was understandable.

"Did you hurt Lucca?" Dante's tone wasn't really accusatory, just curious.

"Yes. Emotionally, not physically."

"The kyros?" Oron's voice squeaked. "You know what? I'm just going to try to pass out for a bit. This is all a little too much."

"Can we get you anything?" Dante twisted to look up.

"No. Go on with the get-to-know-you. I'll be fine."

"He is brave," Ona said. It had to be painful in there.

Dante agreed. "What does my brother have to do with the kyros?"

"The Empire deemed Seren, Kyros Meric's wife, the new kyros when he died. She is the reason the Invaders lost."

"Did she come up with those exploding containers?" Dante swallowed.

"Along with an engineer, yes."

"Genius." His voice was grim.

"She and Lucca truly care for one another."

Dante's eyes widened and he looked at his lap.

She didn't blame him for being amazed that a Silvanian mercenary could attach himself to a kyros. "It is pretty shocking. A lot of the higher ups weren't too thrilled with the affair."

"I can imagine. Lucca doesn't seem like a kyros's spouse."

"I disagree. He isn't overly authoritative, but he is a good leader when he has to be. He has a level head and an open mind. I guess it comes from reading all those books."

"He still does that?" Dante grinned and smoothed a hand over his knee, toying with a tear in the fabric. "I was never much for books."

"You and the old me would've got along nicely."

"Not the new you?"

Ona touched the closest rune on the end of the sword. Two slanted lines came together above a circle. "Maybe. I'm just not sure who the new me is."

"I understand." He stared into the grove as the mist thickened around them. "I thought my life was set in stone, that I would be who the Invaders wanted me to be until I found death. But now," he touched the place where his brand once was, "the world is open and I'm lost on what to do with this second chance."

"Exactly. I thought I was dead on that battlefield. I've lost my will to fight and I was a mercenary. I've never been anything else. What good is a mercenary who can't chant?"

"You can chant."

"So can Lucca."

"I would've liked to see him do that."

"You will. You can return to Akhayma with me. If we get out of here alive."

Dante's face changed. His light brown eyebrows moved toward his hairline and his eyes sparked. "You would travel with me? After we tried to kill you and my brother?"

"The Invaders tried to kill us. And it's not like you had a choice, Dante."

"You always have a choice," Oron mumbled.

Ona scowled. "I thought you were asleep."

"I am."

Dante waved a dismissive hand at Oron. "So you don't hate me, Ona?"

"You saved my life."

"Not at first. At first I was your captor."

A horrible thought sprinted through her mind. "Were you the one who ran me through?"

"No. I didn't see you until the end. We gathered you up."

Ona exhaled. "So you didn't try to kill me. Not directly. And I think that's as good as it can get in our situation." Ona laughed to herself.

"What's so funny?"

"Lucca and I make up terrible mottos for ourselves sometimes. That one would be a solid choice. *As good as it can get in our situation!* Great motivator right there."

Dante chuckled. "I think my brother still has his sense of humor."

"He definitely does."

"Does he look like me? I haven't seen him in so long and he was just a boy when I ran away…"

Ona's gaze slid over Dante's strong, dimpled chin and his furrowed brow. "Some, yes. But your eyes are light and his are dark. His hair is nearly black. Your hair is lighter and has a load of other colors in it like copper…" She reached out to touch a strand, then realized what she was doing and pulled her hand back.

He grabbed it gently. "It's all right. It's amazing to have someone being kind to me." His jaw tensed. "Sorry. I'm acting like a child."

"You're not. I'm sure those Invaders weren't real sweethearts."

He laughed a little. "No, they were not."

She ran her fingers down the side of his face. His eyes closed. "You are among friends now, Dante. I may not be able to help you fight, but I am here. Whoever I am."

Opening his eyes, he smiled. "I'm glad."

12

KINNERET

Kinneret led Calev up the small rise, climbing over tree roots and hoping she wouldn't hear that voice inside her head again anytime soon. She'd much rather meet this forest god and talk to him face-to-face. She'd negotiated and/or stolen almost everything she'd eaten or possessed since birth up until this past moon cycle and this creature skulking around in her head wasn't about to get the best of her. Haggling was as natural as swimming.

"What do we have to bargain with?" she asked. Brainstorming with Calev always produced good ideas.

"With all the talking he is doing inside your head, it seems like Runnos wants you, specifically, to do something for him. I wonder if he ends up having to force you to do whatever he wants, if it might mess with the magic of whatever it is."

"That's a load of whatevers. So you think he might need to persuade me to do this mysterious whatever willingly or it won't take?"

"Maybe."

"Do you think the farmer who originally cleared the land is dead?"

Calev shrugged. "That would be my guess."

"Maybe we can threaten Runnos with more clearing?" The fog snaking around the trees lessened and sunlight speared the leafy canopy. "Other landowners would be interested if we word things in a certain way. Silvania doesn't have a lot of land to divvy up, right?"

"True," Calev said. "But Runnos might say he can strike down those who try to cut more of the forest."

A root tripped Kinneret, and she hissed at the pain in her toe as she regained her footing. "There are a lot of humans in Silvania. He can't possibly kill them all."

"We have numbers on our side." Calev set a hand on a pine and climbed over an outcropping of mossy rock. "And persistence. Motivation. We aren't giving up Oron or you. We'll die first."

Kinneret snorted. "But will the rest of Silvania sacrifice themselves for us? I don't think so."

"Of course not. But Runnos doesn't have to know that," Calev whispered, tugging at Kinneret's skirt.

He *had* learned a little about negotiating from her, she thought proudly. "We also have that sword with the runes inscribed on it. Dante's sword."

"It slices through these cursed trees like a hot knife in butter."

Kinneret rubbed her hands together, getting excited. "Exactly. He won't want us waving that thing around."

Her fingers caught on one another and she paused, staring at them and turning them over and over.

Her skin was changing again.

Her fingernails faded into tapered ends like branches and a tiny bud pressed out of her wrist.

She sucked a breath.

Calev grabbed her and looked around for what might've injured her. "What is it?"

"My hands. Look." There was no hiding this now.

Calev's lips parted as he touched her fingers gently. "My Kinneret. My fire. What is he doing to you?"

Tugging her hands away and trudging onward, she raised her chin and fought tears of panic. "We will fix it. We've been through worse than this."

Behind her, Calev took a loud, strengthening breath before he started walking.

"We certainly have." His words were steel and blood. "And we have won."

WATER BUBBLED from a slide of rocks near a slender path between ferns. At the start of the trail, Kinneret bent to look at a footprint. It was small, the toes bare and rounded.

"This has to be the boy's. I think we should follow the path and see if we can find him."

Calev nodded, and after drinking some of the cold spring water—he tested it first, taking just a drop on his finger and finding no strange feel or taste to the liquid—they began the trek through a less dense area of the wood.

Beech trees rattled their leaves. Chipmunks scurried from the undergrowth. With the sun glowing green through the leaves and the scent of sweet pine in the air, it was almost beautiful. The beauty of the cursed forest took hold of Kinneret's senses like poison. She moved slower instead of running. Her limbs grew heavy, and she longed to fall to the pine needles and forget the world.

"Kinneret." Calev took her by the shoulders. "Are you all right?"

She blinked to clear her head. "Yes. Fine. About the boy. I wonder how he survived in this place. Why haven't the tree men claimed him?"

Still watching her, Calev walked by her side. "Did Oron say how long the boy had been here?"

"No, but if the boy knows about Runnos, he has to have been hiding for a while, right?"

The path turned east and widened at a clearing. A hut of stone, sticks, and moss huddled beside a twisting pine that reached toward the sky. Under a simple, square window, a pine sapling grew from a wooden bucket. Thick ivy crawled up the hut's side and onto its roof, but the area around the shelter was clear and nicely cared for. Someone lived here and lived fairly well. Kinneret was still trying to understand how that could be true when the door opened and a boy who looked about eleven or twelve years old walked into the hazy, forest light.

"Greetings. I'm Miach." He smiled shyly, then turned as a tiny goat trotted around his feet. "And this is Ethus."

Miach's innocent beauty struck Kinneret as hard as the forest's strange charm. His skin was so clean and young that it nearly seemed luminescent. He was thin, but looked well enough. She had an overwhelming urge to pick him up like she used to do with Avi.

Kinneret traded a look with Calev, who stepped forward.

"Miach, can we come inside and talk to you about this forest?" Calev asked.

The boy patted the goat's head and said quietly, "Yes." His words sounded furry or disjointed...wrong somehow. Like they began in another language and grew into something Kinneret could understand. "Come in. Stay awhile."

Calev shivered beside Kinneret. "I'm not sure about this."

"Me either. But how could a little boy be a danger?"

The inside of the hut showed the same kind of tidiness as the outside. The packed earth floor had been swept as clean as was possible for dirt. A small hearth in the far wall held a seasoned log, but no buildup of ashes. Small piles of acorns and berries lined the two shelves near the window and a small bed of moss and leaves sat in the corner.

Miach sat beside the hearth, pulled his knees up under his long tunic, and cuddled the goat under one arm.

"Did you call for help yesterday?" Calev knelt beside the boy.

Kinneret watched out the window, fully expecting a tree creature to come crashing down on them at any moment.

"I did. That's my job. I'm the lure."

Oh. Kinneret did not like the sound of that.

Calev froze in the act of scratching the baby goat's chin. "What is a lure?"

Kinneret tugged on Calev's sleeve. "We don't have sun to chat. Sorry. Time to go."

But Calev held back.

Miach stood, tears glistening in his big eyes. "I don't like it, but Runnos says it's the only way I can stay alive. He keeps my Ethus alive too. I have a debt to pay, Runnos says. My father was the blacksmith."

"We can help you escape," Kinneret said. "Tell us everything, and we'll come up with a plan."

She saw the moment Miach noticed the bark-like skin that had crept up her fingers over the last few hours as well as the pine needles sprouting from her wrist. He tensed, then seemed to absorb the information like he'd seen this happen. Like it was no surprise. The urge to question him about what might be happening to her pushed at the back of her throat, but she shoved it down. First, they needed to get him talking about himself. They needed to know what they were dealing with.

"Please, Miach," she said. "Tell us how you ended up here."

The boy crossed his legs, and the tiny goat crawled into his lap. "I'd like to tell my story. I haven't told anyone in..." He looked out the window, dazed.

"When did you come to the forest?" Calev asked gently.

Miach blinked. "My father made a sword. Our village was strong with magic. He etched symbols of power and control into the weapon and the Silvanian king offered to buy it. Father said we wouldn't have to eat only bone marrow during the dry days anymore. He said we'd have enough silver to buy chickens. I love eggs."

"He has to be talking about Dante's sword." Kinneret gripped Calev's sleeve.

"But that weapon looks brand new. There isn't a sign of exposure anywhere on it. And Miach has obviously been here for...how long have you been here, Miach?" Calev scratched the goat again and it bleated sweetly.

"I don't know. We don't get old."

Kinneret traded yet another loaded look with Calev. This child was mad. He made no sense. If he couldn't even remember his age or how he came to be here, how was he going to help them resist Runnos and save Oron? "How old are you?"

"I used to be ten years old. Now I'm still ten years old."

A chill slithered down Kinneret's arms. "Still."

Miach met her gaze. "Still."

"Kinneret." Calev's voice was low and wary.

"Do you know the name of the Silvanian king?" Kinneret balled her skirt in her sweating hands.

"It's a funny name. I had an uncle with that name. Alfonso the Second."

Calev stood very slowly.

Kinneret took hold of his fingers.

"You must be mistaken, Miach." She smiled but she felt like vomiting. "Alfonso ruled one thousand years ago."

"Yes. That's it!" Miach hopped up, the goat with him, and started toward the shelves. "Would you like some berries before you die? They are very good for a last meal."

All right. Enough. "Calev, grab the goat." Kinneret gathered the boy up and hurried out of the door, ignoring his protests.

"Kin?" Calev's eyes went wide.

Kinneret looked over her shoulder. "We're getting out of here."

The sun slipped behind clouds above the forest as they headed back down the fern-lined path. Miach punched at Kinneret's back. He was surprisingly strong for a one thousand and ten-year-old.

"Stop that. We're going to help you escape this cursed forest. Whether you like it or not. You've been cursed yourself so you don't know what's good for you."

"I can't. I can't! He'll kill Ethus!"

"He won't. Calev has him. And Calev is from Old Farm, a place where animals are practically revered."

"Not exactly," Calev said. In other circumstances, she would've thought his adherence to absolute truth was adorable, but in this case...

637

"Yeah. Yeah. You treat them seas better than the rest of the world anyway."

"True, but…where are we going and what are we doing?" Calev asked.

"You're turning into one of them." Miach's little fists pounded against Kinneret's shoulder bone. "You've already lost. Just let me keep Ethus alive!"

Kinneret forced herself to speak calmly. "We're going to take Miach and Ethus back to Ona, Dante, and Oron, then figure out a plan to break out of this wood," she said in answer to Calev's question. "Everything is going to be fine. We might use your father's sword, Miach. He was a fine craftsman, wasn't he?"

Miach was crying a little, but at least he'd stopped with the punching. "Yes." His words still sounded odd, like someone was translating them inside Kinneret's head. She didn't like it one bit. "He also made a shield, but it's even more lost than the sword."

"A shield?" Calev trotted up beside them, the tiny goat in his arms. The creature seemed perfectly happy to be carried. It closed its little eyes and almost seemed to smile. "The sword has runes. Magic runes. Does the shield?"

Miach lifted himself a little to look at Calev. "Of course."

"Of course it does, Calev." Kinneret helped Miach move to a more comfortable position on her back. He'd stopped fighting her for now, but she wasn't about to let him down so he could run off and tell his friend Runnos all about them. "If the sword can kill green men, what can the shield do?"

"Protect a human from Runnos's commands. From his voice and—"

They passed under the branches of a spindly pine and an array of deep green needles brushed Kinneret, then Miach.

The boy went silent and very still.

Kinneret stopped and maneuvered Miach around so his belly was near hers and she faced him. "What is it, Miach?"

His eyes glazed and his lips parted.

Calev put the little goat between Miach and Kinneret. "Here is your friend. Talk to Ethus. Are you all right, Miach?"

Miach didn't seem to notice Ethus at all. "Runnos calls for my silence in this. I must be silent. He calls for your death." The boy's head spun to face Calev and the unnaturally quick movement made Kinneret feel sick. Miach looked to Kinneret then. "And you are chosen."

Then Miach's eyes fluttered shut and he fell against Ethus and Kinneret.

Before she could utter a question, a vibration buzzed through her fingers, the fingers gripping Miach's bare little legs.

638

Her view of him and his goat went black.

"Calev?" she called out, still feeling Miach and Ethus in her arms, but unable to see anything.

She couldn't hear Calev's answer or feel anything except her flesh contact with the boy and his pet through her altered fingertips.

Then the black lightened to gray. Shapes grew. Light filtered into view.

A group of men and women wearing long shirts in shades of ruby, vermillion, sage, and sunlight gathered around a sparkling waterfall. The water fell from a cliff well above their heads and kept on falling into the earth, a distance Kinneret couldn't quite make out. The spray cooled her face as she studied these people. They were dressed unlike anyone she'd ever seen. Ankle length cloaks clasped with intricate pins partially hid their loose, multi-colored pants. Bushy-haired children threaded back and forth through their elders.

The children were dressed like Miach.

He wore the same odd necklace and simple tunic like the other young ones. Though they spoke to one another and sought attention by pulling on their parents, they were too quiet for children. Something was wrong.

Kinneret looked down at herself and saw Miach's body.

She was Miach.

This had to be a memory.

Shuddering at the strangeness of it all, Kinneret walked toward a tall man, the one closest to the waterfall. His dark beard was wet from the spray.

Father, her mind said.

The wind kicked up and leaves blew hard against the group, twigs too. The ground rumbled with thunder.

"The forest god knows," Miach's father said, voice strong but strained.

He was obviously their chieftain. A weapons-maker as chief. That told Kinneret how ancient this memory was. Now, chiefs, kings, and kyros were politicians and warriors. Never craftsmen. But long ago, things were different.

"We must hide this shield," he said. "Then we'll find another place for the sword. We can go to the king, tell him the tale, and he can use his mighty forces to retrieve the objects. I won't let my family die for this."

Murmurs of agreement flowed through the group, then they hurried around the back of the waterfall. Kinneret followed, feet slipping slightly on the rocky path behind the sheet of water.

Miach's father waved the group on. "The green men will not pass into this space." He held out a hand to Kinneret. "They hate strong water."

Kinneret's—Miach's—foot shot out from under her and she slid toward the ledge. Miach's father neatly grabbed her up and steadied her on the ground. A woman with long, thin braids walked up and put a gentle hand on Miach's shoulder. *Mother.*

"Be brave, my fine boy," she said.

Miach's father led the group into a damp cave behind the waterfall. Several men and women clapped their hands together and said a word that couldn't untangle itself in her mind. Light sprang to life between their fingers.

What magic they had! Where had this power gone over the centuries? Kinneret wondered if this was how it was in the Northern Isles where magic was still very strong.

The cave's pathway tightened to a space just wide enough for a child. The wet walls housed many-legged creatures Miach didn't want to touch. Kinneret wondered where Ethus was. He could've comforted Miach. But there didn't seem to be anything in his thoughts about the baby goat.

Miach's father rubbed his beard, then reached his glowing fingers through a small opening to survey what was on the other side of the cave wall. He leaned back out again and studied Miach. "Son. Are you brave enough to take this shield and tuck it away to save us all?"

The boy's trepidation echoed through Kinneret like a snake's rattle. "Yes, Father."

The man removed a round shield from his back and set it against a rock. "Solid ground lies past this opening. Set the shield there, then climb back out. I doubt the tree spirits will ever manage to find it."

Five bronze circles decorated the shield and each of the shapes showed runes similar to the ones on the sword Dante found. Fitted leather edged the shape and regularly spaced dents in the metal between the circles showed off the tribe's craftsmanship. Stones had been set into the shield too, inside each of the bronze circles. One was a pearly white, another almost transparent—three more of differing colors winked in the torchlight.

Kinneret put her hand to her head, the scent of cave mud and fresh water in her nose. Miach's nose.

This was so disorienting.

Miach's father lifted him and set him on the rock outside the small opening that led deeper into the hill. Then the man handed the shield over. It was heavier than Kinneret had expected. Maybe it was because she only had a young boy's strength instead of her own at the moment. She wedged the shield through the oval of darkness, keeping one hand on the smooth, leather strap.

"Don't let it fall now." Their leader gently patted Miach's back with his illuminated hand.

"I won't, Father."

Kinneret moved her feet so they hung on the other side of the opening, then slid to the ground. Darkness blanketed the area, heavy and flat. Using only touch, Kinneret settled the shield on the cave floor, then turned to feel her way out. Strong hands helped her return to the family and the woman —*Mother*—cocooned Kinneret in her wiry arms.

They headed out of the cave, beyond the splashing waterfall, only to meet nine great tree men.

Scooping Kinneret up, Mother turned to run back into the cave to safety, but a vine, thick as a spear shaft, curled around her neck and yanked her to the ground. Kinneret was torn from her arms. Her heart sputtered like a dying candle as she watched a green man pull Mother into its trunk, where she disappeared.

Gone. Forever.

"Mother!" Tears tore down Kinneret's cheeks and she fell to her knees.

Father raised the rune-etched sword to slice off that same tree spirit's largest limb. The creature roared and grabbed the weapon. Hissing, it dropped the steel. The sword hit the ground beside Father who'd been knocked to his back. Father reached for the sword, but the green man's roots crawled over his middle and squeezed him until Kinneret had to turn away. Vomit burned her throat, mouth, and lips.

"Mother! Father!"

Then all the horror and fear crashed over Kinneret and the pine needled forest floor rose to meet her.

The world disappeared.

Darkness swamped her.

Kinneret woke to the feel of a gentle nudge to the head. She opened her eyes. Ethus wore a tiny goat smile. The small animal climbed onto Kinneret's chest and nestled its chin under hers. Love washed the desperate fear away. Dizzy, Kinneret saw two images lying on top of one another. Ethus on Miach's chest and Ethus on her own chest. She blinked and finally she was in her own body only instead of Miach's memory.

She sat up, dislodging Ethus as gently as she could in her state. Miach was now in Calev's arms. They knelt beside her.

"I saw his memory," she said to Calev, her voice rough with emotions she was never meant to feel. "Miach's memory."

"What did you see?"

"The shield. Miach put it in a cave. Behind a waterfall. His father was the chief and they died and…"

She was shaking and couldn't stop. Calev and Miach put arms around her. She closed her eyes and let them hold her. Ethus nibbled her left thumb and bleated loudly as if he wanted to tell her something.

Finally, they started in the direction of the grove. Miach wasn't fighting it, but Kinneret kept one hand latched to his tunic just in case he decided to run. She felt so differently about the boy now. She knew his pain. She'd felt it.

"I'm sorry about your family," she said, her words tiptoeing out of her mouth. She didn't want to wake the grief in him.

He held up her greening fingers. "You saw through these." His big eyes were such a frightening mix of cunning and innocence, if such a combination could exist. "Runnos and his green men can watch your life."

A shiver ran through Kinneret. She couldn't question him about the shield. Not yet. She had to let that experience wash over her first. Miach stumbled on the path and yawned widely. Maybe what she'd accidentally done to him had drained his strength. He stopped, eyes dropping shut.

Kinneret helped Calev gather up Miach. She tucked the baby goat under one arm gently. The animal bleated softly, but Miach made no sound aside from deep breathing.

Kinneret shook her head. "I don't like any of this. We obviously need to find that shield. But if Miach can't tell us where the waterfall is, it might take ages to find. And what does Runnos want with me? Miach said I'm becoming one of them. I'm assuming he doesn't simply mean I'm becoming a Silvanian," she said wryly. "I'm growing into a green man."

Calev's throat moved in a swallow. He wouldn't meet her eyes and she knew it was because he was hiding unshed tears. "I won't let that happen. We won't let that happen."

The path gave way to the darker area of the wood where fog tangled in the undergrowth despite the sun that tried very hard to pierce the thick leaves overhead.

Kinneret held up a hand and splayed her fingers. They felt stronger. Like she could steer a boat in the worst of storms without breaking a sweat. But her fingers didn't look like hers anymore. They were someone else's. Some*thing* else's. An itch like she had some horrible disease spread over her neck and down her arms. She scratched at the bark growing along her ring finger and thumb until the altered flesh burned and bled.

Calev was suddenly close. "Stop that. It won't help." Keeping the sleeping

Miach close to his chest, he reached out his own hand and cupped hers. His eyes were fierce and dark and she loved him so much. "I am here with you. I will not give up on you. We will win this. No matter what. We will get back to Avi. We will sail Ekrem's ship. You are Kaptan Kinneret and nothing is going to stop you."

Emotion surged through her chest and made her heart beat too quickly. She gripped his fingers hard. "I know. We will."

She kissed him like a promise made and they traveled deeper into the darkness.

13

ONA

"I wish I could get my head on straight."

Ona tried to separate herself from the pain of her two wounds so she could think. While Dante sipped watered wine from his flask and searched the grove for edible plants, she took three breaths. Her injured ribs didn't want her to breathe deeply, but she did her best. Oron had been quiet for the last hour, so she kept her voice down.

"When Lucca and I raided an enemy's stronghold, we always sent at least two of our party into the heart of the set up. In the war room, or the keep, or the master's bedroom if it was late at night. We need to find this forest's heart and strike there to win." She realized Dante was staring, open-mouthed. "What?"

"You don't sound unsure of yourself right now. You sound every bit like a mercenary."

He wasn't wrong. Maybe strategy was removed enough from the actual violence that her broken mind could handle it. "Well, let's enjoy it while we can, hmm? Who knows when I'll become a mess of tears and snot again?" She rolled her eyes at herself.

Dante handed her some dark, black berries. "They're safe. See?" He popped two between his lips and Ona tried not to gape.

"I'm going to wait and see if you die."

"Good idea." Dante chewed and stared up into the canopy. The tendons in his neck stood out. He had a tiny birthmark under his left ear.

"It looks like an arrowhead."

"What?"

"Your birthmark. It has the shape of an arrowhead."

He put a hand over it, then let his fingers slide away. "Lucca thought it was an *older brother mark* when he was little. He said all older brothers had them." Dante chuckled. "He thought he knew everything."

Anger flared inside Ona, sudden and unexpected. "Weren't you worried about him when you left? What if your father had decided to beat Lucca in your absence? And what about your mother?"

Dante had the decency to look ashamed. "I was a child. Thirteen years of age. In my mind, my father hated only me. The family didn't function because of me. I thought leaving would make everything better for them all."

Ona's anger cooled. She remembered feeling like that as a child. Like every problem centered on her. Dante had been too young to understand that his father was the problem and he himself was not at fault.

She touched his hand and gave him a sad smile. "But you know better now."

"I still wish I hadn't left them."

"It does no good to beat yourself up about it. It was an awful situation. You did what you thought was right."

"Maybe you need to say some of those things to yourself."

Ona shut her feelings off. They'd talked enough. Now was the time to plan.

"Back to our strategy. Where could the heart of this forest be?" Ignoring the pain, she stood and walked around the grove. "This could be it. That fog and the animals and Oron here...this seems like an active place."

"True. But you'd think Runnos would be present in the heart of his sacred wood. If he only speaks here occasionally, I don't think this is it."

"I disagree. He might be wise enough to keep his most vulnerable spot hidden."

"He might not have a vulnerable spot."

"Everyone has a weakness. Something they hold highest and would die without." For her, it had been avenging her aunt. Now, it was somehow, some way, to reunite with Lucca. Lucca and Seren were her priority, her heart—her weakness and her strength in one.

"I don't." Dante's voice cut through her thoughts. He pressed the tip of his blade against his palm, not hard enough to draw blood, but just to pinch the skin.

"At the least, you care about not feeling pain."

He cocked his head, then nodded. "Yes. I guess you're right. That's pretty sad though. I only care about my own well-being. I need some new priorities."

His gaze locked with hers. A strange heat flooded Ona's body. He held the sword at an angle, the tip digging lightly into the forest floor. He'd tied his hair back and his cheekbones stood out. She remembered exactly how gentle his hands had been during their journey with the Invaders.

She turned away, swallowing. "I think my wound is healing. Kinneret's abilities are better than she guessed."

"I'm glad." Dante went to Oron's tree and spoke into the opening. "Sailor, sorry to wake you, but would you like some watered wine?"

Oron grunted. "If you can manage it, that would be good."

Dante did as Kinneret had earlier, wetting the end of a cloth he had stored in a small bag on his belt.

Oron sputtered. "Wait. I hear them. I caught something in their whispers."

Dante pulled the cloth away.

Oron said something else, but Ona couldn't catch it. She scrambled up the side of the tree, leaning in as close as possible to Oron's face. But she still couldn't hear his strangled words.

"Let me help." Dante lifted Ona with one arm and she braced herself against the rough pine bark. Pine sap permeated the air and stuck between Ona's fingers.

"Oron. Say it one more time. Please. If you can," she touched his head lightly, the half-broken trunk scratching her skin and making it ooze blood.

"I heard them. The sword."

"Yes." Dante, eyes fierce, held up the weapon so Oron could glimpse it. "We have it, sailor. Is there something you think we should do with it specifically?"

"No. There is also a shield. The smithy made a shield too. If you have both—"

Coughing broke off his sentence.

"Oron!" Ona's heart pinched at the sight of tears streaming from the brave man's one visible eye.

Dante held the dampened cloth to Ona. "Try giving him a drink."

She took the cloth, but Oron's eye had closed. He breathed shallowly like someone very sick and nearing death. She shook her head at Dante. He lowered her down, then tucked the cloth away.

"Did I hear him mention a shield?" Dante sheathed the sword in his belt.

"He said the blacksmith who crafted the sword also made a shield to go

646

with it. If the sword is the only weapon the green men truly fear, then what might the shield do?"

Dante linked his fingers behind his neck and breathed out, his gaze going from Oron's tree to the ground. Circles were beginning to color the soft skin below his light eyes. Old Ona would've demanded that he snap out of his fatigue and fight on, but new Ona considered things differently.

"Why don't you sleep for a while? I'll keep watch. Give me the sword and rest. Then we can think together."

Dante looked reluctant, but he gave the weapon over. "Are you certain you feel strong enough?" He eyed her wounded side and shoulder.

"I am. I promise. Just for a little bit. Pushing through fatigue is stupid and I'm done with being stupid when I can help it."

The corner of his handsome lips lifted, and he lay flat at the base of Oron's tree, hands resting on his flat stomach.

He was asleep in five heartbeats. He was definitely a soldier. Warriors could sleep at will. Ona knew the feeling well.

"Get those dreams while you can, warrior," she whispered, standing guard over him. "This is for Lucca. And also, a little bit, for you."

She couldn't help but enjoy the look of Dante's sleeping form. She could almost see the thirteen year old boy in him, the one who had run away in hopes of fixing everything in his broken home.

Raising the sword and clearing her wistful thoughts away, she waited for the attack that would surely come. It had been far too long since a tree creature made an appearance.

KINNERET

Kinneret and Calev crashed into the grove with Miach and Ethus, surprising a sword-wielding Ona and a sleeping Dante. Ona looked ready to pass out. Probably from her many injuries. She was a tough one, that was for sure.

"How is Oron?" Kinneret went immediately to the tree. The trunk had grown. Now she could only touch half his head of hair rather than the whole expanse. "Oron?"

A hand touched Kinneret's arm. It was Ona. "He has been…asleep for a while," Ona said.

"I will get you out of there, friend," Kinneret whispered.

Then she filled Ona and Dante in on how she'd accessed Miach's memory and the way Runnos seemed to stop the boy from telling them about the shield.

"Runnos did the same thing to Oron," Ona said.

"So is this the boy who called for us?" Dante took Miach from Calev and set him carefully on a patch of mossy growth in the center of the grove.

"What is the story with the goat?" Ona cocked an eyebrow and bent to pet the goat gently. Kinneret thought maybe she was about to cry. The woman wiped her eye with the back of a hand roughly, then stood. Why would the sight of a goat make her want to weep?

Kinneret gave Oron's head one more touch. Her heart weighed a ton. They had to get Oron out of there. "Ethus is Miach's friend. They are immortal."

Calev picked up where she left off. "Runnos gave the boy and his pet eternal life in exchange for luring prey to the wood."

Dante shook his head, disgusted.

Ona kicked a tree root, then sat down, cross-legged, beside the boy. She took his little hand in hers. Kinneret wondered what she was searching for in those fingers. Evidence that he was a working part of the cursed forest?

"He isn't the only one falling into Runnos's plans." Kinneret showed her own hands. They were so much worse and her feet were feeling strange too. Eyeing her sandals, a sweat broke over her forehead. Her toes seemed to be melding into one and were oddly flexible. Her stomach turned. "I think I'm becoming a green man, as you call them." Ona's eyes were pitying and Kinneret loathed the look. "I'll fight it. I'll be fine. What did Oron say before Runnos put him to sleep?"

A branch snapped beyond the grove.

Dante was standing, runed sword poised, before Kinneret could move an inch. They all stayed still, listening. A crow called, and they all jumped a little.

Dante glanced at Kinneret. "Oron told us there is a shield that was made alongside this sword. It seemed like he thought if we had both, we'd stand a better chance of surviving this."

"That goes along with what Miach said before Runnos stopped his tongue."

Calev ran a hand over the boy's head. "Can you tell us where the shield is, Miach?"

Miach's eyes fluttered open. He looked like himself again, the foggy look gone. He reached for Ethus and the goat snuggled up beside him.

"I can't tell you. Runnos will take our lives away. He won't let me tell you even if I wanted to. His power...it's in my mouth. I can feel it." He moved his tongue and crinkled his immortal nose.

Kinneret punched her thigh, frustrated.

Dante came up beside her. "Couldn't you simply go into the boy's memory again? Maybe you'd spot some area details that would help us locate the waterfall and the cave."

"It wasn't simple. Miach blacked out after I did that. We need to let him rest. Just for a short time. Don't we?"

Ona shrugged. "I really don't know."

"He's immortal, right? It's not going to kill him," Dante said. "And staying here with Runnos and his henchmen might be the end of the rest of us."

"He makes a good case," Calev said. "If we are injured or killed, Miach and Ethus won't have anyone to help them escape."

"We're not escaping," Miach said. "I've told you. Eat some good berries. Death comes." Miach didn't look at them. He scratched Ethus's ears and set his cheek on the goat's bumpy little back. "It's better if you don't think about it."

Kinneret and the rest of the adults swapped horrified glances. This little boy definitely needed their help whether he knew it or not. "Let's take some sun to rest and eat those greens and berries you've gathered there, Dante."

Dante doled out handfuls of edibles as the group arranged themselves in a circle, backs to the center where Miach and Ethus settled down for a nap.

"I'll keep first watch." With Dante's sword, Ona began a slow circuit around the grove. "Your healing worked wonders, Kinneret. Thank you. I won't hesitate to defend you this time. I swear it. But maybe someone should join me."

Kinneret could tell that admission cost Ona quite a bit. "I'll join you," she said, taking her dagger from her sash. "Sleep, Dante and Calev. We'll need you soon."

Both men nodded and lay on their sides.

The sun through the trees dimmed and turned greener as the afternoon faded into evening. Watching the trees, Kinneret and Ona shared stories about friends and family, treasure and victories, and their best days.

Kinneret's smile faded. "What is one thing you would change if you could move the sun back?"

Ona switched her grip on the magic-infused sword and didn't meet Kinneret's eyes. "I would side with Seren, not her enemy. I can't even imagine what she and Lucca think of me now. Well, they think I'm dead, but I guarantee they're cursing my ghost."

"I doubt it. You surely had some good reason for going against them. You were all fighting the same larger threat. The Invaders. Right?"

"Yes, but the reason I sided against Seren and Lucca was to win. Defeating the Invaders and killing as many of them as I could, that was my only focus. I let that thirst for revenge ruin the one thing I still had. Lucca will never forgive me. But I'm going to ask anyway. It's the least I can do. That and reunite him with his brother."

"That'll score you some points, surely." Kinneret nudged Ona with an elbow, trying to cheer her. "It won't hurt that Dante thinks you're amazing. He'll speak well of you to them. Of how you've changed."

Ona's head whipped around to look at Dante. "He doesn't think I'm amazing."

Dante snorted and rolled over, snoozing soundly despite being in the middle of a forest of monsters. Kinneret longed for his brand of courage. Or was it stupidity? Well, she wanted whatever made that enviable sleep possible.

"Yes, he does," Kinneret said. "He watches your every move and can't keep the admiration out of those blue eyes of his."

"They're actually more of a steel color. And his—" Ona's mouth hung open as she realized Kinneret was smirking. "Oh shut up. Fine. We might be fond of one another. It's just because of our shared love of Lucca."

"Sure."

A low growl rumbled from the south side of the forest.

Kinneret whirled around only to come face-to-face with a tangle of red-tinged ivy.

She thrashed at the vines as they spun around her ankle. The dagger had little effect, but Ona was behind her in a flash. She drove the runed sword down, slicing the ivy in a clean strike as the men woke.

"Get Miach." Kinneret ignored the fact that the ivy didn't burn her skin like it had the first time she'd been wrapped in its red-green leaves.

Calev grabbed the boy, who remained unnaturally asleep.

Dante took the sword from Ona, who was sweating like she was fevered. She obviously couldn't fight for long with the injuries suffered by both her body and her mind.

They braced for another attack, but the ivy slithered back into the sun-dappled forest.

"Oron?" Kinneret hoped he was still alive. She couldn't bear to think of losing him. So far, she'd refused to let her mind even consider that outcome. "Oron?"

Running to the half-broken tree that held him, she peered inside. The tree now grew over his entire head and both shoulders. Only one spot of his jawline was visible. Chest tight, she pressed her knuckle against the skin there. Oron had been there for her ever since she lost her parents. He was the reason they won over the oramiral at Quarry Isle. He won over the slaves there. He was the reason she'd never truly felt abandoned when death took her parents. Forcing her tears back, she turned to face Ona, Calev, and Dante.

"He's dying. We can't stay here and rest anymore. And guarding him is doing nothing. Runnos is still taking him."

Calev pressed his hand against the tree and whispered Oron's name along with an Old Farm prayer.

"We have to find that shield," Kinneret said, "and figure out how to use both of Miach's family heirlooms to destroy Runnos. That is the only way we can save him and escape this cursed forest."

"All right." Dante sheathed the sword and spread his hands wide. "Since there is a spring northeast of here, near Miach's hut, like you mentioned, then there may be a convergence of water, leading to a creek, which could produce a waterfall south of here."

Kinneret squeezed her eyes shut to recall what she had seen in Miach's memory. "The waterfall dropped into a deep crevasse. Anyone know of a fault line near here? A place where the earth shakes sometimes?" She'd heard of such things from Oron, who'd traveled all over the world as a trader before working for her.

"Oh yes!" Ona pointed excitedly to the South. "I've never been there, but my aunt used to talk about a town that was eaten up by the earth before Silvania was even a country. All that was left of the town was a great scar in the ground."

"Outside the wood?" Calev handed Miach off to Kinneret, who'd tucked her dagger away.

She hated how her tree-like fingers looked against his skin and hoped she wouldn't be thrown into any of his memories again. She'd hate to hurt him. "Are you sure I should hold him? I might do that thing again."

"If you do, we'll know more."

Ona nodded. "He is immortal."

Kinneret swallowed and held the boy carefully.

"Is the crevasse outside the wood then?" Dante asked. "Will we even be able to access it? Runnos might not let us out."

Kinneret started southward. "We won't know until we try."

THE FOREST DARKENED as Kinneret led them through more pine groves, oaks with trunks wide as her old boat, and paths riddled with mossy roots and thick ferns. Branches cracked in the distance every once in a while, putting them all on alert. Dante kept his sword poised and Calev had his dagger ready. Ona's gaze watched movement that Kinneret couldn't even see.

Kinneret's sandals rubbed her changing skin and she finally had to stop.

Miach woke and went right to Ona like he knew her. Ethus had been circling Ona's ankles since the sun began to set. "Where are we?" he asked Ona.

Kinneret sat and tore off her sandals. Her stomach rolled. She tried not to look at her feet. They felt very wrong and staring at them wouldn't fix anything.

"We're headed to the waterfall to get the shield," Ona answered, her gaze on Kinneret's ripped up shoes.

Miach went pale. "We can't. He'll find out. Runnos will kill Ethus." He grabbed the baby goat and held it tightly.

Calev put a hand on Miach's shoulder. "We won't let that happen. I'm good luck."

"He is." Kinneret managed a smile as they started forward again. "I'd be dead long ago if it weren't for his good luck."

"See? We'll be just fine." In the gathering dark, Calev graced the boy with his best smile.

Ona came close. "Good luck? I thought that was all your salt magic? That's the way everyone tells the story anyway."

Kinneret waved her off. "Without his luck, I wouldn't have had a chance to use it."

"Really."

Kinneret nodded.

Dante clapped Calev on the back. "I don't pretend that bad luck was the reason my life has been the horror it's been. That's all me and my bull-headedness. But I'd love to think some of your good luck might find its way to me."

Calev smiled even as he kept an eye on the trees hulking over the animal trail they walked. He took a shamar yam shell from his sash and handed it over to the wide-shouldered, former Invader. "Take this. Say a prayer into it and you may find more than luck. You might find faith."

Dante took the purple-striped shell and kissed it. "I'll do that. Faith is something I've never found, but I wish for it every day."

Calev laughed. "That *is* faith, Silvanian. If you didn't believe it was going to happen, you wouldn't continually wish for it."

Pocketing the shell, Dante blinked. "I never thought of it like that."

Kinneret's own laugh was cut off when Runnos began speaking inside her head.

She jerked to a stop and Ona smashed into her back.

Come to me. Come to me. Come. To. Me.

The words were like hands, warm and smooth, gliding through her hair and down the back of her neck. Her breath left her and goosebumps rose along her arms.

We will be one. My power is your power. My darkness is your darkness, strong one. Come. To. Me.

653

The path faded into a dull green. The trees around her glowed a deep blue-green. She whirled and saw a flame of orange and red in the shape of Ona.

"Kinneret?" Ona's voice warbled like she was underwater.

Another flame came close. This one touched Kinneret, and her flesh ignited with a fierce need. A hunger.

This was so wrong.

She screamed.

The world returned.

There was Calev standing in front of her, eyes full of worry, his hand on her arm. Ona, Dante, Miach, and the little goat circled her.

"Runnos took my mind..." Her head pounded like his voice knocked on the door of her thoughts. "No." She gripped her head, branching fingers digging into her scalp. "Go away!"

The pulsing echo of Runnos's power disappeared.

Calev took her in his arms. "You fought him off, didn't you? See? You're going to beat him at his game. You are far too strong for him. You are Kinneret Raza, salt witch, full-ship kaptan to an amir, and the best sailor the world has ever seen."

She sucked a breath and swallowed. "I saw you as a pillar of fire. Ona too."

Ona grimaced. "You looked like you enjoyed it a little bit. I hate to say it, but maybe you should be aware of that."

"No, you're right. I did." Kinneret's cheeks heated. "Runnos is disgustingly tempting. It's awful."

Dante held out the hilt of the magic sword. "I wonder what would happen if you tried to hold this? Maybe it would drive that god out of your flesh."

It wasn't a horrible idea. She took the sword.

The moment her hand curled around the hilt, her entire being caught fire. At least, that was how she felt. The pain roared in her aching head and she threw the weapon with surprising force across the path and into a clutch of ferns.

"Well, that didn't work." Ona went to fetch the runed steel.

Calev crossed his arms. "Understatement."

The night weighed down Kinneret's shoulders. With every step closer to the edge of the forest, with every snap of a branch in the distance, with every whisper from Runnos, she sank deeper and deeper into a mood that fit the darkness. She was almost certain the god wouldn't let her leave the forest's boundary line. How she knew that, well, she wasn't sure. That would mean the rest of them would go on to search for the waterfall and the cave without her. She'd be left to Runnos. Left to his temptation. And she didn't know whether she could shake him off again so easily. Someone could stay with her, she supposed, but then they'd be at risk if she lost her mind. Who knew what she'd do? She couldn't ask someone to risk that.

She'd have to grit her teeth and hold on and fight the god herself.

15

KINNERET

Thick trees blocked any trace of moonlight. Only a faint glow in the distance showed where the forest ended and the sky showed itself. Darkness had always made Kinneret's hands sweat. After all, at sea she rarely experienced full dark. Even intense cloud cover let a haze of moonlight through somewhere over the water and the waves reflected it. But now, with the dense leaves and what must've been a cloud bank over this forest, there was no light except for that distant goal—the end of the wood.

Suddenly, pricks of pain stopped her.

"Halt." Dante's voice called out to her left. "I think we've wandered into a patch of thorns."

Everyone was making noises of discomfort around her.

"Well, let's back up." She gripped the thorns crowding her feet and legs, enduring the burn of their sharp ends to yank them away.

"Don't pull on them," Calev said.

Before she could ask why, the thorns crushed against her skirt, piercing the fabric to plunge into the flesh beneath. She howled in pain and surprise.

"When you fight them, they just grip more tightly," Calev said.

Ona grunted. "I'm trying my dagger." An owl's call covered the sound of her attempts. "It isn't working. It seems to grow back right away. Maybe the runed sword will make a dent."

"I'm giving it a go," Dante said through what sounded like gritted teeth. "I can't...I can't even lift the sword, let alone use it. They're everywhere."

Something flapped overhead and tossed Kinneret's hair. "I'm hoping that was a bat."

"What?" Miach asked, his voice trembling.

"Nothing. All right. I can get into my salt pouch. Maybe my magic will do something. Anything. Who knows?"

As she reached into her bag, a thorn dragged itself up her arm like a tiny knife. The pain was impressive considering the size of the thorn. With a pinch of salt held awkwardly in her fingers, she whispered.

Blood of the sea,

Free me.

Hear my call,

Free us all."

The salt fell easily from her fingers. She held her breath.

Then the thorns pulled away from her.

"It worked! I can lift my arm. Hold on, I'll—"

The plant lunged at her, this time holding her closer and impaling her in one hundred different spots.

"Kinneret?" Ona's voice was gentle and wary.

"I was wrong. All the thorns came closer. It worked for a moment like the plant was trying to decide if it accepted Salt Magic."

A crunching sound carried on the breeze.

"What is that noise?" Calev asked.

"Ethus is eating the thorns," Miach said. "I think he likes them."

"Sadly, I doubt that little fellow has enough stomach room to eat a way out for everyone," Dante said.

They all gasped as the plant tightened its grip.

"Help!" Miach sniffed and moaned pitifully, tugging at Kinneret's heart.

Calev cleared his throat. "I...I have an idea." He hissed in pain. "I'm thinking this is a darkthorn bush. It can take these plants ages to get this large. This is truly an elder and maybe it deserves some serious respect. Maybe even a sacrifice."

Dante snorted.

Kinneret glared at the warrior even though it was black as pitch and he'd never see it. "Listen to him."

"Aye, aye," Dante said.

The thorns squeezed Kinneret's waist and crept higher.

Calev coughed. "This won't feel wonderful, but repeat after me if you're up for trying my plan."

Ona called Miach's name. "Are you listening? Calev is a good man. Follow his directions and the pain will be over soon."

"All right, Ona," Miach whispered.

Thorns reached up Kinneret's back. Pinpricks of heat flayed her skin under her shirt.

"Elder," Calev said, "we respect you and offer our lifefluid to show our earnest apology for breaking into your land and crushing your growth beneath our feet. Everyone, grip the thorns in your less useful hand. Let the points prick you. Let the elder see we are genuine."

"This is ridiculous," Dante whispered.

"Just do it," Kinneret snapped.

They repeated Calev's words as best they could, stumbling over the phrasing here and there. Then Miach yelled as Kinneret gripped the plant in her left hand. Hot blood pooled around her fingers and the vicious spines of the darkthorn bush. She clenched her jaw and kept her hand in place, hoping it wasn't too terrible for the others, especially Miach.

Insects chirruped in the trees and more bats fluttered past.

Ona sighed raggedly. "I don't think—"

The thorns retreated with a dragging sound and Calev whooped in delight. Finally, Kinneret could move without jabbing pain. She hurried toward the light marking the end of the wood, grabbing whomever was closest. "Let's get out of here before that plant decides it wants a finger or two."

"Agreed!" Calev took her arm.

"Nice work back there," she said.

"At your service, Kaptan."

Dante's deep voice called Calev. "Apologies for my continued lack of faith, Old Farm. In the future, I will trust your instincts."

"Thank you." Calev stopped to clap Dante on the back. Kinneret could just barely make out their silhouettes.

"Enough sweet talk," Ona barked. "Like Kinneret, I'd rather not lose any body parts to this forest if I can help it."

THE FOREST abruptly stopped at a moonlit meadow dotted with boulders that looked like sleeping beasts.

The last time Kinneret had seen this place was in Miach's memory. And it had been colored in his family's blood.

Miach released Ona's hand and stood staring.

Kinneret touched his shoulder. "You honor them with your courage. With the way you show love to Ethus."

She heard him swallow. He nodded jerkily, then went back to clutching

Ona's fingers. Dried blood showed on his wrist. He was one thousand and ten years old, but he seemed like any sweet, little child that had lost loved ones. From what Ona had told Kinneret during their watch, those two had a great deal in common.

She said a silent prayer for Oron, her own family that she was in danger of losing. Pressing a hand against her heart, she drew courage from the fierce need to save him.

Ona and Miach started toward the forest's last trees.

A new thought occurred to Kinneret. "Will Runnos allow you to go past the boundary, Miach?"

"Yes." His voice was small and shaky, his gaze on the field where he'd watched his kin fall to the green men. "I have a little distance I can walk before I get sick. That way, I can call out to travelers who don't come right up on the wood."

Calev's eyebrows knotted. He whispered something sharp under his breath about Runnos.

"Well, maybe I'll be able to go too," Kinneret said.

Calev cocked his head. "You didn't think you could?"

Kinneret shrugged, tears burning the corners of her eyes. She willed them away, then stepped into the meadow with her strange feet. "I feel the same. I can do this."

Dante started into the low grass, Ona behind him with Miach and Ethus. "We should hear a waterfall of that size if we get anywhere close."

"What if the waterfall isn't flowing anymore?" Ona asked. "Miach's family was here so long ago."

Kinneret walked beside Calev, grateful beyond words that she was able to stay beside him during this nightmare of an adventure. She was so glad Avi wasn't here. Her sister had been through enough. "There should still be a crevasse and a cave."

"True." Dante pointed. "There. See the line of paler ground? I'd bet all my silver that's it."

"You don't have any silver, do you?" Ona eyed him.

"Oh. No. I don't. And come to that, I don't have any more dried meat or bread either. Does anyone else have any food?"

They'd passed the fresh water from the spring that Calev and Kinneret had gathered in their waterskins, but no one had shared a bite of this or that in hours. Kinneret realized she wasn't even hungry. Not for meat or bread.

That strange darkness swarmed around her mind and she shook her head harshly to clear her thoughts. Calev put an arm around her shoulders and gave her a squeeze.

"I think we're out." Ona closed up the pouch on her belt and scrunched her mouth. "Dante, after we nab this shield, and if we live through it, do you think you can scrounge some more of those berries or leafy greens for us?"

He bowed his head. "I certainly will try."

Kinneret touched the puncture wounds the thorns had made on her hand. As they walked on, she wondered when Runnos would discover what they were up to and how much they would bleed when he did.

16

ONA

Half way between the supposed gigantic crack in the earth and the wood's boundary line, Ona paused, Dante coming up beside her. Miach still held her hand. A sudden thought had occurred to her and she wondered why she hadn't considered it earlier.

"Dante."

"Ona."

"Why aren't we escaping right now?" she whispered.

He rubbed his lip with a knuckle.

"I mean," she said, "Runnos doesn't seem to be sending any more green men out here. The old me would've already been gone. Well, I might've dragged you along for Lucca's sake and maybe for the pleasure of your handsome company, but I'm telling you, I would've been gone already. Why aren't we taking off?"

"You really were pretty terrible before your injury, weren't you?"

"I was."

"So answer it yourself, Onaratta. Why aren't you high tailing it out of this hell with me in tow already?"

Behind them, the line of pine trees swayed in the wind and the scent of night rose. Water, danger, animal scents. She shivered. "Because there is a man trapped in there. He'll probably die anyway, but we still have a chance to save him."

"And?"

"And Kinneret. We have to try to help her. She doesn't seem quite as

661

innocent as some, but I like her. She made herself a legend in spite of ridiculous odds. Like Seren. I admire her."

"What about…" He jerked his chin toward Miach and Ethus.

Ona's throat tightened. "He is the enemy," she whispered in Dante's ear. "He is. If you think about it. He spies for Runnos, works for Runnos."

"You still want to save him." It wasn't a question and Dante was right.

"He lost them." Ona's aunt screamed in her memory, beat her hands against the Invaders. "I would never, ever leave him. I know how it feels to lose that much. In that way. I won't leave him. Or any of them."

"Then we're of the same mind."

Ona nodded, feeling oddly at ease. Her brush with death, her aunt's memory, and that last look at Lucca on the walls of Akhayma had smothered the flame of selfish, over-focused revenge. She didn't know what would drive her now. But doing her best to save these people—this was something she could latch on to.

Kinneret and Miach paused in unison. The boy's hand tugged at Ona's and he held his stomach. Ethus bumped his leg, then circled him three times.

Kinneret doubled over. Her skin was taking on an eerie greenish tone. What would happen if they couldn't stop her from changing? Would they be forced to cut her down with Dante's sword?

"You all right?" Ona asked Miach.

"We can keep going." He grimaced, then spoke to Kinneret, his partner in discomfort. "It will get a lot worse before we pass out."

Dante squatted beside Miach. "So you've tried to escape and Runnos knocked you out?"

"Yes."

Dante ruffled Miach's black hair. "Brave man."

A sad smile pulled at Ona's lips. She hoped with everything in her that she'd be able to reunite Dante with Lucca.

Miach grinned up at the large warrior. "Will I someday have muscles like yours?" The boy poked at Dante's impressive arm.

Dante looked at the ground for a breath. For all they knew, Miach would never grow up. He was stuck in this…strange suspended age of ten years. If they took down Runnos, he might die. Would he become a pile of one thousand and ten-year-old dust?

"Of course you will, boy. Of course you will." Dante stood and strode forward, shoulders bent and head tipped down.

Ona could see the cost that lie had reaped from Dante. He'd had to tell it though. Why scare the little fellow more than he already was? No point in that. Miach's father had doomed his son the moment he began crafting that sword and shield.

The moon rose high and bathed the meadow in light. The smoother areas looked much like the silver pool of magic water in the wood. What was the purpose of that strangely spelled body of water? Had it always been there? It was most likely Runnos's doing, but it didn't seem to serve his needs very well. Surely the god could've done a little better than leaving the effects to chance. Wouldn't he want everyone who entered the pool to be turned into a green man to serve him or something like that? Why bother with blessing some people like he had Dante? And the water had healed Kinneret's boils at the same time that it began her transformation into a spirit of the wood. Why did the magic there seem at war with itself?

The group had been quiet since Dante's sad lie, and Ona didn't care to break it now with a question about a silver pool they'd hopefully never have to visit again. Miach might know about it though. She'd ask him later. Maybe she'd question him after they had the shield and were on the search for the sacred grove, for the heart of Runnos's home here in Silvania.

One more rise of ground, and the great crack in the earth appeared at their feet.

Ona stopped the stumbling Miach from going too close. Tufts of short grasses hung over the edge, and it was too dark to see how far down the break in the ground reached. The main stretch of the abyss ran roughly northeast toward the wood, but a long branch of it broke off here and wriggled north.

"But where's the waterfall?" Kinneret's voice was a croak. She and Miach were obviously feeling dizzy and sick.

"I suppose the flow of the waters did change. But look at that wall of rock there." Calev pointed beyond the chasm's northward trek to a dark patch in the moonlight. "That could very well be a cave."

"And we'll need to cross this death trap to get to it." Dante began searching behind boulders and in the few clumps of small trees. "We need a bridge. Or a vaulting pole."

Kinneret leaned against a jagged rock. A sparkling line of white crystal spanned the front corner. Her pointed fingers curled around the crystal like vines around a tree branch. Ona fought a shiver.

"I'm not going to be leaping over anything right now," Kinneret said. "I doubt Miach is very excited about that either."

"I'll stay with you." Miach and Ethus joined Kinneret on the boulder. Ethus nibbled at Miach's tunic, and the boy gently nudged him away from the cloth. He picked some grass and fed the tiny animal from his outstretched palm.

Dante gripped a small tree's largest limb and yanked hard. Calev grabbed a hold to help.

"One, two, three!" Dante's arms bulged as he and Calev forced the branch down, snapping it away from the tree.

Ona bent to look into Miach's face. His eyes were as big as the moon above. He had to be remembering what happened in this place and the loved ones he'd lost in such a violent manner. She knew how that felt.

A sudden memory attacked her.

She saw her aunt laughing, sketching charcoal in hand. Two goats about Ethus's size stood on the table beside her paints. They'd tipped one jar over and blue ran down the table leg to puddle on the tiles.

Then the memory flashed forward and the Invaders were crashing into the room.

Her aunt lay on the tiled floor. Blood. Blood. Blood.

Breathing heavily, Ona realized Miach was shaking her arms. "Ona. Ona!"

"I'm fine. It was a long time ago." She breathed in slowly, trying to calm her frantic pulse. "They killed my aunt. She was my only family."

Miach drew her into a fierce hug. "I know. Shhh. I know."

He didn't know a thing about it, but here he was caring for her all the same in the best way he knew how.

She hugged him back, then drew away to look into those big eyes. "You do understand, don't you?"

He nodded, lips quivering and gaze darting around the meadow. His memories of this place still lived in his head and heart.

"We'll be strong together, all right?" Ona whispered.

"All right." He smiled and Ona felt something stir inside her.

Something that felt oddly like power. Like she was about to chant.

She pushed the feeling away. This was no time for violence. What was her body doing? Why had she thought of chanting at this moment?

"It's going to reach," Dante said.

He finished positioning the tree limb while Calev and Kinneret piled rocks on either side of the limb to keep it from rolling. When had Kinneret left the boulder? Ona's mind must've been truly gone for a moment. They tore three more limbs from the small trees near the crevasse and attempted to make a bridge.

After one last hug from Miach, Ona joined Dante. "This is not going to be fun."

Kinneret snorted and headed back to Miach. "No. But it won't be dull."

Calev's smile was there and gone in a blink. "That's my fire," he said quietly.

"I'll go first." Dante stepped onto the makeshift bridge.

The wood cracked ominously.

"Dante." Ona stepped closer. The scent of wet earth rose from the great crack in the ground. "Careful."

"I don't think any more of you should go across this." Eyes squinted in concentration, Dante paused about three-quarters from the other side. "I can get the shield."

"No, you can't." Miach shook his head. He tried to say more, but it looked as though his mouth wasn't working.

"He's right," Kinneret said. "I remember seeing the small hole Miach climbed through to hide the shield on the other side of the—"

Kinneret's face froze.

A gurgling sound came from her throat like she was choking. Calev ran to her and quickly untied his waterskin. He put the vessel to her lips, but she pushed it away, gasping.

"I'm not choking. Runnos just won't let us talk about…it." Kinneret did take a drink, then she kissed Calev's wrist.

Ona turned away to see how Dante was doing. His arms wheeled in a circle. He was only a step from the other side. Her heart hung limply in her chest. "Just jump it. Go on!"

He glanced at her, then flung himself toward the cave side of the chasm. Ona held her breath until his body rolled onto the earth, safe and whole, his hair and white teeth shining in the moonlight.

"I made it!" He brushed himself off and stood. "So I won't fit. All right. I'll hold the bridge from this side, and you, Ona, come on over with me. You're small and strong. You'll be able to fit I bet. Miach, what do you think?"

The boy nodded, lips white and pinched. Ethus bleated loudly in Dante's direction.

"Thanks for the affirmation, Sir Goat." Dante tipped his head to Ethus, then got onto his knees to support the bridge.

"Sir?" Kinneret looked to Calev like she didn't understand Dante's meaning.

"It's a label of respect. Of nobility," Calev said. "It doesn't translate well." He picked up one of the smaller branches they'd torn from the larger limb and began fashioning it into a torch.

Ona nodded at Calev's description. Thankfully, she and Dante spoke the trade tongue well enough to avoid too many confusions. The last thing the group needed was more of a challenge.

Calev handed Ona the new torch. He'd wrapped a ripped piece of his fine tunic around the end and smeared it with some plant growing at the base of the boulder where Kinneret and Miach sat. It burned hot and bright white.

A torch in her hand and her knife on her belt, Ona started across the makeshift bridge. The limbs shifted with her weight and the moon cast deceitful shadows across the uneven surface. Her wounds burned. The one from the battlefield throbbed in time with her heartbeat. It was a serious distraction and threw off her normally above-average balance. Three steps. Four.

One limb snapped.

Ona jerked. She fell straight down, through the branches until one leg was trapped between two of the tree limbs. She let out a very nasty curse.

"I was hoping that wouldn't happen. Too many bowls of Kurakian chicken with Seren…" she whispered to herself in Silvanian, trying to laugh off her fear.

Shaking and pleased she had managed to keep a hold on the torch, she tried to breathe deeply to calm herself. If fear took her here, it was over. A drop from this height was death. The ground was nothing but a great hole of darkness. There would be no getting out of that alive. Her knuckles whitened around the torch.

"You can do this, Onaratta." Dante's voice rumbled in their native tongue. "You are a chanter. A true mercenary of Silvania. This little chore is nothing to someone like you."

Her heart swelled at the compliment even though she knew she didn't deserve it. "You never even saw me fight." She gripped the unbroken limbs and began lifting her body to draw her leg from its trap.

"Didn't I?"

She stared at Dante. "You said you found me half dead at the end of the battle." She felt oddly exposed, imagining this kind man watching her chant and strike and take the enemy down—his own fellow warriors down.

"That was the truth. But I also saw you. Right when you came onto the field."

Ona's foot found a solid surface behind her other foot. She stood slowly, face burning with the effort and concentration. The earth scent from below wafted into her nose and she wondered for a moment whether or not one could smell distance.

"Ona." Dante's voice was sharp. "Hurry up now, and I'll tell you exactly what I saw on that field of blood."

Swallowing, she took a tentative step. Another. "Did you hear the chants I used?"

"I did. I will never forget the image of you that day."

"Oh. I'm sure. Small mercenary falling on a sword. Very inspiring."

"That is not what I saw."

"Then tell me what you saw. A monster enraged beyond reason? A beast who defied her friends and let revenge take her straight into death's arms?"

Five more steps.

"No."

"Tell me."

"Keep walking."

Ona glanced down.

"Please," Dante said.

She leapt into his hands and they tumbled to the ground. The torch went flying.

Rolling, he held her gently on top of him. "I saw a goddess of protection, there to keep that city of innocents safe from Invaders and their desperate swords." His lips curved into a vicious smile. "You were stunning. You were so quick. You were the Empire's strongest weapon."

It wasn't true, but Ona couldn't seem to argue. She was all too aware of his strong body under hers and the feel of his hands on her hips.

Calev, Kinneret, and Miach waved their encouragement from the other side, and Ona spun away from Dante to find her feet as well as the torch.

"If we didn't have living trees and their heinous god after us, I'd have stayed there on that ground with you for a while." Ona grinned, feeling for once like herself.

Dante barked a laugh. "If I still have a proper body when this is all over, I'd be happy to give you a second chance."

And there it was. Ona was flirting properly again. A smile pulled her mouth wide, and she took out her dagger to spin it like she used to do when walking with Lucca in the forest.

The weight of the weapon was as familiar as her own fingers, but the handling of it didn't give her the same feeling it used to. Now, it was a blade that she might have to use against those who might hurt her or her friends. There was joy in the skill of wielding it—the spin and the clean striking movement—but she had no desire to drive it into anyone, even an enemy. She gripped the weapon tightly, then stopped and stared at the thing.

Was this how Lucca had always felt about fighting? Was this the feeling he had and why he explained the reasons for each skirmish or battle to himself as they rode into a fight? No wonder he kept his books with him. Knowledge was what drove his soul. Not violence or rage or fierce pain.

What drove her soul?

The mural she'd started in the Napo Chapel flashed through her memory. The charcoal lines of wings, sunlight, and grape vines swirled in her mind's eye. She had brought the scene from Silvanian history to life with her own hands. The proud tilt of the queen's chin. A rock dove lifting into the sky. She'd brought that to life.

Her soul pulsed inside her chest, bringing her strength and driving the pain in her wounds away.

The knife glinted in the moonlight.

"I wish it was a paintbrush."

Her admission shocked her as much as it obviously did Dante. His look of confusion was comical to say the least.

"Don't wear that face too long," she said. "It might stick and then you'd have a hard time talking me into that *second chance*." A laugh floated from her lips.

The rocky ground led them to a flat area. An opening yawned in the hill and musty air blew from inside.

"I'm sorry, but did I hear you say you wish your knife was a paintbrush? Am I going mad?"

The dark thickened inside the cave's entrance. Ona held out the torch and felt a moment of regret as Dante pulled a flint and stone from his pouch to re-light it. She would still be by Lucca's side if she hadn't turned to the wrong leader before the battle. What would he say about her wish to turn her knife into a paintbrush?

"I used to be an artist," she said. "Before the Invaders killed my aunt. Before I ran to the mercenaries and gave my life to revenge." The torch's light illuminated spider webs on the ceiling and strange charred markings that might've been art from Miach's time. "I painted murals."

"That's impressive."

"Are you being sarcastic?"

"I'm not. Art is the key to civilization, if you ask me."

Ona tried not to chuckle, but she couldn't hide it. Dante frowned, facing her.

"I'm sorry," she said, still laughing. "But you're all *I'm the big warrior man and I'm a tracker and look at all my muscles* and now you're going on about art and civilization."

The light flickered over Dante's proud nose and the frown in the light-colored beard he'd grown since their flight from the other Invaders. Complicated shades of chestnut, copper, and wheat shone brightly in his tied-back hair. "Did you think Lucca was the only one with a brain in my family?"

"No. No. I'm so sorry." The old Ona would've hit him in the stomach and told him to get over it. New Ona actually realized she'd hurt his feelings and felt bad about it. "Really. You have proven your smarts over and over again. I'm a horse's arse. Sorry."

"You're fine. Just remember the cover doesn't always tell the story."

A shock of recognition flew through Ona. "Did you just quote Lucca?"

"Ah. No. That was originally from our mother. She gave Lucca his love of books."

The cave path turned left. Ona lifted the torch to keep them from losing their footing along the edge of the crevasse where the waterfall once fell. Now the area was dry as bone though the air had a musky dampness to it. Far off, drips of water echoed every several minutes.

"Lucca told me your mother wasn't overly...cozy."

Dante sniffed. "No. She wasn't horrible like our father, but she didn't seem to care too much about children. She was always running off to parties with nobles and other wealthy families. Most women seem to have children fairly young, but our mother had us when she was well past average childbearing years. I'm quite sure she is gone by now."

"I'm sorry."

"Don't be. I mourned her long ago and we were never close."

"Still."

Dante nodded, then paused. "Eh. Look up there."

Ona raised the torch, and a rough circle appeared in the cave's wall. A large point had grown down from the top of the opening, maybe from the small drips of water depositing minerals.

"Maybe little Miach could slip under that point, but I can't. Not without losing some skin." She banged the bottom of the torch against the stony growth

Dante took the torch. "Maybe let's not get lost in a dark cave, hm?"

She smiled. "But I can't get through there without breaking that point out of the way."

Dante handed the torch back to her, his fingers rubbing hers. She had the fleeting desire to curl her hand over his and—

He removed the sword from his belt and flipped it to show the hilt. "If this thing can take down those tree monsters, I doubt it'll have too much trouble with a stalactite."

"A what?"

"Stalactite." He banged the hilt against the stone. It did nothing.

"Well, it doesn't seem to want to leave its happy home."

Dante sighed. "You're going to cut yourself pretty good getting in there." His years with Invaders had affected his accent in interesting ways. Ona had to remind herself that he wasn't one of them. He was a good man and he'd saved her more than once since they'd met.

"I don't have much of a choice. Your big self definitely won't fit."

"Did anyone ever tell you that your ability to compliment is severely lacking?"

"Let me rephrase. That tiny space can't possibly handle the magnificence of your extremely well-muscled and manly body."

"She can be taught, folks."

Ona punched him lightly in the stomach. "That felt nice." She popped her knuckles. "Maybe I'm not entirely finished with violence. It's so succinct. The light sock to the gut says it all."

He grinned. "And yet you're still talking."

"Heft me up there, please."

"You're sure?" His light eyes reflected the torch's flickering yellow. "Because this is going to hurt. We could maybe—"

Ona looked away from his beautiful eyes, from the fire reflecting in their depths. "There's no other way. We don't have time to be clever."

"As you wish." Dante got on all fours and jerked his head at his back.

Ona used the torch to study the opening once more before propping it against some rocks. Dante's back muscles tightened under her boots. She slipped a bit, but managed to get her head through the circle of rock, then her arms and most of her torso. The stalactite bit into the back of her arm as she scraped through. Tumbling to the ground, darkness fell over her like she'd dropped into a giant ink pot.

"Little light, please?" She dusted grit from her clothing and stood to see Dante's face, peering at her alongside the torch.

"All right? How's the arm?"

Blood ran hot down to her elbow. "Not a problem."

Dante extended the torch through the opening and Ona took it. The orange light flickered along the uneven ceiling where a few tiny, dark green bats hung. Most of their friends were probably out hunting. That was just fine. A funny memory hit her. Lucca actually liked the flying rats. He'd spent one summer spouting facts about them after reading some monk's journal he bought at a market in the south.

The musky air didn't allow for a nice, deep breath like Ona's body needed. She tried to stay calm as the torch dimmed. Her feet stood in a few inches of dust.

"I don't see a shield."

"Maybe he tucked it into a corner?" Dante's voice echoed off the walls.

"You all right out there in the dark?"

"Yes, but I do think the bats are on their way back home."

Before she could say a thing, a flurry of wings exploded through the opening and crowded the ceiling. The creatures squeaked and swooped low. Ona's heart knocked against her teeth, and she ducked.

"They're luminescent!" Dante called out.

Ona reluctantly raised her head. Indeed, dotted lines of glowing green ran down the bats' sides. "Focus. Where should I look? And how long is this torch going to last?" She squat-marched to the left, to a corner. "Any good guesses on that?"

"Calev smeared it with a root that should burn a bit longer than oil would. That was a good find. I may need to visit Old Farm with this new life I've been given. They know their plants."

Ona waved a curious bat away from her head. "Great. Sounds good."

Then her boot hit something.

She shoved her fingers into the thick cave dust and found a cool lip of worked metal.

"Dante."

"Yes?"

"You'll want to prepare a celebratory dance. I think I just found the key to defeating Runnos."

There was a roar. A crack.

The cave shook.

Something hit Ona and the world went black.

KINNERET

The ground shifted under Kinneret's feet.

Miach shrieked and clung to Ethus. "I told you he would know. He is going to kill us!"

But this couldn't be Runnos, could it? They were past the boundary. This might've been the earth shaking like it did sometimes in this area. Like the activity that altered the waterfall and took the town Ona had mentioned.

The earth jerked again. The cave across from the branching chasm expelled a cloud of dust in the moonlight.

"Calev!" Kinneret was already running toward the chasm and the bridge.

Miach pulled at her hand, but his strength was nothing to hers and no matter how much she did indeed worry about what Runnos would do to them during this whole thing, she couldn't let something happen to Dante and Ona—they'd risked their lives to save Oron, a man they didn't even know.

Calev joined her at the bridge, and they panted as the earth calmed and the dust cleared. A cloud whisked past the moon, then scant silver light drifted over the mouth of the cave.

The opening was gone.

The cave was nothing but a pile of rock.

Miach was sniffling quietly. His goat sat on his feet. "I hate this meadow," he whispered.

Kinneret's heart tilted and pressed against her side. "I know. Me too. Calev, I can't let them die in there."

"Certainly not." He wiped his hair away from his face, then seemed to realize he'd lost his headtie at some point. "I'll go over. Maybe there is a path out that we can't see. I can call out to them and maybe help them move in the right direction."

But Kinneret knew who was the strongest here. Even with the dizziness, it was her. With this curse running through her veins, she held power in her arms, legs, and hands that she'd never even imagined. Knowing full well Calev would argue, she didn't ask his advice before vaulting over the crevasse in one graceful leap.

The only sounds were Calev's gasp of surprise and water rushing somewhere far, far, far below her morphing body.

She landed with a thud and hurried to the cave. The rockfall had no obvious room for escape. "Dante! Ona!"

Calev said her name once, but then both he and Miach kept quiet on the other side of the abyss so she could hear, but no voices answered except the distant whisper of the forest and the green men's buzzing like gnats she couldn't shake out of her ears.

The rockfall consisted of mostly large, slanted cuts of rock that had sheered from the outcropping above the cave. After a quick glance back at Calev, she curled her branching fingers around one of the rocks. It was nearly the size of her own torso, but it was light as a bundle of wheat in her new arms. She turned and threw it into the chasm.

She didn't want to see what Calev's face showed right now as she removed another rock. He had to be shocked at the change in her. This strength—more than the pine needles growing along her temples and flaring from her eyelashes, or the spindly look of her fingers—said very clearly that she was no longer human.

Swallowing panic, she worked up a sweat heaving rocks from the former opening and calling out for Dante and Ona like her life depended on it. Because it did. Her human life would be gone soon if the shield and sword didn't beat Runnos down. Oron would die. Avi would be without a sister. Calev, Miach, Ona, Dante, and probably even poor little Ethus, would all die an ugly death at the hands of the green men. Pulled apart. Absorbed into the trees for their lifeblood.

She couldn't think about that now. She would succeed in this. Everyone needed her and she flat-out refused to fail. She was Kaptan Kinneret Raza, and she would not go down this way.

Flinging the last of the rock away, she rushed into the cave's dusty mouth. "Dante! Onaratta!"

"Here!" Dante's voice was close. He coughed in the darkness.

A torch. Why hadn't she brought a new torch? Of course theirs was out. She kept her back against the wall and walked over fallen rocks, heading deeper into the hill.

"Wave one of those long arms of yours toward the ceiling," Dante said.

"What? Why?" What possible purpose could there be to that? It might even damage the cave further. Maybe he'd been hit on the head.

"The bats. They're in here. I can hear them. Listen. They're luminescent. If we disturb them, I think they'll light up."

Kinneret frowned, but did as he said and reached high to run fingers above her head. The ceiling exploded into a flurry of wings and a green glow. It didn't amount to much light, but a circle of stone showed above the place where Dante stood.

Blood ran down the warrior's cheek and under his chin. "She is in there." He pointed a thumb toward the circle in the cave wall.

Kinneret stepped over another pile of rubble and leaned in through the circle. A point of rock scraped her skull lightly. No moonlight or light from the bats reached the space beyond the opening. "Ona?"

Ona coughed, and Kinneret jumped, knocking her chin on the rock. "I'm here," Ona said. She sounded terrible.

"Did you find the shield?"

"Yes. I...here...hold on." There was a scraping sound and the shield appeared. Ona wedged it through the space sideways.

"Here, let me," Dante said, taking hold of the shield.

Even in the dark, Kinneret could tell the shield was dented and very dusty. Dante worked the circle of metal through the space.

"You ready to crawl out of there, Ona?" Dante's voice was strong and direct, like he was doing his best to make Ona feel like it was a surety that she would actually be able to get back out of that other room. "How can we help?"

"My entire body hurts like I've been run over by a very large creature with too many legs. But I think I can manage."

The dark hid her progress, but with the grunting and scraping and occasional cursing, Kinneret was fairly sure she was getting through.

"Take a swipe at those creepy bats again, will you?" Ona asked. "I need to see where to drop what with all these new rocks."

Kinneret waved her hands high, ignoring the fact that her arms were distinctly longer than they were supposed to be.

The tiny flying mammals bloomed into light, and Dante hurried past Kinneret to help Ona to their side of the cave. Using mostly feel and the small splash of moonlight the cave's new look allowed, the group worked their way outside.

Calev's smile was bright in the low light. But Kinneret knew most of his good mood was forced. He had to have been struck by how she leapt across the crevasse earlier. "I am *very* glad to see all of you."

"How about this?" Ona held the shield up proudly, and it flashed moonlight across Miach's face and Ethus's hooves.

Calev clapped. "We are well armed now, friends. Now, how are you going to get back across?"

Kinneret swallowed the disgust she felt about her changing form, grabbed Ona and Dante in one arm each, then vaulted over the chasm as easily as if it was a mud puddle in the Jakobden marketplace.

18

ONA

The one-thousand-year-old shield may've been the dustiest item Ona had ever held, but under its layer of dirt, it was glorious, just like the sword. There were several dents beside one of the bronze circles set into the steel but the runes etched in each circle were clear-cut and practically hummed with power. She ran her hand over one of the stones set into the bronze circles. Most of them felt relatively the same, but even in the near dark she could tell they were different colors.

"How will it work exactly?" Dante asked Miach as they crossed the meadow.

"We shouldn't have it," Miach said. "He will hate this."

"But you do know how it works." Ona smiled encouragingly.

"Father set the stones for a clear mind, focus, blocking negativity, and grounding. Malachite, smoky quartz, clear quartz, hematite, and amazonite."

"So the stones are what blocks Runnos's influence on the bearer?"

"Yes, but it won't work. It will only protect those under it. And not all of us can fit. Besides, the green men can still grab you. The shield doesn't stop that."

"Are you a sorcerer like your father was?" Calev's gaze was on Kinneret even as he spoke to the boy. His eyes were always turned in her direction. "I've never met a sorcerer."

"Yes, you have," Kinneret said gently. "At the dock in Verita. You met that Northern Isle seithr. They are sorcerers, right?"

676

"I didn't realize they were the same thing. I suppose you could be deemed a sorcerer too, my fire."

Miach wrinkled his nose. "Aren't there sorcerers in every town?"

"Not anymore," Dante said. "My mother once told me the northern air somehow gives such powers. But it must not blow around like it used to, because there are only people who do amazing things with runes and stones in the Northern Isles now, and they can only work their magic near their homeland. Mostly. At least, that's what my mother told me when I was little."

"My grandfather was the most powerful sorcerer ever." Miach beamed, but then his smile faded. "But he died long before I was even born."

"What killed a man that strong?" Kinneret asked.

Miach scratched his head. "I don't remember. My father told me, but I... can't remember the story."

"It must've been a great story." Calev gave Miach a sad smile.

"It was. And father used his caster to show it to me."

Ona handed the shield to Dante. Her injuries were throbbing. "What is a caster?"

"It's a length of woven thread," Miach said. "Done in threes and sevens."

Kinneret stopped. "Like a wraith lantern's wick."

"Yes. Exactly." Miach grinned up at Kinneret.

"The caster showed Father's story in the colors of the weaving. It was all in blue and white so I didn't get to see it like true life, but it was amazing anyway. At least, I think it was..."

"What's wrong?" Ona pulled his finger from his mouth. He'd started chewing a nail.

"There is a blank spot in my own memory. I can't remember the casting Father did of Grandfather's death. I think he showed it to me. Maybe I...I don't know."

"It's all right," Calev said gently. "Just rest. Maybe you'll remember tomorrow. We should stop to sleep."

"I agree that we should stop," Ona said. "I can barely put one foot in front of the other."

GUIDED by Calev and using his flint and dagger, they built a small fire solely out of fallen, fully dead branches and old logs. Dante and Calev stood watch while Kinneret, Miach, Ethus, and Ona found spots around the fire to shut their eyes for a bit.

Ona couldn't seem to sleep

Mostly because of the monsters just waiting to attack from the green shadows, but also because the woman next to her was quickly growing into one of those monsters. Kinneret dozed, her forehead wrinkled in the firelight. Tipped in long pine needles, her eyelashes brushed over her cheeks. She'd tucked her knees up and her feet moved slowly as she slept. But they weren't feet. They'd become roots. Each toe had elongated into a searching twist of woody root and Ona wouldn't have been surprised if they plunged into the earth right now to soak up nutrients from the ground.

How long would it be safe to be around Kinneret?

The woman's hands were frightening too. Ona shut her eyes to stop staring. Those hands had saved slaves, rescued a sister, and worked salt and prayers like no one in history. It was so sad that this might be her end. With a heaviness hanging on her heart, Ona's body finally overruled her mind and she fell into a deep, dreamless sleep.

A shout woke her. It was nearly dawn.

Ona jumped to her feet, body responding properly for once. A green man with a beard of oak leaves snarled and his branching arm reached for Dante's leg. As Dante fell, he threw his shield to Ona. Her hands moved to catch it. She slipped her arm through the leather strap and had one fleeting thought about the magic that held leather in one piece for one thousand years.

Dante struck at the bearded tree spirit with the runed sword. The creature dropped back.

In the pre-dawn light, Calev threw dirt into a tall, thin green man's eyes, then rushed to the fire. He grabbed up a burning stick.

"Good thinking!" Ona went for her own piece of flaming wood.

Kinneret stood and held her hands over her ears, tears streaming down her cheeks. "The entire continent. All the forests and all the towns. You can't. No!"

There was no time to figure out what Kinneret was talking about.

Ona gritted her teeth against the pain in her wounds and teamed up with Calev to light the tall green man's shoulder and torso on fire. The thing shrieked and spun, nearly toppling onto Miach and Ethus, who'd tucked themselves behind Dante. Dante was up and fighting again, the sword moving quickly but not quickly enough.

Ona pulled her flint from her belt.

Then the voices of the wood shouted into everyone's heads. Ona heard it too.

Give in to us. We are your life. You are our life. Rest. Rest. Rest.

Miach pointed at the shield with a tiny finger. "Ona!"

She lifted the shield above her head. The voices disappeared. All she heard was the hiss of roots sliding over the ground, the moaning of the green man who they'd burned, and the cackle of the bearded tree spirit.

Kinneret was tossing her head violently and crying like she'd lost everything already.

Dante wasn't using that sword of his the way she could. The way she used to.

It was time to see if she still had her skills buried deep inside of her. "Calev! Flint please!" He tossed her the stone. "Dante! Sword!" She reached out a hand.

He blinked, then tossed the weapon hilt first.

Catching it neatly, she began a chant.

"Your enemy is my enemy,

Let him feel my wrath."

Her lips trembled as she struck the flint on her sword.

"I strike like the snake."

A flame leapt from her hands, and she clutched the flint in her shield hand as she spun and dragged the runed sword across the tall green man's scorched middle. He screamed and crumpled to the ground.

"I bite like the wolf."

She ran at the green man coming at Dante, her knees like jelly. The creature raised a leafed hand as she jabbed the sword under his arm, deep into his trunk-like torso. The thing roared. She dropped the weapon and the shield both.

The green man bled sharp-scented sap as he dragged himself toward her. Her hands shook so hard that she couldn't even try to pick up the blade. She was going to die here, taken down like she'd never fought a day in her life.

"I'm no warrior," she said, somehow needing to voice the truth. To accept it.

A large hand darted forward, grabbed the runed sword, then plunged it into the green man's back. Dante stood over the thing as it curled and twitched, dying beside the smoldering fire.

Sweating and flushed, Calev grabbed the shield and held it out to Kinneret. She was still wailing and covering her ears. "Try this, my fire. Try this." Tears welled in his eyes.

She twisted to look at him. Now, she stood taller than he did. Her strange fingers reached out for the shield, desperation plain on her face.

"Runnos showed me it all," she whispered. "He isn't only enforcing his

679

rule here, in this wood. He is somehow connected to all the other forests. Everywhere." Her face paled. "All the green men are waking. Runnos will destroy every city in Silvania, Jakobden, Old Farm—the entire Empire."

Bile touched the back of Ona's throat.

The entire continent.

That's what Kinneret had been screaming during the fight. Runnos planned to overtake humankind completely. Ona's mind flew to Lucca and Seren.

Would Seren see this possibility in the Fire? What would she do in Ona's situation?

Calev was very obviously shaken. He glanced at the surrounding trees, then held the shield out to Kinneret again.

She took it.

The moment her flesh touched the shield, her mouth fell open into a silent scream. Dropping the shield, she went to her knees and Calev wrapped his arms around her.

Dante swallowed hard, also moving his gaze away from Calev and Kinneret, and offered his hand to Ona. She took it, but didn't stand. Instead, she pulled him down next to her to sit. Miach and Ethus snuggled up behind her and began playing with sticks in the fire.

"Could Runnos truly take over everything?" Dante asked quietly.

"Who knows? Maybe." Nausea poured through her. "We have no way to warn anyone." The wind tugged her hair, and she let it, too weary in body and soul to care about much of anything. "I...I thought I could chant again. And save you all. I couldn't even hold a weapon."

"You killed that one." Dante nodded toward the scorched and dead tall green man. "And nearly offed this one too. You just needed a little back up. Get it? I stabbed him in the back so...?"

Ona smiled warily, too overwhelmed to let him cheer her up with terrible jokes.

"Eh, Onaratta. Come here." Dante opened his arms.

Eyes burning, she went into them gratefully. Dante waved for Miach join their small circle. They huddled together for a few quiet minutes.

Ona tried to imagine a way out of this, but she just couldn't. Not with Oron alive, Miach freed, and Kinneret as a human again. Dante met her gaze. She traced the sweep of his eyebrows and the turn of his cheek. She touched his bottom lip, wishing she could mix a color to match the exact shade of his handsome mouth, wishing she was far away, paintbrush or chalk in hand.

This situation was hopeless.

Runnos wanted a war, and Ona had realized her passion didn't lay in being a warrior. She was, and always had been, an artist.

19

KINNERET

Kinneret's mind finally eased and Runnos left her alone again. The quiet was wonderful. She pulled it in desperately, almost like she breathed air after a deep, deep dive. Without the terror and seductive tug of Runnos in her head, she could think through what she'd just experienced. There was almost too much to untangle. She clenched her hands together.

Runnos was going for all of it. The human world would fall under his roots.

Unless they stopped him. Here. Now.

If she were to organize a group to take down an age-old god, this wouldn't be it. Yes, they had Dante and Ona, but the rest of them were simply a boy, a farmer, a sailor, and a goat. But Ona…

During the fight, Ona had moved faster than anyone should ever be able to move. When she spoke those Silvanian words—her chant, she'd called them—she'd practically flown over the ground to attack the green men. She'd only been a blur most of the time.

"Ona. You are amazing."

Ona closed her eyes.

Kinneret let her be. The mercenary was obviously not pleased with her performance during the fight, but Kinneret remained completely impressed. If that was disappointing, she couldn't even imagine how the woman fought at peak level.

Miach scooted toward his father's shield and began touching each stone in turn. "Malachite." The swirling green of the rock reminded Kinneret of the water around Old Farm's dock. "Clear quartz and smoky quartz." Miach's thumb bounced along the stones. "They help with keeping your thoughts to yourself and keeping his thoughts away." He breathed warm air onto a silvery stone. "Hematite. My favorite. Which one do you like, Kinneret?"

"That last one." She pointed. "The one that looks like the Pass when the sun filters through it."

The memory of the day she, Oron, and Calev dove into the Pass to look for the wine jug and the map to Ayarazi washed through her. She could almost feel the cool water against her sand-worn skin. The sound of Calev's feet kicking through the waves. Oron's shout under the water because they didn't leave when he thought best.

She smiled and swallowed against the pain.

Oron was still trapped.

Did he know they were trying to save him? Doubtful. If Runnos wasn't sure what they were up to, Oron wouldn't catch wind of it. But what if Runnos simply didn't think they could pull it off? They had the sword and the shield. How long until Runnos brought down his entire army of green men?

Miach clicked an opaque, blue-green stone with a knuckle. "That's… ummm. It's a hard word. Sounds something like Zonite."

"Kin," Calev whispered into her ear, tickling her. She longed for simpler times when that was all she needed in the world. "Ask to look into his memory again. We need information."

He was right. "Miach? Would you mind if I peeked at your life again? At your memories? I promise to stop if you ask or if it makes you feel bad."

He took a heavy breath, then plopped into Kinneret's lap. "All right." He faced Ona. "But Ona, please watch Ethus until we're done."

"Will do." Circles hung below Ona's eyes, Dante's too.

They were all exhausted. Ona stared at the fallen green men. Kinneret refused to look at them.

"I'll gather some more food." Dante stood and began eyeing the surrounding area. "Calev, you want to join me?"

"I'm going to help Kinneret and Miach. Just in case."

Dante nodded and began picking his way into the brush, sword in hand.

Kinneret smiled at Miach, then placed her hands on his bare forearms. She closed her eyes and Miach's family appeared. They stood beside a large hut made of stone, moss, and sticks.

A fire snapped beside his father, who laughed at something Miach's uncle had said. Then his father held up his hands.

"Come close, kin. This is the only casting you'll see me do for a long while. I grow tired of the drain of magic. The air…it changes."

Miach-Kinneret toddled forward on chubby legs. He held onto his mother's brightly-dyed skirt. "What will you show? The ships? Show the ships."

Miach's father touched his nose. "No ships today. I will show you something far more important. This is the casting of the day my own father gave his life to contain Runnos."

Whispers ran through the small crowd of dark-headed cousins and siblings.

Miach's mother chewed her lip and the boy pulled on her skirt. The fabric was coarse and familiar.

"Don't you like this story, Mother?"

"I don't. I miss that man. Your grandfather."

Miach hugged her leg, bunching the fabric, as his father turned a large loom to face the group. The thick woolen threads woven from end to end, side to side, held two colors—a soft blue and an ivory shade. The chieftain spread his fingers wide and touched the yarn. The loom shivered. The wool almost seemed to spark in the firelight. Father stepped to the side a little, then traced shapes with his thumbs against the weave.

Runes.

Then Kinneret was struck with an invisible force. The memory flew away from her mind. Calev and Miach stared, saying something, but she couldn't hear them over Runnos's words in her head. The words echoed, purred, sucked at the marrow of her bones.

No. Listen to me. To me. Come to me.

There was a flash of movement, then Runnos's voice disappeared, and Calev's voice became clear.

"Was Runnos interrupting the memory?" Calev took her hand and stroked it gently like it was still her same old hand and not one twisted by a god.

"Ona fixed it." Miach grinned and pointed up.

Ona held the shield above Kinneret and Miach like a roof. She smiled over the edge. "Try to see the memory again, Kinneret. I'll hold this here."

Kinneret drew up her courage and accepted little Miach from Calev. The boy smiled sadly and pressed a hand to her throat. His skin was warm and soft.

The memory flooded into her senses.

The scent of a fire. The jostle of people standing beside Miach on that day. The excitement running through Miach's blood as he watched his father cast.

The chieftain stepped out of the way of the loom and spoke in low, powerful tones.

"I cast the tale of my father. Great sorcerer. Strong father. Sacrifice for our safety."

The weaving began to move.

First, it was just a ripple that could be dismissed as wind moving the wool, but then the small movements became the shapes of a man and a deep valley filled with pines and bluebells. At the widest pine—a massive tree unlike any Kinneret had ever seen—the man lifted a staff and spoke, his voice unheard.

Miach's father spoke for the casting, explaining the images. "'I challenge you, Runnos, god of the wood, to do your best to kill me with your own breath.'"

The weaving showed five green men rush at the sorcerer.

"'Do not send your henchmen to do the job, Runnos!' my grandfather said, 'Use your own breath. Can you not do it, powerful god of the wood?'" Miach's father smirked and watched the woolen green men flinch from the sorcerer.

A huge wave of movement rolled through the weave. Miach's father took on the voice of Runnos. "'You are nothing to me.'"

The limbs of the huge pine in the center of the valley stretched. What looked like a cloud billowed from the shadows hanging from the tree.

The sorcerer held up a staff. He quickly dragged the tip of it through the air to form a complicated series of dips, loops, and slashes as the cloud tumbled toward him.

Miach held his breath, fingers tightly gripping his mother's skirt.

The cloud hit the runes his grandfather had drawn in the air.

The plumes of power froze, then shattered into shining pieces.

The brilliant white specks of the former cloud overtook the sorcerer, and he crumbled at the base of the pine. Filling the entire valley, the sparkling cloud morphed into a strange liquid that increased and increased until the entire weaving was the pale white of the moon.

Miach's father faced his family. "And that is how my father died. He battled the great Runnos, shook the god well, but in the end, lost that fight."

The memory slid out of Kinneret's head. She blinked, then saw Miach's sweet face, older than he was in the memory, and Calev just behind him, eyes fierce with worry.

A sharp knowledge swept over Kinneret. "I know where the sacred grove lies."

Miach's mouth dropped open. He tried to speak, probably to confirm what Kinneret had put together from the memory and the information they'd already gathered.

"Where is it?" Dante walked up, holding two fistfuls of green plants.

Kinneret closed her eyes and wished Runnos's heart—his sacred grove—was somewhere other than the place that would forever haunt her nightmares, if she lived long enough to have nightmares.

In that silver pool, she had started her transition into a monster. The moment her toe hit that cursed water, she'd lost her entire life and everyone in it.

"The sacred grove..." She coughed, then cleared her throat. "It's under the silver pool."

Calev stood. "The place that cursed you?"

Kinneret nodded.

Miach nervously twirled the longer hairs on Ethus's foreleg with a finger.

Kinneret set a gentle hand on his back. "Miach. Don't feel bad about not knowing. It's not your job to know everything. You already told us so much. You are the reason we found the shield. You are the reason Runnos is going to lose this fight with us."

The side of Miach's mouth lifted and he kissed Ethus right between the goat's tiny horns. He whispered something to his little friend. They both jumped up, Miach grabbed the shield from Ona, then he and the goat disappeared into the forest.

Dante ran after them.

Ona's eyes were wide. "I just let him have it. I didn't know he was going to run."

Calev started after Dante, calling out Miach's name.

"Why would he leave like that?" Kinneret trailed Calev. "Or if he was going to betray us, why not take the sword too?"

Ona followed Kinneret through a thicket of thorny undergrowth. "He's a boy. He would barely be able to lift that sword. It's much heavier than the shield."

Low tree branches swayed in Dante and Calev's wake, Kinneret ducked low to avoid a larger pine's branch, and Ona climbed over a fallen log.

"Miach!" Kinneret's voice was lower and scratchier than it should've been.

Beyond a stretch of beech trees, Dante knelt. He touched the ground, then turned. "They're headed east."

"But why?" Ona squeezed her hands into fists. She'd messed with her hair at some point and the two knots she wore were neater and more tightly wound. Mud still showed on her face and her eyes were bloodshot. "He's going to get himself killed," Ona said.

"Not killed. Punished maybe. Runnos can't undo making him immortal, can he?" Calev grabbed Kinneret's hand as they hurried under a tangle of mossy, oak limbs.

Dante and Ona zipped through the wood ahead of them, crouched and ready to spring at whatever might come at them.

"Who knows?" Kinneret said in answer to Calev's question about Runnos snatching immortality away. "He gave it. Why couldn't he take it away?"

"We should've worked harder to convince him we're going to win against Runnos and free him."

"That would've been difficult considering I'm seriously doubting it at this point. How can any of us get through that silver pool to the grove hiding underneath? The water," she stopped to swallow her fear, "takes over your mind and nearly paralyzes you."

Calev rubbed at the beard trying to grow over his sharp jawline. "But if the person who tries to breach the watery boundary holds the shield, maybe they'd be protected."

"Like the shield protected me as I watched Miach's memory."

"Exactly."

"It's not a bad idea, Master of the Harvest." Kinneret grinned teasingly. When Calev explained things or gave orders, his voice deepened and sounded more like his father's. Kinneret teased him about it, but really, she liked the sound of it. The authority inside the tone was like a special power. And anything that gave Calev power was fine by her.

Calev rolled his eyes. "I was not using that voice."

"You were."

"No."

"Definitely." She ran a finger along his arm, pretending not to notice how her skin no longer looked like her skin at all. It'd do no good to fall apart right now. It was better to joke and plan and grit teeth than to moan and wail about what she'd lost. Once she was fully a green man, then she could mourn.

Calev huffed and shook his head. "Fine. Back to the point. One of us will enter the silver pool and—"

Ona ran back toward them. "Calev, may I ask you something? Privately?" She made an apologetic look in Kinneret's general direction.

Kinneret froze, anger ready to fly but reason holding it back. "Why?"

Ona breathed out slow as Dante continued on, his form just a small mark of light in the emerald trees. "You're turning into one of them. Runnos speaks to you through thoughts. Who is to say he can't take everything Calev is telling you about possible strategy right out of your head?"

It was like falling to the ship's decking and knocking her chin on the planks.

She stepped toward Ona, chest heaving. "So you've given up on me, have you? Think I'm already one of them? Well, I'm not, and I know how to protect my own thoughts."

Ona backed away, chin high to look up at Kinneret. "You have to admit Runnos has full access to your mind some of the time."

Calev worked his way between them. "Ona, give us a moment?"

Ona sighed and started the way Dante had gone. Kinneret was very, very glad to see the back of her. The mercenary scared her a little. The way she'd moved during her attempt at chanting when she fought the green man attacking Dante…

"Kinneret, I can see you're weighing the idea of knocking Ona's head from her shoulders."

"She is a really great fighter."

"And that's the only thing holding you back."

"Pretty much."

"Not the fact that she risked her life to save us."

Kinneret glared. "She also thinks I'm going to betray you, the love of my life, to Runnos."

"She doesn't think you'll do it on purpose."

A grinding sounded in Kinneret's jaw. "Kind of her."

"You did lose your control for a moment earlier."

"And I fought him and won it back."

"What if it takes longer for you to win it back next time and he picks around in your thoughts and beats us before we even have a chance to try a plan, any plan?"

He was right. Of course he was right. But Kinneret was not in the mood to say so. She stormed away, her hair longer now and trailing pine needles. Sprigs of the same green growth emerged above her elbows, on the back of her arms. Swallowing, she tried to tug them off. It hurt like they were another appendage. Like she was trying to pull her own arms off.

Heat swirled inside her middle and crawled up her throat. Anger crashed over her like a wave. She thrashed in the current of her fear and outrage and frustration, ripping at the needles in her hair and kicking her root-like legs and feet. Great mounds of earth flew from the piles of dead needles as she tore through the wood toward Ona.

"I won't let him take me! I refuse!"

One sound stopped her, reined in her rage.

"Kinneret." It was Oron.

They had returned to the grove where Oron stood trapped inside a broken pine. She and Calev ran to the tree. None of Oron was visible, but they could hear his wheezing gasp and the one word he managed to utter.

"Kinneret."

Her anger poured out of her eyes in the form of tears. "Oron. We're here. We're going to get you out. Stay strong. It's almost over."

She gripped Calev's wrist, then hurried to follow Dante and Ona. They could talk all they wanted without her. As long as they let her stay to fight as long as she was still in control of her body. The insult and hurt Ona's comment had caused was nothing compared to the panic that hearing Oron had raised inside her.

As they picked their way through the unnaturally darker part of the forest, Kinneret turned to Calev. She memorized the fierce glint in his eyes and the firm set of his jaw.

"Do whatever you think is best," she said quietly. "You and Ona and Dante. Keep me out of it if you think you should. I don't care. We just have to get Oron out of there."

Calev paused to touch her lips, her cheek, her eyelids. "You are an amazing woman."

Before she could respond, he tugged her gently, urging her to move quickly.

Soon they'd caught up to the two warriors.

They stood a good distance from the silver pool. The water lay utterly silent. Not a ripple despite the chilly, resin-scented breeze. Ona had one hand on Dante's shoulder.

In front of them, close to the pool and beyond arm's reach, Miach held the shield above his head. His little arms hardly seemed substantial enough to do the job. Ethus stood beside him, preternaturally still for a baby goat. The sun that fought its way through the canopy and the forest's heavy gloom glinted off the stones of the shield—green, clear, gray, silver, and blue.

Miach and Ethus walked into the pool of cursed water.

20

KINNERET

Hands grabbed Kinneret's hair and dragged her backward, her strange feet digging rows into the earth. She screamed and heard Dante shout something.

Green men were everywhere.

An oaken man lashed a leafy paw at Ona. Blackish green leaves scattered into the wind as he knocked her off her feet. She began to chant in Silvanian as she lunged at the thing. Despite her speed, it slipped to the side of her blade. Her chant faded, and she stood there like she was frozen.

"Just stab him and be done with it!" Kinneret shouted, her own scalp burning as the tree spirit pulled her to standing.

Another green man, with pinecones framing his face, ran at Calev.

Kinneret's heart beat sickeningly in her throat. She swung at the green man holding her, but couldn't reach his face. One finger caught in the branches sprouting from its shoulders and snapped out and back into place with a shot of pain.

The green man rammed his head into Calev's side. Calev flew several feet before crashing into another tree. He stayed down.

Kinneret swayed. "Calev?" Her voice, like her body, felt sick and wrong. Calev was fine. He had to be. Avi needed him. She needed him.

Three green men raised woody legs to splash into the silver pool after Miach and Ethus, who didn't seem to notice.

The water slid up Miach's arms and hit his chin.

The tree spirit holding Kinneret jerked her to the ground, then lifted one massive root to smash her into the ground.

Kinneret had a fleeting thought. Avi was safe in Jakobden. She'd go to the Gathering soon and meet with the boy who'd helped her during her visit to Akhayma. She'd be happy. At least there was that.

Because it was now certain that Kinneret was about to die.

Dante flipped a different green man over his back. The creature landed beside Kinneret, green-black eyes rolling in its jade-tinted face. Dante slipped between Kinneret and the massive root. Grimacing, he drove the runed sword upward. The steel pierced the monster's foot. It howled and listed left as Dante pulled Kinneret to standing. Calev was up and fighting again. His dagger moved like small bolts of lightning in the storm of branches coming at him from all angles.

Two green men had him surrounded.

Kinneret coursed over the ground, fire in her veins. She reached for the first green man tearing at Calev and wrapped her new fingers around its neck. Her strength had increased, but she still couldn't pull the thing away from him.

Dante was there slashing the other green man's legs out from under him.

Kinneret gritted her teeth and tugged at the green man and finally, finally pulled him a step away from Calev. Two lines of blood leaked from Calev's nose.

Ona kicked a smaller green man away from her. She stood at the lip of the silver pool, hands cupped at her mouth and her hair in her eyes. "Miach! Behind you!"

The green men in the pool had only to reach out and they'd nearly have Miach. The milky water rose over Miach's black hair. It lipped over the shield. Covered Miach's knuckles.

And then the boy and his friend and the shield were gone.

The old sorcerer's broken spell—the silver pool of blessings and curses —swallowed them whole.

Kinneret yanked her victim back a step more, then squeezed as tightly as she could, choking the thing. Did it need air? The green man's face darkened. His lips went black. Bile rose in her throat as the fight left him, and he tumbled from her grasp. She was growing stronger every minute.

Yesssss.

"No!" she shouted at Runnos's voice in her head and dove into the fight with Calev and Dante.

Calev threw his dagger and missed. Kinneret ran for the blade. Found it stuck in the ground. Ripped it free and tossed it, end over end, to Calev. He threw again and this time it hit the target. The knife drove straight into the tree creature's eye. It shrieked, the sound like a murder of crows in Kinneret's ears. Dante's runed sword whipped low, then high. He jumped and twisted at an angle, slicing the back of the green man's neck. The creature fell to its knees.

Now, my new one. My strong one. Now. Be with me. We will rule the forest as one.

Sudden as a storm at night, Kinneret's mind fell under the god's sway.

Wholly.

Completely.

No space left untended, untouched.

Runnos's words spilled down Kinneret's temples like warm oil. They slid over her neck and down her body. She shivered. It felt as though the god's request, his demand, soaked into her. His will was her will. There was no fighting it.

"Kinneret!" A familiar voice broke through Runnos's continued whispering.

She shook her head hard and tried to form Calev's name in her mind and on her lips.

A hand touched her, and she looked down to see him. Her love. She smiled, and Runnos's voice faded a little.

Dante raised the spelled sword and the light hit her eyes like arrows.

In her momentary blindness, Runnos's voice grew louder.

My strong one. My powerful soul. Fate brought you here.

The scent of pines billowed over her. Her body seemed to light up from the inside out. The sounds of rain on leaves and of trees creaking in the wind filled her ears to bursting. She was the forest. The forest was her. She felt every insect crawling just under the ground, along the roots. Each move of the night wind shifted her limbs. The oaks, beech, and pines sang for her, deep and dark and beautiful. The forest swamped her senses in a lush tangle of sound and feeling.

Let go. Fall in. Let go. Let go. Let go.

When she opened her eyes, she saw as Runnos and the other green men did. There were no fleshy, small creatures who thought and loved and had a purpose outside feeding the forest. There were only flames of life that made her mouth water for want of them.

Take them. Yes. They are all yours. Then, you go into the water.

The buzz and heat of power rushed over Kinneret's limbs and through her chest, to her heart. She opened her mouth. A roar that sounded like a great tree cracking open poured from her lips. Flinging her right hand out, each digit a bendable branch of dark green leaves and spiny twigs, she caught up one of the bright flames of life.

She was so thirsty.

Yes. Feed. Feed on these.

So very thirsty for life.

The moment the flame touched her toughened skin, she knew she'd never be satisfied. She could feast on these flickers of lights for an eternity and never, ever stop. Drawing the life toward her body, her trunk-like stomach tensing, she heard something just beyond the din of Runnos's smooth permission to continue feeding.

"Kinneret," a voice said from far, far away. "You are my fire. You are Avi's sister." Something in the voice reminded her of something… "You are a beautiful, strong salt worker who loves the sea. Remember. Please, my fire, remember."

Tears choked this strangely familiar voice. Kinneret's heart curled around the sounds from this flame of life. She paused. He was special. But she wasn't sure why. If she absorbed his life into her, she'd no longer hear his words.

Runnos spoke louder in her mind. *If he confuses you, break him and take him later. I need your power now, my strong one.*

The life in her hands struggled and cried out her name. Her name?

"Kinneret!"

Yes, it was.

She released the flame.

Runnos thundered inside her skull. *Then another of my green men will take him. He cannot be released.*

They would absorb the man's familiar light. His name…he was called… Calev! Calev. How did she know this flickering light's name? What was this? If one of the others took him, fed on him, Calev would be no more.

The thought bent her in half, and she coughed, hands going to her neck. Her skin was so tough, sharp, wrong. Nausea swam through her middle. She stumbled.

Then she was herself again.

Calev stood below her, hands raised. "We will beat this, my fire!"

She started to reach for him, smiling and weeping.

Runnos gripped her mind. *We will create a fresh earth.*

Images of bloodied swords and fighting men fell under a carpet of bright green grasses. In her mind, saplings burst through the ground. A parent hit a child, then the child tore the wings from a butterfly. A wave of leaves crashed over them, leaving only a peaceful land of birdsong and sunshine, of a forest as wide as the horizon itself. Again and again the images, like paintings, moved through Kinneret's head. Blood and gore and hate and evil—all washed in green.

This is what the land is. This is what our land could be.

Then she saw the continent, stretching from the far West to Verita's bustling port, from the ports north of here to the most southern reaches, beyond Jakobden and Old Farm. The entire landform rolled and shook like a great beast, crumbling cities with powerful tree limbs and thick vines of red-tinged ivy.

And though it was horrible, though it filled her with such terror, this new heat inside her knew it was beautiful.

Calev called her name. "Don't forget your sister, Avigail. Avi, who plays games and reads too much and loves you and needs you. Think of the night we were Intended. The love between us." He touched her, and she knew he was right.

She focused on Runnos's presence in her mind. "There is great beauty in us too. In humans."

She brought all her greatest memories to mind.

Small Avi, long ago, flinging herself at Kinneret for a hug after a long day at sea. Her little arms were so strong even then, and she wore her lion look, as Mother called it, all fierce about her love. Kinneret imagined Calev grinning, teeth white and dimples showing, as she took his arm during their Intended ceremony. In her head, she saw Oron braving the Pass's most powerful waves and expertly working the sails, once again saving her life and Avi's too.

"We are also good," she shouted into the air, defiance roaring through her heart.

But darkness trampled her memories and ground them into dust.

Runnos spoke. *You are mine.*

Her thoughts slid out of her mind like quick little fish, lost to the ocean of languid sensation and Runnos's dark, dark sway. The god ruled her. She loved him for it.

And she was very, very hungry.

One of those flames of life threw himself against a green man nearer to the pond. He moved like sunlight on wet leaves, unpredictable and quick. He struck the other green man's chest and face quickly enough not to be absorbed in any way.

Brave. That flame of life was brave like the familiar, most beautiful flame at her feet.

"Kinneret!" the familiar voice shouted. What was its name again? Ca...

She looked down to see him bleeding life onto the pine needles that had fallen from her tangled hair in the fight. She had broken him in some way she couldn't see. Not his body. His soul. His heart.

"Calev?" His name rose in her mind like the sun. She strained to understand what it meant. If only she could see his face instead of the blur of life that only looked like the sustenance she needed to satisfy this wild, gnawing hunger under every inch of her new flesh.

"Ona is nearly there. Just hold on to yourself a little longer. Please. Please."

No. Runnos was all she cared about. And feeding. What was this being saying? Why did she care? "Where?" Who was Ona? Her tongue was thick and didn't want to speak this language any more.

"The heart of the wood," the flickering life said. "She will end this suffering."

Runnos shrieked, and it was one thousand crows cawing, one thousand trees snapping in the wind, one thousand new trees bursting into life. Kinneret covered her ears and shrank from the sound, but the words drove straight into her mind like expertly aimed arrows.

Go to my grove. Under the pool. Absorb the woman's life.

"What is he telling you?" the little flame said. "Don't listen. You are one of us. Not them. You don't have to listen to Runnos."

This being didn't understand. Runnos's orders were *in* her. She couldn't fight them just as she couldn't stop breathing. His demands were her demands.

Yes, the god whispered. That sweet warmth of Runnos's presence slid up her calves and over her ribs. The essence of him breathed into her neck, sending waves of heat down her body. The gnawing hunger ebbed away.

She sighed. This had to be the most wonderful feeling in the world.

With the hunger temporarily satiated, she opened her eyes. And saw the being's face. Every detail. His dark eyes. Ebony hair. The love in every feature.

Another green man grabbed the being and swung him into the air, snagged in fingerlike branches.

Kinneret snarled and lashed out at the other green man. "He is mine!"

She lashed out an arm like a whip of sinewy bark and ripped the small flame from her competition. He panted with fatigue and his fear-sweat rose from the coverings on his form.

She lodged him roughly onto her back as her roots rolled over the earth toward the pond.

"We can't go. Let Ona do her work. Please. Don't you remember?"

Runnos drove more orders like sharpened stone into Kinneret's mind. *Now. Destroy her. She is there, at my holy pine. Beyond the old sorcerer's barrier. The pond will not affect you in your form. Go. Dive. Now.*

The oddly familiar flame on her back grew quiet as her roots found the cool, silver pond. She couldn't remember why she had taken him like this. But there was some reason. It tickled her thoughts and she would let him be. Absorb him later.

"Green man." The flame on her back spoke in different tones now. He no longer seemed familiar. Now he frightened her. "The woman in the pond, in the hidden grove, she has a rune-etched sword that will end you if you try to stop her."

Kinneret paused, the silver pool lapping over the bark on her knees. She stared into the water's still depths. Tendrils of silver light danced below the surface.

Go. Now. Runnos sent a storm-scented wind across the pond. The air pulled Kinneret deeper. The orders forced her forward. All sound save Runnos's cooing voice faded as the pool's cloudy water welcomed Kinneret into its soft embrace. The hunger dimmed here, but Runnos's continued command of *Go. Now. Destroy.* pushed her onward.

The life on her back pressed into her shoulders, touched her cheek, then was gone. He had floated back to the surface. A part of her went with him, though she couldn't remember why he mattered so much. She would deal with that after ripping the woman flame apart.

The silvery water tugged at Kinneret's hair and the pine needles growing from the tips of each strand. Her powerful arms surged through the liquid and her roots grounded her, making each step long.

Runnos spoke quietly but firmly. *Keep on. Soon, you will reach the end of the barrier.*

And just as he said, the water began to give way to air at the tips of her roots. She stepped into the most sacred heart of the wood. Her new form grew jubilant at the sight of so many huge pines. The light here was like twilight, green and hazy from the barrier, but the trees didn't seem to suffer from the lack of sun. Something else fed them here. She leaned her mind into the shared thoughts of all the green men.

We feed them, the voices whispered.

By claiming the flames of life lured into the wood, the green men poured growth into this sacred place. Through roots and the very earth itself, Runnos's heart thrived.

The largest of the pines stood proud and dark at the base of a steep incline.

Beside it, a flame of life lifted something that gave off black curls of evil smoke.

It was the woman with the runed sword.

Kinneret sped down the slope, rage and fear rising behind Runnos's command.

Destroy.

21

ONA

From where Ona stood beside the pool, it looked as though Kinneret had grown even taller. She towered over Calev, who shouted her name. He was a fool for getting so close. She could crush him with one swing of a fist.

Ona was torn.

A huge part of her wanted to go after Miach, into the pool, to save him from those three green men who'd followed.

Another part of her had to stay here and fight with Dante and somehow help Calev shake Kinneret out of this change.

Kinneret whipped her branched arms toward Calev like she might grab for him. He slipped away, still calling out to her. The pain in his voice hurt her too. It was so raw and real. He was losing his essence here, now, as he lost the love of his life.

The wind gusted as Dante fought off another green man.

Pine needles and small branches like horns tangled in Kinneret's hair. She roared, the sound thundering through Ona's bones. Now, she was the only one of Runnos's creatures present.

"Ona!" Dante waved a hand, then threw the runed sword in a high arc. "I name this sword Carver and give it to you freely."

The weapon bloomed into light briefly before landing blade first in the ground. Ona snatched it up. The hilt was still warm from Dante's hand. She lifted it, adjusting to the feel of its weight in her hand.

"Carver," she whispered. The runes on the blade flashed in response. She nearly dropped the sword. Northern witches called their staves by that name—carver—because of the blade each held at one end for making runes and drawing up magic.

"Go after Miach! I'll take care of them." Dante nodded at Calev and Kinneret.

Kinneret keened, her wail long and torturous. The sound buried itself in Ona's ringing ears.

Ona traded one last look with Dante, her heart snagging on a beat, then turned to that horrible silver water.

There was no time to worry about whether it would cause her intense pain like it had the first time she'd gone in. Kinneret was about to kill her own lover. Dante would be killed too. Oron was likely dead. And Miach and Ethus were being chased by three tree spirits.

No time for fear.

She simply had to be a warrior now.

There was no other choice.

The water was cool against her ripped clothing.

Sweat rolled down Ona's back, and she curled her spine like it might somehow protect her healing wounds from further injury.

Seren would've leapt right into the pool to save even one of her people. Ona could do this too.

The water slid past her elbows. A shiver rocked her hard.

Yes. Seren would've done this. Lucca too.

She focused on a memory of Lucca in battle. His ferocity and focus. The way he made certain to fight beside her.

Then Dante's face appeared in her mind's eye. He was also ferocious in a fight. But more reckless. More warrior. Less bookworm. Dante leaned on brute force more often than Lucca. But he was still intelligent.

Ona was surrounded by proud warriors of all kinds.

The water rose and swallowed her chin.

It passed over her mouth.

She could do this.

After all, Seren wasn't a warrior first and she handled the tough stuff fine. She was a ruler first. Ona didn't have to focus on the fighting all her life. Just right now. She could be an artist first, soldier second. That was doable.

The water rose over her nostrils.

She held her breath.

Her body shook. From fear? From pain? She wasn't certain.

The cold liquid pressed and touched and scratched against her.

Her eyes opened like they knew better than the rest of her that she'd have to see where she was heading. Feathery, sparkling water made up the whole of her view. She swam down, kicking her feet and keeping a firm hold on Carver.

Her lungs burned.

The water was endless.

She would die here, waiting for pain, striving to save them, longing to be the woman she knew she could be if given one more chance.

Then the water billowed away from her face. A valley opened up below. Great, green pines stretched wide, twisting limbs which cast strange, luminous shadows over a carpet of bluebells. Resin filled Ona's nose, and she gripped Carver in both hands.

The green men who'd chased Miach were moving at a fast clip down the slope that led into the valley.

High above them, Ona forced her legs to run.

Glimpses of Miach showed through the green men's limbs. He still held the shield over his head, and though he seemed to only be walking at a boy's pace, somehow he was far faster than the tree spirits. Maybe the shield was helping him. Maybe this place—sealed in a strange pool of magic the boy's own grandfather cast—recognized his blood and gave him an edge.

"I hope you give me an edge," she said to Carver.

The steel bit into the first green man's back like a fang, going deep. The tree spirit slumped. Ona yanked the sword from the woody flesh just before the thing tumbled down the incline. The second creature turned and howled, reaching for Carver. The weapon sizzled against the monster's hand. Ona twisted and lopped an arm completely off. The green man shrieked and came at her as the third creature joined him.

Ona backed up a step. There was no time for flint or spark, but a chant floated to the surface of her mind.

"I am the fox in the forest.
Clever and quick."

She spun and dragged Carver across the second green man's neck. Thick and pungent sap poured from the wound, but he kept coming.

"I am the bird in the trees.
Light as feathers."

Leaping, feeling the chant's power in her veins, she sprang over the third green man's shoulder.

"I am the stag in the shadows.

Crowned with power."

She bent Carver and drove its point into the green man's side. The blade ran clean through the creature so she rotated the steel, then ripped it back out, tearing the thing's insides apart.

Her stomach turned, but she faced the other tree spirit.

"For you, Lucca, so you'll meet your brother again. For you, Seren, because I want to deserve your friendship. For you, Miach, because I know what it is to lose so much. For you, Dante, because I owe you my life."

"I am the bear.

Clawed and unrelenting."

Muscles coiled and strength surging through her blood, she jumped and flipped the sword.

"Wake, iron, wake!"

Carver blazed white as she gripped it in both hands and forced the runed steel into the last green man.

The tree spirit dissolved into a cloud of green-black mist.

She exhaled in a gust of air, arms shaking.

Below, Miach and Ethus marched toward the largest of all the pines. Its branches stretched slowly, menacingly, toward him.

Getting her feet under her, Ona started down the hill. "Miach! It's alive. Stay back!"

The ground evened out and Ona jumped over a boulder, then launched herself over a small stream.

"Miach!"

The tree nearly had him.

Under Ona's boots, the ground vibrated.

Voices scattered in the valley's wind.

Rise. Defend.

It was the voice of Runnos and his green men.

Miach turned as Ona ran up to him. "This is the sacred pine," he said. "You know what to do."

There was a glow to Miach's eyes that showed the centuries of his existence.

"Miach, come. We must get away from here." She grabbed his arm, but he held firmly to his spot, shield still raised, as the tree's branches creaked and lowered toward them.

"Use my father's sword."

"Carver."

Miach laughed. He actually laughed, and they were about to die. "That is a perfect name."

"What? What do you mean? Come, let's go."

"You are an artist. Make your mark on the tree."

"My mark?"

He took one hand from the shield to touch a rune on Carver's shining blade. "Like those. Close your eyes. Let my grandfather's magic speak to you."

What was he talking about? "Your grandfather lost the battle against Runnos long ago."

"Did he?" That ancient glow in Miach's eyes brightened. "Sometimes the war lasts longer than one man's life."

Goosebumps flew down Ona's arms.

This wasn't just Miach she was talking to. This was his grandfather. The great sorcerer.

Miach rose onto the tips of his toes to hold the shield over them both.

Ona poised the tip of Carver's steel against the huge pine.

The tree froze.

A gust of chill wind blasted Ona's back. Carver slipped from her hand and fell to the ground.

"Ona!" Miach's voice was all boy now. "It's Kinneret! Hurry!"

The fierce kaptan and salt witch had fully morphed into a green man.

Dark emerald green—almost black—cloaked the entire expanse of her eyes, whites and all. Every finger ended in jagged branches, some with pine needles and others with vines tinged in blood red. Her cheekbones and chin had sharpened into vicious edges, distorting her beauty into terror. Two great vines of black and red and green snapped from her back like wings. She used them to grab boulders and earth as she rushed toward Ona and Miach.

Ona had thought she'd known fear.

When the Invaders came to her home and killed her aunt. Then, on the battlefield at Akhayma, when the Invader ran her through and life bled out of her.

But this was a fresh fear.

Kinneret was an angel of horror Ona had never expected or imagined. Soldiers killed with sword, arrow, fist, or spear. She had no idea how this bent creature—woven out of a new friend and a curse—would bring death.

Knees quaking, Ona knelt and grasped for Carver. Her fingers closed around pine needles and dirt wedged itself under her nails.

"The sword. I need the sword."

Miach held the shield upright, arms shaking. "I can't let the shield go.

702

He'll take us even before she does." His gaze flicked to the great pine that had begun to stretch down and bend over them.

Ona found Carver, then did the most difficult thing she'd ever done.

She turned her back on the threat and let the artist in her take over.

Drawing the bright blade over the pine's trunk, she carved a slanted line. Her wrist turned, aching, and she created another line that crossed the first.

"Ona!" Miach bumped against her, Ethus at their feet.

She could feel Kinneret's power at her back and the force of the pine burning in the air all around them.

Carver moved so easily against Runnos's pine. The runes blazed moon-white.

A voice echoed in Ona's ears.

Stop them.

Pain shot through her head and ricocheted down her body. Her battle wound pulsed. She bit her lip to keep from crying out as the heat of new blood leaked from her side and her shoulder. It was the curse again. She kept hold of the sword though. She didn't lose it. Not yet.

Destroy. Destroy. Destroy.

Ona brought Carver's hilt high. One last mark. The sword's power shivered into Ona's arms. Tilting the blade a fraction, she placed the tip under the tree's flesh, then drove the steel down. The pine roared. The last mark became a clean swathe of silver.

The valley shook, leaves dropped to the earth, and roots tore themselves from the dirt. Kinneret shrieked, her arms flailing.

The watery sky—the sorcerer's spell—exploded into a flood of sparkling rain.

Miach shouted something, grinning, and gripped the shield to his chest. "Farewell, Ona! I see them and I'm going to them now!"

Ona blinked. "Miach?"

The solidity of his face, arms, and legs began to fade. Ethus was disappearing too.

Kinneret ran her palms over her head and raised her face to smile. No pine needles showed in her hair or along her eyelashes. The branches that had protruded from her skull and back fell to her feet. She touched her arm tentatively as the flesh resumed its original light brown hue.

Ona ran to her and clasped Kinneret's human fingers in her own. "You're back, Kaptan."

Kinneret's joyful look dissolved into one of horror. She twisted away to run up the hill, out of the valley. "Calev!"

Ona turned to see not Miach or Ethus, but only the shield. It sat quietly beside the great pine. Runnos's pine. She bent to touch the quartz stone on the shield. "Be well, Miach. Be well. Ethus, you take care of him, all right?"

Sunlight warmed Ona's left side as she stood. The rune she'd carved into the great pine glowed lightly. The tree was just a tree now. The air around it was simply forest air. None of the foul power of a bent god tainted its presence any longer.

With the immediate danger gone, Ona had one thought.

Dante.

Carver in hand, she sprinted up the hill, marveling at how her wounds no longer pulsed in pain. They were not completely healed, but not far from it.

Out of the valley, Kinneret and Dante bent their heads over Calev. He sat up and Kinneret pulled him against her. Dante's chin lifted and he saw Ona.

Ona ran to him, but once she was there, against his chest, breathing, she didn't know exactly what to say. *I just saved the day. Thank you for the fabulous sword. I really need a nap. That adorable boy and his goat passed on to their family and I don't quite know how. I forgot to pick up the shield.*

Dante raised his eyebrows. "You look like you're about to explode."

"I am. Are you all right?" She ran hands over his arms and chest, forgetting for a moment that they hardly knew one another.

He covered her hands with his. "I am."

"That was…madness."

"I'm sure. Where is Miach?"

"He disappeared. Ethus too. Miach told me he was going to them. I can only guess he meant he was passing on to be with his family."

Dante exhaled slowly.

Ona stuck the sword into his belt. "You're certain you're all right?"

"Yes," a different voice said. "I am all right, and thank you so much for asking!" Oron walked up to Kinneret and tapped her on the shoulder.

The kaptan shrieked, this time in delight. Ona grinned as Kinneret and Calev embraced the man. They looked like a family and it made Ona miss Lucca terribly.

"Glad you're not a tree!" Dante saluted Oron, then put his hands on Ona's shoulders gently. "What exactly happened down there?"

The silver pool was of course gone. The whole area had obviously been spelled to look smaller than it was. The valley undulated far beyond where the pool had been. It made Ona a little dizzy.

"It's a long story. How about I tell you on the way to Akhayma?"

"To see Lucca."

"Of course."

"He might hate me."

"That makes two of us. We're going anyway."

"I suppose we are. What is that saying you and my brother have? Your wishes are my wishes?"

"As long as yours don't war with mine." Ona touched the corner of Dante's sly grin and wished she wasn't as tired as the dead.

22

KINNERET

Kinneret lifted her tear-stained face from Calev's tunic, then she kissed him. He obviously wasn't angry with her for losing her part of the battle with Runnos, because he gripped her hips and pressed hard into the kiss. His breath was warm, and he smelled like he always did, like sun-warmed earth and lemons. Lord of the Harvest. And he was hers. Her body heated against his and she dug her fingers into the waves of his ebony hair.

"Kinneret." He spoke into her neck, mouth pressed against her sticky skin.

Thankfully, it seemed that Ona and Dante were busy talking a bit of a ways off.

Then there was a voice. And a tapping on her shoulder.

"Oron!" In her excitement, Kinneret shoved Calev away, but Calev laughed it off. She gripped Oron's wide face in her hands. "I am so angry with you."

"I just escaped a tree. You aren't allowed to be mad."

Her hands went to her hips. "Well, I am. You drank too much. You let your anger take you."

"Fine. You're permitted one full day of being angry with me."

"Good." Dante shouted something at Oron, but Kinneret didn't hear it. She was lost, staring at Oron and thanking Fire and sea that he was alive.

"Ona!" she called. "We need to hear what happened under the water. But first, let's get back to the road and try to rummage up some food and drink."

"I do like your priorities, Kinneret," Oron said.

A shout of greeting came from the trees. Then another. Another.

A group of five men and two women filtered into the small clearing.

"What happened?" a woman in a light-colored dress asked in the trade tongue.

Two men walked beside her, talking to one another in quick Silvanian. The first wore noble livery and the second had a beard far too large for his face.

All of them had dirt on their faces and leaves on their clothing or in their hair. The woman was missing one shoe.

Oron swallowed loudly. "I think these might be people who were also trapped by the green men."

Calev stood slowly. "Maybe these are the people taken recently whose spirits had not yet been fully absorbed by the wood."

Kinneret wasn't sure what to say. "Welcome. Our friend Ona here," she gestured to the mercenary, "somehow stopped the forest god and freed you. At least, that's what I know."

"That's about it," Ona said. "I used the runed sword to bind Runnos."

The man in noble livery scratched his head. "I feel like I've been dreaming for a month."

"More like having a nightmare, wasn't it?" Oron asked.

"Yes."

"We'd offer you food and water, but we have none," Dante said.

"Thank you," the woman said. "I am Rosa. This is my friend Giuseppe." She pointed to the man in the livery. "I'd love to hear how you managed to defeat a god, but I just want to get back to my family in Verita."

"Of course!" Kinneret said. "Travel with us. We're headed there too. We have a meeting with the king."

"Oh!" Giuseppe clapped his long hands. "We work for a member of his court."

The rest of the freed people greeted Ona and thanked her before hurrying out of the forest in pairs. Finally, Kinneret and the rest gathered themselves and did the same.

As THEY WALKED, headed for the charcoal burners' huts to beg some food and a night's rest, Kinneret talked in whispers with Ona and Oron. The horror of Runnos had personally touched each one and Kinneret was relieved to have two people who—at least a little bit—understood. Dante and Calev let them have their restorative conversations, almost serving as

707

guards along the road, Dante with the sword he had named Carver, and Calev with his dagger and keen eyes. Rosa and Giuseppe kept their own company, talking in serious tones nearby.

At a rippling stream, the group stopped and washed the cursed forest off of them. Blood, leaves, magic, and tears. All of it. With no dry clothing to change into, Kinneret shivered a little in the breeze as she took up her discussions of Runnos, the sorcerer, Miach, and the green men with Oron and Ona.

"So Miach's grandfather was actually the reason why Miach was still alive."

Ona tied her hair up into two knots. "Yes, but Runnos twisted the magic and used Miach for his own purposes."

Oron frowned. "But how did the spell get to Miach when the man died before he was born?"

"That, I don't know." Ona shrugged. "Magic?"

"Indeed," Oron said wryly.

"And when you were in the silver pool, Miach took on some of his grandfather's spirit?"

"It looked like that to me," Ona said. "His eyes were…different. Old. Powerful. He showed me a rune to carve into the sacred pine. It was on Carver's blade."

Kinneret was overwhelmed. "I can't help but think you were…destined for the job of taking Runnos down. I mean, you are a warrior and an artist. It's like it was all fated."

"Just as you are a fabulously talented sailor with a fierce heart, determined to get rich, and you found Ayarazi," Oron said.

"It wasn't just about the silver," Kinneret said, "and you know it."

"I do." Oron patted Kinneret's arm.

"It must've been amazing to see the silver pool from below and watch it blow apart."

Ona nodded. "It was. I've seen a lot of things, but that beat them all. You were there, but I suppose you don't remember."

"I don't." Shame heated Kinneret's throat.

"Kinneret." Ona's earnest eyes caught her gaze. "Don't do that. Don't blame yourself. I'm guessing you held out against Runnos's magic far longer than any of us could have."

"Agreed," Oron said. "And from what I've heard, we should be glad Dante didn't lop your head off with that fine, new sword. He is quite the swordsman, hmm?"

Kinneret knew he was trying to change the subject. "I hurt everyone. Most of all, Calev."

Calev walked ahead with Dante. He pulled his dagger and showed Dante the hilt. He was probably telling Dante all the Old Farm legends about the Dagger Dance. Kinneret wanted to be happy, but she only felt really, really sorry about losing her mind in the forest.

Ona's gaze brightened. "Kinneret." The former mercenary's eyebrows flew together in a vicious scowl. "No, you didn't hurt everyone. Runnos did. And we took his tail down. So just stop with the whole *I'm terrible* thing. You aren't and we know it and you know it. You are amazing." She punched Kinneret lightly on the arm.

Kinneret had to smile. "I think I like you."

"I know I like you."

"I'm in love with you both. In an older brother kind of way, that is." Oron hugged them briefly. "Thanks for not leaving me in the tree."

"Avi would've killed me if I had," Kinneret said.

Oron laughed the first real laugh since they were on Ekrem's full-ship. "I will be sure to write her a fine thank you note for her murderous reputation upon our return."

AFTER WHAT FELT like a short journey and a terribly long one combined somehow, Kinneret looked up from Oron's and Ona's faces to see the charcoal burner, who'd let Calev and her rest, coming out to greet them.

The woman raised her hands. "You survived it. I hardly believe my own eyes. And you got your friends with you too. This is a cause for celebration. Hardy, get those eggs you found in the treeline last night. We're having a feast."

It was no feast, but the eggs were very, very good.

The charcoal burner, named Valentina, had talked her fellows into dragging two stumps and a wooden plank in front of her hut. The whole group sat down to fresh water, pine needle tea, and plates of eggs and greens.

"Thank you, Valentina," Kinneret said to the woman.

Valentina handed the bowl of eggs to a woman sitting across the basic plank table. "No. Thank *you*!"

"For what?"

"You set the cursed wood to rights, didn't you?"

"We did," Ona said. Her voice was stronger than it had been since

709

Kinneret met the mercenary. And there was a lightness to her walk despite the sadness that still reigned in her eyes. "Runnos is bound now."

Oron rubbed the back of his neck. He'd shown Kinneret the red marks left by the tree's first grab at him. "That wood is still not the most pleasant spot."

Ona smiled a little. "No. But I think…" She glanced at Carver. Dante had given the sword back to her, saying Miach would've wanted her to have it. "I think he can only scare people a bit now. He can't do anything too horrible."

Oron snorted. "So maybe just some creepy whispering and the occasional tree with a trunk that just sort of resembles a man?"

"Yes. Maybe just that. Probably less than that."

Valentina didn't seem to understand they were joking. "The animals are back. That's what I have seen. The rabbits bothered my garden again today. The deer ran across the road. Things are the way they are supposed to be again. Like they were when my mother's mother was a child."

Dante swallowed a bite of egg, then pointed to a spot between two beech trees. "You should plant some of that woody herb that's growing right there in your garden. Might dissuade the rabbits a little. Not completely. But a little."

Ona shook her head. "Why is it that I'm the one who actually lived in a forest for years with your brother and you're the one who knows all about plants?"

"Guess you were focused on something else during those years."

"I was."

Kinneret wished her younger years could've focused on something other than starving. "And you had someone else to find dinner for you."

Ona had the decency to look abashed. "I did. I was fortunate. The mercenaries I fought with had a cook. She was very good."

"You're a mercenary?" Valentina didn't look happy about the fact.

"I was. Not anymore."

Valentina breathed out and passed some field greens to the charcoal burner next to her at the table. "Good. I didn't think you had the eyes of a killer."

"I have killed many." Ona didn't look proud.

"But you won't anymore. You are something else." Valentina tapped her chin and studied Ona. "Maybe a scribe? You sound learned and your hands look very capable of delicate things."

Ona held them up. "They do?"

Valentina elbowed Dante and winked. "They surely do. Don't they, handsome?"

Dante looked like he'd just been smacked with an oar. "Uh, yes." He grinned and chuckled.

Kinneret could've stayed here for three days instead of one night. Valentina and the rest of her crew were full of laughs and good sense. Kinneret didn't realize she'd miss the humility of spending time with the low-caste type. Well, Valentina would be considered low-caste here in Silvania although the Empire's caste system held no sway here. Silvania still had one. It was simply invisible. Lately, Kinneret had spent most of her non-sailing sun at Amir Ekrem's little court, surrounded by the haughty and the overly educated.

"Eh, Calev." She nudged him with her foot, and he eyed her behind his cup of pine needle tea. "After we marry, can we spend our month going from port to port, down the coast? I need more real folk in my life and fewer highly educated knob-heads."

Calev sputtered, then laughed. "Sounds great to me. First, we have to survive the Silvanian king's court."

Kinneret sighed. "I'm definitely going to need some new clothes." One of her capped sleeves hung limply over her shoulder and a tear ran from the hem of her skirt all the way to her knee. And some of the dirt from the forest didn't come out when they'd washed in the stream.

Across the table, Oron lifted a hand. "Spending silver is one of my greatest joys. I will be happy to help."

"You're hired." She suddenly missed the presence of Miach and Ethus. The moon rose over the road and the charcoal pits. The white light washed over everyone's faces, making them look like ghosts. "I wonder how disappearing felt to Miach and Ethus."

Calev stared at the moon too. "Ona said he was smiling. I'd guess it was better than we can imagine. He'd been lonely for too long."

The urge to kiss Calev's cheek overwhelmed her and she leaned in close. His skin was warm. His growing beard pricked her lips.

"What was that for?" he asked.

"For being you." She gave him one more peck on the cheek, then turned to Rosa and Giuseppe. "Do you work for a noble family then?"

"We do," Rosa said. "And I have an idea. I think you should keep your torn clothing, as we will. We will go right into the court as is, and you can tell the whole story. You and yours here saved our country, if not the entire continent. The king must acknowledge that feat and surely he'll agree to whatever you demand."

Ona leaned in. "I like the sound of that. Dante and I need horses for our trip to Akhayma. Silver would help too."

"I do need to eat." Dante patted his flat stomach.

Oron nodded appreciatively over a heaping forkful of egg.

"I wouldn't want to return Lucca's brother in a state of emaciation," Ona said.

"Of what?" Valentina asked.

"It means he'd be missing all those muscles of his." Ona poked at Dante's big arm appreciatively.

Grinning, Kinneret wondered how long it would be until those two traded more than jokes. Two days on the road. That was her private bet.

When Kinneret and the rest were full of eggs, exhaustion caught up and dragged them all into a deep sleep.

Kinneret dreamed of Miach and Ethus.

23

ONA

Verita blew Ona's hair back. Yes, she was from Silvania, but she'd never gone to the huge port city to see its ornate merchant houses or streets of water where traders rode boats more often than horses. It was a city of islands. And silver. The wealth dripped off the nobility here. Ona and her group did not belong. At all. In torn trousers, tattered shirts, and muddied tunics, they didn't look like they should be approaching the king's castle.

Kinneret had retrieved a harried-looking woman named Ridhima from the dock. She had been guarding the skiff Kinneret came in on. After a quick tale about what had happened and assurances that all was well for the time being, they sent Ridhima off to give word to their full-ship crew about the delay.

At the king's castle, a young woman with black and silver hair strolled out of the archway. A group came up alongside her. She held a bladed staff and inclined her head to Calev, Kinneret, and Oron.

"You retrieved your friend," the woman said. She must've been from the Northern Isles.

"Yes," Calev said. "Thank you for your help."

Oron was stiff, but he nodded a thank you. "I heard you told my friends about my unfortunate situation. I appreciate your break from tradition. Maybe you can enlighten the rest of Snowfallen when you return."

She frowned and studied him. Her group left without a backward glance. "Perhaps," the woman said. Tucking her fine cloak around her, she swept into the road beside the canal.

Ona touched Carver's hilt. "I should've asked her about the runes."

"I can tell you a little," Oron said. "I was born in the isles."

Rosa and Giuseppe greeted the guards outside the arched walls. "We are of the DeLuca household," Giuseppe said in quick Silvanian. He gestured to his mucked-up livery. The silver embroidery and fine fabric didn't match his unshaved chin and blackened eye.

The guards scowled. "Is Master DeLuca expecting you at court? Like this?" one of them asked.

Rosa smiled, indulgent. "We have a great story to tell the king. It will please him. If not, you will have the pleasure of kicking us into the canal."

The guards laughed and waved the group on.

Inside the first gate, a courtyard bustled with boys saddling horses the color of night and gondolas bumping out of a tunnel and up to a dock. Strips of rainbow-colored fabric streamed from the dock's silver-painted poles. Dodging a spirited gelding that Ona wished she could ride to Akhayma, they came to a second set of guards standing at an arched doorway. Voices echoed from the high entrance.

Rosa gave these guards a similar treatment.

"What if the king decides he isn't wild about seven beggars barging into his throne room?" Ona's palms began to sweat. She wished she was on the road, heading toward Lucca and Seren already.

"Then we'll have another night of sleep. Perhaps in a prison cell." Dante shrugged.

"Great."

A hallway of mirrors and windows threw spears of light onto a ceiling covered in detailed paintings.

"I might actually be fine with a night in prison," Oron said. "I'm a walking corpse right now."

As she studied the shape of a painted rock dove above their heads, Ona threw an arm around Oron. "Maybe you can steal a nobleman's wine?" Her fingers itched to paint a better version of that bird on the room's elaborate ceiling.

"If one thing could bring me back to life, that would be it."

"It'd have to be a good red, though, right?" Dante looked very serious.

"Definitely," Oron said. "Bring up my part of the tale right at the beginning of our audience with the king, Ona. Then I'll have a little sun to harvest an unattended glass."

"Can do."

The king of Silvania stood with his back to a massive, silver throne. He laughed—a deep and bellowing sound—before turning around to see what the cat had dragged in.

The servant at the door announced them. "Two of the DeLuca household bring you a tale they believe will entertain the court, your highness.

Ona had told Rosa and Giuseppe everything she could remember from the time in the cursed wood, but they hadn't practiced for this, and Ona wasn't sure if she was supposed to speak up or not.

The king tilted his head to one side. "Hmm. That sounds interesting. Ah. Is that Kaptan Kinneret Raza and Calev ben Y'hoshua I see there?"

Kinneret and Calev bowed.

"I thought we were set to speak yesterday morning. Or was it the day before that? I'm not accustomed to being ignored."

Calev stammered and Kinneret stepped forward. "Your highness, we apologize for the inconvenience. You see, a group of drunken sailors—not mine—stole a friend of ours away and he ended up in a cursed forest not far from Verita. So you'll excuse us, please, if our near death experience made us late for a meeting."

Calev grimaced and took over, hands clasped. "Your highness. This is the story we are here to tell. Please forgive us for causing you any inconvenience."

"And for looking like beggars in your gorgeous court, your highness," Oron said. "I will happily start the tale. A glass of wine might help me speak more clearly."

The king's frown smoothed, and he laughed. Clapping his hands, he said, "Give them food and drink. Then, when they are fully ready, this good man can start the telling."

Oron gave a ridiculously low bow, but the king chuckled, obviously enjoying the expert sailor's whimsical way. If Lucca had been here, he'd have loved Oron. Ona wanted to ask him to come with them to Akhayma, but there was no way he'd leave his job with Kinneret.

Oron downed a glass in what seemed like one swallow. He cleared his throat. "It all began when an innocent and rather intelligent fellow went for a drink not far from here. Yes, he most likely had too many..."

The tale went on and on.

The king and his court gasped and laughed at all the right spots. Ona spilled her end of the story and brought out Carver for all to gawk over.

The king touched the blade. "May I?"

Ona nodded, and the king took the hilt and lifted the sword. He moved well enough—a respectable swordsman if not a little overdramatic with his striking. A lady in red velvet squeaked as the king swept the sharp edge close to her feet. His laughter was infectious though and soon she was joining in.

The telling was over.

Ona needed the king to give her horses and coin. Without it, she'd have to beg off Kinneret and Calev, who had stores on their full-ship. She really didn't want to do that.

"Your highness, did you enjoy the story?"

"I did." He gently handed Carver to her. "This has been the most entertainment we've had since my old jester decided he'd had enough of me!"

The court erupted over what Ona assumed was some sort of inside joke.

"Would you consider a…reward for such a tale?" Ona swallowed, watching the king take a glass of red wine back to his throne.

He stopped, then turned on his heel. "I would! Just tell me what you need, and it will be given to you."

Ona exhaled, relief flooding her. "Two horses. For me and for Dante." She gestured toward Dante, who bowed roughly. "And perhaps a small sum so we may eat and drink during our journey to Akhayma."

"Why do you head to the Empire's capitol?"

"I have a message for the new kyros."

"I heard she is a beauty."

"She is very powerful. The Fire blesses her with visions."

"I will have to be careful then when we meet for negotiations."

Calev and Kinneret stepped forward. "Speaking of negotiations, Amir Ekrem worries that Invaders may come around the southern tip of the continent and attack Jakobden's ports."

"He believes they are capable of doing so much by sea?" the king asked. "They are more of a land army, aren't they? The new kyros destroyed the bulk of that army, did she not?"

"That's the message we received," Calev said. "But there are wanderers. Invaders who have broken from the main force and now travel the countryside pillaging."

The king set his wine on a small, round table. "I can see how that would pose a threat to Jakobden's trade."

"And a threat to those lemons you love," Calev added.

The king arranged his sumptuous clothing around his large body and sat on the silver throne. "I would hate to miss out on that taste." He held up the fingers of his right hand and kissed them loudly. "So delicious! Now, what exactly does Amir Ekrem want from me?"

"If we are raided by Invaders and have at least three witnesses to the event, Amir Ekrem asks that you send two full-ships. Armed. And three smaller vessels to the Pass to stand in defense of the area for one moon cycle. After that, Amir Ekrem will renegotiate with you."

"Agreed."

"You are?" Kinneret's eyes were wide.

Ona snorted. "The man knows what he wants. A true Silvanian," she whispered.

Kinneret whistled low. "Well, then we are agreed."

The king ordered his servants to hand out more wine in celebration and demanded that everyone dance. A flute player began piping and a man with a huge oud strummed his strings vigorously. A boy from the stables was summoned to ready horses and packs for Ona and Dante.

Ona smiled. It was great to hear Silvanian music again.

Kinneret turned to Calev. "Will you dance with me, my love?"

Ona left them to it and found Dante. "Should we try to leave now?"

"Why not have a bit of fun first?" Dante held out a hand and wiggled his eyebrows at the musicians.

Ona took his offered hand and put it on her hip. "Let's see what you've got, big man."

24

ONA

Nearly One Year Later

As Ona rode beside Dante, toward the great walls of Akhayma, she realized that, in her mind, this city hadn't changed in almost a year. She'd frozen the place in time, fully expecting to see pillars of blue-black smoke like mournful ghosts all around the battlefield. Seren would've ordered the people to burn bodies of the Invaders as well as those of fallen Empire soldiers. The air should've been rank with flame and flesh. But that had all happened months and months ago.

Back in Verita, right after the battle with Runnos, Dante and Ona both had run into relatives in the port city.

With the happy reunions, they'd been talked into waiting to return until now.

Ona hadn't fought her cousin's request that she stay because she'd been afraid still, afraid she'd be turned away at Akhayma, afraid her heart and Dante's would be broken by Lucca and Seren.

But there could be no more stalling.

A year. It was far too long already. Seren would've already held another Fire Ceremony as kyros. They'd have long since forgotten about Ona, but she owed them a sincere apology and an explanation and they would have it.

Dante hadn't argued against staying in Verita either. He hadn't even brought up the idea that they send a message to his brother. She recognized her own fear of rejection in his eyes.

So they'd had drinks and visited with cousins and enjoyed the king's continued good will through several moon cycles of gondolas and late nights talking about what their lives might look like now.

That's how they ended up arriving at Akhayma, not right after the battle with the Invaders, but long past that and nearly time for the Gathering.

Soon, people from all over Seren's Empire would descend onto the plains, raise luxurious tents, and compete in a number of archery, racing, and strategy tests for bragging rights—at least that's how Kinneret had explained it before she'd returned to Jakobden with Calev and Oron.

"Do you think they truly believe you're dead?" Dante clicked his tongue at his black gelding and the horse hurried into a trot.

Ona nudged her mount with a bump from her heels. "Yes." What would they say? Would they be happy to see her or horrified?

The horses' hooves kicked up clouds of the sandy earth as they made their way to the front gate. Ona had made this trip with Lucca once. She remembered her awe at the honeycomb structure of the gate and the colors of the stone walls. They were still impressive. She would paint them. Soon. Now, she was the artist she'd never let herself be. Even if she hadn't created a thing yet. It was in her, the artwork. It beat inside her chest like a second heart.

The guards stopped them, their acorn-shaped helmets shining. Rings of gray hung below the men's eyes. This had to have been one of the worst years in the city's history. So much loss.

"Kyros Seren will want to see me," Ona said. "I have news from the king of Silvania."

The first guard called in a few others, and the group escorted Ona and Dante toward the Kyros Walls, inside the city proper.

THE MAIN TENT looked much the same as it had before the battle. Beautiful stars of pale gossamer in the ceiling. Oil lamps, shined to a glow, hanging from the dark, peaked fabric of the tent. Tables lining the walls and one raised table at the end of the room.

And there was Seren.

Dante mimicked Ona as she chewed her provided mint leaf obediently, passed a hand over the Holy Fire bowl, then approached Seren.

"Kyros." Ona's voice faltered.

719

Seren stood. Her ebony hair fell over her shoulder, and the green cosmetics on her eyes twinkled. Her mouth opened. Shut. Opened again. "Ona?"

Ona nodded. "I am so sorry." She dropped to her knees.

Seren hurried around the table, face unreadable. Was she going to hit Ona? Order her to a grisly death? Neither would surprise Ona.

But Seren took Ona's hands in hers. "Stand," the kyros said in Silvanian.

Ona did. She gripped Seren's fingers, afraid that if she let go, she'd never see this new friend again.

Seren blinked. "I can hardly believe it," she said, this time using the trade tongue. Her smile was radiant. "I thought you...I thought you were a ghost."

Dante stayed back, near the door with the guards who were watching closely.

"I felt like I was dead. An Invader ran me through on the battlefield. The only thing that kept me alive was the possibility of apologizing to you. I'm sorry for betraying you, my friend. I will never, ever do it again. Not that I expect you to trust me."

"Why did you go to Varol's side? I have my guesses, but..."

"Because I thought his kind of leadership would win against the Invaders. I thought you were too soft." Ona hated the words, but she had to be completely honest out of respect for Seren.

Seren closed her eyes briefly, and a sad smile crossed over her mouth. "You needed your revenge. For your aunt."

"But that's just it. Even after I killed so many Invaders. Even now, knowing we won against them and you annihilated their army—the feeling didn't satisfy me. All the death hollowed me out. I was a husk. It confused me. I didn't know who I was without that need to avenge my aunt's death."

Ona told Seren everything. About Runnos and Kinneret. About Dante.

"You are Ona the artist," Seren said.

Ona's smile was unstoppable. "I am."

A man emerged from the back door. Curly, black hair. Dark eyes. A walk like a lion.

"Lucca!" Ona threw herself at him.

His breath gusted out as he caught her. "Ona?"

She didn't want to look up from his shoulder, to break the embrace, to see if he was happy or upset by her arrival. She breathed him in, feeling safe and purely happy.

Then his chest heaved. His arms squeezed her tightly. "My friend. My Ona."

Wake. Her aunt's voice, the sound she'd heard on the battlefield the day she'd thought she'd died, echoed in her mind again. Finally, she understood. Her aunt had wanted her to wake from the nightmare of vengeance so Ona could enjoy life again. *Wake.*

I've done it, Aunt, she whispered.

Ona and Lucca didn't say another thing. They just cried and held one another until the storm passed.

When it did, Dante came forward, out of the shadows. "Brother."

Ona broke from Lucca and wiped her face with her sleeve. "I brought you a gift."

"No." Lucca shook his head, his eyes red. "No."

Dante smiled tentatively. "Yes. And I have forgiveness to ask too. I...I never thought our father would treat you or mother badly when I left. He hated me. I had to leave. Please know I wouldn't do it again. If I could go back and change my actions, I would. Now. Immediately. But I was—"

Lucca turned away and cleared his throat. Dante's hands fisted at his sides. He looked miserable.

"You were young," Lucca said. "You were hurt. You thought it was best at the time." His voice was raspy with emotion, and Ona's heart bled for the child he was when his older brother ran away. "There is nothing to forgive," he whispered.

Dante shook his head in disagreement. "When I crossed out of Silvania, near the Green Mountains, a band of Invaders captured me. They trained me as their own. I fought here. In Akhayma. Out there." He jabbed a finger toward the door. "On that battlefield. And I'm sorry. I didn't want to," he said to Seren, "if that's any consolation. I accept whatever punishment you see fit."

"There will be no punishment," Seren said regally. "I too was assaulted by Invaders. I know well what they do to children and families. I will not punish you for simply staying alive and doing what you had to do."

Lucca walked toward Dante. "Brother."

Dante gripped Lucca's forearm. "Brother."

They hugged one another and whispered phrases touched by tears.

Ona's body was light as a feather. She'd done it. She was redeemed.

721

KINNERET

Akhayma's plains held an ocean of tents that rippled in the breeze. Kinneret slipped inside the first of Old Farm's clutch of tents, a green creation that was more of an oak's color than a pine's, which was a very good thing considering her past.

The cloth door adjoining this tent to the next fluttered. Someone was coming.

Please don't be Calev's Aunt Y'hudit, Kinneret thought. The woman was kind, but she was a lot to take in the morning.

But the nosy woman who'd jokingly hounded Kinneret about her first nights as Calev's wife didn't walk through the door. It was Calev himself.

Her heart swelled and she opened her arms.

Calev lifted her and swung her around, burying his face in her hair. "Are you going to compete today?"

Kinneret kissed him, savoring the taste of lemon on his warm lips and loving the feel of his strong arms. She pulled away, and his big, dark eyes opened. His lashes were ridiculously long.

"In the archery contest?" she said. "I'm not nearly good enough to go up against the people here."

"Come on. It'll still be exciting. The kyros herself is competing."

"I can't *wait* to see that. After the stories Ona told about that woman on horseback… If I compete, you have to as well. You're no slouch with a bow. Plus, I'd like to see you up there, in front of the crowd, knowing you're mine."

"You want to show off your new husband, do you?" Calev's hand snaked under the hem of her shirt. His fingers dragged lightly across her ribs.

She shivered. "Definitely." Her body fit against his perfectly. Like he was made for her. His hipbones pressed gently into her and she curled her fingers in his wavy hair.

With one last kiss, she pulled him out of the tent to find Avi, who was supposedly about to meet her friend Radi, a native to this area. They'd been exchanging letters for a long while.

"Avi!" Kinneret kept Calev's calloused fingers in hers as they wove through the Old Farm camp, toward Amir Ekrem's camp.

In the center of three blue tents—a makeshift courtyard of sorts—Avi sat across a gaming board from the boy Kinneret could only guess was Radi. He moved a glass game piece, then Avi laughed. She moved another piece. "I think you let me win."

"I did not," Radi said, appearing insulted. "I would never! I am simply gathering information about how you play. Next time, or perhaps the game after that, I will be the victor."

"We'll see." Avi raised an eyebrow. Then she noticed Kinneret and Calev and stood in one graceful movement. "Sister! Brother! Come meet Radi."

Radi gave them a simple bow. "Your sister has been busy annihilating me on the game board."

"I'll teach you how to best her," Calev said.

Avi stuck her tongue out at him like she was still a child.

Heart warm, Kinneret laughed, then hugged Avi and kissed her sun-colored braid. "Where is Oron?"

"I am here, my lady." The man himself walked out from the pathway between two tents, wine in hand. He lifted it high. "I have a surprise for you!" He turned and held out a palm.

Dante and another man who looked a great deal like Dante walked into the courtyard.

"Greetings!" Dante said. "This is my brother Lucca, the famous mercenary."

"I've heard so much about you all," Lucca said. He embraced each of them like they were kin, Kinneret last. "Thank you," he said sincerely. "Thank you for bringing my brother and my friend, Ona, back to me. Back to life. It is a miracle. I was told what you lived through and how you fought. I am in your debt."

Kinneret's cheeks were hurting from smiling so much. Where was Aunt Y'hudit when you needed to frown? "No, there is no debt," she said. "Ona is the hero. She saved us all, she and Miach."

Miach and his sorcerer grandfather often visited Kinneret's dreams. She often wondered what parts of the dreams were real and what were merely her own inventions.

"Oron, how did you find Dante?" Calev set up the gaming board, his fingers quick on the shining glass pieces.

"Once you've fought a forest together, you have a special kind of link. And before you say anything disparaging about my lazing about a tree trunk whilst you all raised sword and shield, I'll have you know that battles are not always fought and won with the physical body."

"I wouldn't dream of disparaging you, Oron. And I heartily agree." Kinneret shuddered, remembering the feel of Runnos's voice inside her head. Her nightmares brought the god back to full power at least once a moon cycle. She longed to see Ona, the woman who'd fought by her side during that terrible time in the cursed forest. Somehow, Kinneret thought maybe seeing Ona whole and well and strong might chase the remnants of Runnos from her own mind.

"And it didn't hurt that Dante and Lucca were holed up in the wine tent by the gates," Oron said.

Avi snorted. "Special link indeed."

Oron walked into one of the amir's tents, then back out again. He held up a scroll. "I just needed to grab this. Now, let's visit Ona and see what she has been hiding under that tarp of hers."

"Tarp?" Kinneret caught up with Oron while the rest of them walked a step behind.

"Our friend Ona has a big surprise for the kyros," Oron said.

"All right. But what is that?" She pointed at the scroll.

"This is a plan I drew up for Avi's proposed new business. She asked me to do some tallying for her and double check her own findings."

Avi hadn't said a thing to Kinneret. "New business?"

"She thinks it'd be a good idea to start a library. For the Empire."

"She doesn't do anything in halves, does she?"

"With a small donation from the kyros and Amir Ekrem, she claims we could set up a delivery system for literature, philosophy, poetry, and history books between Jakobden and Akhayma. With several stops in between for the smaller towns. I'll go over these tallies with you between archery contests today."

"As you wish."

The tents gave way to an open area at the eastern expanse of the city walls. A massive tarp covered a swathe of the striped stone. A rope lashed to a cart pulled one corner up.

Ona stood on a ladder, hair in two knots and a large paintbrush in one hand.

She turned, saw them, and waved. That was the first time she'd seen a true smile on the woman. Green paint decorated her cheek. She opened her arms to address a crowd that was quickly growing.

"Welcome visitors and friends! Please pay respect to our kyros, Seren, Pearl of the Desert!"

A striking woman in deep purple walked out of the city gates. A crown with little peaks that glittered like flames graced her brow. Kinneret squinted in the desert sun. They weren't actually flames, were they? No, they had to be gemstones. But the effect was dazzling.

The crowd erupted into cheers for the kyros. Children sat on fathers' shoulders. Warriors waved their yatagans in the air, making the sun leap from blade to blade. It was blindingly beautiful.

Lucca was positively glowing beside Dante. The look on Lucca's face answered Kinneret's unspoken question. Yes, Lucca and Seren were definitely still together.

As Calev took Oron's spot beside Kinneret—Oron was chatting with a pretty woman in blue—Seren greeted the crowd fluently in three languages.

"Welcome to the heart of the Empire. During this Gathering, we are all friends, despite any differences. Let us share our cultures, our foods, our jokes, our dances. Remember, the most beautiful weaving boasts the most varied colors. Together, you are the loveliest tapestry my eyes could ever behold."

The people shouted for her again and she silenced them by raising both hands.

"I hear that a friend of mine, Onaratta, has a surprise for me. She asked permission to do something to our walls and I'm as excited as you to see what she has done."

Ona moved the ladder away, then faced Seren. "I dedicate this work to you, Kyros Seren, for your bravery, your friendship, and your mercy." Ona looked up and waved her arms.

Five men and women at the top of the walls worked the ropes. The tarp slid to the ground with a great *whoosh*. When the plumes of sandy earth cleared, an image like Kinneret had only seen in illuminated manuscripts or fine Silvanian chapels bloomed from Akhayma's walls.

Framed in scrolling silver paint, a mosaic-style painting showed rock doves and market stalls bursting with fruit, children playing by a fountain and warriors training on the field. The shapes linked like puzzle pieces, each one leading into the other like a trick to the eye. Roses and those trees that only grew around this city branched wide and reached into a starry sky under which countless flames flickered.

Seren covered her mouth and said something in a language Kinneret didn't know. Then the kyros ran to Ona and hugged her tightly while the people cheered and shouted compliments to the creator of the mural.

"She is truly the artist she wished to be." Avi linked her arm in Kinneret's and gave Calev a smile.

Kinneret kissed Avi's temple, a contented peace flowing through her like a gentle current.

The kyros suddenly locked gazes with Kinneret. "Please join me in thanking the rest of the group who fought the forest god, Runnos, and saved our land!" Seren called out. "Thanks to you, Calev ben Y'hoshua of Old Farm, Oron the Great Sailor of the Broken Coast, Dante the brother to my love and savior of the sword Carver, and of course, the legendary Kaptan Kinneret Raza!"

The entire Gathering roared in applause and Avi leaned toward Kinneret's ear.

"I knew you were destined for great things, sister," Avi said, "but this is a little much."

"Says the girl planning to open an Empire-sized library system."

Seren took a gorgeous, wooden bow from a man and held it high. "Now it is time for me to beat you all in an archery contest!" She laughed with the crowd.

Avi elbowed Kinneret. "I'm sure you have even more plans than I do up your sleeve."

"Oh yes." Kinneret set her head on Calev's shoulder. "Just wait until Calev dazzles everyone with his dancing tonight. While they're busy staring at his handsome face, I fully plan to nab that crown off Seren's pretty head. It would look great on me and I'm certain Seren has ten others just like it." She winked, joking.

Avi slapped her. "Behave."

Kinneret grinned. "Never."

Want a complimentary prequel to this series or Alisha Klapheke's Edinburgh Seer trilogy? Go to www.alishaklapheke.com/free-prequel-1 today!

Alisha also hangs out in the Facebook group Epic Fantasy Fanatics. She'd love to see you there.

Keep reading for a sample chapter of *The Edinburgh Seer*. Magic, ancient prophecies, and romance combine in an alternate Scotland to create an adventure you'll never forget.

94085051R00435

Made in the USA
Middletown, DE
17 October 2018